LESSONS IN MURDER

TRACIE OLIVER

Michael Terence
Publishing

First published in paperback by
Michael Terence Publishing in 2020
www.mtp.agency

ISBN 9781913653057

Cover image
Daniel Cartwright

To Julie, Mark, Debbie and Linda…
for your love, support and encouragement.

Prologue

Tara was lying in bed in a deep sleep when the phone rang. She glanced at the bedside clock. Six a.m. For a split second, she thought it must be a work message, then remembered it was Sunday.

"Hello?" she said in a throaty voice.

"Tara, Tara help me! Help me!" said a distressed woman, between loud sobs.

She sat bolt upright. It was the voice of her best friend Izzy. Only Izzy wasn't making any sense. Tara repeatedly told her to slow down so that she could help her.

"I've done it, Tara," said Izzy in a dramatic whisper. "I've done it, I've killed him."

Tara could not believe what she was hearing and yet she always knew something terrible would happen. Izzy, her dear best friend had been pushed to the brink by this vile man who just used and abused her. A true player, six feet tall, dark hair, blue eyes and gorgeous, in a rough-edged kind of way. He could get any girl he set his cap at and he knew it. And he did, whilst continuing to use Izzy on a daily basis.

Izzy couldn't stop sobbing.

"I'm at home," she said eventually. "I need you to come round straight away." She took a huge gulp. "Will you help me get rid of the body?"

1

Tara switched off the alarms and opened the front door to the office. The sun was shining, at least one good thing to start the day. She wondered which school would need what. No sooner had the thought left her mind when the first call came in. She hurried to her desk. Education Supply had a two-ring policy so she knew it was for her and quickly scooped up the phone.

Key Stage 2, pupils aged between seven and eleven, Jessica Delves for an all-day session at St. Magdalene's Roman Catholic School. Tara groaned knowing that this would be no easy task. Jessica Delves was a pint-sized, 42-year-old, very attractive divorced mother of two. Jessica's teaching ability was second to none but she had one slight problem. She simply didn't like to work. Tara wondered what today's little drama would entail.

St. Magdalene's was run by a super-efficient, School Business Manager Isabella Hughes, aka Izzy, Tara's best friend.

"See if you can dig the lazy cow up," said Izzy, laughing down the phone.

"I'll see what I can do," said Tara gloomily.

"I'll phone you later, I need to tell you something. Bye!"

Tara replaced the phone wondering, not for the first time, how on earth these supply teachers paid their bills. She looked up and watched as Carrie, all blonde hair and mascara, dashed across the office and flounced into her chair, make-up bag at the ready. She was quickly followed by Daniel the office manager, who had a face like thunder hovering above his 6ft 4-inch frame. Tara could not work out if Daniel was gay. He was married with a son but did a cracking imitation of Kenneth Williams.

Tara busily filled in the booking sheet for St. Magdalene's and gave it to Daniel to sort. If anybody could sweetheart Jessica Delves into work, it was him. Mark strolled into the office followed by Val. Poor Mark lived at home with his warring parents, one of whom was a dominant police officer father who terrorised him. Tara looked at Val's miserable face and thought here we go. In her forties, Val had responsibility for all Education

Supplies' accounts but what with being married with personal problems, she was the biggest pain to work with. Tara wondered how any work ever got done.

Daniel came into the coffee room and yawned.

"Busy night?" asked Tara.

"No, not really."

"It's me you're talking to," she said, laughing.

"Well," he said, smiling back. "I was chatting to that girl I met in Starbucks."

Then he started shuffling uncomfortably from one foot to the other.

"Erm," he continued. "And I need to tell you something."

"Come on out with it," said Tara, one eyebrow raised at the unmistakable fact his face had gone bright red.

"I brought her back here," he muttered. "And fucked her in the back of my car."

"How the hell did you manage that?" she said. "You're 6ft 4!"

"With great difficulty," he replied and they both burst into fits of the giggles.

"Well at least," he continued, handing her a cup of coffee. "Jessica Delves has got off her lazy arse."

They both went back into the office and handed out the coffee.

The morning moved along briskly and then the first interview came in. On paper, Jack Baxter looked like a first-rate English specialist so Carrie was looking forward to getting him on board. Jack had filled in all of his documentation and Mark set about verifying it, so Carrie began the interview. Jack Baxter was very good looking, in a used car salesman kind of way. He certainly displayed a nice smiley demeanour but Carrie couldn't work out why he seemed so on edge. The man couldn't sit still. She let that go, continued the interview, shook his hand at the end and thanked him for coming in.

Carrie came back into the office and gave the info to Mark to start reference checking.

"Well," she said. "I couldn't make my mind up out about him. Let's see what comes back for him? On the face of it, he left his last job due to stress."

Tara and Daniel looked at each other. Seen it all before.

Carrie had moved south from Wigan. She'd fallen in love with a chap she met through friends at a party in the Café Royal. Jeremy, a very successful accountant, fell for Carrie in a big way so at last she had taken the plunge and moved to London to be with him. Jeremy had lots of posh high-flying friends whose wives, unfortunately, couldn't stand Carrie.

After lunch things settled down. A few bookings came in and around 4 pm Michael Kelly appeared and plonked himself down in front of Tara's desk.

"Had a good day at English Martyrs, then?" asked Tara, as he yanked off his tie.

"The usual."

Michael taught Design Technology at English Martyrs, on a day to day supply, as and when they needed them. The school was in Brixton and in anybody's book, a tough call. Tara looked at Michael. He resembled a rodent with small glasses, a pointed face and a receding hairline but he had a flair for dealing with challenging schools. He peered over his glasses and proceeded to tell Tara and everybody else in the open-plan office about his day.

"Well," he said. "I had this Year Nine kid who was a little bastard and would not behave, so I picked him up and shoved him head-first in the bin. You're rubbish, I told him, so this is where you belong."

Tara didn't know whether to laugh or cry.

"You did what?" she said, trying not to raise her voice.

Michael looked at her as if she was mad.

"Exactly what I said. I told him he's rubbish and he belongs in the bin. But don't get your knickers in a flap there were no witnesses. Just him and me."

Everyone in the office sat there gobsmacked. Then Michael jumped up out of the seat and waved at everyone.

"Cheerio," he said. "See you all on Friday when I've got my timesheet signed." And off he went.

A call came from the switchboard. Tara answered it praying for someone sensible.

"Ah hello dear Simon!" she said. Simon was Tara's husband.

"I was just wondering what was for tea?" he said.

Tara still hadn't recovered from Michael's outburst.

"If you look over the garden fence, dear," she said through gritted teeth.

"You will see a red fucking cross parcel being parachuted in."

Seriously when did he think she had time to shop?

Simon was eleven years older than Tara. She was sure he had come out of the womb wearing his glasses, a pin-striped suit and carrying a briefcase. Chief executive of a family-run company and the brains behind it all, he had qualified as an accountant then put it to good use running the firm. Tara and Simon had been married for four years, very happily until she decided there wasn't enough sex.

As different as chalk and cheese it worked well. Tara was 5ft2 blonde, full of energy and liked working out. He was 6 ft.1, read the Financial Times and believed people who worked out were clinically insane, whereas his penchant for Porsches and motor racing was perfectly alright. Fortunately, they both loved a decent bottle of wine and fine dining.

2

Izzy needed to speak to Tara. She knew she wouldn't like it but she was torn between feeling excited and needing to be careful. The school bell had long since gone signalling the end of the school day but she remained busily sorting out her desk, which didn't need sorting, then headed towards main reception to lock up. She could not stop thinking about last night. Her friend Tanya had just about begged her to go up West to a trendy new wine bar called Limes.

"See I told you Jonny would sort us out," gushed Tanya as they both jumped the queue.

Limes was fast becoming an exclusive wine bar and they knew they were more than lucky to get in. Jonny Devroe manned the door, 6-foot-tall with dark hair, blue eyes and a body that a champion boxer would be proud of. He was the hottest doorman in London with a reputation to match. He'd served time for grievous bodily harm over ten years ago but rumour had it he'd been set up.

Izzy and Tanya pushed their way through the throng to the bar. Izzy could not believe how busy the place was on a Thursday night. They ordered white wine.

"Do you like the place then?" asked Tanya, scanning the room.

"Yes," smiled Izzy. "It's great, smart people not like the usual skanks we drink with."

"Cheers," they said in unison and clinked glasses.

Izzy had been convinced that Tanya was spinning another story to get her to go out on a school night again. Her friend just could not help herself. Considering Tanya held down a good job in a bank, she was deluded about most things and top of the list had to be her interest in Jonny Devroe. The man had a past and in Izzy's opinion should be left well alone.

Limes was far more upmarket than the usual places the girls frequented and it made a nice change. Izzy glanced around at the beautiful leather sofas, the chrome and glass fittings and then their eyes locked together. Jonny was staring at her. Izzy felt a frisson of excitement. Everything in her suddenly felt alive. It was as if 200 volts had just shot through her. He held her gaze then turned and walked away. Something had just happened and Tanya had clocked it all.

"Well," she said. "He likes what he sees."

"You can forget that," said Izzy. "He's done time. My mother would have a heart attack."

Tanya started laughing and struggled to pull her incredibly short skirt down to somewhere decent.

"There's a lot more fun in the naughty boys."

"Forget it," snorted Izzy, flicking her long dark hair back. "It's not happening he's all yours let's dance."

The girls put down their drinks and moved to the dance floor. Tanya had been right. Limes was good, full of upmarket clientele and Izzy started to relax, getting into the beat. But she could feel his eyes burning into her back. She knew without turning around that Jonny was watching her and she started to move her hips in rhythm to the music. She didn't know what had got into her. She was usually shy, certainly not an attention seeker in any way. The track finished and when the girls moved back to their seats, they found the barman serving up a fresh glass of wine each.

"We didn't order this," said Tanya, catching the barman's eye.

"Compliments of Jonny Devroe," he said.

"Oh, that's really nice of him," cooed Tanya. "I will have to thank him."

The barman moved off smiling. Here we go again he thought. He didn't know how girls fell for it so easily.

"We can't accept it!" shouted Izzy over the music.

"Course we can, don't be silly," replied Tanya.

"He's been in prison. You told me that," said Izzy indignantly.

"Lighten up for Christ's sake Izzy, it's only a drink."

"Look, Tanya, I'm going. I've had enough. I'm not accepting wine from criminals," said Izzy, standing up and grabbing her bag.

Tanya couldn't believe it but she stood up and joined her friend after downing her drink in one.

"Ok then, goody two shoes."

And with that, they headed to the exit and out onto the street.

The cool night air hit Izzy and she realised that she was a nervous wreck. Thank God, he wasn't there when they left. She had never felt anything like it when Jonny Devroe locked his magnificent big blue eyes on her. She swore that her heart stopped. But School Business Manager plus Career Criminal? No way.

Jonny had only gone into the office to speak to his boss for five minutes and missed Izzy's departure. She clearly had no idea of the effect she had on men. Jonny Devroe was an expert on women. He'd had hundreds.

3

Tara started to open the post. Friday, last day of the week. Nearly the start of the weekend. Everyone had their heads down trying to get all of the bookings filled for Monday when the switchboard rang. Daniel took the call then transferred it over to Tara. It was her favourite Deputy Head, Graham Smith, always positive and happy.

"Bit of a problem sweetie," said Graham, coming straight out with it. "Ken didn't turn up this morning."

Tara glanced at her watch it was 11 a.m. Ken Turner's timekeeping as a supply teacher could be deemed at best dodgy but not two hours dodgy.

"That's a bit odd," she said. "He hasn't rung in. Let me make some calls. Do you need a replacement?" she asked suddenly, thinking about the lost revenue.

"No," said Graham with a laugh. "He's only booked for the a.m periods, so no. It would have helped if my department head had told me earlier but they covered it internally, thinking I knew."

Tara wasn't happy. Years ago, before she owned Education Supply, she worked in an admin recruitment agency. One day a Telephonist hadn't returned to a temporary job after lunch and Tara had rung her home number, getting ready to berate her. Only the girl's mother answered, crying hysterically. Her daughter had been run over by a bus on her lunch break. Best go steady, she thought.

When Tara rang Ken's landline number, Sylvia, his snotty, overbearing ex-Head of a wife answered. Sylvia who bore a strong resemblance to Mrs Slocomb from Are You Being Served, was at her best.

"Sylvia Turner here!" she bellowed.

"Morning Sylvia," said Tara, taking a deep breath. "Tara from Education Supply here."

"Yes?" replied the insufferable woman, snorting down the phone like a thoroughbred racehorse. "Yes?"

Tara suppressed her laughter before ploughing on.

"I've just had Sunhill Academy on the phone. Ken didn't turn up this morning for work. Is he there?"

"I assure you he left the house at 8 a.m this morning prompt," she roared, raising her voice a few decibels.

He is there. Oh, God Tara thought to herself, here we go.

"Well," she said. "I have it on good authority that Ken hasn't signed in, therefore he hasn't entered the school premises."

It was like an explosion. Sylvia had always been volatile.

"Are you calling me a liar?"

"No Sylvia," she replied, starting to feel seriously annoyed. "I'm concerned he's been involved in a car crash."

"I assure you," she said, not having any of it. "He's there and the school has made a mistake. Call me back when you have something sensible to say young lady!" and with that, she slammed the phone down.

Tara looked up. Carrie, Daniel, Mark even Val sat staring back at her. Poor Val had her mouth wide open. They'd heard Sylvia's every word.

"That fucking woman," said Tara, slamming her pen down.

She didn't know what to do. He definitely hadn't been on the school premises.

"Should we call the police or the hospitals?" said Val, looking upset.

"No, we fucking should not," said Daniel laughing. "He'll turn up. Let's just wait."

Everyone carried on with their duties and work progressed. At 1 pm Mark looked at Tara.

"Hard hat area. Ken's on line 4."

She couldn't wait for this. Tara grabbed the phone.

"Where have you been Ken?" she asked. "I was worried."

She could hear background noises. He was still in his car.

"Tara, listen," he said. "I couldn't face going into the school so I just sat in the car park then went for a little drive."

Tara heaved a huge sigh of relief.

"Well," she said. "You'd better tell your wife or I will. She thinks I'm lying to her."

"Ok. Will do," said Ken. "If you get anything for tomorrow, let me know?" and he was off.

Tara could not believe what she'd just heard. Never mind about the kids, the school, loss of revenue, even picking up the phone and not letting anyone down. No Ken couldn't face it so that was it. A day in the life of a responsible supply teacher.

A few days later Sylvia turned a mundane day in the office into pure entertainment. She burst through the vestibule, not mentioning a word about the incident with Ken.

"I've come to register for work with you but the kids in Sunhill are vermin so I simply refuse to work in this area. Anywhere else is acceptable but you will have to run it by me first."

Mark took her up to the interview room giving Sylvia the dirtiest look he could muster. Sitting in reception, Lesley Downs one of Education Supply's loveliest and most professional teachers was filling in a timesheet.

"She can't work in Sunhill," she piped up. "She was head of St. Joseph's Primary school and got caught stealing. She had to resign or face being prosecuted."

You could have heard a pin drop. Got you, thought Tara. Just wait until I reference check you. The paperwork was all filed and St Joseph's kindly responded quickly. The reference was ordinary, bland even stating length of service etc. Little did Tara know that this was an agreed reference. Sylvia had stolen from the school but they didn't prosecute. They couldn't face being all over the local press, so she was forced to resign. Then with an agreed reference, here she was, clear to work.

Tara was in a hurry to get out of the office. She had a game of squash booked with her friend Debbie at the health club they were both members of. She gathered her papers together, picked up the work phone as she was on call this weekend and wished everyone a great weekend. She clicked the automatic garage door up and drove out of the garage, her black Porsche gleaming in the sunshine.

Simon was heading to Brands Hatch this weekend with his expensive toy. Tara couldn't wait to say goodbye to him and spend the weekend enjoying a bit of freedom. She drove quickly out of work and reached Pines Health Club faster than anticipated. She found Debbie waiting for her in Reception. Debbie, 5 years younger than Tara at 35, looked very good. Blonde, 5ft 4 married with two children, Debbie was a very happy girl always ready to take any positive out of a negative.

"There's a really hot guy just signed in," she said grinning at Tara.

Debbie knew Tara wasn't happy with the amount of sex that Simon thought constituted an active sex life.

"We haven't even got in yet!" Tara laughed.

Both girls hurried to the locker room and got changed. The courts were booked by the session so if you were late you lost some of the time. Debbie pushed open the door leading into the corridor and Tara, with her head down, walked straight into a solid wall of man.

"I'm terribly sorry," she said, glancing up at this poor chap she'd just crashed into.

It was only when she caught a proper look at him that she realised this must be the 'hot guy' Debbie had referred to earlier.

He smiled at her and laughed.

"Don't worry about it, you can bump into me anytime." He stuck his hand out. "David Foster pleased to meet you."

"Tara Black," she said, shaking his hand and laughing. "Likewise."

She turned and headed to the court.

"Well," said Debbie. "It must be fate. That was the guy I told you about."

"Did he have a wedding ring on?" asked Tara.

Debbie started howling with laughter.

"And what does that mean? You don't wear one."

"Still need to know sweetie," said Tara.

"It hasn't stopped you yet," laughed Debbie.

"And for that, you're going to pay," said Tara, whacking the ball.

Six games later tired and spent, a shower and a swim were on the cards. They went back into the locker room and changed into their bikinis.

"Good job Stephanie did my waxing," Tara laughed, pulling on her bikini bottoms. "I wonder if he's only played squash?"

"We are about to find out," Debbie replied.

They grabbed a towel each from Chloe at reception and wandered over to the pool. No sign of him. Tara felt disappointed. They swam a few lengths and Tara climbed out of the pool. She hated swimming but Debbie kept going. She liked to do her 60 lengths. Tara headed towards the jacuzzi, which lay hidden in an alcove surrounded by potted plants. She wasn't taking much notice but suddenly there he was sitting in the jacuzzi on his own.

"Hello again," said David, smiling.

Tara was mortified she wasn't at her best. Make up all over and her hair had gone fluffy, not the usual poker straight style she preferred.

"Mind if I join you?" she asked, getting in anyway. "I haven't seen you here before, how long have you been a member?"

"I joined about a month ago," he said.

Tara couldn't stop looking at him. Not quite her usual type. She liked them dark, tall and slim. David was 5ft 10 with green eyes and blonde hair but he looked pretty good, that's for sure. They talked and talked. She felt she'd known him for years. Married, no children, his wife was a doctor and worked long hours. He had opened his chartered surveying practice 5 years ago and now had more time to relax. The conversation was interrupted by Debbie getting into the jacuzzi.

"Oh, lovely!" she said, letting the hot water soak into her.

David started to get up.

"Well girls, it was lovely meeting you both. See you soon."

As he left the jacuzzi, neither of them could resist looking back at him as he walked down the side of the pool.

"Nice arse," sighed Debbie.

"I cannot disagree," said Tara. "Come on, time to go home."

They returned to the locker room, showered and changed ready to go home. They said goodbye to Chloe on reception, handed their towels in and made their way to the car park, just as David drove past in a white Aston Martin.

"He's becoming more interesting by the second!" said Debbie.

"See you same place, same time, next week," said Tara, kissing her goodbye.

4

Tara got home just in time to say a quick goodbye to Simon. He was looking forward to spending all weekend going round and round a race track in his fast car. As she switched the TV on to hear the news, her mobile rang. It was her friend Jackie. Jackie was a PA and currently working on an engineering site.

"Hi Tara, are you free this evening?" she asked.

Tara had quite fancied a nice quiet evening alone in the house.

"What's on offer?"

"Well," said Jackie. "A few of us are going to DeLucas for tea would you like to come?'

Tara knew a few of us meant Jackie and men.

"Ok," she said. "What time?"

"Seven pm? is that Ok with you? Because we'll be coming straight from the site."

Tara checked her watch. She had time to sort her hair out.

"Yes, that's good. See you there."

Tara pulled on a short black dress. It was a beautiful night and DeLucas overlooked the beach so it would be pleasant dining outside.

When she arrived, Jackie was already there and as predicted she had four guys with her. One guy stood out a mile. He was so fit, all floppy hair, brown eyes and legs like a racehorse. Tara could not stop looking at him. Jackie introduced Mike, John, Andrew and finally Guy. Tara nearly fainted. Guy had obviously been to the best school money could buy and he stood out like a sore thumb. Tara shook hands with them but when it came to Guy, he held her hand longer than necessary and kissed her on both cheeks.

"Delighted to meet you," he said.

He was all man. He had the deepest, sexiest voice she'd ever heard. With beautiful, curly hair, which he kept flicking back, he looked like a model from an aftershave advert.

They had a great night, laughing and joking. It turned out that Guy surfed. He had worked for a year as an Engineer then spent a year surfing in all places around the world, from South Africa to Hawaii and Tara knew something was going to happen.

The guys wouldn't hear of Jackie or Tara paying and at the end, they all headed towards the car park. Guy had parked next to Tara. He stopped and lit a cigarette, taking a long draw.

"So," he said. "Where did you stay in South Africa?"

"We stayed at Camps Bay," she said, getting her car keys out of her bag.

"It's nice there. That's where we were surfing."

He took one more drag on his cigarette and threw it to the ground. It happened so fast Tara didn't realise what he was doing. He slowly wrapped his arms around her waist and started stroking her hair.

"I'm going to fuck you," he drawled slowly and brushed his lips against hers.

She felt his tongue enter her mouth and her hands instinctively went around his neck. She pressed herself into him. It was a long, slow, lingering kiss.

"I'm staying at the Marriott," he said. "Would you like a nightcap?"

"I'll follow you there."

They got into their cars. The Marriott was a ten-minute drive. Tara was so excited at what was going to happen. She followed him to his suite of rooms and as they walked in, he kicked the door shut and grabbed Tara, kissing her and pulling her dress off. She started unbuttoning his shirt and fumbled for the belt on his jeans. She couldn't wait to feel him inside her. They fell on the bed and kissed passionately. Then Guy entered her. He couldn't get enough of her. Tara thought she was going to explode. He was fucking her slowly and hard and she felt the exquisite pleasure building inside her. They both came together and then lay back stroking each other.

"You are so beautiful and horny," said Guy.

Tara never liked the lying in bed together part, so she quickly recovered and jumped up. She pulled her dress back on and hunted around for her shoes.

"Where are, you going?" he said.

"Got to go." She leant over and kissed him on the lips. "Bye, see you later."

She left him there lying on the bed wondering what the hell had just happened. Tara found her car and drove home. As she walked into the room the telephone was ringing. It was Simon.

"Hello darling, I've done a best time ever," he said.

"I'm so pleased."

"The car went well so I should get a good lap time tomorrow."

Tara smiled. It was so easy.

"That's great," she said. "Let me know how you get on tomorrow."

It was so damn easy.

Tara woke up with the wind and rain lashing at the windows. One of the downsides of living 500 yards from the beach. Simon gently snored beside her. He'd had a lovely weekend at Brands Hatch but he didn't get back until well after 1 pm, which was fortunate for Tara as she was fast asleep and had missed being bored senseless about his motor racing.

The alarm went off at 5.30 a.m sharp. Simon stretched and rolled over onto his back.

"For God's sake, what time is it?" he moaned.

"The usual time the alarm goes off Simon, 5.30."

She didn't give him a chance to go on and on. He didn't mind spending the money she earned, on exotic holidays or quaffing champagne in First Class but he couldn't stand Tara being on call. He thought that work should start at 9 a.m and finish at 5 pm.

Tara took a shower then boiled the kettle and made some hot water and lemon. She took a peek at the beach from the kitchen window. The views were spectacular from their house and every day she realised how lucky she was to live there. The work phone was secure in her dressing gown pocket. It had to be with her at all times, particularly on a Monday, the busiest day of the week for emergency cover. All sorts of mishaps occurred to teachers over the weekend. She ran upstairs, dressed quickly and set off for work.

At six-thirty all hell broke loose. Everyone needed cover. First call was from Ken Turner.

"Morning Tara, err bit of a problem. The dog's run off across the paddock with my false teeth."

Tara counted to ten. She could not believe the crap that was coming out of this man's mouth. The time had come that he needed telling.

"Look, Ken," she said. "It's as simple as this. If you don't want to work just say and we won't contact you."

"No, no I'm telling you the truth," Ken sighed. "Bruno is away across the field with my teeth. You need to replace me."

She got him off the phone and quickly sorted a replacement for him. It was beyond her why Sunhill Academy kept requesting him. His reliability was appalling but still, they wanted him. Maybe it had something to do with the Deputy Head being his drinking partner and best friend. It sort of worked that way in education.

Tara switched on the computer. Matthew James, a supply History Teacher, was scheduled to attend an interview at Moorside C of E academy at 11 am. If he was successful, he'd be securing work through until December. Tara saw his name pop up on the system and started reading. He was terribly sorry but he had a hideous migraine, so he couldn't possibly attend the interview but he had contacted the school direct, to advise them of the situation. Tara hit the roof. Why did she bother? He didn't know the client and had no business contacting them directly. It was Education Supply he should be ringing but as usual none of them took any notice. Top and bottom of it was that he didn't want to go. It made Education Supply look very unprofessional. Tara picked up his application form and rang his number. It rang and rang and eventually the message service kicked in.

"Matthew," she said. "Tara from Education Supply. I've picked up your email. Can you call me back as soon as possible to clarify the situation and for us to reschedule your interview, thanks." She noted the time, 7.15 a.m.

Tara opened the front door ready for Mark and Val to come in at 7.45. Carrie, Daniel and Tara had parking spaces at the back of the building and never used the front door. The phones didn't stop. Quite a few teachers had thrown a sicky, this usually happened when the weather was bad at the start of the teaching week. Good news for Education Supply.

Daniel came in through the back door. Tara heard him click the kettle on in the tearoom.

"Morning sweetie, anything happened?"

"Yes," replied Tara. "I'm ready to kill someone already."

The switchboard rang again and Daniel quickly took a booking from Northolme C of E Academy for a Year Four teacher. He grabbed the standby list and rang Yvonne Brown. Yvonne didn't really need to work. Her husband had retired from being very high up in the Metropolitan police so they were very comfortable and took a lot of holidays. Tara often thought it was strange though, how she could scoff three free school dinners and had on one occasion asked a head if she could use the phone, only to be caught speaking to someone in Florida for twenty minutes. Yvonne agreed to go to Northolme so Daniel began the paperwork.

The switchboard rang again so Daniel quickly grabbed it.

"Good morning, Education Supply," he said only to find a sheepish Yvonne on the line.

"Oh, hi again Daniel, it's Yvonne. Look I'd forgotten that I have friends coming over for lunch today so I can't do Northolme."

Daniel went from 0 to 100. What she really meant was that Northolme was a tad too far away so she'd decided that she would give it a miss.

"Ok, Yvonne," said Daniel through gritted teeth. "Thanks for letting me know."

As she started to speak, he put the phone down on her. He had better things to do on a Monday morning than waste his time messing around plus he had to refill the vacancy. Tara heard what was going on and grabbed the details from him.

"Leave it with me. I'll sort it out. You get the coffee on."

A relieved Daniel was only too happy to let her.

The first interview came in at 9 a.m. A Maths specialist Ray Pringle was surprisingly on time. His dress code, of course, was a typical teacher these days. Jeans and a t-shirt with a leather holdall, at fifty years old his appearance didn't do him any favours. Mark took him up to the interview room to complete the paperwork. Mark was quite a shy 22-year-old, not very confident and certainly no match for Ray Pringle. He came down into the main office and approached Carrie's desk.

"Erm, Carrie?" he said. "I'm sorry to interrupt you but he's refusing to do a DBS check, to see if he's got a criminal record."

"Well he can't go into any school or near children without one so he's fucked," sneered Daniel.

"Daniel, be a love," said Tara. "Go up and have a word with him please?"

Daniel went up to the interview room, sat down and tried to point out the ins and outs of a DBS or Disclosure and Barring Service, check. Daniel had just got his backside in the seat when Ray surprised him.

"Look," he said forcefully. "I'm a serving police officer. I don't need one."

Daniel sighed.

"If you're a serving police officer Ray, you will appreciate that everybody needs an updated DBS. We have to complete a DBS application for everyone that comes into contact with children."

It was Ray's turn to sigh.

"Right," he said. "And I suppose that's another 44 quid is it?"

"Not if you joined the update service Ray," said Daniel, looking him straight in the eye.

It never ceased to amaze anyone at Education Supply how these people thought. All they had to do was follow the clear directions given by the DBS and join the update service then their certificates would be updated regularly. Either they couldn't be bothered or they just wouldn't listen. Daniel came back downstairs into the main office and handed the paperwork to Carrie.

"Over to you," he muttered. "All yours."

"I'd like to say I'm looking forward to this but I won't," she said.

The day progressed nicely after the morning rush and about 11ish Tara decided she'd had enough. Out of courtesy, Matthew James should have explained himself by now. But first, she got Mark to go onto the BT site to see if he had a landline number, as according to him, he did not. Bingo he lived at home with his parents and there was the address listed under his father's name.

Time and time again Education Supply asked their staff for landline contact numbers only to be told that they didn't have one. Tara knew they were lying as it was very convenient to avoid a mobile or use excuses.

On the fourth ring, an elderly lady answered.

"Hello Mrs James, is Matthew there?" said Daniel.

"I'm sorry dear," she offered immediately. "Matthew is at work today."

"Really?" spluttered Daniel. "I'm from Education Supply and Matthew was supposed to be attending an interview today at 11 a.m, for a long-term job through us."

"I know nothing about that dear," said Mrs James. "He received a call at 7 this morning and was showered and out by 7.30."

Daniel felt his face going redder and redder with rage.

"Kindly ask him to call us, please?"

Another day in the life of a responsible supply teacher.

5

The school bell sounded and a pleasant hush descended upon the school. Izzy loved this part of the day when all the children had settled into their classrooms and lessons began. Her phone was lying on her desk and she saw the screen light up displaying the name Tanya. It was a text asking if she was free tonight. Could it seriously be Thursday already? The weeks seemed to go quicker and quicker every year.

"Yes," replied Izzy. "Where did you have in mind?'

She knew the answer before the text arrived: "Limes."

The place seemed to be of great interest to her friend but she could hardly blame Tanya as it was much more upmarket than most of the dives they went to. Immediately Izzy's thoughts moved to Jonny Devroe. There was no doubting he had an effect on her. He made her feel excited and nervous at the same time. She shook herself. Not a good idea she thought. He was dangerous and she knew it.

She tried to look at the computer screen, checking her budget but she couldn't concentrate. Her mind kept going back to Jonny. She replied to Tanya that, yes Limes was good and she would see her there at 8 pm as she had a governor meeting from 5 to 7.

Jackie the Head came in with some papers.

"Can you sort this out, please? I've overspent again on the books that we needed and the damn caretaker has gone mental in B & Q so we need to find the money from somewhere."

Izzy looked at her incredulously. Did the head think she had a magic wand? St Magdalene's was over-budget year in and year out but Jackie didn't seem too concerned. Yet again, as usual, it would be down to Izzy the school business manager to perform some sort of financial miracle and source funds. Either way, Jackie would have to explain herself at the next governors' meeting. Now that would be interesting.

She could hear the children out on the school playing field. It was lunchtime already. Izzy had lunch. She loved school dinners, then sat in on an early year's performance meeting and headed home. She threw open her wardrobe doors and said out loud: "What am I going to wear?" At school, she was the most disciplined person but in private she was a shopaholic. She loved to shop. Her three-bedroom house was crammed with clothes, shoes and handbags of every colour. She opted for a lovely black Ralph Lauren dress, capped with a cream collar and cuffs. She showered, applied her makeup and pulled her long thick black hair into a messy ponytail.

"Not bad," she said looking at herself in the mirror. "For a 40-year-old."

Tanya got to Limes first. She ordered a glass of white wine and sat at the bar. Izzy was the worst timekeeper ever but she wanted to be alone to try and catch Johnny's eye. The place was far quieter than last week which Tanya thought was a good thing, as she could see more of who was coming in. Jonny wasn't on the door but Tanya didn't have to queue. She wondered what was going to happen to Izzy. She had lit up like a Christmas tree when first introduced to Jonny. A spark had flown and Tanya knew from experience this wasn't necessarily a good thing. Izzy, divorced and a failed relationship behind her, wasn't desperate but Tanya thought to a certain degree Izzy was quite needy and Jonny had a past. They were two such different people. Izzy went to Mass every Sunday for God's sake. Nobody would know what Jonny Devroe got up to. He certainly wouldn't be going to confession.

As Izzy approached Limes, she felt that frisson of excitement again. She was on radar alert. Her eyes roamed everywhere looking for him. Good, she thought, he's not here. She tried not to look too interested, whilst wondering if it was his night off. She entered Limes noticing that it wasn't full but not empty either, just right for being able to see around the place. She plonked herself down at the bar with Tanya.

"No queue got straight in," she said.

"You look lovely," said Tanya, noticing Izzy had gone the extra mile and had made a special effort. Had to be for Jonny.

Tanya bought her a glass of white wine and started to chatter away about her day in the bank and the characters from Sunhill, the small town that used it. Suddenly Izzy felt the hairs on the back of her neck stand up as Jonny appeared behind them.

"Hello, ladies. It's lovely to see you again," he said smiling.

Izzy wondered how the hell he did it. He had this animal quality about him almost feral and oh boy did he look stunning dressed all in black. Izzy had to catch her breath and Jonny signalled to the barman.

"Let me get you another drink."

Izzy shot 'a don't you dare look' at Tanya but she completely ignored her.

"Two white wines please."

Great thought Izzy, I can hardly say no while he's standing there.

"It's quiet tonight," said Tanya, trying to make conversation.

"Don't hold your breath," said Jonny, shrugging. "It's early yet. It'll liven up. So," he continued, turning straight to Izzy. "What do you do? I haven't seen you around before."

Izzy's mouth just ran away with her like an express train.

"I'm a school business manager," she explained.

Jonny hadn't decided what he thought she did for a living but somehow hadn't imagined it would involve working in a school. She looked more like a businesswoman.

"So you're in charge of running the school?" he said.

"In theory," said Izzy, smiling.

He wouldn't have a clue what her responsibilities entailed. Schools were run like a business now, not a place of education and Izzy had a first-class finance background. Jonny started walking away but he touched Izzy's shoulder as he turned to leave. Izzy actually felt weak-kneed. One touch and she was like a gibbering wreck. She inwardly remonstrated with herself. Pull yourself together for God's sake. But there was definitely something electric there. She could feel it.

The girls bumped into a few people that they knew.

"Turn around now and face the bar," spat Izzy. "One of our parents has just walked in!"

It was an occupational hazard in any form of education. The parents could behave however they liked but the staff could not and parents certainly did behave badly. It was too late Shelley Riley had spotted Izzy and her friend. Shelley 45 years old, overweight and blonde looked as if she'd been stuffed into the skirt she was wearing and had far too much make-up on. She thought she was gorgeous and her kids, a boy aged 9 and a girl 5 who was a mini-me of her mother, could do no wrong. St. Magdalene's had had running problems with her Jake but they knew any intervention from the head sent Shelley into orbit. She was constantly up and down having meetings with Jackie. Thank the lord he'd be off to secondary school soon.

Shelley marched straight over.

"Out on a school night?" she said pointing her chubby finger directly at Izzy.

"Could say the same about you Shelley," said Izzy, smiling.

That shut the oversized fat woman up. She really looked quite ugly when she scrunched her fat face up like that. Izzy glanced up and noticed that Jonny was smiling at her. He had seen exactly what had happened and appeared to find it funny. It must be written all over my face, thought Izzy, exactly what I think of this woman. Shelley trotted off, balancing her fat legs on six-inch heels and went to join her equally overweight and overdone friend on the opposite side of the bar. She didn't appreciate a member of the school staff answering her back.

"There must be a dress code or ugly list," said Tanya, looking down her nose. "How the hell did those two freaks get in?"

"Her husband is loaded," said Izzy, laughing. "He's the local scrap man."

"You've got to be joking," said Tanya. "I thought she must be married to the rag and bone man."

Jonny was still smiling at her so she looked away. Now and again she made a point of checking his movements. She wanted to look at him. She couldn't get enough.

By ten pm Izzy couldn't take the vile looks from Shelley any longer.

"I'll have to go, Tanya," she said. "I'm being clocked by Harold Steptoe's wife over there and it is a school night."

"For fuck's sake!" shouted Tanya over the noise of the music. "You're a grown-up."

"I know, I know but I'm knackered. Let's come back on Saturday and make a night of it?"

Tanya shrugged.

"Ok, Saturday it is."

They headed towards the exit with Tanya leading the way. Jonny was there and he stopped talking to the other doorman.

"Leaving so early?" he said, putting his hand on Izzy's arm.

"Work tomorrow," she replied.

Her friend looked at both of them.

"We will be here Saturday though to make up for it."

"Good," he replied.

Izzy gathered up her handbag, looped it over her shoulder and walked out the door. It wasn't until she got home when she was rummaging through her bag looking for her house keys, that she noticed a scrap of paper. It was a note with a mobile number on.

'Ring me if you want lunch or a drink, Jonny.'

She hadn't noticed him putting the note in her bag. Izzy wasn't sure if she liked it or thought it was underhand. No way, she thought. I will tear it up and ignore him but she didn't. Somehow, she just could not part with Jonny Devroe's mobile number. She kept turning the note over and over in her hand.

6

Tara was just about to leave the office on Friday afternoon when Jack Baxter sauntered in without a care in the world. He stood in reception beaming at Val.

"Has my DBS arrived yet?"

"It only went off two days ago Jack!" she said laughing. "I'll check and see what stage it's up to. You are in a hurry."

"I'm keen to get out to work Val. Bills to pay," he said.

"Well take a seat in reception, while I check the system for you."

Jack did as he was told and took a seat in the reception area. Daniel glanced at Tara. They were both thinking the same thing that he was in a hell of a hurry.

Tara thought back to when Jack originally came in to register with Education Supply. He already had a DBS from the previous school he worked at. The document showed no previous convictions but had been processed two years ago. Obviously, Jack knew the system. Each time he changed schools he needed to complete a new DBS application unless he was on the update service which of course Jack wasn't.

Val joined him in the reception area.

"It's only at Stage One, Jack," she said. "They've only just received it."

Jack made it clear he wasn't happy with the situation in fact, he became quite agitated. Then he managed to pull himself together and headed for the door.

"Ok, thanks," he said. "Keep me posted." And left.

Carrie looked up.

"We need to call his ex-head and get that reference in," she said. "He's in too much of a hurry. We told him at the interview that a DBS can take up to two weeks."

Tara and Daniel agreed. Red flags were being raised all over the place concerning Jack Baxter. Tara collected her squash bag from behind her desk and assured Carrie that she'd deal with it first thing Monday morning. At 4.30 on a Friday afternoon, she didn't have a cat in hell's chance of pinning down a head.

Tara made her way over to the Pines Health Club to meet Debbie for their weekly game of squash. She hadn't given much thought to Daniel Foster but now she found herself recalling their meeting the previous week. David was definitely not her usual type but if you liked that kind of thing, he was attractive. Tara preferred tall, slim, dark brooding kind of men and David was the opposite blonde, stocky, lovely eyes and great fun.

As she pulled into the car park, she immediately noticed both his Aston Martin and Debbie's BMW convertible. Well, she thought to herself, it makes a game of squash a bit more interesting. Chloe at reception gave her a towel and told her that Debbie was already getting changed. When she entered the locker room, she found an uncharacteristically flustered Debbie, in the process of getting changed.

"Hi," she said, plonking her bag down.

"Hello," said Debbie. "I can't stay after the game sweetie, my little boy's poorly so the mother-in-law's got him and you know what she's like!"

Debbie's mother-in-law was a right old bag. She loved to be difficult and make Debbie think that she abandoned her two kids at the drop of a hat. The stupid woman failed to appreciate that her perfect son worked in Manchester Monday to Friday and that he would pick Sean up as soon as he got home. Not to mention that Debbie worked nine to three Monday to Friday at a small accountancy firm in Sunhill.

"I don't know how you do it," said Tara, who really wasn't into kids and playing Mummy. "Thank God I didn't want them."

"Come on let's get cracking," said Debbie laughing. "Did you spot David on your way in?"

"No. I saw his car and I've noticed that court 1 is being used so I'm presuming he's in there."

"He's really nice," sighed Debbie, secretly wishing she was single again.

"He is," agreed Tara. "But not really my type. I'm not sure if I fancy him," she said lowering her voice in case he could hear from the next court. Then started to laugh. "I sound like a fifteen-year-old!"

"Nothing wrong with that sister. You're never too old for a man to stick his hand up your skirt."

"Sure, makes a girl feel good," said Tara, who couldn't stop laughing. "I'm forty Debbie maybe it's time to start behaving myself?"

"No, no," cried Debbie. "I'm a lost cause so I have to live my life through you, so you go girl."

When they got on the court, Debbie couldn't concentrate and needless to say Tara slaughtered her. Her mind went back to Guy and the Marriott Hotel room. She would definitely sleep with him again. Jackie had texted her a few times but as yet Tara hadn't found the time to reply. They came off the court and Debbie quickly shoved her work clothes into her bag.

"I'm sorry," she said. "I haven't even got time to shower. Will you book us in for next Friday? I have to fly."

"Of course. I'm going to stay and have a swim. See you next week."

"Of course you are!" said Debbie with a wicked wink, as she headed towards the door.

Debbie knew that Tara was rather hoping she might bump into David, again. Her friend had never changed where the opposite sex was concerned.

Tara had a quick shower to remove the sweat and then put her new bikini on. A bit much for the Pines but David would like it. She gently eased herself into the pool and wondered why the place was so quiet. Very unusual for a Friday night. She swam a few lengths then got out of the pool and bumped head-on into Chloe, armed with a cleaning brush.

"Is there a fire? Where is everyone?"

"Don't speak too soon," said Chloe laughing. "I'm having a lovely quiet shift. There's a black-tie boxing event on in Sunhill and most of our male members are going. A few have played squash but they've gone home to get changed."

Chloe started to walk away, then turned.

"Oh, by the way," she said. "David Foster told me to say, he's sorry he missed you."

"Thanks, Chloe," said Tara, her voice a pitch higher.

Did he really now, she thought. Well, he can bugger right off. I'm not coming here for the pleasure of seeing him.

On the drive home, she realised it had seriously irritated her that David had left early. To be honest, she had been ever so slightly looking forward to seeing him. A bit of male attention never went amiss. Oh well, there was always next Friday.

When she pulled into the drive, she knew Simon was already home. His Porsche stood there gleaming and where it went, he went. He would set off again soon for the ritual Friday night drink with his brother Tim. Tara wondered how he didn't get bored rigid with Tim. They worked together every day, not that Tim did much because he was never there. Simon ran the company and Tara thought Tim seemed quite happy to take a back seat and of course take the money. It was a very successful company. Simon had doubled its size in the last five years and the expansion wouldn't end there. Whereas Tim's education amounted to just about leaving school at the required age, Simon had gone on to become an Accountant so he made all the decisions.

She clicked open the garage door. May as well put the car away she thought and entered the house via the kitchen where Simon was putting the fish and chips into the oven to keep them warm. Poor man, thought Tara, I should try harder on the food front.

"Good day?" he asked looking up.

"Just the usual," she replied jogging up the stairs to get changed.

Simon was still in his shirt and tie. He wouldn't get changed until he went out. He had to read the Financial Times cover to cover before he moved anywhere. It always made her chuckle because every Sunday she had the Sun on Sunday delivered and every Sunday she'd get the 'how can you read that crap it's utter rubbish' and the minute Tara was out of the room she knew she'd come back and catch him reading it.

"Don't forget dinner at eight on Saturday with John and Melissa!" he shouted up the stairs.

"Ok I won't," she shouted back.

Another boring outing to look forward to. John had screwed half the girls in his company but Melissa had used her pea brain and got herself pregnant so John's divorce from his current wife was turning out to be extremely acrimonious. She was a physiotherapist and didn't take too kindly to being usurped by a 25-year old blonde bimbo. The huge age gap between John and Melissa was almost embarrassing, especially for John's two children. But Simon and John were best friends so dinner had to be done.

Simon disappeared at 8.30 and after a long soak in the bath, Tara decided to return Jackie's texts. She didn't get much sense from her as she was out with colleagues, which meant all of the men she worked with and was probably legless by now. Her replies were indecipherable. Tara poured herself a large glass of red wine and had just settled down to watch some TV when her mobile rang.

"Hi," said a deep male voice. "Why aren't you here?"

Tara glanced at the phone screen and saw Jackie's name but she couldn't recognise the voice, what with all the background noise from what sounded like a pub rammed to the rafters with desperate Friday night revellers.

"And this is?" she asked.

"You could freeze ice on your arse you're so cool!" said the voice, laughing.

Tara recognised him. Guy of the Marriott Hotel bedroom.

"I'm not there," she said. "Because I wasn't invited."

There was a moment's pause.

"Well I'm inviting you," he said.

"And you're out of luck," she replied. "I don't think my husband would like it."

"Shame," he tutted. "Have a good weekend."

And there the call ended. Tara smiled and remembered what he felt like and his lips on hers. The smell of him.

She had an early night and only vaguely heard Simon come in but then went straight back to sleep. At 5 a.m she was wide awake. Time to get up and go for a run, no excuses. She looked out at the beach. Perfect and the sun was just coming up. She grabbed her trainers then found her phone and waited for it to boot up. She liked to know what was going on and if she had missed anything. A text was waiting for her but the number was not logged onto her contact list and she didn't recognise it. As soon as she read it, she knew who it was from.

'I've spent all night thinking about you.'

Guy had sent it fifteen minutes ago. I wonder? She thought and started typing.

'Did you now?'

He replied in a matter of seconds.

'What are you doing now?'

A smile played on her lips and she considered what he may have in mind. Her fingers hit the buttons.

'Just got up and I'm going for a run.'

The screen flashed.

'Meet me at the lost children shelter on the promenade in 20 minutes.'

Tara's heart started to beat excitedly and she texted back immediately.

'Ok.'

He was staying at the Marriott for the duration of his engineering project. The hotel stood at the opposite end of the beach from Tara's house, about a mile away. She ran down from her garden onto the cliffs and started a slow jog onto the sand. Then it dawned on her that she hadn't given Guy her mobile number so Jackie must have done. She made a mental note to kill her. All her friends knew that they could not give out Tara's mobile number. But hey ho, maybe just this once.

She neared the old shelter and saw him waiting for her. There he was not a bead of sweat on him. He looked like a fit marathon runner in his shorts and Nike top and was extremely well tanned. The moment she came up to him, his arms were like an octopus everywhere. He didn't even speak to her but turned her to face the wall. Tara submitted. She liked the way he took charge. She felt one of his knees part her legs and his hand pulling her shorts down. She could hear him tugging at his shorts and his breathing became erratic. He started to kiss the back of her neck then he entered her fucking roughly from behind. Tara had never felt so alive she was desperate to come. She pushed back wanting him to go deeper and deeper until she felt him shudder as he came. All of the noise of the crashing waves had been drowned out by the intensity of their lovemaking but she suddenly came back to the real world.

He turned her around, pulled his shorts back up then kissed her on the lips.

"Got to go," he said. "See you later." And ran off in the opposite direction.

Tara couldn't believe it. 5.25 in the morning, she had been fucked and left with her shorts round her ankles in a lost children's shelter. It was exactly what she had done to him the night they met at the Marriott. The irony wasn't lost on her. She started to laugh no way could she be bothered to run now. She pulled herself together and headed home.

7

Monday morning again. Tara had been lucky so far as no standby emergency calls had come in really early. This gave her time to be at her desk and settled. It worked better this way but Education Supply could never predict what time the first call would arrive. Tara reflected that it was odd that Izzy hadn't communicated and this usually meant she was up to something. Note to Tara, she thought, text Izzy. As it happened Izzy was the first call.

"Hey you," she said when she heard Tara's voice. "I've forgotten what you look like!" and laughed down the phone.

Tara smiled. Izzy was her best friend and she missed her even after a couple of days.

"I need Jessica for Year One, honey. Can you sort it?" she continued.

"With a bit of luck, yes," said Tara. "I'll get back to you. And I shall call you tonight for a catchup. I just know something is on the boil with you, Izzy. You're far too quiet!"

Izzy howled with laughter.

"You know me so well and yes I have news."

"Excellent," said Tara. "I'll call later when Simon's out of the way."

Tara didn't feel up to Jessica Delves this morning. She couldn't be bothered with the circus her life had become, or rather not become, as Jessica loved a bit of drama. Fortunately, Carrie came in early and offered to sort it.

Tara kept wondering what Izzy had up her sleeve. Something was brewing which usually meant a man. Then she was thrown off track by a call to John Baxter's head. Mr Brown took Tara's call straight away which was unusual in itself. Normally it was difficult to get past a head's PA. They could give any doctor's receptionist a run for their money. Tara thanked him for taking the time to speak to her and explained the nature of her call.

"Which agency did you say you're calling from?" asked Mr Brown.

"Education Supply."

"You are the only agency to contact me about this," he said. "And I'm aware that John Baxter has registered with a few. It's a very onerous situation. I'm not surprised he needs the DBS quickly. He's been arrested, currently awaiting a trial date."

Tara felt quite shocked but couldn't think why as the incidents she had experienced over the years amounted to epic proportions.

"John was responsible for our school trip to America," continued Mr Brown. "And allegedly, he borrowed from the deposits paid upfront by the parents. It only came to light when a parent had to cancel because his son broke a leg and he asked for his money back. John, allegedly, had already spent the money and couldn't repay it. The parent notified me and I had no alternative but to call the police. The bank account had been emptied," sighed Mr Brown. "Two and a half thousand pounds gone. I'm now tearing my hair out because if the school can't replace the money, the trip will have to be cancelled and that, as you can imagine, simply cannot happen."

Tara began to feel sorry for the man.

"And to make matters worse," growled Mr Brown. "The little fuckwit is trying to push his DBS through before the trial and inevitable conviction so that the DBS certificate comes back without a conviction. It beggar's belief!"

Tara really didn't know what to say because it had now become very clear what John Baxter had been intending to do.

"I'm so sorry Mr Brown," she said. "What an awful predicament he has put your school in."

"I know," he said. "But I am impressed by your agency. You're the only one who has bothered to check him out correctly. I assume you smelt a rat?"

"Yes. He's been in twice demanding his DBS and that alone told us something was wrong. We informed him at the interview it would take up to two weeks, not two days."

"I'm going to have a word with our cover manager. We'll start using your company from now on," he said. "I'm extremely pleased with your vetting procedure."

Tara thanked him then relayed the information to the rest of the staff. Nobody could believe it. Taking money from the kids seemed an all-time low. As it happened a week later John Baxter appeared on the front page of the local paper, the Daily Echo. He would never work in a school again that was for sure and true to Mr Brown's word he gave Education Supply a long-term History position. A positive from a negative if ever there was one thought Tara.

8

Izzy needed to get the story straight in her head before speaking to Tara. Saturday as planned, she had met up with Tanya at Limes. She watched the groups of girls in front of her with naked interest. They didn't have a clue. They were dancing around the men like predators and looked so desperate. Each one fought to outdo the other on the dance floor. Izzy had never really noticed before now just how stupid they all looked. She slyly got out her compact mirror, making sure nobody saw her and reapplied her lipstick. Her hands were shaking so much, it took longer than she hoped. Jonny wasn't on the door but she knew he was there. He made her feel nervous and edgy.

Tanya could sense that Izzy was hyper. She looked gorgeous. She had a black and white jumpsuit on with high heels. Lots of men were looking at her. Tanya felt slightly jealous of Izzy. Most girls felt the same, except of course Tara. But Izzy had no idea how stunning she looked, nor the effect that she had on men. Now Tanya began to regret introducing Jonny to Izzy. She hardly knew him but she'd been in Limes previously with her friend Steph and he told her then she'd never have to queue up while he was around. At the time, she loved it. Now she'd made a few enquiries and it seemed Jonny had been quite a bad boy in his time, not to mention the dubious company he kept. Apart from the prison sentence, he had his fingers in some dodgy pies. Maybe he's a bit older and wiser, thought Tanya. Little did she know what an evil, ruthless bastard Jonny Devroe could be, especially when he believed for one moment that he'd been crossed.

Izzy and Tanya managed to do a bit of catching up, shouting over the loud music. The place was heaving. Then, out of the corner of her eye, Izzy saw him appear. He didn't come over straight away but she thought he would at some point. Tanya stood up.

"Two mins," she said. "I'm popping to the loo." And headed off.

Izzy turned her back on the dance floor and started talking to Mitch the barman. Suddenly Mitch stopped mid-conversation and moved away rather quickly. Izzy hadn't seen Jonny approaching.

"You didn't ring me," he said putting his hand on her shoulder.

Izzy felt quite intimidated and didn't like his tone at all. Who the fuck did he think he was speaking to? She flicked her long, thick black hair back and picked up her wine glass.

"I don't go out with criminals," she said.

As soon as the words were out of her mouth, she regretted it. If looks could kill, she'd be fifty feet under. He gritted his teeth and squeezed her shoulder a bit harder.

"That was a long time ago," he snarled, then spun around and headed back to the door.

When Tanya came back from the Ladies', she knew immediately something had happened.

"Alright, what's going on?"

When Izzy explained, Tanya looked very worried.

"He's only a doorman Tanya, who cares what he thinks?"

Tanya nodded and ordered more drinks. She could feel Jonny's eyes burning into them. She only hoped her friend knew what she was doing. Jonny's world was a place that Izzy had never set foot in.

Jonny stormed into the office. He liked his women with a bit of backbone but nobody spoke to him like that. He was buzzing. He didn't know whether he wanted to slap her or fuck her but it turned him on. She didn't have a clue who she was dealing with. One of the other doormen came looking for him.

"Phone call Jonny, it's the boss."

Jonny took the call and listened.

"No problem," he said eventually. "Gives me the details and I'll sort it."

He left the club and ordered Stevie to bring the car round the back. He gave the driver instructions to go to the local pub. Micky Jones had overstepped the mark. He was at the low end of the market, selling drugs in and around pubs. Jonny had timed it perfectly, they arrived just as Micky was leaving the Four Bells, cigarette dangling out of his mouth and legless. Tonight had been a good night for him, he was meant to keep his drug pushing low key so as not to step on other dealers' toes but he wasn't big in the brain department. As soon as he saw Jonny approaching, he knew he'd stepped on the wrong toe, the one belonging to Jonny's boss. Micky headed up a dimly lit back lane which was a mistake in the current circumstances.

"In a hurry Micky?"

Micky stopped dead in his tracks. He could feel the sweat running down his back and he thought it best to front it out.

"Alright Jonny?" he said.

"I'm fine Micky. Busy night?"

"Just been for a few pints, Jonny."

"So it's not true what we've been hearing about you then, is it Micky?"

Micky tried to keep walking but Jonny pinned him against the wall.

"We've heard you're selling gear at the club again and that isn't happening. You've been warned once and that was a friendly warning."

Micky started to tremble. He was no match for Jonny. Jonny looked at the pathetic sight in front of him. People like Micky were just vermin in his eyes, who didn't care what was in the low-grade shit they peddled. But Micky had been peddling it at Limes and that could cause big problems. All it took was for one of their customers to collapse and the police would be there. Micky dealt very low-grade cocaine.

Jonny continued staring at Micky like something he'd trod in. Micky had dug his own grave and he just wouldn't listen. The greed had got to him.

"Clearly the friendly warning last time didn't work, Micky," he said and smashed his fist into Micky's face.

He felt his nose break and slumped to the floor. Full of drink he didn't know what had hit him. There was blood all over the place.

"Final warning," said Jonny and casually strolled back to the car as if nothing had happened. "Let's go, Stevie," he said and the car roared into life.

Stevie glanced at his watch. It had taken ten minutes to sort Micky out. Jonny got back to Limes, had a wash and combed his hair. He reported back to his boss Tony Adams that this time Micky had heard the friendly advice he'd been given. Then he returned to the door as if nothing had happened.

The girls had a great night. Izzy didn't even notice Jonny wasn't around, due to the number of cocktails she had consumed.

"Time to go," announced Tanya who was now legless.

When they reached the exit, they saw Jonny. Izzy full of bravado, brought on by the drink, gave him a smile. He pushed his way past a group of girls trying to chat up one of the other doormen and just as she turned to say goodbye, he went to touch her face. Izzy noticed his knuckles were all scuffed and one of them had been bleeding. He followed her glance and immediately pulled his hand away. Just then his mobile started to ring in his pocket and he turned away. Saved by the bell.

In the taxi going home, Izzy couldn't stop thinking about Jonny. He was so good looking but her mind kept flashing back to his hand so she decided to see what Tanya thought.

"Did you see the state of Jonny's right hand?"

"Yes, I did. He must have done it at work maybe on some bottles. He didn't leave the club all night."

"That's what I thought," said Izzy. "We'd have noticed if he'd gone out."

Izzy decided then and there to dismiss it.

The girls didn't live in Jonny's world and it would never have occurred to them what caused that scuffed and bleeding hand.

9

On Sunday morning Tara had a nice lie-in. Sundays were always spent at Simon's parents for lunch, 1.30 prompt, which Tara looked forward to. His parents Giles and Dorothy were very interesting people, who had started the business from nothing. Tara collected the newspapers from the front door, put the coffee on then had a quick look at her phone.

There was a text from Izzy. *'Fancy a catch up later, 4-ish at the Pantry?'*

Tara decided the timing was perfect and replied, *'See you there.'*

The Pantry was a small coffee shop in the village that Tara and Simon lived in, which meant Tara could walk there after consuming a lot of red wine at lunch and Simon could sprawl on the sofa and sleep it off, without being disturbed.

After a pleasant and delicious lunch, she walked up to the village to meet Izzy. The little bell chimed on the door as Tara opened it making Izzy look up from her paper. Tara started laughing.

"Now this is a first, you're actually on time!"

Izzy was notorious for being late but she just smiled. Izzy ordered a latte and Tara ordered her usual macchiato.

"Come on then let's have it?"

"Well," started Izzy. "I've sort of met this guy."

Tara settled in for the long haul.

"He's so gorgeous and I can't stop thinking about him."

"What does he do and where did you meet him?"

Izzy took a deep breath this was the bit she was dreading.

"I met him at Limes, he's the head doorman."

"Are you seriously serious? A doorman?"

"He's not rough or anything the exact opposite. He's older than the usual type, well-spoken and really friendly," gabbled Izzy feeling an overwhelming need to explain.

"Izzy sweetie, really all doormen are bad news and you know nothing about him. Most clubs allow drugs and God knows what. He will be into all sorts of things and more importantly know some seriously dangerous people."

Izzy sighed. This was just what she expected Tara to come out and it wasn't what she wanted to hear.

"Look he's not like that Tara I'm sure he's a really nice guy," she said.

Tara drained her coffee cup.

"Be it on your own head but you're well out of your depth here. Be very careful."

Izzy smiled and perked up a bit now the lecture was over.

"I will, I promise."

She remembered Johnny's bloodied hand and thought there's no point mentioning that. Tara would only freak out and anyway she was sure he must have done it moving crates around for the bar staff. They chatted about work for a while. When Tara went to pay the bill, Izzy took the opportunity to check that Jonny's note was still in her bag. The girls kissed goodbye on both cheeks and Izzy promised to keep Tara up to speed.

When Izzy got home, it was only 6 o'clock and she felt bored. She had nothing to look forward to except work and the odd night out. She needed some excitement in her life. She opened her bag and found his number. She turned the note over and over in her hand wondering if this was the right thing to do. It's only a drink for God's sake what harm can it do? Sod it, I'm ringing him

Jonny answered on the third ring. He sounded furtive as Izzy had dialled 141 first so the call would show up as number withheld. When she heard his voice, she dried up and went blank. She was more nervous than she thought. Then she plucked up the courage and found her voice.

"Hi Jonny," she said. "It's Izzy from Limes."

Jonny smiled. He knew she'd ring. They always did.

"Well hello you," he said. "You fancy that drink then?"

"Yes, that sounds great, if you're free tonight?"

He was and they agreed to meet at the Speckled Hen at eight. Unusual she thought because the Speckled Hen wasn't in town it was way out in the suburbs. Maybe Jonny lived out there? She really didn't know anything about his private life. Then came the problem of what to wear. Casual or quite formal? After an hour she decided that black jeans, ankle boots, a nice crisp white blouse and black jacket would look smart but not too over the top. Casual would suffice for the Speckled Hen.

Izzy drove there but it did cross her mind that he hadn't offered to come and pick her up. Perhaps he did live near the pub. She decided not to question it as she wasn't prepared to let him know where she lived at this point.

Jonny was sitting in the corner waiting for her holding a bottle of beer. He stood up when she walked in and bought her a glass of white wine. He knew what she drank at Limes.

"You look lovely," he beamed and he meant it, she really was stunning.

"Thanks," she said and started to giggle like a silly teenager.

The night flew by. She felt she had known him for years. He was such good company, charming and funny. Tara had no need to feel concerned. He was a genuinely nice guy. Izzy was having such a good time she didn't want to leave but she knew she must.

"It's a work night Jonny, I'm going to have to go."

"That's a shame," he said. "We're having a lovely time."

"I know but can't go into work knackered!" she laughed.

"Come on then I'll walk you to your car," he said and took her hand.

In the carpark, her heart was pounding, wondering if he was going to kiss her. She didn't have long to wait. He turned her to him, locked his hands behind her neck and gave her a long, deep, smouldering kiss. God, he's good thought Izzy. She'd never been kissed like that before by anyone.

"Until the next time," he said and walked back into the pub.

She was beaming like a Cheshire cat all the way home. When she got in, she went into autopilot and it wasn't until she was lying in bed that she thought back to what a great night it had been. But she kept remembering how people were constantly coming up to him saying 'Hi' and asking how he was. Like everyone seemed to know him wherever he went. Izzy leaned over and turned out the bedside light. Well, he's a doorman, she thought. He must know thousands of people. So what? He's popular and everybody likes him.

Jonny walked back into the Speckled Hen. He liked Izzy but he was pleased she had gone. He had a little bit of business to take care of and not the sort a school business manager would understand. What she didn't know wouldn't hurt her and surely she realised he was a doorman.

Izzy stood at the school gates on Monday morning. It was part of her job to ensure the safety of pupils and parents, as they entered the school property, especially given the number of cars that ferried the kids in and out. The poisoned dwarf parent Shelley Riley parked her Range Rover as thoughtlessly as ever, blocking everyone in, then stomped up to Izzy. What a vulgar woman Izzy thought, even at 8.30 she's got her tits on show. She was wearing the lowest top imaginable for a school drop and her make-up looked like it had been applied with a trowel. But this morning, she was looking at Izzy in a really strange way, smirking and clearly dying to say something.

"My, my you're keeping bad company these days," she said, the words bursting out of her botoxed duck lips.

Izzy looked down her nose at the woman not having a clue what she was talking about.

"I beg your pardon?"

"Jonny Devroe?" Shelley flew on. "Does the head know who her school business manager is busy with?"

Jesus Christ fumed Izzy, one drink and this poisoned dwarf knows all about it. The Speckled Hen isn't even in Sunhill.

"He was in trouble a long time ago Shelley," she said. "Jonny isn't like that anymore."

Shelley laughed uncontrollably.

"One born every minute!" she cried and rushed off get her kids into school.

Izzy was left standing there furious. Other parents must have heard the exchange. Anyway, what did Shelly Riley know about anything? She only listened to gossip in the schoolyard. If Izzy could have stopped for a moment and joined the dots, she would have remembered Shelley's husband was a scrap dealer. He wasn't averse to stepping out of the box occasionally and illegally disposing of hot cars. He would definitely know the likes of Johnny Devroe. Unfortunately, Izzy did not live in this world and was far too naïve for her own good.

10

Carrie was trying to sort out her desk. It had been so busy that morning. She looked at the clock, five to ten. She wondered if the primary teacher who had booked an interview for ten o'clock would be on time. Tara was away with Simon in London. He had a business meeting and she'd fancied tagging along for a night away and a bit of shopping whilst he was busy. So now the office was a man down and Carrie had to maintain the works phone on standby.

Sunhill Academy rang in requesting a Music specialist and by the time Carrie had sorted that out, it was ten past and still no sign of the interviewee. It was common these days for teachers to break interview appointments without even bothering to let anyone know.

Carrie found the woman's contact details and rang her. No reply so she left a voicemail asking why she hadn't turned up. Carrie knew it was a waste of time but it made her feel better that she'd drawn attention to how ignorant and rude she was. She knew for a fact that the candidate wouldn't get back to Education Supply but at least in a roundabout way she'd been pulled up.

After lunch, Daniel was tearing his hair out. An allegation had been made against David Noble, Education Supply's most popular primary teacher. He was always requested back at every school he was sent to, so Daniel found this a bit odd.

"Wish Tara was here," he said, loud enough for Carrie to hear but he knew he'd have to deal with it.

It was quite a serious allegation and the police may have to be called. David was accused of kicking a football in the classroom and it had bounced off the ceiling and struck a child in the head. After getting off the phone from the head Daniel turned to Carrie.

"Surely he couldn't be that stupid, not David Noble? Do you think it really happened?"

"No way not David," she said, shaking her head. "Well, I'd like to think he didn't do it. We have other teachers I could name who might be that stupid but not him. He's one of our best teachers."

Daniel wrote all of the information down that the head had given him and Education Supply's safeguarding procedure sprang into action. The head removed David from the school and told him to go home pending further action. Daniel had a bad feeling about this one as the incident had been referred to the general teaching council as a safeguarding issue. An allegation had been made of unacceptable professional conduct. Education Supply would be informed later that day when the meeting would be scheduled. In the meantime, Daniel called David as he needed to get him into the office to write out a statement of what had occurred that day.

David answered the phone when he heard Daniel's voice and started crying. Yes, it was all true. Daniel wanted to kill him. The trouble he had caused was spectacular. A grown man, 42 years old and married with one child behaving like the school clown. What was he thinking of? Daniel knew David was really a bright and kind human being, so he had clearly lost the plot but he was struggling to hold onto his temper with the man.

"We need you down the office asap so that we can ascertain from your point of view exactly what happened this morning. This is a very serious allegation and it looks like the boy's parents are going to involve the police."

They agreed to meet at two o'clock. Education Supply had a duty to find out all of the facts regarding each incident. Nine times out of ten allegations turned out to be made by a troublemaking kid who didn't like being told what to do. However, Daniel sensed it wasn't the case with this one. David was far too upset. Daniel gave Tara a quick ring. She didn't answer so he left a voicemail filling her in on what had happened. If a fly farted in the office when she wasn't there, she wanted to know and went crazy when notes weren't left for her keeping her informed. But she was right. Their business survived on communication and who knew what, where why and how.

David arrived at two o'clock on the dot and had already written a statement of the events. He looked terrible, deathly pale and his eyes red raw from crying. Daniel despised him on sight. It never ceased to amaze him how on paper these people were bright and well educated but acted sometimes worse than the children that they were supposed to be in charge of. He was old enough to know a lot better. He'd been with Education Supply for four years and they'd never had one problem with him. In fact, it was the exact opposite the schools loved him and always requested him back.

"I'm so, so sorry," he kept saying to Daniel but Daniel could not be bothered to listen to him and told him to calm down.

"Listen, David," he said quietly. "This is very serious. I will hold onto this statement but if the parents do involve the police it will go to a higher level. The head is speaking to the parents now."

David held his head in his hands and started blubbering, snot running down his face.

"I can't remember doing it."

Daniel looked at him dumbfounded.

"You cannot recall kicking a football in a classroom and it bouncing off the ceiling striking a child?"

"No, no I can't," wailed David.

Daniel decided to draw the meeting to a close. He couldn't get any sense out of him but he had the written statement and that was all he needed at this time. There was no merit in pursuing this any further until all of the facts had been gathered. He sent David home but he was furious and so was Carrie. Education Supply's reputation would be shot to hell if this made the papers. The atmosphere in the office sank to an all-time low.

When Tara came back the next day, Carrie filled her in regarding the incident that had occurred yesterday then she read David's statement. He'd stated in black and white that he'd had the week from hell, starting with his friend being killed in a car crash. His grandmother had died on Sunday and then as if that wasn't bad enough, his wife had left him. He was so distressed that he'd paid a visit to his GP who'd instantly prescribed Valium. Tara could not believe her eyes. How in God's name did a professional teacher think it was alright to be in charge of children when he was pumped full of Valium? She had no way of verifying anything, other than possibly contacting the GP but one thing was clear, David was on his way to the general teaching council and would be formally interviewed to see if he was fit to teach.

One thing that was abundantly clear in David's statement was that he had mentioned twice that he had no recollection of the incident because he'd taken the Valium. That was convenient she thought. Tara checked with Carrie that Daniel had spoken to the head at Grangewood Primary School. Carrie told her that the head was quite upset as it was out of character for David to behave in this manner. He'd been in and out of this school for over three years and up until now, the head confirmed he was the best supply teacher she'd ever had.

Tara made a silent prayer that the rest of the day would be 'normal' or as 'normal' as any day owning a supply agency could be. Another day in the life of a responsible supply teacher. Tara was earmarked for a 3 pm interview but that teacher also failed to turn up and Tara made a mental note to phone another ignorant person and ask why they'd failed to contact the office. It was getting worse. In all walks of life, people had no manners but Tara often thought that teachers should know better when they were trying to set an example to the kids they were supposed to be teaching. It constantly surprised her.

She was just about to leave when Daniel arrived, falling about with laughter. He'd just interviewed a Teaching Assistant who'd worked as a team leader at Santa's grotto. The whole office erupted into laughter. How anyone could add that onto an application form as employment history was beyond them.

Tara left the building and got into her car, still smiling. Then the car phone rang and Izzy launched into the information regarding her drink with Jonny. Tara listened, giving the obligatory yes and no.

"Just be careful," she said when Izzy paused for breath. "You don't know anything about him."

Izzy agreed and promised to let her know what was happening. The smile had vanished from Tara's face and once again that red flag went up, the one that went up every time Jonny Devroe's name was mentioned. Tara had asked Izzy when she would be seeing him next. She didn't know as he didn't have her mobile number, she only had his. Tara thought that was strange but hopefully, Izzy was old enough to know what she was doing.

As Tara clicked the garage door up and started to drive out, she saw Max Armstrong getting out of his car. Now there was a sight to warm a girl's day. His office backed straight onto hers and they saw each other most days pulling in and out of their garages. Max was a lawyer and very, very attractive. He wasn't very tall maybe 5ft 10 but he was as lean as a whippet. Tara had been told that he ran for Sunhill Harriers three times a week. He closed his car door and walked over to Tara's driver side. Tara immediately put the window down.

"Hi," he said. "I need to pop over to see you. We are all getting together on the traders' association to argue with the council over the business rates and we need your signature."

She didn't need to think about this longer than a nanosecond.

"Okey dokey, I'm in all day tomorrow," she said cheerily.

"Right," he said. "I will ring first but it should be in the morning. I'm in court all afternoon."

Tara thanked him and drove away. She had noticed the wedding ring but she knew he was interested in her. He had predator written all over his face. Tomorrow should be interesting. At least he was something to look forward to. She'd have to wear something tight and clingy she thought nearly going through a red light. She'd liked him for a long time but they only met once in a blue moon in the back lane. Five years had passed since she bought the building and he certainly appeared very friendly whenever they coincided in the car park.

Max also thought tomorrow would turn out interesting. He picked up the audio machine and started dictating his court notes for his PA but his mind fixed on wearing his navy-blue, pin-striped power suit to impress the lovely Tara. Everybody around their offices had noticed her but she kept herself to herself and didn't even frequent the local coffee shops so no excuse to bump into her until now. Frankly, he couldn't give a fuck about the business rates.

The next day Max phoned Tara's office to warn her he was coming. She decided to entertain him in the interview room. No intent there then, she thought. Just because it was totally private and away from prying eyes. He came into the office like a human dynamo and Tara led him up to the interview room. She'd opted for a Prada, black, skin-tight pencil skirt, huge heels and a crisp white shirt, her long blonde hair in a ponytail. She looked like sex on legs and he couldn't keep his eyes off her, appraising every inch of her body.

He went through the paperwork and they both had a giggle together about some of the celebrities in their street and did a fair amount of slagging off the local businesses around them. Finally, Max placed his elbows on the desk, rested his chin on his hands and commenced a steady stare deep into her eyes. She couldn't help notice that he had the most divine long eyelashes framing his hazel coloured eyes and apart from everything, he was beyond confident.

"You're gorgeous," he said.

This caught her unawares. So she put her head on one side and smiled. He half stood up and leant over the desk, cupped her face in his hands and started to kiss her. She returned his kiss and they moved round to the corner of the room against the wall and really started to kiss each other deeper and deeper. His hands strayed to her bottom then moved upwards caressing her breast. She felt off the scale of exhilarated. He knew how to kiss and she was so excited and turned on. He had the most unique smell as if he'd just got out of the shower. Tara didn't wear underwear and she knew he'd discovered this and it seemed to turn him on. She could feel how hard he was hard as he pressed himself closer and closer to her. They both stopped and stepped back from each other.

"You're a great kisser," he murmured. "I've been dying to do that for years."

"You're not shy," said Tara.

He asked for her mobile number and promised to be discreet. Tara opened the desk drawer and found one of her business cards, then quickly scribbled her mobile number on the back and gave it to him.

"Right I have to go. I'll be in touch," he said, brushing his lips briefly against her business card.

They went downstairs to the main office together and she showed him out. Daniel looked at her. Everyone was out so they had the office to themselves and Tara couldn't wait to tell him what had happened.

"You lucky bitch," he said. "You've fancied him for ages, go for it!"

"I shall, don't you fret about that," she laughed.

Her phone blipped and it was a number she didn't recognise but she knew at once it was Max. *'you feel so good'* said the text. She didn't reply. It wouldn't hurt him to work for it.

11

Tara believed not many people knew just how early she started work in the morning. But the next day, as she drove up the back lane of her offices and clicked the garage door, her mobile beeped. The message:

Get the kettle on gorgeous.

She hadn't saved his number yet but she knew it was Max.

Ok.

Just as she replied, his garage door opened and there stood his black SUV still hot from driving. She parked up, unlocked the back door then quickly deactivated the alarms and took the divert system off the phones. She heard his footsteps, the slam of the back door. Her heart beat faster and faster with the anticipation of what was going to happen. Max led her up the stairs and stopped on the landing. He started to undo the buttons on her blouse and greedily licked her nipples. She cried out with pleasure and moved straight to his belt. In two seconds, his trousers were down. He was so hard. They fell to their knees and Tara took him in her mouth. Max groaned. He hadn't bargained on that. He felt himself coming into her mouth. Too soon. He lay Tara on the thickly carpeted floor and unzipped her tight black skirt then spread her legs and thrust his tongue deep inside her until she could take it no longer. Shuddering from head to toe she reached a tremendous climax just as they heard the garage door go up. They both jumped to their feet, sorting out their dishevelled clothing. By the time Carrie walked in, they were sitting at Tara's desk downstairs in the main office. Fortunately, at that moment the switchboard rang and Carrie answered the first call of the day.

The day flew past. Tara had no idea what the time was, she felt as if she was floating on air, even more so when the flowers arrived. No card but she knew they were from Max. In his office, Max checked the time too and wondered if she'd received the bouquet. He'd also sent his wife flowers just in case she spotted the name of the florists on their joint bank statement. After all, it was Kate that earned the money. He couldn't stop thinking about Tara and could feel the familiar heat between his legs when he pictured her lying on that expensive carpet waiting to accept him. She was so horny.

12

Izzy finished work and went home. Three days had passed and once again the note was going around and around in her hands. She couldn't decide if it would appear desperate if she rang him. Then it occurred to her that Jonny had no way of contacting her, so bugger it. She keyed his number and this time did not withhold hers. Jonny picked up.

"Hi," she said nervously.

"Here she is, the girl of my dreams!" he said, recognising her voice.

Izzy loved that and it went straight to her head. She couldn't stop giggling. Jonny was at Limes and what she couldn't see, he was in the middle of a business meeting and coked out of his brains.

"Come and pick me up," he demanded and Izzy agreed.

The meeting over, Jonny and his friends took turns at swilling vodka from the bottle and crushing ecstasy pills which he proceeded to take with another gram of coke. He was in the mood for entertainment and he knew Izzy lived on the road between Limes and his house. He was lying on the office couch when Stevie the driver knocked on the door.

"Jonny there's a bird at the door for you saying she's picking you up."

Jonny smiled and galvanised himself into action.

Izzy had worn a long skirt with a slit up the side and made sure that Jonny got a flash of bare skin on her lovely long legs but she couldn't work out what the hell was wrong with him. He was all over the place, very animated so she assumed he was drunk.

"Let's go to your place," he said putting his arm around her shoulder.

At first, Izzy wasn't too sure about him coming back but as soon as she had him in her car, all doubt flew out the window. She revved the engine and took him home.

Sleep had been impossible so as soon as the light began creeping into her bedroom, she jumped up and pulled on an oversized t-shirt. Jonny lay there snoring softly. Izzy couldn't stop staring at him, he was so handsome but she couldn't believe what had happened the night before.

When they got back to her house, he had started kissing her and asked her where the bedroom was. As soon as he reached it, he collapsed onto the bed and passed out, fully clothed. However, when Izzy woke up the next day, he was naked under the covers so at some point he must have woken up and undressed. Izzy smiled he probably hadn't wanted to wake her up. At least he was thoughtful she told herself. She quickly showered and got ready for work then placed a cup of coffee on the nightstand and tried to wake him. He mumbled in his sleep and turned over so she left him there in her bed and went to work.

On the way, she rang Tara from the car phone.

"You've left a complete stranger in your fucking house?" raged Tara. "Are you out of your mind Izzy?"

Izzy started to feel a tad apprehensive.

"I do know him. He's Ok. He'll just get up and leave."

"Seriously Izzy," said Tara. "I'm starting to get worried about your state of mind. Did you hide all your jewellery?"

"Tara, you're over-reacting!" fumed Izzy, unable to keep a lid on it any longer. "Of course, I didn't hide my jewellery. It will all be Ok I promise."

"Well," sighed Tara. "Just let me know your house is in one piece when you get home tonight." Then exasperation got the better of her. "He's a fucking doorman Izzy!"

"It will be Ok I promise," repeated Izzy and disconnected the phone.

Tara realised there was no reasoning with her stupid friend while she was under the spell of the great Jonny Devroe. Meanwhile, Jonny yawned and stretched stroking the luxurious bedding he found himself wrapped up in. Put his flat and belongings to shame that was for sure. He'd heard her trying to wake him up but couldn't be bothered to talk to her, knowing she'd have to go to work anyway. He touched the coffee cup which was now stone cold and got up. He had a little look round the bathroom and decided to have a nice, long soak then he got dressed. He sat on the bed and the room began to spin. He'd done too much gear the night before which was becoming a bit of a habit.

He couldn't believe he'd ended up at Izzy's house. Jonny raided the fridge and made himself a bit of breakfast then patted his pockets, looking for money for a taxi. Realising he didn't have any, he found Izzy's number and called from his mobile. Normally at school, her phone was on silent but she noticed the screen light up and recognised the last three digits of Jonny's number. She grinned from ear to ear thinking he must be ringing her to thank her for last night.

"Any chance of a lift home?" he said. "I've got no money."

Izzy thought he was joking.

"I'm at work Jonny. It's not that easy to get out."

"It's only a school for Christ's sake," muttered Jonny under his breath. "But you're only ten minutes away. Surely you get a break?"

Izzy was irked but when she thought about all the hours she'd stayed behind at school, she decided to do it. She told him to make himself at home and she'd be there in half an hour.

Izzy made her way to Jackie's office and told her that she thought she'd left her straighteners on. Jackie was mortified and had visions of Izzy's house burning down so told her to go immediately. Jonny did as instructed and got the frying pan out for more breakfast, assembling the butter, bread, bacon and red sauce. He had a nice little appetite from the coke he'd consumed and didn't think it necessary to do any of the clearing up, that being woman's work.

He was waiting at the door when she drove up.

"Sorry about this," he mumbled. "I'll go to a cash point later."

He gave her directions to his flat and as they ploughed deeper into one of the seriously least desirable areas Sunhill had to offer, Izzy thought he must have made a mistake. But no, this was where he lived in a council flat. She could not believe he lived there. Somehow, she thought he would have at least owned his own home. Trying desperately to make conversation, she asked him if he drove. He told her he hadn't passed his test yet, which at the time she didn't really take on board. As they stopped, she thought he was going to ask her in but he just unclipped the seat belt, kissed her on the cheek and was off.

Izzy decided it was prudent to swing by her house on the way back to school, just to check everything was in order. When she arrived, she wished she hadn't. It ruined her day. It was like a bomb had exploded in her lovely kitchen. Dirty dishes left everywhere, frying oil all over the floor and the cooker and the worktops and everything.

Later that day, Jackie, her boss and the head of the school, asked her to go with her to pick up an iPad she was borrowing from St. Joseph's, a school close to St. Magdalene's. As they stopped at a red light, Izzy happened to glance over to speak to Jackie and couldn't believe her eyes. Jonny appeared beyond Jackie's head and behind the wheel of a shiny black Mercedes with two guys in the back. She could not take this in. He'd told her he couldn't drive. What was he doing behind the wheel of a car? There must be some sort of mistake she must have misheard him. It bothered her all day then it suddenly dawned on her that perhaps he had felt bad that he had no money and had inconvenienced her by calling her at work. She decided to mention it the next time they met. Jonny hadn't spotted Izzy as she was in the passenger seat of Jackie's car. If she'd been driving, he would have seen her straight away. He was driving Tony Adams's motor, his boss, on the way for a pickup.

Izzy desperately wanted to share all of this with Tara but she kept thinking there had to be a logical explanation. Suddenly she had a vision of Shelley Riley's fat mouth telling her there was one born every minute.

After the pickup, Jonny hung onto Tony's car. He wouldn't miss it for an hour. He drove over to his friend Donna's flat. He'd arranged the night before that he would be at her place for 1 pm and he was always such a good timekeeper. The door was on the latch so he let himself in. Donna used to be a model but at twenty-nine they called her over the hill so she worked at Limes as Tony's right-hand girl. She knew where all the bodies were buried and over the last two years had become indispensable to Tony's setup. She was lying in bed waiting for him so Jonny slid into bed beside her and edged up against her smooth body. Jonny momentarily thought about Izzy but switched his attention straight back to Donna. She was gorgeous, streetwise and most important of all lived in the real world, their world. A lethal and irresistible combination.

"I'm here," he whispered in her ear.

He could feel himself getting harder by the second.

"What took you so long?" she said, turning to face him.

His hands began exploring her body, touching her in all the places she liked to be touched. Then he kicked off the sheets and was between her legs. She gave herself up to the moment and came like an express train. She forgot all about their boss Tony Adams ever finding out. He didn't like any of his staff to fraternise with each other but what he didn't know wouldn't kill him, thought Donna.

Izzy couldn't concentrate all afternoon so when the bell rang to mark the end of the school day, she was straight out the door. On the way home, she decided she would ring Jonny. She needed to speak to him. But as soon as she opened her front door, she caught the smell of frying oil, most of it coming from her kitchen floor. The place stank and it took her ages to sort out. She knew she would never be able to tell Tara about this.

Meanwhile, Jonny had got back to his little council flat, showered and was just drying himself on one of his threadbare towels when he caught sight of himself in the chipped mirror. He posed, turning this way and that and reassured himself he was one good-looking man. The hours he spent in the gym were clearly paying off. He wasn't classically handsome but he had an edgy quality, a ton of attitude and he certainly knew how to present himself to the ladies. He savoured the view in the mirror for a moment then started to get ready for work.

He only worked three nights a week on the door at Limes and this suited him right down to the ground, as it left him plenty of spare time to carry out other duties for Tony. He heard his mobile ringing but by the time he found it in a jacket pocket, it stopped. He saw that it was that bird he'd pulled from Limes. He groaned and thought to himself that he would have to stop doing so much coke, as he remembered how he'd ended up at her place last night. He glanced around his shabby flat and cast his mind back to her lovely home. She must have thought he was drunk and he sure as hell couldn't remember a thing about last night. She didn't go mad or even kick him out but then again, she was a nice, innocent girl. He threw the phone back into his pocket. He couldn't be bothered to ring her back. Izzy replaced the receiver but it did cross her mind that he should be ringing her, thanking her for her hospitality. But hey ho, he must be busy.

Tanya and Izzy giggled hysterically, getting out of the taxi at Limes. Jonny was on the door and spotted Izzy immediately.

"Straight in ladies," he said, removing the red ropes and letting them pass.

"You look gorgeous," he said to Izzy.

He took her to one side and put one arm on the wall blocking her escape.

"Thanks for last night," he smiled. "It was great."

"Don't worry," she smiled back. "I will catch you later," and ducked under his arm.

It didn't seem an appropriate time to discuss the state he'd left her house in. Both girls had downed a few cocktails at another bar before getting to Limes and Izzy had fessed up to Tanya what had happened with Jonny. Tanya being well drunk and without any clear vision, told her not to worry and even suggested they go to Limes. Izzy had intended giving the place a miss but after four Cosmopolitans thought it was a cracking idea. However, Jonny disappeared for the rest of the night which suited her as she could forget all about him and enjoy herself. They both became steadily drunker.

13

Tara had received an obscene amount of texts from Max. In fact, there were so many she'd lost count. Not sure whether to be worried about this or not, she decided to be flattered. After all, she got zero attention at home. Perhaps if she had a Porsche badge between her legs, Simon would pay her more attention. The texts ranged from I'm going to fuck you, I can't wait to fuck you or I'm falling in love with you, which Tara found a bit too much and way over the top. Meanwhile, Max played the dutiful husband and father, screwing the wife from time to time and taking his little girls pony-riding, even if he did end up flirting with the stable girls who all thought him wonderful and charming. Simon, on the other hand hardly ever made love to Tara so she decided to fuck Max at every given opportunity. He was married so he wouldn't want anything other than just sex. It would certainly cheer up their working days.

Tara was on interview duty today but first, she had to deal with the David Noble incident. Thankfully the parents had decided not to involve the police and Tara guessed this was more due to good work on the part of the headteacher. If the General Teaching Council found David responsible, then he deserved everything that was coming to him. She rang David to give him the date of the proposed hearing. Thankfully he didn't answer so she left him a voicemail explaining that the GTC would be writing to him with confirmation of the meeting that was scheduled to take place. She quickly dictated a letter to Val for David, creating the paper trail just in case David pretended that Education Supply had failed to notify him.

The new candidate arrived for his interview and Mark walked him through the main office, towards the stairs leading to the interview room. Carrie tried really hard not to stare. He was small, stocky, white and wearing a Barbour. Nothing wrong with that but he also sported one of those flat caps that farmers wore and the weirdest thing for a forty-year-old, huge expanders in both ear lobes. In fact, his lobes were stretched to the maximum, huge and dangling. He looked ridiculous. Tara knew it was a complete waste of time interviewing him as under no circumstances would

Education Supply employ anyone who looked like that. What was the teaching profession coming to? They don't even care what their appearance is like. Setting standards in front of the children was fast going out of the window. To make matters worse this chap was a Geography specialist. Perhaps if his chosen subject had been Art he just possibly may have got away with the expanders.

His name was Liam Hussain which everyone in the office thought was strange for obvious reasons. However, he had worked for four years at Redmount Secondary School, certainly no walk in the park. In fact, it was the area's most challenging school. That's how he got away with his appearance, thought Tara. No-one would have batted an eyelid there. As the interview progressed, she could hardly stand the arrogant, full of himself, jumped up little shit a moment longer. It was embarrassing the way he conducted himself. He even bragged about his much younger partner who was having their baby. Paedophile thought Tara. Little did she know how old his partner actually was.

She got him out of the building and gave his application paperwork to Mark insisting he was vetted and checked quickly. She made a point of telling Mark that she felt he was dodgy and a story was going to come out. After years of interviewing teachers, she could spot it a mile off. Tara knew that they would never employ him but it was still their duty to check everyone out.

When Tara told Daniel that Liam was an arrogant little fucker, Daniel burst out laughing. He loved to see Tara getting edgy. Daniel also informed her that her phone had been blipping over and over again and he winked at her, knowing it was Max. Daniel secretly thought that the man was needy and was contacting her far too often. Tara quickly read the texts which mainly asked when could he see her again.

She cast her mind back to one morning when she had spotted him in the back lane after her garage door had been left open. She remembered watching him chatting to a group of lawyers from offices in the same streets. Their two streets were full of lawyers, insurance brokers and estate agents. He was holding forth with an attentive audience hanging on his every word. He loved being in the spotlight and certainly knew how to play to the gallery. A force unto himself she thought. Tara had found herself wondering then what his wife looked like. She knew from other people that Kate was a GP. Tara giggled to herself back then imaging a woman all twin set and pearls. As it happened Tara was quite right. Kate, bless her was frumpy and overweight but she did earn a lot of money and

Max did like to spend it as fast as she could hand it over, poor cow. On the face of it though they were the perfect power couple.

As it happened Max had a plan. All the other partners were in court that afternoon so he was the only one in and that meant empty offices upstairs. He waited until Sandra his PA had popped to the ladies, then hurriedly inserted the name Jennifer Brown into his diary, scheduled for 1 pm. Next, he sent a text to Tara inviting her over, instructing her to use the name, Jennifer Brown. He knew she'd make up some imaginative excuse to get out of her office.

At 12.45 Max had a good look in the mirror and satisfied with his image, started to look forward to their meeting. Right on 1 pm, his internal phone rang and Sandra announced that Jennifer Brown was in reception. He asked her to bring Jennifer to his office. The minute Sandra got back to her desk, she texted Angela at Finch Brown and told her that Tara from Education Supply was in with Max under an assumed name. Every girl in the adjacent streets knew Tara Black and was well jealous of her looks not to mention her flashy Porsche. They were sure her husband must have bought it all for her. How little they knew. Simon wouldn't lend her a fiver if she was desperate. He would tell her to go earn it.

Today, Tara wore a beautiful black and cream Chanel suit which clung to all the right places and she strode in on huge Louboutin heels. Max took one look and couldn't believe his good fortune. She was the horniest woman he'd ever laid eyes on and yes, he'd forgotten all about the woman he'd been shagging at his running club this morning and all the false promises he'd made to her. Tara didn't need anything from him other than sex and he could handle that.

"You look fantastic," he drooled.

"You're only flesh and blood," she said and started to laugh.

He almost prowled out of his chair and bent her over his desk. Her face was pushed against some legal documents and she did her best not to get lipstick on them. No foreplay for this one she thought. She'd been turned on the moment she'd entered his office. Max Armstrong wanted it and he was about to give it to her hard. He navigated his fingers into her and she felt his hard dick entering her. Pens, pencils, paper clips went flying as her hands scrabbled to grip and push back hard into him. He came really quickly. It was almost too exciting for him Tara thought. She stood up and pulled her skirt back into position then kissed him goodbye.

"I'll see myself out," she said, leaving him standing at his desk with his trousers down and expensive Boss shirt flapping.

As she wandered back to Education Supply the thought did cross her mind that her dry-cleaning bill was about to double.

"Carrie sweetie, what's going on this afternoon?" she asked as she settled back at her desk. "Anything I should know about?"

Carrie smiled. Everyone knew that Tara put her heart and soul into the business not to mention all her savings.

"Two interviews and Daniel is out visiting a school that's using one of our competitors."

"Right then," said Tara. "I'm off home for a run. I'm on call tonight so I'm taking the works phone. See you all in the morning."

Shed only driven fifty yards down the back lane when her mobile blipped.

'Where do you think you're going?' read the message.

She knew it was Max before she'd even read it.

'To fuck my secret lover,' she replied instantly.

He was way too clingy for her and what was the silly man doing watching her out of the window? She now knew that his office was on the other side of the building so how the hell did he know that she was leaving?

'And I'm going home to screw my gorgeous wife'

'Enjoy!' she struck back.

Quite frankly she couldn't give a toss if he was screwing Miss World. It was just fun they were having and she crossed her fingers that he wasn't going to be the needy type. She couldn't help smiling. One minute she was lecturing Izzy over Jonny and the next minute she was having sex with Maxwell Armstrong about whom she knew bugger all. Perhaps a solicitor would be better behaved than a doorman?

The next morning Tara had just made herself a coffee in the office when she heard Carrie reversing into the garage. At the same moment, her phone blipped.

'I'm coming over' texted Max. He'd clearly missed Carrie's arrival.

'company staff in no can do'

'I have to see you'

This sounded like he'd gone into a huff, so she ignored it. Anyway, she could hardly make an excuse to Carrie to go over to his office at 6.40 in the morning. Her phone blipped again.

'Back lane five minutes'

Tara decided to tell Carrie that she had left her purse in the car and go and find out what on earth was so urgent. As she closed the back door, she heard the switchboard ring, so that was Carrie taken care of. He was waiting at the front of his garage for her and waved her across the narrow back lane. Neither of them noticed the little silver hatchback tucked around the corner of the building next to Max's. There was no doubt in Kate's mind that Max was up to something. He obviously hadn't factored into his thinking, the stupid man, that he hardly ever got his head off the pillow by eight a.m., never mind six. So this behaviour was completely out of character. Then there was all that time he was spending preening himself in the bathroom mirror. She didn't believe the crap that was coming out of his mouth when he said he needed to catch up at work. Now here, before her very eyes was the gorgeous reason that Max could suddenly get out of bed. She was starting to despise him in fact at that very moment she hated him more than she could say.

14

Izzy was fast approaching the end of a very trying day at St. Magdalene's. She often thought the teachers behaved more childishly than the children. The threat of an Ofsted inspection loomed so all hell was about to break loose. Every contract statement, in fact, every piece of paper in the school would have to be checked and double-checked mainly by Izzy. Her workload had doubled. It was a lot of responsibility for any school business manager and tempers became frayed. A lot rested on a below-par Ofsted inspection. She was just about to put her coat on when her mobile blipped. It was Jonny asking if she had any plans for the night. She immediately felt alive. She would love to see him again. She loved being in his company.

'What did you have in mind?' She quickly texted back.

He replied that he'd like to take her for a drink. She agreed to pick him up at 8 pm and they'd go to the Speckled Hen, the pub that they'd met at previously. She still thought that the Speckled Hen's location was odd as it was out of town, bearing in mind he said he didn't drive. Interestingly she decided to put all of the questions she'd wanted to ask him to the back of her mind. Why spoil a good night? It never crossed her mind either why he wasn't taking her into town where everyone knew him.

Unusually for Jonny, he was feeling slightly apprehensive about what to say to her. They were from different planets but he was desperate to have her and tonight was going to be her lucky night. He paced up and down. She was fifteen minutes late but just when he was about to call her he heard a car pull up, a door slam and the intercom buzz.

Jonny was big on charm, he'd used it all his life to get his own way but he was also quite a mystery. When the charm offensive wore off he appeared cold and had a real disregard for women. They were playthings to be used. He certainly didn't want one as a feature in his life. Izzy would never understand him the way a girl like Donna did but she was a good-looking woman and he was going to have her.

The charm button was switched to high and Izzy couldn't believe how attentive and flattering he could be. She enjoyed a great night with him but still, lots of men kept coming up and talking to him. She thought that it must be his local somehow and he usually took a taxi there. At the end of the evening, he talked her into going back to her place so that she could have a drink. She parked up switched the house alarm off and poured out two Baileys. Her hands were shaking as he was staring at her. It was unnerving but she knew he was going to kiss her. Nothing was going to stop the inevitable. She wanted him so badly that she felt totally overpowered as his big hands started to stroke her hair and he began kissing her. She thought she might faint.

He slowly removed her clothes and began to make love to her as she easily fell into rhythm with him. He was enormous and all man. Izzy couldn't believe how strong he was. She closed her eyes and as she felt herself coming she dug her fingers into his back. She could feel the sweat running down it. Jonny also felt himself coming. Her long colt legs were wrapped around his back pinning him into position.

After a few minutes, they disentangled themselves and Izzy made a dive for her clothes. She was by nature a shy girl and didn't want him to see her naked.

"Quite a little goer," he said laughing but she was already on her way to the spare bedroom to make herself decent.

She could hear him pulling on his jeans.

"Make yourself a drink," she called out.

"No thanks. See you later."

She heard him run down the stairs. Then the front door slammed. She looked out of the front bedroom window. Where the hell was he going? He hadn't even ordered a taxi. Izzy felt her anger rising. She'd been used. He'd fucked her and didn't even say goodbye properly. What the hell was that all about and where was he going at one-thirty in the morning?

Jonny strode nonchalantly down the road. Her house was quite handy as it was very close to Sunhill centre and could easily be walked but en-route was a garage that he needed to be at for 2 a.m. He'd kill two birds with one stone he'd planned before picking up the phone earlier to Izzy.

15

Tara tried to ring Izzy at work. The call was semi work-orientated but she also felt concerned about her friend and wanted to monitor the situation with Jonny Devroe. The receptionist explained that Izzy was in a budget meeting and didn't have a clue how long it would go on for. She made a joke that it would probably be a week as the head had been going mad on the spending front, so Tara left a message for Izzy to get back to her.

Daniel pulled up a chair in front of her desk.

"I'm not sure if this is good or bad," he said, handing her an email and a wad of papers.

She started to read the information but couldn't quite grasp the context of it. The Professional Committee of the General Teaching Council had decided in David Noble's absence, that the allegation of unacceptable professional conduct had not been established, as the evidence presented to the committee was insufficient to satisfy them and that Mr Noble's actions had not been deemed inappropriate. The committee's decision was final and Mr Noble had been found not guilty of unacceptable professional conduct.

"Dear God," said Tara. "He admitted kicking a football off the ceiling, which then struck a kid in the head. He also held his hands up to teaching a class while full of fucking Valium. How did he get away with that?"

"Well he did, said Daniel shaking his head. "And God knows what the head of the school thinks?"

So that was the end of the matter. David Noble remained free to continue teaching without a blemish on his career.

"Don't let him know yet," said Tara. "Let him sweat and wait for the GTC to inform him."

"Now we have Liam to deal," said Daniel. "You were right Tara, one of his references needs further investigation."

"What the hell's he supposed to have done?" she groaned.

Daniel shrugged his shoulders. They'd all grown sick of the minefield, recruiting so-called professionals.

"He was dismissed from his last school but the head isn't saying why. He's written a note on the front cover of the reference, advising us to contact him."

All Tara's company's private calls were made from the accounts' office upstairs for data protection. They couldn't risk anyone walking into reception and overhearing sensitive information. So after Daniel had made the call, he asked for everyone's attention so that he could explain what had been said. It turned out that Liam had been teaching English and had arranged a theatre trip for his class. He took the money from the parents and then went on to forge his credit card statement to say that the tickets had been purchased when they hadn't. When the head had asked him for the tickets as the date of the show approached, Liam found himself in big trouble. The head had backed him into a corner and Liam finally admitted when they threatened to call the police, that he'd pocketed the money. The head instantly dismissed him.

"Wait a minute," said Tara. "Why didn't he involve the police?"

"Same old, same old," laughed Daniel. "He didn't want the school all over the papers. It's a behavioural unit and he reckons they get enough flack. But hold your horses, there's more. The head wouldn't say why but he strongly advised I contact Liam's last employer, Redmount. It seems a bigger story's unfolding at that school which will involve possible legal action."

The switchboard rang and Val signalled to Tara that Izzy was on the line.

"I'll take it in the interview room. Val," she said and made her way up the stairs. This call was best kept private.

"Izzy, are you Ok?"

"Yeah I'm good just trying to figure out this Jonny Devroe guy," she said.

"Why what's wrong?"

"I can't fathom him out," she said with a huge sigh. "He seems really interested in me but the other night, well you know, we erm, well you know."

"Fucked," said Tara, trying to speed up the conversation.

"Well yes," said Izzy. "But then he left straight away. In fact, he just shouted through the bedroom wall and I heard the front door slam. It was really off-putting and I was quite annoyed."

"Look, Izzy," said Tara. "He's a fucking doorman, probably one step away from a gorilla, you need to stop seeing him."

Izzy knew she was right but she felt so alive around him. He was like a drug and she wanted more and more each of him. He was her fix.

"I know you're not going to listen to me Izzy but he's dangerous, be very careful."

Tara wasn't telling her what she wanted to hear and it was getting on her nerves.

"Come on Tara, stop being so dramatic he's not a murderer."

At this point, Tara knew it was pointless and inevitable. Whatever was going to happen would happen.

"Ok," she replied. "But don't come running to me when you're in trouble. And please remember what type of job you have," and she hung up the phone.

Izzy just stared at the receiver. Never in all the years they'd known each other, had Tara hung up on her. But it still didn't sink in that her friend was genuinely concerned about her, or that Jonny Devroe could turn out to be very bad company indeed.

When Tara went back downstairs, she found six missed texts on her phone, all from Max. Instead of being pleased and flattered it annoyed the hell out of her. He was far too needy and she couldn't be bothered to return them. Izzy had put her in a foul mood. She realised that it wasn't up to her to tell her friend how to conduct her life but Izzy lived in a sheltered environment and she was sure that her friend wasn't giving her the full story.

She decided to take her angst out by dealing with the Liam Hussain case. She smelt a rat but as it happened Daniel had got to the bottom of it whilst she'd been upstairs. Liam had been seeing one of his pupils at Redmount. This was over a year ago. Now the girl said she was pregnant with his baby and they were living together as a couple. Big trouble for Liam and Education Supply would be shredding his details directly after filing a report, to be kept in case he tried to register again. Another allegation surfaced of his calling a movie star 'an arrogant ugly bastard' in a classroom situation. He obviously hadn't looked at himself in the mirror lately, Tara thought.

Poor Carrie wasn't faring any better, as she trawled endlessly through the internet search programme that Education Supply paid for, to recruit teachers looking for work. Every single person she rang didn't want to work. Their reasons were ludicrous and Carrie was fed up to the back teeth.

"Why the fuck do they put their CVS's up there if they don't want to work?" she shouted, slamming down the receiver. "And why go to University and qualify if you don't actually want to fucking teach? How do they pay their bills?"

At this moment, the vestibule door swung open and Billy the window cleaner walked in. Billy was a bit of a character. He looked like a fat, jolly Friar Tuck and walked everywhere with his ladders over his shoulder and swinging a bucket.

"Alright everybody?" he beamed as he came in for his money. "You all look sick of your lives!"

Carrie looked up but she did smile.

"We are," said Carrie. "We can't get anybody who actually wants to fucking work." She did manage a smile, for Billy's sake.

"It's alright man," he said. "I could do it."

This made everybody laugh. Then Daniel noticed that Billy's feet were covered in sand, odd seeing as the beach was about two miles away. Billy started to tell them the story in all seriousness. His friend had been given a snake as a present and he didn't want it so the two of them hatched a plan, involving taking the snake down to the local beach and releasing it. This was too much for Carrie as a mother, who instantly thought of her children making sandcastles on the beach and coming across a real live snake. Daniel and Tara howled with laughter and didn't really think Billy was serious. Until the next day, when the Daily Echo carried the story on its front page. A snake had been found alive and kicking and a team of reptile experts had been brought in to capture it, at great expense to the local council.

Max was desperate to clap eyes on Tara but she wasn't replying to any of his texts. He wanted her badly, or at least to see her. Every morning he leapt out of bed as if he couldn't wait for the day to start and get to work and the amount of aftershave he absorbed was frightening. Kate of course noted everything. He grew increasingly irritated in the evening, except when he went for a run. But of a morning it was like a light bulb had gone on. Max didn't pay her any attention. He couldn't be bothered with her any more. As long as she paid the bills and looked after their kids, he didn't give a flying fuck. Nothing compared to spending time with the gorgeous Tara.

Last night he told Kate he was going for a long run. Then he signed in at the running club, spoke to a few people, proving he had shown his face and promptly jogged off to Susan's house. He'd promised Susan, whom he'd been shagging for two years, all sorts of things: he loved her; when the kids were older, he'd leave Kate; they would move abroad and have a new life. He didn't mean a word of it. She was very handy. She lived one mile away, in a scummy little flat on her own and worked as a shop assistant in another town, therefore unlikely to bump into anybody Max knew. Susan liked to smack him on the bottom during sex with a wooden kitchen spoon as she knew he loved it. The harder the better but unfortunately for Susan, she was on her way out. Max had to drag himself there last night and had even lied to her, saying he couldn't make their usual Thursday arrangement because he had to take the girls to a party while Kate was on call. Susan sensed immediately that her position was in jeopardy. Max never missed a Thursday. If he was seeing another woman, she Susan would do for him. Max had no idea the lengths she would go to, as a woman scorned.

Max decided to text Tara again, asking if she fancied a coffee around the corner from their offices. Tara noticed the phone light up on her desk and quite frankly, considered it perfect timing. She welcomed an excuse to escape for half an hour. She found him already there in Barney's, waiting. As soon she came in, he jumped up to kiss her. Tara stopped him. He needed to calm down they were both married and couldn't be doing that in public. They sat down and the waitress took their order.

Tara noticed a man sitting at the next table. He lowered his newspaper and greeted Max. She thought he looked about sixty, fairly nondescript, just an older guy who happened to be sitting near them. But Tara couldn't quite leave it at that.

"Who's that, Max?" she asked casually.

"Davy Robinson," he replied, lowering his voice.

She knew the name then it hit her. Davy had murdered someone years and years ago and now he ran one of the biggest pub protection rackets in town. He'd been all over the papers recently regarding some trouble in a pub, after which it had burned down. She took a slurp of her coffee, looked at her watch then told Max she had to go a forgotten appointment. She left Max sitting there wondering what the hell had just happened but there was no way she was sitting at the next table to a murderer.

She realised she had to take on board, that Max was a lawyer. He may have gone to the best school money could buy, speak with the correct accent, but he also knew all the criminals in town. She wouldn't be going for coffee with him again. He got back to his office and texted.

'are you ok?'

'yes I'd forgotten I had a rep coming to see me so I had to go'.

Max knew this was a lie and it annoyed him that he didn't seem to have any control over her like he did with Susan and Kate. She just did what she wanted, when she pleased and he didn't like this one bit. He had to bring her round to his way of thinking and take total control of her. He decided to treat her so spectacularly well, she wouldn't be able to live without him.

Tara pushed the murderer to the back of her mind, as Daniel walked into the office laughing and shaking his head at the same time.

"Well," he said. "That gives a new meaning to a school visit."

"Why what happened?" asked Carrie.

"When I got there, I saw a woman standing on the school reception steps. As soon as I parked, she came over to me. So I put the window down and she asked if I was Daniel? Then she explained that she had to take some kids to a nature reserve, so she'd speak to me while I sat in my car." Daniel started laughing again. "I could see four children sitting in her car waiting for her to finish, so I quickly explained about our service, gave her our information and her Education Supply mug and off she went."

Tara and Carrie just looked at each other with their mouths open.

"So," said Carrie. "You conducted a meeting with a school business manager through your driver's side window in the school car park with four children waiting nearby in her car?"

"You've got it," said Daniel.

"How unprofessional is that?" said Carrie, shaking her head and looking at Tara. "What is it coming to?"

Tara had watched education slide ever lower in the fifteen years she'd been involved in the profession. All of the older, more experienced staff were starting to retire or get out early and the new wave coming in didn't have a clue, never mind a work ethic.

16

Izzy had popped round after work, to make sure her elderly parents were Ok, then headed home. It had been a long day and at seven pm she was ready to relax. But as she put the key in her front door and pushed it open, she found a stream of water pouring along the hallway towards her from the direction of the kitchen. Izzy started to panic and reached for her mobile. The first person she thought to phone was Jonny. She felt sure he would know a plumber.

He was quite surprised to hear her from her but realised she was in trouble and needed help. He looked at his watch, he had nothing else to do so twenty minutes later he arrived at her house in a cab. She opened the door and he smiled at her.

"I don't specialise in plumbing, mind," he said. But he did have a bag of tools with him.

She felt so reassured to see him. He headed straight for the kitchen sink, where the water was coming from. He stuck his head in the cupboard underneath and got busy.

"You need to switch the water off at the mains," he shouted. "Do you know where the stop cock is?'

"Er no, I don't know."

"Ok," he replied, sliding back under the sink.

She put towels all over the place trying to soak up the water, while Jonny was on his knees struggling to turn off the valve to shut the water off. His jeans were soaking but he managed it and the steady stream of water slowed down then stopped.

"You're brilliant!" cried Izzy, jumping up and down with excitement.

"It's far from sorted," he said. "All I've done is switch the valve off, which anyone could have done. You still need a plumber."

She went upstairs and brought down a huge, white, fluffy towel and then put his soaking jeans in the dryer. When the jeans were dry and after five cups of coffee, she handed them back to him and thanked him for his help. They went into her lounge and sat down on the couch together. He reached out for her and their lips met. She wasn't sure if he had kissed her or she had kissed him. It no longer mattered. He knew exactly which buttons to press, their rhythms matched perfectly and their bodies fit as one. They both came together with what felt like an explosion. Afterwards, she lay in his arms savouring the moment.

"I've been waiting for you for a long time," he whispered in her ear. "I always knew you were out there somewhere."

Izzy was in seventh heaven. She was so happy. She felt that something had suddenly clicked between them. She had him in her life and in every nook and cranny of her body. He'd become part of her forever. They moved to the bedroom and lay in her bed, both falling into a deep sleep and woke up the next morning fully satisfied.

Jonny got into the shower and Izzy joined him feeling totally comfortable with him. They ate breakfast together, talking and laughing with each other than dressed and went for a long walk on the beach. It was the best Saturday Izzy could remember in ages. When they got back to her place they climbed back into bed and made love again. Jonny stretched and yawned. She knew he had to go to work but she didn't want him to leave her. It was Saturday night the busiest of the week in pub and clubland.

"If you like I can give you a lift into work?" she said.

"That's great," he replied. "I'll go straight to Limes. I have clothes there I can change into."

He didn't seem to be in any hurry to leave so she fussed around him, clearing up the dirty dishes. He came up behind her, enveloping her with his big strong arms. She sighed and nestled into him. It was just so perfect.

"I'm knackered," he chuckled. "I could do with a change of scenery, a holiday or something but hey ho, to work I go."

He took one final look at himself in the mirror before they left and got into her car. Izzy drove him to work and he promised to call her later.

When Izzy got home she was grinning from ear to ear wondering what it would be like to go on holiday with Jonny and have him every day, all day to herself. She couldn't stop thinking about him. She'd never met anyone like him before in her life. He was so exciting. Izzy switched on her computer. No harm in having a little look she said to herself. Half term was fast approaching and after all, she had been thinking about a holiday. Why not take a peek to see if any good offers were out there?

Donna was busy in the office at Limes when Jonny arrived. She'd spotted Izzy dropping him off outside and she'd clocked the posh, white Audi.

"It won't last," she smiled at him as he filled in his timesheet. "She's too normal. You'll be sick of her in a week."

Jonny started laughing.

"I'm getting old and I don't want to die alone, honey."

He took a long look at her black, high heeled boots and her black leather skirt and couldn't help himself. Donna was more than willing, so he fucked her against the wall.

Meanwhile, at home, Izzy rang Tara.

"I'm thinking of going on holiday at half term," she said. "And I've found a really good deal with Jet 2."

"Excellent," said Tara, pleased her friend would be getting away from that arsehole. "It should be nice and warm by then. Who are you going away with?"

Izzy took a deep breath.

"I'm going to ask Jonny."

Tara took a deep breath. She could feel her heartbeat getting faster and faster.

"Oh no Izzy, seriously no. You don't even know him."

Izzy had braced herself but she was fed up with Tara's attitude and lost it.

"You're just not used to seeing me so happy, are you?"

"Are you happy?" interrupted Tara immediately.

"Am I happy? Well yes Tara I am very happy," shouted Izzy, with a defiant toss of her hair.

"Well, you didn't look it the last time I saw you!"

Izzy tried to hold her temper in check. Who the hell did Tara think she was talking to, her best friend or not?

"Look, I've got to go, Tara," she said abruptly. "I'll speak to you later." And slammed the receiver down.

Tara made a cup of coffee and tried to calm down. She was upset at the state her friend was in and hated to see that bastard taking advantage of her. She knew full well Izzy would be paying for that holiday and Tara couldn't bear the thought of witnessing the inevitable disaster. Izzy didn't even know him or had spent enough time with him. The doormen in Sunhill had a terrible reputation and it only took one look at Jonny Devroe in the flesh to see exactly what he was about.

Meanwhile, Izzy started writing some notes on the great deal she found on Tenerife as the go-to destination. She wondered if Jonny would want to go with her and if he could actually make it. Her thoughts flashed back to Tara. She wished her friend would stop being so dramatic. It was only a holiday and it would be so exciting having Jonny all to herself for the whole week. What better way was there, to get to know him than a holiday together?

Izzy awoke in the middle of the night with a deep sense of foreboding and didn't know why. She couldn't put her finger on it. She and Jonny had enjoyed a fantastic evening together with great sex and a special kind of love. She had felt it. She had not imagined the sparks that flew between them. They were so in tune with each other and everything was perfect. Fuck it, she thought. I'm going to book that holiday. She was sick of being Miss Goody Two Shoes with her boring life. For once she was going to do something rash and if it backfired then she'd have to live with it.

She found her mobile and called Jonny. The phone rang and rang but he didn't pick up so she left a voicemail asking him to call her back. Izzy tried to get back to sleep but he didn't return her call. Four hours later he still hadn't rung her back so she rang again and left a quick message asking if everything was ok and could he call her back. As the rays of daylight started to burst around the sides of the curtains, Jonny still had not returned her call. She was not happy but told herself that he must have been really busy so she decided to text him.

'Are you free for a week in Tenerife mid-June my treat?'

Then she got up, making sure to pop her mobile into her dressing gown pocket so that she could hear it ring.

Jonny was on the way back from a pick-up of cocaine for his boss Tony when he received the text. He showed Stevie the driver his phone and let him read Izzy's message. Stevie couldn't stop laughing. They both knew that June or anytime would be convenient for a free holiday. They dropped the car back off at Limes then Jonny called a taxi. Last night, his boss Tony had introduced him to a fabulous looking Russian girl, wearing black silk pants and a little white bolero that was wide open with nothing underneath. Everyone in the bar had got a great view of her fantastic breasts. The girl had sat with them all night with her breasts hanging out and didn't bat an eyelid. She was stunning and thoroughly enjoyed the sensation she caused around the bar. By one-thirty a.m she had danced with Jonny enough, but before leaving she handed him her number. Jonny jumped in the taxi and headed home for a shower.

Later that day Jonny rang the Russian woman and made arrangements to meet her at Mal Maison at eight pm for drinks in the bar. He also took the liberty of booking a room for them there. Jonny loved it. As far as he was concerned the only way to handle a woman was to find a dumb, good-looking one, keep her at arm's length, then take what you can get and move on to the next one.

It didn't take him long to get the Russian into bed. He couldn't pronounce her name so he didn't bother to try but the night cost him a fortune as she only drank champagne. He could taste it on her lips as he kissed her in the huge luxurious bed. He tugged down her underwear which was all that was left on her.

"Tell me you want this," he whispered in her ear.

"I want this please," she begged in her broken English and he felt himself instantly get hard. He loved it when they begged. He pushed his huge dick into her and she pushed back hungrily against him. He could feel her coming and he felt the waves wash over him as they came together. After that, they lay together for a while and he poured her another glass of champagne from the minibar. She nestled into him and fell asleep.

Jonny reached out to the nightstand and found his phone. He re-read Izzy's text then typed:

'that will be lovely but are you sure?'

'of course I am it will be fun' came the reply within seconds.

Jonny smiled to himself. He liked plenty of fun.

'Great that will be lovely,' he sent back. *'I'm knackered so going to grab some sleep now text you later'* and switched off the phone.

He snuggled deep down into the covers and reached for the gorgeous Russian girl's bare flesh. He was grinning from ear to ear and getting harder by the second.

Izzy, on the other hand, was just about doing cartwheels. It must mean something that he had accepted. He was hers all hers. She just knew it.

17

Tara had received a text from Max the previous evening. He wanted to see her and all of his usual flattery but he explained that at 11 a.m he had to visit one of his clients, on remand at Her Majesty's pleasure. So he wondered if she fancied a trip out with him.

'to a prison??' Tara had texted back.

Max explained that the prison was in the next county and very close to a small rural village so he could drop her off there and pick her up after the meeting. What Tara didn't know was that Max had booked a room at the local Travel Lodge at the great expense of twenty-five pounds, which he deemed as far too expensive for the hour that he needed it for but hey, it was worth it. He couldn't stop thinking about lying in bed naked with Tara, a real treat and more comfortable than his or her office.

All went according to plan. Tara told Daniel exactly what she was up to and he made excuses for her absence at work, just in case Simon called. Then when Max mentioned the Travel Lodge, he saw Tara's face.

"Do you want me to catch a verruca?" she asked.

Max couldn't see what was wrong with the place, after all, he stayed in them regularly when travelling with Kate and the kids. Eventually, Tara conceded. After all the sex was good and at least it would be more comfortable and private.

Tara irritated Max by refusing to put her bare feet on the floor of their room. She even popped to the loo in her heels. Then after they both enjoyed a good few orgasms, Tara looked at her watch and said she had to get back. Max was not happy. Why did she always have to leave straight after sex? Could she not cuddle up for a while? They both got dressed and got back into Max's 'van' as she called it. Definitely a family car. In fact, she looked stupid in it but on a positive note, nobody would recognise her.

When she got back to the office, she pulled Daniel into the tea room and told him everything. He could not stop laughing.

"You in a Travel Lodge? Could he not have done better than that?"

"Clearly not," said Tara, trying to stop herself laughing.

When she returned to her desk, her phone had lit up with a barrage of texts from Max, proclaiming just how much he had enjoyed himself. All this achieved was sheer irritation from Tara.

"For fuck's sake," she said to Daniel. "How needy is this man?"

She read out some of the texts to him. *'I've never met a girl like you, the sex is unreal, please I need to see you'* and so they went on. Daniel had a worried look on his face.

"Fuck me, Tara, you need to go steady there," he said. "I'm not being funny but have you seen those marks on his wrists and have you asked him about them?'

"Yes," said Tara and sighed. "He said he burnt them putting a pizza into the oven for the girls. Burns can look like wields."

"'I agree they look like burns but he just seems really needy that's all," said Daniel, closing the subject.

The day continued as normal, the usual interviewees not turning up and the continual ringing of people who didn't want to accept any work. Tara told three teachers that if they didn't want to work just say and she wouldn't bother calling again. But she always got the same response, they did want to work just not today. This succeeded in wasting everybody's time and resources not to mention the phone bill. The Liam Hussain scandal was dealt with. His last employer was taking him to court for breach of trust with a pupil. The girl was now seventeen and having his baby any day, so the General Teaching Council would have no qualms in striking him off the teaching register.

Max found the receipt from the Travel Lodge, tore it up into little pieces and tossed it into the bin. Good job he found it and not Kate, he thought. He was sure she went through his pockets but now he almost didn't care if she did find out about Tara. He was in love.

Susan, on the other hand, presented another problem altogether. At fifty-three she was twelve years older than Max but she'd looked after herself and appeared quite attractive, five feet two, blonde and divorced with no children. Perfect for Max but the biggest plus, she lived conveniently less than a mile away from his home. She'd got so used to Max texting and popping in for sex on tap that without even realising it, she'd completely put her life on hold for him. Of course, he had promised her the earth when the kids got a bit older etc., etc., etc. Susan didn't have much money and lived on the edge of the rough end of Sunhill. Again, this worked to Max's advantage as nobody other than the odd lurking criminal would know him there and he could come and go as he pleased.

However, Susan harboured a strong feeling all was not well. She hadn't heard a word from Max for two days. She suspected she had ceased to exist in the forefront of his life and it didn't help when she arrived at work that morning and her friend Hayley sidled up to her with disturbing news.

"Hi, Susan! Who's the gorgeous blonde I saw Max sharing a coffee with yesterday? Just across the road from where he works."

This riled Susan no end.

"I don't know," she snapped. "It could be anyone from his work."

Hayley hadn't meant to upset her. She realised she'd somehow put her foot in it.

"Look, sweetie, I'm not trying to cause trouble," she said, gently putting an arm around Susan's shoulder. "But it didn't look like a work-related meeting to me and the woman got up and left very quickly as if they'd had words."

"Oh Hayley," she sighed. "I don't know but something's wrong. I haven't heard from him for two days. It's almost as if he's gone off me."

"But he promised that you guys would be together soon?"

"I know," said Susan. "But it's all bollocks isn't it? Three years of my life wasted. Let's face it, he's been lying to me just for a regular shag really."

Hayley didn't know what to say as Susan started to cry. She hustled her friend into the tea room, away from the shop front and prying eyes.

"Look," she said. "We need to find out exactly what's going on."

Susan wiped her eyes on the tissue Hayley had just found in the bottom of her handbag.

"I know," she said. "I've left three voicemails, sent God knows how many texts and he hasn't replied to a single one."

Hayley felt furious on her friend's behalf but kept a lid on it. She knew all along that it would come to this. After three years, it was obvious he was using her just for sex and Hayley had repeatedly warned Susan that this may happen. It was also obvious that Susan's house was far too convenient. He could pop round whenever he felt like it, plus they saw each other twice a week at the running club. Max often told Kate that he was going out for a long training run which usually meant the mile to Susan's and two hours in bed. He didn't take Susan anywhere and after three years something should have happened in their relationship.

"Let's keep an eye on him on our days off," suggested Hayley. "And see if we can find out what's going on?"

Susan perked up. At least if she could find out what she was up against she had a sporting chance she told herself. She'd invested far too much time at her age, just to throw it all away. What Susan didn't know was that Max had listened to her voicemails and texts and decided that he had no intention of returning any of them. Was she stupid or something? He asked himself. Did she really believe he'd leave a doctor for a shop assistant and spend the rest of his life with her? Women always read far too much into sex.

Four days passed and Susan decided to take her balls into both hands. She couldn't sleep or eat and felt ill. It was starting to affect her work so on her day off she decided to hang around Max's office about the time she knew he usually set off for court. However, she didn't know he was already attending a court hearing in Dagenham city centre, about twenty miles away. After an hour of skulking around on the corner, she had attracted too much attention so she went home and cried her eyes out. She was so upset. She felt like a discarded dishcloth, all rung out. Max, on the other hand, had been saved by the skin of his teeth. Never the less, Susan would be back. That was for sure.

18

Izzy worked out that she had two months, eight weeks to be precise, to lose a stone in weight before Tenerife. Jonny looked so fit because he spent a lot of time in the gym. She was damned if she would let herself down. She needed to be absolutely beach fit for this holiday. She trawled through the websites on her computer at work, trying to find a local Zumba class. She couldn't join Tara boxing or running. Tara looked so much fitter. The head was out again so she'd had a lovely stress-free morning until her phone blipped. A text from Jonny. She smiled instinctively and felt the same warm sensation spread through her body, that happened every time he communicated with her.

'Any chance of a lift to Dagenham tonight? Meeting the boys'.

Now Izzy really smiled and thought this is it. We're getting closer. He's actually asking me to take him to meet his friends. Must be the holiday she told herself and smiled. Izzy decided that they were now a couple and texted back:

'Yes what time do you want me to pick you up?'

She carried on with some finance work and about an hour later, received the answer.

'Eight.'

Izzy decided she would wear something really nice. Her thoughts were interrupted by having to deal with a dispute between a dinner supervisor and one of their cleaners since the head still hadn't returned from her meeting. Izzy was certain the head buggered off home whenever she felt like it.

At eight on the dot, Izzy pulled up outside Jonny's flat and tooted her horn. She never had been invited up into his home. Jonny sauntered out dressed up to the nines. He looked gorgeous and once again Izzy couldn't believe that she'd pulled him. He had on black jeans, a chic, expensive shirt and a designer black leather three-quarter jacket.

"Wow!" said Izzy, as he got in the car. "You look good for a night out with the boys."

Jonny kissed her cheek.

"Thanks, thought I'd make the effort. It's not often we can all get together like this."

Izzy set off and smiled at him.

"Do you want a lift back?"

"No, no," replied Jonny a bit too quickly. "We'll club together and get a taxi back to Sunhill as I've no idea what time it will be."

She drove him into Dagenham city centre and he told her to drop him off at the railway station, where the boys were meeting. She wished him a great night and he promised to ring her the next day. Jonny smoothed down his leather coat and set off in the direction of Mal Maison, to meet the Russian girl again for a drink. There were no boys. He had a date, Izzy had a car. He knew she'd jump at the chance to be in his company. On the way home, Izzy's car phone started to ring and she answered when she saw Tanya's name come up.

"Well," said Tanya, laughing. "Clearly you're alive and kicking."

"I'm really sorry sweetie, I've been so busy. What have you been up to?"

"Just the usual' she said. "I've been to Limes a few times. It's getting seriously good, you need to get your arse down there."

Just the mention of Limes and Izzy couldn't help herself.

"Have you seen Jonny?" she said eagerly.

Tanya sensed that one coming and only admitted to spotting him once, working at the door. Izzy checked the time. It was only eight-thirty.

"I'm on my way home from dropping Jonny off," she said. "Why you don't come round and I'll put the kettle on?"

Tanya agreed and said to expect her at nine. Izzy promised to tell her all about Jonny. Tanya put the phone down. She was shocked at the way her friend had glossed over Jonny Devroe. Izzy clearly adored the man. It was palpable even over a telephone line.

"Oh God," she groaned. "What have I done introducing those two?"

How could she tell Izzy she'd spied Jonny kissing a girl on Saturday night at Limes? Even worse, he'd seen her watching him. It was almost like he was daring her to say something to Izzy but he knew that she wouldn't.

When Tanya arrived at Izzy's house, she decided to keep her mouth shut and even when Izzy told her how she was paying to take Jonny on holiday to Tenerife, Tanya still felt that she couldn't say anything to her friend. On top of not wishing to upset Izzy, she didn't feel like crossing Jonny Devroe either.

As Tanya drove herself home afterwards, she repeatedly asked herself what kind of friend am I? Surely Izzy had a right to know that Jonny had been kissing another girl? But in the end, she came down on the side of best not to meddle in other people's affairs.

The next morning Jonny woke up next to the gorgeous Russian, once again in the bare flesh. He could feel himself getting harder just remembering what he'd done to her last night but then his phone started ringing. Irritated he grabbed it from the bedside table.

"Where are you?" demanded his boss, Tony.

"Mal Maison," he replied.

"Stevie's on his way, job on," said Tony.

"Ok, I'll be at the front door." Jonny cut his phone. "Got to go, babe," he whispered in the Russian girl's ear.

"Now?" she asked, laughing and gliding her hand down onto his hard dick.

"Well perhaps not this very second," he replied and started to kiss her.

Within fifteen minutes he was standing at the front door of the hotel, as Stevie drove up to take them to their next job.

The next morning at work, Izzy checked her e-mails. The booking confirmation had arrived for Tenerife. She printed off a copy for Jonny, so he could keep it and have all their travel details together. She was so excited, ecstatic even, her hands were shaking as her fingers tapped away on the keyboard. She came quickly back down to earth when Jackie, the head, popped her head around the door and asked Izzy to locate one of the teacher's contracts for her. This teacher had caused untold problems and they needed to discuss it at a meeting.

After locating the contract for the head, Izzy got busy putting together an e-mail to be sent to all parents dealing with the recent plague of head lice, wreaking havoc in Year One. The head had felt it necessary to explain that there really was no way of discovering which individual child had started the epidemic and could the parents please stop trying to find out? Both Izzy and Jackie were fully aware that it was Shelley Riley's daughter who'd started scratching first but as much as they detested Shelley, it was hardly the poor little girl's fault.

On a lighter note, Izzy set herself off laughing because she'd seen Shelley dropping the kids off earlier and noticed her top lip looked very red and angry. She'd obviously had her upper lip waxed the night before and her beautician must have used the wrong astringent. It had brought Shelley out in a rash so she was now sporting a full-on, scarlet handlebar moustache. Sarah, the head of Year One, said at least it distracted you from looking at her usual low-cut top with her breasts on show. At least they had something new to look at. Shelley Riley was the talk of the school.

Izzy kept checking her mobile throughout the day to see if Jonny had contacted her but so far, no word from him. She told herself again that he was a very busy man, even though she knew he only worked three nights a week at Limes. But then he had mentioned on more than one occasion that he did part- time jobs as and when required, for his boss Tony Adams, the owner of Limes. When she asked what he actually did, Jonny had become very vague and said he moved things around. She didn't know the nature of those things but she got the distinct impression he didn't want to discuss it further, so she stopped asking. The best news of the day, she had found an exercise class in a gym, with no less, a Greggs the Baker, right next to the car park. Perfect.

19

Tara got to work early on Monday morning, praying not to find Max lurking in the shadows. He'd been away at the weekend visiting the in-laws. She was fast becoming sick of Simon and had started to wonder again what her life would be like being single. She knew she was headstrong and Simon, the complete opposite had been a good match for her as he kept her on the straight and narrow so to speak. Still, Tara knew she couldn't carry on behaving the way she did. Simon would find out about the extramarital stuff one day and that wasn't right. But she reasoned with herself, the lack of sex in their relationship could hardly be laid at her feet. She loved sex and he simply didn't provide enough of it.

Tara glanced down at her desk and her mood plummeted even further on reading the first message, left for her late on Friday afternoon.

'Gordon Hall only wants us to contact us on his landline if it's an emergency and to use his mobile, as his wife wasn't very happy when we woke her up on Friday morning.'

Daniel came into the office and took one look at her face.

"The Gordon note," he said.

"Are these people for fucking real?" she asked. "Is getting work, not an emergency?"

"I know. You wouldn't dare would you," said Daniel, sitting at his desk. "You'd think she'd be pleased that we had work for him."

"Coffee, that's what we need," said Tara, leaping up just as the phones started ringing.

While she stood waiting for the kettle to boil, she realised Izzy was bothering her too much. She felt very concerned about her. She knew she needed to stop having a go at her and just be there as a friend. Nothing could stop Izzy seeing Jonny, so Tara knew that if she didn't stop acting like Izzy's mother, they would fall out big time and Tara couldn't allow that to happen over a man. She just constantly worried about her, so when she got back to her desk, she texted Izzy:

'is everything ok?'

She was surprised when Izzy replied really quickly.

'Everything great. Am taking Jonny to Tenerife at half term. Really looking forward to it.'

Tara nearly dropped the phone. She craved to send a real broadside, like are you being serious? But in the end, she wrote:

'right, something to look forward to.'

She couldn't do any better than that, but she soon found it had opened up the floodgates. Izzy could not have felt more overjoyed by her text and even better not to receive a lecture. So everything was Ok with them again.

Tara's phone bleeped again.

'Happy Monday gorgeous' she read. Tara smiled a bit of flattery from Max felt quite welcome at this moment. He asked if she could meet him for coffee at the same place around the corner from their offices before he went off to court. He also texted:

'no murderers this time.'

Tara smiled.

'Ok 9.15. Let me get the morning rush out of the way first.'

Max got to the café first and ordered for them but he didn't see Susan's best friend, Hayley, sitting in the corner as she had her back to him. When Tara walked in, Hayley's friend Janice, who'd accompanied her to the café, couldn't help herself.

"Wow," she said. "She's good looking!"

Hayley turned around to see what Janice was talking about and nearly had a heart attack. It was confirmed Max was seeing another woman and as much as she loved Susan, Hayley realised she was going to have to tell her the depressing details. The longer the coffee conversation went on between Max and Tara, the closer Hayley came to actually committing murder in broad daylight. From her viewpoint, Max was all over the blonde woman sitting opposite him. He kept trying to get hold of her hand. Hayley just wanted to walk right over to him and call him a lying bastard. She just about managed to contain herself though and planned to follow the blonde to find out all about her.

Hayley timed it perfectly. Her friend Janice had already asked for the bill and they popped the money down on the table. Hayley said goodbye to Janice then slowly and leaving a good bit of space, she watched Max kiss Tara on the cheek then walk away in the opposite direction heading back towards his office. Tara turned and left. Hayley followed her but they only went as far as the next street. Then Hayley carefully tailed Tara as she proceeded down the back lane, produced a garage fob and clicked one of the garage doors open. It was directly opposite Max's office and Hayley noted she could see his car in the unsecured office driveway.

What really focused her attention, however, was when Tara unlocked the gleaming, black Porsche. Hayley felt sicker with every step she took. How was Susan going to take this? Not only had she been dumped but she'd been traded in for a very good looking and obviously successful businesswoman, with a Porsche! No wonder Max had dropped Susan like a hot potato. What a bastard, she kept saying to herself over and over again. How dare he lie to her friend like that and more importantly not even have the balls to tell Susan it was over? He hadn't even returned any of her calls. It was a mess and Susan would need her support, but right now Hayley was determined to find out everything she could about this woman.

Looking at the entrance Tara had taken, Hayley counted four garages at the back of the office buildings. Then she went round to the front and did the same. The plate on the fourth front door said Education Supply. That was a start. She would Google their website when she got back to find out who Max had kissed and had coffee with. Hayley felt close to tears. How could he be so cruel to Susan? She still didn't know how she would begin to explain this to her friend.

As soon as Tara got back to work, she started opening the post. Boring bills and timesheets, except for one envelope, which contained an invitation to an employment law course at the beautiful, old stately mansion, Windleston Hall. Tara toyed with the idea, then decided an excuse for a night away might be a good idea. She wondered if Max could get the time off, so she sent him the details. He received the invitation, whilst sitting at his desk trying hard to concentrate on work when all he could think about was Tara.

'Yes!' he replied instantly.

He didn't give a toss what he was going to say to Kate. All night spent in a bed with Tara sounded like a dream come true and he wouldn't be turning that down for anybody. But he did hope her company would foot the bill. He was a bit strapped for cash.

20

Izzy still hadn't heard from Jonny and felt peeved, to say the least. She had all the paperwork for their holiday and she wanted him to have it and see how excited she was. It was only three weeks away now and she'd only seen him twice, and that was to give him lifts in her car. He told her they would be spending a lot of time together on holiday and that he was very busy. So when she texted him, she didn't expect a reply. But to her surprise one came back straight away.

He asked her if she fancied going out for tea and if so, could she pick him up at 7.00 pm? Izzy replied YES and after four outfit changes, arrived at Jonny's place. She decided to try to beat him to it, by ringing his buzzer but Jonny was one step ahead of her and headed down the internal staircase of the block of flats, reaching the front door more or less at the same time as her.

They got into the car and Jonny smiled at her comfortably, a smile that indicated all was well with the world. He noticed the paperwork on the passenger side of the car floor and bent down to pick it up. Izzy was like a kid in a chocolate factory, smiling and gushing, hoping he liked the hotel she had chosen for them and that the flight times worked for him. Jonny flicked through the papers and said that everything looked fine and pointed her in the direction of a local Indian restaurant.

He took the papers into the restaurant but barely looked at them whilst Izzy banged on about the hotel. She was irritating him but he decided to try to join in. After all, she was paying and he'd look great with a tan. Izzy had noticed a bruise on the side of his face. It was old as it was turning yellow but she couldn't help asking him about it. Jonny was surprised that she'd noticed it but told her that he'd done it at the gym with a weight. Izzy asked a few more questions but it was clear that she believed him and she happily changed the subject, especially when he asked how many pools the hotel in Tenerife had.

After the meal, he said he was tired and she dropped him off at home. As she drew up at his block, she wondered if at last he was going to ask her in but he leant over and pecked her on the cheek. That was all she got for her trouble. As she drove away Izzy started making excuses for his behaviour as always. But at least he had paid the bill this time and after all, he was going on holiday with her soon. When she stopped at a red-light Izzy glanced down at the footwell on the passenger side and noticed that Jonny had left the travel documents on the floor. Izzy wondered if he needed them and decided to go back.

Meanwhile, Jonny got in and decided he did need an early night. He looked at the yellow bruise on his face and smiled, still amazed that she had noticed it. It was the very reason he hadn't seen her. He and the boys had received a bit of retaliation on an enforcing job Tony had sent them on and Jonny had been on the floor at one point, taking a kicking from a guy wild on drugs. However, his crew stepped up to the plate and Jonny's aggressor landed in Intensive Care, thus Jonny had laid low for a while. Izzy, of course, didn't need to know any of that and the sun would help clear the bruising up. She believed anything he said. Most of them did.

Izzy pulled up at his flat. She did a recce of the flats and knew that he lived at the front, on the third floor. She could clearly see lights on and reckoned it was number 24 so she rang the intercom button. Inside his flat, Jonny heard the buzzer and thought to himself how does she do it. He knew he hadn't told her which flat, but her job had been made easier because all the other flats on the third floor were in darkness. He ignored the ringing getting severely more irritated by the second. "Why doesn't she just fuck off?" he said out loud. Then the buzzing stopped and his mobile rang. He let it ring and then she sent him a text explaining he'd left the paperwork for their holiday and she thought he may need it. By now, Jonny believed he'd found the local bunny boiler. She was too full on for his taste and he certainly hadn't given her many green signals that he was love's young dream.

Izzy realised he wasn't going to answer the door or the phone so when she got in she rang Tara.

"Something's not right," she told her best friend. "No sex, not even a kiss! But when we do have sex it's been fantastic. I just don't know what's going on."

"Well you're not in a full-blown relationship with him, so I'm not sure why you booked this holiday but it's done now so try to take it slowly," was all Tara could bring herself to say.

"I just want to be with him, he's so exciting!" sighed Izzy.

"Just slow down, take it easy one step at a time," said Tara, groaning inwardly. "A man like that will be difficult to pin down."

Tara changed the subject and told her about Max and how bored she felt with Simon and that she'd decided to leave him. This had the desired effect and Izzy asked Tara a barrage of questions. She liked Simon and thought Tara could be making a mistake.

By the time Izzy put the phone down, she thought maybe Tara was right. She looked at the dishes in the sink and pushed her hand into the now cold water. She'd missed a wine glass on the counter and went to grab it, but the rim bounced off the counter and shattered on the tiled floor below.

"Bugger it!" she shouted.

When she knelt down to pick up the shards of glass, a sliver of glass cut sliced into her hand. She turned on the tap and let the cold water pour over her hand. Then her vision became blurred and tears welled up in her eyes. She was starting to feel a bit silly over Jonny. She knew that the relationship, if you could call it a relationship, wasn't right but no one was around to ask her why she was crying, so she just let the tears fall. She took a tissue out of the box on the window sill and wiped her eyes. She started to doubt all her thinking about Jonny but it was too late now. The holiday was happening and he had agreed to go with her.

Tara once told her that the really mean guys couldn't stop circling once they smelt blood in the water. Izzy's hostility seemed to ratchet up a notch but there was no point upsetting herself like this. Hopefully, the holiday would bring them closer. She wrapped a piece of kitchen roll around her hand, catching the leftover trickles of blood. Then she got the brush out and swept up the glass. Her kitchen was a mess. She'd been so busy recently that housework had gone right out of the window. In fact, she'd been so consumed with Jonny Devroe that she seemed to spend every waking moment thinking about him.

When her mobile started ringing, she ran to the lounge to find it, like an anxious schoolgirl. She expected it to be Jonny but she was disappointed again when she saw Tanya's name on her mobile and didn't answer it. Tanya would know that she was upset and she didn't want to answer any questions. Tanya heard Izzy's voicemail but didn't leave a message and hung up. She was worried about this Jonny situation but it would keep.

The next two weeks flew by but Izzy only saw Jonny twice and began to fear he wasn't even going to bother turning up for the holiday, the amount of interest he was showing her. Then her phone blipped and his name came up. She grabbed the phone, it was a text asking if she was free that evening and could he come over to her house to sort out the travel arrangements?

Izzy immediately felt the cloud hanging over her vanish as if a great weight had been lifted from her shoulders. She joyfully replied yes to everything and he agreed to be there by seven. Out came the clothes and the three outfit changes as Izzy wanted to look her best for him. Just as she felt she looked good enough for him, he knocked on the front door. She threw it open, beaming and hugging him like her long-lost friend.

"Whoa, steady on!" laughed Jonny, pulling back from her but Izzy just tutted and ushered him into her lounge.

"I was beginning to think that you weren't coming on holiday with me," she said.

"Of course, I'm coming on holiday!" he said. "I'm looking forward to spending some time alone with you."

He watched her delighted reaction to his words. It always amazed him what happened when you knew the right buttons to press with a woman. Izzy spouted all the flight details and agreed to pick him up at seven a.m. She would leave her car at the airport. It was beyond him why they just couldn't make it simpler by getting a taxi but she was paying. When she asked him how much spending money he was taking, he suddenly became very vague and eventually said that it would probably be about the four hundred mark, as he thought the holiday was all-inclusive.

"Is that all?" asked Izzy, surprised.

When Jonny said that he thought it was sufficient, she got the distinct impression from his tone she'd better not argue with him. They lay on the sofa and watched television with a few kisses and cuddles thrown in. As it approached midnight, Izzy imagined he would stay the night. But he leaned over her to look at the clock and stood up.

"I'm going to head home now I'm knackered," he said.

"Don't you want a lift?" she asked but he declined and headed to the front door.

It was pouring down with rain when she opened the front door and again offered to give him a lift but Jonny said he needed the exercise and preferred to walk. He didn't even have a coat. He'd get drenched. It was just like before Izzy thought to herself, no sex and the disappearing act and now Izzy came to think about it, it had been at about roughly the same time of night. But the holiday was fast approaching, there'd be plenty of time for all that.

As Jonny walked away from her house he couldn't help smiling. He was en route to the garage, on his way home to pick up his thousand-pound pay packet from the last job he'd done for the people who owned the place. Four hundred of that would do for his holiday spending money.

The next day Izzy still wasn't feeling right about the whole Jonny situation but she called Tara to say goodbye, as she was flying on Saturday. Tara could hear in her friend's voice that something wasn't right.

"Izzy, promise me you'll be careful?"

But Izzy just laughed.

"Nothing is going to happen to me. I told you, he's not a serial killer."

Tara managed to stop herself saying anything else that would upset her friend or burst her bubble.

"Well then promise me that at least you will stay in touch when you get there?"

Izzy promised that she would. When Tara replaced the receiver, she felt nothing but worry for her friend.

Saturday came around very quickly. Izzy hadn't slept the previous night at all. Firstly, she had packed and then repacked, adding clothes into her suitcase then taking them out again. In all, she had twelve outfits for the night times. She felt so excited and nervous, she couldn't have slept even if she'd wanted to.

As usual, Jonny was already coming down the stairs of his flat as she drew up. Izzy was stunned to see him with only hand luggage, just a small holdall, in fact.

"Morning!" he said as he threw the holdall onto the back seat of her car.

"Where's your suitcase?" she said, staring at him.

"I'm only going away for a week. I don't need that much. It's not as if I'm going to Ibiza and need to dress up."

Izzy swallowed hard. She didn't like that remark at all. If he wanted to go to Ibiza he should have paid to go there. There's nothing wrong with Tenerife. She saw him having a good look at her overweight suitcase, bursting at the seams. She just threw him a dirty look back to let him know that she knew exactly what was going through his mind.

At the airport, they settled themselves into the lounge, Izzy had paid an extra eighty pounds for. As she relaxed, she noticed how much Jonny was drinking. He also started texting all the way through a story she embarked on about her work. The more she described the work situation, the more he drank and played with his phone. By the time their flight had been called he was on the verge of seeming well drunk and had only spoken about two sentences to her since they arrived. Izzy became more infuriated when after getting seated and settled on the plane, he promptly fell asleep and only woke up when they landed in Tenerife.

Izzy was livid. Jonny complained about having to get on a coach with other travellers. He couldn't think of anything worse than doing all of the drop- offs at different hotels so he turned on Izzy.

"You've got to be joking!" he almost shouted at her. "I'm not sitting in one of those in this heat."

Izzy couldn't hide her feelings. This was a great start to the holiday she had so lovingly planned.

"Ok, Ok," she said eventually, putting her hand on his arm. "Calm down let me find out how much a taxi costs."

She walked off across the terminal and went outside to find the taxi lines, amongst the throng of the people. It was so hot she thought she was going to faint but came back minutes later and told him to follow her to the waiting taxi. They arrived at their hotel, the Excelsior and she paid the driver thirty-five Euros. It never entered her head that Jonny should have paid for the taxi as she had been quite happy to get on the bus. She just thought it was easier to keep the peace and keep him happy. Jonny smiled as he watched her pay and patted the thousand pounds he had in his pocket.

21

Tara got into work on Monday morning and found Daniel already at his desk. He had been on call all weekend because Tara had been away motor racing again with Simon. Daniel had been so busy booking teachers out that he thought it prudent to get in early. His face looked as if it was tripping him up.

"What's up sweetie?" she asked.

"Well it's not me who's up, that's for fucking sure," he snapped. "Emma fucking Carr, that's what's up. I knew this would happen."

Emma had badgered the office for weeks, constantly ringing up and emailing to ask why she wasn't being offered any work as a Teaching Assistant. Then every time Education Supply offered her work, she gave a reason why she couldn't do it. Then finally, she accepted a two day per week position, working on a one-to-one basis with a special needs child who had severe autism. Daniel had pitched really hard for this job and had seen a few other agencies off so he was really pleased that he'd managed to get the work in the first place. After interviewing three applicants, the school had decided on Emma.

From the get-go, there were problems with her. The hours weren't right. She'd booked a holiday without telling anybody. She had a child with severe diabetes and basically, the lazy bitch just didn't want to work. Now, Daniel had switched the computer on and there was an e-mail from Emma sent at six a.m to say that she was ill and couldn't go in. Daniel was fuming. Tara tried to calm him down.

"She has no intentions of going back Dan," she said, only succeeding in making him feel a whole lot worse. "The two weeks she spent there have nearly killed her."

"I know," snapped Daniel. "But it's a bit more complicated than just the lazy cow letting everybody down. The school loves her and she's also built up a great relationship with her student. He's settled in with her really nicely. It's him she's letting down big time."

"Since when did that matter to the likes of Emma Carr?" replied Tara. "These days half of them don't give a flying fuck about the kids."

Tara was right. The new standard of teaching staff was worrying. For every ten teachers she interviewed, only one would outperform the others and have the right attitude. She even had teachers who refused to do their marking. People in other industries had told Tara that it was indicative of all careers, even doctors and nurses but Tara and her staff couldn't help being appalled by what they were witnessing on a daily basis and it was becoming increasingly difficult to weed out the good ones from the bad ones.

As a great number of Education Supply's more experienced, fabulous teachers were starting to retire Tara could physically see the standards dropping and if she heard one more of the new ones moaning about the workload, she wouldn't be held responsible. It was funny how they didn't mind ringing Education Supply at eight o'clock at night when they had a spare minute. Tara often wondered how teachers thought other professionals worked and the hours they put in. Did they think they worked nine to five and managed to get thirteen weeks off on holiday, on full pay? Frightening. Daniel was always banging on about school, university, then school as a huge mistake. The best teachers were always individuals who had worked in industry first.

Daniel eventually managed to track the head down to explain that Emma couldn't make it. He said he felt extremely disappointed as the little boy she was working with needed continuity. Daniel apologised and promised a replacement. He knew Emma was lying and wanted to kill her. Meanwhile, Emma who was sitting in bed with her laptop at the ready, heard her landline ring but chose to ignore it. She knew it would be Daniel. In the end, she listened to his voicemail asking her to ring in and explain what was happening and tell them if she was going in the next day.

Emma grabbed her laptop and sent another e-mail stating that she'd lost her voice, her husband had left for work so he couldn't speak for her. Tara read the e-mail and was shocked at the woman's unprofessionalism. She was clearly lying. Daniel had found a replacement, a girl who actually wanted to work and had confirmed with the head. Then he sent over the DBS information for the school's records.

"What are you saying to Emma?" asked Tara.

"I'm ignoring her," he shouted. "Let her sit and stew," and with that, he flounced off to make the coffee.

Hours' later Carrie started laughing.

"Oh please," she groaned. "Everybody click onto Emma's latest correspondence!"

Everyone in the office hit their keyboards. Tara actually wept with laughter. Emma Carr had stated she wanted to keep Education Supply up to speed and needed to let them know, that in the last two hours, she had been to see her doctor and had been diagnosed with Bell's Palsy so she wouldn't be able to accept any further assignments.

Tara stopped laughing. They all looked at her.

"Wouldn't it have been much simpler," she said. "To be honest and just say that she really doesn't want to work? Then nobody would have been messed around, particularly the poor kid she was working with, rather than coming out with that shit!"

Everybody agreed and turned their attention to other tasks.

Tara sneaked up to the interview room which was a private area and phoned Max, to make sure he was on for the next evening as they were due to meet at Windleston Hall. He was as excited as a Labrador puppy with the toilet roll in its mouth on the TV advert. He told her that he was planning to be there for seven, in time for dinner. Tara would leave home at around nine in the morning because she was supposed to be on the course. She had left the schedule details of the meeting on the kitchen notice board for Simon to see. She had no intention of attending the course but would check in early, go shopping and have a little look around the small rural town nearby.

Everybody at work also thought she was on the course, apart from Daniel whom Tara had confided in so she was sorted on all alibi fronts. She momentarily wondered what excuse Max had made to his wife but dismissed that notion quickly as she really wasn't that concerned. Later she took off to see Stephanie, to get her waxing done. Stephanie could spot a stray hair a mile off and had her all plucked and oven-ready as she called it, then she had a long relaxing massage.

Tara arrived at the hotel the next day and checked in. As luck would have it, she received a text from Guy who thought she must have died. He'd sent her so many texts and messages but seeing as she was quite busy with Max, she'd ignored him. However, today his timing was perfect as she was all alone in a huge bedroom. She replied, explained the situation and within two hours Guy was lying next to her in the bed. He was unbelievable in the sack, in fact, he could leave Max standing but as time marched on she knew she had to kick him out. She looked at her watch and pretended to panic.

"Jesus! Is that the time? I have to go!"

She leapt out of bed and ran the bath. Guy tried to get in the bath with her but Tara managed to shoo him out and promised to call him tomorrow. Next, she rang room service for a delicious, cool glass of Kir Royale, which she sipped while relaxing in a fragrant, hot bath. She never did get to the shops but Max managed to arrive late with some sob story involving his children. Tara had to tell him that she really wasn't interested whilst unzipping his trousers at the same time. She took him in her mouth and suddenly he forgot all about his children. He and Tara never did make it down for dinner.

Max left at six-thirty the next morning which suited Tara as she liked her own space and was a bit sick of him by then. She hadn't bothered to ask him what he'd told Kate. Max drove home quickly. Kate had been away the night before visiting an old friend from her medical school days and had taken the girls with her. However, he had to be back early in case she rang the landline at home. He hadn't mentioned going missing the previous night. At a push, he could tell her that he was duty solicitor and had been called to the police station in the dead of night but he knew he wouldn't get away with that lie first thing in the morning.

He dashed in and opened the lounge curtains then spotted the answer machine light flashing with one message. Luckily, he'd only missed the call by ten minutes so he hurriedly dialled Kate's mobile number from the landline and explained he'd been in the shower when the phone rang. He even had the television on in the background, as an extra reason he hadn't heard the phone ringing. Kate listened to him banging on about having to go to the police station in the middle of the night. She wanted to interrupt him, go insane and shout and scream but she reined herself in, remembering that revenge was a dish best served cold. The stupid man didn't realise, she had a private detective following him. She knew exactly where he was last night and with whom.

22

The weather in the Old Town was fabulous, everything Jonny could have hoped for in the quest for acquiring the perfect tan. However, Izzy was irritating him half to death. She couldn't relax or even just lie and sunbathe. She talked nonstop when she wasn't going back and forth to the room, or bringing drinks and more annoyingly she kept replenishing her lipstick every ten minutes. His only consolation had been pretending to pass out drunk last night and avoided having to sleep with her. He still sort of liked her but she was way out of his division. All she ever talked or moaned about was her job and the people she worked with and they sounded like the most boring people on the planet. So when she mentioned hiring a car he turned on the full charm offensive. Anything was better than listening to her and he quite fancied a trip around the island.

Izzy infuriated him further when she kept changing her mind about which days to hire it but with some gentle persuasion on his part, they delivered it at noon. A nice little Suzuki jeep for them to play with. Izzy was the named driver as he repeated the fact that he couldn't drive. Izzy fought hard with herself not to mention the time she saw him behind the wheel of a car but something inside her told her to stop. He was clearly lying but if she came out with it now, the holiday would be ruined so she bit her tongue and they set off to fill up with petrol.

From the moment she switched on the ignition, Jonny criticised her driving skills pushing her nerves to breaking point.

"What the fuck are you doing?" he shouted as she drove too close to the kerb.

"Nothing," she replied. "I've never driven one of these before and you're making me worse."

But he couldn't help himself and when she tried to reverse into a parking bay, he really lost it and began screaming at her.

"You can get a fucking bus in there for fuck's sake!"

Izzy was so upset that she jumped out of the jeep and stood with her arms waving around like a windmill.

"Well if you can do any better," she yelled. "Be my guest and you fucking drive!"

Jonny stomped out of the passenger seat, slammed the door and got behind the wheel.

"Get in the fucking car," he said and Izzy clambered into the passenger side.

Not one word was said as he drove away but all Izzy could think about was the fact that he said he couldn't drive and for sure they weren't insured. However, they continued driving along the coast, stopping to look at some stunning views and visit places of interest. By the time they headed back, it was if nothing had happened. Izzy knew better than to confront him.

They reached the hotel at around seven. Jonny jumped into the shower then announced he was starving and wanted to go straight down for dinner. This put Izzy is a bit of a state and it took her ages to get ready and she didn't want to be hurried. Two hours' later, she could just about see the steam coming out of his ears, so she told him to go down and she would meet him at the bar. Izzy was nearly in tears. She just couldn't decide what to wear.

Jonny sat waiting for her at the bar. The Russian had texted him and for the thousandth time, he asked himself what on earth he was doing in Tenerife with Izzy but quickly reminded himself that it was all free. He promised himself to work hard on his tan tomorrow. He wanted to look good when he got back. Everybody would be saying how great he looked and asking where he had been. He'd say he'd been away with some of the boys.

Izzy didn't know what she had said to Jonny to annoy him so much but as he got drunker and drunker, he kept mimicking her and generally having a go.

"Oh, you're in finance, are you?" he kept saying and Izzy began to get upset.

"And what exactly do you do Jonny?" she snapped back.

This made him worse. His eyes narrowed into little slits.

"None of your fucking business Miss Goody Two Shoes."

Everyone in the bar could see and hear everything. It was so embarrassing. Izzy had enough and abruptly stood up, pushed her chair back and stormed out of the bar. When she reached their room, she was still fuming and couldn't work out what had turned him into such a different person. Then she heard a tap at the door and reluctantly opened it to find Jonny standing there looking shame-faced.

"Look, I'm sorry there was no need for me to speak like that. I don't know what came over me," he said putting his arms around her. "Let's find a bar and get out of this place?"

Izzy just wanted to curl up into a ball and cry her eyes out. She was so unhappy and now felt trapped with him. She wiped her eyes and tried to pull herself together.

"You're not speaking to me like that again Jonny."

"I know," he replied, softly.

As they left the hotel, Izzy sighed with relief that she didn't have to walk through the bar area.

They found a taxi easily outside the hotel. Neither of them had any idea where the bars were, so they asked the taxi driver to take them to the best bar Tenerife had to offer. Five minutes later they stopped outside a place called Frankie's. As soon as they got out of the taxi, Izzy could hear the pumping music and she noticed that it didn't look too exclusive but they were there now, nothing she could do and Jonny seemed happy as he strode up the stairs at the entrance, leaving her to follow on behind.

As soon as they walked in, Izzy decided she didn't like the look of the people lining the bar, at all. The clientele was rough, to say the least, and she found it difficult to tell them apart. All the men resembled each other with their bald heads, huge biceps and sleeve tattoos. The girls standing around also resembled each other in bad fashion and appalling makeup. However, Izzy did notice two really pretty girls, standing on their own in a corner, away from the other people.

All eyes were on her and Jonny as they found a place to sit at the bar. Izzy couldn't help noticing how women always drooled over Jonny. He was very aware of it and Izzy could tell that he loved it as he started shaking hands with everyone and introducing himself. Izzy felt mortally uncomfortable but knew that she was going to have to keep her opinions to herself. In fact, she would need to get very drunk to get through this. The night wore on and Jonny continued throwing the drink down his neck. He was in his element with these people, lording it over them, telling them stories about the famous people he had met and knew in Ibiza which was all news to Izzy as he hadn't told her any of these stories. It was like he needed to play the big guy and it was working because even all the men in the bar were hanging on his every word. It made her skin crawl. In fact, it was pathetic.

Izzy noticed that one of the girls sitting in the corner was really pretty. She had a figure to die for and beautiful, long, dark hair but more to the point she kept staring at Jonny. She dismissed it as the girl could clearly see that he was with her. Izzy touched Jonny's arm and told him that she was popping to the ladies. The last thing she expected to see when she came back was the girl standing next to him with her arm around his waist. Jonny had his back to her so didn't notice she'd returned and at this point, he bent down and pecked the girl on the cheek.

The girl had noticed her approaching and gave Izzy a look that said I can have him if I want him. Izzy felt a red-hot rage instantly burn through her body. She was livid. How could he humiliate her like this? So she changed direction and headed straight for the front door. She was leaving and he could go and fuck himself she thought. She got straight into a waiting taxi and went back to the hotel. She was sure that Jonny would follow her so she quickly glanced at her watch and noticed the time, eleven-thirty. She decided that she'd give him twenty minutes to follow her and if he didn't, she'd pack up and get a flight home. She wasn't putting up with this type of behaviour.

She paced around and couldn't calm down but after an hour decided that it was over and she got into bed. She was so upset that she was shaking and felt sick but must have fallen asleep because she woke up when she heard the apartment door open. She glanced at her wristwatch. It was one o'clock and she could hear him crashing about. He was obviously drunk again so she pretended to be asleep. She felt the bed give way as he got in and within five minutes, heard him snoring his head off. Izzy was so upset. He hadn't tried to say sorry or make any amends at all, it was as if nothing had happened. It did cross her mind that this was probably normal behaviour in his world but she had made her mind up she was going home tomorrow. Tara had been right about him.

Izzy woke the next morning still feeling very annoyed but as he lay beside her still snoring, she decided to wait to hear what he had to say about last night. He clearly wasn't going to wake up any time soon so she showered and headed down for breakfast. On the way out, she slammed the door so hard it nearly flew off its hinges. That should wake him up she said to herself smiling.

She ate breakfast alone and decided that she had better text Tara. It was day four and she knew her friend would be worried so she needed to touch base with her. She didn't want to admit to her friend how wrong things really were, because she knew Tara would worry. So she just texted that the weather was brilliant and everything was fine. Tara replied within seconds.

'Ring me when you get back'

Izzy knew that her friend had sensed all was not well.

Jonny didn't join her at all for breakfast so reluctantly she went back to the room and grabbed her bathing gear. She made plenty of noise getting ready, applying her makeup again and pulling out clothes from the bedroom wardrobes but Jonny just lay in bed like a beached whale snoring his head off so she left for the pool, once more almost removing the door from its hinges on her way out.

Izzy lay at the side of the pool and noticed that she was the only single person there. Everyone else was in a couple, applying each other's suntan lotions, smiling and happy together which only intensified her unhappiness. She'd been shouted out and then belittled in front of people and to boot, she had paid for everything so far, even the drinks and taxi last night. He hadn't offered to pay for anything. He just expected she would get her purse out.

Her brain was working overtime when Andreas the hotel manager on his rounds, stopped to ask her if everything was Ok? Her eyes filled up with tears just because he spoke kindly to her. He was such a gentle man and clearly concerned about what had occurred in the bar the night before. She assured him that everything was fine and attempted a dazzling smile. Just then she looked over Andreas's shoulder and saw Jonny looking for her. As soon as he saw her, he waved and make his way over. He chatted away to Andreas as if nothing had happened in the bar. Izzy was mortified but Jonny was busy putting his towel down on the sunbed next to Izzy's and chatting away.

When Andreas wished them a great afternoon and left, Jonny started talking away to her, again as if nothing had happened. Izzy couldn't stand the charade any longer.

"So you're not going to mention what happened last night?" she snapped.

"What about last night?" he sighed as if carrying the weight of the world on his shoulders.

"Are you for real, Jonny? That girl you were kissing?"

"Kissing?" he scoffed. "It was a peck on the cheek for fuck's sake. She knows somebody who knows me."

"That's alright, then is it?" she said exasperated.

Jonny started to raise his voice and Izzy became very aware they had attracted the attention of the other sunbathers.

"Nothing happened," he growled. "She approached me."

"Yeah, sure," replied Izzy. "Only when I left you alone to go to the ladies. Why didn't she come up to you when I was there?"

Now Jonny was starting to get really riled up and his eyes narrowed viciously.

"How the fuck do I know? Why don't you ask her that question?"

He rolled over onto his stomach so that he could start tanning his back, dismissing her, conversation over. She didn't know what to do or say or even how to handle him. In all her years, she had never met such an ill-mannered man in her life. It didn't seem to bother him that she had made her own way back to the hotel in the dark and in a foreign country. Izzy lay thinking about her options. They had only two full days left, followed by a full day's travelling home and eventually, she reasoned with herself that he was right, he hadn't approached the girl. She had willingly gone over to him maybe to say that she kind of knew him? Plus, it had been just a friendly peck on the cheek and he had come back to the hotel room. It wasn't as if he'd stayed out all night with her.

Jonny lay next to her, wondering what the hell he was doing there with her at all. He had zero in common with her other than feeling happy about her paying for him and quite frankly he'd had a much better time in the bar last night with complete strangers who didn't talk about schools all of the time. He'd had a really good laugh with the guys at the bar but he realised he was going to have to be nice to her and put on the famous

Devroe charm just to survive the last few days on holiday. He had to admit, she looked attractive today but Jonny wasn't attracted to that look. He liked club girls, tits and teeth, nice short skirts and the slutty look. Izzy always looked immaculate and very well dressed but not dressed like a club girl in any way, shape or form. He really didn't have much in common with her except that she was one of the few straight people without a criminal record that he knew. She hadn't even had a parking ticket. She might actually come in handy one day he thought.

23

Tara had read Izzy's text and knew something was wrong. She showed the message to Daniel first thing on Monday morning at work, to see what he thought.

"Well that speaks a thousand words," he said, passing the phone back to Tara. "Don't you think you should ring her? It wouldn't do any harm to let that gorilla know someone's checking up on her."

"You are right," she said. "But I think she'll go spare if I do. Something's not right so I might make the situation worse. I'm sure she'll tell me when she gets back and then hopefully it will all be over."

Daniel agreed and shoved an application form in front of her.

"Here," he said. "Have a look at this and take particular notice of the medical history section."

Tara glanced through the details of Andrew Hodgson's history and thought so far so good. He was a science specialist. Her mood dropped when she reached the medical section. He had ticked the autistic box. Tara looked up at Daniel.

"Is he being serious?" she asked.

Daniel nodded.

"I don't understand it," she continued. "He's been working for two years at a really tough academy. How the hell did he manage that if he's autistic?"

"Probably because that school can never get staff. Beggars can't be choosers but this is the best bit, he's handed his notice in to become a carer for his sick father."

"But if he's autistic he may need a carer," said Tara. "And for insurance purposes, would we employ him in a science lab handling dangerous chemicals, surrounded by children?"

"I agree," said Daniel. "But let's see what his references have to say first? He only wants work for two days a week."

Max inundated her with texts all morning which she ignored. Then she decided to open the post because Val was waiting for timesheets to come in. She immediately noticed a hand-written envelope, marked strictly private and confidential, to be opened by addressee only and thought that it looked interesting so ripped it open. She settled down to read it as it was pages long but felt her heart hammering in her chest when she read the opening line.

'I know that you're having an affair with my husband.'

It was from Kate, Max's wife. Tara read and reread the letter with her heart hammering even harder, wondering what to do and wanting to throttle Max for being so stupid as to get caught. The letter went on to explain to Tara that Max had problems. She had no intention of informing Simon about what was clearly going on but that she was very worried about her husband's state of mind. She would like to talk to Tara. She had left her mobile number at the bottom of the letter.

"No fucking way!" said Tara out loud.

"What's wrong?"' asked Carrie.

Tara hadn't realised she'd spoken out loud.

"Oh, nothing," she replied and got up to go to the interview room, where she could speak in private.

Carrie watched her leave, realising something had seriously rattled her.

Tara felt so angry, she could barely press Max's number on her phone. When he answered and she said she needed to see him urgently, he was too stupid to detect the urgency in her voice and started to come on with the sexy jokes.

"This is serious Max," she said cutting him off.

He agreed to get out of work in twenty minutes and meet her at the usual coffee shop, around the corner from their offices. Meanwhile, Tara called Daniel up to the interview room.

"Look at this for fuck's sake," she said handing him Kate's letter.

As Daniel read the letter, he turned whiter and whiter.

"Fucking hell, she knows!" he spluttered. "What are you going to do?"

"It's his fucking problem, Dan. He'll have to sort it out with her. I'm presuming since she's writing to me that she wants to save her marriage and scare me into not seeing him anymore."

Tara could see Daniel's mind working overtime.

"I'm concerned about the part where she tells you he has a lot of problems and she's very worried about him. I mean what kind of problems has he got that you don't know about?"

"I don't fucking know," she snapped. "He's needy, I know that much. More importantly, how did he manage to get caught? I have to leave. I'm meeting him in five minutes. I'll show him the letter that's for sure."

Tara headed off to the coffee shop, while Daniel sat there feeling more and more concerned about her. He always thought Max was trouble. In fact, he couldn't stand him.

Max knew something was wrong as soon as Tara arrived and sat down opposite him. To say he nearly had a heart attack when he read Kate's letter was an understatement. He turned into a little boy, shaking all over which irritated Tara immensely. She just wanted to yell at him to man up and pack it in. Kate had obviously written to Tara first without saying a word to her husband. Suddenly, he grabbed her hand.

"I don't want to lose you," he mumbled. "I love you."

"For fuck's sake," said Tara, feeling she was just about to go into orbit. "We are both married and you have kids. It was just a bit of fun Max. It was never going to go anywhere. Now just go and sort your wife out and get on with your life."

To her horror, Max burst into tears. Everyone turned to look. So she stood up, separating her hand from his and glowered at him.

"Get a fucking grip you fuckwit," she said through gritted teeth, then threw his wife's letter at him and stormed out of the café.

With perfect timing, Hayley and Susan appeared walking down the street towards her.

"That's her!" said Hayley, nudging Susan sharply in the ribs with her elbow.

Max came out of the café in such a distressed state, he careered straight into them. He didn't know where to put himself but fell on Susan's neck and wrapped his arms around her.

"I've missed you foxy!" he cried into her shoulder.

Hayley could not believe her eyes. He'd obviously had a row with the blonde and now Susan was hugging him back.

"Oh Max," she wept. "Where have you been?"

This was exactly what he expected to happen so he kissed her full on the lips.

"Can I come to you tonight?" he whispered in her ear. "I've missed you so much and I need to talk to you."

"Of course, you can," said Susan from Cloud Nine and he kissed once more, full on the lips.

Hayley had clenched her fists so tightly she'd almost drawn blood. When Max walked away, Susan dried the tears from her eyes looked at her friend.

"Do not say a word," she warned.

So Hayley clamped her mouth shut and said nothing.

Max walked around the block a few times to compose himself, then returned to his office and sat down at his desk to read Kate's letter. He couldn't believe Kate had found out and written to Tara without mentioning it to him. She had appeared fine at the weekend, in fact perfectly normal. He didn't want Tara to know about his problems and he felt annoyed that Kate had even hinted he had some. Those kinds of things shouldn't be shared with anyone outside of their marriage. He rang Kate at the hospital but she told her PA to tell him she was busy and they would speak tonight. She knew exactly why he was ringing. She wondered if Tara had realised yet what a weak creature her husband really was.

When Tara got back to work, she told Daniel she'd dumped Max and thrown the letter at him.

"I didn't fucking want it," she said. "I told him it was just a bit of fun but if people are going to get hurt it has to stop."

"What worries me," said Daniel. "Is that Kate knows something about him that you don't. I feel that may not be a good thing. When she tells you he has problems, I'd be inclined to believe her. It must have taken some balls to write that letter."

"I agree," said Tara. "He's way too needy but it may be something else. On the other hand, she could be making it up to finish us. It's Ok though because I've dumped him. I'm not risking getting into trouble over him."

Daniel didn't tell her what he really believed that Max Armstrong wouldn't go away easily.

Max had planned in advance everything he said that night. As soon as Kate came home, he started crying.

"I'm so sorry Kate," he said. "Tara means nothing to me. It's just that you always seem so busy but I know I should be more understanding. I love you, I really do. It's finished with her. I don't want to lose you, our family."

Kate slapped him hard across his face and told him he was pathetic but at the back of her mind, she couldn't forget what happened the last time she told him she was going to divorce him. She felt enough had been said and decided to leave it at that.

Later when the girls were in bed and everything had calmed down Max put his running gear on and told Kate he was going for a run for about an hour-ish, to clear his head. Kate wanted him out of the house for a while so thought that this was a great idea and a very healthy choice. So off Max went jogging straight to Susan's house, less than a mile away. Sex he thought would definitely clear his mind. He couldn't stop smiling to himself as he got closer and closer to Susan's dingy flat.

Tara had been reflecting all evening about what had happened that afternoon. Simon was in Brussels on a business trip for two days so she didn't need to worry about him. She called Debbie who came straight over and freaked out when she heard what had happened.

"I hope you got shot of him after that?"

"Dumped him, big time," said Tara.

They both agreed that she couldn't continue conducting her life in this manner because eventually, Simon would find out, no matter how discreet she thought that she was. Debbie joked that Tara had had a good run for her money and she should quit while she was ahead. Tara had thought that was hilarious but on reflection agreed. In fact, she wasn't sure how she hadn't been caught in the past.

24

Izzy woke up on day five a very happy woman. Jonny had taken her down for dinner last night then made love to her for over an hour. He'd wrapped himself around her and fallen into a deep sleep and she'd never felt as content as this for a long time. She wondered if there would ever come a point in time when life would feel normal again, the way it used to be when a phone call from Jonny brought her happiness, instead of feeling like it was dragging a piece of her heart out of her chest. She felt tears sting her eyes. Then, as she lay beside him, she decided there and then to write off all the mood swings and bad temper tantrums he'd shown throughout this holiday, put it down to the fact that he would need time to get used to being in a couple. He was so used to being by himself that he must have found it a struggle.

They spent their last day lounging around the pool and soaking up the last of the sunshine. Jonny was being so lovely to her the only downside was he couldn't take his eyes off a pretty, young blonde who had checked in the previous day. Izzy subconsciously felt pleased that they were leaving.

Jonny had worked up a great tan and was starting to think about going home. His phone had never stopped and Tony advised him to get in touch the minute he got back, as he had a job for him. He checked his cash flow while Izzy was in the shower and was very pleased with himself that he had only spent fifty euros. Not bad, he thought, not bad at all for a week in Tenerife.

He was looking forward to getting home and had already texted the Russian for a date. He was dying for some real sex. Izzy wasn't very exciting in the sack, it was a bit like having sex with a headmistress but at least he'd worked out that once he'd had sex with her, it was enough to keep her mouth shut, payment for the free holiday. So he got so drunk on the last night, passed out and pretended to be fast asleep the next morning. He'd felt her hands stroking his back but it did nothing for him so he continued to snore and she got out of bed and started to run the shower.

She coughed up for the taxi back to the airport so he scored there and as they drove away from the hotel, Andreas the manger watched them leave.

"What a lovely girl," he said to Maria his second in command. "What is she doing with that moron?"

"You know," sighed Maria. "She paid for everything, including the hire car and the taxi. He didn't pay for anything."

Andreas sighed. He saw it all the time in the hotel industry.

"She's got everything going for her and he's just a bad guy. He's got it written all over him," he said.

"She'll find out soon enough," said Maria and they went off to greet the new arrivals from the latest holiday flight.

When they reached the airport, Jonny started moaning about the small terminal building and how basic the facilities were. To shut him up Izzy booked them into the private lounge, costing her a further one hundred and fifty euros. It was worth every penny just to get some peace. Jonny smiled as she went to fetch some drinks. He loved testing her to see how far he could go. He thought this was great. After all, he was only used to going to Benidorm with his pals and there wasn't a private lounge there. In fact, he'd never set foot in one before.

Finally, they were home and Izzy dropped Jonny off but not before she'd had to stop for petrol, which set him off moaning again about having to wait. As she approached his flat, she began to feel a tad nervous, wondering what he was going to say. She needn't have worried as he jumped straight out of her car as soon as it stopped, grabbed his bag, pecked her on the cheek and left.

Izzy cried all the way home. What a thoughtless bastard. He didn't even thank her for the holiday. As soon as she got in, she dropped her suitcase, grabbed a bottle of water and phoned Tara. Tara could barely hear a word she said, she was so upset. So Tara jumped in the car and drove straight over to Izzy's house. The whole saga poured out.

"The ungrateful twat," said Tara. "Who the fuck does he think he is?"

But she knew she had to try and calm Izzy down who was still terribly upset. She made her some of her favourite tea and eventually Izzy agreed that it was over. She was done with him. Tara let out a huge sigh of relief.

"Thank God for that Izzy. He's nothing like us and he doesn't know how to behave or even how to treat you."

What Tara really wanted to say but couldn't was that Jonny had used her friend for a free holiday. It would have been like rubbing salt into the wound and that wasn't on so she stopped herself from going any further. To shake Izzy out of her devastation Tara decided to change the subject and tell her about Max and the subsequent letter from his wife Kate. She was in full flow explaining that she'd dumped him when Izzy started to laugh uncontrollably.

"So you're lecturing me?" she spluttered. "Your solicitor's no better than my doorman!" and they both fell about laughing. It was like they were still kids and had survived getting out of another scrape together.

Meanwhile, Jonny dumped his holdall and called Stevie the driver to let him know he was back at his flat and to come and pick him up. He quickly pulled on a pair of old jeans, he didn't want to get blood all over his good pair and set off with the baseball bat he kept by his front door. No scraped or bruised knuckles for him this time. It would clash with his lovely tan.

Days went by and Izzy heard nothing from Jonny. At first, felt pleased because she didn't want anything to do with him. Then as time wore on she couldn't stop thinking about him, wondering where he was and what he was doing. She even contemplated getting in touch with Tanya and popping into Limes. Then after a week had gone by, she was sitting at her desk at work and her face lit up when she saw a florist coming into the school with a huge bouquet of red roses. Oh my God, she thought. At last, he's going to say thank you for a great holiday. But her hopes were dashed when the florist asked for Jackie the head. It was her wedding anniversary. Izzy could feel the tears welling up.

Jonny was thinking about Izzy but only because he needed to sort his driving problem out. He had no licence and needed to apply for a provisional. He was hopeless at anything official and was sure that if he asked Izzy nicely, she'd jump at the chance to help him sort the paperwork out.

'Hi you. You ok?' he texted.

He waited. Of course, she may have lost interest in him but he seriously doubted that. Women loved him. When Izzy saw the text, she was quite surprised to hear from him but she could feel the heat going through her body. She felt ecstatic, he did want her after all, she told herself so she decided to stay as casual as possible and replied only:

'great thanks'

To her surprise back came the message:

'fancy a curry tomorrow night?'

And that was that. She had jumped straight back in. He told her to pick him up at 7.30 pm.

The next day Tara was really busy but checked to see how Izzy was doing. She felt quite surprised to hear her friend sounding like her normal, happy pre-Jonny self. Izzy didn't say a word about her date with Jonny. She knew Tara wouldn't understand.

That afternoon Jonny attended a meeting with Tony. Tony wanted him to go to Leeds on Saturday and pick up a few packages for him but it was proving difficult on the transport front. Stevie needed the car for another of Tony's pickups so they had to find a spare motor. Then Jonny had a brain wave.

"I know someone who will drive me to Leeds," he said. "As long as you're cool that the driver's a bird and a civilian?"

Tony smiled, knowing exactly whom Jonny meant.

"That silly bird who paid for you to go to Tenerife?" he laughed. "What a mug. I don't know what it is you do to them Jonny but it clearly works." And they both laughed. "Yeah it's cool," continued Tony. "She won't ask any questions, take her shopping or something just make sure you get the gear. Here's the pickup address."

Jonny knew she wouldn't have a clue what was in the packages and if anybody was watching them, they would never in a million years suspect her of anything. So while they were sitting eating the curry, Jonny asked her if she fancied a trip out to Leeds to do some shopping. Izzy couldn't believe it, her heart was racing. He wanted to spend some time with her and have a lovely day out! She jumped at the chance. When she popped to the ladies, Jonny texted Tony:

'Saturday sorted' and then he smiled to himself. Women were so stupid and gullible. He'd never met one yet who wasn't.

25

Tara and the whole team were having a bitch of a day. Everything that could go wrong did go wrong and to make matters worse someone kept ringing in then dropping the receiver. It was becoming very annoying.

"I bet it's that arsehole across the road," said Daniel quietly to Tara who had also thought exactly the same thing.

Then come mid-morning the bouquet arrived with a card, message: *'I miss you, I love you, please ring me there's so much I want to say to you'.*

"Here we go," said Daniel.

There wasn't much she could do with the flowers. She could hardly send them back without drawing attention to the situation, so she rammed them into two vases and put them in the office upstairs so that she didn't have to look at them all day. She and Daniel had started frequenting the same coffee shop that she and Max had, on the pretext they needed to talk shop but Dan was about the only person she could confide in. Using the café so much, the regulars started to say hello to them but they did notice, now and then, the same two women who always sat as close to them as possible. In fact, every time they came in, they moved closer and closer. Both Tara and Daniel hushed their voices as they were sure the women were listening in.

Daniel asked Tara if she knew them but she'd never met them before. Then one morning the blonde woman's phone rang.

"Hi Max," she replied loudly.

"Coincidence," said Daniel as Tara looked at him.

Whilst Izzy was busy preparing to drive to Leeds and Tara was away that weekend motor racing with Simon, Daniel went with his wife and son to a women's charity fun run. Daniel clocked Max straight away. He was with two little girls and a hefty blonde woman who wasn't particularly obese or slim but unfortunately had the physique of a shot putter. Daniel presumed correctly that this was Kate, Max's wife.

When Daniel's wife Anna went off to the start line and the shot-putter moved out of sight, Max let go of his little girls' hands and they moved in front of him to play with the ball he'd just given them. He was busy watching them chase the ball around when suddenly a short, blonde woman appeared out of nowhere and dashed up to him. The starting pistol made a loud bang to signal the start of the race and the runners all moved off together but the blonde woman didn't miss a stride. She ran up to Max, linked her hands behind his neck and kissed him full on the lips. Daniel had his camera in his hand and at the same time as the kiss, the shutter clicked. He took another one for good measure. He was sure that it was one of those women from the café who had been taking far too much interest in their conversations.

Max appeared quite shocked. His arms remained stiff and straight at his sides. He didn't touch the woman and after having a brief exchange of words, he moved away as quickly as possible. Daniel couldn't believe that his girls had not spotted what was going on but as the firing pistol had gone off their attention had been drawn to the start of the race, probably trying to spot their mother.

After the race, Daniel couldn't get Anna home fast enough so that he could find somewhere to get the shots developed ready for Monday morning, ready to show Tara. He didn't want to say why he wanted to get the pictures developed so quickly but Anna thought that it would be nice to have a record of her fabulous fastest time. Daniel had photographed her crossing the finishing line. Susan watched Hayley finish the race and congratulated her. Hayley thought it was odd that Susan didn't do the run but as she looked over towards the other competitors and noticed Max and Kate and one of their little girls proudly displaying her mother's race medal swinging from her neck, that explained it. Hayley wondered how desperate her friend was. Max must have told her Kate was running so they would be able to steal a few minutes together, even with his wife in the background. Max, on the other hand, had been very concerned that someone might have witnessed Susan kissing him but he'd taken a very good around and saw nobody who really knew him. He didn't recognise Daniel, after all, he'd only met him the once.

26

Izzy was beyond excited as she drove to Jonny's flat to pick him up for their day trip to Leeds. She was really looking forward to a day's shopping and of course spending quality time with him. Jonny, on the other hand, had the address of the pickup written on a note in his pocket. The pickup was in the city centre so shouldn't cause too many problems for them. So on the journey down Jonny broached the subject.

"I've been asked to pick up a couple of packages for a friend whose mate lives in Leeds. is that ok?"

"Yes, of course. Where is it?" said Izzy considering it only a minor distraction.

Jonny typed the address into her satellite navigation.

"It won't take long," he said. "Then I'll take you to Harvey Nichols for a cocktail."

That perked Izzy up no end. He knew he'd got her totally on side. Well, that was easy he thought to himself.

The pickup was from an old warehouse near the city centre so it didn't take long. It never occurred to Izzy to ask why the packages were coming from an old disused warehouse. In fact, it didn't enter her head to ask Jonny about it all. He proceeded to load all six into the boot of her car. She did think to herself that they looked very heavy and resembled bricks. However, all she could talk about was shopping and where they could go for lunch.

She was starting to drive Jonny round the bend with her constant banging on. He could feel himself getting tenser and he had to fight with himself to keep his mouth shut, especially when she nearly reversed into a post when she finally found the multi-storey car park. He couldn't cause a scene, what with the gear in the boot of her car so he bit his tongue.

They found a lovely little bistro for lunch and when the bill came Izzy offered to pay so Jonny let her. They went into Harvey Nichols but Izzy could feel the atmosphere between them getting thicker and after one hour of taking different outfits into the fitting room, none of which she could afford, she asked Jonny if he wanted to go to the roof garden for a cocktail. Jonny checked his watch and indicated that they should be getting back if they wanted to beat the rush hour traffic. He had lost the will to live.

Izzy felt hugely disappointed. She'd been looking forward to the cocktail all day and it had been fun trying on the clothes but she knew he'd had enough so they went back to the car. On the way home Jonny could barely be bothered to speak to her and fell asleep for most of the journey. Izzy looked over at him. She loved spending time with him but she wanted to chat and get to know more about him. Maybe it was a compliment she told herself that he felt so comfortable with her that he could relax so easily.

She dropped Jonny off at his flat and as usual, he didn't invite her up, just said he'd be in touch and that was it. He got into his flat pleased to be away from her and rang Tony to let him know that he was home and the goods had been delivered. Twenty minutes later Stevie turned up to collect the merchandise. He handed over an envelope to Jonny with fifteen hundred pounds in it in used notes. Stevie told him that one hundred of it was for the petrol. Jonny smiled whilst he counted every single note. He loved cash nearly as much as he loved women.

Izzy got in, popped the kettle on, kicked off her shoes and slumped onto the couch. She'd had a lovely day apart from her shopping time being cut short. She glanced down at the floor where her bag was lying and decided to take a look in her purse. She quickly totted up the eighty pounds for petrol, another eighty quid for lunch and the thirty-three pounds for the parking and suddenly realised that Jonny hadn't contributed to anything all day. She actually blushed as she felt so stupid. She started to get angry with herself as on top of everything, he had just sat there in the passenger seat like she was his personal chauffeur. She made a cup of tea and then started to think that it was her car and petrol but he really should have paid for the lunch. After all, she had paid for his holiday.

27

Daniel noticed that he was sweating as he clicked the roller shutter up to get into the office that Monday morning. It got worse when he saw Tara's car. She was already in. He had the photograph in his suit pocket. After getting the film developed, he'd removed the picture and kept it in the glove compartment of his car so that Anna wouldn't see it. She would find it very strange that her husband had taken a photograph of two strangers kissing. He strode into the office but Tara was on the phone sorting out a booking so he waited until she replaced the receiver.

"Remember I told you Anna was taking part in that charity race at the weekend?"

Tara looked up wondering why Daniel was looking so shifty.

"Yes, how did she do?"

"Look who else was there," he said, propping the photograph up in front of her.

Tara picked it up and had a good look.

"That woman's familiar so it can't be Kate as I've never met her but I have seen this woman before."

Daniel watched the cogs turning followed by the dawn of recognition.

"Fucking hell," exploded Tara. "It's one of those women from the coffee shop." Then she looked up nervously. "Did she see you?"

"No," he said laughing. "She was far too preoccupied with lover boy to notice anyone. She took a hell of a chance what with Kate there but I don't think it bothered her that much."

"So he's been seeing her at some point," said Tara. "There's nothing secretive or furtive about her behaviour there. She's full-on."

"Who knows with that fuckwit," shrugged Daniel. "But it's pretty obvious that Kate doesn't know about her."

Tara studied the picture again.

"He was looking after their girls but I have to be honest and say that he looked very uncomfortable when she was kissing him. She turned up out of nowhere and he got a big shock when he saw her."

"I'm not surprised," said Tara. "Hell of a risk that Kate might spot them."

"I got the impression that's what she wanted to happen," said Daniel. "Look at his body language, he's not exactly throwing his arms around her."

"Well," said Tara. "Our next café visit is going to be very interesting if she's there."

"You had to know," he said.

"I did, thanks. But how sad that this woman has to follow me around and sees me as some sort of threat to her relationship with him. That suggests it's been going on a long time and he's promised her everything, poor cow."

Daniel shook his head.

"I see it differently," he said. "I think you're right it's been going on for years. Then he met you and something happened and he's dumped her. That's why she sees you as the threat."

"Oh God," she sighed. "Why are women so fucking stupid. I didn't even know she existed. It's his fault. She should be following that dick head around, not me."

The rest of the staff came in. Tara was itching to get out of her seat and go to the café but when they got there, she was disappointed. Susan was on the early shift at work that day and couldn't make it.

Meanwhile, Max was beside himself. He wanted Tara so badly. He missed her and especially missed the sex. He'd never met a girl like her before but he had stupidly somehow given the game away. He should remember that Kate wasn't stupid. He had underestimated her. So he figured if he could get Tara back, he was going to have to treat Kate like a princess and convince her into thinking that their marriage was back on track.

Now that Kate knew Tara had received the letter, she correctly assumed that she had dumped her errant husband because his face had been up his arse all weekend. He didn't check his mobile every five minutes any longer, so she knew the contact had ceased and he had taken the screen lock off too, so he clearly had nothing to hide.

When Kate got into work, she instructed her PA not to disturb her for fifteen minutes. Then she got busy googling Education Supply, quickly located the telephone number and rang it. Carrie answered the call and asked her to hold. Carrie didn't have a clue who Kate was and went off to find Tara, who happened to be in the tearoom talking to Daniel.

"Tara, sorry to interrupt," said Carrie in all innocence. "There's a Kate Armstrong on the phone for you."

Daniel and Tara stared at each other.

"What does she want?" asked Tara.

"She just said it's personal and you would know who she was."

Tara couldn't believe it. She was a hostage in her own building, first a letter and now a phone call. Was the woman mad, she'd made her point. She thought quickly.

"That's a great line for a sales call. Tell her I'm not available please?"

As soon as they heard the door close and Carrie went back into the main office, Daniel went mad.

"For fuck's sake, she's fucking brave wanting to speak to the other woman!"

"Or stupid," said Tara.

Daniel felt concerned again.

"What is it that she's so desperate to tell you, Tara?"

Tara didn't want to know. She already had her mobile in her hand and was texting Max.

'What is your fucking wife doing ringing my office? Deliver her this message Max we are finished and there really is nothing to say.'

Max, on the other hand, was simply overjoyed when he saw her name light up on the screen of his mobile. He had been sitting at his desk thinking about her. He felt ill and couldn't concentrate on anything. He wanted her back. In his mind, even if she was arguing with him it was a form of communication. He replied:

'hi baby great to hear from you, can we meet? miss you so much but I have no idea why she has contacted you'.

Tara showed the reply to Daniel who raised his eyebrows nearly as far as the tearoom ceiling.

"You're going to have problems with him, sweetie."

"No, I am not," she snapped and texted back:

'don't be a stupid fuckwit'.

Max felt so upset. She was being vile to him and he really didn't know how to proceed with her. Tara was a different proposition to Susan or even Kate. He had those two eating out of his hand but Tara was very much her own person. But then, taking a positive out of a few negatives, he still had Susan back on track after a bit of slavering and Kate's reaction boded well. She hadn't screamed for a divorce again. All he practically had to do was get Tara back on-side then happy days all round for him, back to business as usual.

When he arrived home, he found Kate already there so with a nice quiet, child-free house, he took Kate by the hand and led her upstairs. Kate didn't know what had hit her. It was the fastest, hardest sex she'd ever had and Max came like a steam train. She believed he was desperate for her. But of course, the only one he was desperate for was Tara, not Kate. All the time he was screwing Kate, he felt he was punishing Tara for not wanting him. Afterwards, she lay cuddled into him on top of the bed covers and he looked up but immediately wish that he hadn't. Why didn't she take that fucking huge cross down from the wall above their bed? It clearly wasn't working. The poor woman would need more than divine intervention to deal with her wayward husband.

The next morning Tara could not wait to get into the café to see if the two stupid bitches were there. She had decided she no longer felt in any way sorry for the stupid cow who was following her around. She clearly needed medical help. It was embarrassing for a woman to sneakily follow someone about like that. She grabbed Daniel and as they passed the shop front, she elbowed him in the ribs and pointed. They weren't disappointed. Susan and Hayley were coming down the street towards them so Daniel and Tara got in first and Tara made a point of facing the front door. Daniel felt a tad nervous. He had no idea what Tara had in mind. However, whatever it was he felt sure she'd be discreet. Tara never made a public exhibition of herself.

As usual, the two women sat as close as they could to Tara. Daniel hadn't really taken much notice of them before but now he had a good look at them and was surprised to find them slightly down at heel. In fact, the blonde one's friend had greasy, filthy, dark hair that wanted cutting and she looked as if she needed a bath. Tara got halfway down her macchiato and then suddenly stood up. She walked over to the women and held out her hand to the blonde.

"Hi," she said. 'I'm Tara Black and you are?"

The blonde woman went all the colours of the rainbow. Daniel could see this was the last thing she had expected. The woman stammered and stuttered then managed to get it out.

"Susan King," she said.

"And you are following me around because?"

Susan really did not know what to say so Tara helped her out.

"I hear that we have a mutual friend Max Armstrong?"

Any minute thought Daniel, she's going to faint.

"Erm well, yes."

"And I'm a problem to you because?" Tara ploughed on.

Susan could not have felt more embarrassed at being outed and her friend just sat there with her mouth agape. Then Susan managed to pluck up the courage to speak.

"We are going out together," she announced.

As soon as it came out of her mouth, she knew how ridiculous it sounded. The woman standing in front of her was way out of her league. She was so formidable, not to mention gorgeous, that Susan felt like a church mouse sitting there. It didn't help that Tara was standing looking down at her. Then to make it worse, Tara started to laugh.

"Well, you just keep on going out with him. It's nothing to do with me. Oh, and nice kiss at the fun run on Saturday."

Tara returned to her seat.

"Feel better for that?" said Daniel.

"I do," she replied and they both watched as Susan and her filthy friend left the café.

Susan was very close to tears as she walked quickly up the street. She felt belittled and humiliated by that woman speaking to her like that and she had to admit she was in awe of Tara. The woman was way out of

Susan's league and that made Susan hate her. She had money, a flash car, she had everything going for her and she'd even taken Max, the only person that really mattered to her.

Tara went happily back to her office, satisfied that she had put that stupid bitch in her place. She still could not understand what made women behave like that over men. He'd clearly been lying his head off to her and she was stupid for believing him. Daniel agreed, the woman was making herself look stupid.

Susan got home and could not pull herself together. Hayley tried to help but her friend stayed in an absolute rage.

"Who the fuck does that stuck up cow think she is?" she shouted. "Speaking to me like that!"

However, Hayley was more interested in how Tara knew about the fun race and the kiss.

"I don't give a fuck," wailed Susan. "I hope his wife did see us."

"You don't mean that Susan, her kids were there."

But Susan proclaimed that she did mean it. Max was going to have to leave Kate. They had been together for long enough now so the time had come that he was going to have to do something about the situation. He told her often enough that he loved her and wanted to be with her. Hayley couldn't get out of the house fast enough. She knew her friend would fall from a great height, but there was no telling her. Even Hayley knew Max would never leave Kate for Susan.

Tara popped up to the interview room and rang Izzy to tell her about the café incident. They were on the phone for ages discussing various scenarios and ended up giggling like kids. Izzy tried her best to feel sorry for Susan, after all, she knew exactly how the poor girl felt. But quite frankly she didn't stand a chance up against someone like Tara who was going at the situation like a dog at broth. Tara kept hammering the case, Susan was pathetic letting a man run her life for her. It wasn't until Tara went to bed that night and lay there running the day's events through her that she inwardly groaned. How could she have been so tactless? Izzy was Susan and Jonny was Max.

28

Izzy had a manic day at work. The head had been overspending year on year and all hell had broken loose. Jackie had been summoned to a meeting with the diocese to explain herself. Izzy as the School Business Manager was worried that she would be implicated so as soon as Jackie left, Izzy picked up the phone and explained her fears to Tara. Tara decided that her friend needed some tough love. As usual, Izzy was off on a tangent so Tara went in guns blazing.

"For fuck's sake Izzy, will you grow a backbone! The head sanctions everything so how can the School Business Manager be held responsible for her overspending?"

"Well, they may think I'm just buying things."

Tara started to laugh.

"You can't do that without the head's say so, plus you had a governors' meeting on Tuesday concerning the budget so the governors are fully up to speed on the whole school's spending."

"I know you're right," sighed Izzy. "I'm constantly telling her to stop but she just doesn't listen. She sanctioned five grand last week on supply staff and books. God knows where I'm going to find the money, plus you should see our wages bill. We are way over-staffed."

Tara started her usual rant that all of the schools should go back to being under one organisation rather than controlling themselves. The Local Education Authority wasn't perfect but Tara heard far too many horror stories concerning how some of the schools were being run and where the money actually was going. Heads she thought are not business owners, they were meant to teach. And schools are places of learning, not businesses. Daniel was forever pontificating that it was all going wrong because the wrong people were in charge and had too much control.

Izzy felt much better and more confident after getting a bollocking from her friend. Tara was right, she was far too soft. She glanced down at her desk and noticed Jonny's provisional license paperwork. She'd paid the money for it and as she sat wondering if he had received the actual license yet, her phone started to ring. Usually, mobile usage was banned in schools but seeing as Jackie the head was out again, she answered it and was surprised to hear Jonny's voice.

"I've received my provisional licence!" he said, sounding very chipper indeed.

"That's good," she laughed. "You can drive legally now."

Immediately she sensed the chill coming down the phone line.

"What's that supposed to mean?" he barked.

Izzy needed to think about what to say quickly. He was really annoyed with her so she started laughing again as if nothing was wrong.

"Jonny I was joking."

How could she have been so stupid she thought but she now had confirmation that driving was a very touchy subject. Jonny thawed out.

"Oh right," he said. "Well I didn't think that was very funny and you need to be careful what you come out with. Anyway, I thought we'd celebrate. Do you fancy a curry tonight?"

Izzy liked that idea very much. She agreed to pick him up and began to work out what to wear.

As she drove over to his flat that evening, she started to wonder if he would give her back the forty-three quid it had cost her to send away for the licence. She knew what Tara would say, just ask for the money. But she couldn't do that, not with Jonny.

Throughout the meal, he was a very happy man and it was infectious. He felt excited about driving which Izzy thought a bit crazy at his age. Surely, he could have been driving years ago. Seeing him in such a good mood, she plucked up the courage to ask him.

"Why didn't you learn years ago?" she said.

"Never really needed to drive," he said smiling. "But I fancy it now."

As usual, Izzy thought that explanation sufficed. Loads of people didn't drive until they were older. He was never going to tell her that he'd been prosecuted twice for driving without a license and no insurance.

People seemed to be coming and going in and out of the restaurant. She started to wonder where they were going. She asked Jonny but he didn't appear to know. He just shrugged off her question and carried on eating. Then one distinctive looking chap came in and went straight to the bar, was given a package and left again via the door leading to the corridor for the toilets. He didn't come back.

They enjoyed their meal and had a lovely chat. Izzy excused herself and headed off to the ladies. As she opened the door into the corridor, she felt a gust of fresh air and noticed the fire doors hadn't been closed properly. She pulled them together and made sure they were shut. Then she realised she'd forgotten to bring her handbag with her from the restaurant. She didn't really need the loo, she just wanted to refresh her lipstick.

When she came back in, she saw Jonny standing at the bar and was just in time to see him hand over quite a large package to the man who ran the restaurant. Jonny didn't bat an eyelid.

"That was quick," he said smiling at her.

"I forgot my bag," she said, retrieving it and heading back to the ladies.

As she stood in front of the mirror reapplying her lipstick, she could feel her heart hammering. She knew she had just walked into something but what it was she had no idea. It had made her feel very uncomfortable. Something else was bothering her. The package that he was handing over, she recognised it as something she'd seen before. It was the wrapping that looked familiar.

She got back to her seat and finished off her drink. Jonny was still in fine form and still, she kept wondering if he was going to offer to pay her the forty-three pounds that he owed her. She could hear Tara's voice: will you please grow a backbone and stop people walking all over you. But she was too embarrassed to ask him.

"You looked rather busy at the bar earlier," she said.

"Well, not that it's any of your business," he said, glaring at her. "I was paying for the party the Limes staff had here last weekend. They prefer cash so is that alright with you?"

Izzy felt herself going red and made a mental note to keep her thoughts to herself in future. But still, random people came in, gave the guy behind the bar some money, received a small item in return then off they went out through the fire door because they never did come back. She also noticed that the bar staff kept their eyes on her. Izzy thought that they had noticed she was paying too much attention to the people coming in but she really didn't have a clue what was going on. Izzy nearly fainted when Jonny got up to pay the bill. That was a first but the chap behind the bar, who appeared to be in charge, shooed him away patting him on the shoulder and refusing to take payment.

"No, no," he kept saying to Jonny. "You are a very good customer, have this one on us."

Bugger Izzy thought. The one and only time he was going to pay and he got out of it. She drove him home and this time didn't expect anything which was just as well because he pecked her on the cheek and set off up the steps to his flat.

On the way home, Izzy rang Tanya. She felt that the subject of the package was not for Tara's ears. She should have known then something wasn't right if she felt she couldn't discuss it with her best friend. Izzy felt it in her bones that something was going on, which she shouldn't know about. But Tanya wasn't much help.

"It was probably exactly what he said it was," she said and the more Izzy probed the more Tanya backed off.

Izzy rang off and decided that Tanya was right, she was probably just overreacting. Meanwhile, Tanya poured herself a stiff drink. It was clear to her what had been going on but Izzy did not live in that world. Tanya realised that she should never have introduced Izzy to Jonny but she never thought in a million years that Izzy would go anywhere near someone like him. He certainly wasn't Izzy's usual bag and in fact, it was Tanya who fancied him. She could handle his lifestyle. She needed another drink and poured herself a large glass of red wine. This situation wasn't good. Tanya couldn't help wondering how naïve Izzy could be. Obviously, he had been handing over either drugs or cash for drugs but either way, Izzy shouldn't be involved. It was also blatantly obvious that the people coming in and out of the restaurant were buying drugs. Tanya had heard on the grapevine, through the bank where she worked, that Tony who owned Limes also owned the Indian restaurant. So it made sense that the package Izzy had spotted was a stash of cocaine. It was all worrying and she just prayed he didn't get her friend into any trouble. However, no way was she going to forewarn Izzy or get involved. Jonny was a very dangerous man.

Izzy lay in bed but sleep just would not come. Something was niggling away at her but she couldn't put her finger on it. She always thought with Jonny that he was having a big party somewhere and she wasn't invited. She played the evening over in her head. She knew Jonny thought she was stupid but something had been going on tonight and she still didn't understand where all of those people went to. She was also thinking that Tanya hadn't been upfront with her like she was holding something back from her. Izzy knew that Tanya spent a lot of time going out in Sunhill and through her job at the bank, received a lot of information concerning where money was going and who was investing in what. To be fair to Tanya, she had warned Izzy about Jonny. She had said on more than one occasion that their worlds were totally different and she shouldn't get involved. That's when it hit her like a ton of bricks. The package in the restaurant that he handed over was exactly the same wrapping, but a slimmer version, of the packages he put in the boot of her car in Leeds.

29

No doubt about it, Max was obsessed with Tara. He begged her morning, noon and night to see him so that he could explain things to her. She decided to agree. She wanted to see his face when she told him about Susan and her silly antics. He came over to her office, strutting around like a peacock and she took him up to the interview room. The staff, apart from Daniel who looked horrified, thought Max had come about the trader's association and didn't bat an eyelid. Max was determined not to appear weak in front of her. He began to ask her how she was, just as Tara threw the photograph of Susan kissing him across the desk. Max steeled himself for one of his Oscar-winning performances. He really had missed his true vocation.

"Jesus Tara that was over a long time ago. She just happened to be at the race because her friend was running in it,"

"It looks like it's over," she said staring at him incredulously. "Have you told her?"

"Of course," he sighed. "She knows it's over it was ages ago."

Tara didn't really care one way or the other but one thing was for sure, Susan hadn't told him about their little meeting in the coffee shop. Tara thought it was remarkable how the women in his life didn't quite keep him in the picture. Max got up and wrapped his arms around her. He was all over her telling her how beautiful she was and how he missed her. It felt so good that Tara decided then and there that she liked fucking him and as long as he kept Kate reined in, then maybe she'd continue to have sex with him when she felt like it. She could feel his erection pressing into her and thought it would be rude to waste it.

Tara came back downstairs and showed Max out of her office, trying to ignore Daniel's raised eyebrows.

"What have I missed?" she asked, making herself comfortable at her desk.

Daniel was clearly in one as he was trying hard not to raise his voice.

"We have a science specialist in the interview room who I'm about to twat, he is being so difficult. He hasn't even brought a CV in."

"Way of the world with teachers these days," she sighed.

Just then they heard a noise on the stairs as the interviewee ran down. He came into the office clutching his application form and announced that he had completed it. Everybody knew that he simply had not been in the interview room long enough to complete the paperwork. Tara got out of her seat and approached him.

"Excellent," she said, holding out her hand for the form. Then scanned the details. "You haven't completed sections five six and seven."

"I know," said Abdul, smiling at her. "Because I'm going to email my CV to you tonight, so I would be repeating myself."

"Well," said Tara, returning his smile. "Without any employment history Abdul how do you think I can interview you? You haven't even completed the reference section."

She pretended to study the application form but was really stalling for effect.

"You live in London is that correct?"

"No," sighed Abdul. "I live in Sunhill."

"It states here on place of residence that you reside in Ilford, London?"

She could tell it was all getting a bit too much for him.

"I'm telling you that I live in Sunhill."

Tara watched him squirm.

"It states here that you live in London. So you can see the problem I'm having? Your paperwork has not been completed correctly."

At this point everyone in the office downed tools. They knew she wasn't going to take any crap from him and she started again.

"The small part you have completed states the agency in London. I'm not sure how you would like me to proceed with an interview with so little information. Also," she said pointing to the back page of the form. "This is a declaration that you have neither signed nor dated. And that's very important as you're stating that the information you are giving us is true."

This seemed to tip him right over the edge.

"And how long will this take?" he snapped.

"About an hour," she replied.

Abdul stifled a groan. He was seriously starting to get sick of her.

"I've never been in a teaching interview that has taken an hour."

Tara looked him straight in the eye.

"I'm surprised at that," she said. "It takes forty minutes to fill in the paperwork. You apparently haven't got time to register with us, so how about I reschedule your interview and you can squeeze us in some time?"

He just about threw the Education Supply pen back at Tara.

"Yes," he snarled. "That will be a very good idea."

As Tara turned to get the diary from Carrie's desk, he stormed out of the office and slammed the door.

"And I'm never coming back," shouted Tara.

Everyone started laughing. It happened every day. These people just could not be bothered to prepare themselves correctly for an interview. They failed to bring a CV, which made interviewing them very difficult. Tara picked his paperwork up again. He had written the name of one school in London so Tara asked Carrie to do a reference check on him. She couldn't do anything else as he'd failed to even write his teacher reference number down.

Tara went to the tea room and popped the kettle on. She heard the door open and knew Daniel had followed her.

"I take it you and lover boy are back on?" he said.

"As long as he keeps Kate in check," she grinned.

Daniel thought she was crazy.

"Jesus Tara, bit of a risk and far too close to home don't you think?"

"It will all be Ok. Don't panic. I like the sex and the action around work makes my day a bit more interesting."

"As long as you know what you're getting yourself into."

At lunchtime, she went off to meet Max for a coffee, business as usual but when Tara got back Daniel was waiting for her.

"There's been an allegation made against Sarah Grey," he said.

"Sarah? You've got to be joking. She's our best primary teacher where is she placed?"

"Denton Primary Academy."

"Fucking hell," said Tara, flopping into her chair. "It's like a fucking zoo there."

"I know," he said. "The head wants to speak to you."

"Does Sarah know anything?" she asked.

"She wouldn't say anything to me, she wants to speak to you. I think it must be a secret," he said pulling a face at her.

Sarah was Education Supply's most professional and experienced primary teacher. She'd had a fantastic career in teaching and came very highly recommended. Sarah had only resigned from her last position because her daughter had bagged a job with British Airways. She was based in New York and flying all over the world which meant she could book her mother free seats. Sarah had the time of her life flying over to New York whenever the whim took her. Education Supply knew they were very lucky to have someone of her calibre so Tara wasn't going to take this situation lying down. She rang Denton Primary and asked to speak to the head, Paula Taylor. The phone was answered by a girl who was clearly some sort of halfwit. She could barely string a sentence together and was speaking the most appalling common drawl. Again, Tara thought, this is what it's coming to. Halfwit told Tara to hold or Tara thought that's what the halfwit had said and then Paula came onto the line.

"There's been an incident concerning your supply teacher Sarah Grey," she said.

"I'm sorry to hear that but can you tell me what has happened?" said Tara.

"No, I can't," snapped Paula.

"Well, how can I deal with it if I don't know what's occurred?"

Paula wasn't having any of it.

"I will investigate this matter further and come back to you. I'm happy to keep Sarah in school for the rest of the day. I will call you later." Then she literally slammed the receiver down.

Daniel was sitting on the desk next to Tara and had heard most of the conversation.

"It can't be too serious then if they're keeping her for the rest of the day. Usually, teachers are frog-marched out of schools like criminals."

"I agree," said Tara. "It doesn't sound like a safeguarding issue."

Tara heard her phone blipping with a text. She opened the phone.

'I love fucking you'.

Tara smiled but didn't bother to reply. Daniel glared at her as he caught her smiling. He knew it was from Max. She knew Daniel only had her best interest at heart and she also had guessed that Daniel saw Max as a weak man and didn't have much time for him. He would have to get over it.

The rest of the day flew by and Tara was beginning to think that nothing was going to happen concerning Sarah. But at three o'clock Paula phoned.

"I've looked at the CCTV in school and I'm happy to report that nothing untoward has happened and I will deal with this in school."

"That's great to hear," Tara sighed. "But out of interest, what was the accusation?"

"I repeat," said Paula. "I cannot discuss the matter with you but what I will say is that Sarah Grey is the best supply teacher I've ever had. Her classroom management is first-rate."

Tara decided not to press her any further.

"Excellent, we must be doing something right. Thanks for getting back to me." Then she realised that the head had already rung off. Ignorant cow she thought to herself.

Tara told everyone that the panic was over and they could all relax. Nobody liked an allegation. Tara decided to go home then go for a run. She clicked the garage door to open before she left the office which had given Max enough time to shoot over from across the back lane. He pulled her behind the wall so that nobody could see them and started to kiss her. His hands were all over her tight skirt and he slipped one under it to feel her. She gasped as his fingers touched her. She was so wet and wanted him badly. This dangerous sex was so exciting but she stopped him. It was too close to her staff and she'd never get over it if Carrie or Mark caught them.

Tara waited for Simon to go out for a drink with his brother then picked up the phone. She needed to keep in touch with Izzy after the Tenerife fiasco. Of course, Izzy was proclaiming weeks later that they'd had a lovely time but Tara knew differently. The girl was deluded.

"I need an update," she said to Izzy as soon as she heard her friend's voice.

"Well hello to you too," she laughed. "Not much has happened really, except he took me out for a curry and also a little day trip to Leeds which was quite nice."

Tara felt surprised to hear it seemed to be going well.

"So everything is Ok?"

Izzy hesitated. She couldn't go as far as to say everything was Ok, there were a few issues that she definitely wasn't happy about but she wasn't sure if she should confide in Tara. Then she decided to press ahead with the most pressing issue.

"We haven't had sex since Tenerife."

Tara counted to ten before she opened her mouth.

"That's odd, why do you think that is?"

Izzy sighed so loudly, it sounded as if she was thoroughly sick of her life.

"I don't know he just seems to want to take me out now and again. He doesn't drive so I had to do the driving to Leeds."

Tara was quite taken aback at that piece of information.

"What? He doesn't drive at his age?"

"No," said Izzy. "I don't mind but I've just sent away for his provisional licence for him."

"Can he not read or write either then?" interrupted Tara.

"Of course, he can. He's just not very good at filling out forms, so I offered to do it for him. He's going to take lessons."

Izzy was dying to tell Tara that she'd seen Jonny behind the wheel of a car but felt she was being disloyal to him so shut up. Tara knew she had to change the subject. She could feel the words dying to spew out of her mouth. The man was a complete using fuckwit. Why could Izzy not see it? He wasn't even having sex with her so what exactly was she getting out of it? Was he using her for something else? Nothing was going to stop Izzy seeing him so she just had to be there for her and wait for something to go horribly wrong. Which of course it would.

She told her all about Max and hadn't realised she was doing it until Izzy pointed it out.

"You're taking the piss out of him. Have you heard the way you're talking about him like he's a commodity?"

Tara thought about this and agreed.

"I am just using him for sex, sweetie. No need to get your knickers in a knot."

"That's terrible using him like that," said Izzy, always the nice guy.

"Well he's not doing any complaining," laughed Tara.

They chatted for a bit about work and promised to do a catch up later in the week.

Tara had been trying to make a few enquiries about Jonny. His conquests were legendary around the Sunhill nightlife scene. Izzy had to know something or at least have heard a rumour. It was clear why he wasn't sleeping with her. He was too busy sleeping with everybody else. Tara decided that she was going to try to get hold of Tanya. She couldn't stand the woman because she represented everything in Sunhill that Tara despised. She was still going to the places she had frequented since she was eighteen, the only difference being that some of the nightlife had changed names. She had never settled down. In fact, it hadn't dawned on Tanya or any of her mates that they would never meet anybody interesting swimming around in that gene pool. Most people gravitated away from it.

Tara lay in bed and watched the sun streaming through the gaps in the curtains. Simon didn't stir as usual so she got up and started to get ready for work when the work mobile began ringing.

"For fuck's sake!" she said out loud. It was six twenty a.m. Years ago, she had been taught to smile when she picked up a receiver but this morning she simply couldn't be bothered and all the caller got was a sharp "Education Supply." She heard a squeaky, young sounding voice on the other end.

"Hello, I'm Lucy Best. I can't work today as I think I've caught tonsillitis from my little girl."

Tara went straight into orbit.

"You can't catch it, Lucy, as it isn't contagious. If you don't want to work just say and we won't contact you."

Tara thought that Lucy was going to start crying.

"Well I can't go in," she squeaked. "I'm ill and I've got a temperature."

Tara was sick of them treating her and the staff as simpletons all because they couldn't be arsed to go to work. She slammed the phone down knowing that she'd have to get into work to replace her. It was always the same on Monday mornings. Some of them had too much to drink at the weekend and couldn't quite manage to get into work. Again, Tara wondered how they paid their bills.

Daniel came in already in a mood. He'd been fighting with his wife Anna all weekend so Tara teased him as he moaned on about her. They all had a really difficult morning. It was always the same when the weather was good. The permanent staff all skived and took sickies and the supply staff wouldn't work. Daniel needed a secondary teacher urgently for a day's cover in one of their local schools that used a lot. He must have made over twenty calls but only three people picked up and they all had excuses why they couldn't or wouldn't work that day.

"It's like a fucking waste of breath in those interviews that we do," he said. "We ask them and explain to them that they must tell us when they are not available so that we do not waste our time ringing around and this is the fucking result. We haven't got a crystal ball. What a waste of fucking time."

The switchboard rang and Tara answered it.

"You've just rung me," said a woman.

Tara couldn't help herself.

"And you are?"

"Err it's Emily," she answered.

"We were just wondering if you are free to work today Emily?"

"Nar," she replied as if Tara had just asked her to fly to the moon. "I'm getting my highlights done."

Tara just could not be bothered to say that it was common courtesy to keep the office in the loop as to her availability, in case one of her regular schools needed her. Not for the first time, Tara thought it was time to sell and get out. Education was changing and not for the better. The phone rang later and Tara answered.

"Good morning, Education Supply."

"Are you Tara Black?" asked a voice in the commonest slang she had heard in a long time. At first, Tara wasn't sure if she should confirm her identity or not.

"Yes, I am."

"I'm Chantelle from Denton Primary. I'm ringing on behalf of the head. She doesn't want Sarah back in from tomorrow."

"Hang on a minute, can I speak to the head?" said Tara, thinking it must be a joke.

"She's told me to tell you that she's not available," said the halfwit and the line went dead.

Tara was left holding the receiver. To put it mildly, she hit the roof then immediately rang the school back and was again told that the head wouldn't take her call.

"I can't believe that education is coming to this," she shouted. "I spoke to Sarah privately and she told me that the Year five pupil had called her a fat, fucking cow and she had dealt with situation. That child has had her successfully removed from the school. I don't suppose the little twat is concerned that she's now out of work."

"The parent or guardian or social services will have been in," said Daniel. "He'll be telling all sorts of lies, so it's easier to get rid of the supply teacher."

Tara was now shouting and at full throttle.

"Well, they should show them all the fucking CCTV. The head's viewed it. If he gets away with this, he'll be a lost fucking cause."

"You are right," sighed Daniel. "It's still easier to get shot of our teacher."

"I know all of that," said Tara. "But what's it coming to when a child can get away with behaviour like that. The head is doing him no favours. Fucking broken Britain," and she stormed off to the tearoom leaving Daniel to break the news to Sarah, who couldn't understand what on earth she had done wrong.

30

Jonny had earned his place in Tony's family. When Tony said jump, Jonny asked how high. If Tony singled someone out it was assumed that the person had done something very wrong and had it coming. Tony had eyes and ears everywhere and as Jonny glanced at himself in the bar mirror liking what he saw, he realised the creds that he got by working for him. Tony had rewarded Jonny well over the years and tonight would be no different.

He noticed Izzy with her friend Tanya sitting at one of the low tables. She was chatting away and hadn't noticed him. She looked good, by far the best-dressed woman in the place. She always looked well-groomed. He was sure that she wouldn't even answer her front door without full makeup on. He also knew that she needed him and he was sure he could make her depend on him like all the others. He caught her eye and she trotted over to him.

"Didn't know you were coming in tonight," he said.

"A last-minute decision," she said smiling.

"Well it's lovely to see you and you look great. I'm just off to sort a few things for work, catch you later."

He headed off in the general direction of the office. Izzy was bursting with excitement. She loved being near him.

The security upstairs in Tony's office was huge. He'd had the windows bricked up years ago as a lot of cash was handled in that room. Jonny stood looking at the impressive safe. The door was open and he could see thousands of pounds in used notes stacked up on the shelves and wrap after wrap of cocaine waiting for dispatch. Jonny was the only other person there. Tony didn't trust too many people but they were stopped by a knock on the door. Tony closed the safe door and pushed a few numbers into the combination, locking it firmly.

"Yeah?" he shouted.

"It's me, Stevie."

Tony clicked the security button for him to come in. Stevie was Irish, a huge man but everyone knew he was as soft as butter but if the shit hit the fan Stevie would wade in with the best of them. Tony employed him only as a driver and that's where his skills lay. Stevie had been one of the best getaway drivers in the business and had never been caught by the police. Tony always said Stevie could teach Lewis Hamilton a few tricks behind the wheel of any car. Stevie lived with his mum. He adored her and she often made cakes for all the boys, who she thought were Stevie's best friends.

"What can I do for you Stevie?" asked Tony.

"It's that Tommy McCabe," said Stevie looking uncomfortable. "He's causing trouble Tony, talking out of turn, slagging you off. I just thought you needed to know."

Tony liked that. Stevie was showing absolute loyalty to his boss but Tony already knew what was going on and that was why he'd called Jonny up to his office.

"Thanks, Stevie but I already know. For what it's worth that little fucker is going to be taught some respect."

Stevie felt relieved. He was on the best money he'd ever earned and didn't want anything to fuck it up. Tony had the monopoly on the local drug business so he needed to teach McCabe a lesson and further demonstrate by actions, what happens if you cross him.

"Trouble coming, big trouble," said Jonny.

He knew Tommy McCabe had been trying to muscle in on Tony's patch but the McCabe lot were no shrinking violets. Tommy had a brother Barry who had the IQ of a snail so Tony wasn't about to be ripped up by those two fuckwits. Jonny could see Tony's anger barometer rising.

"Ok Jonny," he said. "Nothing too drastic a good hiding will do and a few broken bones for good measure."

"You're right boss," he said smiling. "He needs sorting out."

Tony gave Stevie an address where Jonny could find Tommy.

"It's a new boozer. used to be the Nags Head. My snouts have told me he was in there an hour ago."

Jonny got into the Mercedes with Stevie. Nobody said a word. They waited outside in the car for Tommy to come out of the pub and Jonny smiled at the divine intervention, as the stupid man half-cut walked into the back alley to take a leak. He didn't know what or who had hit him as Jonny surprised him from behind. The problem was Jonny didn't know when to stop. He loved showing people the error of their ways a little bit too much. Once he started punching him, he dropped to the floor like a sack of potatoes and then Jonny started kicking him. He could hear his ribs breaking then he pulled out a small lead cosh that he'd tucked into his jacket pocket and walloped Tommy in the knee caps. He didn't scream much at that point. Tommy was semi-conscious from the beating he'd already taken.

Jonny left the man in a pool of blood then casually strolled over to the pickup point that he and Stevie had agreed on.

"Everything Ok?" asked Stevie.

"Perfect, his own mother wouldn't recognise him."

Stevie handed over some cloths to protect the car until Jonny could get cleaned up at Limes. Stevie and Jonny worked well together.

Tony was already putting the word out on the street and started hearing the whispers coming back about what had happened to Tommy and why. The police wouldn't be too fussed either. Tommy was nothing but a pain to them. They would be thankful someone had taken him off their hands for a while.

Meanwhile, Izzy and Tanya were having a great night and hadn't noticed that Jonny was missing. Izzy assumed he was still busy in the office as he'd said earlier. It did cross her mind that he was a doorman and couldn't understand why he wasn't on the doors now. The other two doormen had their work cut out, the place was heaving. Jonny made his way back into the bar after getting himself cleaned up. Everyone looked at him and he lapped it up, he knew women found him very good looking.

He spotted Izzy and Tanya and made his way over to them. Izzy felt her heart skip a beat. She was the envy of the room. Catching her eye Jonny nodded for her to move away from Tanya with him and they stood at the bar together.

"Fancy some company after I finish work?" he asked her but Izzy wasn't sure what he meant as he wouldn't be finished until the last person left the club.

He noticed her frown and put his arm around her.

"I meant I'd come around to your house," he said.

"Just knock," she said to him. She felt chuffed to bits.

"It will be late mind," he said but Izzy just confirmed that anytime would be Ok as she didn't have work the next day.

She returned to her seat and brought Tanya up to speed on what was happening. They decided to call it a night shortly after that and Tanya warned her to be careful. Izzy wanted to have a bath and put her make up on again so when Jonny arrived, she would be as fresh as a daisy. Jonny noticed them leaving and also paid attention to the leggy blond who had just walked into Limes. She was a stunner and every man in the room was leching after her. Jonny hadn't seen her before but occasionally, if any minor celebrities were in the area, they would turn up at Limes as it was one of the smarter clubs. So he assumed this was the case. She looked like a model. She was wearing a silk cream catsuit that didn't leave much to the imagination as it was skin tight. She looked stunning and all thoughts of Izzy went out of his mind.

Simone loved the reactions that she got from men when she walked into a room but she had clocked the tall good-looking man in the corner who was staring at her. Jonny wandered over to her and her friend and ordered her a glass of champagne without asking her what she wanted to drink.

"Compliments of the club," he said to her.

Simone accepted the glass and just smiled at him. She didn't say a word and Jonny turned and walked away.

Jonny waited for her to leave the club and then introduced himself. Twenty minutes later he was in her bedroom. It had been as easy as that. They wanted each other. Simone slipped out of her catsuit. He loved the conquest as much as he loved the sex. The room was beautiful. In fact, it wasn't a normal hotel room but a suite which confirmed that she must be a model. Jonny handed her a glass of wine from her mini bar, he reckoned she wouldn't be paying for it, not with a room of this standard. Simone thought he was beautiful. Much better looking than the wimpy models she worked with. He was all man.

Jonny stared at her taking it all in. She looked as if she should be on a Californian beach with a surfer, he picked her up and carried her to the bed, kissing her hungry lips as he gently lay her down on the bed. She loved the feel of his huge hands as he stroked her smooth young skin. She wanted him so badly. She behaved like a feral animal locking her long legs around his back. She felt him enter her and let out a deep moan as he thrust deeper and deeper into her until she felt herself coming all over his huge manhood. She felt Jonny climaxing as soon as she had started to come and afterwards, they lay beside each other exhausted. Jonny rolled over and gave her a long deep kiss.

"I'm going to have to go," he said.

Simone was pleased and leant over to grab her cigarettes.

"See you around," she said.

She watched him get dressed and then quietly close the bedroom door on his way out. It was five a.m. and he was knackered. Fighting and screwing all in one night was a great combination but very tiring.

Izzy lay in bed and for the hundredth time looked at the bedside clock. She didn't deserve the grief that he was giving her and she could feel her eyes welling up. She had been looking forward to him coming over but she couldn't help herself where he was concerned. Her mother had always told her to aim high and now she seriously wondered what the hell had become of her. She had sent him a text but she knew he wouldn't reply. A job must have come up she reconciled to herself. Surely, he wouldn't just not turn up? She rolled over and tried to get some sleep.

Jonny woke up at noon the next day. He ached a bit but apart from that, he felt great remembering the time he'd spent with Simone. He smiled to himself because he hadn't given her any of his contact details. He made coffee then noticed his phone flashing with missed texts and groaned when he saw that they were from Izzy.

"For fuck's sake," he said. "Why doesn't she just fuck off?"

She could irritate him from six miles away at the other end of town. Jonny's jaw clenched. He was going to have to have a word in her shell-like. If he didn't turn up then so what, get over it. The next night Tony had given him the night off and Jonny and the boys hit Dentonham city centre with a vengeance. He was drunk but they'd had a great night. It was ages since all of the guys had been on a night out. Towards the end of the evening, Micky Moran and some of his crew had turned up. Micky was Declan Docherty's right-hand man, Tony's biggest competitor but they all knew where the battle lines were divided and didn't usually step on each other's toes. Jonny was as surprised as Declan to see him so he knew it wasn't a setup. Both gave each other a cursory nod and stayed at opposite ends of the club, but everyone could feel the tension building.

31

Tara couldn't believe how quickly the weekend had gone but here she was again, Monday morning 6.30, at her desk or rather waiting for Max to get himself over before Daniel and Carrie arrived for work.

"You have given Kate a good excuse for this early start I presume?" she asked, as he plonked himself down at her desk.

"Of course. She thinks I'm off to a prison visit," he laughed.

Twenty minutes later, Kate observed him leaving Tara's office and cross the lane back into his office, straightening his tie up as he walked. She had parked her car around the corner this time just in case he was looking for it. She felt furious and considered knocking on his office door but then she glanced at her watch and realised it would have to wait. She had a very tight schedule to meet at the hospital today.

Tara dealt with the morning rush and then rang Izzy to have a chat, which Izzy had to cut short because she couldn't talk. The head had dropped a bombshell that morning. A proposal had come up to turn their school into an academy and nobody was happy at the situation so she promised to ring her back later. Tara only half believed her friend. She had known Izzy for years and could tell from her voice that she was fed up to her back teeth which meant Jonny must be involved in some way.

Five scheduled interviews didn't bother either to turn up or cancel but the office was really busy and time flew. A small problem did crop up with one of their Teaching Assistants who had a mouth like a docker and a face like a shipyard worker. Aimee had worked with Education Supply at the same school for over two years. It was a tough school but because of Aimee's disposition, the children loved her. She shared the same background. She had been on the school's annual trip but an incident had occurred and she needed to tell Tara what had happened. She appeared and flounced her great bulk down into the chair in the interview room.

"I've gotten wrong of Mrs Carruthers on the school trip," she sighed as if it was all too much effort.

Tara was finding it hard not to laugh.

"Well tell me all about the facts of the matter and we will go from there," she said.

Aimee gave another huge sigh making Tara want to slap her.

"Reet," she said eventually. "We went to the bird island up North and the weather was terrible. Gale force winds and lashing it down, so Mrs Carruthers said reet, there's nowhere for the kids to get out of the rain so we will have to press on up the hill to the castle." She squirmed her huge bulk around the interview chair then carried on. "So it's a force ten gale and them little bairns are only eight, bent double they were trying to get up the steep hill. We were doing the Vikings and they were trying to chatter away with each other but they couldn't even hear each other over the wind when little Davey Smith said to me: 'How miss they must have been reet hard cunts them Vikings.'"

Tara was fighting the urge not to laugh. She had this mental picture of little Davey dragging his parka closer to him to protect himself from the elements realising that the Vikings only wore sackcloths.

Aimee went on to explain that she had told him off immediately but had then turned away sniggering. Unfortunately, Mrs Carruthers witnessed the snigger and reported her to the head on arrival back at the school.

"Davey Smith did not see me laughing, no way," Aimee repeated about three times for effect. "I had completely turned away from him."

"For God's sake Aimee," groaned Tara. "Look, I'll speak to the head and sort it out. Go home. I'll get back to you after I've spoken to him. I'm sure it will be Ok."

Aimee removed her huge bulk from the chair and Tara heard her thudding down the stairs. Then Daniel joined her.

"What's happened?"

Tara explained.

"For fuck's sake," he said. "She's working in the most challenging school in this area and the kids love her. They see her as one of them. I believe her that she turned away. She's quite professional and she has been there for two years so it's not as if she's a stranger."

"But it is very funny," said Tara and the two of them fell about laughing, "I've told her to leave it with me and to be careful next time but at least they haven't told her not to go in. I'll give the head a ring."

"They must have been reet hard cunts them Vikings!" said Daniel one last time, throwing them back into hysterics. When they went down to the main office, he had tears running down his face.

Simon had gone away again, testing his racing car so Tara spent ages in the bath relaxing. It wasn't until much later that she realised Max hadn't texted fifty times. She smiled, thanking God for a break from him. He must be busy doing husband and daddy things so she switched her mobile phone off.

Meanwhile, Max had got home at tea time and noticed Kate's car already on the drive. Unusual for her to finish that early he thought. He had gone inside and just settled himself into a chair with the local paper when all hell broke loose. Kate stormed into the lounge and slapped him straight across the side of his face.

"Listen to me, you vile bastard," she screamed. "I saw you this morning going in and then out of that fucking woman's office!"

Max just sat there speechless. He didn't know what to say. He had never seen Kate so angry in all the time they'd been married. He felt physically sick. He'd been caught fair and square but he had to try and get out of this. God knows what further action Kate would take. He stood up and put his hands on her arms to try and keep her still.

"Kate, listen to me," he said. "I went over there to tell her that it's finished, she's been pestering me all week."

To his amazement, Kate started to laugh.

"You're pathetic!" she raged. "Really pathetic. Women like Tara Black don't pester men like you, you fuckwit. Take a look at yourself."

Max now knew he had to do something drastic to get out of this and abruptly jumped back away from her.

"It's not true!" he shouted and ran up the stairs taking two at a time.

Kate heard the bathroom door slam and the lock turn. She ran up to the bathroom door and started banging on it.

"For fuck's sake!" she shouted through the door. "How fucking old are you?"

She stopped as she heard a horrible, loud thud and then Max cried out. He was a skilled enough manipulator to know when he was losing his audience and started shouting back through the door.

"I'm not lying to you. You never believe anything I say to you and I was never good enough for you!"

But Kate had already gone back downstairs. She had lost the will to live with him and couldn't be bothered to listen to any more crap coming out of his mouth. She waited for a while but when she couldn't hear any noises coming from the bathroom, she grew a tad worried. She knew from past experience what he was capable of. She climbed the stairs again and rapped softly on the bathroom door.

"Open the door, Max," she said.

Kate could hear him sobbing for a while. Then she heard him move and he slowly unlocked the door. To her horror, she saw the bathroom covered in blood. It was everywhere from one end to the other. Kate put her hands to her face taking in the shocking scene then stared at her husband. His face was covered in blood and he bent over the sink trying to stem the flow from his lacerated eye. It had swollen so much it was almost closed and already turning black.

Kate paused for a moment trying to take it all in and work out what exactly he'd done to himself. She had never seen so much blood anywhere.

"Why Max? Why do you do this?" she shouted, scared and furious at the same time. She could only thank God that the kids were out.

Max dropped down from the sink and propped himself against the wall, sobbing like a baby. He held his hand to his eye as the blood streamed through his fingers.

"I'm sorry Kate," he sobbed but Kate was too busy trying to get the towel up to his face to stem the bleeding.

"You idiot!" she shouted. "You need stitches. What am I supposed to tell them at the hospital? I work there."

Kate blinked rapidly sensing that this was her crossroads. Behind her, she had this life and in front of her, she could have a much better one, without him. She reached forward and helped him to his feet. As she turned around it dawned on her what he'd actually done to himself. He had smashed his forehead against the metal towel rail, a direct hit with his brow bone onto the metal join. He couldn't have connected his head with a worse part of the towel rail if he had tried but that was Max all over. It had to be maximum effect. It would need a lot of stitches to close the gaping hole in his head which ran the full length of his eyebrow.

Kate managed to get him into her car after replacing the saturated towel with another one and drove him to Accident and Emergency. She drew up in the designated parking area, left the engine running, jumped out and dragged him out. As soon as he was upright, she leapt back behind the wheel. Max couldn't believe what she was doing.

"Kate please come in with me?" he cried but Kate was already making a fast getaway.

"Ring Tara," she shouted. "I've had enough. You need to be in an asylum."

She left Max standing alone on the pavement with blood streaming down his jacket to the floor. He watched her car disappear out onto the main road, then patted his jeans pocket to check he had his mobile on him and headed into the hospital reception. After waiting for two hours, to his surprise, the doctor kept him in. He had a significant head wound and had been sick a few times so to be cautious the doctor said he wanted to keep him in for the night under observation. The doctor knew he had seen Max before but couldn't quite place him. He also didn't believe a word of Max's story that he had tripped in the bathroom. On a good note, thought the doctor, at least the patient was sober, unlike many other head wound cases.

When they had cleaned him up and stitched his wound, Max settled himself down in his hospital bed and started to play on his phone. An hour later a panic-stricken Susan rushed into Ward c42. She was in such a state of worry about him that she nearly tripped going up the stairs two at a time. It was inevitable that Kate would eventually hurt Max, she knew that this was going to happen. The woman was a drunken idiot and shouldn't be treating the sick. The fact that she was a practising doctor beggared belief. She should be reported.

Kate slept surprisingly well and only woke up when the alarm sounded. She had seen more drama with Max than anyone deserved. He was like a little boy always trying to attract attention. But self-harming and blood all over the bathroom? It was definitely time to get out of her marriage for the sake of the girls. At nine a.m., she was on the phone searching for the best divorce lawyer in the area. She needed the very best. After all, Max was a solicitor and would have plenty of legal friends to help him out.

32

Tara was busy chatting away to Daniel in the main office. Two of their teachers who lived together had insisted they wanted all the work they could lay their hands on because they were getting married. However, they hadn't bothered to answer their phones this morning. Daniel felt really upset as the client particularly wanted both of them both back. It would be the same classes as before. He had spoken to them last night and they insisted they were both available and wanted all the work Daniel could put their way to pay for the wedding. Daniel had wasted at least half an hour ringing and ringing them to no avail. At the time of their registration, Daniel believed Petra would prove the most reliable. He was wrong.

Suddenly the office vestibule door opened and Max Armstrong stumbled in looking like the victim of a car crash. He staggered across the office, his face bloodied and black and just about made it to Tara's desk, where he seized both her hands and squeezed them together. Tara and Daniel were transfixed.

"She's finally done it," stammered Max. "She attacked me."

"Upstairs Max," said Tara immediately. She couldn't have him in the general office in this state.

She sat him down upstairs and closed the door, determined to get the truth out of him.

"She hit you? A doctor assaulted you?"

Max confirmed this by nodding his head. She knew things were bad between them but this was phenomenal.

"How many stitches have you had?"

"Fifteen," said Max and started to weep. "They kept me in overnight because I had concussion but I've discharged myself to come and see you."

Tara couldn't believe this was happening.

"This can't go on Max."

"I know," he said. "I'm going to have to sit down and talk to her tonight."

"Where is she now?" asked Tara.

"Probably at work," he said shrugging his shoulders.

Tara found herself hating him at that moment. He was so weak.

"But what was it about?"

"You," said Max, managing a faint smile on his smashed-up face. "She followed me and saw me returning across the back lane from your office."

"Could you not have made something up for fuck's sake?" exploded Tara.

Max sat there looking shocked for a moment.

"I thought we could be together?" he pleaded.

Tara could feel her face turn puce.

"Are you fucking mad? It was just a bit of fun Max. In fact, get out of my office and sort your fucking life out, especially your crazy wife."

Tara sat in silence whilst he started to weep again and she wondered what the hell she had got herself into. She baulked at any violence but a doctor attacking someone was hideous.

"Look, Max," she said a little calmer, but with steely determination. "You are going to have to leave. I'm not getting involved in any more of this. God knows what my staff think. I want you to leave right now. So off you go."

Max pushed the chair back and stood up.

"I know," he said. "I just wanted to see you and tell you what had happened."

Tara was already out of her seat and heading down the stairs back into the main office. He left the building without her saying goodbye.

Daniel was waiting for her.

"Can I have a word in private please, upstairs?" he said and they both went back up to the Interview room.

He closed the door and turned to face her.

"Please tell me that you don't believe one word that has come out of his fucking mouth?"

Tara considered her reply carefully.

"Honestly, I don't know Dan. It's so appalling, how could he be lying about it?"

"She'd be struck off Tara, no doctor would behave like that. The man's unstable, you must know that."

"Are you suggesting he inflicted that head injury on himself?"

"I wouldn't put anything past him sweetie, he's not right in the head. Please stop and think about this. You're married, he could cause all sorts of problems for you."

Tara nodded her head as he spoke. She knew he was right. She'd already made up her mind that Max was a liability and in all honesty, this episode had frightened her. She didn't know anybody who lived like this. He was an attention-seeking little boy, the exact opposite of the person he portrayed in court.

Meanwhile, Max had arranged to be at Susan's for ten-thirty that morning. Once the tea and sympathy were over, in the hospital last night, he had wanted to get rid of her. Now Susan cleaned her little cottage from top to toe in anticipation of his arrival. She also changed the bedsheets just in case he wanted to lie down. She heard him knock at the door early for once and smothered him with kisses asking him how he was feeling but Max insisted on going straight to the bedroom to lie down as he had a shocking headache. He was too weak to have sex he told her, so Susan obliged with a blow job, knowing that would make him feel better. After he came in her mouth Max smiled slyly to himself. Beats aspirin every time. Then he got up and drove himself home, leaving Susan standing at the front door realising, yet again, that he had used her.

Tara ignored his texts all day. She needed to think. The next morning, she woke up more tired than when she went to bed. She ran a hand through her long blonde hair and stared at her reflection in the mirror. She looked like Myra Hindley dug up. Despite the heating being on, she felt a shiver run through her. This situation had to stop. Max no longer amused her and people were already getting hurt. The situation had become very serious indeed. Tara got to work then sat at her desk rubbing her tired eyes. She checked her mobile. Thirty-five texts the idiot had sent her. Wasn't he even slightly concerned that Kate could get hold of his phone? Then the switchboard rang breaking her train of thought.

33

Six miles away Izzy who for once was enjoying a deep sleep, woke up to her alarm ringing. As she switched it off, she noticed Jonny had sent a text.

'Fancy tea at 6.30?'

'Yes great! I'll pick you up at 6!'

Izzy was thrilled. She knew there was no point expecting him to pick her up, she knew the drill. Izzy's taxi service. She listened to the pitter-patter of rain starting to beat against her bedroom window and thought how wonderful it would be if he was here with her right now, all snuggled up comfy in bed. She could feel his strong arms around her. Never mind. She wouldn't let anything spoil her day. She was on cloud nine. Jonny wanted to see her and that was all that mattered. The effect he had on her was both exciting and humiliating, mostly because she had no real idea how he felt about her. Was he curious or was he interested in something deeper? She knew the hours he kept and working on the doors but she felt sure she could make him happy and give him a life he would love. She shook her head. She couldn't keep flying off at tangents. She had to take this in steps and be realistic. Jonny lived in a completely different world from hers.

Izzy eventually got into work. She heard the bell ringing as she drove up. But she was seeing Jonny tonight so she couldn't care less if she was running late. She stayed behind for plenty of meetings. On the way into school just at the reception door, she bumped into Shelley Riley. Rats, she thought, too late to avoid the parent from hell. What with her pursed lips and pronounced underbite she reminded Izzy of a frustrated bulldog. Shelley was in a hurry herself so only had time to give her a passing sneer.

Izzy chuckled away as she took her coat off and sat down at her desk. Jackie wasn't in again for the morning session, she allegedly had another meeting with the diocese. Izzy had no way of checking without dropping herself right in it but Jackie had been banging on about her highlights being desperate. For a bright woman, she did let herself down. She couldn't resist telling everyone what she was up to.

Izzy worked solidly on staff figures. She wanted to get it just right as Jackie needed a report listing all the wages, to see where cuts could be made not to mention possible redundancies. It was a horrible job but she had to do as she was instructed so she needed to get it spot on. Every time someone came into her office, she had to quickly turn papers over as it was highly confidential. Sure enough, at one o'clock, Jackie breezed in, complete with new hairdo. Well there's one staff cut that should be made, thought Izzy. If Jackie was using school time to get her highlights done, they clearly didn't need a full-time head.

At six-fifteen, following four outfit changes, Izzy drove up outside Jonny's flat and tooted the horn. She glanced up at this social housing complex he called home and shuddered. It was a dump from the outside and she could only guess at the inside since he'd never asked her in. Again, she wondered how the hell he'd ended up living there. He must have earned some money from the job he had at present. He strode out of the communal front door looking exceptionally fit, his body lean and muscular. Jonny got into Izzy's Audi and immediately started chatting with her.

"Fancy a curry?" he said.

"Lovely!" she replied, smiling. "The same place we went to before?"

Jonny nodded. He was in a very good mood, even whistling along to the song on the radio. He hadn't kissed her or praised her appearance and for a split-second, Izzy wondered why she bothered. Then she realised he would come round in time. After all, he'd invited her out for tea so he must like her.

Almost against her better judgement, which kicked in every now and then, Izzy had a great night. Jonny regaled her with stories from the past, some of the famous people he'd met and worked with. Izzy just smiled and went along with it. She was dying to tell him that he'd told her some of these stories before. He just loved hearing the sound of his own voice. However, she did concede, the one about being on Rod Stewart's security team was new to her.

"Let's go on holiday again," said Jonny, breaking her train of thought.

At this point, she knew he was lying, not only to her but himself. She sat with her mouth open momentarily unable to speak, then leant across the table and hugged him tightly.

"Stop being so clingy," he said and shrugged her off him.

She didn't care if he knew how much she liked him. She started to ask him where he wanted to go. They chatted for ages and Izzy promised to have a look on the computer the next day and sort out maybe Greece for the next school holiday, in about five weeks. Jonny said that he was flexible and by the time he pecked her on the cheek goodbye, she could not wait to get her hands on her computer at home. She knew that she would be on it all night searching for a great holiday for them both. She didn't care about sleep. In fact she was far too excited to sleep.

The next day her eyelids felt too heavy to keep open but her mind was strangely alert. She had searched for hours and had at last texted Jonny the details of four holiday deals, she had selected and was awaiting his thoughts as to which one she should book, then they could make the travel arrangements.

Jonny had been hearing his phone blip all through the night and had become so sick of her texting that he eventually switched it off. If Tony needed him at short notice, he would ring the landline. She was irritating him to death but thank the lord he hadn't given her his landline number. He couldn't recall one meaningful conversation he'd had with her since the day she had been introduced to him but if he played his cards right, he knew he could bag himself another holiday.

Izzy paced back and forth across her office floor. She had the most terrific holiday in Santorini on hold and it was such a great deal but she really needed an answer from Jonny to see if he was on for it. He was doing his usual non-communicating act. Eventually, her phone blipped and she nearly broke her neck grabbing it from her desk. It was a curt:

'Yes, Santorini great and the dates convenient.'

Not wanting to lose such a great deal, Izzy retrieved her credit card from her bag and went ahead with booking the holiday. She put two and a half thousand pounds on her credit card. The holiday was five weeks away so it would give her time to get some weight off. She texted him to let him know the holiday was booked and confirmed and that she would catch him later. He didn't reply. That afternoon she couldn't stop thinking about him so she texted him to ask if he wanted to come around to her house for tea and in the meantime, she would print out the holiday details for him to keep. He replied to say that he had to work but could make Thursday at six pm. Izzy confirmed and asked him to bring his passport as she needed the details from it to enter onto the booking confirmation.

The week rattled on with no major incidents other than a child persistently wetting himself at school and when the parents were informed, they blamed Jackie the head.

"It never happens at home," bellowed the father in Jackie's office.

Thursday arrived and Izzy grew excited all over again because she was going to see Jonny. She went to great lengths to make him a curry. Her house stank to high heaven but it meant nothing if Jonny liked the food, she had lovingly prepared for him. The whole evening passed and he didn't turn up. She rang him and texted for hours but he didn't reply. Izzy was so upset. She ranged from thinking he'd suffered an accident, to believing he was the most ignorant person that she'd ever met. Three hours later he did text to say that he'd been called into work for a job. He told her that he would be at her house tomorrow, Friday for six o'clock but he couldn't stay long as he started at Limes at nine.

Izzy was devastated but what choice did she have? She'd just splurged two and a half thousand pounds on a holiday for them. Jonny stretched across Donna and switched the phone off. She managed to catch a glimpse of his messages to Izzy.

"Arsehole," she muttered, tutting at his behaviour.

But then as Jonny slid his fingers in and out of her she got wetter and wetter. She was moving against his hand tensing with each stroke of his fingers. He unzipped his trousers and pushed himself inside her. She tightened against him and he pulled her up onto her knees forcing her to open up wider for him. Donna started to moan as Jonny rammed in and out of her. He didn't care if he broke her but she finally came holding onto him with all of her might. They lay there spent for a couple of minutes, then as usual Jonny pulled his jeans back on, sorted himself out, kissed her goodbye and left. Job done.

Izzy spent all day Friday worrying if Jonny was really serious about this holiday she'd booked. At the same time, she wrestled with her conscience, telling herself that if he had to work, there was nothing he could have done about it. Still, she kept remembering his awful behaviour. He didn't even ring to say he wasn't coming. All of the food had gone in the bin. She was snappy with everyone at work but she managed to get out at a decent time.

Fifteen minutes after she got home, Jonny knocked on her front door. She didn't bother to kiss him but smiled as he sat himself down on her sofa. Izzy fetched him a beer.

"Did you bring your passport?"

Jonny got up to find his coat.

"Here it is," he said handing it to her.

Izzy sat down with the laptop and started to load the information in but there was some sort of problem.

"Oh my God!" she shrieked. "It's out of date!"

Jonny looked at her and took the passport out of her hands.

"It can't be," he said.

Izzy could feel her heart sinking and the holiday slipping from her grasp.

"If we go over to the passport office tomorrow, we can get an express form and you can complete it while you're there," she said pointedly.

Jonny sighed. He couldn't be arsed to sit in the passport office all day with her going on at him.

"Look," he said. "I'll get the forms from the post office and pay for the express service. It'll only take two to three weeks."

Izzy was about to argue but knew not to. He had made his mind up.

"Ok, just let me know when you have the forms and I'll help you fill them in," she said.

"Look, I better be going," he said fetching his coat. "I'll ring you when I have the forms tomorrow," and he made his way to the door.

Izzy was sick of him and just wanted him to go. Everything turned into a chore with him and now she imagined the ghastly prospect of going on holiday by herself. What about the money she had just shelled out? She noticed he hadn't mentioned giving her half, or giving her anything at all.

The next day Jonny did go and get the passport form which perked Izzy up a bit as she had honestly thought he wouldn't bother. He texted to say he would come over for her to fill them in for him as he was crap at that type of thing.

When he turned up at her house, he seemed rather pleased with himself and started taking an interest in Santorini. It wasn't until he left that Izzy realised he had left the completed forms with her to post. She read the information list that went with the forms and looked for the address to send it to. Then reality dawned on her. She would be paying the one hundred and twenty-eight pounds required to purchase it. She instantly flew into a rage. How could she have been so stupid? He had deliberately set her up. Jonny, on the other hand, thought that if she was that desperate to be with him, she could pay for his passport. He knew it had run out six months ago.

34

Tara was at home on Friday evening when her work phone rang. She was on call but it was well after five pm so she started to wonder who wanted what. Then as she picked up the phone, she sensed trouble. Nobody ever wanted to talk about school on a Friday night.

"Education Supply," she answered cheerily.

It was Paula Levy from Baxter Grove Academy one of the largest schools in the Sunhill area.

"Hi Tara," she said. "I'm really sorry about this but we have a problem."

"Paula," said Tara, almost laughing. "It's 6.30 on a Friday night, what could possibly have happened?"

"It's very unfortunate. One of our parents has made a complaint against Adrian Everton but in spectacular fashion. He's only gone directly to the Local Education Authority and by-passed our safeguarding team."

"Oh for God's sake Paula," groaned Tara. "Why didn't he speak to your school first?"

"No idea but he's not a happy bunny."

She went on to explain that the alleged incident had occurred in January and that Adrian had sworn at the kids. Paula and the safeguarding team had disciplined Adrian as it was considered a matter of conduct and he'd apologised profusely. Apparently, he had meant to say for God's sake but in actual fact, it had come out as for fuck's sake. The matter had been dealt with and it was all over and done with. However, a further incident had come to light when a group of girls accused Adrian of putting pictures of women under his bed so that his wife couldn't see them.

"But it's June now," said Tara, overcoming her shock. "So if this was dealt with in January, I'm not sure where this allegation can go. He's been in your school teaching for five months after the fact."

"You're right," said Paula. "The kids were accusing him of having the pictures and there's no truth in it. The only mistake Adrian made was in not reporting it to his team leader, as it was happening but we sorted it out in January. Unfortunately, this parent got wind of the story five months later and said he doesn't want Adrian teaching his son. Now he's gone one step further and reported it to the Local Education Authority."

"Well, that takes it right out of your hands. They'll have to follow their procedure now and investigate the matter."

"Yes, that's true," sighed Paula. "But as far as we're concerned it's still a conduct matter and we've already dealt with it."

Tara thanked her for putting Education Supply in the picture but they both agreed that the Local Authority Designated Officer Team would be in touch on Monday to review 'the case'. They wished each other a happy Friday and ended the conversation.

Simon had come into the kitchen during the call so Tara had to explain what was going on.

"So, all that happened was Adrian swore and that happened in January?" he asked looking at her as if she was stupid. "What a complete waste of time. No wonder education has no money. That father is probably on the dole and sitting in the house all day watching Jeremy Kyle."

He went off to get ready to go out for a drink with his brother, the usual routine on a Friday night. Tara quickly rang Daniel to keep him in the picture.

"Wankers got nothing else to do," he said and wished her a good evening.

Tara tried to get hold of Izzy. She was far too quiet for Tara's liking but the mobile just rang and rang. Izzy had heard it but when she saw who was calling, decided to ignore it. She felt too anxious to answer any questions from Tara at the moment. She felt stupid and guilty, not only for paying for the holiday but coughing up for his wretched passport as well.

Monday came with its usual flurry of early morning calls but the Local Authority Designated Officer, or LADO, team had emailed to invite Education Supply to a review meeting on Wednesday at 2.00 pm.

"Review exactly what?" asked Daniel, glancing up from his computer. "Something that was dealt with in January? What a fucking waste of time."

Tara nodded in agreement but either way, they would have to attend the meeting.

Max rang a few times but Tara ignored him. Work was more important and he needed to sort Kate out and keep his marriage on track. Tara just didn't feel happy at the moment. She had been enjoying the casual sex with Max but that situation had grown far too volatile and dangerous, so she decided to give him a wide berth. Maybe they could pick up again later when he had sorted himself out.

She was also on the verge of telling Simon that their marriage was over. Their relationship had run its course, ten years wasn't a bad batting average she often told herself. Daniel cheered her up and they were so busy that day that she didn't have time to think about any of her personal problems. Then in the afternoon one of their teachers came in and asked Tara if she could have a word in private. Tara took Frances upstairs into the privacy of the interview room.

"Thank you for seeing me," said Frances, plonking herself down in the chair. "I've just come in to let you know I'm getting divorced. So I'm not going to be available every day as I will have to sell my house and I need to be around for viewings."

Tara's antennae shot up immediately. Frances and Tony lived eight doors away from Simon and Tara and in fact, their house had a much better view down the coastline. Tara had never made a faster decision in her life.

"Don't advertise it. I'll buy it," she said as Frances sat gaping at her.

"Please keep this confidential but I'm going to leave Simon. We live in such a beautiful place, I'd really like to stay in the area."

Frances couldn't believe what she was hearing. It would certainly make her and Tony's divorce a lot simpler and quicker if the house didn't have to go on the market.

"Ok," she said. "I'll get it valued and let you know the market price. One question Tara, are you serious?"

Tara told her she'd never been more serious about anything in her life. It was as if a weight had been lifted from her shoulders. She wanted to be single and not have to answer to anyone again. Her mind was made up. Simon would have to be told but he surely wouldn't be that surprised. They hardly saw each other and had slowly drifted apart over the last few years. She was leaving him and that was that.

What a day it had been she thought later on but it was funny how things turned out. Daniel rang upstairs to interrupt Tara.

"Giles Haversham is in the main office to see you."

"Ok Daniel, Frances and I are done I'm coming down."

Tara shook hands with Frances and they promised to keep in touch.

Giles Haversham had the hots for Tara. He was very, very posh and one of Education Supply's most popular secondary teachers. He had moved from London to Sunninghill and all the kids thought he had been born at Downton Abbey he was so posh. In fact, Giles had attended one of the most prestigious boarding schools in the UK and in Tara's opinion had been wasted in the teaching profession.

She walked into the general office and found Giles sitting in front of her desk. Being a gentleman, he instantly stood up when he saw her and they shook hands.

"Hi, Giles, lovely to see you. What can we do for you?"

He looked very uncomfortable and started to blush bright pink.

"Well it's a bit of a difficult one," he said.

Tara glimpsed Daniel glued to the conversation but Giles carried on regardless.

"It turns out that my wife has become a lesbian and she has moved her partner into my house so I'm having to move back south to live with my mother."

Daniel got up and left the office but Tara had to front it out. She was struggling so hard not to laugh that she could feel the sweat running down her back.

"I'm so sorry," was all she could manage to say but Giles appeared to be quite resigned to the fact that his wife had just become a lesbian.

"These things happen," he said. "But I came in to thank you for all of the work that you have given me over the years and of course the support."

He didn't hang around he just shook hands with Tara again and left. Daniel waited till the coast was clear before sneaking back in.

"Thank you very much for the support there Dan," she said as he kept on laughing.

"You're welcome," he spluttered, enjoying himself immensely. "As of interest, how does one's wife suddenly become a lesbian?"

This made the whole office laugh and nobody could give him the answer. Unfortunately, the day only got worse. Tara was just getting ready to leave because she was on call that evening and wanted to sneak a quick run in before five pm when Neil Turner walked in with his two little girls. He was the last person she expected to see. Neil had emigrated to Australia two months ago with his wife. He was beaming from ear to ear and bounded over to Tara's desk after leaving the two little girls in the reception area.

"Can I re-register?" he said.

"But you've moved to Australia!"

"I've left her and she's staying over there," he said.

All eyes moved to the two cute little blonde girls in reception.

"I've kidnapped them," he said. "The girls are staying with me."

You could have heard a pin drop.

"You can't do that Neil," said Daniel, the father in him coming out. "Your wife will be distraught."

Tara saw Daniel had gone white in the face and looked as if he was going to have a coronary. Neil stared at him with naked aggression.

"I can and I have. My two girls are staying with me."

"But why have you come back?" asked Tara.

Neil told them the whole sorry saga. When he caught his wife in bed with one of his friends, he booked the first flight home and left. His parents were helping with the girls. Tara sent him away and told him to come back and re-register when he had sorted himself out. After Neil had gone everyone just sat staring at each other.

"It's like working in the local lunatic asylum today," was all Tara could say.

"These people are in charge of our children's education, their futures even and they can't even fucking look after themselves."

Nobody disagreed with him.

Tara managed to catch Izzy on the phone and tried to make arrangements to meet her for a drink but Izzy was flat out with Jonny. It was all she could talk about Jonny this, Jonny that and Tara had to admit to herself that as much as she loved Izzy, she just couldn't listen to much more of it. They decided to get together in a few weeks, before the Santorini trip.

When Tara put the phone down, she realised that Izzy hadn't even asked her how she was. She had talked for over an hour nonstop about Jonny and Tara found that worrying. She acknowledged that Izzy had always been one of the most selfish girls she'd ever met. It was always about her but that would never change. Tara had tried everything she could to warn her about Jonny Devroe and she wouldn't listen. In the end, Tara thought, she'd just have to be there for her when it all came crashing down.

35

Izzy was counting down the days. She had lost so much weight, probably due to sheer excitement. Jonny had stepped up the contact but hadn't really taken much notice about the travel arrangements. He was happy to leave it all in Izzy's hands. He had taken her out a few times but only for tea, his excuse for not staying over was that he had to work to make up for the time he would be on holiday. In her quieter moments, Izzy did consider her relationship, if she could call it a relationship, wasn't exactly conventional. Was he actually having a relationship with her or were they just friends? It also troubled her that he had not offered her one red cent towards the holiday, nor the passport she paid for. Was he seriously expecting her to pay for everything? She had meant to bring this subject up but every time she went out with him, she had such a nice time, she didn't want to put a damper on things.

She had so wanted to discuss this with Tara when she phoned the other night but she knew she could never admit to what was going on. Tara would think she'd lost the plot. Her phone blipped. Izzy had invited Jonny round to her house for tea and had texted him asking if he preferred lamb or chicken? So she was quite surprised to read his message:

'I fancy going out for a drink tonight'

'great where do you fancy going?' she replied, imagining he was taking her out for a drink.

It took him a while but he replied:

'thought I might go out with my friends for a pint.'

Izzy was not happy. She had paid for a holiday and his passport and he would rather spend time out with his friends after arranging to have tea at her house. No, she wasn't happy so picked up her phone.

'Thought you were coming around to mine for tea' she texted and she got the answer that she didn't want within five second.

'Well I'm not now, I'm going out with my friends.' Izzy was furious. No apologies, nothing, he was simply informing her that he now wasn't coming for tea. Something inside of her snapped. He was using her like a

doormat. She paced around her lounge wondering what to do. She knew he was looking forward to the holiday so she texted:

'See you at the airport then.'

No reply. By the time she went to bed she didn't know what to do. She couldn't sleep, couldn't talk to Tara. In fact, she couldn't do anything. She was completely at his mercy and she knew it.

The next day Izzy got up and checked her phone. Nothing. She realised she'd put her own back against the wall saying seeing you at the airport. All she could do now was wait and see what transpired. She felt anxious, worried and tearful. One minute she was on cloud nine and the next all of her hopes could be dashed and she was back at rock bottom. It wasn't healthy living like this. With only two weeks to go until the holiday, she now had no clue as to what he was thinking, let alone if he was even going to fly but Izzy was determined not to contact him.

She went to work and had a dreadful day. She couldn't concentrate on anything. All she could think about was Jonny. She convinced herself that he must have another woman. She repeatedly checked her phone to see if he had texted her but in her heart of hearts, she knew he wouldn't get in touch. He would be expecting her to crawl to him. She got home and thought that she was having a panic attack. Her chest felt tight and she couldn't stop the tears from flowing. How could he be so cruel to her? Nothing else for it, she would have to ring Tara and confess everything.

Tara was surprised to see a call coming in from Izzy. Izzy rarely contacted anybody these days. When she answered the phone, all she heard was her friend bawling like a baby.

"Jesus Izzy, who's died?"

"Tara, I've been such an arsehole!" she cried.

"Come on then, it's obviously a Jonny attack," said Tara, bracing herself.

"I've said the wrong thing to him and now I don't even know if he's coming on the holiday with me."

Tara popped the kettle on whilst balancing her phone on her other hand. She sensed a long-haul conversation coming.

"What's he done?"

Izzy took off with the bit between her teeth. By the time she'd finished, Tara felt quite insane.

"Are you for fucking real Izzy? Seriously I'm taking you to see a doctor, you need medical help."

Izzy couldn't reply she was crying so hard. She knew Tara would go mad and maybe it was what she needed, someone to make her see sense. She didn't know what it was about Jonny but the man could do anything to her and she just let him.

"'I know," she said. "I'm stupid and it's not going to happen again."

"Why did you pay for his passport let alone the fucking holiday?" said Tara, who couldn't leave it there.

"It's just the way it happened. He kind of filled the forms in at my house and just left them there for me to post."

Tara hadn't realised just how needy her friend had become.

"He's using you and you're getting nothing back. Please tell me the sex is good?"

"We've only done it twice," sniffled Izzy.

"Let me get this straight. You're not even, actually shagging each other?"

"No, not really," said Izzy, between sobs.

There was a silence on the line then Tara inhaled deeply.

"I don't really know what to say to you other than please stop, you are making yourself look stupid and needy."

"Do you fancy going to Santorini with me?" said Izzy, brightening up. "I've checked how much it will cost to change the name on the ticket and it's do-able so if you're free to fly I can change it?"

Tara asked for the dates out of courtesy. She didn't really fancy listening to Izzy banging on about Jonny for seven days on a Greek island. Fortunately, she was scheduled to fly to Dublin with Simon then, for his motor racing at Phoenix Park.

"That's a shame," said Izzy. "But it's over now Tara I promise you. I'm being stupid and it has to stop."

When Tara put her phone down, she prayed to God Izzy meant it. Otherwise, things were set to get a damned sight worse.

Izzy poured herself a glass of wine and reflected on what Tara had said. She knew she would get it in the neck but all she could think about now was who she could take on holiday with her as a backup plan. Jonny still had time to communicate.

Meanwhile, Jonny was swigging alcohol with his mates in the departure lounge of Dentonham airport. They were already on their way to being drunk like excitable little schoolboys waiting for their flight to Ibiza. Jonny raised his glass and made a silent toast to Izzy. It was very kind of her to have paid for his passport.

Izzy had hatched a plan to take one of the girls from her office on holiday. Michelle was single and as far as Izzy knew, she hadn't booked a summer holiday yet. Izzy waited until they were on their own and told Michelle what had been happening and asked her if she'd be interested. All she would need was her spending money. Izzy knew that she shouldn't be doing this as after all she was the school business manager but all of her friends had kids and their holiday plans were set in stone so it was either Michelle or go it alone. Michelle snapped her hand off but Izzy made it clear that if Jonny got in touch, she would have to cancel her. Michelle didn't mind. All of the girls knew about her Jonny situation and knew that Izzy didn't have a cat in hell's chance with him. They all went around the town pubs in Sunhill and most of them knew about his reputation. The only person that didn't was Izzy.

The week dragged on with zero news from Jonny. She was so tempted to contact him, especially after a few glasses of red wine one night but something had stopped her. What she didn't know was that Jonny, on the other hand, was having a great time. The weather was scorching and the women were even hotter. He had loads of contacts in Ibiza because Tony his boss had business dealings out there. Jonny had very nearly moved there a few years ago but at the last minute, Tony had changed his mind. He needed Jonny's talents back at Sunhill.

Jonny joined his mates at a hip new nightclub, owned by Tony's best friend Sergio so the whole group got in for free and received a royal welcome. The champagne flowed. Big Stevie, Tony's driver was in the group. Jonny had managed to drag him away from his beloved mother who rang Stevie about five times a day to make sure he was eating properly. Jonny wondered what she would do if she knew what Stevie really did for a living. On the face of it, he was only Tony's driver but any sign of trouble and big Stevie waded in to give the boys a hand. Stevie was having the time of his life and had a lovely little auburn girl wrapped around him at the bar. Jonny was heavily engaged in talking to the most beautiful brunette that he had ever seen and giving her the full charm offensive. He was going to have her.

A famous boxer entered the club and the whole place stopped. He'd just won a huge world championship belt in Vegas and was very hot at the moment. People kept trying to talk to him but he spotted Jonny, waved and went to join him and his friends. Stevie thought he was drunker that he actually was when he saw the boxer making his way over. He thought he was hallucinating when he saw Mike shake hands with Jonny. He didn't even know that Jonny knew him, but more champagne appeared from behind the bar. Stevie was developing quite a taste for Crystal.

The brunette loved meeting Mike the boxer. She'd obviously chosen the right man in the bar to flirt with and in her view, the night could only get better. Jonny finally managed to get her name. She had been reluctant to tell him at first but when it became clear she was coming back to his hotel with him, he insisted. Sophia. A beautiful name for a beautiful girl. Then Sophia insisted she would feel more comfortable if they went back to her place, a private villa. Jonny couldn't take it all in. The villa was palatial.

"Are you staying here all by yourself?" he asked.

"My brother is staying with me," she said, smiling at him. "But he's off to Old Ibiza town tonight and he's not coming back so we have the place all to ourselves."

She led him upstairs to the most opulent suite he had ever seen and it did cross his mind to wonder where the money came from. But he was only interested in fucking her not appearing on This Is Your Life with her. He ended up collapsed on top of her on the bed. They were kissing like they couldn't get enough of each other and his hands slid all over her body. She was so fit and Jonny felt himself getting harder, wanting her more and more by the second.

He rolled off her and she put her hand under his shirt then slowly started undoing the buttons as he pulled the zip on the front of her dress down. Her breasts spilt out into his hands and he kissed her long and hard both of them panting with desire. She was so wet and as Jonny felt for her underwear which didn't exist, he easily slid three of his fingers into her and Sophia moaned loudly as she could feel him pushing his wet fingers in and out of her. Jonny stopped and pulled off his jeans, releasing his huge dick, which Sophia started stroking. He lay back and felt her soft, warm mouth envelop the end of his dick and he thought that he was going to come.

He was so excited to be in a bed with such a beautiful horny woman that he was struggling to keep it together so he gently pushed her back onto the bed and mounted her. Sophia let out a small moan as he plunged deep inside of her. They both came together and then lay exhausted in each other's arms. Jonny couldn't believe how beautiful Sophia looked lying there against his shoulder. He almost changed the habit of a lifetime. But as Sophia leant over to the nightstand to retrieve her cigarettes Jonny got out of bed and put his jeans on. Sophia propped herself up on the pillows and took a deep drag from her cigarette.

"Will I see you again?"

This was the part that Jonny hated.

"Yeah of course," he said. "I'm sure we will bump into each other." Then he leant over the bed and kissed her goodbye.

He got back to his hotel which was nowhere near as flashy as the villa Sophia was staying in. The sun was coming up, ready for another red-hot day and Jonny felt all was right with the world. Stevie was busy in the kitchen area brewing up which Jonny found hilarious.

"Want a cuppa?" he asked Jonny.

"Yeah go on, I will. I can't believe you brought tea bags, bet your Mum packed them for you."

"She did," he grinned. "And I even went to the shop last night to buy milk. She's got me well trained."

They sat down with their brews on the balcony looking out over the sea. Suddenly Stevie threw Jonny an interesting question.

"I'm presuming you know who that bird is that you fucked last night?"

"Yeah, she's called Sophia."

"Do you know anything about her?" said Stevie.

"Not really except she's got great tits!"

Both men laughed.

"She's Darren Reid's daughter."

Jonny's blood ran cold for a moment.

"You are joking?" he said.

"I'm sure as hell not my boy," said Stevie, shaking his head slowly from side to side.

"Fucking hell," said Jonny. "I didn't realise who she was."

He put his head in his hands and wondered why on earth he hadn't checked her out before going back to her place. Now the villa added up. Her father owned it. Darren Reid was a notorious gangster who controlled half of London, not a man to mess with.

"I wonder if she knew all along who you were, Jonny?"

"I don't think she knew anything about me, Stevie. She just wanted the same thing as I did but I'm praying she isn't going to tell her father because I bet he's very protective of her."

As Jonny sat there, worrying about his survival prospects, Stevie got up and put his empty mug into the sink for the maids to sort. Then as an afterthought, he turned to look at Jonny.

"Darren probably had one of his men tailing her to make sure she was safe."

"Well I didn't notice anybody and nobody stopped her getting into bed with me. Is her father here?"

"Not that I know of," replied Stevie.

Jonny made a mental note to give Sophia a wide berth now he knew which family she belonged to. He didn't want to cause any trouble for Tony. They all knew each other and avoided stepping on each other's toes. Fucking one of the biggest gangster's daughters in the country probably crossed every code in the book.

Izzy had three days to go until her flight. She found it hard to muster up any enthusiasm for the holiday as Jonny had made no attempt to contact her. It didn't help having Michelle buzzing around her full of excitement at her free holiday and Izzy began to wonder if she had done the right thing. Perhaps she should have listened to Tara and gone on her own, give herself time to sort her head out.

As she came out of the main office, heading towards Year 6 to pick up some forms for the Senior Management Team, she bumped into Joanie one of St. Magdalene's kitchen staff. Izzy said a quick hello and attempted to walk on when Joanie stopped her dead.

"I was talking to your ex last night," she said.

Izzy felt her stomach hit the ground.

"He's got a tremendous tan."

Izzy knew she would faint, any second now.

"Tan?" she muttered.

"Yeah," said Joanie enthusiastically. "Yeah, we were in Limes last night for a birthday party and he was on the door. He's been to Ibiza. Reckoned they had a fabulous time but he fell asleep in the sun and he's very sunburnt."

Izzy could feel herself paling. The bastard had allowed her to book and pay for a holiday that he clearly had no intention of going on as he was already booked to go to Ibiza and had let her pay for his passport. The penny well and truly dropped. That was what it had all been about. He needed her to pay for his passport. He really didn't have any money, or was that a lie too?

Izzy got away from Joanie as fast as she could, ran back to her office and slammed the door shut. She sat at her desk for a minute then jumped back up again and hung the 'do not disturb' sign on her door. She needed to think. The tears were running down her face. Yet again, she felt hurt and used. She phoned Tara. As soon as she heard her friend's voice Izzy burst into tears. Tara couldn't get any sense out of her so told her to at the local café in twenty minutes.

Izzy made an excuse to Jackie that her mum needed her help and took off. At that point, she didn't give a shit if Jackie sacked her. She managed to pull herself together by the time she sat down in the café with Tara and explained what Joanie had said. Tara did feel sorry for her.

"Oh, Izzy he's just using you. You have to stop this yo-yo behaviour with him. You are not having sex with him or having a proper relationship so you need to get out of it and stop feeling sorry for yourself."

"But I love him!" wailed Izzy as the tears plopped down into her untouched skinny latte.

"You do not love him!" Tara hissed, deciding to get really firm with her. "You do not love him, it's the fucking drama you love. The two of you have got zero in common and more to the point he treats you like shit!"

"I paid for his passport Tara. How could he let me do that?" she said between hiccups and sobs.

"Because he knew that you would, you silly b…, I mean, girl. He saw you coming you are so desperate for him and that's the bit I cannot get. He does nothing, no wining and dining, no sex. In fact, you're lucky if he takes you for a curry once a month. What is there to like for God's sake?"

Izzy shrugged her shoulders. It was one thing Tara coming out with it but it was another putting it into practice.

"I know what you are saying is right," she started but Tara interrupted.

"It's like some movie going on in your head. He's a petty criminal, not some huge godfather figure and quite frankly Izzy it's hard to watch you go through this. You look ill, it's not good for your mental health and you are doing it to yourself!"

Izzy couldn't take anymore. She looked at her watch, took a swig of her now cold coffee and stood up.

"I'm sorry Tara, I do agree with you but I'm going to have to get back to school. I lied to get out."

"And normally you would never do that," said Tara. "See Izzy those are the depths that you are lowering yourself to, all because of that fuckwit."

That part hadn't occurred to her but Tara, as usual, was right. She had lied to cover herself because of something that Jonny had done.

"And did you think he was never going to use that ten-year passport you just paid for? It's obvious he would be travelling somewhere so why are you getting so upset about it?" Tara was on a roll. "You should never have paid for it."

Tara paused and looked at Izzy's face. She had turned a funny grey colour but she needed to live in the real world otherwise Jonny would destroy her.

"You know what my mum always said, Izzy? If you want to look at a man, look at his friends first and she was right. It's the best indication of a person's character, who they hang out with."

When Izzy got back into her car, she looked at her image in the vanity mirror. Dog's vomit. Tara was right, this had to stop but she had her phone in her hand. The hurt had morphed into anger. How dare he go away on the passport she had coughed up for. Who did he go away with, another woman paying for him? She turned the phone around and round in her hand working out what she was going to text the horrible bastard and then it came to her.

'Enjoy your memories of Ibiza. When are you giving me my 128 pounds back?'

'Who said I was in Ibiza?' came the instant reply.

That sent Izzy even further into orbit. Never mind the 128 quid he owed her, all he cared about was how she'd heard about Ibiza.

She threw the phone onto the passenger seat, feeling worse than she did before. Had she really expected him to offer to give her the money back? Or was she more upset that he had been on holiday having a great time without her? Which one was it? She asked herself. She should never have contacted him. Wrong move, another knee jerk reaction. She turned on the ignition and headed back to school. She was so upset, it was almost as if he had died or she had caught him in bed with her best friend. Actually, not much chance of that happening, Tara wouldn't look at him twice. Still, she couldn't shake off the feeling of utter despair he had caused.

By the time she reached the school gates, Izzy tried to pull herself together.

"Fuck you Jonny Devroe!" she shouted out loud in the car. "My turn to go on holiday and enjoy myself without you."

It never entered her head that Jonny really didn't care if she went to Barbados with Brad Pitt.

36

Tara had tried unsuccessfully to contact Izzy over the weekend so ended up sending her a text to wish her bon voyage. She received a curt 'thanks' in return but Tara had known her for a very long time and in all of those years, Izzy had never changed. The minute she knew that she hadn't handled a situation correctly or acted accordingly or was even in the wrong, her back was up and she went straight on the defensive. God help the messenger. In this case, it was Tara and she knew she was well and truly in the firing line. Hopefully, the sun would shine every day in Santorini and her friend would come back a bit more chilled than when she left.

Tara turned her attention to her other problem. Max had texted her nonstop over the weekend. She hadn't replied but she got quite a shock when he appeared in reception on Monday morning. He looked better. The stitches had been removed but his eyebrow was still swollen and looked very painful. She felt odd when she saw him but realised it was the sex that she was missing, not him, so when he asked her to go for a coffee, she accepted much to the surprise of Daniel whose one eyebrow shot up almost to the ceiling. Val to her credit pretended not to notice either of them and kept tapping the keys of her computer.

Max failed to tell her he had spent most of the morning at Susan's flat. The other two women in his life wouldn't have sex with him so he'd have to make do with her until he got Tara back on side. They sat down with their cups of coffee.

"I've missed you," he said holding her free hand.

"Your situation is too volatile Max. Kate's clearly watching you and after all, I don't want to be with you, it was just sex."

"Well it wasn't just the sex for me Tara," said Max looking hurt.

"What is going on with you at home now anyway?"

"I have apologised," he said with a huge grin. "And I'm trying very hard to put things right."

Tara couldn't get to grips with the head wound incident. Surely no marriage could survive domestic abuse on that scale? She finished her coffee and stood up.

"'I have to get back, Max."

Then he stood up and grabbed her by the hand. She shrugged him off.

"When will I see you again?" he said desperately.

"Max, we can only be friends. You need to sort your life out and I need to do the same."

"What do you mean," said Max, pouncing on the information. "How are you going to sort out your life?"

Tara realised she had said the wrong thing. She was transmitting straight to him that she couldn't keep living like this either.

"Just go and sort yourself out Max," she repeated. "I'll send you a text at some point."

When she left the café, she looked back and watched him heading to his office.

At her desk again, she knew by the look on Daniel's face, he wasn't happy.

"Only a coffee," she said and the eyebrow flew straight up again.

Tara couldn't wait for three o'clock. She had a secret arrangement to view Frances' and Tony's house. She had been in the house before but they were going to talk money and set the ball rolling. Tara felt really excited, but then the post arrived and she noticed the unmistakable handwriting on the envelope, 'to be opened by addressee only. Kate again.

Tara slowly opened the letter and started to read, trying hard to digest all the information. The letter read like War and Peace, but Tara couldn't help feeling sorry for the poor woman. She was obviously trying her best to salvage her marriage, probably for the sake of their kids. The only person Max was going to salvage was himself. The letter was quite matter-of-fact, explaining to Tara that it had come to Kate's attention that he had been spinning the story that she had assaulted him. She quite categorically denied this but went on to say that Max had ongoing problems and that he had at last promised to get help. She also went on to say that she was very worried about him as his behaviour was becoming increasingly destructive and self-harming. Other incidents had occurred in the past that

Kate didn't really want to go in to but nothing as significant as him striking his head against the metal towel rail in their bathroom and the subsequent head injury. She went on to explain that the bathroom door had been locked at the time that Max had struck himself.

When Tara finished reading the letter she was in shock and passed it straight over to Daniel. He read it and passed it back.

"Confirms everything I've said. You need to be very careful with him. In my view he's an attention seeker and mentally unstable," said Daniel and returned to his keyboard.

Tara had already half-suspected he had given himself that head wound, though how anyone could inflict such pain on themselves was beyond her. Trust her to find someone for great sex who was turning out to be the village idiot. She decided not to say anything to Max about Kate getting in touch, then nearly had a heart attack when she saw the time. She jumped up and grabbed her coat. She'd arranged to meet Debbie at two forty-five, who'd kindly offered to view the house with her for a second opinion. At that moment, a text arrived from Izzy, saying what a great time she was having without Jonny. Tara didn't believe a word of it.

Tara woke up the next day with the work phone already ringing.

"For fuck's sake," muttered Simon from the other side of the bed.

It was six o'clock and from then on, all the time Tara was trying to get ready to leave the house, it never stopped. She was down to her last secondary teacher Jennifer Garland. Tara rang her and a sleepy sounding Jennifer picked up.

"Morning Jennifer, Tara here from Education Supply, are you available?"

"Oh yes," replied Jennifer and took down the details of where she needed to be that day. "Mind you," she added just as Tara had finished. "I haven't got my DBS."

Tara knew it had all been too easy.

"Why?" she said. "Where is it?"

"I think I left it in one of the schools I was in before. I'll have a ring round and see if I can find it."

"You can't get into a school without the certificate," Tara reminded her.

"I'm on the update service so as long as I take in my passport as photo ID and you send your part over, it should be Ok. They can check it."

"If only it was that easy," said Tara. "But we will give it a go."

It wasn't an ideal situation but Tara agreed and made a note for Val to send the information off so that the school had a record for identification purposes. Then she quickly got ready for work. At this point Simon was also getting up with a face like a horse's behind, moaning about being sick of the bloody phone ringing at ungodly hours. Tara smiled to herself, he wouldn't have to suffer much longer.

By the time she got into work, Daniel and Carrie were already hard at it so she popped the note on Carrie's desk regarding Jennifer and sat down at her desk. Tara noticed Carrie was straight on to the information that she had just given her. Then she heard Daniel on the phone.

"I do appreciate that Julie, but Jennifer is on the update service and has brought her photo ID in for you to look at and record. You can check immediately that she is on the update service yourself by typing in the certificate number."

He was trying to keep a lid on it. Tara could hear him growing more annoyed by the second and realised that Jennifer had beaten her to it and had already arrived in the school's reception area. Daniel slammed the phone down.

"She's sending Jennifer home as she does not have her DBS," he snapped. "She's on the fucking update service for God's sake but Julie the Cover Manager is not having any of it."

Tara smiled trying to lighten the load.

"But there is some good news," she said, staring at her computer screen. "I've won the lottery."

"No!" said Daniel.

"An email has just arrived from the LADO team. No further action is going to be taken regarding the swearing allegation so Daniel you can ring that little fucker and tell him if he swears again in a classroom, I will personally chop his balls off."

Everybody starting laughing then settled down again to wade through the paperwork from the morning's activity. Tara deleted all the text messages from Max from the night before. She couldn't be bothered to read them. He peppered his messages with so much useless information that Tara felt the need to list them in bullet points before her head exploded.

37

Izzy had been home now for two days but still no word from Jonny. Her resentment was beginning to grow into healthy measures. She looked at herself in the mirror admiring the fabulous tan she had worked hard to get and had an overwhelming desire for him to see what he was missing. The weight had dropped off her and even if she said it herself, she was looking good. Michelle had driven her crazy and Izzy had realised by day two that they had nothing other than work in common but by then it was too late. Izzy was going to have to keep her mouth shut and just get on with it. She had spent every waking moment hatching a plan to get Jonny's attention but by the time she was through thinking it out, she lost interest and moved on to a different idea.

All her ideas had seemed half baked until Friday afternoon. Izzy had popped into school, as usual, she had to let the caretaker in during the holidays, so he could get on with the remedial work. When her phone vibrated on the desk, she made a grab for it, still subconsciously thinking by some miracle it could be Jonny but it was her friend Tanya.

'Haven't seen you for aeons girl. Are you back??' If yes Limes tonight???'

Izzy suddenly felt alive. Decision made. She would go to Limes and ignore him, have nothing to do with him and he would be staring at her because she looked so good and he would want her all over again when he saw her.

'Sounds great. Pick me up at nine, I will be ready' she replied.

Izzy was fully aware that Jonny started at nine, so by the time they reached Limes he would be working on the door and she could make her grand entrance. Only a fool thinks he can fool other people Izzy thought. Tanya read her reply and was happy Izzy had agreed to come out but she knew it was just for Jonny's benefit. She also knew there wasn't a cat in hell's chance that Izzy would be ready on time.

When Tanya arrived, as she had guessed Izzy still wasn't ready. She was now a nervous wreck at the thought of seeing him, but she wanted to look her very best. Tanya had to step over the piles of clothes Izzy had discarded on the floor plus as Tanya noticed, she had been drinking, probably for Dutch courage. Izzy was as high as a kite. Tanya looked around at the mess and remembered the last time she had been away with Izzy, she had wanted to kill her, the mess she made in every room she entered. It was just as well she lived on her own. She was constantly leaving the bath running and forgetting all about it. Twice, to Tanya's knowledge, Izzy had flooded out her kitchen, which was directly under the bathroom. She was always breaking things, dropping make up all over the carpets and she never could put anything away. It always went on the floor.

This evening, her bedroom was a disaster area but Tanya helped her straighten her hair to hurry proceedings up and whilst she did this Izzy filled her friend in with the passport and holiday gossip.

"Oh my God," said Tanya, aghast. "I am so sorry that he treated you like that."

"It's not your fault," she said smiling.

By now Tanya had a feeling of dread in the pit of her stomach. That's why Izzy had wanted to go to Limes. Tanya could smell a scene coming on.

"He's dangerous Izzy, don't cross him. In fact, let's go somewhere else tonight?"

"I have no intention of speaking to him tonight or ever in fact."

But Tanya couldn't shake the feeling that fireworks were about to go off and she certainly didn't want to get involved in any of this shit going down with Jonny Devroe. Tanya wanted to cancel the night out completely but it didn't really matter which way it went now. Izzy was always the same, she went for the same type of guy who constantly treated her badly then got shot of her. Then she would meet another one who would promise her the earth, was lovely to her then once the honeymoon period was over, he would turn into a complete arsehole. It had been going on since Jesus lost his sandals. She would never change so what was the point in wasting a good night out?

Finally, Tanya managed to get her out of the front door and the taxi dropped them off right outside the front of Limes. Izzy's eyed darted all over the place looking for Jonny but she couldn't make her grand entrance as he was nowhere to be seen. Izzy was gutted but she told herself that he must be working somewhere inside. She was so disappointed not to see his first reaction at how good she looked with her deep golden tan and weight loss. She had replayed this little scenario in her head all day long. He would smile and tell her how gorgeous she looked and that he had missed her. The other two guys on the door who knew her through Jonny, waved them inside so they didn't have to wait in line with the other party-goers.

The two girls headed straight to the bar. Tanya decided she needed a drink quickly to settle her nerves. Izzy was acting very strangely. She was searching high and low for Jonny with her eyes but he was nowhere to be seen. Izzy felt unsettled and wanted to go to the ladies to check on her makeup so that when he did present himself, she would be looking perfect. As Tanya got the drinks in, she headed off to the ladies. As she neared the corridor where the loos were situated, she heard some noises from around the corner. Out of curiosity, she went to have a look.

Whoever said curiosity killed the cat got it spot-on. Jonny was leaning against the wall with his shirt unbuttoned and his jeans down at his ankles. His eyes were closed and all she could see was a mass of auburn hair between his legs. The head was moving and she was using her left hand and mouth on him whilst he held her right hand. Izzy thought she was going to throw up when she realised what they were doing. His eyes flew open when he heard her sharp intake of breath but then he just looked at her, mouthed the word 'Hi' and closed his eyes again whilst auburn head carried on not missing a stroke.

Izzy was mortified and just about made it back to the bar with tears streaming down her face.

"I've got to get out of here," she sobbed to Tanya who was smiling away busily drinking her Bacardi and coke.

"What on earth is wrong?" she said putting her arms around her distressed friend.

Izzy had to make a decision fast. Stay and let him see that it didn't bother her or run away.

"Fuck him," she said suddenly.

Izzy plonked herself down and started necking the wine her friend had got in. She told Tanya what she had just witnessed but Tanya wasn't fazed by anything Jonny might do and well believed her. Ten minutes later Jonny strutted across the bar smiling easily at Izzy and Tanya.

"Evening ladies," he threw in their direction but he didn't stop to talk and promptly disappeared.

The girl with the auburn hair had disappeared too. Izzy wanted to see what she looked like. Tony had summoned Jonny up to the office.

"I want my two best men on this," he told Jonny who had spotted Stevie sitting at the back of the office.

"Ok boss," said Jonny.

"Stevie will fill you in on the way there," said Tony. "He didn't want to interrupt you earlier when you were consoling that bird beside the ladies' toilet."

Stevie started to laugh but Tony carried on.

"It's a simple clean up job. Phone me when it's sorted."

Jonny headed to the car but he knew that nothing was simple where Tony was concerned and wondered what he was going to be faced with. They made their way to a building development. Some of it was completed but other floors were still very much under construction. The top four floors were taken but the lower two were still being fitted out. As Jonny made his way onto floor three, he could smell the blood. Stevie had sensibly suited and booted them so that no fibres would be left at the scene. He'd even thought to bring a huge plastic sheet.

When Jonny saw the body, he went up and gave it a kick to make sure he was dead. He could see it was definitely a he. The prostrate shape was as big as a barn door. Jonny peered at the body. He had one bullet hole in his head that Jonny could see but someone must have been very angry as the dead man had slash wounds, some of them quite deep, all over him. That accounted for the amount of blood all over the concrete floor. The man had obviously tried to defend himself and move away because the blood trailed off in different directions.

He had a black suit on that must have been expensive and his shoes also looked handmade. He was young, early-forties and he had one splash of blood on his face which was why Jonny and Stevie didn't recognise him straight away. Then as they started to haul his dead weight onto the plastic, they both looked at each other. The dawn of recognition. This was no simple clean up. This was Jimmy Calvert.

"Fucking hell," said Stevie. "I'm expecting big dollars for this." Then he lay the plastic sheet out, ready for Jonny to roll the dead cop onto.

Jonny and Stevie returned to Limes after disposing of James Calvert. They both stayed silent in the car coming back. It didn't need to be said but they both realised that their involvement in this matter had sunk them to an all-time low. A dead cop was going to cause ructions if he was found and people would start asking a lot of questions.

Jonny looked over at Stevie who was driving slowly trying not to attract any attention on the quiet country road.

"This is trouble, Stevie," he said.

"Whatever happened to him," sighed Stevie. "It wasn't our fault."

Some people were prepared to share their feelings rather than bottling them up but Jonny knew that's all he would get out of him. He couldn't help wondering if Tony had finished James off himself. What could possibly be going down, involving the old bill? James Calvert must have well and truly trodden on the wrong shoes.

Stevie swung the Mercedes into the car park at Limes and Jonny checked out his appearance in the rear-view mirror. They parked up and headed towards the entrance of Limes pushing through the smart glass doors and headed straight to the boss's office. They knew Tony would be waiting for them. He was sitting at his desk with his feet on it looking far too casual for Jonny's liking.

"Usual place?" he asked and for once Stevie did the talking.

"Yes, it's done and the fucking car is covered in mud."

This set them all off laughing. He was more bothered about the precious car being filthy than the dead body they had just disposed of, let alone it being police. That's why he employed them. They always carried out his orders to the letter and more importantly could keep their mouths shut. He opened the safe, pulled out wads of cash and gave them two grand each. A job well done.

Meanwhile, Izzy and Tanya were still sitting at the bar, laughing and drinking. Izzy was trying not to notice that Jonny wasn't around but it was like she'd had radar fitted. Her eyes were everywhere, searching for him. She immediately perked up when she spotted him coming from the direction of the office. He headed towards them and ordered two glasses of wine.

"These are on me," he said smiling.

"Even though your boss is really paying," she said, smiling back sarcastically. "But thanks anyway for two free drinks."

Tanya just looked at her and waited for Jonny's reaction but was surprised when he started laughing.

"Now, now," he said tutting. "Enjoy." With that, he turned and headed back to the stairs.

Tanya knew that Izzy was drunk and she needed to get her home quickly before Izzy said something that would get her into trouble and she would later regret.

"He's still gorgeous," said Izzy, slurring her words.

"And still a dangerous man my friend," muttered Tanya, to herself as she bent down to pick up her bag.

It was one o'clock in the morning and the club was really starting to come to life. The staff were busying themselves trying to serve as many people as possible and making sure that everything stayed looking as glamourous as possible. Tanya wasn't really ready to go home but she managed to get Izzy to the front glass doors. Izzy propped herself up against the reception wall giggling whilst Tanya went to find a taxi but she nearly had a heart attack when the guy next to her turned around with a dazzling smile. She hadn't noticed Jonny and she felt the blood rush to her face at the shock of finding him that close to her.

"What the hell are you doing here?" she slurred.

"Er I work here?" he said laughing.

Oh God, he only had to smile at her and she was ready to roll over. Tanya came back through the glass doors to fetch Izzy but she slowed her pace as she saw Jonny and Izzy staring each other out. She could feel the sexual excitement in the air.

"Come on Izzy," she said, grabbing hold of her arm. "Taxi's waiting."

"I'll take her home," said Jonny, waving Tanya away like she was some servant at his beck and call.

Tanya could see where this was going and she felt her face burning. It was a very bad idea but Izzy smiled at her like a Cheshire cat, delighted he was making a play for her. Jonny smiled back. He liked it when women shared his bed but never his life. Izzy said goodbye to Tanya and left her standing in the reception area of Limes with her mouth open. Meanwhile, she and Jonny stepped straight into the taxi Tanya had hailed. She gave her address and the car sped off into the night.

Tanya was furious. Her friend had just left her there. She'd been used just so that Izzy could be in the same room as Jonny. She also knew it would all end in tears, again. How could Izzy forget so quickly? She went back outside and re-joined the taxi cue.

Izzy stumbled out of the taxi holding onto Jonny and dropped her bag. Everything spilt out onto the road and Jonny suddenly realised that this was a bad idea. She was irritating him already but it was late so he pressed on looking for her keys. He found them and unlocked the front door of Izzy's house, leaving her sprawled on the ground trying to pick everything up. She managed to get herself into the house, fell headfirst onto the sofa and promptly fell asleep. Jonny was thrilled. All he wanted was a good night's kip in her comfy bed. After the night's events, he was knackered and didn't want to be at home just in case anything had gone tits up. She would be his alibi and he was certain she would say anything he told her to.

As he undressed, he noticed some dried blood on his shirt so he headed downstairs and stashed it in the washer. Izzy didn't even raise her head. She was flat out. He'd get her to iron it in the morning for him.

Izzy woke up to the sound of Debbie Harry singing Rapture. For a split second, she hadn't a clue where she was until she realised that Jonny was sticking a mug of tea in her hands. She knew she must look terrible. She could feel the makeup smeared down her face and her head was banging like a steam engine. Jonny sat in the chair opposite her and listened to her rant on about how ill she felt and that someone must have spiked her drink.

"You were hammered," he pointed out.

Izzy just shrugged. There was no point denying it but she was kicking herself for wasting such an opportunity to spend time with him. Jonny finished his tea.

"Any chance of you putting my shirt in the tumble dryer? I had beer on it and washed it when you were flat out."

Izzy felt terrible but somehow got herself off the sofa. It felt like raising the Titanic but she shoved the shirt in the dryer for him. Then she made a monumental effort to pull herself together but as she took the shirt out of the dryer, she knew he would be off. As she watched him leave, she did wonder why the hell he had bothered to come around. Of course, she had no idea she was his alibi. She was perfect. She didn't even have a parking ticket.

38

Tara got into work on Monday morning without any of the usual circus activities. She laughed hysterically at the note Daniel had left her from Friday. One of their teachers, a geography specialist John Cornely had been given permission to take the kids on a field trip. So far so good but the trip hadn't been to any of the usual geography highlights but to his mother's grave. Whilst he sat on his knees at the headstone bawling his eyes out, he left the kids to write a report on the rock formations adjoining said cemetery. The head had gone berserk but Tara could not stop laughing and when Daniel arrived, he knew instantly what she was laughing at.

"It's terrible isn't it?" he asked but Tara could only shake her head and wipe the tears from her eyes.

"I cannot believe he could be so stupid!" she said still laughing. "How did he not think that the kids would shop him?"

"He's adamant Tara," said Daniel in all seriousness. "That it was a genuine geographical site and he will be personally marking the kids' work."

"I don't know what it's coming to Daniel," she said, shaking her head and they started filling the bookings that came in.

Tara glanced at her phone. Max still hadn't given up the ghost. He kept declaring his love at every given opportunity and she was sick of him sending her flowers. God knows who was paying for them and it did cross her mind that Kate may be checking the bank statements. Tara had to admit to herself that she was missing the sex with Max. She'd had quite a long conversation with Debbie on the telephone about the situation and was halfway into deciding that she might start it up again, purely on a casual basis. Debbie, of course, thought that she was as clinically insane as Max was for even contemplating it. However, Tara tried to convince her that if it was just the sex then he would handle the situation. Debbie told her in no uncertain terms what she thought but now, Tara picked up the phone and texted him just a quick:

'I'm fine thanks' and within seconds her mobile blipped.

'Can I come round??? I've missed you so much'.

Max was grinning from ear to ear. He loved Tara in an inexplicable way and he could not stop thinking about her. Tara knew that she could possibly be opening another can of worms but sex was sex and she liked doing it so she typed:

'Yes.' and pressed send before she could change her mind.

She explained to Daniel that Max was en route and she would need the interview room to 'talk to him in private' but all Daniel could do was raise his eyebrows skyward as if to say here we go again. Max walked into her office beaming. He was delighted to see her and she took him straight up to the interview room so that they could be alone. He was dressed impeccably, as usual, the pin-striped suit he wore must be a designer label she thought. It certainly didn't look like a Marks and Spencer job. Tara gave him the look that she usually reserved for children and stupid people. He was far too keen gushing all over her but she couldn't help taking him all in. His legs were lean and strong, he looked like a runner. His shoulders were wide and she knew that underneath the suit his abs were of a premiership footballer quality. It wasn't just the way he looked though. His hands knew exactly where to touch her and his mouth was so soft and his tongue knew where to probe. In fact, sex with Max was fabulous.

Tara's moral compass went out of the window. She knew exactly what she wanted and it was there for the taking. He bent her over the desk, pushed her skirt out of the way and guided himself into her. She was so wet with anticipation that she almost drowned him. Tara closed her eyes as he pushed into her deeper and deeper and she could feel herself coming as he explored the back of her neck with his tongue, caressing the lines and indentations.

They both heard the nearby accounts' office door open and close. Max shot backwards yanking his hands away from her and zipped himself back up. His heart was thudding against his chest.

"Who is that?" he said.

"Calm down," said Tara giggling. "It will be Carrie."

They were like two kids nearly caught in the back of a parked car. Max struck up a conversation with Tara that was utter rubbish as the footsteps got closer. By the time Carrie put her hand on the door handle, the poor girl jumped back with fright when she saw Tara and Max. She hadn't realised that anybody was in there and embarrassed, she asked Max how his kids were. Max was a lot more embarrassed than Carrie. He had guilt written all over his face. He stood up and couldn't get out of the room fast enough, leaving Carrie and Tara staring at each other. When they were sure he had gone, they both burst out laughing.

As Tara went back downstairs to the general office she thought to herself 'poor man' but at least she'd managed to orgasm.

She took a call from her solicitor. The house sale was moving along nicely and she was starting to feel the impending dread of breaking the news to Simon that she was leaving him. She did think that she had no need to worry about his reaction. A blind man on a galloping horse in the dead of night could see that their relationship was over and she felt sure he would agree and be pleased even, that she had the courage to be the one to say it's over. She had also picked up the phone to Izzy who was far too quiet for Tara's liking but the call was work-related so she did have to speak to her. Tara knew her well enough to realise that the shutters were down so Tara gave up. Izzy never changed. It would be a big secret until the shit hit the fan then Tara would be the first person she called for help and that's what friends were for she supposed. She knew that it would involve Jonny but Izzy would come clean and fill her in when she was ready.

Daniel came back from lunch and plonked his huge frame on the edge of her desk.

"I had a very interesting interview earlier whilst you were having your G8 summit upstairs," he said. "Do you remember the incident with Sarah Grey at Denton Primary a few months ago?"

"I do," said Tara. "I remember feeling furious at the time because I wanted to speak to the head, Paula Taylor, after she'd instructed a vile, common, little minion to do her dirty work for her."

"Well," he continued "I interviewed a decent behavioural mentor earlier. He was recruited by Denton, at about the same time they disposed of Sarah. He was to work one-to-one with a Year 5 boy who had severe behavioural issues."

"It has to be the same pupil," she said.

"Well I think it is the same pupil," said Daniel. "Ben, the guy I interviewed had a terrible job with the kid. He was bitten, kicked, slapped, spat on even by this feral child. His job description included never to leave the boy's side, not even in the playground, he was deemed so violent."

Tara shook her head.

"Was he statemented or disabled to have such problems?" she said.

"Oh no," replied Daniel. "He was just really naughty. His parents couldn't care less about him."

"Well it will be down to the school to sort him out as usual," she said. "Nothing to do with the idiots that spawned him. I bet the taxpayer paid for an outside agency to come in and write a report about him and 'talk' to him."

"You've got it."

Tara was starting to get annoyed.

"How come these so-called appointed agencies don't go to the kids' homes and make whoever looks after them responsible for the kids' actions? Why is it the school's responsibility these days?"

"You're preaching to the converted sweetie," said Daniel, putting his hands up. "But this situation has got a whole lot worse. The boy beat another pupil up in the playground. He banged the poor boy's head off the ground. Hospital was involved. Ben had to drag him off. The kid is now permanently excluded. He fractured the other kid's skull."

"I don't get it, Dan. A teacher's job is to teach. Every morning when the kids come in, they should be ready to start work. Since when were all of these other issues allowed to creep into the classroom? It's all at home and it makes my fucking blood boil that an innocent child has been hurt by that feral git."

"Well Ben lost his job when the kid was excluded but he will now go to a Pupil Referral Unit and they'll have to deal with him. When does it stop Tara? When are these kids punished for their behaviour?"

"No," she felt her anger boiling over. "No, when are the parents, parent, guardian or grandmother brought up to the school and forced to remove them and be held responsible for their fucking behaviour, and if they don't go to school the court should step in. Stop their fucking benefits and I would guarantee they will stop their kids acting in this way. Stop leaving it to the schools to sort out when their hands are tied. Whatever problems the kid has, biting, spitting and fracturing skulls is not on. I wonder how he would feel if a big boy came up to him and did the same thing? What was the head's uptake on all of this?"

"She thought the best option was to take him into her office and talk to him," said Daniel, laughing. "Especially when he kept disrupting classes by running up and down the corridor kicking the doors and shouting fuck off."

Tara didn't know what to say.

"We are doing these kids no favours you know," she said eventually. "He will end up in prison or stabbed and all because he didn't know the difference between right and wrong and wasn't held responsible for his actions."

They both agreed on one thing that in hindsight, it was good that Sarah had been pulled out. God knows what may have happened to her. Plus, the boy was saving the council a fortune. One-to-one teaching was expensive. Now he could join the other feral animals at the PRU.

"Do you know why they do finger painting in primary schools, Dan?"

"Why?"

"To collect their DNA from an early age, so they can use it when they're arrested."

Daniel and Carrie started laughing. Poor Mark being a bit slow didn't get it.

Max sent her a text that she 'owed' him one but Tara had a secret little giggle to herself as she deleted it. She couldn't care less that he hadn't had time to finish what he started. Debbie had pointed out to her that the way she behaved and talked about Max, she wasn't really sure if Tara actually liked him. This gave Tara food for thought and had admitted to Debbie that she was just using him for sex she didn't want to be with him.

Tara got home and walked from room to room. She was going to have to start packing and more importantly tell Simon the news. She heard the garage door go up and the throaty sound of his Porsche engine. Tara wondered what sort of mood he was in. She didn't have long to wait. He came in, flung his tie and jacket over the bottom of the stair rail and barely grunted in passing. She was sick of him.

Tara blinked a few times then took a deep breath,

"Sit down Simon, I need to talk to you."

He realised by the tone of her voice that this was serious but slumped onto the sofa disagreeably.

"For fuck's sake, Tara not now. I've had a very busy day and all I want to do is read the paper."

Days' later, when she thought about it, she realised that he had done her the biggest favour reacting like that. It had annoyed her so much, it galvanised her into action.

"State of my life with you Simon," she yelled. "You would rather read the fucking paper than talk to me. If I had a Porsche badge between my legs you might show me more interest!"

Her mouth was open and a thin line of spittle dangled from her top lip. She badly wanted to slap his arrogant face. Simon's eyes were nearly popping out of his head at this stage. He was so taken aback by her outburst.

"No easy way to say this, I'm leaving you and filing for divorce and I'm also in the process of buying the house five doors up."

When she saw the look on his face it crossed her mind that he was going to faint. He was in shock. He'd turned ashen.

"You are joking?" he stammered and the tears started to roll down his face.

Now it was her turn to be shocked. In all the years that they had been married Tara had never seen Simon cry. Not even at his Uncle's funeral whom he'd been so close to.

"I'm sorry that it has come out like this but there is no easy way to do this," she said.

He got up and was so visibly shaken, Tara felt guilty, as if this was all her fault. He clearly hadn't expected anything like this to happen in their marriage.

"You seriously can't expect our lives to go on like this, no sex, your temper tantrums. I've had enough. You're more interested in your racing car than you are in me."

"That's not true, I really love you, Tara," he said, weeping openly.

Tara did not know where to put herself but the ball had started rolling and there was no stopping it. This was obviously Simon's biggest nightmare. She could see the pound signs rolling around in his head. He sank back onto the sofa.

"When are you moving out?" he asked.

"Next Friday, so I'm going to do us both a favour and move into the Marriott for the week and come back tomorrow to get some more of my things."

Simon just stared at her. He was totally floored and for once in his life completely out of control.

"There's no need to move out. Stay here until Friday, I will help you."

That was the last thing she wanted.

"It's for the best Simon," she said quickly then dashed up the stairs two at a time to collect an overnight bag.

"What shall I tell Julie?" he said, shouting up from the bottom of the stairs.

Julie was Tara's housekeeper and she paid her.

"She's coming with me," she called back.

She could hear a mumbled voice and realised that he was on the phone in the lounge but all she heard was something like 'father she has left me.'

Tara checked into the Marriott and managed to get a discount on a Junior Suite for the week's booking. A bargain was a bargain she chuckled to herself. She hung her clothes up then grabbed her trainers and went for a long run along the beachfront to clear her head. After a long soak in the bath, she felt a huge weight had lifted from her back. She hadn't realised it but the thought of actually telling Simon had pressed very heavily on her mind. Now she had done it, she knew it had been the right decision. She could not help going over and over his reaction though. She felt bewildered because she honestly thought that he would have agreed and secretly he would have been pleased, relieved even that one of them had the guts to call it a day. It appeared she was way off the mark. He was genuinely distressed. The look of hopelessness on his face had made her feel like a first-class bitch.

Tara took a deep breath and texted her whereabouts to everyone who needed to know. She didn't phone as she wasn't ready to enter into the shock and horror and all the crap that went with it. Her decision was final. She deliberately left Izzy out of it as she wanted to tell her face to face. Izzy was lying very low at the moment. In fact, she was horizontal on the communication front, so it served her right if she found out from somebody else.

The reactions were mixed but Daniel's was the best. He texted her back:

'For fuck's sake, you're having a midlife crisis, don't be so stupid.'

Tara started to laugh. He always had her best interest at heart and was in total awe of Simon's status and money not to mention the family name and history. All he wanted was for her to be financially secure for the rest of her life. Tara, of course, had other ideas. Life was too short and the thought of living without sex and continuing to play around behind his back had to stop. One day he was going to find out. On that note, Tara reflected that Max now had a problem. If Kate found out then she couldn't tell Simon and break her marriage up. One of them was behaving in some sort of correct manner. She was certainly going to keep quiet about her living arrangements for the moment. Max didn't need to know.

39

Izzy must have been dog-tired the night before because she slept right through and didn't hear her mobile bleep when it received a text through the night. The phone was lying on the bed next to her and the first thing she did every morning was to reach out and check if Jonny had contacted her. She knew it was pathetic but she couldn't help herself. It was Sunday, she felt restless and she had been wondering what to do with herself. The answer arrived quickly.

'Fancy a day out?'

She curled up in bed hugging herself, smiling and felt immediately excited. The thought of him even asking her to spend the day with him sent her into orbit. She felt a huge wave of love for him, so she picked up the phone and asked him where he wanted to go. To her surprise, it didn't take the usual twenty-four hours for him to reply.

'Northumberland, pick me up nine.'

Suddenly she felt irked. How dare he just expect her to jump when he cracked the whip? He hadn't been in touch for ages and then suddenly it was action stations but she knew she would give into him. The chance to spend the day with him was too good to turn down. Maybe he would realise what a good time he could have with her, then they could share more time together. She didn't reply and jumped into the shower.

Five changes of outfit, ranging from very dressy to jeans and a white shirt, and she was ready. She pulled up outside his flat and again wondered why he lived in such a dump but he was already waiting outside for her. He was a big man and obviously trained most days as he looked very fit. He knew he was good looking and he swaggered with an air of confidence as he walked up to her car and got in. He always looked slightly dangerous and had even admitted to himself that he was indeed a very dangerous man but today Tony had warned both Stevie and Jonny to stay out of the way. The heat was on with James Calvert the dead cop and if the police were going to come around asking questions, Tony had wanted them out of the way and lying low.

Tony had also taken the precaution of scrapping the Mercedes which broke Stevie's heart but Tony had decided that the car could be hot. No matter how careful the boys had been, he thought it wise to get rid. He had a mate who owned a scrap yard that didn't ask too many questions. The car had moved the body so Tony was taking no chances with any trace of forensic evidence, no matter how well the car had been cleaned.

Strangely enough, Tony was very well thought of in the serious crimes' unit. He propped up a few of the meagre salaries the higher-ranking officers earned and they in turn kindly warned him that most of the 'names' were about to have their business premises searched for any evidence linked to the disappearance of James Calvert. Warrants had been granted and the police were ready to move. Tony supposed they had to be seen to be avenging one of their own but it was common knowledge that Jimmy was despised by everyone who knew him, apart from his mother. Most of the police officers had breathed a collective sigh of relief when he disappeared. He'd had it coming for years was the general consensus.

Izzy had made a pact with herself not to appear overly keen so when he got into her Audi, she acted dead casual.

"Hello Jonny, long time no see," she said with even a hint of sarcasm.

It was wasted on him as it bounced right off.

"You've lost weight," he said, smiling at her which Izzy really liked but she was soon dropped back down to earth when he followed it up with "But your highlights need doing."

Izzy gave him a look that would have put him fifty feet under but resisted a massive urge to slap the smug look from his face. Then he got hold of her hand and leant over and plonked a kiss on her cheek, which shut her up. She put the car into gear and headed off in the direction of the motorway. She presumed she was heading in the right direction which was North and awaited instructions. Jonny would know exactly where he wanted to be.

Stevie was in his element twenty-five miles away. Tony had made arrangements for him to go and replace the Mercedes, like for like and even left the colour up to Stevie to decide on as long as it wasn't black like the previous model. Stevie had made a day of it and even took his Mum along who was fit to burst with pride as her son commandeered the salesman who fell all over him.

She really didn't know exactly what her son did for a living but as she walked around the plush showroom taking it all in, she thought that he must be doing really well. As far as alibis went, the two of them were nicely sorted for the day.

Jonny was pleased with his life today and he gave a grin of satisfaction as he dished out the directions to their destination, which ended up being a lovely little country pub called The Mouse. They had driven over the moors and through the local town then headed to the pub for lunch. As she pulled into the car park, she looked at the sign 'The Mouse' and giggled looking at Jonny. It should have been called 'The Rat' in his case.

After a lovely lunch during which Jonny was unusually talkative even asking her what she'd been up to. He had never shown any interest in her life before, whatsoever. School life bored him to distraction and she had long ago given up telling him anything but they went for a lovely walk along the river by the pub and he even held her hand. Izzy thought she had died and gone to heaven. Talk about mixed signals, she thought to herself but now she knew that Jonny really liked her. He couldn't behave like this if he didn't. It seemed so natural and when he stopped and cupped her face in his hands and kissed her, she actually could feel her legs trembling. She loved him so much that she thought her heart was going to burst.

Jonny looked at her long and hard before releasing her face.

"You're a good girl," he told her but she knew that a man like Jonny would find it hard to say I love you and she was so sure that was what he had been about to say. Izzy swallowed hard and without waiting for him to say anything further, pulled him down onto the grass beside the river and there they lay for a while in the hot sunshine lost in a world of their own.

Jonny broke the spell that she was in when he looked at his watch. He was bored, there was only so long you could watch water running by so he stood up, brushing the grass off his Armani jeans and told her that he was thirsty. He knew another pub nearby. He could do with a drink and to get out of the sun. It was the hottest day on record. She reluctantly got up and followed him looking for her car in the packed car park.

They found the pub but Jonny wanted to sit inside to cool down so Izzy settled herself at the bar whilst he ordered the drinks. She knew instantly that something was wrong. Everyone had been laughing and talking when they came in but when they saw Jonny, a hush descended. At first, Izzy thought she was imagining it but the barman's eyes darted about all over the place before he served them. It was obvious he knew Jonny and didn't like what he saw. She glanced around the bar and some of the customers were leaving. Jonny seemed oblivious to any of it and carried on quenching his thirst with cold lager.

Jonny started chatting away to her about the last time he had been in The Mill but the atmosphere was terrible and she was astounded that he couldn't sense anything was wrong. Jonny looked at the barman who was by now clearly terrified of him.

"Mr Williams about?' he asked.

The guy looked as if he was about to faint.

"I'm not sure," he stammered. "I'll check."

Just then Jonny excused himself.

"Won't be a mo," he said and headed off to the gents.

Izzy turned her attention to the overhead television showing Sky News. A bomb had gone off in Manchester. She watched the awful carnage playing out on the screen.

As luck would have it for Jonny, he pushed open the toilet door to find Williams washing his hands at the sink. He paled when he saw who had walked in.

"You were sent by Tony?" he asked.

In one stride Jonny walked up to him and crushed his nose with his fist. Williams fell backwards and Jonny jumped out of the way to avoid the blood spurting from Williams' face. Jonny pointed at him.

"Pay what you owe the man or next time it will be your kneecaps."

Jonny calmly washed the blood from his hands, while Williams slid down the wall and started rolling about on the floor clutching his face with both hands clearly in a lot of pain. His nose was flattened. Jonny calmly re-joined Izzy at the bar and finished his drink as if nothing had happened. The barman who had left the bar earlier sensing trouble never did come back. Everyone knew Jonny Devroe.

Tony loved hearing the news when the two thousand pounds that Williams had owed him turned up at Limes like magic. When Jonny later recalled the story to Tony and Stevie, he could not stop laughing and gave Jonny five hundred pounds for working on his own initiative. It had been a total fluke that Jonny was in the right place at the right time and had seized the opportunity to reclaim an arrear. Tony loved the way that Jonny seized an opportunity and Tony was two grand up.

Izzy was deep in thought on the drive back home. She felt something had occurred in the pub but Jonny had told her on numerous occasions that he was as straight as an arrow these days. No way was he going back to prison but his lifestyle went against everything that she stood for. She had always been an upright citizen and had never had any involvement with the police but he assured her she had nothing to worry about. In fact, when she asked him about the atmosphere in the bar, he looked at her as if she was mad and didn't know what the hell she was going on about. He'd even gone as far to say that he thought she was paranoid.

She decided to put her thoughts to the back of her mind. They'd had such a lovely day, no need to spoil it. Izzy took the turning to head towards his house but he stopped her.

"Where are you going?" he asked.

"To your place," she said but he turned in the seat to face her and smiled.

"I thought we would make a night of it and go back to yours?"

Izzy could feel her heart hammering against her chest. She thought it was going to explode. She was so happy that he wanted to spend the night at her house and be with her.

Tony didn't let the boys know that the police had been around to Limes with a warrant to search the premises. The warrant had been executed at nine a.m so the only people present were the cleaners who were so used to seeing people coming and going at all hours, that they hardly took any notice as the officers were in plain clothes. Tony had insisted to his contacts that no uniforms were to attend and that's exactly what happened. They did the necessary merely glancing over paperwork and records but they could find no evidence that Calvert had been anywhere near Limes. They also had checked Tony's Mercedes but knew this was a complete waste of time when they realised it was fresh out of the showroom and he had the paperwork to prove it. A few eyebrows were raised that his old car had been scrapped but he even produced the paperwork to back that up. Tony had enough money that he didn't need to trade in the old one and he had no need to explain himself to the filth.

As he listened to the police officer explaining what they needed to do he fought the urge to tell him to shut the fuck up but instead he murmured the right words. Mike Hughes, the detective in charge had been friends with James Calvert and for all Calvert had been an absolute stupid prick, Mike knew that Tony was lying. He needed to find out what he was lying about and why.

Jonny and Izzy settled themselves on the sofa to watch television. Izzy couldn't have been happier. It was a perfect end to a perfect day but she did notice that Jonny's phone was never far away from him and the minute it bleeped, he replied straight away which was more than he did when she contacted him. It got to about eleven-thirty and Izzy started to think about the sleeping arrangements. Was he going to stay? She hoped so. He had been kissing her all night on the sofa and stroking her back so she was at the point now where she thought something was going to happen. She wanted him.

He put the phone down after replying to yet another text and started kissing her. He manoeuvered her under him on the sofa but his kisses were tapering off. She had felt his hardness earlier against her leg but that had disappeared too. She sensed he was losing interest but wrapped her legs around him pulling him into her. Jonny was thinking about Donna all of the time he was touching her and when he opened his eyes and saw Izzy he didn't want to go any further so he pulled away and was saved by the bell when his phone started ringing.

He untangled himself and jumped up to answer it. Izzy was devastated and tried to listen to the conversation but Jonny only said 'right, ok' so no clues there but she realised it was a work-related matter. He came back into the lounge.

"Got to go," he said and grabbed his coat.

Izzy stood in his path.

"Are you coming back?" she asked.

He threw her the sort of look that made her feel like she was something he had trod in.

"No, this is business, got to go. See you later."

She watched him unlock the front door, slam it and then disappear down the street. He had no transport so where the hell was he going? Jonny got out of the cab that he had ordered to pick him up from the bottom of her street and headed straight for his bedroom. He reached up on top of his wardrobe and retrieved the baseball bat he always kept hidden there. He removed the polythene that he kept it wrapped up in and then waited at the window for Stevie to come and pick him up. He could feel the excitement rising inside him. He loved his job.

Stevie knew where the job was on at and as they parked up and approached the house, Stevie stayed outside to keep watch. Meanwhile, Nick Bennett was lying in bed with his favourite whore when he heard his front door unceremoniously battered into his hallway by two men with sledgehammers. Before Nick could blink, he found Jonny Devroe standing at the foot of his bed complete with baseball bat. Nick calmly lit a cigarette and smiled at Jonny.

"Hello you, what can I do for you?" he smirked taking it all a bit too casually for Jonny's liking.

"Information Nick," said Jonny, smiling lazily back. "What do you know about James Calvert?"

The smile was instantly wiped off Nick's face. Everyone knew on the street that James Calvert was on the missing list and nobody was talking. He tried to scramble off the bed.

"Jesus Jonny. I know jack shit about that arsehole. Nobody knows anything."

Jonny continued smiling.

"Well, you need to be scared very scared because if I ever get wind that you or any of your pathetic little group of boys know anything and you haven't come forward to tell us, there will be blood."

Nick was scared alright and the poor girl lying next to him thought that she was going to witness a murder.

"Of course, Jonny. Tony would be the first to know."

Jonny was satisfied that the message had been delivered and stopped passing his baseball bat from hand to hand. Five minutes later Jonny and Stevie departed but Jonny stopped to ring Tony. He told him and everyone would now think that Tony of all people, wanted to know who had taken Calvert out of the picture. He needed to throw everyone off the scent and he knew that some old informant somewhere would let on to the police that Tony had been asking questions.

Izzy lay in bed. Her insides were clenching and she knew that sleep would never come. She could not understand what had happened. One minute everything was fine and the next it wasn't and she ended up alone again. It was like she was running up sand, she was moving closer yet somehow every step seemed to take her further away. She could feel the tears welling up.

40

Tara was happily chatting away to Alex, one of their supply teachers. She thought it was all running along smoothly until Alex stopped mid-sentence.

"Erm," she said, crossing and uncrossing her legs. "I'm just wondering if I can have an advance on next week's wages?"

Here we go, Tara thought and took a deep breath.

"Sorry Alex, company policy, no can do. We've been stung too many times in the past."

Alex looked as if she was about to burst into tears and then she started to babble on. The long and the short of it was that she had met a Nigerian on holiday. He'd been in the UK with Alex, but couldn't stay any longer on his visa and had to go back. Alex, of course, had fallen in love with him and was devastated. Tara could see Daniel out of the corner of her eye trying not to laugh. When she finally left the office, he let rip.

"For fuck's sake Tara. The world's gone mad. Another needy teacher."

Tara didn't really know whether she should feel sorry for her or think her an idiot. Alex's husband had left her years ago and she'd let herself go. Her hair was long and grey and her spectacles had a band-aid on the side holding them together. She looked like an overweight witch but she taught maths and was rather good at it. The school she was teaching at had held onto her for two academic years so Education supply wanted to keep her happy and on track, Nigerian or no Nigerian.

The conversation swiftly moved on to Tara's new house and Daniel wanted to come around and see it.

"You'll have to give me time to settle in," she told him. "I only moved in on Sunday."

"Have you told Max yet?" asked Daniel, his eyebrow pointing towards the ceiling as usual when he asked one of his probing questions.

Tara glared at him.

"No, no, of course I haven't," she said a little too sharply.

But Daniel smiled and gave her that knowing look of his.

"Mark parks in the back lane and often talks to Max. He reckons Kate has chucked him out."

Tara didn't think he was serious. Max would have been dying to tell her that important piece of information.

"Really?" she said.

"Yeah, he's supposed to be living at River Mews. She's rented him a nice posh apartment."

River Mews was a smart new complex of apartment buildings in the city centre. The location would be perfect for Max as it was fifteen minutes away from their house. Handy for the kids Tara thought to herself. She felt secretly relieved that she wasn't actually within spitting distance of Max during their break up. Tara still wondered why he hadn't said anything in all the hundreds of texts he had sent to her, begging to meet up. Then again, she hadn't told him that she and Simon had separated. The difference being a separation, not a throwing out. She wondered if he believed Kate would take him back. She didn't mention leaving Simon in case Max did manage to get back through Kate's front door.

Tara thought about her own situation and gave a deep sigh. It was as if she had never been married to Simon, she hadn't missed him for a second so she knew that she had made the correct decision. Tara quickly sent a text to Izzy asking to meet up. She needed to let her know what was going on. Then she busied herself with paperwork. She kept looking at her watch and after an hour realised that Izzy wasn't going to hurry back with a reply. This didn't bode well. It meant she was totally in Jonny Devroe's clutches and some drama would be unfolding which would be much more important than her best friend leaving her husband.

Tara glanced over to Daniel who had never been off the phone whilst she had been trying to get her head around a safeguarding paper, she was struggling to concentrate on as it was so boring.

"What's wrong?" she asked him.

Daniel put his head in his hands then looked up at her.

"Can you remember I pitched for ages to get into Rye Hill Academy?"

Tara nodded, he had done so well to get into that school, they'd been using another agency for years.

"And," continued Daniel. "I found them a brilliant Computer Scientist, John Wood."

Tara nodded again. He continued getting redder and redder in the face. She thought he was going to explode.

"Well that job ended and the school tried to find another class for him. Then all of their staff returned to work so he left. However, John is registered with another agency who just happened to ring Rye Hill and ask if they needed any staff the week after John had departed. Guess what? They said yes. That fucking bitch Cover Manager Alison had just been told that their Information and Communication Technology chap had gone off sick again. She mentioned it to the agency and lo and behold they quoted John's name and in he goes so we have lost that work."

Tara's voice rose ten octaves.

"You have got to be joking. We introduced John Wood to that school. They only know how fucking good he is because we sourced him. Why didn't Alison give us a call and ask for him back? And come to mention it, why hasn't John said anything?"

Daniel was too upset so Tara found the number for Rye Hill and tried and tried to speak to Alison but her calls went unanswered.

"Un-fucking-believable!" she shouted. "They do something underhand and then haven't got the balls to face up to it. Did they seriously think we would take that lying down?"

She immediately fired off an email fully knowing that the weak bitch would never reply. Daniel stood up and grabbed his empty coffee cup.

"The worrying thing is that these people are in charge of the kids. They're supposed to be role models and this is the way they treat people? The kids don't stand a chance with people like that in charge."

Tara got up and followed him into the kitchen.

"I know it won't get John back," she said. "But Alison's shagging the Deputy Head. They're both married so I'm going to put a right spanner in her works."

Daniel started to smile. He knew people crossed Tara at their peril. Alison was heading for trouble.

"I am going to drink this coffee and calm down a bit then I'm going to tell John wood exactly what I think of him. Fucker. At least it will make me feel slightly better."

Tara stirred the coffees, realising her job involved putting out fires on a daily basis. The minute she had extinguished one fire another one started and off she went again, dampening down.

Max sat at his desk a street away from her and decided now was the time to let Tara know he was single. He had begged Kate to take him back, even cried in front of the girls which only made Kate hate him more. Nothing would work. She meant it this time. He wished he was on Facebook because even at his age he would derive a lot of satisfaction from changing his status from married to single. He texted Tara:

'I need to see you.'

He popped his phone back down on the desk not expecting a reply but was pleasantly surprised. A message alert. His heart was hammering in his chest praying that it was her. He needed her so badly.

'Ok' she wrote.

He read the text again 'ok' but even one word sent his spirits soaring.

'Dinner tonight Deluca 8 pm? His hands shook typing it.

He didn't hold out much hope. She could never make evenings.

'See you there.'

It did cross his mind that she was going to stand him up but he needed to be fed so it may as well be Deluca's. For the rest of the day, he couldn't wipe the smile off his face. He was beyond delighted that she'd agreed to see him, let alone have dinner.

Tara explained to Daniel what she was up to and could see by the look on his face that he was not impressed. He'd voiced his concerns relating to Max on more than one occasion. None of them were favourable and all ended up with the word wanker. He had also pointed out that you can't light a match then act surprised when the house burns down, meaning Max was trouble.

The day flew by and Tara didn't even bother to get changed to meet Max. When she reached the restaurant fifteen minutes late, she found him sitting in the bar area sipping a beer. He sat with his legs spread wide like his balls needed the extra room. There was almost something tragic in the way he looked at her. His longing for her seemed to pierce right through her skin. She could smell his desperation. He stood up beaming triumphantly, which irritated the hell out of her.

"I never realised how much I missed you until you walked through that door," he said putting his arms around her.

Everybody heard and Tara felt a bilious attack coming on and wanted to run right back out again. She stiffened as she felt his arms tighten around her. She hated any public display of affection and managed to shrug him off. She could hear Daniel's voice, wanker, wanker and at that point had to agree with him. Antonio who owned the restaurant and had known her for years was trying hard to mask the look of surprise on his face at Max's little outburst. Even he wanted to be sick she thought but he took her coat and then showed them to the table.

As soon as they sat down, Max grabbed her hand. He looked so eager and pleased with himself. She knew what he had to get off his chest and decided to burst his little bubble for him.

"So when did Kate throw you out then?"

She watched his face crumble like a little boy having his favourite toy taken away from him.

"How did you know?" he stammered, in shock.

Tara looked down her nose at him, as if he was something she had trodden in. Now she was assured he didn't know about her and Simon. She removed her hand from his.

"You forget Max, I know everything."

"I suppose you've been speaking to Kate," he snarled, rounding on her.

It never crossed her mind that he would imagine such a thing.

"Er, no sweetie," she laughed. "She is the last person in the world I want to have anything to do with."

Max visibly relaxed and picked up the menu. He couldn't bear to think that Kate had told Tara even half of what went on in their marriage.

"I left her three weeks ago."

"And are you happy?" Tara asked him because at that point he didn't look it.

"Yes, I am," he said as he looked up and smiled at her. "It means I can spend more time with you and even have somewhere to take you that's private."

That definitely confirmed it for Tara. He didn't have a clue about her divorce proceedings and that made her smile, she had one over on him. She didn't want him pestering her every five minutes coming around to her new house. She was enjoying her freedom and Julie her housekeeper was enjoying having no more shirts to iron.

"That's good," she said. "You'll get used to it."

She made small talk with him and kept slyly looking at her watch wondering how fast she could get home. At the end of the night, she kissed him on the cheek and said good night. He wasn't happy she could see it written all over his face but on the way home, it dawned on her that he hadn't mentioned his girls once.

Max drove to his apartment gutted that he hadn't even got to the point where he could ask her to come back to his place. He pulled over and started dialling. Susan was out in town with her work colleagues. Fred in the warehouse was retiring and it was their last drink. She was having a lovely time laughing and dancing but she lit up like a Christmas tree when her phone started to ring and she saw it was Max.

"Hi babe," she said cheerily.

"Hey foxy," gushed Max. "I've spent all night with the girls. I miss them so much but I've missed you too."

He babbled on. Susan loved this. At long last, he had actually got up and left Kate but she understood that she would have to keep her distance. She couldn't move in with him until the divorce was settled. It never entered her head that Max didn't have any money. Kate was the major earner so Max having another woman would make no difference at all to the outcome of their divorce.

"I've missed you too," she cooed. "But I'm at this leaving party."

"Ok then," he sighed. "I'll catch up with you later."

He sounded irritated and the last thing she wanted to do was upset him, just when things were going in the right direction.

"No, don't be silly," she said. "Shall I come to your place say in an hour?"

Max was busy looking at himself in the rear-view mirror fussing over his hair and started smiling. He remembered to keep the little boy lost voice on.

"Only if you're sure. I don't want to spoil your night."

"I'm on my way," she insisted.

Max had a leisurely shower, opened a few beers and settled down to wait for her. He could feel himself getting hard anticipating what he was going to do with her. He could always rely on good old Susan when he needed to get laid. She was his best-kept secret.

Eight o'clock the next morning, the private detective lurking in the car park opposite Max's apartment, quickly picked up his camera. He started shooting footage of the same woman leaving, who had arrived the night before, as Max hugged and kissed her at the entrance door. He took at least another ten shots of Max kissing the blonde woman goodbye. She looked as if she had been to a party, completely dishevelled and he wore nothing but his boxer shorts. He laughed at how much he loved his job. He was dying to see Kate's face when he presented his evidence to her and wondered if she knew who the older woman was. He was also anticipating a generous tip as he had definitely caught Max red-handed.

Tara settled down for a busy day at work. It was nearly half term which meant a lot of moving about for supply staff. Max had sent God knows how many texts the night before, saying how much he loved and needed her but he had thankfully stopped around the eleven pm mark and hadn't sent any more until about nine this morning. Wonder what he was up to? She thought as she deleted all of his messages.

Her thoughts were interrupted when a call came through from Alan Banks, the cover manager at the school where Alex Smith was covering a long-term Maths sickness. Daniel looked up straight away when he heard Tara mention Alex's name. He knew it was trouble from the get-go. Stood to reason if she was in asking for a sub on her wages for the Nigerian boy, she was heading in the wrong direction. It was only the previous day that she had been into the office cap in hand.

Tara started to fidget and her cheeks began to flush. Daniel knew this was the first sign of her getting very angry.

"Oh my God," whispered Carrie to Daniel. "What has she done?"

He shrugged.

"She did what?" said Tara, suddenly very loudly.

Everyone in the office knew that the shit had hit the fan.

"I want her here Alan, in my office as soon as possible and I can only apologise for her behaviour."

The cover manager seemed to be saying that neither Tara nor Education Supply could be held responsible but Tara was livid. In fact, Daniel hadn't seen her this angry in all the years he had known her. She slammed the receiver down and started pacing up and down the office. She didn't know where to put herself she was so angry, her Louboutins clicked with every step which only annoyed her further as now her shoes needed re-heeling.

"I'm going to fucking kill that stupid bitch with my bare hands," she shouted.

Daniel stood up but stayed behind the safety of his desk.

"Sweetie calm down, what on earth has happened?' he asked.

"Happened?" she shouted "I will tell you what has fucking happened. That stupid ugly woman has taken leave of her senses, that is what has fucking happened."

She could feel the sweat running down her back, she was so furious. Daniel sat back down hoping Tara would follow suit, which thankfully she did by plonking herself back down at her desk. She took a moment to compose herself and looked around the office at everyone waiting for an explanation from her.

"Right," she said. "Alex decided in her infinite wisdom, due to her landline being cut off, to ask a Year 10 pupil if she could borrow her phone. Then guess what? Yes, you've got it, she only phoned the boyfriend in fucking Nigeria."

Daniel looked like a goldfish. He sat with his mouth wide open as Tara continued.

"The pupil assumed it was a local call but when she realised that Alex had made an international, call she started to panic. Her mum pays her phone bill and she knew that her mum would be asking who she knew in Nigeria and would hit the roof."

"She was that desperate to speak to somebody who's about to take her for a mug that she would risk her job and take a lend off a kid?" said Daniel incredulously.

Tara burst into sarcastic laughter.

"No, no sweetie. He loves her and wants to spend the rest of his life with her."

"Jesus," said Carrie who had stayed quiet till then. "He probably only wants a British passport can she not see that?"

"No, she fucking can't because she's another desperate woman," shouted Tara. "Daniel get her on the phone please?"

Alan the cover manager who was Alex's line manager for the duration of her maths contract had already removed her from the school. She had assured him that she would go straight over to Education Supply's office. Or, if she found a payphone box on the way, she'd at least call them.

After three days with no word, Tara could not contain herself and drove over to Alex's house. She knocked on the door a few times but noticed how echoey the knocks sounded so she got down on her knees and peered through the letterbox. The house was empty. Alex had gone.

Max had rung Tara a few times but she hadn't bothered to answer and he was starting to get a bit fed up with being ignored. Susan always picked up or at least rang him straight back. So he texted Kate and asked if he could go around and see the kids. He was still sick to the stomach that she had thrown him out. The weight was dropping off him and he had no money. She had taken his name off their joint account and even gone as far as cancelling his credit card, which she paid for, so now he was on his own.

Max only did legal aid work so he didn't earn a great deal. For years she had wanted him to stop doing criminal work because there was no money in it but he loved it and just kept going. Kate also wondered how he could spend day in day out with the scum of the earth. He had no high priority paying clients and as long as she was keeping him afloat financially, he was happy to carry on. She had nicely put the boot in, by taking the girls for a week's holiday in Italy.

When he thought about them on holiday without him, he felt very low. He could have done with a break, free at that. She was like his mother looking after him. He cast his mind back to when Kate was at medical school and he was at law school just down the road from her. They had met in a pub and it didn't bother him that she was nine years older, because she had a little soft-top sports car which he basically commandeered. She never did get to drive it after he came on the scene. All-in-all, Max started to feel very sorry for himself so he was surprised to see a reply from Kate saying that she would expect him at six for tea. He shrugged his shoulders realising that at least he would eat.

When he arrived at his old house, nobody seemed too bothered to see him. Kate noticed his disappointment.

"They're not performing seals, Max. You did fuck-all with them most of the time, so they're hardly going to miss you."

Max hung his head, he supposed she was right. He was always busy doing something or somebody else when perhaps he should have been bonding with them. Tea didn't go too well and he soon realised why Kate had been so keen to get him round.

"I've had the locks changed," she just blurted out.

Max felt as if a knife had been plunged deep into his heart. His eyes filled with tears.

"Why?" he asked.

"It's my house, Max," she smiled. "And just in case any of your pathetic little criminals pick it, I've also had an alarm installed."

Max just sat looking at her and it dawned on him that it really was over and she was serious about divorcing him. He heard the girls laughing upstairs and it dawned on him that he would miss his home life. He pulled himself together and glared at her.

"You're right it is your house, but I can look after the girls for you and help out when you're on call."

"What," she said laughing. "So you can bring Susan or Tara around when I'm out?"

"I would not do that," he said indignantly.

Then he started to panic. She knew about Susan. The atmosphere was so thick, you could cut it with a knife so Kate got up and went over to the sideboard, found a large brown envelope and threw it at him. The envelope wasn't sealed and a pile of photographs spilt onto the floor. He bent over to pick them up and nearly had a heart attack when he saw him and Susan kissing. The pictures felt like red hot coals in his hands and he dropped them back onto the floor. Kate gritted her teeth.

"And that was only last night. So, you can get out of my house and don't come back."

Max picked up the pictures, gently laid them down on the coffee table and quietly left her house. He didn't look round or say goodbye to the kids. It was over. As he walked to his car, he could feel the tears welling up. He felt so wretched, no more holidays, skiing and parties to enjoy. He would miss their lifestyle. Back at his apartment, he looked around. Everything was rented, he didn't even have a photograph. How unfair all this felt to him. Surely Kate could have got over it? She should have thought about the children and put them first he told himself. He started to cry like a baby. What had she done breaking up the family unit?

He tried to pull himself together but as the sky darkened into night, his mood darkened with it. He stayed sitting in the same chair for hours. He didn't even take his coat off. Then he remembered the bottle of Jack Daniels Susan had brought the night before and decided to sit drinking in the dark. He had nothing now, he knew he had blown it. Kate would have looked after him forever but maybe there was still a chance. He had an idea.

41

Izzy had spotted Tara's message ages ago and realised that she would have to tell her something. She also realised that Tara would probably bollock and lecture her about seeing Jonny again. It never entered her head that Tara might have something important to tell her. What could be more important than Izzy's life? Johnny had taken her out for another curry but apart from that she hadn't heard much from him until he texted:

'need a favour'.

Izzy sighed why could he not just date her, go out with her like a normal person? They'd had such a lovely day out together. Did it mean nothing to him? Were they in a relationship or not? She was starting to work herself up again. She never knew where she stood so she texted back:

'?'

Much to her surprise, which it shouldn't have been as he always texted back immediately when he wanted something, he wrote:

'I have a car that I don't want to tax and I need it off the road. Any chance I can leave it in your back yard?'

Izzy didn't like this one bit. Why her yard? He must know other people who could take it. But it didn't take long for her to cave in.

'Yes, no problem'

He left her hanging for a while, then:

'Be at yours 6 pm.'

Izzy stared at the phone and shook her head. There was no: when's best for you? Will you be in? Just the royal command, 6 pm. It sickened her to admit it but of course, she would be there.

The other thing that still bothered her was Jonny telling her he couldn't drive, even though she spotted him driving with her own eyes. And why did he need this untaxed car now?

She shook herself. There was no point going on like this. She knew she would give in to his demands. She popped the kettle on and sat down to catch the local news. She was still deep in thought about the car business when a report came on the local news about a man fighting for his life after being kicked and stomped on by a doorman. Her heart was in her mouth. That's what Jonny did for a living. A picture of the guy popped up on the screen and she was relieved that it wasn't him. She knew he couldn't possibly behave like that anyway. She shuddered when she saw the man's face on the television. He looked like the most evil creature walking this earth. His hair was shaven, he looked like a bowling ball but it was all in the eyes. They were like little blackcurrants, pinpricks even, set into his huge head. His jaw was chiselled and it didn't help that he had a teardrop tattooed under his left eye. Izzy turned the television off. What a horrible man she thought. At least he would be locked up for what he had done.

At six-fifteen there was still no sign of Jonny and it did cross her mind that she should go out. Then when he moaned, she could always say well you didn't show up at six, but again she knew she wouldn't. It was never a given that he would stick to his word. Suddenly she heard a car toot and looked out of the window. Jonny was in a Mercedes, with another car behind him, a Jaguar which she didn't take much notice of.

Jonny came to the front door and asked her to open up the garage door for her back yard because he wasn't sure which one was hers. She went back through her house and clicked the electronic gate up and then stopped dead in her tracks. The Mercedes had parked up and Jonny was directing the car that had been behind him, into her yard. It wasn't the Jaguar that caught her attention, but the thing driving it. Behind the wheel of the Jaguar sat the man she had just seen on the television, complete with teardrop tattoo. She couldn't catch her breath, she thought she was going to have a panic attack. That man couldn't possibly leave his car at her house! how could Jonny do this to her?

The huge hulk of a man got out of the car and winked!

"Thanks love."

She wanted to scream at him to go away but no words came out of her mouth. He terrified her. Jonny kissed her on the cheek then she watched them both stroll down the lane to the waiting Mercedes, get in and drive away. She clicked the door back down again and just stood staring at the Jaguar asking:

"Why me?"

Jonny and Charlie left Izzy's place certain that nobody around there had taken any notice of them. When Jonny's phone vibrated, he cancelled the call. He knew it was Izzy and she wasn't happy. He'd seen the way she looked at Charlie but decided to ignore it. What the two men didn't know was that Charlie had been the main event on the local news. It never occurred to Jonny that Izzy knew who the Jag man was. They'd successfully got the car out of sight and Charlie could dispose of it at a later date when the heat died down. His prints were all over it and any forensic examination would flag up all types of narcotics but Jonny assured him it would be as safe as houses parked up at Izzy's. They headed off to the Speckled Hen to meet up with the guys for a celebratory drink.

Jonny kept it at the back of his mind that he would have to keep it fairly low key with Charlie. Tony his boss had always warned his guys to be very wary of Charlie as he was a liability. He loved a fight and thought with his fists, not his brain. He didn't know when to stop which had landed him in his present trouble and if convicted, he would go away for a hefty stretch. Everyone had been gobsmacked when Charlie had got bail and more to the point everyone wondered who was funding the expensive brief from London who showed up to defend him. All Jonny had been able to rely on in the past, was the duty solicitor, a guy called Max Armstrong.

Izzy paced around her living room. She was sweating with nerves and terrified at the situation Jonny had got her into. She needed to speak to someone who could make her calm down and help her out of this mess.

"I thought you were dead," answered Tara full of irony.

"Distinct possibility," said Izzy. "You are not going to believe what has just happened."

Tara sighed. Another Jonny saga coming up. She settled herself down on her new sofa, with a view of the beach, while Izzy told her about the man in the Jaguar.

"Jesus girl," she cut in, alarmed. "What have you got yourself into? You really have lost the plot this time."

"But at the end of the day I do think he likes me," said Izzy, as if Tara hadn't spoken.

"For someone reasonably intelligent how can you be so fucking stupid? That car is hot. The police will be searching for it as we speak. A body could be in the boot and God help you if the police helicopter spots it."

Izzy gave a nervous laugh. She didn't think a body would be in it but she remembered a police helicopter had been out on a regular basis where she lived.

"Just ring that fuckwit and tell him to remove the car from your property, like right now."

Izzy couldn't admit she had already tried to call him but he cut the phone on her. The more Tara went on, the more frightened she became.

"I'm sure it's going to be Ok," she wittered. "It's only the tax that's ran out."

"Then why did they park it in a completely private yard, hidden by huge brick walls and with you as the perfect alibi?" shouted Tara.

That word alibi again. Her friend Tanya told her ages ago Jonny was a very dangerous man and not to let him use her. She had just witnessed first-hand the type he hung around with.

"Listen to me Izzy," continued Tara, trying very hard to be the voice of reason. "He's a doorman. He will be involved in all sorts of shit and you do not need to be involved with him. This is way above your head and don't tell me that teardrop man hasn't got a few hundred quid to pay his car tax? He needs that Jaguar out of sight."

Izzy started to feel sick with worry. She knew she didn't have the guts to tell Jonny to move the car. In fact, it dawned her that she was actually intimidated by him. She wanted him onside and maybe by helping him out he would lean on her, even need her. So where her best friend Tara was concerned, Izzy resorted to her usual, fight or flight mode and came down on the side of fight.

"Look," she snapped back at Tara. "Jonny wouldn't want to get me into any trouble so I'm sure it's not what you are thinking. You'll see, everything will be Ok."

"Oh, I'm sure it will be Ok," sighed Tara, exhausted. "So you ring me up with a problem, terrified that you are doing something seriously wrong and then as usual, when your back's against the wall I end up in the firing line. I'm not sure why you rang me in the first place Izzy but you sounded genuinely scared and in need of advice. Anyway, why don't you just carry on aiding and abetting criminals and I'll be here when you need me."

Tara knew Izzy had no intention of giving Jonny up. She'd just have to wait for it all to go pear-shaped.

"Just remember," she continued. "You called me and quite frankly I don't like the company that you're keeping. Speak to you soon, bye."

Izzy was left listening to a dead phone line. She didn't know if she felt more annoyed at Tara's opinion, or the fact she'd hung up on her. What Izzy didn't realise was that Tara had also caught the local news and had seen teardrop man. Why on earth did Izzy have that particular fuckwit's car hidden on her property? What next, harbouring a criminal? Tara felt certain that if Jonny stabbed her, she'd bear witness it was her own fault for upsetting him. She'd always been the same where men were concerned, she was naïve to the point of mania. But none of the men before had been criminals. Jonny, on the other hand, had already served a lengthy prison sentence. Tara feared if her friend refused to listen to reason, something terrible would have to happen to break this spell. It also dawned on Tara that she hadn't managed to tell Izzy she'd left Simon. Some friend!

Meanwhile, Izzy, full of indignation, poured herself a large glass of red wine. Who the fuck did Tara think she was, lecturing her like she was some sort of imbecile? Did she think that she wasn't bright enough to stop anything bad happening and why couldn't Tara get it that Jonny had feelings for her? She was sure he wouldn't let anything bad happen to her and in any case, Izzy would be able to spot trouble a mile off. Izzy felt better after her little talk to herself. Only one thing bothered her. She hadn't asked Jonny how long he intended to keep the car at her place. She could feel the dread building up in her gut as another thought occurred to her. What happened if teardrop man was sentenced and sent to prison for his latest misdemeanour? The car couldn't stay there indefinitely. She didn't even know tear drop man's name, so she grabbed her laptop and googled the local news station to read the report on him. That would have his name. She was going to have to come up with a story, possibly tell Jonny that her brother needed the space and he would start asking questions as to whom the car belonged to. She would think of something but either way the car made her feel very uncomfortable. It would also have appeased her if Jonny would at least answer one of her calls.

As the night dragged on Izzy considered texting Tanya. They could show up at Limes when Jonny was working then he would have no choice but to speak to her. Teardrop man was weighing very heavily on her mind and she admitted to herself that she was scared shitless of him. She decided that rocking the boat was a stupid idea so she put that thought away. Plus, she didn't want to drag Tanya into any trouble. She was going to have to come up with something to get the dammed car moved.

Jonny was delighted to have the car out of the way. He didn't mind doing Charlie a favour, because now he owed him and that could come in very handy in their line of work.

He had just completed a job in record time and joined Stevie outside in the new Mercedes. He leant back in the plush seat and relaxed as Stevie put his foot down.

"That didn't take long?" remarked Stevie. Remarked. "I'm going to start timing you and we can run a book."

Jonny laughed, reached into his pocket and waved the wedge of fifty-pound notes around showing Stevie that he had got what they came for. Poor Daryll, on the other hand, had been left on the floor of his flat. His own mother wouldn't recognise him with his broken nose. His chest was bruised all over where he had taken a kicking from Jonny and he was finding it hard to draw a breath. The stench of fear coming from him was very strong but he had given Jonny the money that he owed Tony.

"Bet he comes super quick at repaying money in the future," said Stevie, laughing.

Jonny just nodded, there always was a next time with these people. Jonny's thoughts momentarily flashed back to Izzy and that made his grin widen. He really could get her to do anything for him. His phone started to vibrate in his pocket so he opened it up and read the text.

'Hurry up.'

His grin disintegrated. He didn't like being ordered around. Now he felt irritated and his good mood evaporated. His mood swings were legendary and Donna of all people knew to be very careful. Jonny instructed Stevie to drop him off a few blocks away from Donna's flat. Stevie knew exactly where he was going but knew that he had to keep it quiet. Tony would hit the roof if he knew that Jonny was playing around with his Personal Assistant.

This liaison had to be kept confidential but when she opened the door, Jonny felt something snap inside of him and he grabbed her by the throat kicking the door closed. Donna had a glass of wine in her hand when she opened the door and now it lay on the floor shattered around her feet. Donna felt total panic rise inside of her. He hadn't been like this for ages and like a thousand bricks dropping on her head, she now realised why Tony didn't want her having anything to do with him. It might have been the best sex she'd ever known, but nothing was worth this. She tried to turn and get away from him but he was too strong and his grip tightened. She fell backwards and could feel her own temper getting the better of her, so she slapped his face as hard as she could. This only made him worse, he even started laughing and caught her hands together and pinned her against the wall.

Donna just prayed it would soon be over. She could hear the television on in the next room and wished she was still curled up on her sofa watching it, normal life, instead of being under attack in her own home. Their heads clashed together as he violently kissed her. His tongue filled her mouth and she felt sick to her stomach. She realised that this was the end. She hated him and repeatedly asked him to stop but he just laughed in her face. He used one hand to rip open her jeans and she could feel her heart sinking.

"No Jonny, not like this!" she cried out in pain.

She couldn't believe what she was seeing when he spat in his hand and stuck it between her legs, then pushed himself into her. She cried out in pain. He was so hard but he wasn't bothered he was in so deep that it winded her and she had to grip onto his shoulders, begging him to stop, trying to avoid each thrust to avert the pain. He bit her lip and she could feel the blood trickling down her face. She cried out but again he ignored her.

"Jonny please stop, you're hurting me!" she screamed.

He started to call her filthy names, a whore and a slag, each time thrusting harder and harder into her. She clenched her teeth to stop herself crying out in pain. It was so bad. He came and almost collapsed against her. As he zipped up his jeans, Donna slid down the wall the tears flowing down her face and she could feel the blood pouring from between her legs. Jonny knelt down on the floor and gently took hold of her face.

"Do yourself a favour sweetheart," he said, affecting a kind and gentle tone but she felt his grip tighten. "Next time don't tell me what to do."

He left slamming the door behind him. She could not take in what had just happened. He had raped her in the safety of her own home and she would never forgive him. She burst into tears. She was in so much pain and she was lying in pieces of broken glass. Then she stopped and looked at the door that he had just departed through.

"Don't you worry Jonny," she said through gritted teeth. "You won't get a next time."

42

Tara wasn't on call so she arrived at work at about eight o'clock that morning and walked into her staff having a right old laugh.

"Tara," said Daniel. "You'll know the answer to this question."

Tara smiled, pleased that everything was running smoothly and she hadn't walked into aggravation.

"Come on then, I've just used my new espresso machine so I'm ready for anything."

"Right here we go," he said. "When we were in primary school,"

Carrie started laughing her head off as she was a lot younger than both Tara and Daniel.

"And you forgot your P.E kit," he continued.

"Vest and pants!" yelled Tara, getting it straight away.

Everyone laughed, except Mark. He looked at them all as if they were mad.

"Do you mean, you had to do P.E in your vest and knickers?" he asked blankly.

"This is what it's coming to Tara," said Daniel, staring at him in pity.

It was beyond Mark who was only twenty-four and thought any man requiring kids to do P.E in their underwear was a potential paedophile.

Christine French walked in clutching a timesheet. Daniel hated her and referred to her as baldy, as the poor woman's hair was thinning at quite an alarming rate. She plonked herself down in front of Tara's desk and started her usual tittle-tattling, heads, dep heads, other supply teachers or even the cleaning staff. Nobody was safe. When she left the office, Daniel tutted.

"She is so fucking fat she should be in a tank at SeaWorld and we could sell tickets."

Tara was helpless with laughter. She would hate it if she ever lost Daniel. He always made her day feel lighter. Carrie, on the other hand, didn't seem too amused.

"I wish you hadn't said that," she told Daniel.

Daniel did the famous eyebrow raise and flashed a winning smile.

"Yeah, well, I wish I hadn't lost my virginity during a midnight screening of Dirty Dancing so get over it."

"Dirty Dancing?" muttered Mark under his breath. "More like the fucking Dam Busters."

He nearly died when he realised everybody had heard him but they all got on with their work and ignored him.

A little later, Carrie rang down from the accounts office and asked Tara to come up and speak to her about something mysterious. She was worried about one of their supply teachers, Ellie Wilson. She had been at Fordfield Park Academy, teaching English for the last two years on supply but recently her time sheets had failed to appear on a weekly basis to enable payment.

"I'm not too concerned," said Tara. "She's been there for such a long time, it's probably just an oversight. Next time I speak to Steven the Deputy Head, I'll mention it."

Carrie nodded and threw her a 'you're in charge but I don't agree with you look.' Tara spoke to Steven on a daily basis because Fordfield Park Academy had a high rate of supply going in and out. She felt sure he would have mentioned it if Ellie had left, or their teacher had returned to work which was highly unlikely after a two-year absence. Tara dismissed it from her mind and went back downstairs to the main office.

"Your phone's going mad with texts," said Daniel. "At least six so far. We all know whom from."

"Now, now," tutted Tara.

Of course, he was right. It was Max asking if she would like to join him at his apartment for drinks at seven. What he really meant was sex. But at least he still didn't know she'd left Simon so he would be thinking he had to stay out of the way.

"Have you told him yet?" asked Daniel, reading her mind.

"No," said Tara. "I'm just using him for sex. He's asked me to go for drinks at his place tonight. I'll do that. But the last thing I want is him crowding me."

"Shag and go beats wash and go. Watch out you don't need fumigating after. God knows what's been through his place."

Tara ignored him and sent a message to Max confirming seven tonight.

The day moved on nicely and at six forty-five Tara looked up from the safeguarding papers she had been studying. She liked the office with no-one else around it was peaceful.

When she got there, Max's apartment looked more like a pigsty. Empty beer bottles and pizza cartons littered the kitchen from top to bottom. Then there was the smell.

"This place stinks Max, open a fucking window!" she said trying to find a clean space to put her car keys on.

"I know," he said. "I need a cleaner. Kate used to sort all that out."

"Well, start doing some of it yourself. You can't bring your children here with it in this state."

"They haven't been around yet," said Max, adopting his little boy hurt face.

"Why?"

"I don't think Kate trusts me with them."

"Well, that says everything, Max." Tara gave him a good hard look. "You are a lawyer, find a family lawyer and start the ball rolling with proceedings."

He looked horror-stricken.

"No! I'll let Kate sort it all out in the divorce."

Tara felt her brain spinning. Yet again, she asked herself what she saw in him, he was so weak. Then she got it. Max was terrified of upsetting Kate and it was all about the money. Kate earned a lot more than a legal aid criminal lawyer. She may even have to pay him some sort of allowance and that thought made her want to slap him. It wouldn't bother him in the slightest that men were supposed to be breadwinners and provide for their families. Max would expect Kate to look after him. She had been doing so for years and it dawned on her that if she ended up with him that he would expect her to pick up the baton.

He moved across the room towards her. Tara still hadn't sat down, having spotted the beer stains on the cream sofa. Something else was also niggling away at her. When she arrived and pressed the intercom button, she'd glanced up and found him peering out of the window checking to see who was there before releasing the lock.

She continued to cast an eye over the filthy lounge, particularly the overflowing ashtrays. He'd obviously had company because as far as she knew, he'd always detested smoking. Tara was still deep in thought when she felt his arms go around her and he pulled her closer for a kiss. His tongue gently probed the inside of her mouth whilst his other hand slid up inside her shirt and she felt the catch on her bra spring open. When he then reached for her breast, she cried out with pleasure. He undid the buttons on her shirt and his mouth quickly felt for her nipple. He licked it and gently sucked on it making her nipple go hard while the other hand was now free to feel the wetness between her legs.

He manoeuvred her into the bedroom and the moment his hand slid up inside her skirt she could almost feel her legs buckling beneath her. She wanted him and felt for the zip on his jeans then expertly helped him out of them. He was so hard. Max undid the zip on her skirt and she felt it slide to the floor momentarily hoping that the floor was clean. He pushed her onto the bed on all fours and mounted her from behind. When she first felt him enter, they both cried out and Max grabbed her long ponytail pulling her head back as he slid in and out of her from behind. She was so excited that she knew this wasn't going to take long but as he bit the nape of her neck, they both came together and landed in a heap on the bed. Now she knew why she liked fucking him.

Tara was the first to move after waiting for her breath to steady and also trying to ignore the smell of the bedsheets. They obviously hadn't been washed since he moved in. She made a mental note not to return even if he had the place fumigated. She imagined herself wearing an all-in-one ICI chemical suit or the type worn by forensics at a crime scene, just to approach his front door.

She collected herself, put her clothes back on, waved and left as quickly as she possibly could. She vaguely heard him muttering to her but she said a hasty goodbye and she was gone. Max was left standing there wondering what the hell had just happened. He had bought an expensive bottle of the red wine that she liked and thought they could have made a bit of a night of it. However, her timing proved perfect. No sooner did he hear her Porsche rumble into life, when Susan texted asking if she could come around. Max smiled. He loved being single.

Next day in the tea room Tara told Daniel about Max's rank apartment.

"It stank Dan, absolutely stank. Dirty dishes and empty beer bottles all over. You would have thought he'd make an effort before inviting me over?"

"He's probably used to having everything done for him," said Daniel.

"But nobody can live like that," she said, her voice rising. "In that filth. It says a lot about him."

They were disturbed by Mark, shouting down the corridor that Steven from Fordpark was on the phone. He knew Tara wanted to speak to him.

"I'd better take this Daniel. Make mine strong," she said as he reached for the kettle. "I need to find out where Ellie Wilson's timesheets are so that we can invoice. She's already been paid."

Steven sounded as happy as a little sandboy.

"Morning sweetie, I need a mathematician as soon as," he told Tara.

She took the details and passed them onto Daniel so he could start finding someone quickly and she could ascertain what was going on. Tara explained but Steven interrupted her.

"I don't understand what you mean," he said to her.

Tara explained that Education Supply had received timesheets week in and week out for the last two years and suddenly they had stopped but Tara had continued to pay Ellie as she thought Steven must have forgotten but she needed to chase it up.

"Now I'm really confused," he said. "We offered Ellie a contract two terms ago and she accepted."

Tara's jaw dropped.

"Well that explains why our invoices to you went unpaid," she said. "We just thought it was an oversight, our bank's about to chase payment with you. Why didn't you inform us, Steven? I haven't got a crystal ball on the end of my desk and rub it every day to know exactly what thousands of people are up to!"

"Hang on a minute, Tara. This means she's been paid twice, once from you and then Fordpark."

Tara wasn't sure what to say so she thanked Steven and told him to leave it with her. This was serious. Ellie Wilson had knowingly been receiving two salaries.

"This is theft," said Daniel. "We should call the police. You can't take two payments like that, it's completely illegal."

"I know it is. First, we need to get the money back and also inform our sales finance team, otherwise, our bank will threaten Fordpark with legal action. They'll see it as invoices unpaid."

"But how come the bursar at the school didn't see the invoices?" said Carrie. "They come in weekly so she must have noticed a stack of unpaid invoices from us and wondered why. Surely she could have checked and she also would have known that Ellie was on their payroll?"

Everyone agreed. However, something had gone wrong or the right hand hadn't told the left what was going on.

"Why do we bother to interview them?" said Daniel getting annoyed. "At every interview, each candidate is told that they work for Education Supply and they must inform us of any change."

"It's a waste of breath," said Tara. "But how did she think that she would get away with it and we wouldn't find out?"

"More to the point she'll have to pay us back," said Daniel. "She's definitely done this on purpose and thought she'd get away with it."

"I'm sending out a memo to all our staff," shouted Carrie across the office. "Reminding them it is their responsibility to keep us informed, as clearly stated in their interviews. So, from now on, no timesheet, no pay."

"Thanks, Carrie, that's a great idea," said Tara smiling.

Meanwhile, Daniel left a voicemail for Ellie, telling her he needed to speak to her urgently regarding the repayment of money she owed Education Supply.

"It's a bad time for her," said Tara, looking up at the clock. "She'll be teaching. Nice surprise though, when she switches her phone back on, thieving bitch!"

By six o'clock that evening, Ellie still hadn't been in touch. They knew then that they had a problem.

The next day Daniel and Tara met in the interview room out of the way of the main office.

"She's not going to pay it back," said Daniel.

"If it was any other matter," she said. "We'd call the police. "But she's working in one of our schools and that makes it very difficult. I can hardly have her arrested."

"Ok. I'll go to her house after work and knock on her door. She'll find that pretty difficult to ignore."

"I agree," said Tara. "It's not strictly the right way to behave but we've tried every other way of contacting her and she's not having it."

Daniel opened his mouth to speak but Tara put her hand up and interrupted him.

"Thanks for offering, Daniel. But I'll do it. I know that you are familiar with her but at the end of the day, you're a bloke and 6 feet tall so it will look as if we are trying to intimidate her. It's better if I go. Will you get Carrie to sort out, to the penny, how much she's taken from us and all of the payslips. Then I can present them to her."

"Alright," he said standing up. "But any sign of trouble, ring me?"

"I will," said Tara. "Her partner's a doctor and I'm pretty sure she hasn't told him what she's up to and sure as hell won't want him to know."

"Thieving twat," fumed Daniel and headed for the tea room. Strong coffee was the answer to all of Education Supply's problems.

Tara hung around in the office until late. She wasn't exactly looking forward to visiting Ellie's home but it had to be done. She was starting to get angry too. It was obvious what the silly girl's intentions had been. She looked at her watch and decided that now was a good time. Most people would be at home, ready for tea. Ellie had two small children.

She popped the address into her sat-nav but as she pulled up outside the place, Tara was quite surprised. She had been expecting a large, expensive house having a doctor as a partner. Ellie was always bragging about the valuable jewellery he bought her. Instead, she saw a run of the mill, three-bedroom semi on the busy main approach road into Sunhill. Tara sat in her car, looking for movement inside the house. A car stood on the drive, with child seats in the back. Mummy must be home.

She waited a few minutes but could see no signs of life and again her anger started to rise. This was ridiculous, chasing money from a teacher, a professional person. However, she very quickly found herself charging up the driveway to the front door, ready for battle. She knocked on the door a few times but had to concede nobody was in that house. There wasn't a squeak of sound which two children would have made hearing loud knocking on the door. Tara took the letter she had Carrie draw up, threatening legal action and shoved it through the letterbox. The letter stated quite clearly that she needed to ring the office immediately to clear this oversight. Tara drove away thoroughly sick of her job again. What was it coming to? She felt better when she visualised the nice, big glass of red wine she was going to drink whilst lying in her bath, with a view of the beach from the window.

She got to work early the next morning. Daniel had been on call so she waited with bated breath to see if Ellie had phoned, knowing full well she hadn't. For sure Daniel would have let her know. Ellie knew Education Supply had an emergency after hours' service. She'd used it in the past often enough.

"Not a fucking word," said Daniel the moment he walked in.

"She wasn't in last night," she said. "I was so angry I did think about going back at about nine o'clock but by then I think I would have slapped her across the face. I'll go again tonight but I'll make it later when she needs to get the kids sorted for school the next day. I don't think she's going to pay us back."

"You know the thing that pisses me off royally, is the fact that she wouldn't have the fucking job if we hadn't found it for her, and now she's trying to rob us!"

"I know," said Tara, shuffling some papers around on her desk. "It's a disgrace but it's as simple as this. I will take court action if I have to. She's giving us no choice."

"Good," said Daniel, smiling. "That'll embarrass her. But she must think she's got you over some sort of barrel, and you won't want to cause a stink with Fordpark."

Daniel was right and the situation was starting to bother Tara. This should not be happening. It was a first for Education Supply but she acknowledged that long gone were the days when a temp or supply teacher was rare, now it was a way of life. Transient Britain had been born and with it, the standard and calibre of staff in all industries and walks of life were plummeting.

The main door of the office swung open and in bowled Nicki, the Commercial Director of Sunhill Football club. She was a force of nature, you could feel the energy coming from her. Tara liked her very much.

"Hello to everyone!" she beamed and sat herself down at Tara's desk without waiting for an invitation. "I've brought your tickets for the first match, oh and your parking permit."

Then she handed the wine list over to Daniel, knowing he wanted to see what the club had to offer. He had a good scan, champagne for Tara, wine for him and beer when they had Clients in the box.

"You look great," said Tara, as Nicki swished her long dark hair back from her face.

"I will never look as good as you Tara," she said, beaming even more. "We still all think you look like Sharon Stone."

"And on that note," said Tara, laughing. "We will see you on Saturday, three pm kick-off."

Nicki thanked her for the business and literally danced out of the office. Daniel smiled handing over the wine list to Tara.

"This should make us some money and raise our profile," he said.

"I agree," she said. "But remember the golden rule when you're deciding whom to invite. Only schools that we are not already doing business with. That's what the box is for."

"Except this weekend," he laughed. "When we're all going."

He began to prepare a list of the schools that didn't use Education Supply but may be persuaded. Tara looked at the clock. Six pm and still no word from Ellie. Tara was trying to work out if it would be prudent to give the silly cow one more day but she had an awful feeling that if she wanted the money returned, she was going to have to take drastic action. The more she thought about it the angrier she became. So she locked up, got in her car and headed straight over to Ellie's house.

This time she saw a different car in the drive, a gleaming Jaguar. The doctor was home. Bingo she thought and tried to compose herself. She strode up the drive. Lacking confidence wasn't something she suffered from and she held her finger on the doorbell just slightly longer than was necessary. A small, stout chap opened the door, smiling in welcome. He was a lot older than Ellie and not pleasing on the eye but he seemed very friendly.

"Hello," he said. "Can I help you?"

Tara smiled back falsely, struggling to keep a lid on it.

"Yes, I'm Tara from Education Supply. Is Ellie at home?"

He frowned and Tara could tell that he was trying to work out why she would be calling at their home but he smiled again.

"No, afraid not. She's at her yoga class."

Tara went in for the kill. If the stupid bitch didn't mind wasting Tara's time trying to get her money back than Tara couldn't give a fuck about embarrassing her.

"I see, well can I leave a message for her?"

"Of course, dear," he said.

"Ellie owes us three thousand pounds and we would like the funds reimbursed. We have tried many times to contact her but so far, she has ignored us."

The poor man's face dropped, the smile fading fast. Tara was like a steam train at full throttle.

"She failed to tell us that Fordpark had given her a contract. Something she is legally bound to do. She has also accepted payment over a number of months from Education Supply whilst being paid by Fordpark. In effect, she has collected two sets of payments which is highly irregular not to mention illegal."

He paled. Obviously, he had no idea what she'd been up to and he felt extremely embarrassed by this confrontation. Tara produced the paperwork and handed it to him.

"Good God," he said, turning the pieces of paper over. "But why? She must have known you would find out?"

"Exactly," said Tara.

For a few seconds, the silence was overbearing then after carefully reading the last payslip, he looked up at Tara with a more decisive expression.

"Wait a minute," he said and left her on the doorstep.

He came back a few minutes later waving his chequebook, went over to the hall table, wrote out a cheque and handed it to Tara.

"Will you accept this? When Ellie gets home I'll find out what's happened. There must be some sort of misunderstanding."

Tara accepted the cheque first checking that it was for the full amount and smiled at him.

"The only misunderstanding here Sir is that she is a very lucky girl that I didn't call the police. But thank you, this should put an end to the matter."

She turned on her heel and headed back to the car smiling. So, he didn't know she thought, as she drove home and wondered what sort of damage this would do to their relationship. The good doctor looked like a really decent chap, best he finds out now what he's up against Tara thought. I've just done him a big fat favour. He will never trust her again. She quickly called a surprised Daniel.

Next morning Tara waved the cheque around in front of him.

"Well done," he said. "We are now debt collectors, our new service."

`Tara told him the full story.

"Oh my God," he said, the eyebrow flying up. "I would have loved to have been a fly on the wall when she got home."

"At least now I can sign off this month's accounts," said Carrie. "And I'm going to the bank to put this through, express clearance, just in case it bounces!"

Saturday approached and Daniel had come up with the idea to wine and dine clients at the football match. That type of promotion never failed. Everyone in the area was football mad these days since Sunhill had been promoted to the premiership. It would be just perfect for the clients to sit inside in the cold weather and watch the match in complete comfort. Not to mention the meal they would be given.

It was a frenzy to get to the match on time. Tara had invited Izzy but she declined because Jonny wasn't included. Tara had flatly refused to invite him which upset Izzy no end. Tara pointed out that he was a criminal and she couldn't inflict him on anybody else but as usual Izzy couldn't see this point of view at all and went off in one. This was to be a friends-only event, no clients because it was the first time they had tried such a promotion and Daniel and Tara wanted to test run the box before inviting clients. As usual most of her friends had too many Kir Royales, including Daniel who had refused point- blank to bring his wife. He insisted he wanted a nice day out without any grief which said it all.

They met in the Executive Bar and couldn't help being astounded at the type of people attending. The men looked like they were wearing their one and only suit, the one reserved for weddings, funerals and christenings. They also looked as if they had just come out of the workingmen's club but the mood was high, party central as Daniel referred to it. He had brought his Irish friend Declan with him who turned out to be great fun. A Dubliner who had set up an Irish bar in Sunhill which so far it had proved an enormous success.

"Do you mind if I use your mobile please?" he asked Tara in his Irish lilt. "Mine has gone flat."

"No not at all, here," she said, smiling and handing it over.

She overheard him leaving a voicemail and his number then gave her back the phone and she thought no more of it. After the match, which saw Sunhill get absolutely hammered, they all went back to Tara's house for a riotous party.

The next day Tara thought her end had come. She still felt legless and would have to spend the day hanging around the house. She had texted Max from the football ground and told him where she was, after his usual 50 texts to her. He was gutted that she didn't invite him, he was a huge Sunhill fan. When she showed Daniel the replies to her texts, he couldn't stop laughing.

"We don't want that little wanker partying with us now do we?" he said.

No, we do not, thought Tara. I might meet someone else.

Come Monday morning, they were still hungover but all agreed it had been a fantastic day out.

"I thought we might have heard something from Ellie," said Tara.

"No," said Daniel, shaking his head. "She's too embarrassed and we'll never see her again now she's on a contract."

"I don't want to see her again," scorned Tara. "I wouldn't be held responsible for what I might say."

They struggled through the day but Carrie had one bit of good news. The cheque from the doctor had cleared.

`Later that night Tara's phone blipped with a text. She ignored it as she thought it would be Max pestering her. He still didn't get it that it was just sex but later she went to check who it was from and was quite surprised to read:

'Who is this?' and a number she didn't recognise.

Tara felt in a devilish mood so thought what the hell and texted back:

'Who is this and who the hell are you?'

She waited intrigued but no reply came so she poured herself a glass of wine and settled herself comfortably on the sofa. Another text message:

'You have contacted my phone'

Tara hurriedly wrote back:

'Sorry you must have made a mistake. Your number isn't recognised on my list of contacts.' Then added: *'So you can't be that important now can you!'*

She started laughing not understanding what was going on with her. She just fancied a bit of banter and what better than with someone you will never know? Her phone blipped:

'Now who says that I'm not important?'

'I do' she replied, giggling like a schoolgirl.

'You don't know me.'

'And I never will because if you're not in my phone then you are clearly a nobody.'

As soon as she pressed send, she cringed and made a mental note not to have any more wine. The phone went quiet and she took herself off to bed.

When she got into work the next day, she told Daniel about the texts but was surprised when his face dropped.

"What's the matter?" she said.

"Oh God, you're hopeless when you have a drink. Do you remember Declan borrowing your phone?"

"Vaguely," she nodded.

"Well," said Daniel. "One of the Irish players is his friend and Declan was ringing him to arrange to meet up after the match, so my friend you now have a premiership footballer texting you."

"Well, wouldn't that make my life just a tad more interesting?"

"A footballer?" Daniel burst out laughing.

He knew that was never going to be her type. She only went for barristers or accountants. Lawyer Max had struck a new low for her. No, she wouldn't touch a footballer with a stick from fifty feet.

43

Jackie was waiting for Izzy as she pulled into the schoolyard. She glanced at her watch again and felt even more annoyed that Izzy found it so hard to get into work on time. She could hardly comment though, as Izzy often stayed late if the need arose. But it just didn't send out a good message to the rest of the office staff. Izzy had noticed Jackie's car in the car park and put a move on. Her hairdryer had blown up so she had to wait until her hair was dry before leaving the house and that had made her late. By the time she reached her office and got her coat off she felt quite flustered. Jackie gave her time to get herself settled and then went into Izzy's office.

"Good morning," she said, smiling.

Izzy knew immediately that something was wrong and felt on her guard, as Jackie sat down facing her.

"This is difficult Izzy but I need to discuss this matter with you. Father John has received an anonymous letter from a concerned parent about your alleged boyfriend."

Izzy went puce. She felt as if she had been knocked over by a bus. The rage built up inside her and was at a loss as what to say. Jackie could see she'd struck a raw nerve and this was not going to go down well at all.

"The parent is concerned that he has a criminal record for supplying drugs and I need to know if there is any truth in this matter?"

Izzy was finding it hard to respond. She opened her mouth but nothing came out, she was absolutely speechless. What the fuck did her private life have to do with school? She wasn't exactly bringing him in with her. She struggled to contain herself then suddenly sat bolt upright.

"And what does my private life have to do with school Jackie?"

"I shouldn't really have to explain this to my school business manager Izzy, but if he is a known criminal, then it has everything to do with school. You helped write the 'Disqualification by Association' form. Surely you must have realised that it applies to all school staff, including you."

Izzy looked down at the floor. When the government first brought out the new paperwork it had crossed her mind that she should declare her interests with Jonny. at least to Jackie the head. However, she decided that as she wasn't living with him, she had nothing to declare.

Jackie stood up and looked hard at Izzy.

"Well if you're not going to explain the situation to me," she said. "I will have to leave it in the hands of father John."

Izzy didn't know where to put herself. Her mind flew back to Charlie's car parked up in her back yard. Perhaps Jackie had a point? After all, it was the head's job to safeguard the school. Izzy stood up so that she and faced her boss.

"It's no secret," she sighed. "Yes, Jonny served a lengthy prison sentence many years ago for supplying drugs, but he was set up. He took the fall for someone else and he hasn't committed any further offences since then."

Jackie looked back at her with nothing short of utter pity. She could not believe the crap that was coming out of Izzy's mouth. Set up for God's sake! And what she really meant was that he hadn't actually been caught for anything since then. She knew Jonny was a doorman. Izzy hadn't said anything but one of their parents, Shelley Riley had been quite active in letting half the school know what their school business manager was up to.

"Ok, thanks for that," said Jackie, turning to leave. "I'll inform father John and hopefully that will be an end to it. The letter was anonymous so there isn't a lot anybody can do."

After the door closed, Izzy gave a massive sigh of relief. She didn't know whether to cry or stomp around the office in a tantrum. Either way, the whole school now knew about her relationship with Jonny and nothing would stop them gossiping about her. She needed to speak to Tara. She would agree with her and give her some good advice. She held off until lunchtime, meanwhile eyeing up every member of staff, wondering who had written the letter.

She sneaked off to her car, the only place she knew where she wouldn't be overheard and managed to get Tara straight away. She asked her to go up to the interview room so that their conversation would remain private. Tara climbed the stairs dreading what was about to come.

She knew it was only a matter of time before the proverbial hit the fan if she continued to be mixed up with Jonny.

Tara sat down and put her feet up on the desk pressing line one on the switchboard to take the call off hold.

"I'm here," she said to Izzy.

She became festered beyond the point of reason as Izzy explained what had happened.

Izzy heard Tara sigh "oh Izzy for God's sake," under her breath and jumped in straight away.

"I know it's a fucking disgrace, isn't it? I do not know what business my private life is of the school."

But Izzy had sadly misread her friend. Tara visually imagined the spade in Izzy's hands ready to dig herself deeper into a hole but she knew, as her best friend, she had to try and keep her on some sort of straight and narrow.

"Izzy, Jackie is quite correct in what she is saying," said Tara, which was met with stony silence. "You are moving in the circles of dangerous criminals, whether you like what I am saying to you or not."

"Ex fucking criminal Tara!" she shouted, losing it. "I thought were my friend!"

"I am your friend Izzy but your brain's come out of your head, girl. As we speak you are harbouring the car of a known criminal, who is up in court on serious assault charges and he is Jonny's friend. Does that not mean anything to you. Who the fuck are you mixing with? And please don't tell me that you think he is whiter than white!"

"Yes," shouted Izzy. "He is!"

"And what proof do you have of that?" shouted Tara back. "You are imagining that you are in some sort of relationship with the man and you're not."

"This has nothing to do with my work," said Izzy, about ready to explode.

"Of course, it does, you work with children, school business manager or not. Your background is important and you would have plenty to say on the subject if it was one of your teachers."

What Izzy didn't know was that Jackie could see her from her office window. It looked from her body language that she was having a very heated conversation with someone and her behaviour was starting to trouble Jackie. Shelley Riley had filled her in on Jonny Devroe in private and she was not happy that a member of her team was fraternising with such a person. She knew Izzy was needy and craved attention, even at work, but an ex-drug dealer come doorman was really letting the side down as far as Jackie was concerned. She watched Izzy get out of her car, nearly taking the door off its hinges as she slammed it shut and then flounce across the car park back into the school.

Jackie got back to her paperwork but was fully aware that someone had said something to Izzy that she hadn't liked. In fact, Tara had ended the call by asking her:

"Do you not feel crap admitting to the head that you even know someone like him?"

"No, I fucking do not," was the reply before the phone slammed down.

Tara sat for a few minutes and wondered why Izzy could not see anybody's else point of view. All she did was just get her back up and go completely against any advice. Then it dawned on her. Izzy realised Jonny wasn't good enough for her but somewhere in her mind she thought that he was the catch of the century, some sort of big shot and somehow this gave Izzy the kudos of even knowing him. She had only rung her because she thought Tara would side with her but it never crossed Izzy's mind that she needed to be even more careful than ever.

Izzy could not concentrate on the cash flow she had been staring at for the last half hour and at this present moment, she didn't give a flying fuck how much school dinners cost. She decided that she needed to speak to Jonny. His phone was switched off so Izzy left a voicemail telling him that she needed to speak to him urgently. She had tried to keep her voice level but she could not help feeling anxious which she was sure he would pick up on when, or if, he listened to it. As usual, she was wasting her phone bill. Jonny didn't bother to return her call.

When she got home, she stood at her kitchen window doing the washing up but she couldn't take her eyes off the car. Her imagination was working overtime. Maybe they'd hidden a body in the boot. Then she shook herself back to reality and told herself not to be so stupid. She also thought that Tara could go and fuck herself, lording it over her like that on the phone. It was her life and she would live it the way she wished. They all had Jonny wrong. She could not settle so she rang Tanya and left a voicemail asking her if she fancied going out for tea. She didn't have to wait long as Tanya rang straight back suggesting a new Italian that had opened not too far from where Izzy lived.

They decided to drive up in Tanya's car and leave it there. Tanya said she would pick it up the next day so for once Izzy was ready when she heard Tanya tooting the horn. As they parked up and approached the bar area Izzy glanced up noticing a large placard in the restaurant window which read:

'These premises are protected by Charlie Shields.'

She immediately lost her appetite and felt sick to her stomach. She only had one of his bent cars parked up on her drive. Tanya saw her face drop and followed Izzy's gaze up to the notice.

"Did you see his picture on the local news?" she asked but Izzy just shrugged her shoulders. "This is what our area is coming to. It's been run by thugs and I bet these poor Italians haven't got any choice other than to pay protection to him."

"Yes, you're right," replied Izzy. "Or their premises will mysteriously burn down. Come on I'm starving."

The exact opposite was true. Izzy felt ill. She so wanted to tell Tanya what was going on but knew she couldn't. It was better not to implicate any of her friends with Jonny, not to mention the riff-raff he knew and she definitely could not say a word about Charlie Shields and the car. Tanya knew something was wrong with her friend. She was pushing her food around the plate and looked totally distracted but Tanya knew not to say anything as she knew Izzy would clam up.

Tanya noticed a few guys entering the bar area and a lot of back-slapping and welcomes going on. Izzy had her back to the bar and didn't see. Tanya looked up and saw a man waving to her from across the other side of the bar and immediately perked up. She knew Izzy would be delighted that Jonny had just walked in. She soon changed her mind when she saw who was directly behind him. It was the man from the local news and boy you would not want to bump into him in a dark alley. He looked like a mass murderer. The man's size was enough to intimidate anyone but he also looked truly evil. It was too late. Jonny had spotted her and exactly who she was dining with. She prayed that he didn't come over because she didn't want his friend near her but she was saved as Jonny patently ignored them.

Tanya knew at that moment that her friend was deluding herself. He had no time for her, that was pretty obvious. Tanya had seen Jonny draped all over beautiful women in the past introducing them to all and sundry but he clearly could not be bothered to even say hello to Izzy. To make matters worse Izzy could only talk about Jonny.

"He's great company," she told Tanya. "And I think I mean a lot to him."

Tanya felt sorry for her friend and could not let her go on so she put her hand on Izzy's arm.

"He's at the bar, Izzy," she said gently.

Izzy swung around. She couldn't believe he was there and hadn't bothered to come up and speak to her.

"How long has he been there?" she asked Tanya.

"About ten minutes."

She saw Izzy's face and wanted to hug her, she felt so sorry for her.

"It will be business, Izzy, and he can't be interrupted."

"Yeah right," she snorted as the men huddled round listening to a joke that Charlie Shields was telling them.

Izzy tried to catch Jonny's eye. He purposely ignored her, he even turned his back on her and to her embarrassment, she saw that Tanya had clocked it too.

"Just business Izzy, I told you. Don't worry about it," she said trying to make excuses for him.

Tanya thought Izzy was about to burst into tears so got a hold of her hand.

"Please Izzy stop this. Stop seeing him. Look who he's hanging around with."

Both girls glanced at the barndoor standing next to Jonny, the pint glass almost obliterated by his giant fist.

"Look at him," said Tanya. "No wonder people are terrified of him. Has Jonny introduced you to that?"

"Of course, he hasn't," snapped Izzy. "I've no need to know that thug."

She raised her hand in the direction of the waiter and summoned the bill. The only thing that could save her face was to leave. They split the bill and waited until Jonny and Charlie were in deep conversation, before heading out the door.

Outside Izzy gulped in the fresh air. She hadn't realised how long she had been holding her breath. She felt relieved that he hadn't spoken to her. Tanya drove her home as the night had been ruined. She had only managed one drink. When Izzy got home, she feigned a headache. She wanted to be alone to think and she could not handle any questions from Tanya about the car in the back yard. She knew that if Tanya spotted it, she would ask. The car was as clear as day from the kitchen window. She opened a bottle of red wine and sank it in half an hour. She knew drink wasn't the answer but at the time it sure as hell made her feel better. Once she had polished that off, she opened another and started to get very angry.

"How dare he?" she said out loud. "How fucking dare he ignore me?"

She took hold of her phone which was always a no-no when she was drunk and started to compile a text.

'Well, I know what you really think of me after ignoring me. I'm good enough for free holidays or stowing your mates bent car though'

She pressed send. She no longer cared what he thought. It was just as well that she passed out at that point because one of Charlie's men was busy snapping off the lock to her side gate and proceeded to place a huge holdall in the boot of the parked-up car. He closed the boot down very softly, so as not to attract attention. Then he very kindly replaced the padlock with a nice shiny new one and popped the key into his jacket pocket. It would make it so much easier for him to come back and retrieve the bag. Just in case he ran into someone in the back alleyway to Izzy's house, having a key made it look as if he lived there or had permission to go in.

As he was popping the key into his pocket and double-checking that the lock was secured, he felt his mobile vibrating in his jeans pocket. He answered it.

"Sorted?" asked his boss, Charlie.

"Yeah, but are you sure it's safe there?"

"Safe as houses," said Charlie. "Nobody uses that yard so when we need to restock you can pop in and get the merchandise out of the car no problem. Nobody will guess what's in there and as long as we go in when it's dark, it'll be safe."

Frank smiled. Charlie had loosely explained that the house was owned by one of Jonny's birds so it was safe but Frank couldn't help feeling a bit sorry for the poor cow who owned the house. She didn't have a clue. In fact, all of the boys had a real good laugh when Jonny told them she was crazy about him and would do anything to keep him sweet.

Izzy got up the next day with a thudding head. First thing she did was check her mobile for messages. Nothing. Why was she so surprised that Jonny hadn't replied? Every time she picked up the damn mobile she felt sure that he would have responded and she could feel her heart grow suddenly heavier every time she realised he was ignoring her. Two miles away Tanya also woke up and couldn't get Izzy out of her mind. She played over and over in her head Izzy's reaction in the restaurant. It was well out of character for her. She was normally always positive, happy and could see the good in everything. Of late she was edgy, unsettled, bordering on the aggressive even, which was so unlike her. She didn't know what to do and suddenly felt very guilty as she had introduced her to Jonny in the first place. Not in a million years had she thought Izzy would even look at someone like him. They were poles apart.

Tanya got herself up, showered and had a coffee then jumped in the car and headed to Asda for food shopping. She kept trying to work out how she could get Izzy to confide in her and tell her exactly what was going on. She wasn't concentrating, rushing around the aisles, her head all over the place when she heard a clash of trolleys and looked up ready to apologise.

"Penny for them," said Frank, smiling.

She was surprised to find herself facing her brother's friend.

"Sorry Frank," she smiled at him. "I was miles away."

Frank had known Tanya through her brother Colin for years. They had all gone to school together but as they got older Colin had drifted away from Frank as he was starting to hang around with the wrong people. Colin didn't want anything to do with them. Frank had always had a bit of a soft spot for Tanya but he knew she would never touch him with a fifty-foot barge pole, especially after her promotion at the bank she worked for.

"You look a bit knackered," he said jokingly.

"It's the red wine, Frank," smiled Tanya. "I was out last night with my friend Izzy. We went to the new Italian on Dean Road. I think you met her once with me ages ago in town?"

Frank started to put one and one together and started to feel very uncomfortable when it dawned on him that the property he was breaking into belonged to Tanya's good friend. He remembered Izzy. Striking looking girl, very pretty and could not believe that she would go out with Jonny.

"Yes, I remember her. She works in a school, doesn't she?"

"Yes, laughed Tanya. "She's a school business manager."

This sadly confirmed to Frank that another lamb had been sent to Jonny Devroe's slaughter. He did not want any harm coming to Tanya's friend and it surprised him to think how let down Tanya would feel if she found out what Frank was doing.

"I'm a bit worried about her, to tell the truth," she said, knowing who Frank hung about with.

"Yes," he said seriously. "You need to tell her to be very careful who she keeps company with."

Tanya rounded on him and he realised that he had said too much.

"That sounded like a warning, Frank."

He knew he could get his legs broken for this but he had always carried a candle for Tanya and didn't want her, or any of her friends caught up in any shit going down. He took hold of her arm after first having a good look round making sure anybody was listening to them.

"Look, Tanya, I'd appreciate it if you don't repeat this because you will get us both into a lot of trouble, but tell your friend to get shot of the car."

Before Tanya had time to take in what he had just said, he was gone. She left the trolley in the middle of the aisle and went looking left and right to try and spot which direction Frank had headed in but she couldn't see him anywhere.

As she left the supermarket, she knew she had to go straight to Izzy's place. What car? She kept thinking to herself. Izzy hadn't mentioned anything about a car but she was clearly very agitated about something and was acting way out of character. Now Tanya had been told something she was going to have to bring it out in the open. What she couldn't do was tell Izzy where the information had come from. She knew with a drink inside her, Izzy could not keep her mouth shut and after all, Frank was looking out for them so she didn't want to get him into any trouble. Tanya knew that if Izzy blurted anything out to Jonny, he would get the information out of her, so under no circumstances was Tanya going to let on how she knew about a car.

Izzy heard the knock on the door and didn't want to answer it. She felt ill but she remembered she'd ordered a few things online, to cheer herself up so the thought of it being her new earrings forced her to open the door. She was very surprised to find Tanya standing there. Not only that but Tanya barged straight in without being invited.

"I'm putting the kettle on," she told Izzy. "And then we are going to have a nice chat."

Izzy tried to stop her going into the kitchen, which overlooked the back yard but it was too late.

"Who does that car belong to?" asked Tanya, as filled the kettle.

Fuck, thought Izzy, she knows something. She could see by the look on Tanya's face that she meant business and realised that she had no option but to lie.

"It belongs to the boyfriend of one of the girls at work. He couldn't afford the road tax and needed it off the road so I said he could park it up here for a while."

Tanya gave Izzy the most condescending look she could muster.

"Yeah, right," she said, rolling her eyes.

Izzy felt quite shocked that Tanya didn't believe her and was beginning to get upset.

"No really that's all it is," she stammered.

Suddenly, she couldn't keep the lie up any longer, burst into tears and continued to sob her heart out. The stress was too much and she hated living like this, so she told Tanya the full story. Tanya slumped down on the kitchen bench with the kettle still in her hands. She was shocked beyond belief, at what her friend had managed to get herself involved in.

"Are you seriously telling me, that the car out there belongs to Charlie Shields and he actually drove it here onto your property himself?"

All Izzy could do was nod her head as she sobbed.

"Oh my God," said Tanya, putting the kettle down on the floor. "I hope you have not laid one hand on that motor for fingerprints? Are you for fucking real?" she said looking at her friend like she was a five-year-old.

Izzy now looked as if she was having a full-on nervous breakdown but Tanya refused to back off.

"These people Izzy are so dangerous. Did you not wonder why that car needed to be kept out of the way?"

"Of course, I thought about it but Jonny told me there was nothing to worry about."

"And what if this Charlie bloke gets sent down? That car is there for a reason you stupid cow!"

She was pacing up and down, wondering how the hell she'd suddenly become involved in some criminal activity.

"We have to get rid of it," she said.

"Well, we could call the police I suppose," said Izzy.

Now Tanya knew that her friend was clinically, truly stupid.

"Do you want to end up dead in the river? Jesus Christ Izzy use your fucking brains!" screamed Tanya.

Tanya knew she had to calm down. She stopped pacing and took hold of Izzy by the arms.

"You have to listen to me. We need to come up with something that he is going to believe for you to get him to move that car."

She dropped Izzy's arms and peered through the kitchen window.

"My God, there could be a dead body in the boot."

"I thought that," said Izzy. "But it would smell wouldn't it?"

Tanya gave a hysterical burst of laughter.

"Izzy the whole street would know if something had died in there, the stink would be so terrible."

In retrospect, Tanya realised that by going to the sink to fill the kettle, she had made life a whole lot easier for herself. The car was in full view from there and she had been able to remark on it. She'd had it all worked out in her head what she was going to say to Izzy. She felt worried about her. At one point she even questioned the fact that Frank had mentioned the car. However, she had known him a lot longer than Izzy and everything inside her screamed to check the facts at least. If her friend was in trouble, she had to know.

Once the tears started to flow and Izzy confessed about the car, Tanya didn't need to mention why she had called around unannounced. Tanya stared at her friend. She looked like a little girl lost but Tanya had noticed that since Izzy had fessed up, she did look visibly calmer. A problem shared definitely seemed to work. She must have been dying to tell someone all along.

"Does Tara know?" asked Tanya.

"Hell no," said Izzy, turning pale again. "Tara does not approve of the company I'm keeping and has told me in no uncertain terms."

"She's right Izzy. She's your friend and only wants the best for you. You must get rid of that car. It could be stuffed with drugs or used for something illegal, for them to need it out of the way. Why haven't they had it scrapped? I think they must be using it to stash drugs on your property."

Izzy burst into a fresh round of tears, which got on Tanya's nerves.

"For fuck's sake Izzy, will you stop acting like a child?" She shouted. "We need to think. Can you come up with some sort of excuse why you would need the space back?"

Izzy just shook her head, with tears flowing down her face.

"I've thought of nothing else," she said and for once in Tanya's life, she was stumped.

44

Over at Education Supply, Friday morning was moving along nicely with everyone looking forward to the match on Saturday. This time the box was reserved for clients only. Tara couldn't have her friends in it all of the time otherwise David, her accountant would go mad. It wasn't meant to be used as a jolly. This was the first time it was to be used for schools so Tara and Daniel had to be on their best behaviour. They needed to entertain headteachers and the cover managers who gave them the business, plus the clients' guests and forge relationships with them. It was an important day.

Her mobile blipped and she jumped to look at it hoping to find the footballer's number and not Max's, whose constant texting had become very tedious. She got what she wanted as she read:

'You going to the match tomorrow?'

She left it a while. She didn't want to appear too keen. Eventually, she replied:

'Yes, I have a box there.'

'What is the number?' came the reply within five seconds.

Tara smiled. He obviously didn't believe her and she still held firm to the pretence that she didn't know who was texting her.

'16' she sent and waited.

Daniel observed her from across the office. He was pleased this had happened. He could tell she felt excited and it got her away from that prick Max. She was right into the hunt and the excitement of it all and so was he. He desperately wanted to meet a footballer. She waited a few minutes then her phone blipped again with an incoming text.

'I want a picture of you' she read out loud after Carrie had popped out to the loo and Daniel started to get very excited for her.

Tara didn't go in for all that picture rubbish. After all, it may not be the person she thought texting her. She was pretty sure but until she had seen him, she held back. So she sent a picture of the view from her balcony instead, showing the beach at its finest with the setting sun.

'Ha ha' he sent and to her surprise a photo of himself but with a full beard and holding a guitar, standing in what appeared to be a recording studio. She knew for sure it was him now. He looked completely different with a beard, nothing like the pictures of him in the papers or on Sky Sports.

'You look like an axe murderer' she texted back.

In previous messages, she had let on to him where she lived, not the exact address but roughly the street in the village, because she knew it was very close to the training ground where the squad were based and went every day to train. To her surprise he texted back:

'I will be round at yours at 6 pm and I'm going to fuck you.'

Her hands began to shake and she suddenly became very jittery and nervous. Daniel spotted her shocked reaction. When he read it, the eyebrow immediately raised to high heaven.

"My, my," he said and started to laugh. "Go for it!"

He had been in on the banter from the get-go and couldn't resist encouraging her.

"Get some excitement in your life," he said. "We might get free invites to the footie."

But Tara was busy mentally ticking off when she'd last been waxed and when her highlights had been done. Then she stopped and started grinning from ear to ear. Finally, a man had bothered her and she realised it so she reverted to type and texted back:

'6 it is'

She felt so excited. A million things were now running through her head. She waited and waited for her phone to blip and it did cross her mind that she had called his bluff and he may back out as he didn't have a clue who she was or what she looked like. She jumped when her phone blipped:

'address?'

Tara typed in her address and pressed send. Too late to back out now. She passed the phone over for Daniel to read the messages as the staff were all back in the office. He became positively giddy as he read.

"Oh my God," he mouthed. "How exciting. You've never had a footballer before."

"Don't you dare tell anyone," said Tara, raising her finger to her lips.

Carrie left the office to go to the accounts room and Mark was busy with someone in reception so Tara went over to Daniel's desk to whisper to him.

"Footballers are usually vile. So if he's vile I will chuck him out."

"He isn't vile. He plays the guitar, reads poetry and is Irish. He's never in the papers for the wrong reasons."

Tara was not in the habit of keeping company with sportsmen, in particular premiership footballers with bad reputations.

"I'm only using him for sex sweetie, so let's see what happens. Plus, he's a lot younger than I am."

"Don't be ridiculous," said Daniel. "You're gorgeous but please phone me later and tell me in minute detail everything that happens. I can't wait till tomorrow when we're at the match."

"I'm going home now," she said, laughing. "I need to prepare."

By the time she got home her stomach was in knots with nervous excitement. She realised it had been a long time since a man had this effect on her. She needed to turn this game into a seduction, something she was very good at.

She had a plan, knew exactly what she was going to do and was all prepared when six pm arrived. She hovered around her bedroom waiting for the doorbell to ring. She heard a sports car pull up. She could tell by the roar of the engine. In fact, it sounded like a Porsche and then she heard the door slam shut and waited. Her heart was pounding, she was so excited. The doorbell rang twice.

Tara walked slowly down the stairs and stopped in front of the double glass doors. Quinn O'Leary stood there open-mouthed. He couldn't believe what he was seeing. There in front of him appeared this gorgeous blonde, wearing thigh-length, black, suede boots, a tiny g-string pair of knickers, a black bra and the most beautiful long black fur coat that draped itself around her when she moved. He felt himself getting excited, he could feel the stiffness growing between his legs.

She opened the glass door and smiled.

"Hi," she said. "Thank God you're not the fucking Jehovah's witnesses."

They both started laughing. Tara couldn't take in how good looking he was in real life. His pictures didn't do him justice and boy did he look fit in his skinny jeans and t-shirt. He immediately took control of the situation barely giving her time to close the front door as he pushed her back into the wall and started kissing her. He kissed her slowly and she could feel his hands on her breasts not to mention his hard dick pressing into her. She felt her way down to his jeans and unzipped him so that she could take him in her mouth. She got down onto her knees lifting his t-shirt and started to lick and kiss his stomach slowly going down and taking his hard dick in her mouth.

He wrapped her hair around his hands and groaned out loud. When he could take it no more he spun her around and faced her, spread-eagled against her hall wall. She could feel his hands moving her underwear out of the way then she gasped as he plunged deep inside her, going deeper and deeper with every stroke. She could feel herself coming really quickly and tried hard not to but she had to let go as she couldn't put it off one second longer. As she came, she could feel him coming too. It all happened in less than five minutes. Tara put herself back together but Quinn was struggling. He felt like he had just been hit by a tornado but he managed to pull his jeans back in position and zipped himself up.

Tara wasn't sure where to go from there so she kissed him on the cheek as she was opening the front door with her spare hand and to his complete surprise said:

"See you around."

He was dismissed. He hadn't even had time to say a word and found himself ambling back down her drive to his car. As he drove away, he started to laugh. Never had a woman used him before like a piece of meat and he realised that he quite liked it. For the first time ever he'd met a girl, or rather a woman, who did not need him or want to slaver all over him and it was refreshing, for a change.

Tara showered then put her dressing gown on and began to relax. She had really enjoyed meeting Quinn O'Leary, however brief it had seemed and she knew that she had floored him. She picked up the phone and as promised filled Daniel in.

"Will you see him again?" he asked and Tara laughed.

"I don't know. He's probably got lists of birds to keep him company."

But Daniel disagreed.

"There's something very different about you my girl. He will want to see you again and definitely after the way you chucked him out. He won't be used to that."

"Well if he does, he does and if he doesn't then so be it," she said.

Just then her phone had an incoming text message. She held onto the landline with one hand and grabbed the mobile.

"I bet it's him!" shouted Daniel.

He was right.

'Until the next time sexy'

Tara smiled.

'If you're a good boy'

This made Daniel scream.

"Oh my God, you're treating him like shit!"

"He will love it," she said but got no more texts.

Daniel was busy hyperventilating.

"He may come and find you tomorrow at the match?"

"I don't think so," she said. "He'll be busy preparing then playing Dan. He won't have time to see anybody. And really sweetie, it was a fuck, nothing serious. You're bigging it up a bit too much."

"No, I'm not, just you wait and see."

They made final arrangements to meet at the box early on Saturday, ready for the match. Then Tara had a nice restful evening in front of the telly but she did have a huge wide grin of satisfaction all over her face.

Next day, she was up with the larks for a run, then showered and waited for Denise her hairdresser to come and straighten her hair. She would be meeting prospective clients all day so had to make the effort on the presentation front and had advised Daniel to wear a suit. She knew the headteachers would come formal. Daniel was in a right flap. His wife Sandra had gone on and on because she couldn't attend the match. He had told her about fifty times that it was work and he had agreed to do it. When he turned in the business, she would be benefiting from the extra commission he made but she kept whining on. Part of the reason he had agreed to it in the first place was to get away from her on a Saturday. She was a royal pain in the arse and he was sick of her. Divorce was starting to cross his mind on a daily basis these days. Eventually, she shut up as they neared the football stadium and she agreed to pick him up at six-thirty when the football traffic would have cleared.

Daniel bounced out of the car. He was so looking forward to today and even hoped to meet Quinn. Tara told him not to raise his hopes as she hardly knew him. They both laughed when he reminded her that after having his dick in her mouth, she was at least on speaking terms with him. As Daniel got out of the lift on the second floor, he could see Tara ahead of him down the corridor so he called out and they walked to box 16 together. It was weird being in the box. The heating was on full blast and the table was set but outside only a few fans had turned up early to soak up the experience. The stadium had the air of something grand about to happen. She could see the television cameras all set up for action. This was an important match.

Tara knew bugger all about football and asked Daniel if Sunhill stood a chance of beating Chelsea. She got her answer when Daniel couldn't stop laughing for ten minutes.

The first guests arrived from Willow Street Primary. The head David Smith had brought his friend Sam Wright which was good as the wives never liked Tara. Daniel rang the bell for the waitress to take their orders. Twenty minutes later everyone was in attendance so Tara asked for the food to be served. Daniel and Tara were both on water as they had agreed beforehand that no drinking should take place in front of the schools. They would only get talked about as that's the way it was in education. However, Tara ordered a bottle of champagne when all of the guests were outside on the balcony watching the players warm up. She put it at the back of the fridge. Daniel came in and spotted her downing a glass but was pleased when she shoved a glass in his hands.

"Quick drink it," she said, which he did but he seemed quite perturbed.

"Quinn's not out there warming up," he said.

Tara couldn't have cared less.

"So?" she said.

"Really, for God's sake, you must be a bit interested?"

"I think you like him more than I do," she said, laughing.

Daniel downed his drink and went outside to join their guests. Tara had a look around then decided she should go out and at least talk to them but then the door swung open and an army of waiting staff came in with the food. She opened the glass door to the balcony and got everyone in and seated. The food was very good. They had all chosen a chicken curry to keep them warm and it had gone down a treat. Everyone commented on the quality of the food and cheeses and biscuits.

Soon it was time for the match to begin and the crowd roared as the music came on and the players proceeded out onto the pitch holding the little mascots' hands. Tara and Daniel were sitting next to each other. He knew she had a very short concentration span with these people, so at least she could talk to him if she got sick of it all.

"You see?" he said, nudging her. "He hasn't come out with the other players."

Tara didn't know one way or the other.

"Maybe he's a sub and will come on later or at half time?" she said.

But Daniel was adamant.

"I bet he's injured," he said. "What the fuck have you done to him? You've damaged him, put his back out or something."

"He was only there for five fucking minutes. Even I'm not that good!" she laughed.

Daniel huffed and puffed and crossed his arms, obviously not a happy man. The match began and after ten minutes Sunhill were one-nil down. Tara had never been so bored in her life. She kept glancing at her wristwatch wondering when she could escape. Then came a message on her phone. She was surprised to see it was Quinn.

'Which box are you in again?'

Tara didn't want anybody to know about him so she replied:

'Why?' and put the phone back in her pocket.

Daniel looked at her, wanting to know who was on the phone so she handed it to him. The eyebrow went straight up and he leant over to her.

"Why don't you just tell him?"

"Because it's nobody's business, Daniel. This has to be kept quiet."

"But, why?"

"Because I don't usually go out with footballers, Dan. They have such a naff reputation and he is a lot younger than me. You know what people will say?"

"It doesn't usually bother you what people say."

Tara knew he was right but this time she was sticking to her guns. Older woman with premier footballer would smack of her being desperate, and that was not happening. Half time came far too slowly for Tara's liking. The waiting staff had pre-ordered drinks as there was only a fifteen-minute break. Everyone got comfortable in their seats discussing Sunhill's performance when they heard a knock on the door. Tara was the closest, so she opened it and nearly fainted as there stood Quinn in a smart suit and smiling widely at her.

Tara was horrified and put her hand on his chest and pushed him backwards into the corridor.

"Piss off!" she said and saw his face drop, utterly devastated at her reaction.

"What is your problem?" he said, glaring at her.

"My problem is that I don't want anybody to know about you and I have clients in here so piss off," she said and stormed back into the box.

Daniel was grinning as if to say he knew Quinn would turn up. Then Tara had to spend ten minutes fielding questions from her guests as to how she knew him. Everyone had seen him at the door. When the second half started Tara was beginning to think that she had over-reacted, even feeling a tad guilty. She had been vile to him. Another message:

'Meet me at entrance to box no 4.'

Tara showed the message to Daniel who had suddenly become Quinn O'Leary's best friend.

"Go on for God's sake. Nobody is going to miss you here and you have been horrible to him."

Tara left the box, excusing herself, by saying she was popping to the ladies. Then she headed towards box number four, at the other end of the stadium. She felt as if she was on a sponsored walk, it took so long but at the end of the corridor there he was leaning against the wall waiting for her. He looked so handsome in his dark suit that Tara felt herself go weak at the knees. She wanted him like an animal. He smiled at her and stood up straight.

"Are you over your little tantrum?" he asked, smirking.

Tara didn't answer. Daniel was right, you could freeze ice on her arse at the best of times. But he got hold of her hand and to her utter disbelief led her into the men's toilets.

"I do hope you've checked that it's empty?" she said.

Then she turned around, jumped in between the sinks and spread her legs. She was wearing a pair of beige riding jodhpurs and long tan boots and his eyes nearly popped out of his head. But then they heard the door go so made a mad dash into one of the two vacant toilets. Quinn put his hand over her mouth as she started to giggle. They heard the man's flies going down then the sprinkle of water. It went on forever then finally he buggered off without washing his hands. Tara did not have time to mess around so she unzipped him and took him straight in her mouth and did not stop until he came. She used the back of her Ralph Lauren white shirt to wipe the lipstick off his mouth and fixed his tie.

"Got to go," she said and left him again, just standing there. She went back into the box as if nothing had happened. Daniel kept looking over at her but she just smirked back at him leaving him wondering. She knew it would be killing him not knowing what had just happened. She'd fill him in later.

Just before the second half, she received another text from Quinn:

'I can smell you'

Tara ignored him. She had work to do. All in all, it had been a successful day and the clients had loved it. None of them had watched the match from the comfort of a box before so they went home very happy people. When it was just Daniel and herself, she fielded questions from him and he could not stop laughing when she explained what had occurred. Daniel pointed out that he must be injured as he was in a suit. He couldn't understand why Tara had not asked him why he was not playing. Quite frankly, Tara was pleased that he had not been on the field and had kept her amused.

When she got home her phone blipped and she half hoped that it would be Quinn. She felt deeply disappointed though when she read:

'Please can I see you. I miss you' from Max.

"Oh go and fuck yourself Max!" she said and threw the phone onto the sofa.

Max knew that she would ignore him. Somebody in court had told him she had a box at the football. He was shattered that she hadn't invited him. He was Sunhill's biggest fan, so he texted Susan. At least she would come straight over.

45

It was starting to bother Izzy that she'd quarrelled with Tara. They had been friends for a long time and through thick and thin Tara had been her support network. If she was honest with herself, she needed that safety net in her life when things went wrong. She was sitting at work after attending the morning management meeting with the Head which had gone as normal, teachers sniping at each other, and she was toying with the idea of holding out the olive branch to Tara. Otherwise, she would be waiting a long time for Tara to pick up the phone, if she ever did. It was Izzy's birthday on Saturday and it had crossed her mind if Tara had remembered. She always did buy such nice presents. After much deliberation, she decided a text would be the best option. See how the land was lying.

Tara was quite surprised to see a text from Izzy and started to smile. She had remembered it was her birthday on Saturday and knew Izzy would want her present.

'Fancy breakfast at the village café, Saturday am-ish?'

'As long as Jonny Devroe is not the source of conversation.'

This irritated Izzy but she bit her tongue and replied:

'Ok it's a deal see you at ten.'

Tara had bought her a beautiful Tiffany pen but hadn't bothered to wrap it yet, as she was waiting to see if her friend would still be in a huff. She should have known better because Izzy loved anything where the attention was solely on her and a birthday qualified for that. Tara remembered her previous birthday when Izzy had promised to pick her up and drive them both for lunch in Sunhill. She was so late that Tara had no option but to drive herself as she was going to be late for her hairdressing appointment. Tara was still waiting for the apology but that was Izzy.

Tara hurried out to buy some wrapping paper. She already had a card. She was back at her desk when one of their supply teachers, Adam Jones came in looking completely bewildered. Adam had been placed at a Pupil Referral Unit for secondary children, aka feral animals. This was a unit where kids who had been excluded from mainstream education were sent.

However, Adam had refused to go in as a teacher, it was such tough going, but he'd worked on a short-term basis as a Teaching Assistant for Education Supply.

Tara realised something had happened.

"What's wrong sweetie?" she said. "You look as if you've seen a ghost."

"I've just been to court," he said.

Tara suddenly realised that she had forgotten all about the incident he had witnessed. It was well over a year ago and none of the agencies involved, nor Adam for that matter, had made Education Supply aware of the court proceedings. A boy aged fourteen, who attended the PRU, had upturned a desk and hurled it at the classroom teacher. Unfortunately said desk had struck the chap directly on his hip. His injury had been so painful, it required surgery. Adam was in the classroom and therefore privy to everything that had happened and subsequently called as a witness. He looked so shaken, Carrie rushed off to make him a coffee.

He went on to explain that neither the child nor parent had been requested to attend the court hearing, which puzzled Tara and Daniel. The blame had now landed squarely on the Unit's shoulders as the boy's solicitors had pointed out that the desk should have been fixed firmly to the floor. Nobody in the office could believe this. It must have been doubly hard for Adam as he witnessed the whole thing and the aftermath, when the teacher was rushed off, screaming in pain, in an ambulance.

Adam pointed out that the boy had found it all very amusing as did the other wild kids in his class. The boy had now got away with it scot-free, with the blame put on the school. Compensation would have to come out of the school's budget. Adam was so upset for the injured teacher because up until the court date, he'd assumed the boy would be punished for his actions. Now the teacher would be suing his employer. Not a good outcome for any of them, except the boy of course.

Saturday arrived and Izzy woke up with a long stretch and a yawn. She could not believe that she had turned forty-five and more depressingly, was still single. She had gone crazy online the previous evening, buying loads of holiday clothes that she was sure she would need one day.

She started to run the bath and headed downstairs to pop the kettle on. She could not survive without ten cups of tea before leaving the house. She picked up her Ipad for a little look at what was going on.

Twenty minutes later, she could hear drips and suddenly realised she'd left the bath running. She bounded up the stairs. The damage wasn't too bad this time, only half an inch of water on the bathroom floor so she set about clearing up then got into the bath with her cup of tea. She was lazing in the bath when she reached for her watch. It was only nine am, plenty of time.

By ten-fifteen Tara was like a cat with its tail wagging from side to side, by ten forty she was about to lose her temper in public, whereupon Izzy strolled nonchalantly around the corner after parking her car. Tara was sick of it. Every time they met, Izzy would leave her sitting waiting by herself. She could not care less. Tara jumped up and the bag with the presents went flying.

"This is the last time you do this to me, Izzy!"

Izzy wasn't bothered, it was her birthday. Tara would get over it. But Tara didn't, couldn't and wouldn't. After today she would never agree to meet her again. The sun shone down gloriously and people sat outside enjoying brunch. Cyclists came and went and the place was heaving with dog walkers. Izzy started talking about letting the bath overflow which she now thought was quite amusing. Then she described the items she had bought online, followed by another hour going on about St. Magdalene's. Not once did she ask Tara how she was and Tara didn't feel the urge to volunteer the information that she had left Simon, moved house and started proceedings.

Tara mused that in all the years she had known Izzy, her behaviour had become worse than ever. She began to wonder if she really needed a friend like her anymore. Every time they saw each other it was like Izzy sucked all of the energy out of her. There was always a problem and she always turned up ranting about it. Tara would say the right words, sort her out then off she would pop happy as Larry leaving Tara exhausted. Tara would not mind if they were real problems but it was all rubbish, mindless crap that other people wouldn't even mention. It had to be all about her, all of the time.

While Izzy wittered on, Tara sat recalling the time she took Izzy to meet some friends and they stayed in a hotel. Izzy got so drunk she didn't even make it down for dinner. The next day when they set off in the car, Izzy realised she didn't have her Ipad and made Tara turn round and go back for it. They found it tucked down between the twin beds. Izzy admitted playing on it all evening. She couldn't make it down for dinner but she could sit in bed playing on her I-pad. She was lucky then that Tara hadn't wiped the floor with her but she would never change. She was a lost cause. Maybe she did fit in with Jonny Devroe and his pals, better than with real people who achieved by hard work rather than criminal activity.

Tara looked at her watch. She wanted to go and she was determined to leave Izzy there on her own for a change. See how she felt. Tara waited until Izzy had ordered yet another pot of tea, then made her excuses and said goodbye. Izzy grasped that she'd aggravated Tara but soon shook it off. Around the corner from the café was a lovely dress shop. She went in and spent two hundred pounds on more clothes for more holidays which may or may not happen.

When she got home, she threw the bags on the floor and noticed her answering machine flashing, a message from Tanya.

"Hi, Izzy. Have you managed to come up with anything?"

That was it. Izzy presumed Tanya was being careful, in case someone was in with her listening to it. The message annoyed her. No, she hadn't come up with anything. She hadn't even thought about it. She had drunk so much red wine the previous evening that she hadn't even noticed Frank returning to the car and replacing the holdall stashed in the boot. Izzy told herself that Jonny would not want to get her into any trouble.

By three pm Tanya felt so furious that she hadn't returned her call, she drove over to Izzy's house but when she knocked, nobody answered and Izzy's car was missing. Tanya did not know what prompted her to walk around to the back of the house. She wasn't sure which garage was Izzy's but it was a fair assumption when she saw the brand new, gleaming padlock on the side gate. When she walked back towards the street, she saw Izzy parking up.

"Hi you, two surprise visits in one week!" laughed Izzy, as she breezed towards her, with car keys swinging in her hand.

"Come with me," said Tanya abruptly. "I want to show you something."

She linked arms with Izzy, forcing her to keep step. As they approached the padlock Tanya could see the surprise and alarm on her friend's face.

"You had no idea this was here, did you?"

For a splitsecond Izzy contemplated lying to her just to get her off her back but she thought better of it.

"No," she stammered.

Tanya swung her around and they headed back to the house. Once inside Tanya pointed out the obvious.

"They are coming and going to that car, entering your premises."

"I haven't heard a thing," said Izzy, with her hands in the air. "And I sleep at the back of the house."

"You are so pissed of an evening, my friend, you would not have a clue if they broke your fucking door down and marched into your bedroom!"

Izzy slumped on the sofa and put her head in her hands.

"Don't start fucking crying Izzy. You have got to get rid of that car. We have to come up with something."

Izzy just nodded her head but she'd already told Jonny that nobody had used the garage for years. What could she come up with now that he'd believe? Fortunately, Tanya was doing all the thinking.

"You are going to tell him that your brother needs it."

"For what?" asked Izzy.

"Either to put a car there or something else large, because he hasn't got the space at home."

"Do you think Jonny will swallow that?"

"He will if you say it convincingly enough. In fact, you are going to do it right now."

Izzy was now flapping higher than a seagull on a pasty outside the local shopping centre.

"No, no, I need to think about it."

"Do you want to lose all of your friends over that fuckwit, Izzy?" raged Tanya, close to Izzy's face. "You could get into serious trouble and if Jonny likes you, the way you keep saying he does, then it will be no skin off his nose to get that car off somewhere else, convenient."

Izzy took a deep breath. She knew Tanya was right but she was terrified of crossing him not to mention Charlie Shields, the real owner of the car. She took a minute to collect herself.

"Ok, ok, Tanya, calm down. How shall I put it?"

Tanya held out her hand for Izzy's phone and typed:

'Tried to contact you a few times to let you know that my brother needs the space out the back of mine so I need the car moving'

Then she pressed SEND.

"Put the kettle on Izzy. Let's see what comes back."

An hour later, there was still no response. Tanya had fully expected the text to trouble Jonny but in retrospect, she should have known a lot better. People like Jonny and Charlie could not easily be intimidated or told what to do. An hour and a half passed and Tanya was going to have to think about leaving. She couldn't stay there all day.

"The minute he responds, call me," she said. "I'll be at home. My Mum's coming down but apart from that I will be around."

Izzy nodded her head and showed Tanya out. She went to the kitchen window and stared at the car, wondering what the hell was going on with the padlock? She should be furious but part of her would do anything to keep in Jonny's good books. Thank God Tara didn't know, she would probably ring the police personally.

Izzy carried the phone with her everywhere. She didn't let it out of her sight, but still no response to her message. Then at eight pm, she heard a knock on the door. She opened it, fully expecting to see Tanya standing there but to her surprise she found Jonny grinning away like a Cheshire cat. He barged past her telling her to put the kettle on.

His whole being filled up her kitchen and as he lifted the coffee cup to his lips, he turned to look out of the kitchen window at the car.

"What's the problem then with the motor?" he asked.

Izzy was no match for him at all and she started spluttering.

"Well I'm really sorry Jonny but my brother has bought another car and he wants to put the old one here until he decided if he's keeping it."

Her face had turned bright red and she knew that she was giving the game away. Jonny started laughing at her.

"I'm sure you can do better than that. I've got nowhere else to put it and you are really helping me out here, I'm relying on you," he said, giving her that strange, taut grin.

Her brain was screaming out to her to mention the padlock on her gate but she literally couldn't form the words on her lips. She was terrified of him. She felt so small and insignificant standing next to him. He placed the coffee cup down, came really close and put one of his huge hands around her neck. He started to grip tighter.

"I presume you do want to help me out here, being such a good friend who I can count on?"

Izzy found herself nodding like a puppet.

"Yes, yes," she said. "Of course, you can. I'll tell him to sort something else out."

Jonny released his grip on her neck.

"Good," he said. "Thanks for the coffee." And he left her house as fast as he had arrived.

When she heard her front door slam she was still trembling from head to toe. She felt all her nerves were frayed and ready to snap. The slightest thing could tip her over the edge. She poured a glass of red wine, her hand shaking so hard she almost missed the glass. The landline rang. Tanya's number glowed in the small screen.

She had to answer it but she knew what was coming. She tried to do a cheery hello but Tanya was straight on to it.

"I've just seen Jonny come out of your house."

"Oh my God, he didn't see you, did he?" she said in panic.

"No, I'm way up the street. Let me in."

Izzy went to unlock the front door. Tanya was horrified when she saw the state she was in. But as usual, Izzy had already decided what was happening and her jaw was set.

"He's assured me that the car is just parked up there as it has no road tax and I'm happy with what he said."

"And the new padlock on your fucking gate?" screamed Tanya.

Izzy could do nothing but look down at the floor so Tanya spoke for her.

"You didn't even mention it did you?"

Izzy shook her head.

Tanya bent down to pick up her handbag which she had thrown on the floor.

"Right, that's it," she said. "You don't need my help? You deserve everything you get. I've tried. You don't listen. Be it on your own head," and she stormed off, slamming Izzy's front door even louder than Jonny had.

"Happy birthday," said Izzy, to nobody but herself.

46

Monday morning came around a little too quickly for Tara's liking but the early rush hour part had run relatively smoothly. Education Supply was having an ongoing problem with one of their clients, Westhill Community Primary School. They had used Education Supply for years and then suddenly stopped. Daniel had rung on several occasions and Sarah Barnes had assured him that nothing was wrong, they had rearranged classes and staff and had a bit of a shakeup so they didn't need any cover. As time passed and a month became six months, no matter what Daniel did or said, Sarah still didn't budge.

All of that changed when a long-term vacancy appeared and Sarah rang up requesting one of Education Supply's most favourite primary teachers, one Sarah had employed a lot in the past. Daniel rang the supply teacher, Emma. She said she was desperate for work, especially something long term so Daniel sent her to see the school.

A few weeks' later, Daniel could not get through to Sarah. She was avoiding him like the plague. Tara knew something was up. Emma then rang, confirming she had got the job at Westhill and would not be available for the rest of the academic year. Once again Daniel tried to contact Sarah but to no avail and he was becoming exasperated.

"I don't know what else to do Tara," he said. "Short of going up to the school and seeing her face to face."

Tara was dead against this as it would become embarrassing for the school.

"Well," she said. "They can't expect to get her for nothing. We have loads of clients who request Emma and she will be a huge loss to us. Invoice them for our introduction fee."

Daniel agreed. Surely, they didn't expect to get staff for nothing? When the clients signed timesheets it clearly stated under the signature section, that if a teacher who had been introduced by Education Supply was offered work direct by the school, then an introduction fee would be charged. Westhill had signed rather a lot of those forms in the past. Sarah who was the school's business manager would be fully aware of that fact.

"There's obviously a problem here Daniel," said Tara. "She ain't gonna pay. That's why she won't speak to you."

He stood up to file a form away.

"They can't expect to get a full-time member of staff who they have had in, tried and tested, checked out, and all the rest of it, for nothing. It's unprofessional."

"It's unethical sweetie," Tara corrected him.

She searched for their solicitor's number. She would sue them. She waited until Daniel had finished with his paperwork.

"Let's go out for coffee?"

Daniel loved doing this. It was rare but he could sit and talk about Quinn as his life was so boring these days. They popped into a different café because she didn't want to bump into Max. They started chatting about the football match.

"I think the clients had a great day," he said, sipping his coffee. "In fact, I've already had a booking from Deerside Academy. Mind you, that might be because the cover manager fancies you."

"I'm sure he doesn't," she smiled. "But who cares as long as we get the business. We have to cover the forty thousand it cost to hire."

"I'm convinced we'll do more than that," said Daniel.

"Then there's how much we spent on alcohol," said Tara. "But to be fair, none of them took advantageous of the free bar. Most of the people were really nice, not the type you might like to spend a lot of time, with but overall it wasn't too difficult."

Daniel started to laugh. He knew Tara couldn't stand the new wave of professionals coming into the business but she loved her older clients and teachers. It worried her, however, when she kept hearing how they were going to get out before the changes happened and Tara could see exactly what they meant.

She received a text and a huge grin spread across her face.

"Quinn?" asked Daniel.

She nodded and showed it to him.

"I want to lick you," he said out loud and Tara nearly had a heart attack.

She looked all around to see if anybody had heard him but they were safe. Nobody was taking a blind bit of notice so she texted back:

'It will cost you.'

She showed Daniel and they resumed the conversation about Saturday. Tara looked at her watch. She was getting into a rhythm with Quinn. She knew he would just have finished training and the afternoon was his to do as he pleased, unless he had official business for the club. She waited and waited but her phone didn't signal a reply until they were back in the office and he sent:

'It already has.'

The message puzzled her so she showed it to Daniel. Neither of them knew what he meant so she decided to ignore him. About an hour later she looked up to see a courier arrive with the biggest bouquet of flowers known to man. Daniel started the ahh business and Tara had to admit she liked it. She read the message in the card:

'Thinking about you Q.'

"Look at your face!" crowed Daniel. "You're impressed to hell."

She couldn't deny it. That's what he had meant when he said it had already cost him. those flowers would not have been cheap. She sent him a genuine thank you. Daniel was impressed that Quinn had managed to get them delivered so quickly.

"Are you going to make arrangements to see him?" he asked.

"I don't know," said Tara shrugging. "If he asks, yes but only for sex."

Daniel looked at her and narrowed his eyes.

"You must be every man's dream date, no strings attached sex."

"And he doesn't even have to buy me dinner," Tara laughed. "But I do wonder if he's going to invite me to his place."

"Do you have any idea where he lives?" said Daniel, becoming even more interested.

"Strangely enough Dan that subject wasn't something we were talking about," and she started to laugh.

Secretly, she would never admit it, but she did love it when he sent her messages. He was so young, fit and successful. He was at the top of his game but there was no way in a million years that she would ever contact him.

When she got home, she put her trainers on and went for a long run, then had a leisurely soak in the bath. She had decided on a nice quiet night in and briefly wondered what Izzy was up to but hesitated to contact her. It would only mean getting dragged into some pointless drama that only involved Izzy, Jonny or St. Magdalene's and Tara didn't have the strength to listen to the mindless crap that came out of Izzy's mouth.

She climbed into her lovely fresh bed that Julie her housekeeper had changed earlier in the day and watched the full moon beaming over the bay in front of her house. It was like living abroad. The view was breath-taking no matter the weather. Even when it was vile and the sea was churning out huge breakers, the view was spectacular. She didn't realise she'd dozed off until she heard her mobile ringing in the distance. It had stopped by the time she found it somewhere in the bedsheets. Then came a text:

'I've had to show my face with the team at an event and I'm bored shitless. 11 pm your place?'

Tara smiled and stretched in bed. Hell, yes, she thought, beck and call girl suited her right down to the ground.

'Perfect.' She replied.

Then it was all action stations as she showered and covered herself in the perfume he loved. When she was all prepared, she got back into bed and watched some television waiting for Quinn's arrival. At a quarter to eleven, a car drew up in the drive. She didn't hear the sound of his sports car so she reckoned he must be in a taxi. She waited for his usual tap on the glass door then walked slowly downstairs in her bare feet.

All she was wearing was the skimpiest black underwear that he had ever seen. Quinn smiled at her and he could feel himself getting hard. Tara locked the door and led him by the hand to her bed. She watched him stand in front of her and slowly take his clothes off staring at her all of the time. He was so ready for her and didn't mess about with foreplay. He crept into the bed beside her and started stroking her back and buttocks. His breathing became louder.

"I want you," he whispered in her ear.

He gently squeezed her nipple and she could feel the excitement building between her legs. She was so wet and wanted him right now but he traced his tongue from her throat down to her naval and she desperately wanted him to go lower but he was in no hurry. He traced his tongue back up and started to suck her breast. Tara cried out the moment she felt his hot wet mouth around her erect nipple and she felt his other hand reach up and start stroking her. He moved down the bed and slipped his fingers into the soft wet mass between her legs and parted her legs fully with his free hand. He stretched her wide open ready to receive him. Tara could feel his hardness against her leg and she could hear his breathing. There was no warning and Quinn entered her. Her entire body moved up and down meeting him willingly as he fucked her, pushing hard against him accepting each thrust that became deeper and deeper. They came together as one and then lay side by side utterly spent. They were both covered in sweat and she could feel every part of him as his breathing slowed down.

Tara turned sideways in bed, placed her foot under his back and playfully started to push him out of her bed.

"Off you pop," she smiled at him. "Some of us have real jobs to go to in the morning. Put the latch down on the front door when you let yourself out."

Then she snuggled back down into bed turning her back to him. Quinn started to laugh.

"And we wouldn't want the princess to get out of her warm bed now, would we. Even to show her guest out?"

But he collected his clothes together, got ready then bent over the bed and kissed her on the head.

"Night gorgeous," he said.

Tara didn't reply but relaxed when she heard the front door close. Then she enjoyed the best night's sleep she'd had in ages.

The next day Tara was beaming from ear to ear when she got to work. Sex was the best pill any doctor could prescribe. Sadly, her smile was soon wiped off when another job was lost through the behaviour of one of their supply teachers. Daniel had pitched for a new client and had been successful. In fact, from all of the CV's Deanholme Academy had received, they had selected one of his teachers. They wanted to meet the supply teacher the next day to have a look at them before offering them a job with a view to a long-term maths post. There lay the problem. Stephen Ridley never answered the phone. He wasn't working but his wife had a very well-paid job so unbeknownst to her, Stephen liked to sit in the house all day probably telling her that there was no work.

Daniel tried to contact him all day. Eventually, he decided to ring him at 8.30 at night hoping the wife would pick up the landline and Daniel could drop the lazy git right in it. The plan worked and Daniel did drop Stephen right in it. He explained that Education Supply had a year's post available and the school wanted to see him, to carry out a day's supply with a view to keeping him. It was agreed that Stephen would be standing right next to the phone first thing in the morning to await instructions, giving Daniel time to contact the school and get him in ready to teach.

Daniel had contacted Deanholme first thing but unfortunately, their second choice with another agency had been free to go into school and was in there now ready to teach. Daniel hit the roof just as Tara got in.

"I'm fucking sick of this. Why do they come in and register for work?" he shouted.

"Same old, same old Dan," she said. "The wives have good jobs and they lie about not being offered any posts."

"Lazy twats all of them," said Daniel heading for the kitchen. "And I thought the man was supposed to be the breadwinner?"

"Not any longer," said Tara. "That's why some of them spend longer and longer at university. It delays joining the real world and having to work."

The switchboard rang and Tara got to it first. She heard sobbing and it took her a few moments to realise it was Charlotte Vasey one of her long-standing supply teachers. She could barely recognise her voice she was so upset. This put Tara instantly on red alert, Charlotte was never a shrinking violet.

"What on earth has happened?" she asked.

Everyone in the office immediately downed tools when they heard the tone of Tara's voice and gave it their full attention. However, Charlotte was still struggling to speak. Tara grabbed the booking sheets to refresh her memory which school Charlotte was at today and which year she was covering. Then she remembered booking her out on Sunday afternoon, to work with a five-year- old on a one-to-one basis, who needed extra help due to some sort of learning difficulty. After a few moments, Charlotte managed to calm down.

"He came to school Tara, with shit pouring out of his trouser legs. He's not toilet trained!"

She started sobbing again but Tara knew there had to be something more to the story, to phase someone with Charlotte's experience.

"Sweetie, take a deep breath," said Tara. "I need to know exactly what has upset you, so I can help."

You could hear a pin drop in the office.

"Well," said Charlotte. "I changed him and he had no underwear on. He had actually got himself to school. His mum's an alcoholic, pregnant with her fifth child and the fuckwit that she is shacked up with is a heroin addict. But," and the sobbing started again. "It's going to make the news at some point, the evil cow has been keeping her kids locked up in dog cages."

Tara had heard some stories in education but this was so horrific, she wasn't sure she actually believed it and found herself repeating out loud what Charlotte had said. Carrie instantly burst into tears at the other end of the office and Mark, sitting at the next desk, got up and comforted her. Tara took a deep breath.

"Jesus Charlotte, that's bad," she said.

"I know," she replied. "She's had the kids taken away from her on numerous occasions but then returned when she's promised to be mother of the year. More like she knew she would lose her benefits."

But Tara knew that all of the services were at breaking point. She was once told by a friend who worked in the probation service that there were so many bad parents around, that if they scooped all of the children up who were on the at-risk register, they would have not enough places to put them in. Her friend had explained countless times that nothing happened to the parents, they simply had the children taken away and were absolved all of their responsibility. When something terrible did happen, it was always the authorities' fault, never the parents. The sad reality, thought Tara, was that the poor little five-year-old boy would turn into a ten-year-old then eighteen-year-old feral animal with all sorts of problems and become another statistic of crime, all through the fault of the person who had spawned him.

Tara spoke to Charlotte for another fifteen minutes and calmed her down. When she finished, she wondered what the hell the country was coming to and how education would cope in ten years when every other child was dragged up in the way that poor five-year-old had been. She explained to Daniel everything that had been said.

"They have to stop the benefits when young girls get pregnant," he said. If they have no means, why the fuck should we the taxpayer pay to raise or drag up, their kids which they don't really want in the first place. Can you imagine how much money an alcoholic mother gets in benefits for four children, only to spend it on drink?"

"And now she's pregnant with the fifth," said Tara.

The mood in the office descended to an all-time low. Everyone kept thinking about what that poor little boy would be sent home to. The children always suffered. Tara didn't care what anybody said, she knew it was true. The parents promised the earth and all the time the kids suffered. Her night of fabulous sex was a distant memory. She would have to do it all over again she thought, to remind herself that life could be fun when a man was sticking his hand up your skirt.

The next three scheduled interviews didn't bother to cancel or reschedule, they simply didn't turn up. Welcome to supply teacher's world. Quinn sent Tara a message, asking if she had enjoyed last night. Tara decided to lighten her mood by sending him the filthiest message he had ever received. She had grown up being told that she had an overactive imagination or rather she was a dirty, horny bitch and who cared, she wanted it.

47

Jonny had been trying to give Charlie Shields a wide berth. He thought that by doing him the favour by getting Izzy to stash the car on her property, that would be an end to it but Charlie had other ideas. Jonny was now his best mate and Charlie wanted to hang out with him after all he had been banged up for ages and had missed the nightlife. Jonny would only admit to himself that he was very wary of him. Charlie was a loose cannon. He was wired incorrectly. He loved a fight and once he started kicking someone in the head, he had to be forcibly dragged off by more than one big bloke. Jonny had seen him in action on more occasions than he cared to remember and had thought it was only a matter of time before he killed someone. Even a lengthy prison sentence hadn't deterred him. It was almost as if he couldn't help himself. He had to inflict violence on anybody he cared to have a go at. All in all thought Jonny, Charlie was a very dangerous man. The lad lying in hospital on a ventilator machine bore witness to that fact.

The other fact that Jonny had to take into account was that his boss Tony demanded that all of his staff kept well away from the likes of Charlie Shields. Tony needed them to stay well under the radar and Charlie attracted a lot of the wrong kind of attention, starting with the police. He was a magnet for trouble. Jonny would have to keep him at arm's length before it got to the point that he got the call from Tony to come in for a few words. He was deep in thought about this situation when he heard his phone ringing in his inside pocket. He noticed five missed calls from Charlie but decided he was not going to return any of them and jumped in the shower to get ready for his shift at Limes.

Jonny got to work at eight-thirty. He was slightly on edge when he realised Tony was in the office but Tony had only said a quick hello and carried on studying his paperwork so Jonny headed for the main door to relieve Davie who had been there since six pm. The place was starting to buzz and all the half-pissed, bright, young girls were waving and hollering at him like he was some sort of celebrity. He lapped up the attention and he knew he could have any of them anytime he wanted.

He was standing just inside the doorway as it had started to rain and out of the corner of his eye noticed a black Range Rover pull into the side street opposite the club. He clocked the number plate and realised it was Charlie. He knew it was too late for him to disappear, Charlie would have spotted him in full view outside the club. He carried on greeting people but felt on edge and prayed that Charlie would not start any trouble in Limes. If he did, Jonny would have to sort it out and make no bones about it, he would sort it out.

It was possible that Charlie was heading for one of the other pubs, he did protect a few pubs in the town centre. But then he saw Charlie and two of his minders approaching Limes and he slapped a grin on his face. Charlie would have to think twice before starting any trouble. Tony was about the only human being on this earth that Charlie gave any respect to. Tony had once told him that if he crossed the line anywhere even close to Tony's business interests, he would find his mother dead in a ditch. Nobody doubted Tony's word for a second. He was a very fair man but woe betide anyone who stepped on his toes. People had disappeared overnight with no questions asked but everyone knew who had been responsible for the disappearances.

"Jonny, my friend!" smiled Charlie, all bonhomie, as he approached the entrance to Limes, arm outstretched. Jonny shook hands with him and opened the door for them as if they were VIP's.

The loud music just about drowned out any speech.

"Everything Ok?" he asked Charlie.

"Yeah," he replied. "Just enjoying the freedom of being out of the nick. Having a dodge around seeing what I've missed. It's been a long time!" he laughed.

Jonny waved them into the main club but he remained on the front door. Normally he would have got some cover and had a drink but not with Charlie. He knew Tony would find out in about twenty seconds. Upstairs in the office, Tony had been alerted by the bar manager that they had undesirable company. Tony scanned the CCTV monitor. It wasn't hard to spot Charlie, his sheer bulk gave him away.

"Why doesn't he fuck off and go somewhere else?" said Tony. "Keep an eye on him at all times. I presume Jonny is monitoring the situation?"

The bar manager nodded.

"Jonny is far from happy Tony. He wants him out, he's lowering the tone of the place. Half of Sunhill have seen the stupid fucker on the local news."

Tony hated Charlie. He was a thug. But he had no choice, he had to let him stay in Limes for a while. He knew he wouldn't be spending the entire evening there. If he had any sense he would leave after a few drinks. Tony was savvy enough to realise that thugs like Charlie did have their uses, for those occasional jobs other people didn't want to dirty their hands with. However, Jonny had stepped up to the plate where that was concerned and carried out all of Tony's orders without question.

He stood up putting his overcoat on.

"Right I'm leaving. Make sure Jonny is at the front door so that I can have a word with him on the way out. Any sign of trouble, tell me. Bring the car around," he instructed the bar manager who was not happy to be left in charge with Charlie Shields propping up the bar. He left to find Jonny and told Stevie the driver to bring the car around to the front door. Tony seemed to be in a hurry.

Tony had a bad feeling about Charlie. He assumed that Jonny would have the sense to keep him at arm's length. He'd always felt that Jonny could be intimidated by him but knew that Jonny was clued up and felt that he would come to Tony if there were any problems. What Jonny didn't know was that Tony knew all about the car that Jonny had helped Charlie to stash on Izzy's property. He wasn't going to let on that he knew until he needed to use it. Tony knew everything that was going on in Sunhill. Frank, Charlie's man was on his payroll. Tony always did play his cards close to his chest and decided to wait and see what came out in the wash. He went downstairs and stood at the door hesitating momentarily to tell Jonny he would see him later. Jonny knew instantly by the look on his face that Tony was not a happy man and also knew it was because Charlie was there. He sent up a silent prayer that Charlie would just have a few drinks and skip the few lines of coke he usually did and bugger off into the night quietly.

Jonny went off on his break and sat drinking a coffee. He needed to stay alert so turned down the bottle of beer that was on offer. It was on his mind about Izzy pestering him to remove the car and he was starting to get annoyed. He didn't see why he had to put up with any grief just to help Charlie. The car had been there for three weeks now. Surely, he could find somewhere else to put it? Then he made a snap decision. Charlie was there and this was the time to sort it and take the heat from the stupid bitch off him. Yes, he finally decided that was a brilliant idea. He couldn't give a toss about her and it certainly wasn't her fault that she was a bit dim and would do anything for him but credit where credit was due, she must have realised that something was up suddenly demanding it was moved. Of course, Jonny knew nothing about Tanya spotting the brand-new padlock that Frank had fitted on her gate, or for that matter that Frank was going in and out at all hours to the car using it for storage.

When he got back downstairs his timing could not have been better as Charlie and his crew were just leaving. The man was an incredible size, weaving his way through the throngs of young girls who took steps back to avoid him as they were clearly intimidated by him. He was like the incredible hulk, huge and so ugly. The teardrop tattoo on his face did him no favours either. He looked exactly what he was.

Jonny watched him strutting about. He was lucky he'd been allowed into Limes. It was a fairly upmarket club and any celebrities at the local theatre or TV studios always made Limes a destination for a drink. No wonder Tony had not looked best pleased but Jonny knew Tony would be dealing with Charlie if it came down to it. Charlie shouted over to Jonny that he would catch him later but Jonny followed him out on to the street telling him that he needed a word.

"I didn't answer your calls," he said. "Because I was with the bird who owns the house where the car is and she was busy giving me earache about wanting the motor moved."

"And you used your famous charm, my friend," grinned Charlie.

Jonny now realised that Charlie needed that car to stay put and God only knew the reason behind that.

"What's going on Charlie?" he said but Charlie just shrugged his shoulders.

"I am still in the same position my friend. Nobody has got anywhere to put it for me, and after all, you did offer." He looked menacingly straight into Jonny's eyes. "Tell you what mate," he continued, patting him on the shoulder as if to reinforce what he was going to say. "I will have a little ask about and see if anybody has come up with something to help miss school girly out of her predicament."

Jonny narrowed his eyes and glared back at him slightly unnerved that Charlie had made it his business to find out who owned the property where the car was kept. Obviously, something was going on otherwise he wouldn't have bothered. He had done his homework and knew exactly who Izzy and what she did for a living. Jonny only felt guilty for a second. It was down to Izzy for agreeing to take it in the first place.

"Great," he replied. "Save me from getting it in the neck from her."

Charlie moved off. It still bothered Jonny though, that the car had to be kept out of sight. Charlie had to be careful. He had just got out of prison and was on license. Surely, he realised the police would be keeping a close eye on his activities. He needed to keep his nose clean. Jonny started smiling to himself. He really was a heartless bastard but he didn't really give a toss about Izzy. She was a big girl, really nice but very tedious. All she cared about was how she looked and if her lipstick was topped up. He reminded himself, however, that she came in very handy. He even wondered if he could get another free holiday out of her. Why should he pay if she was willing and desperate for his company?

He was still smiling away to himself and his ability to get women when a voice came through his earpiece. There was a spot of trouble brewing in the lounge, so he headed off to sort it out. The trouble would evaporate the minute he turned up, he had a certain reputation in Limes. Everybody needed Jonny Devroe he told himself.

Izzy got ready for work the next day and decided to make an extra special effort with her appearance, for no other reason than she loved it when the rest of the staff complimented her. Whenever she had been shopping with Tara in the city, she had always found lovely pieces that would never be sold in Sunhill where most of the office staff shopped so they were always asking her where she had bought her clothes from and telling her how fabulous she looked and she just loved the compliments.

She locked her front door and stood staring up and down the street. Due to the amount of wine she had consumed the previous evening she simply could not remember where she had parked her car. She was sick of never been able to get outside of her front door. The parking around her house was a nightmare. Eventually, she spotted her black Audi at the top of her street. She started to walk up the hill and the fresh air hit her hangover but she had needed the drink to knock her out so that she could sleep. Otherwise, she would spend every night listening for any noises in her back yard near to that damn car. She thought about Tanya and realised that she hadn't heard from her since she had dragged her down the back lane and showed her the padlock on Izzy's gate. She threw her head high in the air and decided that she was getting sick and tired of both Tanya's and Tara's attitudes. Jonny thought a lot about her. She was convinced he would not get her into any trouble. She would have to keep on drinking every night though, because if she didn't knock herself out flat, she might hear or even worse, see, something she shouldn't.

She stepped into her car, checked her makeup again and pulled out into the oncoming traffic. Izzy drove along thinking about Jonny. She would love to see him again and was so busy conjuring up ideas of how she could engineer a meet with him that she didn't notice the dark blue Ford Focus following her.

Meanwhile, Charlie Shields was in his gym pumping iron when his mobile rang. He put down the weights and answered with one word,

"Where?"

"St. Magdalene's," said Frank, who worked for him and he ended the call.

Charlie smiled. It had been as easy as that. No crappy inner-city sink kitchen for miss Schooley. St. Magdalene's was the most successful school in the Sunhill area and had attracted the offspring of doctors and dentists who did not want to send their children to private schools. His day went on as usual and he was starting to get bored. He needed some excitement in his life. Intimidating people was usually classed as sport for him so he headed to his office and waited for his crew to arrive.

Today was payday. Lots of little shops, bars and restaurants paid him protection money just in case of any little incidents that may occur and of course, they always paid in cash, so no paper trail which suited him. At about three-thirty Charlie's thoughts moved back to Izzy. It was a long time since he had been to school but he reckoned that it was about now that they broke up for the day. Izzy may be just about at the end of her working day too, so he got Frank and another one of his lads and told them they were going for a little drive in the Range Rover.

Frank was getting a bit sick of Charlie. He had been erratic before getting banged up but lately, he was off the map. He wondered what Charlie was thinking of now but he didn't have long to wait. Charlie instructed him to drive to St. Magdalene's and park up in front of the schoolyard where everyone could see them. Frank felt that instant mix of fear and dread in the pit of his stomach. God knows what he was going to do. Tanya was a very old friend and he didn't want her mate to get mixed up any further than she already was.

Meanwhile, Izzy was trying her best to get a report typed up for Jackie the head.

"I've got a dental appointment, Jackie," she reminded her as she was desperately trying to get out of the office.

Jackie clapped her hands together.

"I'm so sorry Izzy I forgot," she said. "Get yourself away this can go off tomorrow. We've missed the post now anyway."

Izzy needed no excuse and jumped up from her desk grabbing her coat and bag. She popped into the ladies and redid her make up as she was bound to bump into someone that she knew in the dentist's surgery. As she crossed the yard, she was busy delving into the depths of her handbag trying to find her car keys. When she looked up, she nearly had a coronary. That huge, ugly man she'd seen on the news, and who owned that car, was sitting right outside her school.

She dropped her bag spilling the contents all over the schoolyard. Her hands were shaking so badly, she could hardly gather up her bits and pieces and to make matters worse, she spotted Shelley Riley, the parent from hell striding towards her. Then the woman actually knelt down beside her and started to help her collect her belongings.

"It's Ok, Shelley, I've got it," said Izzy.

She wanted rid of her. Shelley would know exactly who Charlie Shields was, her husband being in the scrap metal business. Then to her dismay, she found herself looking up at the towering figure of Charlie, who just happened to get out of his car and come across the yard to Izzy's rescue. She was now in a very difficult position. Shelley was the last person on this earth who needed to know that Izzy was familiar with this vile man standing in front of her. Her whole body was shaking. She was absolutely terrified of him but Shelley jumped straight in.

"Fancy seeing you here," she said and to Izzy's horror, Charlie leant over and kissed Shelley. They must know each other very well, she thought. Perhaps Shelley's husband had disposed of a few risky cars in his time for the likes of Charlie Shields. Charlie retrieved Izzy's lipstick from the ground and handed it to her.

"I'm thinking about sending my boy here, Shelley," he said in a matter of fact kind of tone.

Izzy noticed that Shelley wasn't that keen to hang around herself and looked a tad uncomfortable in his presence. She grabbed her brats' hands, made some lame excuse that she was in a hurry and scampered off over the yard to her car leaving Izzy with methandriol man. Izzy was transfixed by his teardrop tattoo etched just beneath his eye. She kept staring at it wondering why anyone with half a brain would do that to themselves. But this close up she noticed his face had all sorts of scars on it even a few on his bald head. The man looked so out of place in this civilised environment but it didn't appear to faze him at all. The one relief was that Jackie their head would never entertain the likes of him at St. Magdalene's.

"There you go Izzy," he said swooping down to pick up her car keys that they had both missed.

Izzy didn't say a word, just scarpered to her car. She sat in the driver's seat and immediately put the keys in the ignition activating the central locking system to make her feel a bit safer. Then the penny dropped. Not only did he know where she lived, he now knew what she drove and even where she worked. Jonny must have told him her name and given him the extra details. He probably did it just in conversation, she supposed it wasn't a secret where she worked but she did feel uncomfortable him having this information about her.

She drove out of the schoolyard and her phone blipped. She was almost too scared to look. He could not possibly have her phone number? Surely Jonny wouldn't have gone that far. But it was Jackie:

'Who was that awful man that you and Shelley were talking to? Do you know him?'

Izzy grabbed the steering wheel and shouted: "fuck fuck fuck." Jackie was the last person that she could talk to and she would definitely never admit to the head who she was hanging around with, let alone minding property for them so she texted back:

'No of course I don't. He was helping me pick up my belongings it's Shelley who knows him'

She waited for a few minutes but Jackie did not reply which was odd. She usually would have made some comment and Izzy didn't know what to make of that, it was as if Jackie did not believe her. Or perhaps she was getting paranoid and reading too much into it. Izzy tried to concentrate on the traffic but her mind kept wandering. Tanya was right. The company that she was keeping was appalling but once again Izzy started talking herself into some sort of misguided reasoning to make herself feel better and more in control. Charlie was Jonny's friend. She excluded the fact that she was storing his car from any sort of reasoning because she thought she was doing Jonny the favour not Charlie. She kept checking her rear-view mirror but the Range Rover wasn't following her.

Charlie drove away from the school satisfied that he had put the fear of God into Izzy. He decided that he was going to have a little fun playing with her. He may even be able to talk her into bed. She wasn't bad to look at and he was pretty sure Jonny wouldn't care as he wasn't really seeing her. He ordered Frank to write down her license number which made Frank very uncomfortable. God knows what Tanya would say. He considered having another word with her but dismissed that thought immediately. He was scared of his boss too.

Izzy's day had been wrecked. She had managed to make her dental appointment and was going to do some shopping afterwards but she was so upset she went straight home. Even a hot bath didn't relax her and again and again, she wondered what the hell she had got herself into storing that car? She had closed her kitchen blinds. She couldn't bear to look at the thing. All she knew was she had to work out how to get shot of it. She needed to come up with a plan, a plan that was good and they could not ignore.

She lay in bed mulling over what had taken place. She felt exhausted with the strain but not once did she blame Jonny for anything. He could do no wrong. Izzy felt so alone. She wished that she could call Tanya and confide in her but she had made her thoughts abundantly clear. She wanted nothing to do with Izzy until she changed who she was hanging around with. At that point, Izzy did need some help because it was right over her head what Charlie was doing. It never crossed her mind that he was trying to intimidate her into holding on to the car. The first thing she would be doing when she got into work tomorrow, was to check out the central admission record and scan it for the surname Shields.

It was very tempting to have a glass of wine but she stayed away from the wine cupboard because she needed all her wits about her. She tucked herself down into her lovely, warm, comfortable bed not realising how tired and exhausted she was and promptly dozed off. Then she was woken up in the dead of night. She glanced at the clock and grimaced, four in the morning. She listened hard for what had woken her but settled herself again when she heard nothing.

She was just dozing again when she heard another noise. It sounded like a chain rattling. She crept out of bed in the pitch dark and headed to the back bedroom. She managed to ease the curtain back a fraction. She heard the rattling sound louder now, there was no doubt it was coming from her back yard. She saw a movement at the back of the car. She couldn't make out any features but the yard had some light shining on it from the lamp post in the street so she waited and waited, straining her neck to observe what was going on through the crack in the curtain.

She had just started to think that she had imagined the whole thing when she realised that the car boot had been opened and the man, or so she thought it was a man by the stature of the black form she could see, was either stowing or retrieving something from the boot of the car. She strained her eyes screwing them up tightly to get a better look but the flash of dark shadow was quickly out of the gate, carrying what from a distance looked like a rather large holdall. Izzy then heard the chain rattling sound again, realising it must be the padlock on her gate being secured. She then could not hear or see anything else. He was gone.

Izzy moved away from the window and went downstairs and put the kettle on. She started pacing around and began to cry. Charlie Shields was storing something in that car and they were using her premises anytime they wanted. Not only that, but he had turned up at her work to intimidate her. Jonny must have told him that she wanted the car moving and Charlie wanted to shut her up. She was fed up, angry and feeling stupid. How could she let these people manipulate her like this? Izzy was now more terrified now she had actually seen with her own eyes someone going into the boot of that car. This could not go on so she grabbed her phone and texted Jonny. She wasn't brave enough to front it out with him in person.

'I've got my neighbour at my door. They have just seen an intruder coming through my back gate and watched him from their bedroom window put a holdall into the boot of that fucking car'

Jonny was highly irritated when he heard his phone blip but it was late so it could be Tony needing a job doing. He put the girl down he was busy shagging and looked at the screen. He read the message, flung the phone on the floor and proceeded to open Sam's legs and go down on her. She was very young and giggled which had already irritated him, then being interrupted by Izzy's text irritated him even more. Izzy was seriously getting on his nerves. He was going to have to speak to Charlie.

The next day Jonny had some sleep, sorted himself out and walked to the nearest phone box to contact Charlie. His intuition was telling him to leave no trace of the call. Charlie was surprised to hear from him.

"Jonny my friend what can I do for you?" he said cheerfully enough.

His manner soon changed when Jonny read Izzy's text out loud to him.

"Look, Jonny," he said. "Fuck her and shut her up. You're doing me a huge favour keeping the motor parked out of the way for a bit."

Jonny sighed. He knew it was not going to be easy but he needed to keep Charlie in the loop and he strongly suspected the car was full of drugs. He thought, well I've told him, there's nothing more I can do. He certainly wasn't going to ask any questions but he didn't want any grief either.

"I am just informing you, Charlie. Her neighbours will now be watching out."

Jonny heard the sharp intake of breath at the end of the line.

"Look," said Charlie. "If someone is going in and out of her back yard with a key, they can hardly be an intruder, can they? She's spinning you a story mate. If someone had seen an intruder, as she's calling it, then she would have said to them I don't know who it is and they would have called the police."

Jonny was losing interest.

"Just as long as you know, Charlie. I have to go now."

Jonny walked down the street slowly, pondering on what to do next. He wondered if it would be wise to inform Tony. But he knew his boss would not be very happy. He went back to the phone box and called Izzy. Izzy did not usually take calls from unfamiliar numbers, but answered it anyway and was surprised to hear Jonny's voice.

"Look," he said almost shouting at her. "I'm pissed off with this grief you're giving me so why don't you just tell your fucking nosy neighbour that your friend had an early shift and he came by to get some stuff out of his car, which you have kindly let him park there?"

Izzy was just about to speak but he continued.

"There is no neighbour Izzy, you're just trying to find a way to get the car moved."

"He came to my place of work Jonny!" she said almost in tears.

"Well why didn't you tell him then to move the fucking car!" he shouted and slammed the phone down.

He was not going to help her. She had been a fool.

'Thanks for nothing Jonny,' she texted and hit SEND.

48

Tara rarely ventured out into Sunhill town centre as it was a dump and most of the general population were awful but she today she needed a cash point. She had spent every spare moment in bed with Quinn and had completely forgotten that she had no cash, so she put her pen down, grabbed her coat, told Dan she'd be back in five and left the office. The cashpoint was only in the next street so she hurried around the corner with her head down not really paying attention to where she was going and walked straight into Tanya, who worked in the bank three streets away.

"Hello there," said Tanya. "I haven't seen you for ages. How's Izzy?"

"I haven't been out with Izzy for ages," said Tara.

Tanya decided to seize the moment but was trying to weigh up in her mind what she could and could not say about Jonny Devroe.

"Fancy a quick coffee?" she asked Tara.

Tara felt she should try to find out a bit more about Izzy and agreed.

"Just give me one minute, I need to get some cash," she said.

They sat facing each other in the café, round the corner from Tara's office. Tanya wanted to say something but she wasn't sure what, without causing massive trouble.

"I know you're Izzy's best friend," she started. "I am really quite worried about her."

The waitress arrived and placed the coffee cups down and the girls both thanked her.

Tara put her hands around the cup as if to warm them.

"You are worried about her?" she said. "I think this time she's lost the fucking plot."

Tara had spoken a little too loudly and the lady on the next table glared at her which made Tanya laugh, especially when Tara gave the woman a snotty look.

"There's not much I can do Tanya. She's got it into her head that Jonny the fuckwit loves her and she's not going to take any notice of me or you. She seems to think she's the godfather's moll or something, when she's not. She's just Izzy, the bent doorman's bird. They're hardly super criminals. They're just bent the lot of them and like to give out the odd hiding. I want nothing to do with any of it."

"She's keeping really bad company, dangerous company. I've had my say. She won't listen. I told her I don't want anything to do with her. I don't need that kind of trouble."

"I am with you, Tanya. I will not put my neck on the line for her appalling taste in men."

Tanya thought she ought to change the subject. There was no way she could mention the car to Tara. They both took a sip of their coffees. Tara knew that if Izzy saw them together, she would go ballistic. She'd think they were gossiping behind her back, rather than feeling genuinely concerned.

It was still playing on Tanya's mind to tell her everything. Then she remembered asking Izzy if she had told Tara about the car and Izzy had nearly burst a blood vessel, saying Tara would call the police. That stopped Tanya in her tracks. She knew that she could not go any further no matter how worried she was. Charlie would probably burn Tara's office down.

"I can't help," said Tara suddenly, as if reading Tanya's mind. "You know what she's like. When it all goes tits up, she'll scream blue murder and call in the cavalry and that will be us."

Tanya's brows were just about touching she was frowning so hard.

"These are very dangerous people," she said again.

"Which people are we talking about in particular?" asked Tara, giving Tanya her full attention.

Tanya needed to backpedal. Tara obviously knew nothing about Charlie Shields.

"I meant Jonny and he obviously hangs about with riff-raff," she said quickly.

"If you play with feathers, Tanya there's a strong possibility you might get your arse tickled," she said and drained her coffee. "I've got to get back to the office. There's not a lot we can do, until she comes and asks for our help."

She kissed Tanya and said it was lovely to see her then left. Tanya sat on for a few more minutes wishing that she could have confided in Tara.

Tara was not stupid and relayed their conversation to Daniel.

"What are you going to do?" he said.

"Nothing. I am pissed off with her dramas and the casual way she treats her real friends. As for the company she's keeping, Daniel, they're criminals and way above my remit so let her get on with it. Do you know," she said. "Izzy doesn't even know that I've left Simon, bought a house and started divorce proceedings?"

"You are joking?"

"I am not. Whenever I've met her it's Jonny this and Jonny that, and everyone that works in that fucking school. Then she leaves me waiting for her for forty minutes. Quite frankly, Dan, I am only there to listen to her voice. I shall not be meeting her again. And I am not in the habit of saying things that I don't mean."

They went about their work. Tara knew Tanya was holding something back about Izzy back but on reflection, if trouble was coming, she would steer well away. She was having far too good a time in her own life. This time Izzy was on her own.

The switchboard started to ring and Tara picked it up. For all she was the Managing Director she still loved answering the phones and helping people. It was Michelle Carlton one of Tara's favourite School Business Managers, the last of a dying breed of sensible educational practitioners. Michelle was clearly upset.

"You sound distracted," said Tara.

"I certainly am. Just had a parent on the phone asking why her daughter, Taylor Dene, came home crying yesterday. So I asked her if she would like to make an appointment to see the head, which is now normal practice and she actually said to me: I am not coming up to that fucking school just find out why you have had my girl in fucking tears."

Nothing shocked or surprised Tara anymore at how any of the so-called parents or things that spawned the poor kids behaved.

"So what did you say?"

Michelle started to giggle.

"I put the phone down on her. I could hear Jeremy Kyle banging on in the background."

"They all have so much to say these fuckwits," said Tara. "But they cannot look after their own children. Why did she not sit down with her daughter and ask her what was wrong?"

"Stop the benefits," said Michelle, still giggling. "Stop paying them to sit in the house all day doing nothing."

Tara agreed.

"And can I have a Year six for all day tomorrow?"

Michelle rang back on the quiet later that afternoon and told her that one of their Year six pupils, who had just left the school in the summer to move up to secondary education had managed to get herself pregnant over the holiday and insisted she was keeping the baby. The rant that Daniel started when told this was legendary.

"Broken Britain! Should be made illegal, who would want to ruin their eleven-year-old daughter's life? Give them no benefits, make the mother keep the baby financially."

Carrie now referred to Daniel as the expert on Broken Britain but Tara came out with the best statement, that education was fucked completely because there are more of them then they are of us and they will never want their children to amount to anything more than they are.

Her phone blipped and Tara smiled as she picked it up. When she realised it was Max, the smile faded from her lips. She looked at her phone and wondered why he couldn't say anything more original than the usual I miss you crap and she leaned over to show Daniel the message.

"God he makes me want to puke," she said. "Wouldn't you think he would get the message by now? I'm not replying. I never, ever reply these days. I cannot be bothered with him. The sex was good but all of that was wiped out by the neediness of him, he's pathetic."

Tara got up remembering that she needed to put the bins out as everybody else had forgotten. She headed out into the back yard towards the electronic gate and clicked the fob. As the huge roller shutter started to rise, Tara saw two legs. Her timing could not have been worse.

"Tara, oh my God, I have been desperate to see you!" said Max.

He stood there, suited and booted with his car keys in his hand.

"I am off to court but will you have a coffee with me later?" he pleaded.

Tara was transfixed by his hair.

"What have you done?" she said, sort of pointing at his head and trying not to laugh.

Max's brown hair had suddenly developed ginger streaks that had definitely not been there the last time she saw him. Max grinned and looked quite pleased with himself, as he ran his fingers through his hair. At this point, Tara very nearly lost it.

"Do you like it?" he asked, proudly.

"Jesus Max you look ridiculous," she said tears of laughter running down her face.

"Oh," he said, shocked at her reaction. "I wanted that sun-kissed look. You know, when you've just come back from a beach holiday. I bought some of that 'sun-in' lotion."

Tara could not speak to him and nearly knocked him flying as she dragged the bin around him, then nearly decapitated him as she clicked the fob to lower the roller shutter.

"Please Tara," she could just about hear him say. "I only want to see you, I need you."

Max could hear her laughter, then nothing as the back-door slammed shut. Feeling totally defeated, he got into his car. He supposed it must be over between them.

Tara was crying with laughter when she told Daniel what had just happened.

"How can that stupid scroat stand up in court, in front of professional people that he sees on a daily basis, with hair like that and expect to be taken seriously?" she said.

Daniel joined in the laughter, wiping the tears from his eyes.

"Never mind that, thank God you don't have to see him anymore."

They carried on working. Quinn sent some lovely texts and hinted that his training session would be finished by 12.30 pm. Tara's house was only five miles away from the training ground so she rang Julie her housekeeper and asked her to bugger off for a few hours.

"You're messing up my routine," complained Julie but agreed to go home for a coffee which was not that difficult, as she lived a mile away in the village.

At twelve forty-five Tara was patiently waiting for Quinn in her bed. She had left the door unlocked and could hear Quinn coming in. Her heart was beating like an express train. It was so exciting and at that moment, she felt utterly alive. He undressed in front of her without saying a word and Tara could see how excited he was. She obviously did for him exactly what he did for her. There was no messing around. He went straight between her legs and licked her making his entrance easier. It was all over in five minutes but both of them were very happy people. Unusually, Quinn jumped out of bed first.

"Got to run' he said. "Press call in…" He looked at his watch. "Fuck! Five minutes ago."

He sprinted down the stairs, dressing as he went.

"Speak later, sorry!" he shouted.

Tara laughed. The shoe was on the other foot today. Usually, she was kicking him out.

Tara got back to work and found Andrea Clark, one of their most experienced teachers, chatting away to Daniel in reception. Daniel waved her over.

"Come and listen to this," he said as Tara pulled up a chair.

Andrea looked upset but carried on.

"I did a day yesterday, in one of the old pit village schools, but I can't do a long-term job there."

Tara frowned, the school did not use Education Supply. Andrea read her mind.

"My friend has just taken over the headship. If I agreed to take the post, she was going to put it through you so I went in for a look."

She put her head down.

"So, what was wrong Andrea?" Daniel gently prompted her. "You need the work now your kids are in full-time education."

Andrea was struggling to tell them. Daniel and Tara waited patiently.

"I cannot tell you which school it is," she said eventually. "But my friend has gone out and bought a washing machine and had it plumbed in, in the staff room. The kids are so dirty that she felt the need to buy spare clothes out of her own pocket. She changes them daily. The kids are filthy but there's also a small group of kids that she's taking home and making them meals. These children are starving and she doesn't know what to do to help them."

Daniel just looked at her. Being a father, it was beyond his comprehension that parents could not feed their children.

"Has she reported this?" he said.

"Of course, she has but after an investigation, the cases are not deemed serious enough so social services are monitoring the situation."

Tara did not agree with the head taking the kids home to her house. This was a huge safeguarding issue. She was pleased that Andrea had not told them the name of the school because this could cost the woman her career. Daniel could see how the head thought it was the only option open to her. However, Tara could not get away from the fact that once again an innocent person was forced to bail out parents, who were completely mistreating their own children.

"Maybe we should bring back workhouses," said Daniel grimly. "At least the authorities knew the kids were secure and not roaming the streets starving. Plus, they would be fed and taught something."

Tara just shook her head and wondered what it was all coming to when the parents were never brought to book for anything.

49

Jonny had tried texting Donna to no avail. She would not reply since the last time where he had to admit, he had gone too far and got a tad heavy-handed with her. Even at work, he could see that she was giving him a wide berth. She hadn't once engineered a situation where she could be alone with him which was a pity. He liked having sex with her but she stayed glued to Tony's side. Tony knew that something had gone down between them but he also knew that Donna could look after herself. She was sensible enough, if things got out of hand, she would come to him. The nights were drawing in and Jonny decided he needed a holiday, some sun on his back. He looked in the mirror and thought he looked a bit pale. He needed some colour for the winter months and he knew just the person to call.

Izzy was busy hoovering and hadn't heard the phone ring. She felt shocked and delighted when she realised that he had actually picked the phone up. She could have kicked herself for missing the call after the hundreds of times she'd checked the damn thing, praying that he would get in touch with her. She rang him straight back. He didn't answer. She never stopped to think that if she had made him wait, he probably would have tried again. Nobody could ignore Jonny Devro, especially when he wanted something. However, all of that went over her head. She was elated beyond belief one minute, in utter despair the next. She couldn't help wondering what he wanted. She secretly prayed it was something to do with the car being moved. Her heartfelt trapped in barbed wire. No doubt about it, he wanted something from her.

Jonny rang her back later and before he got a word out Izzy started gushing.

"I'm sorry I missed your call, I was hoovering."

He didn't give a toss if she'd been shagging the Coldstream guards, all he wanted was a free holiday.

"Right," he responded. "Wondered if you fancy going out for a curry, sixish?"

Izzy thought she had died and gone to heaven. Her heart was hammering inside her chest. He not only wanted to spend time with her but he wanted to take her out for tea.

"Pick me up at six then," he said and put the phone down.

Izzy was left holding the receiver but she wasn't bothered. She made a mental note not to mention the car. She wanted it to be a fun evening and that would only annoy him. It was a closed subject and she just wanted to have a nice night with him and show him what he had been missing. Six outfit changes later she set off to pick him up.

The blue Ford Focus nipped neatly in behind her at the traffic lights but Izzy didn't notice it. She was completely overdressed and over made up. Frank, driving the Focus thought she must be going somewhere really upmarket, not just locally for a curry. Izzy knew she was overdressed but she didn't care. She looked fabulous in the black and white catsuit she had specially chosen.

Jonny was waiting on the pavement outside his block of flats.

"Where the fuck have you been? You're twenty fucking minutes late!" he raged, as he opened the passenger door.

Great start, thought Izzy.

"One of the roads was closed and I had to divert the long way around," she lied and for a split second, she remembered Tara shouting at her outside the village café for her tardiness. "But I'm here now."

She knew that once again she had successfully annoyed him. He took her to the same restaurant they went to before. Izzy tried to make the atmosphere more upbeat.

"I haven't seen you for ages," she smiled at him. "How are you?"

Jonny was still fuming and trying to calm down.

"Bit fed up," he replied. "I hate the dark nights plus it's starting to get nippy."

Tara seized the opportunity and jumped straight in.

"I know," she said. "I'm thinking about going on holiday in the October half term. Why don't you come?"

Jonny perked up. It was like taking chocolate out of a baby's hand, it was so easy. He could not help realising how pathetic she was. He knew she would do anything for him. Izzy suddenly went into organisational mode.

"It would have to be long-haul in October, maybe Mexico or the Dominican Republic."

Jonny turned on the full charm offensive and smiled at her.

"Bit pricey for me, I don't earn much working the doors four nights a week."

"Don't worry," she beamed. She was in her element. "I will sort it all out. Tell me which days you can travel? I'll check some deals out on the computer when I get in."

"Are you sure?" he said softly. "I don't want to be any trouble."

Izzy lapped it up. He needed her to do something for him and she just loved every second of it.

"Of course, I'm sure," she smiled. "Don't be daft. I'll be pleased of the company."

They finished their meals and Jonny kept looking at his watch wanting to leave. Izzy ordered a coffee but Jonny stood up making it clear that time was up. After a lot of back-slapping and hand-shaking from the manager, they left. As they neared his flat, Jonny held on to Izzy's hand, deciding he should put in a bit of an effort. Izzy felt fit to burst. He was different this time she told herself. He needed her. But her hopes were dashed when he didn't invite her into his flat, he just closed her car door, said he would communicate and off he went, no look back, no wave goodbye.

Neither of them noticed the Ford Focus parked up, nor Frank at the wheel observing their every move and giving Charlie Shields a running commentary. Izzy threw her bag on the lounge floor and switched her computer on. She could not stop smiling and went straight for the deals in the Dominican Republic. She had gone off the idea of Mexico. She sorted which tour operator flew from which destination and in particular the nearest airport. By 11 pm she had a seven-night, all-inclusive package from Leeds on hold and was waiting for Jonny's reply to confirm that the dates worked for him. The holiday was Saturday to Saturday. She knew that Jonny worked but she ended up waiting and waiting for Jonny to come back to her which of course he didn't.

When Jonny got into his flat, he received an urgent call from Stevie telling him to be ready in twenty minutes and to get changed. In their language that meant they had a job on for Tony and Jonny was going to get dirty. Stevie picked him up at the corner of Jonny's block of flats and told him on the way that Phil Binder had not coughed up again and Tony was not best pleased. Two grand was a lot of money to be owing someone like Tony and they were going to retrieve it. Jonny could feel the adrenalin rising. He loved a good scrap and even if Phil owed Tony two pence, he would have the greatest pleasure in enforcing Tony's rules.

Phil was having a quiet night at home but when he heard the knock on the door at two am he knew trouble was heading his way. As he opened the door Jonny punched him straight in the face and Phil fell backwards against the hall wall. The blood went everywhere. Phil had actually heard his nose pop with the break and in a reflex moment his hands went up to his face to protect himself. That in itself was a mistake as Jonny kicked him in in the balls. Phil groaned and fell immediately to the floor like a sack of potatoes, now grabbing his balls which he thought were going to burst with the pain. He was rolling over and over on the floor not knowing where to put his hands to soothe the pain that was going through his nose and balls like an electric shock.

Jonny stood looking at him but was distracted by a noise coming from what he assumed to be a bedroom. He turned to face the closed door and could see that it was opening slowly. Suddenly it burst open and a woman started screaming as she ran towards him wielding a bread knife. She held it above her head but Jonny took a step backwards, moved out of reach and punched her right in the face. She also dropped to the floor like a sack of potatoes, legs akimbo, nightie in the air, making Jonny feel quite repulsed as she was no oil painting.

She lay silent on top of Phil. Jonny had knocked her clean out but Phil was too busy trying to stem the blood rushing from his face to worry about her. His eyes were bulging as Jonny grabbed him by the throat.

"The two K you owe?"

"In the biscuit tin, stammered Phil. "In the kitchen," he indicated, pointing with his spare arm in the direction of the kitchen.

Jonny grabbed him by his shirt and dragged him to his feet.

"Go and get it you fucking muppet," he snarled.

Phil stumbled along, trying to make his way to the kitchen, bouncing off the walls in an effort to stay upright. The pain between his legs was indescribable and he knew he'd be heading straight to Accident and Emergency the minute Jonny had left. He tried not to look at his wife, Susan who was now groaning but he did breathe a sigh of relief that she was alive. Jonny followed him after first using his foot to make sure the fat bitch on the floor was not about to get up. He also took the precaution of kicking the knife out of the way of her, just in case she suddenly rallied round. Phil still wasn't sure which part of him hurt the most but he wanted Jonny out, so he gritted his teeth, stretched up for the biscuit tin on top of the cupboard and gave it to Jonny. Jonny counted the money, turned on his heel and left. He did not say a word but made sure he left the front door wide open for anyone to see in.

Phil slammed the front door and gingerly got down on his knees to check that Susan his partner was coming round. He was relieved when she opened her eyes but he also knew that all hell was coming to him for getting them into this situation.

Stevie was waiting for Jonny in the car, nonchalantly reading the Sun newspaper which he put down as Jonny got into the passenger seat and handed him the wad of notes. Jonny started to laugh when he regaled Stevie about the big fat bird that had tried to attack him. Stevie then dropped Jonny off at his flat and gave him five hundred pounds from Tony, as promised if Jonny retrieved the money. Then Stevie sped off into the night.

Jonny glanced up at his kitchen clock as he put the kettle on and flicked the wad of cash over in his hands. Not bad for an hour's work. He checked his phone and had a good look at the pictures of the hotel in the Dominican Republic that Izzy had forwarded to him. Mmm, yes, he thought. That would do very nicely. He decided to confirm tomorrow. He knew even at this late hour, if he texted her, she would reply so he decided to make her wait. She'd be keener. He didn't take much notice of the four-grand price tag.

The next morning Izzy got ready for school highly perturbed that Jonny had not bothered to reply to her texts. She was worried that if he did not get his finger out, they would lose the deal. However, all was forgiven at eleven am when she received his text confirming he would be travelling with her. She went from depression to elation in one split second, without stopping to think he hadn't even said thank you. Then she went straight online to agree and confirm everything. Suddenly she started to worry. She didn't know if she had enough money in her account to cover it. It would have been cheaper if she was just paying for herself.

At lunchtime, she popped over to her mother's, crying that she needed some money to cover the holiday. Izzy's mother wasn't stupid, she knew what was going on. It was the same as last time, her daughter was paying to take a man on holiday who treated her like muck and wasn't even in a relationship with her. She knew that Izzy had also bought Jonny new clothes in the past and could not understand how that man didn't have any money, or could even allow her daughter to keep paying for him. However, she liked to see her daughter happy and smiling so she handed over her debit card. Izzy produced her I-phone and started putting the funds into her bank account. She took the full amount of four thousand. Her mother didn't need it she told herself.

By lunchtime every member of staff at St. Magdalene's knew exactly where Izzy was going on holiday and with whom. One colleague nearly broke her neck to be the first to tell the head, Jackie.

"She's only going on a holiday with a doorman, for God's sake," she blurted out. "God knows what else he gets up to."

Jackie wished the interfering woman hadn't said anything. She wasn't impressed by Izzy's choice of company in any case. Ok, it was outside of work but a school business manager had to be very careful what they did or said. And then there was the Catholic ethos to take into account. Father John would know as soon as the jungle drums started to beat. They all loved a good gossip.

Jackie sighed because she knew Izzy was the wrong type of person to be associating with the likes of Jonny Devroe. She was flighty and quite a silly girl who acted like a teenager at the best of times. She constantly got on Jackie's nerves. More than once, Jackie had seriously thought of getting rid of her. How Izzy looked was more important to her than anything in the world and Jackie couldn't stand all that nonsense. Plus, Izzy believed everybody else was selfish while managing to put herself first at every available opportunity.

Jackie knew Izzy thought the rest of the staff were talking about her. She was right, they talked about her constantly. Izzy gave them more bullets to fire that an arsenal. She never had the sense to keep her mouth shut about her private life and as the school business manager, Jackie thought that was unprofessional. The doorman character had to be the last straw. Izzy spent hours discussing him with the girls in the office. She even told them about the last holiday, when she had paid for him only to have him stand her up. The latest gossip was all about, has she gone and paid for this holiday as well?

Meanwhile, Izzy was on cloud nine, planning outfits and buying new swimwear. She had to look good for him and had stopped eating to shift some weight. She bombarded Jonny with texts which he did not reply to. She didn't clap eyes on him again until she picked him up to take them both to the airport. At one point she wasn't even sure if he was going to travel because of his silence. Eventually, he did reply to one of her more frantic texts, with:

'Of course I'm coming. I'm packed and waiting for you to pick me up, your stupid cow'.

Izzy stared at the reply and could feel her temper rising. How dare he speak to her like that, when she'd stumped up four grand to take him on holiday? It did not enter her head that she was not stumping up anything. It was her eighty-two-year-old mother who was paying just to put the smile on her face. Her mother had even gone as far as to order a taxi to take her to the cashpoint at Barclays, where she withdrew another thousand pounds and gave it to Izzy for spending money. She had never met Jonny but she had that sinking feeling that her daughter would be paying for everything. Thank God they were going all-inclusive she told herself but Izzy was smiling and that was all she cared about.

Izzy and Jonny arrived at the airport, checked in and headed straight to the lounge which Izzy had paid extra for to impress him. But all he did was sit and drink. One passenger even nodded at him as if he recognised Jonny. On the plane, Izzy was hoping they could have a nice chat. It was after all a long flight but all he did was moan about the legroom which again she had paid extra for. Then he fell asleep until the meal came round. Izzy did her best to engage him but he fell asleep again as soon as he got rid of the tray in front of him.

Miraculously Jonny woke again when he heard the plane's landing gear being lowered. Izzy felt pretty mad but tried to put it at the back of her mind. He moaned all of the way on the bus ride to their hotel repeatedly saying they should have got a taxi. Izzy could not believe it when they were the last couple to be dropped off and made a mental note that it was definitely a taxi ride when they were leaving.

It was completely dark when they arrived but the hot night air was starting to relax her and she decided that they would unpack and head to the bar for a nightcap. Jonny had other ideas and said that he was knackered and it was better to have an early night and start the holiday refreshed. Izzy had bought a beautiful, long, midnight blue, satin nightgown but by the time she had reapplied her makeup and emerged from the bathroom, she found all the lights off and Jonny tucked up in bed, gently snoring his head off. She did not know whether to laugh or cry but crept into the bed, trying not to disturb him. She gently put her arms around him but he grunted and shrugged her away. Izzy turned away from him and the tears started to fall. He didn't even want her in his sleep. She dried her eyes and tried to doze off. Things would be better tomorrow she told herself.

The next morning, she woke up and felt the heat burning through the window. She knew it was going to be a gorgeously hot day and looked forward to spending a fabulous day with him by the pool. She could feel Jonny stirring but instinctively forced herself to get out of bed. She did not want to put herself in the position where he could reject her again so she busied herself getting ready for breakfast. She showered and then popped on some lovely white Capri pants and a stunning black and white halter top. Izzy looked in the mirror and admired herself. She rustled a few bags and moved things around trying to get his attention.

"Are you getting up?" she said eventually and finished applying her make up for breakfast.

Jonny rolled over, pretending to be asleep but in fact, he'd been watching the performance of her getting ready. It was beyond him why any woman would go to so much trouble to get dressed up for breakfast and sunbathing. He stretched lazily.

"No," he said. "I'm going back to sleep but bring me something up from breakfast on your way back."

Izzy stared at him.

"You're not coming down?" she snapped, wondering why she had made so much effort.

"That is what I have just said," he snapped back and rolled away from her as if she was dismissed.

Izzy slammed the door loudly behind her on the way out. She was very unhappy but felt worse in the breakfast room, with all the couples staring at her. She wanted to stand up and yell at them, 'I am with someone. He just cannot be arsed to get up.'

Meanwhile, Jonny was happily making a few phone calls and sending texts, telling all the boys that he was going to come home relaxed and with a glowing tan. She walked slowly back upstairs to the room dreading every step. She had decided not to slip anything into a napkin from the breakfast table for him. It was not a five-star hotel that did room service it was all-inclusive and she simply was not going to go around sneaking food for him. Fuck him she thought to herself. If he didn't have the manners to join her then she could not be bothered to get anything for him. She gingerly put the key in the door and pushed it open to find Jonny still in bed. She decided to get her bag ready for the pool.

Jonny lay in bed wondering what the fuck she was doing. Everything took an hour with her. He would have gone mad if he'd seen through the bathroom wall, as she tried and re-tried all the different swimming costumes. Eventually, she came out.

"I'm going down to the pool," she said tartly and slammed the door again on her way out.

Jonny sighed. This may have been a bad idea. She was making him sick already but he decided to get out of bed and read the free newspaper that she had brought up with her. He looked around for the food that she was supposed to bring him, realising that she hadn't bothered and felt very angry that she had disobeyed him.

Izzy had spent three hours on her own when out of the corner of her eye she saw him looking for her poolside. He pulled up a sun lounger.

"God it's hot," he complained and flopped down beside her.

She did not speak until he muttered that he was starving and ordered a waiter to bring him a sandwich. Izzy was still furious but decided that there was no point going on like this, it would end up ruining her holiday.

By teatime, Jonny was olive black. He only had to look at the sun to tan but Izzy was still white. He had made disparaging comments about everyone around the pool, nobody was good enough for him. At one point when he was slagging off a male guest, Izzy glanced down and stared at Jonny's fake Rolex then made eye contact with him. She was clearly saying and who do you think you are? He just gave her a filthy look and continued sunbathing.

By the time they'd had dinner and a few drinks, he wanted to go back to the room and then again, he fell instantly asleep. Izzy knew she had made a huge mistake. He was only there for a rest and a tan. She was bubbling over with fury and wasn't sure how long she could take it before having it out with him. He had made no effort to even kiss her, let alone anything else.

The first few mornings passed in the same way. Breakfast alone, Jonny on his phone having a good laugh with his mates when she wasn't there. But on Thursday, Izzy noticed the car hire people in reception and decided to hire a jeep. She wondered if that might rev him up a bit. She ran up the stairs to their room, key at the ready and walked in as Jonny was laughing his head off on his mobile. He was quite shocked to see her so suddenly but she went straight to the safe and took her driving licence out, went back down and hired the jeep without saying a word to him. Her mother wouldn't mind another three hundred dollars on her card.

When she got back to the room and changed into her shorts, she could see Jonny was wondering what was going on. She did not say a word so he was forced to ask.

"Where are you going?"

"I have hired an open-topped jeep," she said, rounding on him, eyes blazing. "And I am going for a drive. I know you don't like getting out of bed before noon so I will see you later."

She turned on her heel but he was out of bed and grabbed hold of her arm.

"That sounds good," he said, smiling. "I'm coming." And turned away looking for his clothes.

Izzy smiled. Got you she thought. The stupid man thought he was going to miss out on something.

As soon as she drove them out of the hotel complex, Izzy became lost. She could see Jonny ready to go up like a balloon. She was trying to find the seafront so that they could wander in and out of the shops and stop off for a coffee or cool drink. Eventually, she found a car park but Jonny's constant criticism was making her feel very nervous and she fluffed reversing into a bay.

"What the fuck are you doing?" he bellowed at her. Everyone on the promenade turned to look at her. "You could get a fucking bus in there!" he roared.

Instead of retaliating, Izzy burst into tears.

"Oh, here we go!" he said. "Get a fucking grip, you stupid bitch and reverse the car."

Izzy hated herself for crying but she had enough. This was supposed to be the best holiday ever with the man of her dreams and it had turned out to be a living nightmare. She wanted to go home. She managed to get the car into the bay and they set off to look at the shops. After twenty minutes she knew that she was making him sick. She liked to spend a lot of time going over things, whereas he looked once and moved off. They went into one shop that sold designer gear and she noticed Jonny toying with a pair of Prada sunglasses. She felt the need to buy them for him and hopefully cheer his face up.

"Do you want them?" she said.

"Bit out of my price range," he sighed, putting them back.

Izzy had picked up a few things and when Jonny wasn't looking, she made a grab for the sunglasses and paid for them at the till with the other things she had fancied. They found a nice little bar overlooking the sea and ordered drinks. Izzy leant down to her bags and pulled out the sunglasses.

"Here," she said. "See if they will sort your face out." And she handed over the Prada sunglasses.

"Thanks," said Jonny, smiling and instantly popped them on.

She had to admit, he did look gorgeous in them. Jonny was struggling to suppress a fit of the giggles. He knew she would buy them for him. In fact, he'd seen her make a grab for them when she thought he was looking at something else. What a stupid cow she is, he thought, but he still took them from her. All day Jonny kept receiving and sending texts smiling at the odd one or two and she wondered who the hell he was communicating with. She could feel herself getting edgier and edgier and every time she threw a drink down her neck, she came closer to telling him what she thought.

That night Izzy was on fire. First, he wasn't coming down for dinner, then he was, then when he did, he didn't want a drink afterwards but then he stayed for a few.

"Just leave me by myself then why don't you?" she wailed at him.

Jonny grabbed her arm.

"Shut up, everyone is looking at you," he snarled but Izzy laughed in his face.

"And we would not want everyone looking at the Jonny Devroe, now would we?"

At this point, he realised he needed to get her out of the bar. She had been drinking steadily all day and she was only going to get worse or louder. He propelled her out of the bar but Izzy spun around releasing his grip.

"Fuck off!" she shouted. "I haven't finished drinking yet."

By this time, they were in the car park and before he knew it, she had disappeared and she had the key. Jonny went to reception to get a passkey. As he was crossing a quiet courtyard to get the base of the stairs leading to their room, it was pitch black. He heard the click of her stiletto heels behind him and smelled her sweet, pungent perfume before he even saw her.

Suddenly, she grabbed his arm and tried to swing his great bulk round top face her.

"And another fucking thing," she screamed. "How dare you let me pay for this holiday and then treat me like shit. You're just a part-time, ageing doorman with no money and no prospects. Can't even afford to take yourself on holiday!"

Before her drunken brain could drum up the next insult, Izzy felt a sharp burn of pain on her face and some liquid trickle from her lip. She still didn't get what he had done to her. It was as if her brain was struggling to catch up with her body. He grabbed her by the hair with one of his huge hands and the other free hand got hold of her by the shoulder. He dragged her within an inch of his face.

"And you're just a needy, pathetic woman who cannot get a man and has to put up with people talking about you all the time behind your back," he said, through gritted teeth.

He moved his head back from her and spat everything he had in his mouth straight into her face. When he released his grip on her she fell to the floor in a big heap. Jonny did not look back and strode off to the room thinking thank God we are going home tomorrow before I kill her.

Izzy lay on the concrete sobbing and put her hand to her lip. It was blood that was pouring down her face. She felt that her teeth were still there and said a quiet prayer of gratitude. A couple heading back to their room found her on the floor and called the Manager. All Izzy would say was that she had fallen over in her high heels. The Manager said he would go and get her boyfriend not believing one word she said but Izzy became hysterical when he offered to go and get Jonny and she ended up sleeping off her hangover in a spare room.

The next day she dragged herself out of bed and nearly had a heart attack when she saw her swollen lip and blackened face. She did not know how she was going to explain this to her mother or the people at work on Monday. She lay for a while and then plucked up the courage to go back to the room. Suddenly like a phoenix rising from the ashes Izzy found some Dutch courage. It was her room, her holiday, why should she be scared to go and retrieve her things?

She stormed along the corridor trying to get her bearings. Her face hurt like hell. Luckily, she didn't bump into anyone and found her way back to the room. She barged straight in and surprise, surprise, Jonny was still fast asleep in bed. The door opening and closing had not stirred him. Izzy jumped in the shower glancing at her watch. In one hour, they would be picked up by the taxi she had booked, just because Jonny hadn't liked the bus ride. Fuck him she thought. If he doesn't get up, tough he will miss the plane. Jonny did get up. He took one look at her face and actually starting smiling.

"Nasty," he said.

Izzy swung round dropping a dress she was busy folding.

"Nasty?" she said. "Is that all you have to say for your behaviour?"

Jonny looked surprised.

"My behaviour? You were going off, hitting and punching me. You were even trying to get a hold of my hair and you slapped me across the face!"

Izzy could not remember any of that and wondered how much she'd had to drink. Jonny saw her struggling with her memory and found it highly amusing but managed to keep a straight face, suddenly becoming the wounded party himself.

"You went wild Izzy. You were like one of those drunken women we see at Limes on a Saturday night and have to stop them from coming in. You wanted a fight all night. Some of the things you said to me were full-on. The Manager asked me to calm you down and stop you shouting."

Izzy could recall that part and realised it must have been her fault. Then Jonny started laughing.

"I'm going to give you a wide, fucking berth next time you're full of drink. Right trouble-maker you are."

She felt clouded, fuzzy and if she was honest with herself, could not truly recall what had happened.

"What about my face?" she said, pointing at her burst lip.

Jonny gave a long sigh like he was speaking to a petulant five-year-old.

"You did that when you hit the concrete, you stupid woman. You swung at me and then ended up clattering to the floor when you lost your balance. Fucking hell Izzy, you can't even remember what you were like. Why don't you ask the Manager? He'll tell you."

By now, Izzy was dying a thousand deaths out of sheer embarrassment. No way was she going to reception to check out. She would have to give him the key to hand in. She was staying well clear. She had to admit she had been spoiling for a fight with him all night.

As she sat on the plane coming home, her face caked in foundation to hide her split lip, she was sure she could remember Jonny backhanding her. She wondered if she had dreamt him spitting in her face. No, she told herself that was too terrible. He would never do that to her.

50

As luck would have it, though she didn't know at the time when it was arranged, Tara had to go to London on an employment law course. These things were tedious but necessary in her industry. The law changed just about on a daily basis and they needed to keep abreast of changes. Quinn had texted her asking if they could meet up that night. Tara had to decline saying as much as she would like to, and she had never said no to him before, it was impossible. She didn't say why as she liked to keep him guessing but he came straight back asking why so she fessed up and said that she was on a train going to London for work and would be there for forty-eight hours.

Tara had planned on going for lunch with some friends of hers and Simon's who lived in Chelsea. She didn't bother to put the phone down as she knew he would text her straight back. She was correct, but the message surprised her. He was heading to London the next morning straight after training. At first, she didn't believe him. She thought he was testing her to see if she was happy or unhappy that they would be in the same place.

'Don't you look at the fixtures? He wrote.

Then the penny dropped. She googled it. Chelsea v Sunhill.

She didn't really want to confess that she didn't have a clue where he was playing as she wasn't usually that bothered. Then her phone went red hot.

'Who are you with?'

'How long will you be there?'

Then came the golden question:

'Where are you staying?'

Tara never felt the need to play games with him so she answered honestly:

'Alone, 48 hours, the Mayfair.'

Quinn was jumping up and down. The team were booked into the Mayfair at the same time. What a coincidence! His teammates would be green with envy, apart from the few who had women lined up. Tara could not help smiling when he told her the team would be shacked up in the same hotel. It would be quite tricky, he explained as the Assistant Manager patrolled the hotel corridors to make sure the team were behaving themselves.

Tara did not like the idea of sneaking about a five-star hotel like a prostitute but when she phoned Debbie to tell her, Debbie convinced her it would be a scream and very different as he could not leave his room. The Manager sometimes phoned their rooms to make sure they were in them. This was all news to Tara. She had no idea how the world of football operated so she sent Quinn a message, she would await his instructions.

Tara was becoming excited and started planning how little to wear for shock tactics when they finally met at the Mayfair. She also promised to keep him awake all night and see if she could affect his performance on the pitch the next day. Debbie thought the whole thing was hilarious and Tara knew she would keep it to herself. Tara promised to ask Quinn if he had any spare footballing friends but Debbie was having none of that. She was a mother and happily married but she totally got off on Tara's antics.

When Tara checked into her suite, Quinn couldn't enlighten her as to which room he would be in. They wouldn't know until they got there. So, the night was hers. She enjoyed a lovely hot bath and had an early night to appear fresh as a daisy for him the next night.

The next day Tara could not believe how boring the course was and she could not concentrate. She had spoken to Daniel just to make sure everything was Ok at work and told him about the team staying in the same hotel which he knew was a complete fluke. He was also green with envy.

"You jammy bastard!" he said, laughing and demanded a blow by blow account as his was life was so boring these days and he was going to have to live his through Tara. She promised and hung up and went back into the course for the second half. She had her phone on silent but kept checking it. All she wanted to see was a room number. She presumed he would have a room to himself. If not, then it was a huge no for her. She was not letting someone else watch, thank you very much. About three pm she saw her phone vibrate on the table.

'501 xx'

Tara could not believe it. The suites were on the fifth floor and sixth floor and she was 540 so he could not be closer to her if he tried. He couldn't have arranged it, because he didn't know which suite she was in. Now she knew that she could wear what she was planning. Still, a bit risky but not having to go up a flight of stairs or take a lift made it possible. She could not get out of the course venue any quicker if it was on fire. Quinn texted to say that all of them had to be tucked up in their rooms by ten pm, so five past ten would be perfect. Her heart was pounding. Debbie was right. It was majorly exciting sneaking around like a teenager avoiding parents.

Tara had a long soak in the bath and ordered a bottle of champagne from room service, working on the theory that it would get her into the party mood whilst she lay in the bath. Utter luxury, no phones, on her own, no disturbances. She lay there smiling and realised that she was rather looking forward to her evening. At nine-thirty she started to get ready but first, she rubbed Decleor oil into her body, making her skin feel smooth and soft. At ten pm she was all ready and took one last look at herself in the mirror. She had hardly any clothes on and wrapped herself up in her long black fur coat tucking her plastic room card down the front of her g-string underwear.

She didn't bump into one person in the corridor but was aware that they would be covered by CCTV so kept her coat firmly wrapped up. She found 501 and gently tapped on the door. Quinn opened the door in seconds not risking a patrolling member of staff spying her going in. His mouth fell open when he found a near-naked Tara, leaning sexily against the doorframe. She looked devastatingly erotic and beautiful. He could not quite believe his luck. He felt his erection growing immediately beneath the towel tied around his waist. His hair was damp as he had just got out of the shower.

Tara slid her coat off and felt his strong arms around her. In one quick movement, Quinn lifted her up and carried her to his bed. His tongue was probing into her mouth whilst his hands searched and then released the catch on her bra. In one swift movement, Tara felt her underwear being ripped off. She could literally hear the silk tearing in his hands. He was all over her licking, feeling and touching every part of her body. When he entered her Tara came straight away and was actually shocked because that had never happened to her before. He turned her over onto all fours and rode her like a derby winner in sight of the finishing post. She kept saying 'don't come, don't come yet', but Quinn also could not help himself and he felt his release, moaning her name over and over.

Afterwards, they lay in bed but this time they had their arms wrapped around each other which was unusual. It felt different. Neither of them spoke. Suddenly, he sat upright.

"Shh. Don't say anything," he whispered, putting his finger to his lip.

Tara heard a faint tapping on the hotel door. Quinn quietly hustled her into his en suite and went back to the door.

"Yeah?" he shouted.

"Just checking you're in your room, big match tomorrow," said a guy out in the corridor.

Tara suppressed the urge to giggle. He was being checked up on like a little kid on a school trip.

"Where else do you think I'd be?" shouted Quinn back.

"Er, the casino?" said the voice laughing.

Quinn waited until he heard the assistant manager move on to the next room. Then Tara and he got back into the nice warm Egyptian Cotton sheets.

"Do they think you are all school children?" she asked.

"You would not believe what some of the guys get up to," he laughed. "But it's usually a late-night card game and some serious gambling that goes down after lights out. I don't bother getting into any of that shit. The Manager knows that, otherwise he would have come into the room. A few of the boys are now in for a shock."

Tara leant over him feeling for his hardness between his legs.

"Well, we'd better get cracking before we get busted. You'll need all your energy for tomorrow."

Quinn started laughing again.

"Tara, I know that you know fuck all about football but we are shite and are going to get hammered tomorrow."

It did not stop him achieving a full erection and when he felt Tara's soft wet lips around the end of his hard dick, he couldn't care less if the result was ten nil.

Tara realised that they had both fallen asleep. The bathroom light was still on and in the shaft of light Tara could make out the time, three-thirty a.m. She could hear Quinn gently breathing beside her. He was in a deep sleep so she extracted her arm and started to lick him slowly from his neck downwards, then used her knee to part his legs and started to lick and suck his dormant dick until it came alive. She knew she had woken him up and he started to moan and within seconds he was fully up to speed. It was all about him tonight. She still had her little plan which amused her greatly.

By six-thirty Tara wanted her own room and bed back but Quinn stroked her arm.

"Don't go yet," he said. "We won't get called until eight."

Tara kissed him full on the lips.

"I have to go. I have to be in Knightsbridge for nine-thirty. I'm meeting a friend."

To her surprise, he suddenly became quite defensive.

"A man, I presume?"

She did not reply. It was none of his business whom she was meeting but as she gathered her clothes together and found her room card which was by now on the floor, he softened.

"Do you want tickets for the match?" he asked as she reached the door.

She politely declined. She had just closed his door and started down the corridor when an older chap in a tracksuit came around the corner. He couldn't see her face but he must have realised she came from Quinn's room. She suppressed a giggle thinking well that's his problem and carried on.

After she left, Quinn could sense her perfume all over his bed. He loved the smell of her. It was unique, almost like her own identity and for a split second, he admitted to himself that he loved being with her and it was not just the sex. He knew that he spent a lot of time thinking about her, wondering where she was and what she was doing. It was driving him crazy to think she could possibly be meeting another man. He shrugged that feeling off as it was really none of his business. She wasn't his girlfriend, but as he thought it, he started to wonder what it would be like having her as his girlfriend. He had never met a woman like Tara before and knew that she would not take any crap from anybody.

Tara met her friend Jane in Harvey Nichols for breakfast. Jane had moved to London and it was rare the two friends got the chance to catch up. They shopped till they dropped. Tara spent thousands but all of it would be worn in Barbados in January. Not having Simon or a partner was hardly going to stop her annual trip. She loved the island. It vaguely crossed her mind what it would be like going there with Quinn. Then quickly dashed the thought. He would still be working.

Tara settled herself into first class on the train at Kings Cross and wondered what the score had been. She grabbed her phone and googled the premiership results Five nil. Sunhill had been slaughtered but she found it highly amusing to note that Quinn had been taken off at half time due to his below-par performance.

As soon as she got home, Quinn sent a message.

'Eight tonight your place?'

She felt a warm wave come over her. Two nights in a row definitely said something. Shouldn't he be out on the town behaving like a famous footballer? But Tara did want to see him again.

'Of course'.

Normally, she would have made him wait for a reply but decided she was not playing games. He was very welcome to come around. She did not make much of an effort, just tied her long, blonde hair back into a ponytail and wore a pair of raggy denim shorts, which had seen better days. Her bum was half hanging out but she knew he would like that. When she heard him knock at the door, she answered it barefoot and he gave her a long lingering kiss.

It felt different again this time. He did everything slowly. No ripping off her clothes but he made long, slow, lingering love to her rather than the normal frenzied sex that they were used to. Afterwards, they lay in bed together and Tara turned around so she could see him properly. He looked so serious suddenly.

"I want to talk to you," he said, his dark eyebrows, frowning.

Tara did not like the sound of this.

"I want to know why you never say you miss me?" he said almost in a whisper.

This threw Tara completely. He was actually developing feelings for her. So she gave him a jokey, lopsided grin.

"Er, because I don't miss you?" she said.

As soon as she saw the look on his face, she regretted saying it. He looked horrified so she quickly backpedalled.

"Look, Quinn," she said. "You can have any girl you want. You're a premiership footballer for God's sake and I am too old for you. This is great but it is just sex and you do not miss me. You like and miss the sex."

"I do," he said. "Remember when I was on the train to London to see the surgeon about my calf injury? I was never off the phone to you."

"You were on a train," sighed Tara. "Everyone would have been at work and you were bored that's all."

Quinn got out of bed. He wanted to say more, much more but it could wait. Perhaps, he thought when they had known each other for a bit longer, she might develop feelings for him. When he had gone Tara didn't give a second thought to what had just taken place but she was busy selecting a bottle of wine out of the chiller when her landline rang.

"Your timing's good," she told Debbie. "Quinn has just left."

Debbie laughed. Tara was obviously having the time of her life.

"Twice in two days?" she laughed. "It must be love."

"Funny you should say that," said Tara and relayed what Quinn had just said to her.

"Dear God Tara," sighed Debbie. "He's trying to tell you that he really likes you and he misses you and you have just thrown it back in his face, poor boy."

"Don't be ridiculous Debbie. I'm far too old for him."

"No, you are not. Have you had a look in the mirror recently? You're fit and gorgeous and he's no spring chicken for a footballer. He won't have long left. Plus, the girls he meets are only interested in their fake tans and teeth whitener. They haven't got a brain between them. You're a real woman."

"It has to stay behind closed doors, Debbie. He is twenty-eight for fuck's sake. People will think I'm a madwoman and he must be desperate."

Debbie now really started to laugh at her friend. There was no point having a debate with her. If Tara felt that way, nothing would change her mind. Debbie also knew that much of this stemmed from Tara's crazy mother. She married someone twenty-five years younger than herself and Tara had to live with the embarrassment.

"And history is not repeating itself," said Tara, as if she had read Debbie's mind.

"Anyway," she said. 'I am really ringing to let you know that I bumped into Izzy in town today."

"That's nice for you, how is she?"

"Well, she has a bit of a tan, looks scrawny and as if she has not slept in a year. Oh, and she has the scarring and bruise from a split lip."

"Split lip?" repeated Tara, almost shouting.

"Yes, she said she and Jonny had a great holiday but when I enquired about the lip, she confessed that she had been drunk and tripped and fell in her kitchen, whacking her face on the kitchen bench."

Tara could feel her pulse accelerating. The fuckwit hit her she could feel it in her bones and that stupid girl was covering for him.

"Are you still there?" said Debbie.

"Yes, yes. I was just thinking."

"She's lying of course. She couldn't look me in the eye, tried to avoid me by changing direction in the shop."

"I can't believe she went on holiday with him. She will have paid for it, that's for sure," said Tara.

"I asked her if he had hit her and she went crazy in the middle of Debenhams. Total overreaction."

They chatted for a while but concluded nothing could be done about the situation. Izzy would not have a bad word said about Jonny Devroe. They both agreed to keep an eye on the situation from afar.

51

Izzy had been dreading Monday morning and it arrived with a vengeance. She did not know what she was going to tell the people she worked with. They weren't fools but she had to say something. Her face had now turned from black to purple and her split lip still had not gone down. She had a story half-formed that it was a drink-related incident and decided to stick to that. They all knew she liked a drink and had been known to fall over, which she was not proud of but it hadn't stopped her.

"What have you done to your face?" asked Ken the caretaker.

Izzy fixed a huge false smile on her face.

"Oh, Ken don't make a fuss!" Then she looked both ways before answering as if she was telling him the world's greatest secret. "Fell over drunk in the Dominican Republic, on holiday."

"Only you could do that," he said, laughing. "Good effort." And slapped her on the shoulder.

Ken was one thing. Unfortunately, the rest of the staff was a different matter and that tale did not go down well with Jackie the head.

"You look like a road traffic accident," she said with a horrified expression.

Izzy promptly burst into tears. She had been dreading lying to Jackie but now she had to pull herself together. Normally Jackie would sympathise but when Izzy had explained what had occurred Jackie knew she was lying and she was sick of it. She also had a fair idea of what had really gone on.

"I want you in the back office, Izzy," she said. "Away from the children. I cannot have you anywhere near them looking like that nor the parents for that matter. You look terrible."

Izzy cried even harder but she could only stick to her story. She didn't want Jackie to think Jonny had used any sort of violence on her. Apart from anything, Jackie's husband worked in CID. The gossip spread like wildfire around the school and people kept making the flimsiest of excuses to keep coming into Izzy's office, gawking at her like an exhibit in the zoo.

By late afternoon Izzy started to do her usual and the temper started to rise. She had spent half the day crying and feeling sorry for herself but then bam, up it came.

"Fuck them!" she said loudly.

She believed that Jonny had been telling her the truth when he said she had landed on the concrete. Then Joan, the cleaner, came into her office and started sweeping around her desk.

"Didn't take him long then?" she said to Izzy without looking up from her sweeping.

"I beg your pardon?" said Izzy and put her pen down.

Joan did not miss a beat.

"Bit of a boy, our Jonny," she said, still not looking up from her work. "I knew his mother years ago. They used to live in our street until the council evicted them. He was always fighting, even then."

Izzy could not believe how forward Joan was being. She tried to assume some air of authority. She was the school business manager in case anybody forgot.

"He was in a young offender's institute for two years," persisted Joan. "For biting off the end of his teacher's nose in a classroom fight."

"He's not like that now Joan," she said, from on high.

But Joan stopped sweeping and leant on her broom, staring at Izzy.

"No, of course, he isn't love, that's why he's still working for Tony, like they all work in a library!"

She left Izzy's office in peals of laughter. Izzy was furious at being spoken to like that. It never entered her head that the cleaner knew more about Jonny Devroe than she did. But it could all be lies, she kept telling herself.

When she got home, she started to fill the kettle at the kitchen sink. She looked out at that car and something snapped. She picked up the first object that came to hand and threw it violently against the kitchen wall. When she opened her eyes and stopped crying, she realised it had been a bottle of brown sauce, all of it now spread from one end of the kitchen to the other.

She had heard nothing from Jonny since their return from the Dominican Republic. Meanwhile, he was loving the compliments he got on the door at Limes.

"Nice tan, you look good," the young girls kept telling him.

Jonny knew he looked good and lapped it all up. He was even going around telling people he had been to Ibiza with the boys, no mention of Izzy nor the fact he had not once put his hand in his pocket to pay for anything.

Izzy desperately needed to speak to Tara or even Tanya but she did not know what to say, nor where to start. She knew she looked a mess, so seeing either of them was out. Bumping into Debbie was probably not a bad thing. Debbie would tell Tara. She had half expected her to call to ask if things were Ok. But Tara meant business this time. She was sick of picking up the pieces every time Izzy railroaded through her life so the silence had prevailed. They would not believe one word of her story anyway so what was the point?

She sat down to concentrate and try her best to remember what had happened the night she was supposed to have hit the concrete. She had a faint recollection of a biting sting of pain on her left cheek but try as she might, she just could not remember what happened next. However, she did remember Jonny shouting at her and spitting in her face. She wished that she had not drunk as much but she was so unhappy at the way he went on. All was well though when she dropped him off back at his flat. Again, it never occurred to her that he was happy because he was getting shot of her. She'd noticed how handsome he looked with his tan that she had paid for.

The days moved on slowly and Izzy's bruises started to fade. Her mother had not believed one word that had come out of her daughter's mouth about being drunk and falling over. She knew she was lying and protecting that man but there was nothing she could do to alter her daughter's stupid opinion so she let the subject drop. Then one morning she was looking through her list of telephone numbers as she needed Tom the plumber, and she came across Tara's number. She ran her finger over and over the number. She sighed, she had always liked Tara, she was good for Izzy, she put the brakes on her.

She picked up the telephone receiver to call her. She wanted Tara to know what her suspicions were and about the terrible bruising on her daughter's face and her odd behaviour. She nearly dropped the phone when she heard Izzy coming through the front door and limped stiffy into the hall to greet her. At ninety-two she was not the woman she used to be.

"What are you doing here at this time?" she asked Izzy who by now was banging around, taking her coat off with steam coming out of her ears.

For a split second, she thought that Izzy had been sacked. The girl was livid.

"I've been sent home!" she shouted at her mother.

"Why?"

Izzy threw herself into the lounge chair and kicked off her shoes.

"Because, Mum, we have an area safeguarding meeting and Jackie doesn't want my bruises on show."

"Oh dear, this is now affecting your job Izzy," said her mother, visibly upset.

Izzy was straight back on her high horse.

"I told you what happened. It was an accident."

Her mother put her hands in the air.

"Alright Izzy, calm down I just hope you know what you are doing with that man. Nobody is believing you and I can feel it in my bones, he's a wrong un."

"I'm putting the kettle on," said Izzy and headed for the kitchen thinking that even her mum was on to her.

However, what her mother was thinking was why her daughter failed to show one shred of embarrassment about the situation. For the head to send her home was terrible and normally Izzy would have been mortified.

52

Tara sat at her desk, beavering away with a huge grin on her face. Life sure felt good these days. It was as if she had never been married to Simon and felt a tad guilty that she had almost not given him a second thought, apart from the solicitor's letters but all of that was going smoothly. Daniel told her that she was as young as the man she was feeling and that made her laugh out loud. Quinn was certainly a lot younger than her.

They decided to sneak out for coffee. They didn't do it very often but Tara found Daniel hilarious and liked spending time with him. Daniel proclaimed that schools were becoming like football teams. If they didn't like the head, they had the power to get them out with whispering campaigns.

"Plus," said Tara. "We live in an age now, where the head has to crawl up the parent's arses or they will get them out too. Who would want to be a head?"

"Have you heard from Izzy?" asked Daniel, changing the subject.

Even hearing her name annoyed Tara.

"No, I haven't and I am not contacting her. I think this may be it, Dan. I am finally sick of her."

"No way," he said frowning. "You've been friends forever."

"She is not my friend. I have just come to realise that. Your friends don't constantly use you, or upset you, leave you waiting. Oh, and then send you crappy text messages like a huffy little girl. Remember when I took her away for the weekend and my car had a fault? It was broken and I had to limp it home?" Daniel nodded. "Well, I will never forget what she said to me: I cannot believe on a bank holiday weekend that I am heading home. My car was fucked and all she could do was huff and puff that we were going home. I should have told her then and there what a selfish individual she was."

"She's always had an agenda," agreed Daniel, sipping his latte. "Everything is a movie or a drama and she's far too interested in the nightlife of Sunhill and that vile doorman world. It's not healthy."

"Exactly, I'm staying well away from it. She's as false as Jonny Devroe these days, with her fake Rolex and Armani watches and she really does not need to go like that, she never used to."

Daniel started nosing for information about Quinn but Tara was keeping her cards close to her chest where he was concerned. She did tell him a few funny footballing stories, which got him off the scent and had them giggling like kids. They drained their cups and headed back to the office.

Suddenly Tara felt Izzy was in trouble. It was like a sixth sense, she felt it in her bones. Izzy never listened. But something was brewing. It was like when you could smell the rain coming in the air. The rain was coming.

Back at the ranch, as Daniel liked to call the office, all hell had broken loose. Booking after booking came in and they literally did not stop. Even all of the interviewees turned up and they registered some really good, experienced staff who seemed to be clear-minded people who did actually want to work.

Nicky Taylor came in with her spaniel, Flight, to drop off her timesheet. Unfortunately, Flight was of a nervous disposition and cocked his leg up against the photocopier which Tara thought was highly amusing but even funnier was Daniel's face. As Flight was relieving himself, Tara's phone had been ringing and she was surprised to see a missed call from Tanya. When the office quietened down Tara rang her back and Tanya got straight to the point.

"Have you seen Izzy?"

Tanya's anxiety was palpable. Tara felt it coming down the line in waves.

"I know somebody who works in the school," Tanya ploughed on. "And when Izzy came back from holiday…"

"What holiday?"

"She took that arsehole to the Dominican Republic," said Tanya.

"You are joking? Where is she getting the money from?"

"I am not joking," continued Tanya. "And she came back with a blackened eye and a split lip."

Tara took a deep breath.

"Tanya, I'm sorry but she has made her bed, let her lie in it."

Tara sensed there was a whole lot more Tanya wasn't saying. She was right. Tanya was weighing up the odds of telling her all about the car parked up on Izzy's back yard.

"Look," said Tara. "You're ringing me to sort this out. I reckon you've already tried and failed. I don't know why you think she'll listen to me. I do not like the people she's hanging around with and I am not sticking my neck out just because she is being fucking stupid. I do not move in those circles and neither do you."

Tanya knew she was right. If she told Tara about the car, she would only be implicating her in an already dodgy setup.

"I don't even like the way she treats me anymore Tanya. I have finally had enough of her so she can crack on," said Tara, trying to shake off her sense of foreboding. "Do yourself a favour Tanya and stop trying to save her from herself."

"'I have tried, I don't know how many times, to speak to her and she won't have it," said Tanya.

"Well, there you go. If she can accept him hitting her what the hell can we do?"

"The head told her to stay in the back office. She looked so dreadful. She didn't want the parents or children to see her."

"And I bet even that wasn't enough to make her feel crap. She will think it's totally her fault that the great Jonny Devroe hit her. I have said this before, if he stuck a knife in her she would say it was her fault for goading him."

"Well let's pray it doesn't come to that!" said Tanya, laughing nervously.

They said their goodbyes and put the phone down. Tara shuddered as if a chill had descended. It's coming she thought.

She went back to her desk and just shook her head at Daniel. He had an idea it was about Izzy and he felt a little bit scared that Tara could get involved, even indirectly, with these criminals. Hopefully, she meant it when she said she'd finally had it with Izzy. But Tara could not stop thinking about her. The situation must be bad for Tanya to ring her. Then again, if Jonny had got to the stage where he was backhanding Izzy, wasn't it wrong for Tanya to try and involve her?

Tara's thoughts were interrupted by the arrival of a huge bouquet of her favourite flowers, white roses. She couldn't help smiling, that is until she read the card.

'I miss you, please talk to me Max xxx'.

"For fuck's sake!" she burst out. "Take these home, Daniel!"

"No, you should take them home," said Daniel with a wicked laugh. "Quinn will ask who they're from and get all jealous."

That's a good idea she thought. Shame to waste them. She tore up the card and threw it in the bin.

53

Quinn and Tara had decided to get a take-away. The weather was horrible and staying in seemed the better option so they had a great night, eating, drinking and having lots and lots of sex. His staying and recovery power was the best Tara had ever been lucky enough to experience so she was extremely relaxed by the time they ended up in bed all warm and cosy.

Just as she started to drift off to sleep, listening to the steady beat of the rain on the windows and feeling his gorgeous body beside her, her mobile rang. She had left it downstairs. It started to grate on her nerves, ringing, ringing off then ringing again in a matter of seconds.

"That sounds urgent Tara," murmured Quinn.

She glanced at the bedside clock. Six a.m. For a split second, she thought it must be a work message, then remembered it was Sunday and decided to ignore it. Next, the landline started, right next to the bed.

She leant over Quinn, her breasts accidentally on purpose brushing past his mouth. She grabbed the phone as Quinn wrapped his arms and legs around her. She could feel his hardness pressing against her. He wanted her all over again and she felt herself becoming aroused.

"Hello?" she said in a throaty voice.

Tara sat bolt upright. All she could hear was a woman sobbing and crying hysterically down the phone line. The person sounded like a wounded animal. When she realised it was Izzy, she knew something terrible had happened.

"Help me, Tara, please help me!" she screamed.

Now Quinn sat bolt upright.

"Tara what's going on?" he said.

Izzy's voice deteriorated almost to a whisper.

"I've done it. I've killed him."

Tara was staring at the telephone receiver as if Alexandra Bell had just invented it. She couldn't comprehend what Izzy was saying. She sounded like a mental patient, nothing like Izzy's normal voice. Slowly the hysteria began to subside and her friend Izzy returned.

"I need your help," she said in a strangely matter of fact tone. Then resumed sobbing.

Tara knew she had to get rid of Quinn.

"Did she just say she's killed someone?" he asked, alarmed.

Tara summoned up her best Oscar-winning performance of the decade and started giggling.

"No!" she laughed hysterically. "She said she *wanted* to kill him. He will have done the dirty on her and she's probably only just found out. I am going to have to go to her, you can hear the state she's in."

Quinn got out of bed reluctantly. He knew what he'd heard and this had nothing to do with a fall-out with a boyfriend. He could feel the gravity of the situation but she obviously didn't want to involve him. He decided to scarper. With his career, he could not afford to get messed up in scandal, even for Tara.

Tara told Izzy to hold whilst Quinn got ready and disappeared. She did not start talking until she heard his sports car start up.

"Ok, tell me again slowly, what have you actually done?"

Izzy started crying again.

"Ok, put the phone down," said Tara. "And call the police."

"No!" Izzy screamed back at her. "Please come over and help me, Tara. I don't know what to do."

Tara was at panic stations. By rights, she should just tell Izzy to get lost.

"Stay there," she said. "I'll be right over."

Tara drove slowly to Izzy's house. She felt stressed out and nauseous, getting stopped by the police for speeding wouldn't help the situation so she tried to stay as calm and collected as she could.

Izzy stared down at Jonny's prone body. She stood transfixed at the scene around her and then started to go over and over how this could possibly have come about. When she heard the soft rapping on the front door, she instantly felt relief. Tara had come to help her.

Izzy hugged Tara and hung onto her for grim death, sobbing. Tara was still in the hallway but she knew for sure something terrible had happened. The dining room door stood half-open, she crept forward and peered inside. Her breath literally caught in her chest as she stared at Jonny's huge frame flat out on the floor.

"Dear God Izzy, what have you done?" she whispered, not quite believing what she was seeing.

The crying stopped.

"He attacked me, Tara. I am going to have to tell you everything."

Tara felt herself automatically leaving the room and headed for the lounge, where she almost fell into the chair. Her hands were shaking as Izzy proceeded to re-live the evening's fateful events.

It had all started when she downed a whole bottle of red wine and texted Jonny:

'I want the car removed'

When he did not reply, the texts grew more aggressive:

'I want that fucking criminal's car removed from my house now!'

When she was still ignored, she upped the ante:

'If you continue to ignore me, I will have no alternative but to call the police and report it. We both know he's stashing drugs in the boot'

Bingo! He called.

She opened her mouth to speak…

"What the fuck is your problem?" he yelled.

She sobered up in a hurry, he sounded really scary. But at least she had his full attention, which only confirmed she was right about the car. Her anger was back on the rise.

"What is my problem? Well Mr Big, aka Jonny Devroe, my problem is that your criminal mate is stashing drugs on my property. You may think I am stupid and I was, for getting involved with the likes of you, but I am fully aware that every now and again a man is coming through my property and removing, or replacing, a huge holdall into the boot of the fucking car. He's even put a lock on my back gate. My back gate, Jonny, that I don't even have access to any more. I want it stopping, right now!"

Izzy could hear her voice going up an octave, the angrier she became.

Jonny took a beat. Charlie would not like this one little bit and as usual, he was right in the middle. Charlie would go off on one that he couldn't control 'his bird'.

"Look, Izzy," he sighed as if she was only vaguely irritating him. "Just calm down. It won't be drugs. I don't know where you got that idea from."

"Of course, it's drugs!" Izzy exploded. "Right that's it, I'm calling the police."

Jonny realised that this time she meant business. He could hear the odd slurring of her words and remembered that when she drank heavily, she was capable of doing anything irrational.

"You treat me like something you've trodden in and I've had enough. I am sick of it, not to mention the trouble I could get into. I'm finished with you Jonny! Free holidays, free clothes, stuff for your manky flat oh and the free taxi service. And now I'm looking after a bent car for your vile mate. It stops right here."

Jonny began to think on his feet.

"I'm coming over to yours right now!" he barked and hung up on her.

He could feel his rage mounting. She needed to remember he was a very dangerous man. Izzy stood there and realised that something had given. In a moment of pure clarity, she understood that everyone had been right. If she was honest, his coming to her house now was the last thing she wanted. She truthfully never wanted to see him again, ever. A few weeks ago, she'd be in the shower, fixing her hair, wondering what to wear. Right now, she did not give a flying fuck. She could see him in wide-screen glory for what he really was. Bad news.

She heard a car screeching to a halt outside, closely followed by a deafening banging on the door. Izzy flung it open, with a huge tumbler of Jack Daniels in her hand and allowed him to enter. He looked a mess. He was unkempt and grubby as if he'd been lying on a sofa for a week like one of the great unwashed. He followed her down the hall and into the dining room, kitchen area.

"You look a mess," she said, stating the obvious.

Jonny just fixed his evil stare on her. It made her blood go cold. Then, realising he'd come there to lighten the situation and bring her back on side, he switched to that lopsided grin, he knew she found boyish and attractive.

"Thanks," he said, still grinning.

Jonny knew that she was drunk but he had never seen this super-aggressive side to her before and he found it quite interesting. He knew how to calm her down, he always did. He plonked himself on the easy chair in the dining room and made himself quite comfortable, which irritated her. She had other ideas.

"Don't make yourself cosy Jonny. You won't be staying, once you've arranged to move that piece of shit out there," she said pointing in the direction of her back yard.

Jonny put his hands out in front of him.

"Whoa, Izzy. It's not that simple. Charlie's abroad at the minute and won't be back for a week."

Izzy snorted and threw her long, black hair back. Another lie and she wondered if he could actually lie straight in bed.

"Arsehole, I saw him two hours ago bowling along in his Range Rover."

Fuck, thought Jonny. Charlie in his car was a bit difficult to miss so he knew she was telling the truth. He shifted around in the chair, trying rapidly to figure a way out of this situation and then made a decision. It was Charlie's problem, not his. So reluctantly he decided to side with her.

"Ok," he said. "I'm going to try and get in touch with him but it may take a few days to get shot of the motor."

This only threw Izzy into another rage, pacing up and down the dining room.

"Oh no!" she roared, not caring if the neighbours heard her. "Make the call now Jonny, or you know what is going to happen."

He so wanted to strangle the stupid, drunken bitch. All he had to do was snap her neck, he could almost feel his hands on her throat and thought that he was going to burst if he didn't do it. But it was too risky. He watched her bordering on hysteria and knew he would have to make the call.

He picked up his phone, which quietened her down a bit, and searched his contacts for Charlie, who was listed under another name. Jonny pressed the green button to make the call but Charlie's phone just rang and rang and Jonny realised that there was no answering service. He closed the phone.

"Now what?" he asked her. "There's no reply."

Izzy had fully expected Charlie to pick up so now she had a problem. She plopped down into the other chair.

"We will wait and see if he rings you back, or try again in twenty minutes," she stated as if she was in charge which made Jonny snigger.

"Have you any idea who you are dealing with?" he asked her.

Izzy did not give a toss if he was the godfather. Something had snapped inside her. How dare these people treat her like this?

Jonny fidgeted for a while.

"You going to make me a drink then?" he asked, with that stupid grin, aimed to charm the birds out of the trees. It had zero effect on her anymore. "May as well have one while we wait," he smiled.

She got up and put the kettle on. She needed a strong coffee. She thought it would just take a simple phone call and the car would be gone. Her plan was not going to plan. The kettle seemed to take ages to boil, so at the last minute, she went over to the drinks cabinet and poured two tumblers of Jack Daniels. Her glass was full. She nearly threw the other one at him.

"Here," she said roughly.

"Steady girl. Calm down for fuck's sake," he sniggered.

Izzy was standing right over him, waving her glass around.

"Do not snigger at me, you fuckwit," she snapped.

Nobody, but nobody spoke to Jonny Devroe like that and he narrowed his eyes and glared at her. His lips thinned into little lines as he struggled to maintain a hold and control his temper.

"Careful Izzy," he almost whispered.

Whether it was the drink, she did not know. She simply could not care less about him nor what he said to her anymore. Her life was a mess. Her friends had deserted her and all because of him. Everyone at work was laughing at her behind her back, calling her stupid. Someone had said something to the head Jackie, even she had changed towards her. Izzy decided, she had nothing left to lose and it was all Jonny's fault.

"Go fuck yourself, Jonny. Look at the state of you. Not exactly the Godfather. More like Sunhill's finest uneducated peasant."

She'd lit the fuse. Jonny's rage had just seconds to erupt.

"Taking free holidays, clothes and meals from a girl? You're not exactly successful in your chosen field, now are you? You're just a pathetic loser."

He flew out of his chair. The glass he'd been holding crashed against the wall, spraying Jack Daniels all over the dining room and he had her by the throat. Izzy dropped to her knees, trying to drag his hands off her. She couldn't breathe.

"Is that so? You stupid little slag!" he roared, tightening his grip on her throat. "Crawling after me all the time, desperate and needy for a man. Nobody wants you!"

He suddenly saw the colour in her face change and decided she wasn't worth doing time for. He released his grip and Izzy fell to the floor coughing and spluttering. He leant over her and gently put his hands back around her neck. Oh, how easy it would be to finish her off, he thought, then stood up.

Izzy leapt out of his way. Unbelievably she wouldn't shut up. That last insult had stung.

"Nobody wants me? At least I pay my way, vermin. You think you're so special? You're not. You're vermin and so are your friends. You should all be fucking locked up and kept away from decent people."

He lunged at her. She had gone way too far and he wanted to kick the shit out of her because somewhere in there she had touched a raw nerve, he almost felt like crying. He knocked over a glass dish, lunged at her and struck her in the face. Izzy closed her eyes, everything was spinning. Again, she felt her lip burst and blood was pouring out of her mouth. The pain was excruciating. As she tried to wipe the blood away with the back of her hand the room started swaying and she staggered around like a newborn lamb taking its first steps.

"Stupid cunt!" Jonny screamed at her. "Who the fuck do you think you're talking to?"

She felt him dragging her up from the floor. She hadn't realised that she had slid down the dining room wall when he struck her. Waves of nausea flooded over her. Izzy collected herself and swerved out of the way. She swung around and dashed as quickly as she could towards the kitchen, intending to lock the kitchen door and ring the police from the phone on the wall. Jonny in his panic to get hold of her somehow tripped over the rug and ended up flat on the floor.

Izzy looked down at him and laughed, thinking she had a moment of safety.

"Wanker," she muttered to herself and turned to leave.

Instantly, she felt the red, hot grasp of his hand on her ankle. She thought it was going to snap, then lost balance and crashed to the floor, half in and half out of the kitchen. He tugged on her ankle and pulled her towards him.

Now she was terrified and near hysteria but as Jonny tried to put his weight on his left leg, it gave way. He had obviously torn something when he tripped over the damned rug. Izzy started to wriggle and kick herself free and to his total surprise, he was beginning to enjoy himself. He decided then and there that she was going to get a hiding she would never forget. He was trying to get upright and test his leg out to see how much weight it could take, but in those seconds, Izzy was off to the kitchen like a greyhound out of the traps.

"Come back you stupid little bitch!" he yelled, then laughed. "Because the vermin is going to teach you some fucking manners and the car is staying put, so what are you going to do about that then?"

Izzy froze in her tracks. She could feel herself shaking with anger, he was openly defying her. She picked up the first thing to hand, a hammer. She'd innocently used it to bang a nail in the wall earlier, to hang a painting. She turned almost in slow motion and faced a half upright Jonny. He was using the chair he had been sitting on to try and get the rest of the way up, grimacing at the pain in his leg. Izzy stood right in front of him wielding the hammer.

She looked ridiculous in his eyes and he could not contain himself. He started laughing at her. He laughed so hard that he sat back down in the chair.

"Do me a favour your stupid slag," he said laughing. "Yeah right," he said, pointing at the hammer.

Izzy was losing control and afterwards admitted that she loathed him so much, that she had not thought twice as she raised the hammer high and brought it down with all of her strength on his head. Jonny saw it coming but try as he might he just could not get up in time. He put his arms up to deflect the blow but his reactions were too slow and he felt a terrible, juddering thud as it connected with his skull. He made a funny gurgling noise and as he slumped down to the floor, Izzy could not stop kicking him, she just could not stop. It felt so good to be finally calling the shots. She hated him and fell backwards after an almighty kick to the back of his head. She wanted to gauge his eyes out. All of the months of pent up hatred kept her going until exhausted, she stopped and surveyed her work.

Suddenly, he groaned and twitched his hand towards her. She decided that she may as well get it right, so she stood over his legs holding the hammer way above her head and brought it down with another sickening thump to his head. She heard a distinct cracking sound as the hammer met bone and bone and bits of flesh went flying through the air.

Satisfied with her achievement, she slumped into the other chair still firmly holding the hammer as if Jonny was suddenly going to wake up and she would need to defend herself. She hung onto it for grim death. Sweat was raining off her and she looked at the prone Jonny and prayed that he was dead. She chuckled at the thought that his friends would laugh at him for letting 'a bird' get the better of him. Then his mobile rang, startling the life out of her. She searched his pockets and found it. It was Charlie returning his call. The name flashing up was a silly one so she knew Jonny had entered him under an alias. She stared at the phone until it stopped ringing. Nothing she could do about that now. She had more important things to do and started scrolling through his texts.

Looking at the dates made her very happy that she had finally dealt with him. The texts were nearly all from his adoring female fans wanting to buy things for him and curry favour. She read them and felt sick. That was exactly the crap she had sent him. One text even went as far as offering to buy him a car. That was from a girl called Chelsea and that made her smile. Eventually, she put the phone down. Nothing was going to be gained by reading that rubbish and upsetting herself. She thought he had been in love with her and now she knew he'd never been in love with anyone but himself.

She could not stop staring at him. She felt for a pulse and was surprised at how warm he felt to the touch but he had only been dead for a few minutes and she was never any good at any of that medical stuff. Again, a huge smile wreathed her face as she realised he was dead. It was almost like a weight had been lifted off her shoulders and she was glad. As she thought to herself, if I can't have him nobody can, it did cross her mind that she had become insane.

She went off to the kitchen and made herself a coffee and again sat staring at him wondering what the hell she was going to do with him. Then she became very, very afraid, realising she would go to prison for life for his murder. What about her parents? Her job? Tears trickled down her cheeks. It was all his fault. The bastard had ruined her life and he was solely responsible for turning her into what she had become, someone she hardly recognised. After weeping for quite a while, she stopped. She needed to think and think straight. The only person who could help her was Tara.

Izzy stopped talking. Tara stared back at her. The deafening silence seemed to go on for an eternity. Suddenly Tara blinked.

"Was it self-defence?" she asked.

Izzy couldn't lie to her, much as she wanted to. It had felt like self-defence after everything he had put her through but in her heart of hearts, she knew it wasn't, so she just sat there shaking her head.

"Because if it was," Tara pressed onwards. "We could call the police and explain to them."

Izzy shot out of the chair like a rocket.

"I hit him with a fucking hammer, Tara. Look at him. It was no self-defence!"

Tara also stood up.

"I am trying to work out a solution here for fuck's sake so do not shout at me."

Izzy burst into tears and sat back down. Tara knew enough about the law to realise her friend was in deep shit and had now unfortunately, involved her in the same shit.

"You could lose everything," she said.

Izzy put her head down and nodded, her vision blurred by a fresh fall of tears.

Tara seized the glass Izzy had been drinking out of and took a huge gulp of Jack Daniels. She honestly did not know what to do. One thing was for certain, she would be spending her entire future visiting her friend in jail if they didn't come up with something fast. Was Jonny Devroe seriously worth a life sentence? Tara told herself that he had hit her friend and treated her appallingly. She felt her brain kick into gear.

"Right," she said. "The first thing Izzy is we have to get him out of your house and as far away as possible. Any idea where we can get shot of the fucker?"

Izzy was busy hugging herself, thrilled that Tara was on board.

"I know of an old place about twenty miles away. It's well off the beaten track and we could put him in the river there. It's in the middle of an old estate. The big house is in ruins and the river has high banks. That would hopefully conceal it?"

Tara scrunched up her brows in deep thought. That seemed a bit risky.

"We could always bury him in your back garden?" she said.

As soon as the words came out, she realised the risk factor of the neighbours seeing them digging a huge, Jonny-sized hole.

"Right," she said. "Let's go with plan A."

"I can put the back seats down in the Audi," said Izzy, eagerly. "We can shove him in there. It would have been easier if the fucking drug courier car wasn't there but with the roller shutter open, I can reverse halfway in and nobody uses that back lane at night. Its pitch black because there are no street lights."

"We need a plastic sheet to put him on or some type of large blanket," said Tara.

Izzy produced a folded, thick, plastic sheet from when she had the flood.

"I'd better cover the inside of the car as well," she said.

Tara went back into the dining room, half-hoping that Jonny had woken up and this situation would be sorted, even though he would probably then kill them both. She prodded him with her foot, nothing. And he'd now turned a horrible colour as if the blood had drained away from his face.

"What are you doing?" asked Izzy, coming back into the room.

She noticed that Tara's mouth had formed into a thin line of contemplation.

"I'm trying to work out how much blood there is and how the fuck we are actually going to possibly move him," she snapped.

Izzy immediately felt guilty. She needed to remember that Tara didn't have to help her. Then the two of them started to lay the huge plastic sheet on the floor next to the body. Both girls tried to avoid looking at his face. Thank the Lord his eyes were closed.

"Do you think anyone will come looking for him?" asked Tara.

"Well," giggled Izzy. "If they did, this would be the last place they would come. He hardly ever turned up!"

As Tara busied herself with the sheet, she started imagining wailing sirens and flashing blue lights, police cars screeching to a halt outside. Then told herself to stop it and get on with the job in hand. It also crossed her mind about the new procedure, she'd implemented at work, Disqualification by Association, and started to giggle. By association, she was assisting a murderer.

Together they managed to get the sheet out flat and every now and then Tara kept an eye on Izzy but the hysteria appeared to have dissipated. Once everything was prepared the two girls stood staring at the prone body not really wanting to touch it with their bare hands. Then Izzy disappeared into the kitchen and came back with two pairs of pink Marigolds.

"Hide any DNA," she smiled.

"Right," confirmed Tara. "Good idea."

Then she grabbed hold of Jonny's arms and told Izzy to take his feet. After much pulling and tugging, they managed to drag him onto the plastic sheet.

"Wrap it over him and we need something like Gaffer tape to bind it together," instructed Tara, parcelling up the dead body as if she had done it every day of her life.

It felt like it had taken forever just to get to that stage. He was a big man. Now they had the next problem. Tara could not see how the hell they could get him down the garden path and onto the back seats.

They sat down for a minute, sweating and exhausted. Eventually, the two girls managed to drag him to the back door and then Izzy appeared with the detergent and franticly began scouring the floor, soaking up the blood and spilt drink. Tara flicked the kettle.

"We'll have to wait now until its really dark. Tea or coffee?"

"I'm not trying to worry you, Izzy," said Tara, as they sat with mugs in their hands. "But seriously have we got the strength to get him down the garden path?"

"Bingo!" said Izzy, jumping out of the chair. "I should have remembered."

She went out of the back door and headed to her garden shed.

Tara was pleased she was gone. She needed a few minutes to herself but then she heard a metallic squeaking sound coming up towards the house and went to investigate. She found Izzy at the back door holding onto what looked like a metal trolley, with small wheels.

"It's my dad's," she said proudly. "I'm keeping it for him as he's run out of room. I am sure this will do to get him down there," she said, pointing towards the garage door.

"It will do nicely my friend," said Tara smiling at her. "Once we get him on it."

Darkness fell and after much huffing and puffing and almost another hour, they managed to get him onto the trolley then dragged it down the concrete hill, the angle of slope helping to propel the weight towards the garage door.

"Quick," whispered Tara. "Bring the car round. I'll wait here."

While Izzy was gone, Tara felt petrified that a neighbour's light would come on and someone would poke their head out to see what was happening.

Tara heard the garage door rising and Izzy backed her car up as far as she could without hitting the other car, which she could cheerfully set fire to at that precise moment. She lifted the tailgate of the Audi. Moving Jonny from the trolley and into the back of the car seemed impossible.

"Talk about a dead weight," hissed Izzy.

"Never mind that, pull the hardest you can, one, two, three!"

He slid off the trolley and remained half inside the car. Pulling his legs up wasn't that difficult. When they slammed the tailgate closed, they both leant back onto the car absolutely exhausted. Tara was convinced she had pulled a muscle in her back but didn't say anything. At least he was in. Izzy straightened the car and Tara got into the passenger seat.

"We have to get a move on," she said anxiously.

"I just need to lock up, five minutes," replied Izzy but she was back in two and jumped into the driver's seat with two bottles of water for them.

"Do you know exactly where this place is, Izzy?"

"Of course, I do. Let's go."

They headed for the motorway in a northern direction.

"I hope I got all the blood up," said Izzy but Tara was turning around checking that the body was covered up with the picnic blanket.

"They would need to be looking for it first," she replied. "You're not on any police database. He certainly will be."

Izzy sighed and thanked God that Tara was her friend.

The two girls spent most of the journey in silence. Tara deep in thought and Izzy trying to concentrate, as the street lights got fewer and fewer until at last, they were heading deep into the countryside.

"What's the name of this place?" asked Tara.

"Upton Hall," said Izzy. "It sounds grander than it is. The main house has all but gone and the grounds are in a terrible state but people walk it in the summer. We used to go for picnics there when we were small."

Tara gave her a worried look.

"How long is it since you were last there?"

Izzy thought for a moment.

"Roughly about ten years?" she said.

"It could be an industrial estate by now!" shouted Tara. "I'm driving around with you and your dead ex in the back of the car. Are you for real?"

"Stop panicking, I'm sure it will be in the same state as before and completely deserted at this time of night."

Silence hung over the two girls again and Tara noticed that the roads were becoming narrower, which could be dangerous if they had to stop and give way. Izzy started to slow down and Tara saw they were heading towards what had once been the grand entrance to a driveway, except the stone posts were all but gone.

Izzy drove through the rusty old gates and Tara could hear gravel crunching beneath the tyres. Startled rabbits ran out in the headlights. Majestic trees hung over the driveway making it seem even darker than it already was. Tara wished for the umpteenth time that this was not happening. She couldn't go back now, whether she liked it or not, the two of them would be forever linked in the mystery of whatever happened to Jonny Devroe?

Izzy stopped the car but left the engine running. Tara looked over to Izzy wondering if this was the place. It was hard to know what was going through her mind. She looked wild, moving her head from left to right.

"I'm a bit lost," she said. "I can't get my bearings it's so dark." She hit the steering wheel in frustration.

Tara's heart began pounding.

"Think Izzy," she barked.

"I know but it's pitch black."

"Well get out of the fucking car and have a look," Tara shouted. "Or we dump him right here and now."

Izzy turned the car slowly to the left.

"It's this way I'm sure."

She steered the car away from what had once been the Grande Drive onto what appeared to be a dirt track. Fortunately, it hadn't rained, otherwise they would have got stuck. They drove slowly in silence, Izzy still looking to the left and right trying to find the spot she had imprinted in her memory. Tara thought she now knew what people meant when they said pitch black. It sure as hell was darker than dark here. Without the headlights, you could literally not see your hand in front of your face.

"Look Tara!" said Izzy suddenly, pointing to the right. "I think that's it."

Tara noticed a low wall.

Izzy stopped the car.

"Keep the engine running, we need the lights," said Tara.

Izzy was already out of the car. They had stopped in a small break in the woods and like music to their ears, they could hear the sound of water bubbling away at the bottom of a dark ravine, which Tara was trying to peer at over the low wall. The embankment looked pretty steep and she realised that the river must be at the bottom of it.

"How big is the river?" asked Tara.

"Big enough and deep enough," said Izzy, opening up the tailgate.

She passed Tara her pink Marigolds. Then Tara caught the expression on her friend's face as she removed the tartan picnic blanket and stared at Jonny's prone body. It was almost like she'd forgotten what she had done and she took a few steps back away from the car. For a split-second, Tara wondered if Izzy was finally going to snap, or worse still, run away into the night and leave her with the problem. But she seemed to recover and both girls stood contemplating the task at hand.

A tree rustled in the wind and a bird made a squawking sound which made them both jump.

"Are you Ok?" Tara asked.

Izzy sniffed a few times.

"Yes, yes. I'm sorry for getting you into all this trouble, Tara."

Tara put her arms around Izzy and gave her a big hug.

"Come on," she said. "We're just going to have to drag him out."

They both grabbed hold of his legs and began to pull his dead weight. It was easier with both of them pulling in the same direction and they were quite surprised at how easily he slid out. His head bumped the bumper and Izzy giggled.

"Oh dear," she laughed.

They sat on the ground for a moment to get their breath back. Jonny's face was visible but the two girls looked away.

"We're nearly there," said Tara, trying to make Izzy focus.

They stood up and searched along the wall trying to find the lowest point.

"This is the best bit," said Izzy.

Somehow, they managed to drag him through a gap where the wall had completely fallen and reached what looked like the top of the ravine.

It took ages before they finally got him into position, stopping more than once for a rest. Before Tara knew what was happening, her friend gave out a little shriek and pushed his body off the top with her hands and then feet. It was so dark they could not see his body tumbling over and over, like a child playing roly-poly on a hill but they could hear the plastic sheeting flapping madly all the way down. Then after what seemed an age, they heard an almighty splash and looked at each other smiling. Mission accomplished. He was in the water and for one crazy moment, Izzy wondered if he had ever learned to swim.

Tara was bathed in sweat and in dire need of her luxury wet room but Izzy just kept staring over the ravine praying that he would sink.

"Right then," said Tara. "As the shepherd said to the sheep, let's get the flock out of here."

They returned to the car and Izzy performed a slow U-turn. Streaks of light began to appear in the night sky, as they found their way back to the main road. As Izzy floored the gas and propelled them back to their normal homes and normal lives, she realised that she would never be able to repay Tara for her loyalty and friendship tonight. Tara had always joked with Izzy that you knew who your best friend was when they helped you bury the body. In a million years she never thought it would happen.

Over and over the body had rolled, on its way down the steep ravine, crashing into boulders and fallen limbs from barren trees. The plastic wrapping gave way with every rotation until after flapping wildly, it worked its way free and was left discarded halfway up the ravine. Eventually, the body fell into the water which wasn't freezing, but at that time of night still decidedly chilly. The body landed on its back, face-up in the water. Its shoulders were slightly submerged but the feet and face were out. At that point, Jonny opened his eyes. Everything around him was black.

It took him a while to focus. He did not know where he was and he wasn't even certain if he was alive or dead and this was hell. It was so dark and he could hear running water but as the clouds lifted, he pictured Izzy's face and the adrenaline surged through his body. He started to gather himself together. He felt so cold and his head ached like hell as if it had been cracked open like a shell. He moved his arms and legs and put his hand to his face. He could feel blood and spittle coming from his mouth but he realised nothing appeared to be broken, apart from his head, so he pulled himself up onto all fours and crawled out of the river. Again, Izzy's face popped up into his imagination and it all came flooding back what had happened. He managed to reach a grass verge and patted his coat pocket looking for his mobile. When he realised it wasn't there, he felt his temper surge again. It beggared belief that the stupid bitch had actually wanted to kill him. He did not have a clue where he was but again the adrenaline kicked in. He was obviously in the countryside, no light pollution in the sky. He had to find a house or a phone box and she would not know what had fucking hit her when he found her. Jonny Devroe was alive and kicking and she was going to pay. Big time.

Acknowledgements

A huge thank you to my editor Caroline Mylon. I would never have been able to put it all together without her patience and guidance and to Daniel Wainwright for his input on the cover.

About the Author

This is the debut novel in the Tara Black Series by Tracie Oliver. After setting up and running one of the leading teacher supply agencies in the North East of England for twenty years she decided it was time to pursue her ambition to write her first novel. After retiring she decided to write seriously after spending years being fascinated by teachers and their personalities.

She lives in a beautiful village by the sea and spends her free time travelling to the Caribbean.

Printed in Great Britain
by Amazon

65493709R00208

Cologne

INSIGHT *City* GUIDES

Edited by Nina Köster
Photography by Wolfgang Fritz and others
Translated by David Ingram

APA
PUBLICATIONS

Cologne

First Edition

Printed in Singapore by Höfer Press Pte. Ltd

ABOUT THIS BOOK

Long gone are the days when it was Cologne's stench more than the sweet smell of its toilet waters that established the city's reputation abroad and prompted William Thackeray to comment: "Cologne… is in size considerable, in aspect unpromising and in smell odious". On the threshold of the 21st century, the city is more attractive than ever. The cranes and building sites that dominated the skyline for so long after the devastation of World War II have disappeared. New parks have been created. The museum complex next to the cathedral, initially so controversial, is now accepted as an architectural masterpiece.

The Writers

Apa Publications assigned *Cityguide Cologne* to the sociologist and journalist **Nina Köster**. Having contributed articles to such Insight Guides as *Düsseldorf* and *The Rhine*, her experience stood her in good stead when it came to portraying the unique symbiosis between past and present that Cologne represents. Her fascination for the city's history is reflected in her contribution to the book, describing developments from Cologne's first cultural heyday during the Roman period to its emergence as a modern metropolis after the devastation of World War II.

The history of a city has a great impact on the character of its people. Cologne has its very own rich cultural tradition; confronted by their carnival and cuisine, the locals' piety, pubs and pretty girls, all garnished with copious amounts of the proverbial *joie de vivre*, the visitor will certainly want to know what makes them tick. An answer has been provided in this book by the great German writer and Nobel laureate **Heinrich Böll** in the article "What is Kölnisch?". Böll was in a good position to know: he was born in the city and lived there until shortly before his death in 1985.

The phenomenon of Heinrich Böll himself is the subject of an article by local literary critic and travel writer **Michael Bengel**, who has also contributed to other Apa guides. Bengel deals with literary figures in his article "City of Poets". Having also taken a look at the attractions of the opposite bank of the Rhine (the right) and discovered some of the monuments that the Romans left behind, he takes a look at what's on offer at the Cologne Trade Fair, before finally satisfying his thirst for the city by sampling its famous beer, known locally as *Kölsch*.

Renate Bach, who has observed the theatre scene in Cologne for more than 15 years, covers the topic in this book, including a feature on the life of Cologne's stage institution Willy Millowitsch. **Dr Wolf Bierbach** of the WDR (Western Germany Broadcasting Corporation) describes the city's importance as a media centre in his article "Cologne Calling".

The delights of the Carnival are revealed by **Engelbert Greis**, the director of a local TV news programme *Kolnische Rundschau*; since the mid-1980s, he has reported for the ARD on the spectacular carnival parade on the Monday before Lent and has often written about this famous Rhenish folk festival.

The art historian **Klaus Hardering** is particularly interested in Gothic architecture. You can't get any more Gothic than Cologne's cathedral, which he has helped to administer since finishing his studies.

Born in nearby Düsseldorf, **Dr Günther**

Köster

Böll

Bengel

Bach

Henneke has lived in Cologne for 30 years. He provided the article on Cologne's Neustadt (New Town). Having worked for a long time as editor of the *Neuer Ruhrzeitung*, he is now press officer of the Rhineland Countryside Commission and writes reviews for the Zurich-based *Neue Zürcher Zeitung*.

Marie Hüllenkremer looks at the art scene in the city. Before she took over as head of the editorial on the *Zeit* magazine in Hamburg, this art connoisseur managed the cultural section of the local *Kölner Stadtanzeiger* and worked as a correspondent for the magazine *Art* in New York. In addition, she is the editor of a highly respected book on art in Cologne.

Petra Pluwatsch writes travel articles, features and reviews for children's books. She studied German and history and now works for the *Kölner Stadtanzeiger*. In this book, she reveals the delights of the local cuisine in a city famed for its gastronomy, and also explores the possibilities of cruising on the Rhine.

Dr Gérard Schmidt went to school in Cologne, but rediscovered the attractions of the city only after landing here again after his world travels. He became a journalist for the *Kölner Stadtanzeiger*, then directed the National Theatre and now has a career as a publisher and author of successful theatre pieces in the local dialect. He provided the chapter on the city centre.

Rainer Sattler grew up in Baden in southwestern Germany, came to study in Cologne some 20 years ago and never left. He works as a journalist and photographer and here presents the attractions of the city's green areas, goes shopping and looks at Cologne's contribution to rock music.

Hannelore Schubert, who has worked as a journalist since 1954, now freelances for the WDR cultural department, specialising in architecture and the protection of ancient monuments. Here she writes about what's on display in the city's museums, takes us to the suburbs on the left bank of the river and out into the countryside to discover attractions within easy reach of the city.

The sports scene in Cologne is dominated by ice-hockey and soccer. The changing fortunes of the city's teams and the sporting aspirations of the city as a whole are outlined by **Bernd Stemmler**, sports editor of a private radio station in Koblenz. **Dr Werner Strodthoff** is one of the city's best known architecture critics and edits the arts pages of the *Kölner Stadtanzeiger*. He takes us on a tour of the wonderful Romanesque churches which have now all been superbly restored after the war damage of the early 1940s. Last but not least among the authors comes **Karin Hackenbroich**, who as journalist and photographer, has followed developments in her home city for 20 years. She compiled the extensive "Travel Tips" section, which was translated into English by **Susan Sting**.

The photographers

Cityguide: Cologne maintains Apa's high standard of photography. Most shots are the work of **Wolfgang Fritz**, who has made a name for himself through his contributions to numerous other Apa guides, and of **Margarethe** and **Günther Ventur**.

The book was translated into English under the direction of **Tony Halliday** and produced in Apa's London editorial office under the supervision of editorial director **Brian Bell**. The proof-reading and indexing were undertaken by **Mary Morton**.

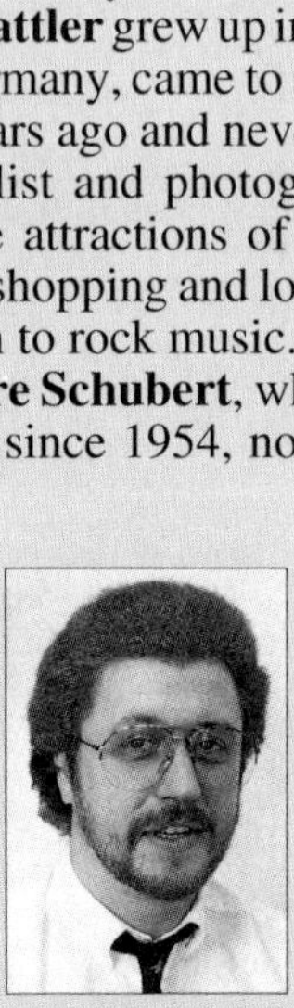

Greis

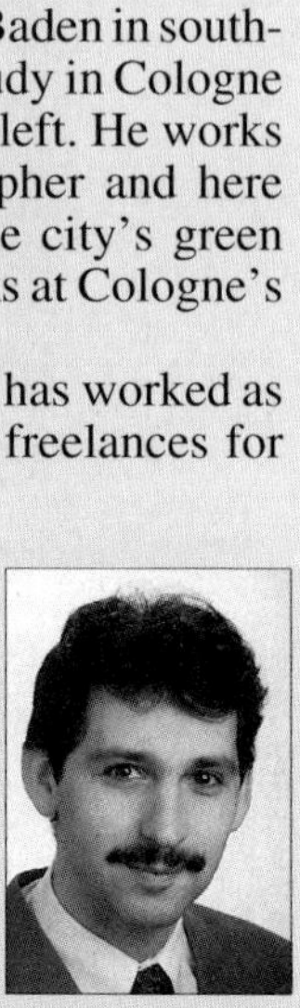

Hardering

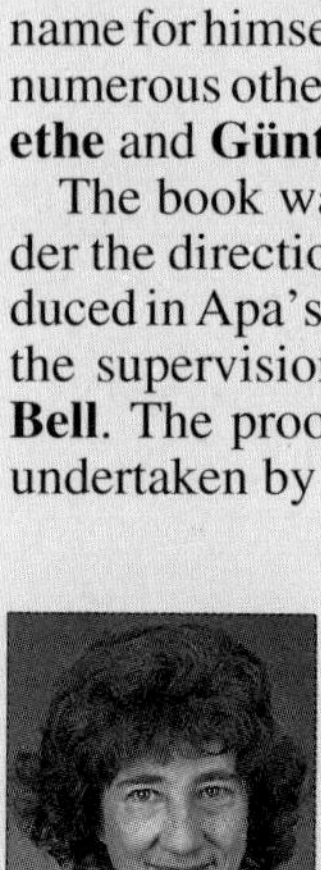

Hackenbroich

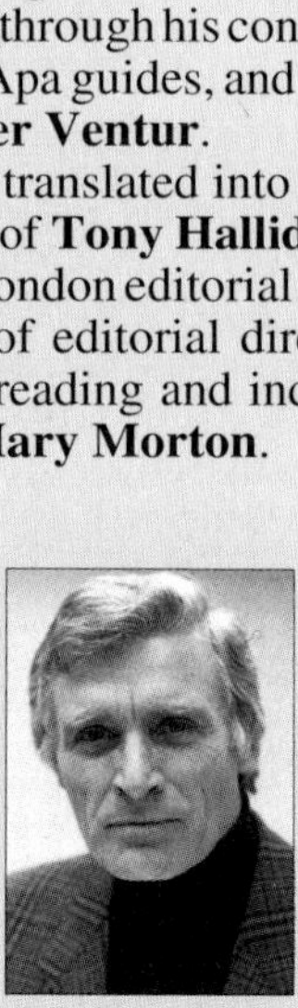

Hennecke

History and Culture

21 **A City of Saints and Salesmen**
—by Nina Köster

25 **Roman Cologne**
—by Nina Köster

29 **Under the Bishop's Crook**
—by Nina Köster

33 **Civic Autonomy**
—by Nina Köster

37 ***Nikolaus Gülich***
—by Nina Köster

40 **Cologne goes Industrial**
—by Nina Köster

45 ***Eau de Cologne***
—by Nina Köster

47 **Destruction and Reconstruction**
—by Nina Köster

51 ***Konrad Adenauer: A Cologne Legend***
—by Nina Köster

55 **What Does "Kölnisch" Really Mean?**
—by Heinrich Böll

61 **A City of Writers**
—by Michael Bengel

63 ***Heinrich Böll***
—by Michael Bengel

65 **The Theatre Scene**
—by Renate Bach

67 ***The Millowitsch Family***
—by Renate Bach

69 **The Music Scene**
—by Rainer Sattler

71 ***Rock 'n' Roll Cologne-Style***
—by Rainer Sattler

73 **Calling Cologne**
—by Wolf Bierbach

78 **The "Fifth Season" of the Year**
—by Engelbert Grels

83 **The Stuff of Champions**
—by Bernd Stemmeler

Places

89 **Introduction**
—by Nina Köster

93 **The City's Major Landmark**
—by Klaus Hardering

101 **The Romanesque Churches**
—by Werner Strodthoff

113 **On the Trail of the Romans**
—by Michael Bengel

119 **The Museums and their Patrons**
—by Hannelore Schubert

126 ***Art and Commerce***
—by Maria Hüllenkremer

131 **Shopping in Cologne**
—by Rainer Sattler

135 **Rhenish Gastronomy**
—by Petra Pluwatsch

141 ***Kölsch***
—by Michael Bengel

143 **In the Heart of the City**
—by Gérard Schmidt

151 ***The City of Tomorrow***
—by Gérard Schmidt

157 **Cologne's Ancient Districts**
—by Gérard Schmidt

167 **The Rhine**
—by Petra Pluwatsch

173 **Cologne's New Town**
—by Günther Hennecke

180 **Excursions on the Left Bank**
—by Hannelore Schubert

193 **The Right Bank of the Rhine**
—by Michael Bengel

199 **Cologne's Trade Fair Centre**
—by Michael Bengel

205 **The City's Green Belts**
—by Rainer Sattler

211 **Into the Country**
—by Hannelore Schubert

Maps

25 City Development from the Romans to the Middle Ages
90 Greater Cologne
92 Cologne City Centre
204 Cologne and Environs
226 Cologne Public Transport

TRAVEL TIPS

220 *Getting There*

221 *Travel Essentials*

221 *Getting Acquainted*

224 *Communications*

224 *Emergencies*

225 *Getting Around*

228 *Where to Stay*

230 *Food Digest*

234 *Nightlife*

234 *Things to Do*

239 *Culture Plus*

243 *Shopping*

245 *Sports*

246 *Special Information*

247 *Useful Addresses*

For detailed information see page 219

Infotec
Opto-
Elektronische
Systeme
fürs Büro

A City of Saints and Salesmen

"Cologne has lost its 'holy city' image: these days its main significance lies in trade and industry", was the complaint in a guidebook written in the second half of the 19th century. Commerce versus the church? Hardly. From time immemorial, the people of Cologne have known all about secular business, despite the reverence they have for their saints. If the two could be combined, then so much the better. In the Middle Ages, the clergy were just as pleased as the merchant classes to see the pilgrims stream into the city. These devout "tourists" swelled the coffers of Cologne's businessmen, and the bishops profited in turn. Indeed, the "Rome of the North" would never have existed had it not been for the generous contributions of its wealthier burghers.

And today? Even in the 20th century, Cologne's appearance is still characterised by a mixture of bourgeois piety and bourgeois prosperity. Its garland of restored Romanesque churches is unsurpassed, its Cathedral unique.

Naturally, industrialisation and the economic upturn after World War II have left their mark on the city's appearance. In the 19th century factory chimneys were built rather than church towers, and in the 20th century huge administrative structures, chic hotels and striking-looking public buildings such as the museum complex next to the Cathedral have all created new architectural accents. But wherever you are in the city, the Cathedral, with its mighty twin towers, is always in view; something doubly fortunate for visitors, in that it provides them with a document of perfect Gothic architecture while at the same time helping them get their bearings.

The people of Cologne forget all about church and business just once in the course of each year – at Carnival time. What the church does for the soul and commerce does for well-being, the Carnival does for the heart. The origins of this "festival of fools" go back to Roman times. Since then, the manner of celebration has altered, but the Cologne Carnival still remains very much a genuine folk festival.

It is seldom that one experiences such unrestrained merriment in the city's inhabitants as in the "fifth season", but that doesn't mean that they don't know how to enjoy life the rest of the time. Cologne's 4,000 restaurants, pubs, bars and discotheques speak for themselves. Indeed, no other city in Germany contains as many restaurants in relation to its population. Cologne's theatre and music scene, too, compares favourably with that of other cities, and as a metropolis of art, it is famed the world over.

Preceding pages: the Wallraf-Richartz Museum bows before the cathedral; reflections of a long history; the swing bridge at the Rhine Harbour; the Hohenzollern Bridge with the cathedral. Left, dressed up for Carnival.

TEPLV MARTINI MAGNI
DO⁹ SENATOR
AD MINORES
S BRIGIDA
S⁹ GEREON
LAVRECI⁹
S.CLARA
die eich porte

TEMPLV S. PETRI ET S. TRIVM REGVM.
AD PREDICATORES
SENT LVPVS
FRANCKÊ TORN
AD MARIE GRADVS
S. MAXIMIN

Cologne has no less a person to thank for its foundation than Roman emperor and general Julius Caesar. Marching eastwards in 53 BC, he very quickly wiped out the tribe of the Eburones, who lived on the left bank of the Rhine and had dared stand in the way of his urge for conquest. Another Germanic tribe was more intelligent, however: the Ubii. Instead of fighting their conquerors, they formed an alliance with them, and the Roman general Agrippa moved the Ubii from the right bank to the left bank of the Rhine, which had been depopulated after the slaughter of the Eburones. The fortified settlement of the Ubii, founded in 39 BC and known as *oppidum Ubiori*, was the seed from which Cologne sprang.

The site of the new settlement was chosen with great care; it was, after all, to form the capital of a province named Germania extending as far as the Elbe. In an area free from floods, on a plateau situated right next to the river, at the intersection of two important trading routes, and also equipped with its own natural harbour because of an island in the river, the "city of the Ubii" had every chance of becoming an important trading centre. Although the Roman plan of conquering all of Germania never came to fruition, Cologne, even in its capacity as a frontier city and later as the capital city of Lower Germania, still assumed a great deal of importance.

The rights of a Roman city: In AD 50 Emperor Claudius, at the instigation of his niece, Julia Agrippina the Younger, who had been born in Cologne and whom he had recently married, granted Cologne the rights of a Roman city. Thereafter it bore the name "Colonia Claudia Ara Agrippinensium" (CCAA), meaning a city with Roman rights (Colonia) founded in the reign of Emperor Claudius (Claudia), the site of an important altar (Ara), and initiated by none other than Agrippina (Agrippinensium). Now Romans from all kinds of different social classes – retired soldiers, traders, artisans, officials and officers – mingled with the Ubii, and they all left their own individual mark on life in Cologne.

Left, the Tomb of Poblicius, now housed in the Roman-Germanic Museum.

The city was then given its first defensive wall. It enclosed an area of roughly 1 sq. km, and it had nine gates and 19 defensive towers. The city streets were laid out like a chessboard, from east to west and from north to south, and the main traffic arteries were the

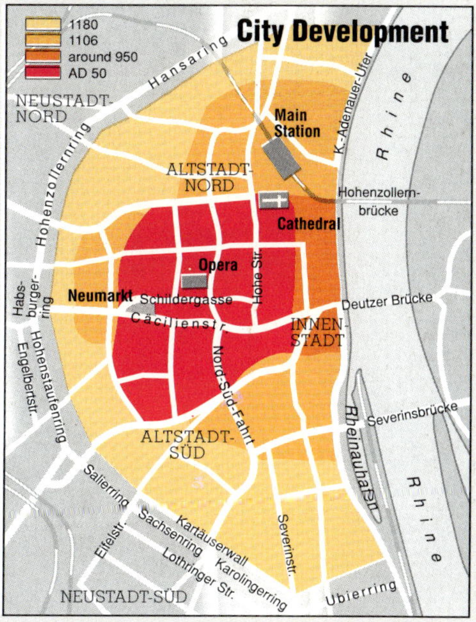

cardo maximus (today's Hohe Strasse), running south, and the *decumanus maximus* (today's Schildergasse), which ran west. The city was provided with fresh spring water via an 80-km (50-mile) long aqueduct from the Eifel Hills; there was an underground sewage and drainage system; and half-timbered and stone houses lined the city's paved streets and generously-proportioned squares.

The interiors of the Roman villas must have been a magnificent sight. Floor mosaics, such as the 70 sq. metre (80 sq. yard) Dionysos Mosaic, which today is the main attraction of the city's Roman-Germanic Museum, were not isolated cases. Even the smallest houses had artistically decorated walls. Excavations have also revealed that some buildings even had heated floors.

No wonder, then, that the Ubii quickly learnt to appreciate the Roman way of life, and in AD 70 they fought on the side of their newfound allies against their Germanic blood-brothers. Germanic tribes rebelled against the Romans on several occasions, and successfully at first. To save their own skin, the Ubii swore an oath of allegiance to these new lords. But when the rebels then ordered them to pull down the city walls and to murder the Romans, they refused. They argued that the Teutons could not expect them to kill their own fathers, relations and children. There again, the Ubii were quite unscrupulous once the tables had been turned and defeat was looming for the Teutons; any rebels still left in the city were murdered on the spot.

However, it soon transpired that the Ubii had made the right decision. Rome's decision to divide up the occupied territory on the Rhine into two provinces meant that Colonia became the capital of the province of Lower Germania in AD 90. As a result, the city flourished. In its heyday, Roman Cologne had around 20,000 inhabitants. The city also played an important role politically and economically within the Roman Empire as a whole. Vitellius, the popular general, was being proclaimed emperor in Cologne by the Lower Germanic army as early as AD 69.

Thirty years later, Trajan, the Roman governor of Cologne, ascended the imperial throne, and one and a half centuries after that, the city was the capital of a splinter empire ruled by Postumus of the Rhine, comprising Gaul, Britain and Spain. The remains of the enormous Roman governor's palace, the Praetorium, can still be seen beneath today's Town Hall.

A trading centre: Cologne, situated at the intersection of several important traffic routes, became a trading centre for goods from many different countries. Brisk trading even took place with the Teutons living on the right bank of the Rhine. Soon the Roman upper classes would only rest their heads on pillows filled with Germanic goose-down, while the women of Rome preferred to wear blond wigs. In return, the Teutons discovered the delights of Italian wine and olive oil, and exchanged natural products such as grain, animal skins, honey and wax for fine glassware, clay bowls, exquisite jewellery and elaborate weaponry. Cologne's artisans were unsurpassed when it came to ceramics and glass-blowing. Production took place outside the city walls to avoid the danger of fire; most houses were made of wood.

The dead were also buried out beyond the city walls, along the highways, as a warning and a reminder to the living. The largest and finest of the tombs were often situated right at the roadside. Many of them were commissioned by their occupants during their lifetimes, and banqueting and battle scenes were popular motifs. Just how magnificent these tombs actually were can be seen from the enormous monument to the legionary Poblicius, on display today in the Roman-Germanic Museum. Poorer citizens were buried behind the ornate tombs of the wealthy, and extensive cemetery areas thus arose, which the first Christians also used for burying their dead.

Tolerance towards people of differing beliefs was a matter of course in Roman Cologne. Roman temples to Jupiter, Mars or Mercury stood peacefully alongside Germanic shrines to goddesses of fertility. The Syrian soldier-god Jupiter Dolichenus was worshipped just as much as the Egyptian goddess of love, Isis, or Mithras, the Persian god of light. Soldiers and merchants from all over the world brought their various deities and beliefs with them to Cologne.

The Christians: A Christian community existed in Cologne probably as early as the 2nd century, and by the 4th century, in the Roman cemeteries outside the city, the first Christian chapels were being built above the tombs of St Ursula the martyr and St Gereon; another chapel was later consecrated to St Severinus. There are still traces of a Christian assembly room not far from the Praetorium. The first reference to the city as a bishopric dates from the year AD 313. It was at that time that Maternus, representing the Christian community of Cologne, took part in the Roman synod.

Meanwhile, the Roman Empire was beginning to show signs of decline. Its frontiers were seething with unrest. At first, however, the Romans successfully managed to defend themselves against the onrush of tribes from the right bank of the Rhine. In AD 310, in order to protect the border, the emperor Constantine the Great founded *Castrum Divitium* (today's Deutz) on the right bank, and had a permanent bridge built across the river to connect it to the city. But in 355 the Frankish general Silvanus, who had been sent to Cologne to protect the Roman borders, sided with his own tribal brothers and had himself proclaimed emperor of Rome. He didn't enjoy his imperial reputation for very long, though: Roman revenge was swift and Silvanus was put to death. That same year, however, the Franks plundered and devastated the city.

Left, the arch of the Roman North Gate. Right, brickwork designs on the Roman Tower.

Roman Cologne never really recovered from this shock. Julian did have Cologne rebuilt a year later, but after the Roman legions were recalled from the Rhine border in 401 it was only a question of time before the Franks took over the city completely. They did so in 450. It soon became the residence of kings of the Ripuarian part of the Frankish kingdom, and the Roman era, which had brought the city such prosperity and security, finally came to an end.

UNDER THE BISHOP'S CROOK

With the arrival of the Franks, Cologne sank into centuries of obscurity. The former cosmopolitan city of tradesmen and artisans became a city of farmers once more. The fact that the Ripuarian Frankish kings had their residence here – as did the Merovingians for a while – did nothing to change things. It was the Christian church that came closest to filling the vacuum left behind by the Romans. Long before the bishops were officially appointed lords of the city they still had it very much under their thumb, and Christian chapels were being built over Roman ruins; one such was St Mary's in the Capitol, built on the foundations of the Roman temple to Jupiter, Juno and Minerva.

A new role: Cologne began to flourish once more under Charlemagne. The Carolingian made the city an archbishopic in 795, and nine years later, after conquering the Saxons, he moved it from the edge to the very centre of the Frankish Empire. His victory not only gave new impetus to the city's economy, it also strengthened Cologne's new role as a religious centre. The influence of the archbishopric of Cologne now extended from the Meuse as far as the Elbe. At the head of the new ecclesiastical empire was Charlemagne's adviser, Hildebold, who first became bishop of Cologne in 787, pontiff at the imperial court four years later, and then Cologne's first ever archbishop in 795. Hildebold started on the construction of a new episcopal church, the forerunner of today's Cathedral, as a symbol of his power.

His successors, too, knew how to preserve and increase Cologne's newly-won influence and wealth. An important role in Cologne's rise to becoming the largest city in Germany was played by archbishop Bruno: he was the youngest brother of the emperor Otto I, and in 953 he became not only archbishop of Cologne but also duke of Lorraine, thus putting combined spiritual and secular power into the hands of one person for the very first time. He also laid the foundations of "holy Cologne" when he had two extremely valuable holy relics transported to the city from Rome.

Extending the city: It was during Bruno's rule that Cologne was first extended, something that was to prove of great economic importance for the city. The trading suburbs which had grown up on the old Rhine island after the former Roman harbour, full of silt, had been filled in, were incorporated into the city and fortified during Bruno's rule. This new trading district was then given the monastery church of Great St Martin's as a spiritual focal point. The collegiate church of St Andrew also owes its existence to archbishop Bruno. But Bruno's main interest was the construction of St Pantaleon's, the first monastery church to be added to the garland of collegiate churches outside the city – St Ursula's and St Gereon's to the north, and St Severinus's to the south. Archbishop Bruno was also buried in his favourite church.

In 1020, a third collegiate church was consecrated under archbishop Heribert on the site of the former Roman camp at Deutz. It was here that Heribert was laid to rest one year later. The valuable gold shrine containing his remains can be admired today in New St Heribert's Church. During the rule of his successor, archbishop Pilgrim (who made more of a name for himself as a military leader than as a man of the cloth), the collegiate Church of the Holy Apostles, begun under Heribert, was completed.

Archbishop Anno II, who ruled from 1056 to 1075, went down in the annals of history for a very different reason. It was during his rule, in 1074, that the people of Cologne – whose self-confidence had grown along with the wealth of their city – first rose up against their bishop. Archbishop Anno II had a lucky escape from the enraged burghers, though their uprising was soon quelled by the superior strength of the archiepiscopal army. However, the conflict continued to smoulder, and little by little the burghers of

Left, the magnificent Romanesque Church of the Holy Apostles in the Neumarkt.

Cologne succeeded in squeezing more and more rights out of their bishops.

Their first real opportunity as far as this was concerned presented itself at the beginning of the 12th century, when the burghers took the side of the Emperor during the Investiture Controversy and thus went against their archbishop; the Emperor rewarded the people of Cologne by conferring on them military sovereignty. After that, in 1106, the city succeeded in incorporating the suburbs that had sprung up beyond the former Roman walls to the north, west and south within its belt of fortifications.

It was just six years later that the burghers banded together to form a "sworn alliance for freedom", in order to protect themselves against interference from the bishops. It was at this stage that the so-called *Richerzeche* was formed, an association of rich burghers for the control of craft and trade; it held its meetings in the "Burghers' House" (Bürgerhaus), the forerunner of the city's Town Hall.

Sancta Colonia: Cologne continued to flourish, despite the friction between its burghers and its bishops. In the summer of 1164 Rainald von Dassel, archbishop of Cologne and a successful military leader, brought the holy relics of the Three Magi back from defeated Milan to *Sancta Colonia*, thus finally making the city the most important place of pilgrimage in the western world next to Rome and Jerusalem. Nicholas of Verdun, a goldsmith from Lorraine, then created the magnificent Shrine of the Three Magi to house their sacred remains, and apparently on feast days up to 100,000 pilgrims would converge on Cologne, thus providing the city with yet another lucrative source of income alongside its craft and trade: tourism.

By the 12th century, the population of Cologne had risen to over 35,000 and so in 1180 the medieval city had to be extended

for a third time. The city contented itself at first with enclosing the settlements that had sprung up around the large monasteries and churches beyond the fortifications within a large semicircle, made up of a wall and a ditch. Around the year 1200, construction work began on a huge stone wall, which on completion was 5.5 km (3 miles) long on the land side and 2.8 km (1.7 miles) along the Rhine bank, and enclosed an area measuring a full 400 hectares (1,000 acres). Cologne was now the largest city north of the Alps. Twelve gates – just as many as "Holy Jerusalem" – provided land access to the city, while there were more than 30 entrances along the Rhine. Cologne's city boundary was now placed so far out that its wall was to last for another 500 years before finally being forced to give way to the hectic pace of 19th-century development. Sections of medieval fortifications do still exist, though, and the course of the wall can still be followed, from the Severinus wall in the south all the way to the Thürmchen wall in the north.

Building boom: The Cologne of those days must have resembled nothing more than one vast building site. And not only because of the new city wall – church building was flourishing, too. Dominicans, Franciscans, Benedictine monks, Benedictine nuns – all of them were busy building. Within the space of 100 years (from 1150 to 1250) almost all of the large Romanesque churches of the city assumed their present-day appearance. The last to be consecrated was the collegiate church of St Cunibert, in 1247.

One year later the foundation stone was laid for the Gothic Cathedral which was to put all the other churches of the city in the shade. Based on the great French cathedrals, a mighty house of God was created, rearing up into the sky; the choir was consecrated after 74 years of construction work, but the completion of the Cathedral as a whole was to last for centuries.

The only reason all this building activity was possible in the first place was because wealthy burghers were donating large sums in order to finance it. Cologne's merchants and artisans, who assumed that they were assuring themselves of a safe place in heaven, could afford to support church-building with generous contributions. Cologne had long since regained its former role as a trading and manufacturing metropolis. It had begun exporting wine to England quite early on, and – alongside Bordeaux – was gradually developing into Europe's largest centre of the wine trade.

Wine wasn't the only major product: the city's merchants were also doing good business with salt and herring, wool and cloth, swords and jewellery, and basalt and slate.

Left, Archbishop Englebert on his shrine in the cathedral. Right, St Severinus's Gate.

Trade was given a further boost in 1255 with the introduction of the so-called "Staple Right", whereby non-local merchants who transported their wares by cart or by boat via Cologne had to pile them up and leave them in the city for at least three days, offering them for sale to the people of Cologne.

No wonder, then, that the burghers, rich and getting even richer in the second half of the 13th century, were also striving ever more energetically for political hegemony. However, by cleverly playing off merchants and artisans against one another, the city's archbishops successfully managed to fend off the burghers' claim to power on several

occasions. However, the showdown arrived on 5 June 1288: the archbishop and the burghers, each with their respective allies, stood facing each other on the battlefield at Worringen. After the largest battle ever fought on Rhenish soil was over, the archbishops had lost their role as the city's rulers once and for all. They were forced to leave Cologne and renounce their claim to power. From then on they resided in Bonn, Brühl or Zons. The only privilege left to them was their right to pronounce death sentences. From that day on, Cologne was *de facto* a Free Imperial City.

CIVIC AUTONOMY

After the Battle of Worringen, Cologne's leading families, or *Geschlechter*, assumed control of the city. Most of them were rich and distinguished merchants, and had already been calling the tune in the city's first autonomous bodies such as the *Richerzeche* or the City Council. Essentially, 15 patrician families in Cologne shared power among themselves.

The university: The merchants ran the city self-confidently. In 1359 they had the old "Burghers' House" replaced by the "Hansasaal". In 1388, they founded the university, the first ever institute of higher education on German soil to be opened by someone other than emperors or princes. The Dominican Order had laid the foundation stone for the university a good century previously with the construction of a college for novices, which attracted several famous medieval scholars to the city. The first ever head teacher at the college was the renowned theologian and scholar Albertus Magnus, or Albert the Great, and his most famous pupil was no less a person than the celebrated philosopher Thomas Aquinas.

The merchant families were more than familiar with finance, and in the 14th and 15th centuries Cologne went on to become the richest city in the German Empire. It was a prominent member of the mercantile Hanseatic League, and its merchants probably had the most extensive connections and the most varied trade of all the cities in Germany. The merchants were only one pillar of Cologne's prosperity, though: the other was formed by the city's artisans. "Made in Cologne" stood for quality and guaranteed good sales. Not surprising, then, that Cologne's artisans also wanted to have their own say in the running of the city.

The artisans had begun organising themselves into guilds relatively early on, initially as a result of religious and charitable motives and only later for professional rea-

Left, the Jan von Werth Fountain in front of the late-Gothic town hall tower.

sons. The most important guild was that of the weavers, and related activities such as wool washing, dyeing, spinning, twining, and cloth-cutting. Gunsmiths, too, as well as goldsmiths and silversmiths were also held in high regard. Even today, street-names such as Weberstrasse (Weaver Street) and Streitzeuggasse (Armourers' Lane) still reveal where the various guilds once traded.

The weavers' uprising: Since the wealthy patricians were rather enjoying being in sole control of the city, and were showing no intention of voluntarily giving the guilds any share in their power, the result was inevitable: the guilds were forced to resort to open warfare. Leading the uprising were the city's weavers, who constituted what was by far the largest and most important guild. The rebellion in 1370 ended with the dissolution of the *Richerzeche* and the admission of the guilds onto the City Council, where the weavers immediately took control. However, in the autumn of 1371 the merchants took the reins in their own hands once more. After a bloody battle, the weavers were beaten, and banished from the city.

So the patricians were again in charge. But not for long. The city's families kept on arguing among themselves, and in 1396 the artisans took advantage of this in order to overthrow the authorities, who were only concerned with themselves, once and for all. The families that were prepared to relinquish their claim to sole right of representation were allowed to remain; those that were not were hounded out of the city and their property confiscated.

Under the terms of a new municipal constitution, the *Verbundbrief*, a division of power was agreed upon between the artisans and the merchants. Every fully entitled citizen of Cologne – which meant roughly 10 percent of the population – was allowed to vote and be voted for. The following were, however, excluded from the very start: women, day labourers, beggars, bondsmen, journeymen, clergymen and Jews. The City Parliament was organised into 22 subdivisions known as *Gaffeln* which, depending on their importance, were allowed to choose two or four out of a total of 36 councillors. The City Council voted for another 13 council members from whichever *Gaffeln* they wished. All 49 councillors thus elected then appointed two mayors. The period of office was one year, and re-election was only possible after two years.

Nepotism: Although well meant, this new

arrangement was all too easy to abuse. Very soon it became quite commonplace for just a few councillors to take turns at being mayors. In the intervals between their terms of tenure they took on other lucrative posts. Corruption was rife. In February 1482, the burghers could no longer contain their wrath, and they rose in rebellion. But the storming of the Town Hall ended with the rebel leader being beheaded. Thirty years later, in December 1512, there was more unrest. This time, heads rolled in the city government. In the *Transfixbrief*, an addendum to the *Verbundbrief*, the burghers' rights were extended, and further controls were imposed upon the City Council.

In 1407 the guilds had begun work on the construction of the Town Hall Tower, as a symbol of their victory over the city families. The construction work was probably financed with money confiscated from the banished patrician families. A few years later, the Town Hall complex was further extended. On the site of the former Synagogue, the Town Hall chapel was built, containing the famous Altar of the City's Patron Saints painted for it by Stephan Lochner. Today this fine example of late medieval painting of the Cologne school can be admired in the Cathedral.

Persecution of the Jews: Just before the Town Hall chapel was built, the Jews had been driven out of Cologne once and for all. Jews had been living in Cologne as early as Roman times. In the 10th century, many of them settled in the area around today's Town Hall. From that time onwards they were subjected to repeated pogroms. The persecution reached its peak with the pogrom of 1349: there was an outbreak of the plague in Cologne that year, and a rumour was circulating that the Jews had poisoned the city's water supply. The Christians' rage was appalling; at the end of what came to be referred to as "Bartholomew's Night", not a single Jew was left alive in Cologne.

A few years later, Jews were re-admitted to the city under the auspices of the archbishop and the emperor, who in so doing were both more than conscious of the income they would generate. But the Jews were no longer needed: the Christians were just as good with money now, and the newcomers

Left, council session in the town hall. Above left, baroque ostentation in the former Jesuit Church. Above right, the Gürzenich, Cologne's oldest banqueting hall.

just meant troublesome competition. In 1424 the Jews were banned from Cologne for good. They were denied right of domicile in Cologne for centuries, and it was only finally restored to them in 1797, after the city had fallen to the French.

But however hard they were on the Jews, the burghers of Cologne were far more progressive when it came to their treatment of women. Even though women were not allowed to vote, they still enjoyed a comparatively large degree of independence in relation to other medieval cities when it came to trade and commerce. Woman merchants and woman artisans contributed a great deal to the prosperity of their city. They were allowed to sign contracts, bring debtors before the courts and make statements under oath; other women in other cities could only dream of being accorded such rights.

There was scarcely any business in which women did not do just as well as men. Stina Waveren, for example, controlled nearly 20 percent of the Cologne cloth trade in the 15th century, and Cathringin Broelman occupied a similar leading position in the steel market. Many women in Cologne were also eager and industrious artisans. They had equal rights in many of the guilds, and in some they even called the tune. In important businesses such as threadmaking and silkmaking, women were left entirely to themselves. Here they were responsible for fixing wages, checking goods, and training employees.

Witch-hunts: This early economic independence did not, however, protect the women of Cologne from being persecuted as witches, just like women everywhere else in the 16th and 17th centuries. Cologne, which liked to portray itself as so liberal, actually played a leading role – on paper at least – in this sorry chapter of German history. The infamous *Malleus Maleficarum*, or "Hammer of the Witches", written in 1487, which provided the ideological basis for witch-hunting as well as being the textbook for torture and executions, was actually the work of two Dominican monks from Cologne: Henricus Institor and Jacob Sprenger.

The city only became really active as far as witch-hunting was concerned in the 1620s. Cologne had not pursued the practice all that eagerly until then. But during the Thirty Years' War, around 30 women were burnt to

Above, Cologne Cathedral took centuries to complete; the state of progress in the 15th century. Right, bronze bust of Nikolaus Gülich.

NIKOLAUS GÜLICH

Favouritism, intrigue and gossip exist all over the world, but the nepotism known as *Klüngel* is a typical Cologne phenomenon. Nepotism in Cologne is nothing to be ashamed of; it's as much a part of the city as the Carnival or the Catholic church. Little tricks to gain personal advantage are the spice of life as far as the citizens of Cologne are concerned; that's what makes life really worth living. Everybody "pulls strings" as best they can, tricking others and getting tricked themselves. And nepotism in Cologne isn't limited to an elite, either; it's practised all over the place.

Civic anger at excessive nepotism has been a recurring phenomenon throughout Cologne's history, but no event has remained more firmly fixed in the memory of the population than the uprising led by Nikolaus Gülich roughly 300 years ago. Gülich, a ribbon merchant, became one of Cologne's historic figures when he rebelled against the nepotism that was rife in the city. At the end of the 17th century, mismanagement, and the preferential treatment of a handful of ruling families who were lining each other up for influential posts in the civic administration, and generally abusing the constitution, had reached such proportions that it took very little for the burghers' dissatisfaction to break out into public fury.

The rebels found their spokesman in Nikolaus Gülich, who had himself been a victim of the authorities' nepotistic practices, but was unwilling to accept that fact without protest. Gülich voiced what many people had been thinking but none dared publicly admit: that the machinations of the ruling clique had to be stopped, and the constitution made relevant once again. Unwavering in the face of repression, Gülich managed in 1680 to have an independent commission of enquiry appointed, and the first conclusion it reached was that certain persons in high office should be immediately dismissed from their posts and brought to trial.

If the City Council had been hoping to take the wind out of the opposition's sails by making this concession, then it was very soon disappointed. The verbal attacks by Gülich and his supporters on the corrupt civic authorities only became more intense after this initial success. The Council finally resorted to arresting Gülich, but it had misjudged things yet again: Gülich's popularity had grown so much by then that the Council soon saw itself compelled to release him.

With more support among the population now than ever before, Gülich continued his fight against the civic authorities. The burghers' resistance became more organised, and in the summer of 1683 they succeeded in putting an abrupt end to the entire City Council.

But the promised reforms still hadn't arrived. The city had new rulers, true enough – but their method of ruling had not changed a great deal. Gülich had settled in comfortably in a new and influential post, and seemed more concerned with having the new civic authorities sanctioned after the event by the emperor than with fulfilling the population's hopes for justice and equality for all.

The emperor, however, far away in Vienna, who had been following all the unrest in Cologne with disfavour now for quite some time, had no intention of giving his official approval to the new authorities. Quite the reverse, in fact: in August 1685, Gülich and two of his leading comrades-in-arms, Abraham Sax and Anton Meshow, were put under the ban of the Empire. In the same month, they were arrested: Gülich and Sax were sentenced to death by the sword, while Meshow was given a whipping and sent into exile.

On 23 February 1686 in Mülheim, the executioner did his duty. Afterwards, Gülich's head was placed on an iron spike up on the Bayenturm, his house was demolished and a pillar of shame, with a bronze effigy of his head on the top, was erected on the site.

In November 1685, by imperial decree, the former City Council and all the other members of the former authorities had already been restored to office. Nepotism was back in the saddle and, as for the constitution, it remained what it had always been from the very start: a paper tiger, its stipulations having very little in common with reality.

death. Even members of the city's leading families fell victim to the madness: Katharina Henoth, for example, the daughter of the city postmaster, was burned alive as a witch in 1627 at Melaten Cemetery. Usually all that was necessary was a simple accusation to set the gruesome machinery of torture, self-incrimination, trials and executions into motion. It could be a coincidence, but it is still remarkable that witch-hunting reached its peak at a time when the city's economy was suffering a rapid decline, and women were no longer playing an important role.

When Cologne was officially raised to the status of a Free Imperial City by the emperor Frederick III in 1475, it had reached the zenith of its development in every respect. Trade and craft were flourishing, and the emperor held the city in great esteem. But less than a century later, Cologne had already begun to show unmistakeable symptoms of decline.

Economic decline: In 1560, construction work on the Cathedral was suspended, for what had once been a steady flow of donations and contributions had now degenerated to a mere trickle. This was partly due to the Reformation, however. True, Protestantism had failed to find a foothold in Cologne, but Luther's theses had dealt the sale of indulgences a sharp blow. Thus, the Cathedral's only provisionally completed choir and the unfinished southern tower with its huge wooden construction crane were to determine the city's appearance for the next 300 years or so.

But Cologne hadn't yet lost all of its grandeur. In 1561, the Staple House beside the Rhine was completed, in 1573 the Town Hall received a magnificent Renaissance Loggia, and the city's Arsenal (Zeughaus) was finished around 1600. Cologne had already been given its most important municipal building, next to the Town Hall, in 1444: the magnificent Gothic banqueting and festival hall known as the Gürzenich. Emperors and princes were frequent visitors to this "grand and marvellous dancing hall", as one contemporary described it. Emperor Frederick III enjoyed holding banquets here just as much as his son Maximilian, or the emperor Charles V. Splendid gatherings, often with more than a thousand guests, were quite a common occurrence in the Gürzenich.

The only church worthy of note to have been built at that time was the Church of the Assumption (St Maria Himmelfahrt), begun in 1618 and consecrated in 1678, one of the most important Jesuit buildings in Germany and the largest Baroque church in Cologne. With this magnificent construction, the Jesuits – who had become a spearhead of the Counter Reformation in Cologne – succeeded in giving physical expression to their religious credo: its Gothic and Romanesque elements bear witness to the traditions of earlier epochs.

The Thirty Years' War: Displaying their characteristic inclination to avoid major confrontations if at all possible, the burghers of Cologne succeeded in keeping their city out of the turmoil of the Thirty Years' War (1618–48). While half of Europe was being reduced to ashes, Cologne did good wartime business: it provided the troops with weapons, provisions and clothing. But even this could not stave off the city's decline.

Cologne, spoilt by success, was unable to find any recipe for dealing with the continual shifts in the world's economy; its merchants were helpless as long-distance trade shifted to ocean-going traffic after the discovery of America, and its artisans were helpless too, in the face of new products and new production methods. So, instead, they clung stubbornly to outmoded customs and habits, dodged anything involving any kind of risk, and steered clear of all innovations.

In the 17th century, as the city's trade and craft became less and less important, corruption and the proverbial Cologne brand of nepotism known as *Klüngel* increased as never before. Under the leadership of ribbon merchant Nikolaus Gülich, the City Parliament succeeded in having an impartial commission of inquiry set up, which went on to drive the mayors, councillors and several administrative officials out of office before placing itself in charge of the city. Gülich's attempts at reform did not meet with the approval of the emperor, however. Gülich and his colleagues were declared violators of the peace, arrested, and then publicly beheaded in February 1686.

A full century was to pass before this "rebel against nepotism" was done proper justice, albeit rather too late: Gülich was posthumously honoured as a freedom fighter by the French when they entered the city in October 1794, after the Revolution. The arrival of the French, however, also marked the end of Cologne's era as a Free Imperial City.

Left, the "Cologne Farmer" at the Eigelstein Gate. Above, the old arsenal (Zeughaus) now houses the municipal museum.

COLOGNE GOES INDUSTRIAL

On 6 October 1794, the day the French entered the city, everything changed. The event marked not only the demise of Cologne's long period of civic autonomy, but also the end of the Middle Ages. Liberty, equality and fraternity were the watchwords of the French Revolution. The Tree of Liberty became the symbol of the new era. Just three days after the French marched in, the first Tree of Liberty had already been set up during a ceremony in the city's Neumarkt. Bit by bit, the old order disintegrated.

In place of the special courts customary until then, a standard system of justice, Napoleon's *Code Civil*, was introduced. The city's economy was also given a boost with the dissolution of the guilds. Moreover, the right to practise their religion without hindrance turned Jews and Protestants, after centuries of persecution and discrimination, into fully-fledged Cologne citizens, and this also found its expression in the economic life of the city, where Jews and Protestants were soon occupying leading positions thanks to their readiness to innovate and to take risks.

Secularisation: Most far-reaching of all, however, was secularisation, which shook the Catholic church – until then it had occupied an all-powerful position – to its very foundations. Convents and monasteries were expropriated, their treasures sold or destroyed, their buildings torn down or turned into warehouses, factories or hospitals. A few parish churches remained unscathed by secularisation, which is the reason why some collegiate and monastic churches hastily passed themselves off as parish ones, thus escaping destruction. The reason most people in Cologne don't like to talk about those 20 years of French rule is probably largely because of the rough treatment the Catholic Church received.

Nevertheless, while the French era had begun promisingly enough, the same cannot

Right, the equestrian statue of King Frederick William IV at the east end of the Hohenzollern Bridge.

be said of the start of the Prussian era. The decision taken at the Congress of Vienna in 1815 to award the left bank of the Rhine, and thus Cologne as well, to Prussia was not well received in the city. The mentalities were too different: the Rhinelanders, such lovers of life, on the one hand, and the duty-conscious Prussians on the other. The fact that not Cologne but Koblenz had been made the centre of the Prussian province on the Rhine in 1822, and that Cologne's university, closed by the French, had not been re-opened since, only served to fuel Cologne's resentment. Nevertheless, the Prussians had big plans for Cologne. Within just a few years it had been turned into the most important fortified city on the Rhine. Forts and other defensive installations sprang up around the medieval city wall, and large barracks were built in the Neumarkt and in Deutz.

Full steam ahead: However, a crucial role as far as the development of the city over the next decades was concerned was played by something else entirely: the invention of the steam-engine. In June 1816 a steamer moored in Cologne for the very first time; in 1828 the first industrial steam-engine began operations in a Cologne corn mill; and in August 1839 a steam train made its first-ever trip from Cologne to Müngersdorf. By mid-century there were already several dozen steam engines in operation in Cologne. The modern era had arrived.

Visible signs of the new age, apart from the tall factory chimneys everywhere, were the railway station, which was built right next to the Cathedral, and the first permanent Rhine bridge ever to be constructed since Roman times, completed in 1859. At the request of King Frederick William IV the road and rail bridge – the forerunner of today's Hohenzollern Bridge – was aligned precisely with the choir of the Cathedral.

From 1842 onwards, the Cathedral was a building site once more. As he laid the foundation stone for the extension work, the King said that the main body of the great Cathedral was to be completed as a symbol of "German unity and strength". In 1880, the work was finished. But what should have been a triumph for the Catholic church instead fell victim to the general quarrel between church and state that Bismarck had provoked: the great celebration in the Cathedral took place in the absence of the city's archbishop – he was living in exile.

But not only the Cathedral was surrounded by construction cranes in the mid-19th century; new tenement blocks and new factories were springing up all over the place. Many of the city's artisans saw their chance, and switched over to mass production. New technology quickly gained a foothold, above all in the textile industry, the breweries, sugar refineries, mills and metalworks, and it brought several Cologne citizens wealth and respectability.

Nikolaus August Otto became world-famous when he developed the world's first four-stroke internal-combustion engine at his factory in Deutz. The internationally famous firm of Klöckner-Humboldt-Deutz developed from this factory, which was founded in 1864. Another firm of international importance, the cablemaking firm of Felten & Guilleaume, was founded by master ropemaker Theodor Felten and his son-in-law Carl Guilleaume in 1826. Franz Stollwerck, a confectioner, made his fortune with the industrial manufacture of cough sweets and cakes. Sugar refineries made Carl Joest the richest man in Cologne.

Mass misery: This economic upswing was paid for dearly, however, by mass misery. Up to 16 hours' work a day, preposterously low wages, women and children being forced out to work, dark and damp tenements – this was the harsh reality facing most of the working people of Cologne in the 19th century. Considering these conditions, it is astounding that no blood was shed in the city during the revolutionary year of 1848.

Perhaps the strong presence of the Prussian military nipped any inclination to start an armed uprising in the bud. Even Karl Marx – co-editor of the *Neue Rheinische Zeitung* with Friedrich Engels in Cologne at that time – who called upon the populace in the Gürzenich to begin the class struggle was unable to bring the revolution to Cologne.

After the failure of the 1848 revolution the city experienced an unparalleled surge of growth. It was not long before the last remaining open spaces within the medieval city walls had been built up. New housing estates and factory areas thus began to appear beyond the fortifications, out in front of the city gates. Cologne's first suburbs developed along the major arterial roads to the north and south: Nippes and Bayenthal. Ehrenfeld grew up in the west and, on the right bank of the Rhine, Kalk and Mülheim.

Left, the French left their mark on the city – street names were written in both languages. Above, the erection of the tree of liberty in the Neumarkt.

The New Town: The old city wall, nearly 600 years old by then, was proving more and more of a hindrance. In 1881, after lengthy negotiations, the city finally managed to acquire the area beyond the walls, fortified by the Prussians, for 12 million gold marks. In June of the same year, work began on dismantling the wall. Only St Severinus's Gate in the south, the Cockerel Gate in the west and the Eigelstein Gate in the north were allowed to remain, along with a few other smaller structures.

It then took less than 20 years for the New Town (Neustadt) to be built according to plans drawn up by city architect Joseph

Stübben; it was based on the Ring Roads of Vienna, and extended around the Old City in a semicircle. Cologne was now roughly 236 hectares (600 acres) larger in size.

Only a few years later, the city expanded yet again. On 1 April 1888 the communities surrounding Cologne were incorporated into the city itself. The new city limits on the left bank of the Rhine now extended along the Militärringstrasse, and, in addition to encompassing the Old City and New Town, they also included the new suburbs of Ehrenfeld, Nippes, Bayenthal, Lindenthal, Sülz and Zollstock, as well as the older rural parishes of Müngersdorf, Longerich, Bocklemünd, Mengenich, Volkhoven and Weidenpesch. On the right bank of the Rhine, Deutz and Poll were also included.

The city's surface area had thus increased tenfold to more than 11,000 hectares (27,000 acres), making Cologne, in terms of the land it occupied, the largest city in Germany – just as in medieval times. The number of inhabitants increased by around 80,000 to more than 260,000.

The fact that the population of Cologne actually doubled before 1910 makes it clear just how rapidly the city grew during the years that followed. No wonder the city authorities were already considering incorporating even more suburbs. In 1910 Cologne swallowed up the towns of Kalk and Vingst, and in 1914 Mülheim and Merheim. For the first time ever in the city's history, the areas to the right and left of the Rhine were now roughly the same size. At the outbreak of World War I, Cologne covered an area of 20,000 hectares (80 sq. miles), and had a population of over 630,000.

Left, complete but still a building site: inspecting damage to the cathedral. Right, a French corporal numbering house No. 4711 in the Glockengasse.

EAU DE COLOGNE

Johann Wolfgang von Goethe thought very highly of it, Wilhelm Raabe attributed life-saving powers to it, and Napoleon Bonaparte's officers gave it its name: Eau de Cologne. No other Cologne product is so inextricably linked to the city as this subtle mixture of ethyl alcohol, orange, lavender and other essential oils matured in wooden casks, and its precise recipe has been a rigorously well-kept secret for generations.

The city may contain more important firms – the automobile manufacturing company of Ford, for example, Cologne's largest employer, or the mechanical engineering firm of Klöckner-Humboldt-Deutz, responsible for the historic development of the Otto engine – but you'll find that the famous perfume is still always the only name to be mentioned all over the world in the same breath as the Cathedral.

Strangely enough, the mixture was originally created as a medicine – good, it was claimed, for curing heart trouble, gout, coughs, the plague and all sorts of other nasty diseases. The reason it didn't remain one is thanks to Napoleon: in 1810 he issued an imperial decree ordering the recipes for all medical remedies to be handed over.

This created a thorny commercial dilemma. Faced with the choice of either having to reveal their secret or to sell their product as a perfume in future, the makers of *Kölnisch Wasser* – and there were several of them at the time – decided to switch to the camp of toiletry article manufacturers and have their product struck off the medical list altogether. This was how the Eau de Cologne so familiar to us today was born, and it soon became incredibly popular with Napoleon's officers. Its aromatic perfume was just the kind of amorous souvenir to suit French tastes.

Today, roughly 20 different firms in Cologne produce the famous perfume. Only two of them, however, were there from the very start: the firm of "Johann Maria Farina opposite the Jülichs Platz GmbH", founded in 1709, who were the first to put the *Eau Admirable* on the market, and the firm of "Ferd. Mülhens Eau de Cologne and Perfume-factory No. 4711 Glockengasse opposite the mail-coach station in Cologne on the Rhine", founded in 1792 and known as 4711 for short.

As for the origins of the perfume, nobody is all that sure. Farina is supposed to have obtained his recipe from an Italian compatriot named Giovanni Paolo Feminis, and at No. 4711 the story goes that the banker's son Wilhelm Mülhens was given the precious formula as a wedding present by a Carthusian monk. Since that time the newer firm has successfully drained off a lot of "Eau" from the older one, and the French had their share of responsibility here, too.

For it was a French corporal who wrote the house-number 4711 on the Mühlens' home in the city's elegant Glockengasse while the French were numbering the city's buildings, thereby giving Wilhelm Mühlens the brilliant idea of labelling his flasks with precisely this number and providing his perfume with an unmistakeable brand-name. No wonder that the descendants of the banker's son are still retaining the legendary 4711 number, even though a whole range of new products – among them "Tosca" and "SIR" – are also making the cash-registers ring these days and have already achieved the status of classics.

Anyone who wants to contact the most famous firm in Cologne by phone only needs to dial 4711, and for anyone interested in the firm's history, No. 4711 Glockengasse is definitely the right address. Here, the Mülhens family has painstakingly reconstructed its original headquarters, destroyed in World War II, according to the historic plans.

Even though production has now been shifted to the Cologne suburb of Ehrenfeld, the neo-Gothic building in the Glockengasse has remained the outward and visible symbol of the firm. Here, visitors can savour the swell smell of success by trying out the Mülhens' very latest perfume creations, lose themselves in appreciation of the remarkable art and architecture, or just observe that memorable French corporal as he rides into the Glockengasse to the tune of the Marseillaise – all electronically controlled, on a carillon built into the facade of the 4711 building.

DESTRUCTION AND RECONSTRUCTION

The outbreak of World War I was greeted in Cologne with much enthusiasm. However, as the hunger and the cold resulting from the British naval blockade became more and more unbearable, as the initial news of success at the Front gradually turned into news of defeat, and when even a few bombs were dropped on the city at Whitsun in 1918, people changed their minds. The discontent made itself felt shortly before the end of the war. Spurred on by the German naval mutiny in Kiel, the people of Cologne, too, rose in revolt. On 8 November 1918, a Workers' and Soldiers' Council took control of the city. The revolution only remained a brief episode, however – when the British occupation forces marched in that same year it quickly came to an end.

The mayor of the city at that time, Konrad Adenauer, was a lot more successful in realising his ideas. In 1917 Adenauer, who until then had been deputy mayor, assumed his predecessor's official duties and despite the British occupation, which lasted until early 1926, succeeded in putting his own individual stamp on Cologne's post-war development. In June 1919, the university was reopened at his instigation. Today, with over 50,000 students, it is one of the largest institutes of higher education in Germany. And in 1921 Adenauer ordered the construction of the Müngersdorf Stadium, which at that time was the largest in Europe.

In 1922, helped by the Provincial Parliament, he succeeded in having the municipality of Worringen made part of Cologne. The incorporation of what until then had been a primarily agricultural municipality made it possible for a huge industrial harbour to be constructed between Niehl and Merkenich, and for accommodation for those employed there to be built in neighbouring Worringen. In the same year, construction work was begun on the trade fair complex in Deutz, where the historic Millenium Exhibition of 1925 was held, as well as the international Press Exhibition (PRESSA) in 1928, with its 5 million visitors.

From 1924 onwards, Adenauer took advantage of the removal of the Prussian fortifications stipulated by the Treaty of Versailles to lay out, under the supervision of Fritz Schumacher, the 7-km (4-mile) long Inner Green Belt and the 30-km (19-mile) long Outer Green Belt, with their children's playgrounds, sports facilities, meadows and ponds, thus creating a local recreation area that is the envy of many other large cities even today. The National Socialists put an end to Konrad Adenauer's work in 1933. True, they were the strongest party in the local elections held on 12 March that year, gaining nearly 40 percent of the vote, but they still remained without a majority in the City Council. This did not stop them, however, from grabbing power for themselves and from bringing the administration and the whole of public life "into line" with their policy of *Gleichschaltung*.

The cells in the basement of the former Gestapo headquarters in the El-De-Haus bear witness to the horrors inflicted under the Nazi regime: the walls still bear inscriptions scratched there by suffering prisoners. Today, an exhibition in the building documents the history of Cologne during the Third Reich. The city's synagogues were burnt down on 9 November 1939, shops and houses belonging to Jews were looted and destroyed, and the Jews themselves tortured and murdered.

The National Socialists had shown their true face in 1936 when they had their soldiers march across the Hohenzollern Bridge to the left bank of the Rhine, thus breaking the terms of the Treaty of Versailles. Eighteen years after the end of World War I and the demilitarisation of the Rhineland it had helped to bring about, the barracks in Cologne were being filled once more, and preparations for war were in full swing.

World War II began on 1 September 1939, when Hitler attacked Poland. On the night of

Left, the girders of the destroyed Cologne-Deutz bridge were raised in 1974.

31 May 1942 Cologne suffered its first massive aerial bombardment at the hands of the Allies. Many more were to follow. When the German Army High Command took its leave of the city on 6 March 1945 with the phrase "The wreckage of Cologne has been left to the enemy", there were still roughly 40,000 people living in Cologne, compared to a figure of 768,000 at the beginning of the war. 20,000 of the city's population had been killed, buried beneath the rubble.

More than 90 percent of its housing had been destroyed or damaged beyond repair, and most of the churches and almost every civic building lay in ashes. All the Rhine bridges had been destroyed.

But new life soon began to stir among the debris. By the end of 1945 over 400,000 citizens of Cologne had already returned to their native city. Reconstruction began on a provisional basis at first. People settled in, removed the rubble and repaired anything that could still be repaired. Then, after the currency reform in 1948, plans for the city's reconstruction were drawn up. Bit by bit, historic buildings were either restored, such as the city's garland of Romanesque churches (1985), or completely rebuilt, like the Gürzenich (1955). Modern structures such as the "Vier-Scheiben-Haus" housing the WDR radio station, or the Severinus Bridge, supported by its single pylon, gave the city a new look.

The reconstruction phase has now come to an end. The last extension of Cologne took place in 1975, when it gained another 18,000 hectares (44,000 acres), thereby increasing its surface area to more than 400 sq. km (150 square miles), and its population to nearly 1 million.

Taken together with its surrounding communities, today's Cologne is an industrial centre with over 2½ million inhabitants, making it the third largest industrial area in Germany. In 1987 the working population of 420,000 in Cologne alone managed to achieve a gross net product amounting to more than DM 42 billion. The city's industry, exhibitions, banks and insurance companies, traders and artisans all contributed to the economic upswing.

Leader in car manufacturing: The service sector has gained an enormous amount in importance in Cologne over the past few years, but this has had little if any effect on the city's industry. In 1989, industrial turnover totalled DM 33 billion, with nearly one in four members of the population employed in industry. Leading the field is the car manufacturing industry, responsible for one quarter of the city's industrial turnover.

American car manufacture pioneer Henry Ford had recognised Cologne's advantages as a production centre as long ago as 1930. Nowhere else, in Ford's opinion, were the transport connections so ideal as in Cologne. This is even truer today than it was then.

Over 1,000 trains a day thunder over the Hohenzollern Bridge. Ten autobahns connect with the autobahn ring around Cologne, and 12 major federal highways in every direction complement the transport network. There are eight bridges across the Rhine, and the Rhine itself is an important transport route, too: nearly 14 million tons of goods are traded in the city's harbours annually. And Cologne is also connected to all the world's major industrial centres by air via the Cologne-Bonn airport – the second largest air-freight centre in Germany.

The Ford company workforce, which

originally numbered around 600, has grown today to over 25,000. Ford is by far the largest industrial employer in Cologne. 1,200 new cars a day roll off the production line at the Ford plant in Niehle. Meanwhile, other firms such as Citroën, Mazda, Renault and Toyota have also taken advantage of Cologne's ideal location. The city also produces tractors and farming machinery.

The chemical ring: The chemical and petrochemical industries are of immense importance to the region. Dozens of refineries and chemical works extend in a kind of ring around Cologne. They have almost 70,000 employees, and their combined turnover totals more than DM 20 billion every year. Further pillars of industry are the machine-tool and electrical industries. The traditional firm of Klöckner-Humboldt-Deutz is the world's largest producer of air-cooled diesel engines. Also well-represented in Cologne is the food, beverages and tobacco industry. Cologne sugar, too, has been famous since the last century, and chocolate produced by the firm of Stollwerck was much appreciated by previous generations. And there are also far more breweries in Cologne and its environs than anywhere else in Germany: a total of 24, to be precise. The famous Cologne beer known as *Kölsch* belongs as much to the city as marzipan to Lübeck or *Weisswurst* to Munich. But of course it was another product that made Cologne famous throughout the globe: Eau de Cologne.

"Learn a trade and you'll never starve" goes the saying, and Cologne's 6,500 craft businesses are proof of it. Alongside trade, it is the city's most traditional branch of industry, employing a total of 65,000 people. Most of the inhabitants of Cologne earn their living in the service sector, however. In 1987 the figure was 230,000 and two years later it had already risen to 240,000.

As the headquarters of 60 insurance companies, Cologne ranks as one of the most important European insurance centres, and it is certainly one of the oldest. Even the ancient Romans made payments during their lifetime in order to be given a decent burial, and in the Middle Ages merchants also insured themselves against losing their ships or cargo. Banking in the city also has its roots in the Middle Ages. After all, businesses

Left, a memorial to two world wars: Barlach's "Angel of Death" in the Antonite Church. Above, symbol of the new beginning: Cologne's trade fair centre.

needed to be financed back then, too. Today, there are 29 credit institutions in Cologne, including several large private banks. Alongside banks and insurance companies, quite a few associations, too, have chosen Cologne as their base of operations – 350 in all. They include the Federal Association of German Industries, the German Congress of Municipal Authorities, the National Housing Association and the Central Association of the German Retail Trade.

A media centre: The West German Radio Company ("Westdeutscher Rundfunk", known as WDR for short), the largest of Germany's broadcasting companies, is based in Cologne. The "Deutsche Welle" (the German equivalent of the World Service), the "Deutschlandfunk" and the satellite TV station "RTL-Plus" all broadcast from here too. Cologne's reputation as a media centre is further enhanced by a full 80 film and TV production companies, plus over 130 publishing companies and more than 200 printing firms. The "Media Park" is sure to strengthen the city's reputation even further; it is presently under construction, on the site of the former Gereon freight depot.

Cologne has enjoyed steady popularity for years as a tourist destination. The city receives over a million visitors every year, nearly half of them from abroad. New luxury hotels are bringing in an increasing amount of money to the city.

The boom in visitors has also been highly profitable for the city's restaurants. No other city in Germany has as many pubs and restaurants in relation to its population as Cologne. One clever person once estimated that if all the counters from all the bars in Cologne were placed end to end, they would extend for 10 km (6 miles). Not only Cologne's restaurant owners, but its retailers too have been very happy about the soaring increase in tourism. As early as 1985 their cash registers were taking in 30 percent more money per customer than the national average – and the trend is continuing.

The people of Cologne would be even happier, though, if their guests stayed a little longer; most of them pack their suitcases and leave after only one or two nights. The reason for these "flying visits" to Cologne could very well be the city's Trade Fair Complex in Deutz: by the beginning of the 1990s, it had more than a million visitors.

Above, Cologne in ruins. Right, Konrad Adenauer was once lord mayor of the city.

KONRAD ADENAUER: A COLOGNE LEGEND

"To be successful in politics you have to be able to remain seated for longer than anyone else." Had this phrase not been uttered by Konrad Adenauer himself one might have been inclined to consider it an evil insinuation on behalf of some of his rivals. But Adenauer, mayor of Cologne for many years before later becoming the Federal Republic's first ever Chancellor, was never too fastidious in his choice of methods, and openly admitted that the end justified the means.

He thought nothing of using his own vote to elect himself Chancellor in 1949, and even during his term as mayor in Cologne he was never afraid of achieving his objectives, even if the manner in which he did so was often rather unusual, to put it mildly.

The story of the Rhine Bridge at Mülheim is an outstanding example of Adenauer's political style. Adenauer was in favour of a suspension bridge, but a specially formed committee of experts, and also the City Parliament, decided in favour of an arch bridge. Anyone else would have accepted this decision. Not so Adenauer. In order to achieve his original aim he adopted a strategy that was effective, if somewhat time-consuming: in a series of private meetings, he took each of the city councillors to task individually.

He had so much success among the communists that one of their representatives, named Knab, had himself brought into the decisive meeting on a stretcher just so that he could vote in favour of Adenauer's suspension bridge (Adenauer had convinced the communists with an enthusiastic portrayal of the beauty of Leningrad and its suspension bridges). At the end of the meeting, the representatives decided on a suspension bridge after all.

A few years before this, when he was nurturing his dream of surrounding Cologne with a "Green Belt", Adenauer hadn't even bothered to ask the City Parliament at all. Its representatives only learned of Adenauer's plan after their mayor had already convinced the British and the Prussians, single-handedly, of his ideas, and had had an expropriation law from the National Assembly in Berlin tailored to his needs.

His methods might not always have been democratic, but his success usually proved him right in the end. Adenauer left more of a mark on his native city than anyone else before him. He restored glory and greatness to weary Cologne.

He had not been destined for a political career by any means, though. Adenauer was born on 5 January 1876 in Cologne's Balduinstrasse, the third son of a minor civil servant. His childhood and youth were marked by piety and thrift. Financial problems almost resulted in his being unable to study. But then events moved quickly.

In 1894 he began studying law at Freiburg University, in 1897 he took his law examinations in Bonn and in 1901 his assessor examinations in Berlin; in 1906 he was working as a lawyer in Cologne, in 1909 he was deputy mayor of the city, and in 1917 he became lord mayor of Cologne, the youngest in all Germany. He remained in his post until 1933. Years of persecution at the hands of the Nazis then followed, before he was eventually reinstated as mayor by the Americans in 1945.

And Adenauer might even have ended his career as mayor of Cologne had it not been for the British; they removed him from office in October 1945. Adenauer's reaction to this was typical: he added a new file to the one in his archive that read "removed from office by the Nazis" – the new one read "removed from office by the Liberators". Then he turned his attention to fresh tasks. He was 70 years old when he started to build up the German Christian Democratic Union (CDU), and 74 when he was elected Chancellor in 1949. He retired at the age of 88, having left an imprint on the Federal Republic as lasting as the one he had previously left on his native city of Cologne.

The integration of the Federal Republic into the West was his achievement, and the decades-long separation of the two Germanies was the price paid. On 25 April 1967 Konrad Adenauer was buried at the cemetery in Rhöndorf. He had become a legend in his own lifetime.

6
16

WHAT DOES "KÖLNISCH" REALLY MEAN?

Heinrich Böll assesses the spirit of Cologne.

The non-*Kölner* probably tends to associate the word *kölnisch* with something dark, devout and bourgeois; something consisting – in varying degrees – of the Cathedral, the Carnival, the Rhine, Wine and Women. As far as the people from the surrounding areas who stream into the city on Saturdays and Sundays are concerned, Cologne's attractions are varied and full of contrasts. Cologne is still a pilgrimage city; for many people its places of pilgrimage are of a discreet and often only apparently conflicting nature. Will anyone ever manage to put things together in such a way that piety, common sense and human nature can coexist without colliding with one another?

Some paintings by Max Ernst show a human ear in the foreground; the mouth that goes with it is off hovering in a distant corner of the picture. Max Ernst, born in the Cologne area, fell under the city's spell; its holy mysteries were a kind of magic for him. In the cool of the Cathedral, the father confessor performing his duties; an ear that hears and yet doesn't; a mouth far removed from that ear, able to absolve what not every priest can absolve. The Cologne saying "*Der muß im Dom beichten gehen*" ("He'd better go and confess in the Cathedral") conveys a mixture of reverence and terror similar to that experienced in prison by small-time confidence tricksters, thieves and opportunists in the presence of genuine gangsters.

I often used to watch my father's helpers poring over the plans for confessionals, trimming the wood and assembling the whole thing with its individual sections; in the remarks they made about communists and atheists they were as outspoken and as critical as only former Catholics can be, but there was still a kind of invisible limit that no-one would have dreamt of crossing in the presence of a child; even in the Carnival, at the point where it feeds off the very depths of vulgarity, this limit is never violated either; in fact the only time it does is when something as untypical of Cologne as *Fasching* gets confused with the Carnival; the Carnival is vulgar, with all the majesty and horror that vulgarity entails, but it is never frivolous; Fasching is a Bohemian invention, while the Carnival has its roots in the people; it is classless, and like an infectious disease it knows no class barriers. Fasching isn't a noticeable part of city life; it can be ignored; but it would be useless to try to ignore the Carnival in Cologne; all one can safely do is remove oneself from the zone of infection.

The Carnival is unthinkable without that ever-present ear, that Max Ernstian ear, hovering above it; if I ever had to come up with a suggestion for a new coat-of-arms for the city, the ear would be an integral part of a rather complex piece of heraldry providing information about the character of Cologne; the mouth to go with it would certainly be visible, too, up in another corner.

The Cathedral wouldn't be in my coat-of-arms, though; the fact that it was so obviously spared by the bombs – something the magnificent Romanesque churches were considered unworthy of – belongs among the sentimental errors as to what Cologne really represents; the Cathedral is a lot less characteristic of Cologne than its other churches; indeed, it's never really suited the city at all, even as an episcopal church.

Cologne argued with its bishops for centuries; battles were fought, tricks were devised, papal bans were proclaimed in Rome, and the city was deprived of priests and sacraments; and all largely because of money, property and privilege. After all, most of Cologne's bishops were more secular princes than bishops, and most of the princes in those days were princes with debts to pay. The city only began to tolerate its bishops when the latter renounced their princely role; this tolerance is only just 150 years old, and not without a certain irony;

<u>Preceding pages</u>: escaping the guests. <u>Left</u>, enjoying a cruise on the Rhine. <u>Following pages</u>: *Brightening up her day.*

everyone knows only too well that the bone of contention has now been removed, for there was no bone more worth fighting over than the good old Cologne *thaler*. The bishop has been back in the city for just 150 years, and since then all the pastoral letters and sermons have had a reconciliatory, almost canvassing tone to them, and this in a city where almost 20 percent of Catholics fulfil their church duties; the bishop still has not lived long enough in the centre of the city, and his church, the Cathedral, is unfavourably located, on a slight rise, surrounded by huge hotels, next to the station, in the windiest part of the city which must have been cursed for its draughtiness by Romans on sentry duty all those years ago.

No, the Cathedral wouldn't suit my imaginary coat-of-arms. St Gereon's, on the other hand, would do the job nicely: a church of martyrs, a church of mutineers. It was named after a Theban who rebelled against Rome, and its chief architectural point of interest has such a cosy-sounding name to it, too: "decagon". A small ear, a tiny mouth, and St Gereon's in my imaginary coat-of-arms; half a bishop's crook, and then to wind up the clerical and religious emblems, a picture of the Madonna. Seen on so many posters, printed in so many brochures, the Madonna among the Ruins and her sister in Lochner's painting still have a freshness about them that is utterly typical. And they keep turning up, too, in all ranks of society, rich and poor: in the tram; at the wheel of a sports-car; selling lipstick at Woolworths; listening to lectures on existentialism. There aren't too many of them but they're somehow always around: those faces that are so *kölnisch*; the serious ones have a slight hint of mockery to them, and yet – the perfect Madonna. The others are gentler, friendlier and yet – the perfect Madonna as well.

Ear, mouth, St Gereon's, the bishop's crook and a Madonna; that's probably enough religious emblems to be getting on with. Then we'd need some secular ones: an insurance building, perhaps, or a bank. And beside them we'd certainly have to have two hands, one of them washing the other; the rest of the world can keep its compromises and gentlemen's agreements, its corruption and bribery – *Der Klüngel*, Cologne's particular brand of nepotism, is something else entirely; it's the Cologne version of "being Nice". If someone asks you Nicely for a loaf of bread, and you can't give it to him, you do have the power as well as the right to say no

– but if you give him three slices of bread and he throws them at your feet, and insists on the entire loaf, then he's just not being Nice, or typically Cologne, about things.

If the ancient wisdom of this city is anything to go by, he'd probably be surprised and overwhelmed at being given those three slices at all in the first place. And hovering above the two hands washing each other we'd need to have the *Grielächer*, the person whose back gets scratched and who sometimes scratches other people's; the *Grielächer* takes nothing seriously, not even those things that need to be; everything's like one big Carnival to him; male voice choirs,

women's rights, education reform and deportation; it's all just another chance for him to tell jokes and insist on everyone being Nice to each other; if we had him between the two hands we could give him a vulgar-looking face, and dress him like a patrician, with Schäl's winking eye and with the nose of someone with circulation problems, like Tünnes; delicate hands and plump feet, or vice versa; he has a horror of things intellectual which can sometimes even make him forget his basic characteristic, his sense of humour; when a *Grielächer* starts getting serious, it's not a pleasant feeling; he's sensed the presence of his arch-enemy, the intellect, and he gets filled with apprehension as he realises that something Not Nice is going to be unavoidable – and if it's not Nice, then Cologne ain't Cologne any more, and what's a feller to do then? *Grielächer* is a word that's impossible to translate.

Left and right, two pleasant faces of the city.

And those certainly aren't all the ingredients, by any means, that make *Kölnisch* into a true adjective that can lay claim to being a word in its own right. Although every city has a prison – and some even have suburbs, Roman walls and the Rhine – the city prison at the Klingelpütz would still have to be mentioned as being typical; it's a horrible-looking building, everyone is familiar with it, it's permanently overcrowded, it hasn't been brought "up to date" for years, and yet the plans presently under way for a new building are filling both its former and its potential inmates with a certain sadness; what the experts refer to as crime is so widespread in Cologne, for reasons as yet unexplained, that it's only really comparable to the crime level in harbour cities.

The expression "*Er sitzt im Pütz*" ("He's doing time in the Klingelpütz") usually refers more to a case of bad luck than real misfortune, and the number of people in Cologne who've experienced the *Pütz* from the inside is so high that one can safely speak of a certain familiarity. I wonder whether as many people know the Cathedral as well from the inside as they do the Klingelpütz? However, I shall attempt to remain Nice. One thing's certain, though: the prison chaplain has the largest congregation in all of Cologne. There they sit now, those who knew not how to practise nepotism, that complicated instrument, those whose Not-Niceness had to be put on the record.

Come to think of it, a little wrought-iron grille, evoking plenty of associations – park gates, prison bars – might rather suit my imaginary coat-of-arms.

From: Essayistische Schriften und Reden, Volume I by Heinrich Böll, Cologne 1979. Reprinted by permission of the Cologne publishing house of Kiepenheuer & Witsch.

A City of Writers

"My ambition is," said Thomas Mann in 1926, "to prove that Lübeck... can be found in all my writings, from the beginning to the end, and that the city both decisively determines and controls them." Cologne is often associated in a similar manner with Heinrich Böll, but in fact Böll never cherished any such ambition: "If the Nazis hadn't arrived, and if the war hadn't happened, and I'd become a writer, I expect I'd be living in Berlin today."

"The apple never falls far from the bough" – a metaphor adopted by Thomas Mann, and it is certainly true of Böll. He was born in Cologne. The city's other famous writers only chose to move to Cologne from elsewhere: Paul Schallück (1922–76) was Westphalian, Hans Bender (born in 1919) came from Kraichgau, and Dieter Wellershoff (born in 1925) came from the Lower Rhine. True, Jürgen Becker was born in Cologne in 1932, but he grew up far from his native land: all of them apples minus the bough?

Thomas Mann's apt metaphor has the same problem as all comparisons: it doesn't stand up to scrutiny. Authors can't be compared to fruit, they don't have a bough, and they strike their own roots.

And Cologne is a particularly suitable place to do just that: the city has around 160 bookshops and several more publishing companies, a whole handful of radio stations, editorial offices and educational institutions: all in all, a countless number of places for literary life to meet. Too many perhaps, for Cologne still hasn't been provided with a proper centre for it all, a kind of "house of literature".

Writing tends to be only very seldom pursued as a main profession. Authors are often more inclined to congregate in the media as critics, lecturers and literary advisers – Werner Koch, for example, or Jürgen Becker, who works at the *Deutschlandfunk* but also happens to be a well-known lyric poet; or Dieter Wellershoff, who read manuscripts for many years in Heinrich Böll's publishing house of Kiepenheuer & Witsch before going on to write his own stuff exclusively. The novelist Hans Werner Kettenbach, born in 1928, is today deputy editor-in-chief of Cologne's largest daily newspaper.

Preceding pages: a night at the opera. Left, Cologne's most famous poet: Nobel laureate Heinrich Böll.

It's when they have the safe background of a paid job that many authors are often at their most effective, the best example perhaps being Dieter Wellershoff, who became the mentor of his own "Cologne School" of new realism, with its famous names: Rolf Dieter Brinkmann (1940–75), who also lived in Cologne, and Nicolas Born (1937–79) are the two most notable.

Historically, close affiliation between authors and professions has been quite common in Cologne: Albertus Magnus, or Albert the Great (1200?–80), taught here as a "Doctor universalis", his pupil Thomas Aquinas (1225–92) became a "Doctor angelicus" and also taught in Cologne as well as elsewhere; Master Eckhart (1260?–1327) had a professorship in the city from 1320 onwards; Johannes Duns Scotus (1256?–1308) earned himself the title of "Doctor subtilis" for his perspicacity; and Friedrich von Spee (1590–1635), famed as a poet and as an opponent of witch-hunting, taught at the city's Dreikönigs Gymnasium.

They all had their roots firmly fixed in scholastic life – and not one of them was born in Cologne. Only one other scholar actually was: the famous necromancer Agrippa of Nettesheim (1486–1535). He, however, used to practise his art in Bonn – his creditors and opponents of his cabalistic teachings having forced him to flee there.

Karl Marx from Trier, who edited the *Neue Rheinische Zeitung* in Cologne from 1848 onwards, might have become a citizen of Cologne had the Prussians not expelled him as a stateless person in 1849. But anyone who wants to claim Marx for Cologne and accord the city a progressive tradition should also mention Robert Blum, who was born at the fish market near the church of Great St Martin's in 1807, and shot dead as a revolutionary in Vienna in 1848. One should also mention Heinz Steguweit (1897–1964) and Ernst Bertram (1884–1957); both were born in Cologne, both died there, and both were lyric poets infected by nationalism.

Cologne writers have hardly ever treated their native city as the "intellectual life-form" that Thomas Mann famously considered Lübeck to be. And the anecdote handed down to us by Hans Bender, about Jürgen Becker accusing him of "living in Cologne like a tourist!" certainly reflects the feelings of many. There again, Cologne occasionally turns up as a theme in their work: Dieter Wellershoff has recently written a book on his native city (*Pan und die Engel*) and Jürgen Becker has been on the trail of his old and new home since writing *Felder* (1964).

Publicists Carola Stern (born in 1925) and Vilma Sturm (born in 1928), as well as Günter Wallraff (born in 1942) are natives of Cologne, though the city is not that important to them as authors. And Cologne often forms the background of books: Graham Greene (*Stamboul Train*), Gerhard Zwerenz (*Casanova*) and in the novels of Bernd Sülzer (*Bensberger Zwischenspiel*).

Alongside dialect literature, the songs of Willi Ostermann (1876–1936), or the poems of Albert Vogt (better known under his pseudonym of "B. Gravlott"), only one more present-day Cologne speciality needs to be mentioned: the so-called *Köln-Krimis* ("Cologne Crime Stories") by Christoph Gottwald (born in Cologne in 1954), who has provided his city with a whole genre. The first book of the series, *Tödlicher Klüngel* ("Deadly Nepotism"), however, was shifted to Cologne only when it was certain that it would be published there. "I can write books anywhere, but the only place I ever want to live is Cologne," said Gottwald.

Whether Heinrich Böll would ever have become a "Berliner" now that the post-war era is over is more than questionable. But Werner Kettenbach is quite clear on this point at least: "Even if Cologne had a literary scene similar to the one Berlin used to have, and I had the time as well as the inclination to get involved in it, the fact that I live here in Cologne and that I want to stay here would be based on quite different reasons."

Two writers of the post-Böll generation: (above left) Jürgen Becker and Dieter Wellershoff (above right). Right, the grave of Heinrich Böll.

HEINRICH BÖLL: AUTHOR WITHOUT A NATIVE CITY

Heinrich Böll (1917–85) was born in Cologne. The city would happily have provided him with his last resting-place, too, at the Melaten Cemetery. But he lies buried in Merten instead, in a pretty little graveyard high on the slopes of the *Vorgebirge* (foothills to the west of the city). From here, on a clear day, one can make out the towers of St Severinus's in his native city. For Merten isn't all that far from Cologne; but – and this is the crucial point – it's also just far enough away *not* to be Cologne.

This small distance, though, somehow symbolises Böll's relationship with his native city. It was one characterised by love, certainly, and by a certain amount of oversensitivity too; and certainly never one of unqualified harmony. In 1982 there was a huge fuss made in Cologne when Böll moved house for the last time – almost as if he was trying to stir up trouble yet again just by changing his address – but in fact all he was doing was returning to his family, at his son René's house.

Böll has been criticised often enough: he has been branded a "nest fouler" and a "defeatist", and if not as "a man without a native land", at least as someone without a native city. One only has to read a few of his many essays, though, to realise just how idiotic such accusations are, and to discover just how closely and inextricably involved Böll actually was with "his" native city. At the age of 50 he said: "I believe that in general, that is to say beyond any subjective point of view, that the city in which a person has lived until he is 21 will always have a determining and a decisive effect on him."

Böll was born at No. 26, Teutoburger Strasse, in the New Town area of the city. He himself spent three times longer than his own figure of 21 years in Cologne. His is the story of someone who gradually fell out of love with his native city.

"When we saw Cologne again, we wept", he wrote describing his return home in 1945. His loss of his *Heimat* had of course begun far earlier, with the sight of the brown-shirted ranks marching through the city, "desecrating the streets", as he put it. His way to school, through the area of the city surrounding St Severinus's, took him past the newsstand with its Nazi newspapers. It was at this point that he began to spend his afternoons writing, at No. 32, Maternus Strasse. Years later he was to say: "I do not believe that one can write, paint, compose, or be an artist at all without resistance…"

But even if Böll's motivation to write was based on his experience of life – and thus his experience here in Cologne – his work is far from biographical. He would seek the settings for his books elsewhere, or simply invent them; Cologne is hardly ever the scene of the action.

Böll did erect a literary monument to the nation's capital of Bonn, though, but it was one that didn't exactly meet with approval: *Ansichten eines Clowns* ("The Clown").

His favourite theme was the history of the middle classes – the kind you find everywhere, but particularly in the New Town area of Cologne, where he and his family had lived. His last apartment before World War II began was also in the New Town, at No. 17, Karolinger Ring. It was destroyed by the bombs, and Böll thus became homeless in his own home city.

Years later, when he moved back to the New Town (to No. 7, Hülchrather Strasse, which is where he also received the news of his Nobel Prize in 1972), it was really only a half-hearted attempt at trying to feel at home. He could never come to terms with what he called "traffic Cologne". The "war and the north-south interchange" were two things Böll tended to mention in the same breath from then on.

Nevertheless, Cologne was still his *Heimat*, and there were many aspects of it he loved. At the age of 60, in 1977, he was proud to remember what he had experienced as a 16-year-old: even during the March elections in 1933 (that is, after the seizure of power), the Nazis had still not managed to win a majority in Cologne.

In 1983, just two years before his death, at a ceremony held in the Town Hall, Cologne made Heinrich Böll an honorary citizen.

SCHAU
SCHAU
SPIEL

Visitors to Cologne probably can't help noticing that the city exudes a discreet, and to some extent quite pleasant, whiff of provincialism; this has occasionally been known to cause problems for the city's actors, for provincial attitudes tend to abound wherever you go.

In 1930, Konrad Adenauer, who was mayor of Cologne at the time, censored the first performance of Brecht's *Dreigroschenoper* ("Threepenny Opera") in the city. Certain "political and moral" aspects of it were watered down as a result. Hansgünther Heyme, director of Cologne's Schauspielhaus from 1968 to 1979, got into trouble for taking a collection to pay for terrorist Gudrun Ensslin's dental bill, as well as for his accurate portrayal of a paranoid Martin Luther (*Luther & Thomas Münzer*).

His successor, Jürgen Flimm, placed himself between all political stools with his play *Absa(h)nierung* (a pun on the German word for "redevelopment" and the verb meaning "to rake it in") about the decline of the Stollwerck section of the city. "Crises come and crises go" is the name of another play from the Flimm era.

Before 1900, Cologne had never been an exciting city for theatre. Historic theatre buildings are conspicuously absent. The oldest theatre, in fact, is the one belonging to Willy Millowitsch on the Aachener Strasse, where plays have been staged since 1936.

Even as early as the serious days of the High Middle Ages, people here preferred to concentrate their energies on the Carnival, which at that time provided more than enough visual effect for a city which today has several museums and around one hundred art galleries. Cologne has never been a seat of royalty; princes have never shown off their wealth here, and so stage performances as such never had a chance.

As late as 1592, "English acting troupes" were being driven out of the city. In the 17th and 18th centuries, travelling theatre groups from Holland, Belgium, France, Italy and Poland were only reluctantly admitted into the city, and only under certain strict conditions. The city didn't care for what they did, and made as much plain to them. "*Hängt die Wäsche weg, die Gaukler sind in der Stadt*" ("Get yer washing off the line, those jokers are back in town again"), as the saying went.

Theatre in Cologne developed only very sporadically. In 1783, the people of Cologne were able to proudly announce the presence of the first proper theatre in the city, in the Schmierstrasse (today's Komödienstrasse), right next to the Cathedral. The site has been occupied by a bank building for many years, for the theatre soon went out of business, despite the fact that Albert Lortzing and Jacques Offenbach kept it going for a while.

Then in 1872, finally, there it was: the first respectable "Civic Theatre". It opened its doors in the Glockengasse, right opposite the place where the Opera House stands today. But it was destroyed in World War II. The site of the former Civic Theatre today has a neo-Gothic structure built on it, displaying the city's most famous perfume, Eau de Cologne.

After the war, plays were put on in the assembly hall of the University, in pubs and in community halls. Herbert Maisch, the director in those days, writes in his memoirs: "And so we drove through the villages in a furniture van to show people that plays were being put on once again in Cologne". On 8 October 1962, a new theatre designed by Wilhelm Riphahn opened with a performance of Schiller's *Die Räuber* ("Robbers"). The play was directed by Oscar Fritz Schuh.

Since the beginning of the 1990s – after a five-year-long lapse under helpless director/dramatic advisor Klaus Pierwoss – exciting, committed theatre has been staged here once again, and has made a name for itself outside the region. With Günther Krämer as director, the theatre on the Offenbachplatz has someone who has successfully dissected the weirder sides of human existence with an

Left, the Schauspielhaus and Opera House on Offenbachplatz.

aggressively sharp disrespect, yet at the same time very aesthetically; someone who has brought momentum, colour and an earthy sensuality to all the plays he has tackled, whether by Brecht or Heiner Müller, Goethe or George Tabori, whether in the Schauspielhaus, the Kammerspiele or the Schlosserei. The director crisis, the asbestos crisis, and also the long closure of the theatre have all been forgotten now. What were the magic words in the days of Flimm? – "Crises come and crises go."

Cologne has developed a lot more of a feel for the avant-garde over the last few years. "Squat", "Living Theatre" or Robert Wilson have been welcome guests in the city. Cologne now has its very own, and very active free theatre scene, with around 20 alternative theatre groups.

Alongside the "Theater am Dom" in the "Schweizer Ladenstadt" (near the Opera House) and Millowitsch's "Volkstheater" on the Aachener Strasse, the "Senftöpchen" is another highly regarded place of entertainment, where cabaret, musicals, nostalgia and even travesty shows enjoy great popularity. Cabaret and music are the most popular of all. The "Comedia Colonia" in Löwengasse (near the main police station) is similar, though perhaps somewhat more alternative. The speciality here is highly colourful children's theatre.

Another firm favourite with children and adults alike is the "Hänneschen Theater" in the Eisenmarkt. Founded by Christoph Winters in 1802, it is the oldest local puppet theatre in all the German-speaking countries, and today it is run by the city. Typical aspects of Cologne are parodied here, much in the style of the Italian *commedia dell'arte* – and all of it, of course, in Cologne dialect.

The "Keller Theater" in Kleingedankstrasse stages drama relating to contemporary problems, and has also put on several neglected plays from the 1950s. In "Bauturm", opposite Millowitsch's theatre, the plays are modern and often home-made, but they also do Horvath and Büchner. One oddity is the "Freie Werkstatt Theater" in Zugweg, in the Südstadt. Here, they're really up-to-date in true 1968 fashion, with plays featuring old people, foreigners and the unemployed, and dealing with topics such as cancer or anorexia nervosa.

Left, a performance of Brecht in the Schauspielhaus. Right, cheers! Now over 80 years old, Willy Millowitsch still performs on stage.

THE MILLOWITSCH FAMILY

It's quite possible that we have Liebig's invention of artificial fertiliser to thank for Willy Millowitsch's famous Volkstheater in Cologne. One day Franz Andreas Millowitsch, born around 1790, a *Spezereikrämer* (grocer) by trade, and forefather of Cologne's favourite actor, was unable to sell his fertiliser from Gerberlohe to the local cabbage farmers, because the latter preferred Liebig's artificial equivalent. So instead, Franz Andreas began travelling around as a street-singer and puppeteer – and became quite a character in his own right.

His descendant Willy is continuing the long tradition; wherever he turns up, the crowds go wild. He captivates his audience time and time again with his special Cologne mixture of character comedy and one-liners, and in his role as a *Jrielächer*, which is roughly the equivalent of a rogue.

If it's traditional, it must be good, and over 80 years old now, he remains loyal both to himself and the dynasty as the lovable lad from the "Veedeln" (Cologne's old districts) in *Nacht jackenviertel*, a play written by his grandfather Wilhelm Joseph, or as the worthy citizen thirsty for adventure in the comedies of mistaken identity written by Arnold and Bach, in which morality and family life always win out in the end, despite the odd touch of irresponsibility in between.

In the playhouse on the Aachener Strasse, where the Millowitsch family have been entertaining their audiences since 1936 with their popular brand of theatre, continuity is seen as all-important. *Tante Jutta aus Kalkutta* ("Auntie Jutta from Calcutta") remains a perennial favourite with audiences. And *Fussig Julchen* provided – and still does provide – a great opportunity for all the female members of the family to shine, from Willy Millowitsch's grandmother Emma all the way to his daughter Mariele. Son Peter helps to stage his father's productions.

The most powerful moving force in the history of this old German family of popular actors seems to have been grandfather Wilhelm Joseph, ex-puppeteer and author of around 30 works for the stage. In 1894 he flung his puppets aside and announced: *"Ich will es Euch bekunden, die Puppen sind verschwunden, es war mir zu gewöhnlich, wir spielen jetzt persönlich."* ("There's something that I have to say, the puppets all have had their day, I found them rather boring, in person's more rewarding.")

He then put all his energy into plays starring real flesh-and-blood characters, also bringing those two famous Cologne character-types Tünnes and Schäl, who had originally been featured in the puppet theatre, onto the stage, thereby making them famous far beyond Cologne.

Willy Millowitsch, such a quiet person in private, and such an explosively charismatic individual the moment he's up on stage, had to suffer for many long years from the arrogance of highbrow criticism, which successfully denied him any entry into professional associations as well as a place in works of reference.

But today, that's no longer a problem: he is an honorary citizen of Cologne, he has been awarded the Federal Service Cross as well as the Telestar Prize, and Hollywood, television and "serious" acting have now beckoned. He has played Molière's *Bourgeois gentilhomme* as well as the philosophical gravedigger in Noelte's *Hamlet*.

His daughter Katarina says that he's remained a modest person. She is a teacher, with two children and a doctorate in German studies, and has made what amounts to quite a prolific contribution to the free theatre scene in Cologne. She often talks admiringly of how calm a person he is, of his inner dynamism, of his "positive conservatism", and even of a "certain childlike side" to him.

Cologne's most famous actor is being plagued by ever-increasing sprightliness in his old age. Television and guest appearances in public go on piling up, and on top of all that Willy spends more than 90 days of the year on his own stage. Even when he's on holiday on the island of Elba, the telephone isn't left alone for a second, and he writes hundreds of letters and postcards to his fellow-actors and friends.

Cologne has a long tradition as a musical city, and offers an astounding range of both old and new music. Very few other cities contain so many active musicians and composers, and concerts, performances and live shows take place almost daily. The city has almost 300 choirs, and 100 serious rock and pop groups. Concerts are staged regularly in the Philharmonie and in the Music Academy, and on top of all that there are also the hundreds of performances that regularly take place in the city's numerous churches.

The opening of the Cologne Philharmonie in 1986 provided the city's two biggest symphony orchestras, the municipal "Gürzenich Orchestra" and the "Cologne Radio Symphony Orchestra", as well as the "WDR Big Band", with a new home. The Philharmonie, designed in the shape of an amphitheatre by Cologne architects Busmann and Haberer, could only be built with the support of the WDR, which contributed a third of the costs.

Inside the Philharmonie, the audience and the musicians sit in a circle, with the conductor or soloist standing in the middle. This means an uninterrupted view from each of the two thousand seats in the auditorium. The acoustics are also excellent; in order to insulate the hall from the sounds of steamers chugging past up the Rhine, and noisy railway trains, the entire auditorium was embedded inside a twin-walled concrete cradle which actually floats on the water-table, and is anchored firmly to the ground. The 11-metre (37-ft) high glass cupola above the podium ensures excellent sound quality and makes the auditorium a great deal larger.

For many years the musical centre of the city used to be the ancient banqueting-hall known as the Gürzenich. In 1821 it was Cologne's turn to organise the Lower Rhine Music Festival, and it decided – at first only on a provisional basis – to do up the rooms in the Gürzenich. Since 1832, the room most often used by musicians is the casino hall, where Franz Liszt and Clara Schumann, among others, once performed.

Left, the acoustics are excellent in Cologne's Philharmonie.

Günter Wand did a great deal to promote the "Gürzenich Orchestra"; he conducted it from 1947 to 1974, and made a lasting personal contribution to the musical life of the city. During the course of the orchestra's 100-year history, numerous famous composers and conductors have stood before the musicians and the members of the choir as their guests: Felix Mendelssohn and Brahms, Richard Wagner and Tchaikovsky, and, after the turn of the century, Gustav Mahler, Weingartner and Pfitzner.

For the Cologne Radio Symphony Orchestra of the WDR, too, with its wide range of music both old and new, the new location in the Philharmonie has many advantages. Indeed, the WDR is of immense importance to the city as a whole: as well as being a radio station, it also commissions new works of music on a regular basis – from the Music Academy, for example. The radio station was one of the pioneer centres of electronic music, especially the works of Karlheinz Stockhausen, who still lives in the city. The WDR also acts as a nationwide mouthpiece for composers and musicians, and naturally for music lovers as well. The radio stations "Deutsche Welle" and "Deutschlandfunk" play a leading role in this respect too, one example being the various concert series they put on in their own concert halls.

The city's Opera House, built between 1957 and 1962, with a seating capacity of 1,400 has long earned itself a reputation both nationally and internationally. Guest performances, and co-productions with other opera houses in Paris and London have been extremely successful. The programme features works from Slavonic countries, Italy, France and of course Germany, too. Today's Opera House on the Offenbachplatz was built during the 1950s; the old one, on the Ring, was destroyed towards the end of World War II.

The vocal music scene lends extra strength to Cologne's already excellent musical reputation. The Cathedral Choir, the Bach Choir, the Philharmonic Choir and the Gürzenich Choir are just four of the three hundred choirs based in the city that have won various awards in national and international competitions. The ensembles for old and new music are just as important and varied, too. Keep an eye out for performances by *Musica Antiqua Köln*, who perform Baroque music on period instruments.

Closely associated with a city's musical life are, of course, its music schools. Cologne's Music Academy and its Rhenish School of Music provide a wide range of different training programmes, as well as various opportunities to perform. And the Music Academy was the first in all of Germany to introduce a "jazz studies" course – no wonder, when one considers the active jazz scene in the city, with famous line-ups such as Saxofon-Mafia, Härte 10 and Nana. And the *Jazzhaus* initiative, with its 50 musicians, has done much to promote jazz via its annual festival, which has been going for 10 years now.

Particularly popular on the Cologne jazz scene are the performances at bar owner/pianist Papa Joe's establishments, known as "Em Strechstrump" and "Papa Joe's Biersalon"; concerts featuring Dixieland, Swing and trad Jazz take place there daily – and admission is free. The band at the "Biersalon" plays music from the 1920s, and the pianists, who play in a lot of different styles, change every day. There's a cabaret, too. Jazz performances also take place regularly in the subway, in the "Klimperkasten" and in the Municipal Gardens (Stadtgarten).

The choice of rock and pop music on offer is just as vast. Depending on their fame, the groups play in the Cologne Sports Hall (Sporthalle), in the "alter Wartesaal", in the Stadthalle at Mülheim or in the Life-Musik-Hall (sic!) in Ehrenfeld. The club scene includes the "Luxor" (rock and pop), the "Cauri-Club" (Afro and Latin-American), the "Rose Club" (Punk and Heavy Metal), the "Popocatepetl" (Blues), and the "Underground" (experimental rock).

Anyone interested in hearing Cologne's most famous rock bands, however, may not get the chance to do so: "BAP" and the "Bläck Fööss", who were very successful in the 1980s, only very rarely perform their *Kölsch-Rock* in their native city these days.

Above, female rock. Right, BAP, Cologne's most famous band.

Rock 'n' Roll Cologne-Style

Times have changed. Cologne's dialect only used to really come into its own during Carnival time. No longer: the city's musicians, who wear their "heart on their tongue" (*et Hätz op de Zung*) rather than their sleeve, have used it to lend new charm to their songs, making them famous far beyond the city's borders.

Ever since the group known as the Bläck Fööss (literally: "bare feet") sang *Linda Lou*, the first ever rock song in "Kölsch", the local dialect, at the 1973 Carnival session, the sound of the language has become an accepted part of the rock and pop scene. The Bläck Fööss are now very popular right across Germany, Carnival time or no Carnival time.

What makes them so special is their combination of cleverly-written lyrics, based on everyday situations, and their quite often excellent musical arrangements.

It's actually astonishing that no one thought of it sooner. The fact that the Cologne dialect, Kölsch, flows off the tongue just as smoothly as the beer of the same name was proven by such poets as Willi Ostermann years ago. Kölsch has a vividness and precision that is unparalleled. A common verb in post-war Cologne was *fringsen*, which meant to pinch (as in money); no one is sure to this day whether the archbishop of that time, Cardinal Frings, quite approved.

But the Bläck Fööss were by no means the only group to realise that the adaptable, soft sound of "Kölsch" was far more suited to rock music than the more common and universally accepted "high German". This was more than proven by the overnight success of Wolfgang Niedecken's group "BAP": their winning formula of committed lyrics combined with catchy mainstream rock have since turned songwriter and singer Niedecken, guitarist and arranger Klaus Heuser (alias Major Healy) and a handful of local heroes from southern Cologne into an internationally famous band.

And it was the group "BAP" who were the first to use the term "Kölschrock" on one of their posters in 1978. The breakthrough as far as other linguistic areas of Germany were concerned came in 1981 with their third album, *für usszeschnigge!* ("cut-out"). Since that time they have made eight more successful albums, and all the group have become millionaires. BAP proved that they were not only successful with audiences at home but also abroad when they toured China (where they played eight concerts to a total audience of 120,000) and the Soviet Union.

Jürgen Zeltinger, known as "de Plaat" ("baldy") because of his lack of hair, is another famous name. In his songs, this "underdog" of the scene touches on controversial topics such as homosexuality in the track *Tuntensong* ("Fairy Song"). His song *Müngersdorfer Stadium* has become the national anthem of Cologne.

The German group that goes by the English name of "The Piano has been Drinking" set Tom Waits' music to texts in Cologne dialect, and are considered relative newcomers on the "Kölschrock" scene. This band, too, has had considerable success on radio as well as on smaller stages.

Holger Czukay, a member of the group "Can", which enjoyed international success in the early 1970s, especially in Great Britain, is still a well-known musician today. He is particularly famous for his "radio collage" activities.

Purple Schulz, a singer from Cologne with texts in High German, who also has a penchant for melancholy ("*Ich will raus*" = "I want out"), has sung his way into the ranks of Cologne's rock musicians, as have Wolf Maahn and his "Deserters" as well as Arno Steffen, who used to be Zeltinger's songwriter/producer.

By far the best way of getting to know the estimated 150 groups who took part in the Rock Contest sponsored by the city is to hear them perform live in Cologne's numerous music venues, such as Luxor, Underground, Life Musik Hall, Basement and Wartesaal. The fact that several major stars have recently chosen to live in Cologne makes it clear just how attractive the city has become as a centre of music: artists such as Tina Turner, Herbert Grönemeyer and Ina Deter have all settled here.

3
3
3

Munich considers itself a "media city" as a matter of course, as does Hamburg; and Berlin would love to be one again too. Cologne, though, has been a media city for decades, indeed it may even be *the* media city of Germany. But it's only recently that it has begun emphasising the fact.

Cologne, with its three daily papers, compares very favourably with Germany's other large cities. The biggest paper is a tabloid, *Express,* which, including subeditions, was selling 440,000 copies a day at the start of the 1990s. *Express* has thus long since elbowed the local Cologne edition of the *Bild-Zeitung* into second place. The same publishing house, DuMont Schauberg, also produces the more traditional *Kölner Stadt-Anzeiger*. This liberal paper (circulation 290,000) is one of Germany's most highly regarded regional newspapers.

The *Kölnische Rundschau* (circulation 160,000), from the Heinrich-Heinen publishing house, is generally regarded as the city's "number two" newspaper, and politically is somewhat more conservatively inclined. The "Rundschau" is actually very much in the tradition of the city's former *Kölnische Volkszeitung*, but without the latter's clerical line.

But it is the radio and television stations in Cologne that really make it a media city. The city did lose the "BFBS" (the British Forces Broadcasting Station) to Herford in Westphalia a few years ago, true, but with its five radio stations and numerous commercial production companies, Cologne has now become a centre of the electronic media. The largest radio station by far is the *Westdeutsche Rundfunk* (WDR) which has more than 4,500 employees. Its productions mostly take place in the city centre, at the studios in the radio building on the Wallrafplatz, next to the Cathedral terrace. The WDR transmits more than 135 hours of music and information daily on its four different stations – and a fifth one is at the planning stage. On top of that, there are roughly 20 hours of television daily, broadcast in the First Programme of the ARD as well as in the Third Programme, *West 3*.

Left, filming of the popular WDR TV series *Lindenstrasse*, Germany's answer to *Coronation Street.*

The two federal broadcasting corporations, the *Deutsche Welle* and the *Deutschlandfunk*, are both located in the southern part of the city on the "Raderberggürtel". The "Deutsche Welle" broadcasts 90 hours of programmes daily on short-wave, in 34 different languages (including German!), worldwide. It thus provides an important link for Germans living overseas as well as keeping other countries up-to-date on events inside Germany and internationally. The "Welle" has a staff of 1,450.

Right next door, the 740-strong staff of the "Deutschlandfunk" provide a 24-hour information and music service in German. Another 12 hours of programmes are transmitted in 11 different European languages.

RTL-Plus, one of Germany's two large commercial television stations, has its production centre west of the city, on the Aachener Strasse. RTL has around 700 employees and transmits a good 20 hours of television each day.

Finally, mention should also be made of *Kanal 4*, owned by the Holtzbrink publishing group from Stuttgart. "Kanal 4" produces television programmes with the emphasis on culture – much like its English equivalent, Channel 4. Still in its infancy is *Radio Köln*, the local commercial radio station, financed and run by newspaper publishers DuMont Schauberg and Heinen.

Two factors are sure to turn the city into a "media mecca": the College for Media Studies (Medienhochschule), which started taking on students in autumn 1991, and the Media Park. The aim of the college is to prepare its students for careers in film, radio and television, while the Media Park is a huge studio production complex, on the site of the former Gereon freight depot, housing numerous firms with up to 3,000 employees.

Cologne without the Carnival is unthinkable. The Carnival isn't just a huge folk festival, it's an explosive "happening", an enormous popular movement; the Carnival is Cologne's "fifth season" of the year. On "the 11th of the 11th" – that is, on 11 November each year – the starting pistol is fired at 11 minutes past 11 o'clock, marking the beginning of the Carnival Season. And the "fifth season" comes to an end on Ash Wednesday, at the beginning of Lent.

Hundreds of thousands of people spend weeks celebrating *Fastelovend*, as the Carnival is called in Cologne dialect. Over a million *Jecken*, or "Carnival Fools", gather in the streets for the climax: the *Rosenmontag* Carnival Parade; the parade on the Monday before Lent. Millions more watch the entire crazy event on television.

This "festival of fools" originated as early as Roman times; it has its beginnings in the Roman cult of Bacchus, the god of drunkenness and ecstasy, and the Saturnalia. The customs and rituals of the Carnival have changed continually over the centuries – often quite radically so. The *Fastelovend* assumed its present-day appearance in 1823, when the "Festival Organisers' Committee" was formed. As is clear from the name, the festivities certainly did need to be organised; there had been occasions in the past when the Carnival had threatened to go out of control because of rowdiness and promiscuity – and in "Holy Cologne" of all places, too.

The gentlemen on the committee thus made it their noble task to reform the festivities and also to organise the whole thing properly. Today they would be the equivalent of the "festival management", though in those days, altering the actual content of the Carnival played a major role.

The trade-mark of the new, improved, transformed and thus socially acceptable Carnival was the first ever *Rosenmontag* Parade in 1823. Until that time there had been a variety of sporadic, very easygoing processions throughout the entire city, many of which had had anything but happy endings. The Parade, on the other hand, gave the city a new direction, it united the whole festival in one huge and colourful finale.

And things have remained like that to the present day. The smaller processions in the "Veedeln" (districts) and other suburbs have been retained, however; though less im-

moral than they used to be, they also tend to be far more basic, and potentially explosive, than the "official" Carnival itself.

After World War II, a second Carnival procession through the city centre was introduced: the so-called *Schull- and Veedelszög* (the schools' and districts' procession) on Carnival Sunday. This is the more popular and traditional procession, while the *Rosenmontag* Parade, despite its satirical elements, tends to be a lot more pompous and perfectionist.

The Rose Monday Parade: On the Monday before Lent, all the various guards, corps,

Preceding pages: Carnival partners. Left, "Funkenmariechen". Right, one of the floats in the parade on the Monday before Lent.

traditional associations and clubs that have connections with today's festival committee assemble together – there are over 50 of them altogether. The Parade is one of the most unique and impressive spectacles ever: it's around 6 km long, and takes no less than three hours to pass by.

Around 7,000 *Karnevalisten* wearing colourful costumes and fine uniforms march, ride or otherwise travel along with it. Dozens of oversized carnival floats – which have taken several months to build – satirising contemporary issues with their political effigies, roll through the city.

Several tons of *Kamelle* (sweets), chocolates and *Strüßger* (posies) are thrown from the floats. The whole spectacle costs several million marks, and is financed by the festival committee, the societies, those participating in the parade as well as by a subsidy from the city (which, naturally, the *Karnevalisten* think is far too low).

The highlight of the *Rosenmontag* Parade is the so-called *Dreigestirn* (literally, "triple star" – the "big three" who hold sway in Carnival time). The roles of Prince, Maiden and Peasant are traditionally performed by well-to-do Cologne men, and at the beginning of the Carnival *Sitzung* ("session") in January they are officially inaugurated at Cologne's historic venue for costume balls, the Gürzenich.

The forerunner of the Prince was "Hero Carnival", who was originally the only one to rule with the fools. The Peasant and the Maiden joined him later. The sturdy Peasant represents the historical fighting spirit and loyalty of Cologne. The Maiden symbolises "the untainted and independent city, free from subjection to any foreign tyranny."

When the Maiden is a man: The Maiden in the "big three" has traditionally always been played by a man. Indeed, the Carnival is, and always has been, very much a male affair.

There have only been two occasions in Cologne's history when the Maiden was actually played by a young girl, and both were during the Nazi regime.

Male predominance at the Carnival is obvious wherever you look. Even in the dancing groups of the Corps, men have been dressing as woman dancers for decades. It was only in 1936 that a woman first danced as *Funkemariechen* with the *Rote Funken* ("Red Sparks" – men dressed in 18th-century military outfits). Although emancipation and equal rights are certainly on the increase in today's *Fastelovend*, women have been an accepted part of the *Rosenmontag* Parade and the "sessions" for many years now.

The societies form the basis of the organised Carnival, and no one is really sure how many of them there are. The "Red Sparks", like all the other Carnival societies, are a colourful parody of militarism, which has never been too popular in Cologne. The Prussians and their regimented existence had little in common with the people of Cologne: in 1823 they were in the city during the first ever *Rosenmontag* Parade, and were sent up by the "Red Sparks".

But the original "Sparks" they are based on were anything but brave soldiers. In the 17th and 18th centuries, the *Funken* were actually the Cologne city guard. They were certainly no brave elite troop. Quite the reverse in fact: they used to earn a bit extra on the side, on top of their soldier's pay, by knitting and babysitting, and war-cries were quite alien to them. The *Funken* then rapidly "funked" the moment the French besieged the city in 1794.

The juiciest part of the Carnival sessions are the *Bütenredner*, or "wash-tub speakers", who make their comic speeches, in accordance with tradition, from a wooden wash-tub. Unlike the *Fastnacht* in Mainz, the speeches are not at all intellectual or didactic. The sheer sense of fun for fun's sake, and an earthy sense of humour that verges on stupidity – but in a positive sense – are the chief characteristics of the Cologne *Fastelovend.*

Left and above, dressing up is all part of the fun, for bystanders and participants alike.

A folk festival: Hundreds of thousands of people attend the "sessions" and the costume balls, which of course also make the Carnival important from an economic point of view. One single session brings in over DM 900 million. The Cologne Carnival is a folk festival in the truest sense – a festival for young and old, and rich and poor; it is valued because it does not divide, it unites. It functions as a melting-pot, and symbolises the tolerant side of Cologne, which can best be summed up in the saying *Jeder Jeck ist anders* – best rendered as "We're all crazy in our different ways."

The battle cry of the Carnival is "*Kölle alaaf*" – anyone interested in knowing what that means really has to visit the city during the *drei tolle Tage* ("three crazy days") at the peak of Carnival time.

There are several reasons for Cologne's excellent sporting reputation, and one of them lies over to the west of the city: the only Sports Academy in Germany. It's a research institute just as much as an educational one, with room for 6,000 students, and it has produced many world record-holders and Olympic athletes.

Only 500 metres away from the Academy is the edifice that has made every Cologne sports fan's heart beat faster for the past 40 years: Müngersdorf Stadium, home ground of the first division team "1. FC Cologne". The stadium, constructed on the western edge of the city between 1921 and 1923 at the behest of Konrad Adenauer, who was mayor of Cologne at that time, was the largest sports complex in Europe when it was completed, and even today, with enough covered seating for 60,000 people in the main part of the stadium, it still compares highly favourably with many newer structures. "Hännes" the billy-goat, the stadium's mascot, has already made the internationally famous club German champions on three occasions, and Cup-winners on a further four.

The other main club in the city, "SC Fortuna Cologne", is just about managing to stay in the second division, with varying degrees of success.

The city's hockey-players are exceptionally successful, though: Cologne's red-and-white, blue-and-white and black-and-white hockey stars regularly make the headlines in field and indoor hockey.

The focal point of the city's ice-hockey is the Ice-Hockey Oval on Lentstrasse; the whole place always goes wild when the *Haie* ("Sharks") from the Cologne Ice Hockey Club, known as "KEC" for short, race after the puck in important league games.

The pace is also just as hectic at the Gallop Racing Track ("Galopp-Rennbahn") in Weidenpesch. The track is only part of what is one of the largest horse-racing courses in Germany, and more than a dozen exciting meetings take place here between March and October each year, including the trials for the German Derby as well as the "Preis von Europa", a flat race with Germany's highest prize: DM 400,000.

The annual highlight of athletics in Cologne, the International Sport Festival, is also attended by the world's best. Several world records have been set during the Grand Prix event (in late summer).

Another centre of exciting sporting activity is the Sports Hall at the Trade Fair Grounds (*Messegelände*) in Cologne-Deutz. Here one can find boxing, handball and motocross events as well as the famous "Six-Day Cologne Cycle Race".

No other city in Germany has so many teams in the various top national leagues as Cologne. A total of 29 different clubs represent the city, and they specialise in 19 different kinds of sport, ranging from baseball to underwater rugby.

As far as the disciplines of judo, hockey, athletics and swimming are concerned, top athletes are trained in Cologne for participation in international championships.

Alongside its leading role internationally from the point of view of competitive sports, Cologne also has extensive sports facilities for the general public. Every sixth person in the city belongs to a sports club, and Cologne has 700 of them, featuring around 50 different kinds of sports, ranging from riding and rowing to tennis, golf and flying.

Anyone in Cologne who doesn't feel like indulging in competitive sports can still find what he's looking for: 19 indoor swimming-pools, 10 outdoor ones, three spas and one thermal bath all provide recreation and relaxation. And the city's numerous fitness clubs and bodybuilding centres, with their weights and home-trainers, are also a good way of keeping fit.

Information is available from either the Cologne Municipal Sports Association (Stadtsportbund), Tel. 2401214, or the "Sport-und Bäderamt", Tel. 4983222.

Left, torchlight vigil at a home game of the Cologne ice-hockey team "The Sharks".

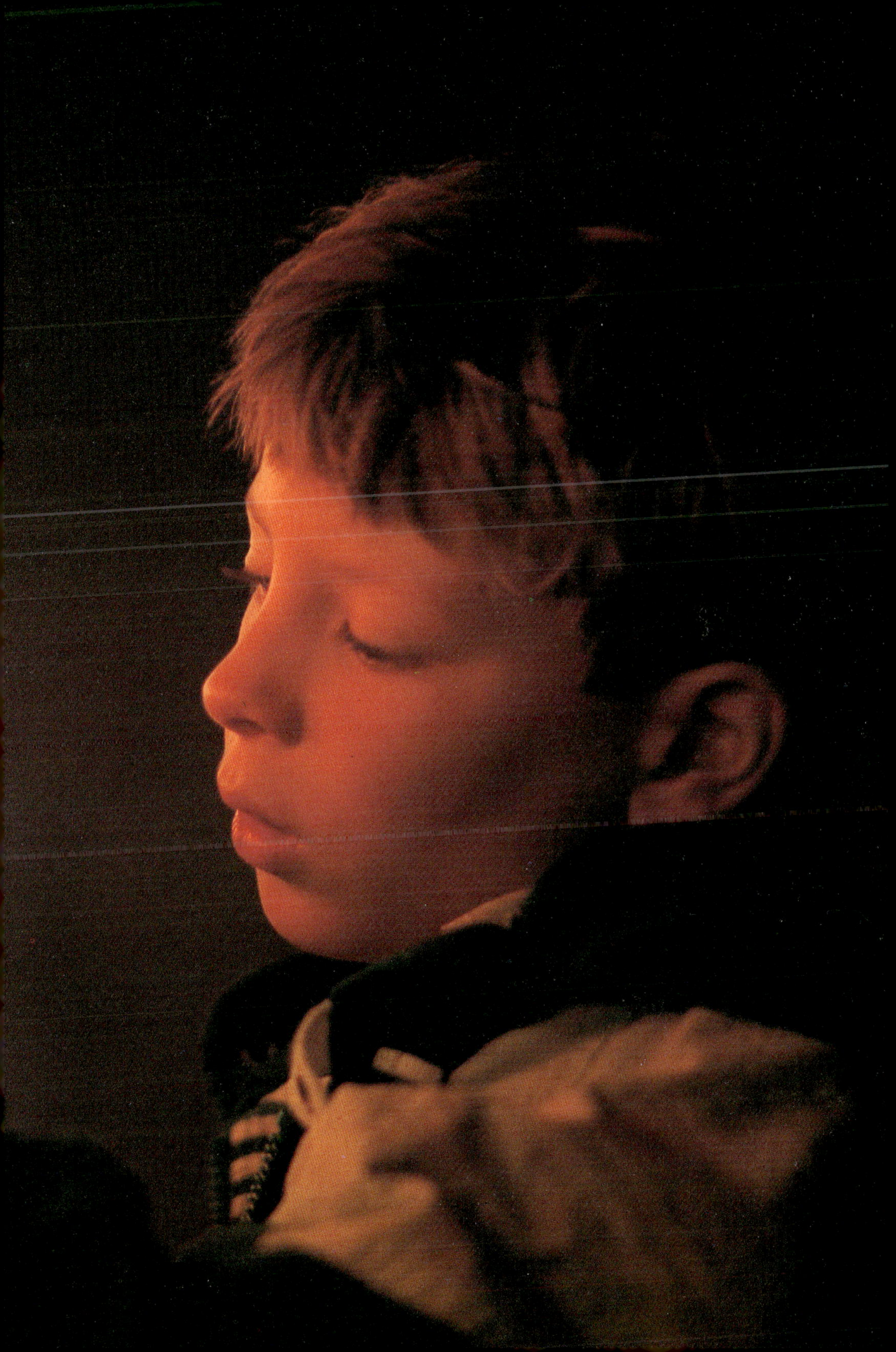

PLACES

Traces of Cologne's 2,000 years of history can be found everywhere in the city. Roman tombs and Romanesque churches, the old Town Hall and the famous Cathedral, a unique collection of museums and the much-vaunted *Altstadt* (Old City): there are things to see wherever you go. But don't try to see everything at once – it can't be done. The Cathedral of course is a "must", but everything else should depend on the time you have to spare, and on your personal preferences.

Don't let the city's fascinating past let you forget the delights of the present: take time off to relax from your journey through past centuries and knock back a *Kölsch* beer in one of the city's highly *gemütlich* taverns, or spoil yourself with a relaxing trip on one of the Rhine steamers. Or why not take a refreshing breather in one of the city's many fine parks? And a piece of advice: Cologne is a very good place to eat out, however bizarre your culinary tastes may be.

Of course, it's not just its buildings and treasures that give life to a city, "it's the people that make the place". It can take a while to get to know them, however, so in the meantime remember that the magic ingredient in Cologne is "leisure". Just take short breaks wherever you happen to be: in one of the museums, in the Old City or in the Cathedral square. It's always easy to find somewhere to sit down and relax.

An even better idea, though, is to leave the beaten tourist track altogether and get a real feel of the city in its traditional districts, known as "Veedeln". You won't need to go far either, for some of the most original and lively of the "Veedeln" can still be found within the city's Rings, in the Eigelstein and Südstadt sections of the city. Anyone with time to spare should also take a quick trip to the sections of the city over on the right bank of the Rhine, or out beyond the Rings.

Modern art enthusiasts can fill an entire holiday just touring around Cologne's galleries. Most of the city's art dealers can be found in the streets around the Neumarkt. One good idea is to combine a stroll through the galleries with a walk through Cologne's shopping streets: the most famous of these are the Hohe Strasse and the Schildergasse. Locals and tourists stroll up and down here today just as the ancient Romans once used to: indeed, the street pattern hasn't changed significantly since those times.

Preceding pages: the choir stalls in Cologne Cathedral; a minister lights the candles. Left, the Corpus Christi procession outside the main portal.

Greater Cologne
1,6 km /1 miles
LONGERICH
NIEHL
STAMMHEI
MENGENICH
WEIDENPESCH
Hafen
Longericher Straße
BOCKLEMÜND
Niehler Gürtel
OSSENDORF
MAUENHEIM
Amsterdamer Str.
RIEHL
Venloer Straße
Äußere Kanalstr.
A57
Flora
Botanical
Garden
Youth Hostel
Lentstraße
Ice Stadium
Zoo
Rhine
NEU-EHRENFELD
NIPPES
St. Agnes
BICKENDORF
Deutz-Mülheimer
Stadt-
garten
51
EHREN-
FELD
Rhine Cable Car
Hansaring
Eigelstein Gate
St Ursula's
Deutz Sports Centre
Telecommuni-
cations
Tower
RHEINPARK
St Gereon's
Cathedral
Trade
Fair Centre
Municipal Museum
BRAUNSFELD
Melaten
Cemetery
3
2
1
5
MÜNGERSDORF
Town Hall
DEUTZ
7
4
Deutzer Brücke
55
Achener Straße
55
6
Müngersdorfer
Stadium
Militärringstraße
Stadt-
wald
Museum
of East
Asian Art
Dürener Straße
Synagogue
55
Severinsbrücke
55
Stadt-
wald
LINDEN-
THAL
University
Rathenau-
platz
Sachsenring
264
Geusen Cemetery
Severinus's
Gate
Volks-
garten
Luxemburger Straße
Vorgebirgstraße
E40
Gleueler Straße
Berrenrather Straße
9
51
SULZ
RADER-
BERG
Bonner
POL
Glueler Straße
Beethoven-
park
265
BAYEN-
THAL
A4
Decksteiner
Weiher
KLETTENBERG
Campsite
Brühler Landstr.
Straße
Efferen
Straße
ZOLL-
STOCK
RADER-
THAL
MARIEN-
BURG
51
Rodenkirchener
Militärringstraße 51
Luxemburger Straße
Berrenrather
E40
51
A555
9
Hermülheim
A4
Forstbotanischer
Garten
265
HÖNINGEN
KONRADER-
HÖHE
HOCH-
KIRCHEN
51
A555
HAHNWALD
Kal-
scheuren

1 Wallraf-Richartz-Museum/ Museum Ludwig /Philharmonie
2 Roman - Germanic Museum
3 Museum of Applied Art
4 Gürzenich/Old St Alban's
5 Opera House/Theatre
6 Hahnen Gate
7 St Cecilia's/Schnütgen Museum
DELLBRÜCK
HOLWEIDE
Bergisch Gladbacher Straße
Gronau
Berliner Straße
MÜLHM.
Dellbrücker
Bensberger
Refrath
Marktweg
Strunderbach
MIELENFORST
BUCHHEIM
Frankfurter
Bruchbach
Mauspfad
BUCHFORST
Straße
MERHEIM
Flehbach
Lustheide
HÖHENBERG
BRÜCK
Brück Game Enclosure
Rather Weg
Brücker Mauspfad
Flehbach
KALK
VINGST
NEUBRÜCK
STAATSFORST
KÖNIGSFORST
UMBOLDT
Rösrather
Straße
Rather Mauspfad
RATH
OSTHEIM
Frankfurter Straße
GREMBERG
Heumarer Mauspfad
HEUMAR
Kölner
FORST
GREMBERG-HOVEN
WESTHOVEN
Straße
Leidenhausen Estate
WAHNER
HEIDE
ENSEN
Hauptstr.
Stein-
Straße
Berger
EIL
Frankfurter Straße
RODEN-KIRCHEN
Campsite
Campsite
PORZ
Hauptstr.
Grengeler Mauspfad
Weißer Straße
WEISS
ADELEN-HÜTTE
URBACH
Airport
GRENGEL
E35
51
A3
506
55
E35
A3
8
A4
E40
A3
E35
A4
A559
8
A59
A3

1 Wallraf-Richartz-Museum, Museum Ludwig, Philharmonie
2 Church of the Assumption
3 St Mary in the Kupfergasse
4 St Mary in the Capitol
5 Josef Haubrich Art Gallery
6 Roman-Germanic Museum
7 Overstolzenhaus
8 Holy Trinity Church
9 Rautenstrauch-Joest-Museum
Cologne City Centre
400 m / 0,25 miles
Old Fort
Ice and Swimming Stadium
KLEINGÄRTEN
State Supreme Court
Güterbahnhof Gereon
Hansa Building
Mediapark
Eigelstein Gate
Ebert-Platz
Theodor-Heuss-Ring
Bastei
Rhine Park
Ursuline Church
St Cunibert's
Medieval City Walls
St Ursula's
Police Station
Dance Foutain
Rhine Cruises
Trade Fair Centre
Rhine ferry
Rhine Round Trips
Chamber of Industry and Commerce
Main Post Office
Main Station/ Exchange Office
St Gereon's
Gerlinghaus
Municipal Museum
St Andrew's
Cathedral
Tourist Informtion Office
Hohenzollernbrücke
Deutz Station
Roman Tower
WDR Broadcasting
El-De-Haus
Museum of Applied Arts
St Heribert's
Guest House for Young People
ALTSTADT
Town Hall / Mikvah/ Prätorium
St Columba's
Great St Martin's
Lufthansa Head Office
Bazaar de Cologne
Käthe Kollwitz Museum
Opera House/ Theatre
Gürzenich / Old St Alban's
Köln-Deutzer Brücke
Hahnen Gate
Church of the Holy Apostles
Richmodis-haus
Antonite Church
Little St Martin's
St Cecilia's / Schnütgen-Museum
St Mauritius'
St Mary in Lyskirchen
Malakoff Tower
St George's
Police Headquarters
Severinsbrücke
St. Pantaleon
Rheinau-Hafen
Church of St John the Baptist
Francican Church
Rhine
Carthusian Church
Urlepforte
St Severinus's
Bottmühle
Bayen Tower
Severinus's Gate
Deutzer Hafen
VOLKSGARTEN
RÖMERPARK

THE CITY'S MAJOR LANDMARK

"The Cathedral Church of St Peter in Cologne is both mother and mistress of every church in Germany"
– Matthew of Paris, early 13th century

The number of titles and names that **Cologne Cathedral** has been given through the centuries could easily be extended, too. In its time it has been called a "papal basilica", and art historians have referred to it as "the youngest and prettiest sister of the great French cathedrals" or quite simply as "the absolute cathedral". "God's battle cruiser" is another name that made the headlines, as did the fondly ambiguous "Rome's dearest daughter". Cologne, despite its unique series of Romanesque churches and its wonderfully varied museums, has really always remained first and foremost a cathedral city.

An early Christian church site: The area around the Cathedral was densely populated as early as Roman times. An early Christian episcopal church with a west choir, atrium and a separate baptistry came into existence after 313 during the rule of Maternus, Cologne's first documented bishop. The edifice was based on Old St Peter's in Rome. In 817, after Charlemagne had appointed his friend and advisor Hildebold bishop of Cologne, and had raised the city to the status of an archbishopric, work began on the new Carolingian structure.

The "Old Cathedral", as it is called, a triple-aisle pillared basilica with two choirs, two transepts, and towers flanking the choir on the westwork is known to us not only from the results of excavations but also from a drawing on the dedicatory picture in the Hillinus Codex (*circa* 1025).

It was when the holy relics of the Three Magi were brought from Milan to Cologne in 1164 by archbishop Rainald von Dassel – a coup that transformed Cologne into one of the most important places of pilgrimage in the West – that plans were drawn up for the construction of an entirely new cathedral. In 1248, archbishop Konrad von Hochstaden laid the foundation stone for the new Gothic Cathedral, which was to be modelled on the great French cathedrals (and on the one in Amiens in particular). On 27 September 1322, the choir was consecrated; it was closed off towards the west by a huge temporary wall.

The wooden construction crane on the provisional roof of the south tower, completed in 1410, was a distinctive feature of the city for centuries. In 1560, construction work on the Cathedral was abandoned. At this stage, roughly 90 percent of the planned total area of the Cathedral could be used for services; a provisional wooden roof above the arcades closed off the inner area.

Late completion: It was not until the 19th century that the Cathedral was finally completed as a "German national shrine". The foundation stone for further construction work was laid on the southern side of the Cathedral in 1842, in the presence of King Frederick William IV of Prussia. Thanks to various advances in technology, the Cathedral was then completed in only 38 years by church architects Zwirner and Voigtel. On 15 October 1880, 632 years after the medieval foundation stone had first been laid, the final phase of construction – the placing of the finial on the south tower – was complete.

The largest medieval section of the building consists of the high choir and the garland of choir chapels, or chevet, with its filigree support system. The facade of the southern transept, designed by Zwirner, is considered a masterpiece of neo-Gothic architecture. The sculptured figures on the portals are the work of Christian Mohr. The bronze doors were built by Ewald Mataré, with the help of his pupil Joseph Beuys, between 1948 and 1954.

The Cathedral is at its most imposing-looking when seen from the west. The two towers rear up above the 7,000-sq.

metre (8,300-sq. yard) facade, the largest in Christendom; its design was largely based on the original medieval plans for the west front. The five axes of the facade find their reflection in the division of the interior into five aisles. Of the three doors, only **St Peter's Door** (to the south) dates from the Middle Ages. A new section built into the northern buttress, consisting of 30,000 bricks, is a reminder of the heavy damage the Cathedral suffered during World War II. At 157.38 metres (516.52 ft), the northern tower is exactly 7 cm higher than its southern counterpart.

Imposing-looking nave aisle: If you enter the Cathedral by the central doorway of the west front, the view stretches right down the complete length of the narrow, towering nave aisle (119 metres/390 ft long). The best place to begin a walk around the Cathedral is in the northern side-aisle. Here, the magnificent stained-glass windows dating from the beginning of the 16th century strike one immediately; the sketches they are based on were executed by noteworthy representatives of the Cologne school of painters. Just before one reaches the northern transept, the **Clares Altar** comes into view; it was created around 1360, and was transferred to the Cathedral from the former convent of Poor Clares in 1821. Twelve Franciscan saints are depicted on the outer sides of the altar wings – the oldest preserved painted wooden panels in the world.

Passing beneath the organ loft, we reach the ambulatory. The mosaic flooring, which covers the full length of the ambulatory, was designed by August von Essenwein between 1885 and 1897, and executed by the firm of Villeroy & Boch, Mettlach. The first large portrait as one enters the ambulatory is of archbishop Hildebold with the model of the "Old Cathedral". On the east wall of the Chapel of the Cross (*Kreuzkapelle*) hangs the **Gero Cross**, commissioned by archbishop Gero (969–76), and showing Christ on the cross at the moment of his death, with

Ordination in the cathedral.

his eyes closed and head bowed. This over-life-size Ottonian sculpture is thought to be the oldest monumental crucifix in the western world. The Gero Cross was incorporated into the Baroque altar in 1683.

Virtues and vices: Separated off by a stone parclose and Baroque choir screen, the **high choir** (which can be entered only on conducted visits) has retained its medieval appearance almost completely: the magnificently carved **choir stalls**, with their depictions of human virtues and vices, were built between 1308 and 1311, and with 104 seats are the largest in Germany. Special stalls were kept reserved for the Pope and the Emperor, members of the Cologne cathedral chapter from the early Middle Ages.

The paintings on the 14th-century choir-screens show scenes from the lives of various saints specific to Cologne. On the choir pillars, the life-size statues of Christ, the Virgin and the 12 Apostles, standing on piers, are among the masterpieces of Cologne sculpture between 1280 and 1290. Angels playing music can be seen above their ornate baldachins. The medieval windows of the clerestory show 48 kings (the 24 kings of Judah and the 24 elders of the Apocalypse), with and without beards respectively, and an Adoration of the Magi in the axis window.

The mighty **high altar**, covered by a single slab of black marble, is decorated with arcades of figures carved from white Carrara marble, representing various scenes, prophets, apostles and saints. It was only after the end of World War II that the **Shrine of the Three Magi** was shifted to its present location in a glass case behind the high altar. Begun around 1190 by Nicholas of Verdun, the shrine, which houses the relics of the Three Magi that were brought from Milan to Cologne in 1164 by Rainald von Dassel, is considered the most outstanding example of medieval goldsmith's work from the Rhine-Meuse area.

The famous Shrine of the Three Magi in the high choir.

Further noteworthy works of art can be found in the seven choir chapels. The second chapel in the ambulatory, **St Maternus's Chapel**, contains the tomb of archbishop Philipp von Heinsberg, with a sepulchral monument that is quite unique: the recumbent stone figure of the archbishop is surrounded by a fortified city wall, complete with towers and gates, reminding us that even though Philipp had his ups and downs with the burghers of Cologne, he finally decided in favour of the construction of the Hohenstaufen wall around the city.

Next door, in **St John's Chapel**, is the tomb of archbishop Konrad von Hochstaden. The recumbent figure of the archbishop, modelled after similar French statues, is considered the most important 13th-century bronze figure in Germany. Moreover, this chapel also contains the so-called *Fassadenriß F*, a detailed architectural plan made in about the year 1300, on a piece of parchment over 4 metres (13 ft) long, of the projected facade with its two towers.

The **Three Kings' Chapel**, the axis chapel of the ambulatory, contains the oldest stained-glass window in the Cathedral. This "Old Bible" window, as it is called, contrasts 10 scenes from the Old and New Testaments respectively. The window was installed around 1260, and is still Romanesque in style. Opposite the axis chapel and behind the choir screen is the tomb of archbishop Dietrich von Moers. Instead of the usual form of tomb, church architect and sculptor Konrad Kuene here chose a group of figures instead, showing the adoring Magi and the kneeling archbishop beside the Virgin on her throne.

The last of the chapels in the ambulatory contains the tomb of archbishop Gero, and also the so-called "New Bible" window, similar to the older one in design but already showing Gothic influence. It was transferred from the former Dominican church to the Cathedral in 1892.

Altar of the city's patron saints: The three eastern arches of the southern nave together form the **Lady Chapel**. The famous **Altar of the City's Patron Saints** by Stephan Lochner has been here since 1856. This masterpiece of the Cologne School of Painters, painted between 1440 and 1445, was originally created for the Town Hall chapel. It portrays several saints closely associated with the city: on the wings we see St Ursula with her companions, and St Gereon with the soldiers of the Theban Legion, who all died as martyrs in Cologne, and on the central panel, the Adoration of the Magi.

The Lady Chapel also contains three more magnificent works of art: just to the left of Lochner's altar is the ornate tomb of archbishop Friedrich von Saarwerden, with a recumbent statue in bronze surrounded by figures inside Late Gothic arcades; to the west, on the outer wall of the chapel, the tomb of archbishop Rainald von Dassel, and in the direction of the ambulatory, the tomb of Count Gottfried von Arnsberg, with a metal grille placed over the recumbent figure – ostensibly with the aim of protecting it from the Count's disappointed heirs.

On the eastern side of the southern transept, the **Altar of St Agilulph** can be seen: it is 5.5 metres (18 ft) high, and was created in Antwerp in 1521. The central shrine depicts the Life of Christ and the Passion.

The most magnificent works of art in the southern side-aisle are the five **"Bavarian Windows"**, commissioned from the royal stained-glass works in Munich and presented to the Cathedral by King Ludwig I of Bavaria in 1842.

No visit to the Cathedral would be complete without a visit to the **Treasury**, which contains a collection of reliquaries, chalices, monstrances and other liturgical objects from medieval times to the present day. The so-called Staff of St Peter (10th–11th centuries), the Byzantine Reliquary (11th–12th centuries) and the baroque shrine of canonised Cologne archbishop Englebert (1632) are especially noteworthy.

The cathedral seen from a different perspective.

THE ROMANESQUE CHURCHES

Contrary to the popular lay perception, churches aren't like simple interchangeable, standardised containers that can just be set down anywhere at random. Churches "grow" rings of stone over the years like the rings in tree-trunks – it's often impossible to work out exactly how old many of them really are. The same applies to Cologne's "garland of great Romanesque churches", all of which, without exception, have now been rebuilt after their destruction in World War II.

The churches – formerly lay canonical foundations and religious institutions for ladies of rank – attracted small clusters of buildings around themselves, made up of collegiate institutions, cloisters and parish churches, right up to the beginning of the 19th century. They celebrated their heyday in the 12th century, however, in the so-called "Hohenstaufen period".

A plethora of churches: The period between 1150 and 1250 has been described as "the greatest century in Cologne architectural history". And justly so, for where else at that time, not to speak of later – and not only in German-speaking countries – could one find such a wealth of massively constructed collegiate and abbey churches within the bounds of a single city? Around the year 1200, the broad, semicircular Hohenstaufen city fortifications were complete.

Before this, for almost a millenium, Colonia had not dared venture beyond its original Roman rectilinear grid. **St Severinus's Church** (St Severin) to the south and **St Cunibert's** (St Kunibert) to the north of medieval Cologne marked the boundaries of the city's historic Rhine panorama, as indeed they still do today.

More churches then appeared in the High Middle Ages: **St Gereon's** (St Gereon), to the north-west, the **Church of the Holy Apostles** (St Aposteln), to the west on the Neumarkt, **St Mary's in the Capitol** (St Maria im Kapitol) on the Heumarkt, **Great St Martin's** (Gross St Martin) east of the Old Market (*Alter Markt*) inside the Old City, **St Pantaleon's** (St Pantaleon) to the south-west, **St Andrew's** (St Andreas) immediately west of the Cathedral, **St Ursula's** (St Ursula) to the north of the old Roman city gate, **St George's** (St Georg) opposite police headquarters, **St Cecilia's** (St Cäcilien) which has housed the Schnütgen Museum of medieval art for decades, and last but not least, the church of **St Mary's in Lyskirchen** (St Maria in Lyskirchen) – incredibly, the 13th-century frescoes on its vaulting survived World War II, the only fresco cycle in Cologne to have done so.

At the turn of the 18th century, the Old City of Cologne contained – believe it or not – 149 churches, with all of 171 towers. Most of these structures, as well as various cloisters and monastery

Preceding pages: the Church of St Martin. Left, relics taken to extremes in the Golden Chamber of St Ursula's. Right, a detail of the portal of St Mary's in the Capitol.

walls were torn down both during and after the wave of secularisation at the beginning of the 19th century.

The large collegiate churches and abbey churches, however (and St Mary's in Lyskirchen was the only church not be counted as one), were spared and were turned into parish churches. Until their destruction in the bombardments of World War II they were restored several times, usually in accordance with the taste of the time – i.e. with plenty of colour, and a great deal of mosaic work.

The spirit of the 1950s: Hardly any of these 19th-century embellishments can now be found in the proud "cornerstones" of Cologne's architectural history, which have been open again to the public since 1985 (Great St Martin's, St Mary's in the Capitol and St Gereon's were all building sites up till then, and St Cunibert's westwork still is).

The incredibly complex reconstruction of this former garland of Romanesque churches was done in the purist spirit of the architects of the 1950s: they loved the simple stonework, and removed what was left of the 19th-century mosaics. In the Church of the Holy Apostles, for example, the open stonework of Speyer Cathedral served as a model, and the Cologne architects of the 1950s still remembered "cryptical" interior concepts such as those practised by Clemens Holzmeister in St George's church during the 1920s.

Alterations: The present trend in Cologne seems to be towards giving one or other of these venerable, and yet also rather "neo-Romanesque" churches more ornate interiors, and the results have been highly controversial. Thus the former Benedictine abbey church of Great St Martin, restored highly sensitively and with graphic bareness by the architect Joachim Schürmann after the war, has now been provided with new and highly colourful windows (very much in contrast to the architect's cautious mode of operation).

At present, Hermann Gottfried is in

The Hohenstaufen westwork of St George's Church.

the process of painting the trilobate choir of the Church of the Holy Apostles in lively neo-Expressionist style; and even the simple coffered ceiling above the Ottonian nave of St Pantaleon's won't be visible for much longer because it is due to be replaced by a new and more colourful one of richer design.

Visitors to St Gereon's, too, should not assume that the relatively topsy-turvy interior of the architecturally magnificent Decagon, which dates from the Roman and Hohenstaufen periods, is the last word in wisdom of design: the window cycles by Georg Meistermann and Georg Buschulte will of course be staying, and yet the Decagon and high choir, taken together, convey a very strong sense of disunity. In itself very beautiful, the Baroque altar that was taken from the destroyed Gothic church of St Columba doesn't fit in very well between the Decagon and the high choir: its style and dimensions seem all wrong. And the blood-red of the cupola clashes with the blue-green walls of the choir.

And yet: whether one is in Great St Martin's, the Church of the Holy Apostles, St Gereon's or even St Mary's in the Capitol (where the magnificently restored Renaissance rood screen has been jammed far too much between the nave and the choir section), the sense of space that is so characteristic of all the Romanesque churches in Cologne overpowers one time and time again.

Most of the churches were first built above Roman and early Christian tombs, St Severinus's and St George's being two examples. St Gereon's was built as early as the 4th century AD, as a Roman imperial building and martyrs' church (for soldiers in the Theban Legion, according to legend). Others, such as St Mary's in the Capitol, for example, with its 11th-century trilobate choir and ambulatory – quite unique in the entire history of western architecture – were constructed above the foundations of former Roman temples.

The splendid dome of St Gereon's.

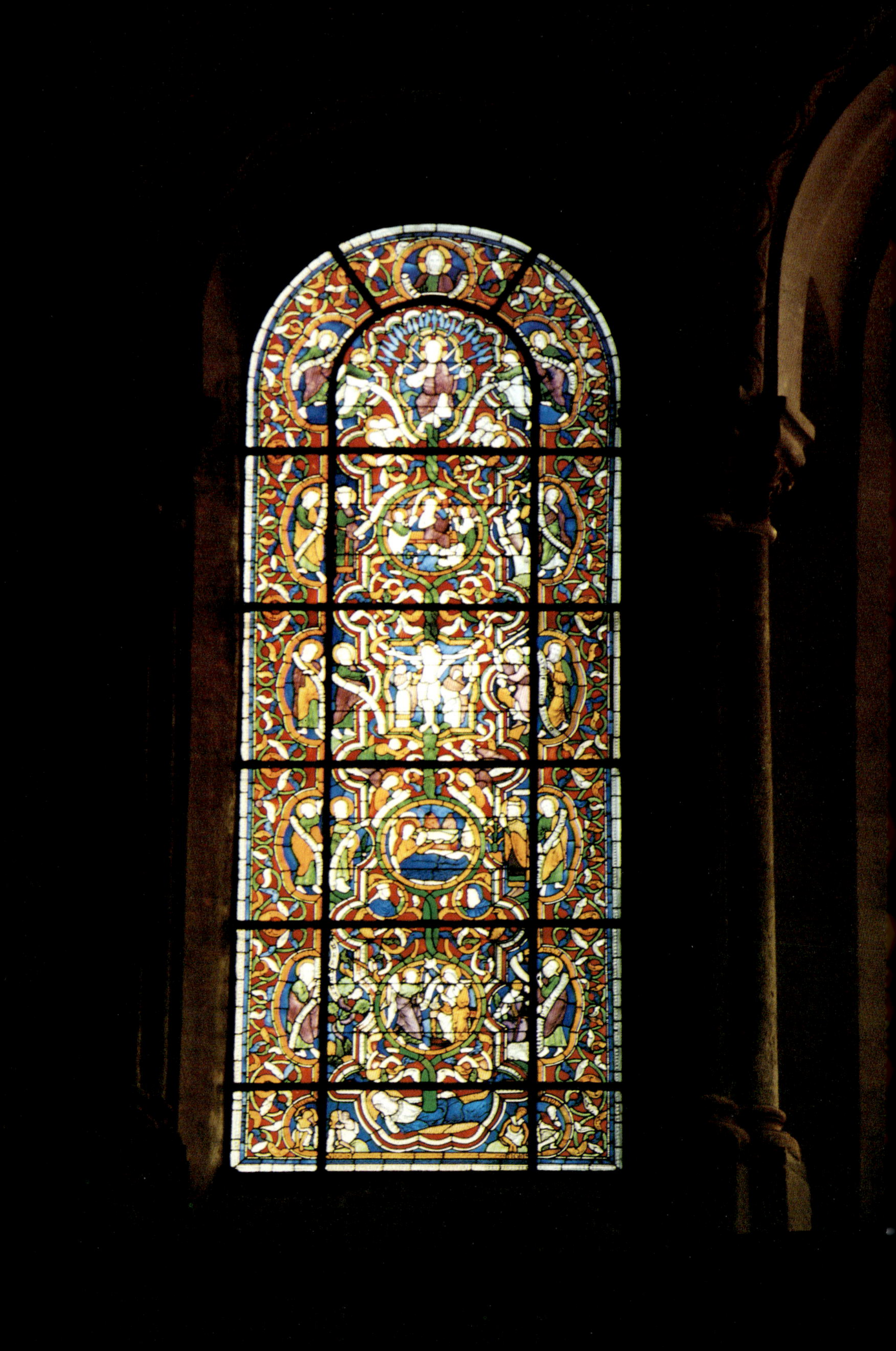

In the case of St Mary's, the church was probably built over a temple dedicated to the Capitoline triad situated above an arm of the Rhine, which in Roman times used to flow directly beneath it.

Traces of "paganism": St Mary's in the Capitol dates back to the 7th century. Plectrude, wife of Pepin of Herstal, the ruler of the Franks, founded a religious house for noble ladies here which managed to raise enough money to pay for the later magnificent trilobate choir. The choir and crypt were consecrated in 1065. Despite the church's destruction and its "purified" reconstructed version, in the stonework one can still make out the Roman remains of the "pagan" temple dating from the 1st century AD.

The nave, before it was destroyed (the crypt, west tower and nave vault collapsed on 2 March 1945), used to be covered by a Gothic ribbed vault. Today the central aisle, rounded off at its western end by a fine imperial gallery, is covered by a wooden "emergency ceiling" dating from 1957. Despite its destruction and simplified reconstruction – the eastern conch has no dwarf gallery – this church still retains much of its former beauty. The pillared trilobate choir is indisputably one of the greatest architectural experiences one can have in Cologne.

The immediate vicinity of this beautifully rounded church, founded in the depths of Roman times, has only very recently been adapted to suit the style of the building (as have the areas surrounding the Church of the Holy Apostles, Great St Martin's, St Cunibert's and St Gereon's).

The trilobate choir in St Mary's in the Capitol provided the inspiration for similar architectural achievements in the Church of the Holy Apostles (choir section with dwarf gallery, built around 1200) and in Great St Martin's (choir consecrated in 1172).

Both of them – the Church of the Holy Apostles with its mighty, fortress-like west end, and Great St Martin's with its eye-catching square tower and its four corner turrets, are among the finest of Cologne's Romanesque churches. All in all, there really was quite a varied collection of buildings in the city just before work began on the Gothic Cathedral in 1248. But now we will take a closer individual look at some more of the more interesting churches.

St Andrew's Church: St Andrew's, that marvellous mixture of Romanesque and High Gothic elements (porch at the west end, nave basilica and high choir), was first consecrated in 974. In the mid-13th century it was restored in High Romanesque style, and in 1420 was given a shrine-like glass filigree high choir, modelled on the choir of the Coronation Chapel in Aachen. The high, Gothic roof had to give way to a simple flat sloping emergency one after the serious destruction wrought during World War II.

Stylistically, the tower with its four turrets draws heavily on the tower of the Minster in Bonn; the crypt was recon-

Left, exquisite stained-glass in St Cunibert's. Right, the nave of St Severinus's.

structed after 1950 by Karl Band. St Andrew's – still the home of members of the Dominican order – with its magnificently structured interior, is one of the most atmospheric churches to be found anywhere.

Church of the Holy Apostles: This church is situated to the west of the Neumarkt, directly behind the site of the former Roman west gate. The Neumarkt is the only large square in Cologne not to have been built over since Roman times, and is thus of great archaeological interest. The church, with its magnificent trilobate choir, made up of three conches, a cupola and a small lantern, and its remarkable rectangular hall at the west end with its open tower, assumed its present shape and size between 1150 and 1230.

Like the eastern choir of Great St Martin's and its tower, the trilobate choir of the Church of the Holy Apostles, too, was also created expressly to be seen – the former for people looking across at the city from the Rhine, the latter giving the Neumarkt its distinctive appearance. The three-aisled nave is impressive for its solid structure (arched nave arcade on tetragonal, cruciform pilasters). Inside the church, bare stone predominates, though the choir section and the cupola are being given a great deal more colour at present by the painter Hermann Gottfried.

St George's: Founded as a lay canonical foundation above the remains of a Roman temple in 1059 by archbishop Anno II, the church was consecrated in 1067, and its nave and choir were vaulted around 1150. The westwork was added as early as 1188, but left unfinished. Constructed as a three-aisled pillared basilica (enriched during the Hohenstaufen period by two central supports), this church is fascinating for its compact plasticity, particularly evident in the Hohenstaufen westwork – a masterpiece of its type.

The walls of the westwork are nearly 5 metres (16 ft) thick, and were apparently planned as the external base for a tower. The restoration work on the church, which suffered heavy damage during World War II, was finally completed in 1964.

St Gereon's: This church is a grandiose decagonal structure on an elliptical ground-plan, built above 4th-century Roman foundations. A canons' choir with two towers was added by archbishop Anno II and consecrated between 1067 and 1069, and renewed extension work took place in the mid-12th century with the addition of an apse. The decagonal Roman central structure was remodelled between 1219 and 1227 to form the present Decagon, with its unique three-dimensional effect; architecturally, it is without a doubt one of the most impressive testimonies to the Hohenstaufen period.

St Severinus's: St Severinus's was built above a Roman cemetery, as a cemetery chapel consecrated to St Severinus. There were several stages of development in its construction, just as with the other churches. Its various sec-

<u>Left</u>, "Death" by Zurich graffiti artist Harald Nägeli, on the walled-up west portal of St Cecilia's. <u>Right</u>, St Ursula's Romanesque west tower is crowned by a baroque cupola.

tions date from the 10th, 11th, 13th, 14th and early 15th century, and elements from the late Hohenstaufen period in the eastern part of the church combine with Late Gothic elements in the westwork to create an overall effect of austere, luminous beauty.

St Pantaleon's: Formerly a Benedictine abbey, the church was founded around the year 957 by archbishop Bruno, on the site of an extensive Roman villa. Bruno is buried here, as is the Empress Theophano (Emperor Otto II's Greek wife), who added the mighty westwork.

Also badly damaged during the war, and subsequently restored, this church still gives one a strong sense of the imposing, imperial nature of Ottonian architecture. Traces of Baroque alterations and additions can still be found in the choir section (high altar and chancel), and the rood screen dates from the early 16th century.

The massive and imposing westwork is most impressive. The long building with its striking west end is surrounded on three sides by a fine lawn – a reminder of the former monastery's area of sanctuary – creating a restful oasis in the centre of the city.

St Cunibert's: Finally, St Cunibert's, the sepulchral church of canonised bishop Cunibert of Cologne, who is said to have been laid to rest here in 663. After several previous structures, the present building, with its double tier of windows and dwarf gallery in the choir, was only finally erected in the late Hohenstaufen period.

Its foundation stone was probably laid in 1215, and most of the choir completed by 1222–24; the church was then finally consecrated in 1247, one year before work began on the city's new Gothic Cathedral. Although it suffered heavy bombardment in World War II, the church was opened again as early as 1956, with the exception of its west end, which is soon to be restored without its original high spire.

Under cover of darkness: Of all the churches in Cologne dating from the Hohenstaufen period, St Cunibert's is considered to be the most uniform in style. Its interior is surprisingly bright and cheerful. The magnificent windows at the east end date from the time it was built (1220–30). During the war, an unofficial rescue operation took place under cover of darkness, and the windows were shifted to the Siebengebirge (hills on the eastern bank of the Rhine). The Gothic baptistery, installed in the south wing of the eastern transept and decorated between 1260 and 1270, also escaped destruction.

In 1247, construction work had been completed on St Cunibert's, and the mighty Gothic choir of the city's new Cathedral had not yet been built: it was at this point, with the completion of St Cunibert's, that the Romanesque, late Hohenstaufen period drew to a magnificent close, its roots still firmly in the old style, yet presaging Gothic brightness and clarity of contour.

The churches of Cologne are referred to as "Romanesque", but in fact they passed through nearly all the important construction periods from the early Middle Ages onwards, and parts of them even date from late Graeco-Roman times.

The High and the Late Middle Ages as well as the Early and High Gothic periods also left their traces, later followed by the odd Baroque insertion. In the 19th century they were cleaned up and renovated, and received several historicist additions; then they were destroyed during the bombardments of World War II, before being rebuilt in a largely "purist" manner.

Now their doors are open once more to visitors, worshippers and all those interested in art and architecture: a garland of churches with no counterpart anywhere north of the Alps, and quite unique in having been constructed within such a small area; an ancient heritage that Cologne has painstakingly restored over the past 40 years, and has now finally regained.

St George slays the dragon.

SANKT
GEORG
SANKT
ANNO

ON THE TRAIL OF THE ROMANS

"Taking the lift back to Roman times"; seldom has a book-title been so apt as that of the popular work by Rudolf Pörtner. The lift does actually exist: the shaft leads from the new Town Hall down into the Roman Praetorium beneath it. But it's the metaphor in the title that is most significant: the heart of the city is rather like a palimpsest, an old piece of parchment from which the writing has been removed to make room for new writing, thus allowing traces of old texts to be discovered beneath newer ones.

Soil steeped in history: Anyone who descends to these levels – whether he takes the lift or just uses a spade – very soon comes into contact with the city's Roman past. To give a recent example: in the summer of 1990, the medieval quarter of St Alban was discovered between Martinstrasse, Quatermarkt and Gülichplatz, to the north of the famous Gürzenich. Here, traces were found revealing that the area had been densely populated as early as Roman times, and further down, a stone decorated with a floral relief was discovered: it had apparently fallen from a great height, and had once perhaps even formed part of the **Temple of Mars**, which many people think once stood here.

At the other end of the Roman city, the **Roman Tower** (Römerturm) of the city's former fortifications has been visible for almost two thousand years. Street names such as "Griechenpforte" (Greek Gate), "Hohe Pforte" (High Gate) or the "Alte Mauer am Bach" (Old Wall by the Stream) are reliable clues to where the old Roman walls used to run, and the greatest temple of any Roman city, the **Capitol**, built to honour the triad of Jupiter, Juno and Minerva, is both apparent and non-apparent in the name as well as the foundations of St Mary's in the Capitol, one of the city's most important churches.

Preceding pages: evening light falls on the Wallraf-Richartz Museum. **Left**, Roman head of Augustus in the Roman-Germanic Museum.

Around the middle of the 1st century AD, Cologne began its history as *Oppidum Ubiorum*. Caesar had annihilated the Germanic tribe of the Eburones on the left bank of the Rhine roughly 100 years before, and had then established relations with the Ubii. Under Augustus, the Ubii rose to become part of the Roman federation, and were settled on the left bank to fill the vacuum left by the Eburones. Even this first Ubii settlement had its own fortifications.

The so-called **Ubii Monument** still stands; it was probably the corner bastion of the former entrance to the harbour. It was only in 1965, during construction of an apartment building on the corner of "Mühlenbach" and "An der Malzmühle" that the mighty squared-stone masonry – the oldest stone monument in the city – was first discovered and exposed.

In AD 50, the Emperor Claudius, at the request of his wife Julia Agrippina, raised the city to the status of CCAA: Colonia Claudia Ara Agrippiensium. Soon afterwards, construction work began on renewing the city walls, and the mighty **Roman stone wall**, with its 19 towers and nine gates, was completed as early as AD 70. The limestone arch of the **northern gate**, which once lay on the road to Neuss, has been reconstructed in the Roman-Germanic museum. On the side facing away from the city one can still clearly see the proud abbreviation "CCAA".

The wall enclosed an area which some sources say measured as much as one kilometre square. The two main thoroughfares, the **"cardo maximus"** which ran north-south, and the **"decumanus maximus"** which ran from east to west, are still the two main streets in the heart of the city today: the Hohe Strasse and the Schildergasse.

Anyone who doesn't just want to sense ancient Rome in Cologne's streets, but to see it and actually experience it at first hand should take a walk along the section of original Roman wall situated to the north of the city; it runs from the Cathedral – where a good section of it can be seen near the entrance to the Cathedral underground car park – along the street called "An der Burgmauer" in a westerly direction, past various remnants and ruins, all the way to the Roman Tower (Römerturm) one kilometre away.

The slope between "An der Burgmauer" on the one hand, and Komödienstrasse and Zeughausstrasse on the other is a present-day reminder of the former difference in elevation between the walls surrounding the city and the broad ditch that lay beyond the fortifications. The **Roman Fountain** in front of the Arsenal (Zeughaus) with its Municipal Museum dates from 1915 (it was renovated in 1955) and is thus somewhat newer than the **Roman Tower**, which is just as richly decorated as it was 1,900 years ago. The mosaic pictures in its stonework can still be easily detected.

The only non-genuine feature of the tower is its crenellation. One theory goes that the tower was twice as high in Roman times. During the Middle Ages it served as a lavatory for the Franciscan nuns from the convent of Poor Clares; in the 19th century an extra storey was added to provide living quarters; and finally it was purchased by the city and restored.

Truth and legend: During the Middle Ages, people could often make no sense at all of the Roman ruins; instead of the truth, they were far more prone to believe in legends, such as that of Master Gerhard, the architect of Cologne Cathedral, who made a pact with the devil that he would complete the Cathedral before the devil could bring water to the site all the way from Trier, in the Eifel. The devil, it is said, won the wager by making use of the Roman aqueduct, whereupon Gerhard flung himself to his death from the Cathedral's scaffolding.

But the Roman aqueduct actually extended no further than the "Marsilstein", or Marsil Stone, which at that time was outside the city limits. Only

A Roman lion.

very little is known of the water system within the city walls, and what some people take to be a section of Roman aqueduct in Theo-Burauen-Platz (named after the popular mayor and honorary citizen of Cologne from 1956 to 1973) is actually part of the **drainage system** which extends underground here along the length of the Budengasse (the former entrance to the Praetorium).

Inside the city itself, traces of the Roman **drinking water canal** exist only in the form of exhibits: in the park at the Museum of Applied Art, for example; in front of the Stadtsparkasse's "City-Treff" on the Habsburger Ring; in front of the main entrance to the *Fachhochschule* (Polytechnic) in Cologne-Deutz, or at the Geological Institute on Zülpicher Strasse. Many of these sections of stone come from far outside Cologne – just like its drinking water 2,000 years ago.

The local water wasn't good enough for the fastidious Romans, anyway. Very soon after Colonia was founded, an aqueduct was built to carry water from the nearby foothills into the city, and it was then followed in the 2nd century AD by a technological masterstroke: the Roman aqueduct leading from the Eifel Hills at Nettersheim, an area that even today still contains the best water for miles around.

The aqueduct, which was built underground because of the harsh climate, begins at a height of 420 metres (1,370 ft) above sea-level and then, descending very gradually, covers a distance of 9 km (55 miles) – though only around 50 km (30 miles) as the crow flies – before it reaches the Cologne area, which lies 50 metres (160 ft) above sea-level. It's possible to visit the original source, and inspect a reconstructed section of the aqueduct in the Eifel even today, and various parts of the canal have now been exposed; in 1988 the Eifel Association ("Eifelverein") opened its "Roman Canal Footpath" for those interested in studying it more closely.

But at the end of Graeco-Roman

Remnants of antiquity in the Roman-Germanic Museum.

times, when Roman domination of the Rhine area came to an end, the Roman aqueduct, too, sank into obscurity. During the Middle Ages, stone from it was used as building material, and fine pillars for churches were cut from it. Anyone accidentally chancing upon the aqueduct, while ploughing or land-clearing, for example, who didn't immediately believe it was the entrance to hell, was even less inclined to believe that people had once gone to all that trouble just to get hold of drinking water.

The aqueduct gets a mention in the 11th-century *Anno Lied* as a *Steinin Rinnen* (stone gutter). And according to another theory the Romans used this long aqueduct to transport their wine from Trier, in the Moselle region, to Cologne. So much for the expertise of the Middle Ages.

The fact that the Romans buried their dead along the highways outside the city limits, firstly in urns and then later in graves, means that another of Cologne's Roman attractions can be found outside the bounds of the former city, even though it has been incorporated into it today: the **Roman burial chamber in Cologne-Weiden** (1328 Aachener Strasse).

It was originally discovered quite by chance in 1843, during some construction work. The burial chamber was refurbished, and now the urns and niches, busts of the deceased, a marble sarcophagus with fine carvings and, above all, the stone furnishings all combine to give one a good impression of the cult of death in those times, at least as far as the wealthy were concerned.

The imposing remains of the **Praetorium**, in Kleine Budengasse, which were briefly mentioned by Cologne chronicler and councillor Hermann von Weinsberg during construction work on the Town Hall Loggia in 1570, have also been made accessible to the public. The impressive walls of what once used to be the palace belonging to the governor of Lower Germania can now be inspected deep below the Town Hall, which was destroyed in World War II; a scale model gives one a good idea of just how mighty this structure alongside the Rhine harbour wall used to be.

The Roman-Germanic Museum: The best place for anyone interested in Roman history is right next door to the Cathedral: the **Roman-Germanic Museum**. Since it was opened in 1974 this unassuming building has had over 10 million visitors.

One could easily spend days on end here studying what Cologne used to be like; the place has everything, from different kinds of everyday implements right up to some of the most magnificent treasures of antiquity. The sheer amount of exhibits is all part of the original idea behind the museum: "a supermarket of early history" is how the collection's founder, Hugo Borger, referred to it.

One of the most important exhibits here is definitely the **Dionysos Mosaic**, discovered in its present position during the construction of a bunker; it adorned the floor of a room in a Roman peristyle house that stood exactly where the museum stands today.

The **Tomb of Poblicius**, above the famous mosaic, was discovered by two young men excavating a cellar in 1965, and the mysterious *diatreta* glass cups, with their delicate network design, were also discovered accidentally during some construction work – as has so often happened in Cologne.

So the more cautious one is when digging away at the ground in Cologne, the better. It will be a long time before the palimpsest is thoroughly deciphered. In 1987 there was a plan to build an underground car park below the Neumarkt, the new heart of the city, once a densely-populated area in Roman times. The car park would have destroyed a great deal. So, despite a lot of protest, the plans have been shelved for the time being, thus giving future archaeologists the chance to stay on the trail of the Romans.

An enduring monument.

THE MUSEUMS AND THEIR PATRONS

While most of Germany's museums have their origins in royal collections, the major museums of Cologne were founded by the burghers of the city themselves. The priest **Ferdinand Franz Wallraf**, who lived from 1748 to 1824, is responsible for many of the collections in Cologne.

Wallraf, like many other of his contemporaries, collected anything that contributed to the cause of furthering science and knowledge, and managed to gather together a vast assortment of books, drawings, etchings, stone monuments, coins and paintings. After Napoleon's occupation of the Rhineland and the resulting secularisation of the monasteries and churches, he became strongly interested in medieval panel paintings, and did his best to save them from destruction.

On his death he bequeathed his collection to the city of Cologne on condition that it be suitably exhibited. To gain some idea of just how passionate a collector this man was, it must be remembered that he alone donated 1,616 paintings, 3,875 drawings, and 42,419 etchings. Parts of his collection were later included in other ones. The various exhibits can be seen today in the Roman-Germanic Museum, the Museum of Applied Art and the Schnütgen Museum. The Municipal Museum also inherited some of his treasures. The main part of his collection, though, is on show in the Wallraf-Richartz Museum, which – as the name makes clear – has another magnanimous patron to thank for its existence.

The merchant **Johann Heinrich Richartz** (1795–1861) donated the sum of 100,000 thalers to the city in order to house the collection. It took a while before the former Minorite convent was deemed to be a suitable site, and it also took yet another donation from Richartz before the museum – built according to plans by Felten and Raschdorf – could finally be opened in 1861.

During World War II the building was completely destroyed, and yet another citizen of Cologne came to the rescue with a generous donation, giving the museum a new lease of life: **Josef Haubrich**. He was a lawyer, and had saved many Expressionist and Modernist paintings from destruction during the Nazi era. His generous donation in 1946 meant that the first new German museum of the post-war era could be constructed. On the original site, the austere, understated design by Rudolf Schwarz and Josef Bernard became a reality, and was opened in 1957. At that time the building was known as the "Wallraf-Richartz Museum and the Haubrich Collection".

The fact that it didn't remain so is thanks to the entrepreneurial married couple **Peter and Irene Ludwig** from Aachen. In 1976, they bequeathed 300 exhibits from their collection of modern art (with the main emphasis on Ameri-

Left, art appreciation in the Ludwig Museum. **Right**, a detail of Stephan Lochner's *Madonna in the Rose-Garden.*

can pop-art and "new realism") to the city on condition that it would be housed in a new museum. The city of Cologne thus decided to erect a large double museum next to the Cathedral: the Wallraf-Richartz Museum and Ludwig Museum.

In 1986 the original and by no means uncontroversial new building, designed by architects Peter Busmann and Godfried Haberer, was formally opened. Then in 1989, the Museum of Applied Art moved into the "old building" at the Minorite convent. So today, monuments to the honourable benefactors Wallraf and Richartz can be seen standing in front of an edifice with little if anything at all in common with their original intentions.

The patron **Josef Haubrich** has had the **Art Exhibition Hall** (Kunsthalle) named after him: it was opened in the Neumarkt in 1967. It acts as a "shop-window" for other museums, and features alternating national exhibitions.

Before one sets foot in the **Wallraf-Richartz Museum and Ludwig Museum** with the **Agfa-Foto-Historama**, it's best to work out in advance whether one is more attracted by older or more modern art, and then divide up one's visit on that basis. Asking for a plan of the building at the information-desk, which outlines the interior and shows the various possible routes, makes it relatively easy to find one's way about. It is advisable, though, to take a break between the two collections, in the generously laid-out museum cafeteria, for example, or in one of the many restaurants in the Old City (Altstadt) close by.

The highlight of any trip to Cologne's museums is the collection of medieval panel paintings by the Cologne school of painters. The great altars can all be found in one room, standing there at eye-level, some distance away from the walls. The work of Cologne's most famous painter, Stephan Lochner, must not of course be missed (the museum owns a *Last Judgement* by him as well as his magnificent *Madonna in the*

A 17th-century Japanese priest figure.

Rose-Garden), but several other works, such as those by the Master of St Veronica, are worth attention. The two large triptychs by the Master of St Bartholomew are also excellent.

As is always the case with museums founded on donations, not every culture and epoch is dealt with in a balanced manner. The transition to the Renaissance is represented by only a few, though exquisite, works of art: Barthel Bruyn's double portrait of the Salsburgs, husband and wife; Dürer's *Piper and Drummer*; and Cranach's *Judgement of Paris*.

Focal points: 17th-century Dutch art, however, is very well represented in Cologne because the city succeeded in obtaining the Carstanjen Collection in the early 1920s. As early as the stairwell one can already see Rubens' altarpiece The *Stigmatisation of St Francis*. Other highlights include works by Hals, Honthorst and von Heemskerck, and of course there is also the fine *Self-Portrait in Old Age* by Rembrandt.

Another focal point is 19th-century painting. Here we find works by Joseph Anton Koch and Schnorr von Carolsfeld, as well as Caspar David Friedrich and Adolph von Menzel. There is also an important collection of works by the realist Wilhelm Leibl, and Corinth and Liebermann form the transition to the French Impressionists, where Renoir's *Portrait of the Sisleys* is a real highlight.

20th-century art: Munch forms the transition to the Ludwig Collection, and 20th-century art. Going down a few steps at the end of the "Museumsstrasse" one finds post-1960 German art: to the right, in the main hall, Penck, Kiefer and Immendorf, and in the Rhine Halls ("Rheinsäle"), works by Klapheck and Richter.

If one then goes up to the second floor, one passes through a small exhibition room containing works by German avant-gardist Joseph Beuys before reaching a large hall devoted to the work of the German Expressionists, including Kirchner and other members of

A scene from the Ludwig Museum.

the "Brücke" group. A monumental sculpture by Otto Freundlich is particularly eye-catching here, and right beside it is a superb ensemble by Beckmann. Then, via Constructivism and the Russian avant-garde, one reaches Picasso, well represented with works taken from all his periods.

As far as Dada and Surrealism are concerned, the Rhineland has its very own contributor: Max Ernst. He was born in the nearby town of Brühl, and is of course very well represented, above all by his scandalous *Madonna thrashing the Baby Jesus*.

One then comes to abstract art of the post-war era – Wilhelm Nay, who adopted Cologne as his home, has a whole exhibition room devoted to his work (Peill donation). Further on, one reaches "Nouveau Réalisme".

Then it's the turn of the Americans, with work by Jasper Jones, Andy Warhol, Rauschenberg and Lichtenstein. In the stairwell, one is suddenly faced by a very colourful *Nana*. At this point, the two sculpture sections up on the roof deserve a visit; they afford a fine view of the Old City, and from the western one there is a magnificent view of the choir section of the Cathedral, which almost seems to be within reaching distance.

Both museums contain small exhibition rooms devoted to old prints, which, though separately run, can be found in the same area of the building. The reading room, where one can be shown individual pages, is situated on the first floor, close to the entrance to the medieval collections.

A real treat for photography enthusiasts is the **Agfa-Foto-Historama**, on permanent loan to Cologne from Agfa, Leverkusen. One can reach this exhibition – which documents the history of photography from the first ever daguerreotypes to the present day – by crossing over to the other side of the cafeteria, or by going down the stairs at the end of the "Museumsstrasse".

The **Schnütgen Museum**, with its collection of church art from the early Middle Ages to the 19th century, also has a patron to thank for its existence: **Alexander Schnütgen** (1843–1918), a member of the Cathedral chapter, who, 100 years after Wallraf before him, devoted himself to saving valuable works of church art.

He was generally considered a rather odd collector, one who resorted to all kinds of ruses in order to acquire endangered works of art. In 1906 he bequeathed his collection to the city, which initially housed it in a new annexe to the Museum of Applied Art. In 1932, the exhibition was transferred across the river to the former Abbey of St Heribert in Cologne-Deutz. The medieval panel paintings from Schnütgen's collection were then moved to the Wallraf-Richartz Museum.

"Germany's finest museum": The abbey was destroyed during the air raids of World War II, but luckily its contents had been moved out in time. They were given a new home after the war in the

An exhibit from the Schnütgen Museum.

Romanesque convent church of St Cecilia. At the museum's opening ceremony in 1956, Federal President Theodor Heuss spoke of it as being "Germany's finest", and the great attraction of this museum even today is still the marvellous combination of the Romanesque church with the medieval masterpieces. One enters the building from the west, and before starting on a tour of the collection one really should allow a little time for the full effect of the interior and the arranged exhibits to sink in.

The exhibition is laid out chronologically, beginning with Romanesque sculpture and ending with the Baroque Heisterbach Grille. There are some real treasures to be found in the choir area, where the crucifix from St George's dominates the crossing, and the alabaster figures from the *Three Kings Gateway* and also the magnificent altar veil from St Ursula's are on view.

The busts of St Ursula, with their endearing expressions, and ostensibly containing the relics of the saint and her 11,000 virgin companions, are a real Cologne speciality.

One magnificent piece of work is the polychromed console bust of a woman carved by one of the Parler family. The western choir contains the mysterious *Siegburg Madonna* which was only discovered in the 1920s. The crypt, finely restored in 1977, and now re-opened, contains valuable liturgical utensils.

The Museum of Applied Art ("Kunstgewerbemuseum"), originally known as the Museum of Arts and Crafts, also has **Ferdinand Franz Wallraf**, whose collections make up the major part of it, to thank for its existence. Again, it was due to the generosity of another patron that the collection was provided with a suitable location. **Otto Gustav Andreae** bequeathed 400,000 marks to the city, and in 1900 an expensive, neo-Renaissance structure was opened on the Hansaring. Several extensions were later added to the building in order to house the Schnütgen Museum and the Museum of East Asian Art. Thanks to generous contributions from the people of Cologne and the acquisition of the collection belonging to Rhenish scholar Wilhelm Clemens, the building soon became one of the most important museums of arts and crafts in all Germany.

After World War II it sank into almost total obscurity, only managing to draw attention to itself via several minor exhibitions in the Romanesque Overstolzenhaus. Until 1989 it was very much a museum of storage boxes and packing-cases. But then, under the careful supervision of architect Von Lom, the now classic structure by Schwarz and Bernard – the original Wallraf-Richartz Museum – was restored to its original form and adapted for the use of the Museum of Arts and Crafts, which is today known as the "**Museum of Applied Art**".

The collection is laid out chronologically and based around particular themes, but these days it no longer relies

The Rautenstrauch-Joest Museum is devoted to the ethnology of non-European cultures.

on self-contained ensembles; rather, an effort has been made to allow each exhibit to retain its individual aura, while conveying a sense of how it connects with the others. Some of the finest exhibits in the museum are its articles of furniture, ranging from the Middle Ages to the time of the "Vienna Workshops" at the beginning of this century. Some parts of the museum feature collections of jewellery and majolica, and there are also a few pieces of fine porcelain on display.

The entrance to the modern collection is situated on the ground floor beyond the main hall. The museum was founded on condition that it also display a collection of contemporary art. The "Textiles and Fashions" section, housed in a small, darkened exhibition room on the upper floor, is attractively laid out.

There is one other museum which no one visiting Cologne should miss, even though it is not right in the centre of the city: the **Museum of East Asian Art**. It, too, has patrons to thank for its existence: **Adolf and Frieda Fischer** presented the city of Cologne with their collection in 1909 on condition that a museum devoted solely to Asian culture be founded. The collection was thus spared the fate of becoming just another ethnological museum.

In 1913, the museum was opened in an extension building to the Museum of Arts and Crafts, and Fischer then stocked it with all the treasures he had specifically acquired for his collection on two lengthy trips he had taken through Asia in 1909 and 1912.

In 1944, the museum was destroyed during air raids, and it was only in 1977 that it was reopened in a new, harmoniously simple-looking building designed by Japanese architect Kunio Mayekawa, next to the Aachener Weiher (pond). The Japanese garden in the inner courtyard and the terrace facing the Aachener Weiher give the building a calm, Far Eastern atmosphere that is very conducive to meditation. The restaurant here is very popular too, especially during the summer months.

The museum contains works exclusively from Japan, China and Korea. Since many of the exhibits are very sensitive to light, they often get changed. Sometimes, during important exhibitions, whole sections are moved.

Impressive: The Chinese and Japanese bronzes are magnificent, and one particularly impressive exhibit is the wooden figure of *Buddha Amitabha* from Japan. The glass display cases contain porcelain and ceramics from Korea, Japan and China, and of course there are also many fine examples of the lacquerwork for which East Asia is so famous. There are always a few particularly fine examples of the museum's large collection of folding screens on display, and one can always be sure of seeing several of the enchanting scroll wall paintings, with their landscapes and scenes from everyday life.

The **Rautenstrauch-Joest Museum** of ethnology also reveals the names of its patrons. The two Cologne families not only formed the basis of the museum with their collections, they also donated money for the building itself, which was constructed in neo-Baroque style by Edwin Crones and opened in 1906 as the first ever museum devoted entirely to ethnology. Even today it is still the only ethnological museum in all of North Rhine-Westphalia.

The building was badly damaged during the war, and the Museum has been somewhat hampered in its effect by the municipal Little Theatre ("Kammerspiele"), housed in the same building. Plans by Gottfried Böhm for a new building on the Heumarkt are now being discussed, but it is unlikely to be moved into before the end of the 1990s.

At the moment, the following sections are open: Indian cultures – the South Seas – pre-Columbian cultures of America – Khmer and Thai. There has also been a recent addition: a toy collection called "Spielzeugwelten" (Worlds of Toys).

The Schnütgen Museum in St Cecilia's contains a unique collection of church art.

ART AND COMMERCE

Cologne has its art dealers' ingenuity to thank for its leading role as the European metropolis of modern art: in 1967, several of them, including Hein Stünke and Rudolf Zwirner, founded an "Art Market". Back then, the newly-created "Association of Progressive German Art Dealers", made up of 18 representatives from the trade from all over the Federal Republic, put on an exhibition in the Gürzenich of non-establishment, contemporary art. And although the odd connoisseur may have been put off by the light-hearted combination of art and commerce, the exhibition was a great success, with 15,000 visitors in five days.

"Art Cologne", as the exhibition has been referred to since 1974, has gone from strength to strength since then, and was shifted long ago to Cologne's Trade Fair Centre. And this despite fierce competition, for the idea of an art market has now gained acceptance and similar fairs are taking place the world over, from Los Angeles to Basle and Paris to Chicago. But only Basle – because Americans prefer Switzerland to Germany – has been providing any really serious competition.

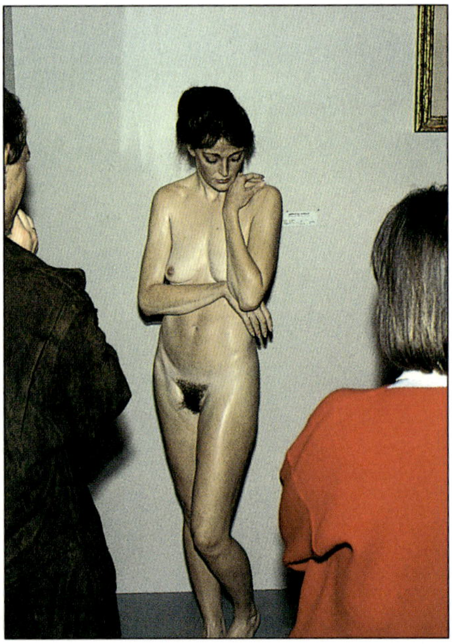

Cologne has reacted to this with fresh ideas: museums and their collections have formed part of the fair since 1978, and there's also room for new talent thanks to a subsidy programme for young artists.

But the main driving force in Cologne's artistic life is less the politicians responsible for its culture than its art galleries themselves. In a city with such magnificent museums, art dealers have been able to set out a selection unparalleled anywhere else in Europe. Anyone interested in art – whether classic modern, constructive, art from the 1950s (when Paris was the artistic metropolis of the Western world), pop or pop art – will find all his heart's desires in Cologne, up to and including the most recent trends.

To make the range on offer even more attractive, the gallery owners have been continually innovative. One example is the "Gallery Weekend" which they stage twice annually, and which brings collectors, artists and museum representatives from all over the world to the Rhine.

But what use are galleries without the artists to go with them? Cologne attracts a lot of artists, and the number is increasing steadily. It's not only the commercial prospects that beckon, either: there's also the basic atmosphere of tolerance here. "*Jeder Jeck ist anders*" ("We're all crazy in our different ways"), as they say in Cologne, reflecting an easy-going attitude towards one's fellow-men, whether or not they happen to come up to accepted norms. On top of this there is also a healthy love of art which the Rhinelanders have retained ever since Roman times.

This unique artistic climate has resulted in a genre that only a place like Cologne could have come up with. Painters, sculptors and video artists do not work separately from one another here; instead, the disciplines tend to blur. Depending on what their subject requires, they can reach for paintbrushes, palette knives or video cameras. This kind of openness and determined lack of narrow-mindedness has resulted in experiments that are making creative art forge ahead. The city plays a leading role in the video arts.

Cologne is not sinking into any kind of regional complacency, though; that is prevented not only by the artists here with international reputations – such as Gerhard Richter, Sigmar Polke, Bernhard Johannes, Ann Blume, Jürgen Klauke, C.O. Paeffgen, Astrid Klein, Walter Dahn and Martin Kippenberger – but also very much by the dealers themselves.

Three gallery-owners in particular had a decisive influence for many years: Paul Maenz, who began by exhibiting Arte Povera and Minimalist art, and was one of the first promoters of "rediscovered painting" (*Transavantguardia* in Italy, and the group "Mülheimer Freiheit" in Germany), took official leave of the business in 1990. Michael Werner, with his consistent exhibition strategy and his mixture of decisiveness and personal commitment, gained international success with his team of artists (Georg Baselitz, Markus Lüpertz, Georg Immendorf, A.R. Penck, Per Kirkeby) and he continues to play an important role. Rudolf Zwirner, really more a dealer than a gallery-owner, still remains one of the great names in the business, not only because of the exhibitions in which he used to mix established names with new ones, but also because of his cultural-political commitment which he continues to display with as much verve as ever, often unsettlingly so. His *Köln Sammelt* ("Collectors of Cologne") exhibition was one of the best in recent years.

Meanwhile, a new generation of gallery-owners is taking the place of the old established names of former years. The dominant figure here is Max Hetzler. Cool and clever, he has built up a gallery in which he co-operates with colleagues in New York. A branch on the West Coast of the USA also means that new talent and new buyers can readily be found. Hetzler represents Günther Förg, Werner Büttner, Georg Herold, Martin Kippenberger, Albert and Markus Oehlen as well as Reinhard Mucha and Hubert Kiecol. He runs his worldwide business from his gallery-house on Venloer Strasse, which was built by renowned Cologne architect Oswald Mathias Ungers.

Roughly 60 different galleries are officially listed in Cologne, but there are actually a lot more, with new ones being founded almost daily. Some of the most important addresses offering a broad range of work in general include: Karsten Greve, with such great names as Jannis Kounellis, Nicola de Maria, Paco Knöller and Lucio Fontana; Monika Sprüth, whose programme also takes in Rosemarie Trockel, Cindy Sherman, Jenny Holzer, Barbara Kruger and Fischli/Weiss; Gerhard Reinz, who with his "Galerie Orangerie" and its works by Picasso, Miro, Fautrier, Ackermann, Nay and Poliakoff, tends to focus on classic moderns and on postwar art in general.

Two major figures among the prime movers are Rolf Ricke, who was the first to introduce the work of American artists Richard Serra and Keith Sonnier to Europe, and Winifried Reckermann with Yves Klein, Arman, Uecker and Calder, as well as several successful young artists such as Thomas Virnich, Dorothee von Windheim and Bodo Baumgarten. Heinz Holtmann has Beuys, Buthe, Banana and Blume on offer, and the Jöllenbeck Gallery looks after Runde Mields, Michael Witlatschil, Rainer Barzen and Frank Dornseif. Several dealers also offer art from the 1920s and 1930s for sale, including the Stolz and Teufel Gallery. And Kicken-Pauseback as well as Johnen & Schöttle both specialise in photography.

Something of a loner on the Cologne artistic scene is the Gmurzynska Gallery. Founded in 1964 by Antonina Gmurzynska, who was born in Warsaw, its clearly-defined, high-quality programme made it one of the top addresses for pioneers of modern art and for the European and Russian avant-garde. Thanks to her excellent contacts, Antonina Gmurzynska succeeded in unearthing key works of the Bauhaus, de Stijl, Suprematist, Cubist and Surrealist movements. Her gallery became a meeting-place from the mid-70s onwards for heads of museums and collectors such as Thissen-Bornemisza and Peter Ludwig. When Antonina died in 1986 and her daughter took over the gallery, many felt that the end was nigh. But Krystyna soon proved she could follow in her mother's footsteps, and the gallery, housed in a new museum-like building, is now in a better position than ever.

Even though no other German city will seriously be able to endanger Cologne's reputation as a metropolis of art over the coming decades, the city will still have to rise to several challenges in the near future. The change in the political landscape means that it will have to re-define its role, and maintain its status as a bridgehead between Paris and Berlin and – thanks to its excellent collection of Pop Art, unrivalled even in the USA itself for size and quality – as a counterpart to New York.

Art and art dealing is thus still very much alive and well in Cologne. And considering Cologne's special mixture of Rhenish cheerfulness, realism, creativity and hard business sense, there really need be no cause for alarm. In the words of Hiltrud Kier, a native of Graz and head of one of Cologne's museums: "The people of Cologne have never been all that concerned with what happens elsewhere, they've always rested safe and secure in the knowledge of their two-thousand-year history." And anyone touring Cologne's museums and art galleries always gets a sense of this relaxed, self-confident feel the city has, along with its cheerful "live and let live" attitude to life.

GESCHENKE
PARFÜMERIE
Schlüssel
KINO
Zuchtperlen FACH GESCHÄFT

Shopping in Cologne

As far as shopping in Cologne is concerned, a very pleasant transformation has taken place over the past few years with regard to quality and variety, and its been lent extra strength architecturally and aesthetically, too, with the reorganisation of the Ring roads between Zülpicher Platz and Christophstrasse, and the construction of well-designed shopping arcades in the city centre.

Whatever you're looking for – fashions, furniture, porcelain, glass, leather goods, cosmetics or jewellery – you'll find it all in the city centre, between the Rings (from Ebertplatz up to the Südstadt) and the Rhine.

The first shopping district most visitors to Cologne get to know is the one around the Cathedral and the Old City. It's certainly worth taking a stroll between the Wallrafplatz and the Alter Markt – top-quality fashions, crockery, jewellery and carpets are all on sale here. Musikhaus Tönger, with its records, CDs and sheet music, is a favourite haunt for classical music enthusiasts. For pop and jazz the best place to go is the highly popular "Saturn" on the Hansaring.

Incidentally, this brick complex on the Hansastrasse was Europe's tallest skyscraper just after it was built in 1925 – something that seems ludicrous today. Another good place for pop music is WOM (World Of Music) on the ground floor of "Hertie" in the Neumarkt.

In the summer, it's very pleasant to sit outside the "Früh am Dom" beer-hall, or the various other restaurants and cafés bordering the Cathedral square, and enjoy a view of the Roncalliplatz, the "Domhotel", the Roman-Germanic Museum and the western facade of the Cathedral. Anyone who still finds the pace of life too hectic here should head down the Stollwerck-Passage for the distinguished "Gartencafé Reichard", with its select assortment of cakes and confectionery.

Preceding pages: faces at a flea market. **Left**, shop-window reflections.

Much of Cologne was destroyed in World War II. The **Hohe Strasse** wasn't spared either, and was rebuilt rather unimaginatively. However, it's still one of the city's most popular and lively shopping streets. Boutiques, jeans shops, fur shops and shoe shops predominate, alongside sex shops and fast-food outlets. At the end of the long, narrow street one arrives at what used to be the Tietz department store, now "Kaufhof"; it has made quite a name for itself with gourmets ever since its new food department opened. Crab, lobster, poultry and game from France, exotic fruit and vegetables from all over the world are permanently available here; at the various "snack-stands" one can sample pasta dishes, vegetarian dishes, fish and meat specialities, and salmon or oysters for a quick meal *en passant*. The range available here should give one more than enough energy to cope with a walk through the next major pedestrian street on the route.

Street performers: The **Schildergasse** got its name from the medieval shield-painters whose guild house once used to stand here, along with some of their workshops. Today the street is lined with clothes shops, large and small; one can buy leather goods, underwear, jewellery and cosmetics, and also find several pleasant places to pass the time of day – in the street café next to the Antonite Church, for example. From spring until autumn this street is a favourite haunt of pavement artists and buskers, as well as mime acts.

The **Neumarkt** was a horse and cattle market as early as the 11th century. Today, depending on the season, this rather unimaginatively designed square is the venue for the "Büchersommer" summer book fair, the antiques market, the wine market and the Christmas market. But market or not, the Neumarkt is still a desirable address.

A further and very recent attraction as far as shopping arcades are concerned is

Richmod's. The tower of the former Richmodis building, with its two horses' heads looking out of the window, is being integrated into the new architecture. Meanwhile, the **Neumarkt-Passage** has already been completed, and it now stretches as far as Richmodisstrasse before connecting three major shopping arcades, including Richmod's as well as the exquisite **Olivandenhof** (named after a medieval building that once stood on the site called the "Haus zum Olivunden" – meaning "elephant").

One of the three very well-equipped bookshops in the Neumarkt area can be found right at the entrance to the arcade, next to the "Kreissparkasse" bank. The interior of the shopping arcade is luxuriously laid-out, with a wholemeal bistro and a gourmet restaurant, and a glass lift travels up to the glass cupola of the Käthe Kollwitz Museum, with its permanent exhibition of graphics, posters and sculptures.

Fashion enthusiasts should definitely check out the expensive and lavish articles of clothing, including leatherware, in the **Mittelstrasse** and **Pfeilstrasse** districts. Here, right next to the **Bazaar de Cologne** (near the northwest corner of the Neumarkt), there is a glass-covered shopping arcade with a whole series of shops, pubs and restaurants, chic fashion firms and several elegant boutiques.

The latest and weirdest fashions: Very different fashions – those preferred by the city's young alternatives – can be found in **Ehrenstrasse**, at the end of which one rejoins Pfeilstrasse. Boutiques, some of which contain extremely weird clothing, alternate with flashy shoe-shops, esoteric bookshops, and leather shops to suit all tastes. Here we find alternative cafés and cinemas, an Asian shop, an excellent poultry and game shop, and also Walther König's artistic bookshop which has a superb selection.

Those keen on seeing something a little more elegant and sophisticated after this should turn off Ehrenstrasse into **St Apernstrasse**. Within this area, surrounding the arcade known as the **Kreishausgalerie**, it's worth taking a look inside the various antique shops and art galleries. And from here it's just a short walk to **Breite Strasse**, in the pedestrian precinct, and to the oldest shopping arcade in Cologne, the **Ladenstadt**. Posters, wine, carpets as well as kitchenware can be found here. There's also the celebrated 4711 building in the nearby **Glockengasse**.

A good old-fashioned stroll: Ever since the tram link between Zülpicher Platz and Ebertplatz was moved underground, Cologne's **Rings** have once again become attractive; it has gone to great pains to restore these streets, once so popular with shoppers and strollers. From 1881 onwards, after most of the medieval city walls had been taken down, the Rings were laid out according to plans drawn up by Stübben, Cologne's municipal architect. The streets of the projected "New Town" (Neu-

Hohe Strasse, Cologne's busiest shopping mile.

stadt) varied in width as well as magnificence according to the kinds of inhabitants planned for them.

Some of this has been borne in mind during the present restoration work, the quality of which is already evident in the magnificent shop and office buildings on the **Hohenstaufenring**, near the Zülpicher Platz. Here one can find expensive furniture, fashions and computers, fine fabrics and a bookshop with a comprehensive selection of travel books and hiking maps (Gleumes). And just around the corner, at No. 3, **Beethovenstrasse**, a fishmonger's, plus snack bar, with what is probably the most comprehensive selection of Mediterranean fish in the whole of Cologne, the "Neptun Fischhalle", opened just a short while ago.

Looking for designer fashions, ultramodern fountain pens, vases made of chromium steel and candlesticks made of perspex? Go to "Rosselli" on the Habsburgerring. On the other side of the Ring, the **City-Treff**, belonging to the "Stadtsparkasse", is a place where anyone can relax, with its bistro and its reading corner.

Form and function in the exclusive Olivandenhof shopping centre.

Hohenzollernring, and **Kaiser-Wilhelm-Ring** in particular have been laid out very attractively with fountains, flowerbeds and groups of trees, creating a park atmosphere. There was a huge festival held in 1988 to mark the completion of the work. Insurance companies settled in the area a long time ago, alongside the numerous street cafés, cinemas, shoe-shops, record shops and smallish department stores. "Pesch" is still the number one address for all furniture enthusiasts, with its unique and highly impressive selection of cupboards, tables, armchairs and living accessories.

A dash of Turkey: The **Eigelstein** is a typical district of Cologne, and it also has a strong Turkish flavour to it. Anyone keen on lamb, mutton, veal or beef will find a fresh as well as comprehensive selection in the half-dozen or so Turkish butchers' shops here. Herbs and spices to go with the food, along with sheep's cheese and olives, good-value vegetables and fruit can be found in several shops. The delicious selection is complemented by Spanish, Italian and Greek shops, all selling products from their own countries, and of course there are also lots of restaurants and fast-food establishments ready to welcome the visitor.

Anyone keen on the "bazaar" atmosphere of fruit and vegetable stands, cheese and sausage stalls, flower stalls and knick-knacks in general would be very well advised to visit one of Cologne's many **markets** ("Wochenmärkte").

The ones in the Old City are of particular interest: there is one in the Alter Markt (Fridays, 8 a.m.– 6.30 p.m.) and at Apostelkloster (Tuesdays and Fridays, 7 a.m. – 1 p.m.), and there are also the markets at the Klettenberggürtel (Wednesdays and Saturdays, 7 a.m. – 1 p.m.) and in the Wilhelmplatz in Nippes (Monday – Saturday, 7 a.m. – 1 p.m.).

RHENISH GASTRONOMY

It's a known fact that the people of Cologne are full of *joie de vivre*. They love a good festival – and not just at Carnival time, either. They're very sociable, they enjoy a good laugh over their glasses of *Kölsch*, and are very keen on culinary attractions of all kinds. "*Jut esse und drinke hält Liev un Siel zesammen,*" as they say ("Good food and drink keeps body and soul together").

Anyone who doesn't believe this should take a look in the – by no means fully comprehensive – Cologne yellow pages. Over 1,800 breweries, restaurants and pubs, along with 80 cafés, can all be found jostling for the gourmet's attention, and these figures don't even include the establishments specialising in *Pommes Rut-Wiess* (chips with ketchup and mayonnaise) and *Rievkooche* (potato fritters) to take away.

A real beer-house atmosphere: Anyone who feels like trying out some of Cologne's gastronomic specialities should head for the city's **beer-houses**: the "Malzmühle" in the Heumarkt, for example, the "Pfäffgen" in Friesenstrasse, "Sion" in the Strasse Unter Taschenmacher or "Früh am Dom" (opposite the Cathedral) in the city centre. These traditional establishments, with their highly *gemütlich* and beery atmosphere, will serve you the kind of food every Cologne granny used to make: large helpings, very substantial, tasty and also good value for money. From midday onwards the wooden tables, scrubbed clean, are already packed with people of all ages.

At the centre of the crush you can see the *Köbes* (waiters) with their blue aprons and their stoic expressions, carrying plates piled high with steaming *Hämchen* (pork knuckle), *Rippchen Rut-Wiess* (cured loin of pork with red and white cabbage), and of course *Himmel un Ääd* (Heaven and Earth), that special Cologne mixture of mashed potato (earth), stewed apple (heaven) and fried blood sausage, also known as *Flönz*, the delicious aroma of which usually reconciles visitors to its questionable appearance.

In all the months with an "r" in, bright-red signs appear in the windows inviting one to sample *kutterfrische Muscheln* (fresh mussels). These can be served with onion rings in a pepper sauce, in wine or in a vegetable sauce, accompanied by delicious black bread with butter. The establishment known as "Bieresel" in Breite Strasse even cooks its mussels *à la provençale*, with garlic and herbs, and also "Vienna style", fried with a coating of breadcrumbs.

A taste of Cologne humour: Let the stranger be wary of such peculiarities as *Halver Hahn*, *Kölscher Kaviar* or *Flönz met Musik*, which actually seem to have been created expressly so as to lead *Immis* (the Cologne word for non-locals) and other unsuspecting individuals up the garden path. The "Halver Hahn" (the literal meaning is "half chicken"), for example, listed under "side dishes" on every Cologne menu, arrives looking very different from the marvellous and delicious bargain you thought it was going to be: it's just a simple roll of rye bread nestling under an enormous slab of Dutch cheese. "Kölscher Kaviar" is nothing more than a small pile of *Flönz* (see above) with a bit of mustard squirted on top, accompanied by a white bread roll. And as for "Flönz mit Musik", all that means is a few onion rings get plonked on top as a garnish.

To wash it all down there's "Kölsch", the city's famous top-fermented beer, which the *Köbes* slams down on the wooden table in small high glasses called *Stangen*. The worst thing you can do to your "Köbes" is to order a glass of Coke, let alone water. "*Jiddet nit*" ("There ain't none") is the usual gruff answer, before the gentleman in the blue apron slams yet another foaming

Preceding pages: a restaurant in the Olivandenhof. Below, not only beer is consumed in Cologne's pubs.

glass of Kölsch onto his astonished customer's beer-mat.

Things are very different in the city's **elegant restaurants**, such as the "Goldener Pflug" in Cologne-Merheim, which has been the city's top address for years now, or Madame Rachel Silberstein's velvet-upholstered "Chez Alex" in the Old City. Kölscher Kaviar? *Jiddet nit.* Why not try *Jakobsmuscheln Noilly Prat*? With lobster parfait, perhaps? Cologne, with its "Halver Hahn" and its *"Hämchen"*, has a surprisingly large number of gourmet restaurants, but in the end it's all just *"jut esse un drinke..."*

Other top establishments include the Italian restaurants "Alfredo" in Tunisstrasse, and "Rino Casati" on the Ebertplatz; there's also the elegant "Wack", belonging to Romain Wack from Alsace, in Benesisstrasse, and the pigeon-grey "Ambiance am Dom". The people of Cologne certainly know how to eat well, and don't mind paying for it either. The main evening menu in the "Goldener Pflug", which has just enough room for 30 diners at any one time, can cost as much as DM 200 a head. Anyone who finds this too expensive just has to content himself with *Canard Nantais aux Raisins* for around DM 100, or a plate of *Turbot et Crème de Cellerie* for a modest DM 65.

Traditional food *à la maison*: If there's one thing common to all the top gourmet cooks in Cologne, whether they come from Italy, Belgium or Alsace, it's their love of consistency. They don't like to experiment. Indeed, why should they, if traditional food tastes so delicious anyway? *Babylotte* served with strips of zucchini, and fillet of sole with herbs have been firm favourites on the menu in "Alfredo" Carturan's 40-seat restaurant for years now, and fillet of beef *à la maison* is still an integral part of the menu at Madame Silberstein's. Quite different, though, is the "Graugans" restaurant in the Hyatt Regency Hotel in Cologne-Deutz. The chef de cuisine there has spiced up his

***Kölsch* tends to level the social differences.**

dishes by borrowing heavily from Asiatic cookery, much to the astonishment of Cologne gourmets, and steams his strips of salmon on lemon grass.

Perennial favourites in Cologne are those living-room-sized French and Italian restaurants with seven or eight tables, house wine and a menu that changes daily, featuring such delicacies as Saddle of Lamb *à la provençale*, Fillet of Beef Strips in Gorgonzola Sauce or Quail in Port Wine Sauce. A main course like this usually costs no more than DM 35.

On Friday nights and at weekends these little rooms are packed to overflowing, guests can wear jeans if they like, and be prepared: when space is at a real premium you can often see right into the kitchen. And the cook at "Il Bagutta" on Heinsbergstrasse, in the student area around the Zülpicher Strasse which Cologne refers to as its "Kwartier Lateng", may even seat himself at the piano as midnight approaches and hammer out a few popular Italian tunes, making everyone's *Mousse au Chocolat* tremble in the process.

Fish soup and fried duck: A few streets further on, the "Tapabo" (Kyffhäuserstrasse), a small bistro with nine tables covered with paper tablecloths, hasn't changed its menu for years. The fish soup here is superb – at DM 10 a plate, too. And situated behind the railway embankment in Krefelderstrasse is "Moissonnier", an attractive restaurant with a very respectable wine-list. *On parle français*. The menu is also in French, but the waiters patiently explain to all the guests that a *Consommé de Queue de Boeuf*, at 8 marks a bowl, is oxtail soup, and that a *Parmentier de Canard* is actually a piece of fried duck.

There are several other similar establishments: the "Artischocke" on Moltkestrasse, for example, with its cosy, old-fashioned decor. Or there's the excellent "La Baurie" at the People's Gardens (Volksgarten). Not to forget "La Barrière", situated far out in Müngersdorf, where the sauces are as dark as the ink from octopus, and taste just as if one were seated somewhere deep within France, instead of next to a level-crossing on the Aachener Strasse.

There again, the astonished visitor really feels he is in Ankara, Istanbul or Anatolia when he enters the Weidengasse, a narrow street with quite a shady past, in the north of Cologne. Oriental music drones monotonously out of the open doors of the snack-bars with their huge pieces of meat revolving on spits, and a heavy aroma of garlic hangs in the air. The Weidengasse, not far from the Eigelstein and the city's Rings, has been taken over completely by the Turks.

The most popular restaurant in the street for years now has been the "Bizim", an elegant and rather cool, though still cosy establishment, where one can find the best in **Istanbul cuisine**: puff pastry rolls with sheep's cheese and parsley, for example, and saddle of lamb with aubergine rolls. To go with it, of course, there's Turkish coffee. On the opposite side of the street there's the "Bandirma", and also the "Baba" and the "Bosporus" a few houses further up.

A gastronomic trip round the world: Or how about a Burmese meal? Persian? Mexican? Cologne can provide you with a gastronomic trip round the world. Just a few tips as you go: Mexican food tastes best at the "Café Especial" Mexican restaurant on Neuhoffer Strasse, opposite the main station in Deutz. Fans of Asian food are recommended to eat at the "Mandalay" restaurant on Brüsseler Strasse. The menu at Cologne's only Burmese restaurant is enticing, and anyone who feels like it can eat his *Fisch à la Mandalay* with chopsticks. A few steps up the street, in the "Bali" restaurant on Brüsseler Platz, huge pieces of fried duck and strips of carrot cut incredibly thin are served on black plates. Haute cuisine, Indonesian-style.

A word about Cologne's **cafés**. They are at least as varied as the city's restaurants, if not more so. Some of them, full of knick-knacks and comfortable up-

When the weather's nice, the tables are put outside.

holstery, serve cream cake, and also *Gulaschsuppe* with a roll at lunchtime. One good example is the "Trödelcafé" (near St Agatha) opposite "Kaufhof". The tiny, comfortable interior is packed full of old pieces of furniture and antiques which can actually be bought on the spot by guests.

Others are very much in the good old coffee-house tradition. Their furnishings haven't changed for centuries: pastel-coloured walls, subdued lighting, tiny tables. Old ladies with blue rinses and housewives who've just completed their morning shopping tend to congregate in the "Café Franck" on the Rudolfsplatz, or in the "Café Schmitz" on Breite Strasse, for a slice of fruit cake with cream. Connoisseurs, however, patronise the "Café Reichard" (Unter Fettenhennen) next to the WDR, which is so luxuriously furnished that it's hard to believe you're not in Vienna, even though the spires of Cologne cathedral can be seen through the windows. The cake is incredibly delicious.

The alternative café scene: And of course there are also those unusual establishments which first started livening up the café scene here at the end of the 1970s, and now have absolutely nothing in common with the usual café image: "Café Fleur" (Lindenstrasse/Engelbertstrasse), "Café Krümel" (Zülpicherstrasse/Weyertal), "Café Moka" (Weyertal) and "Kaffeeböhnchen" (Kurfürstenstrasse), among others. They have a sort of ramshackle, comfy look to them, with a touch of Parisian bistro. Crowded into these places are students, schoolchildren, alternatives, painters, musicians and all those who simply appreciate a good cappuccino and fresh croissants for breakfast.

Which brings us to the "alternative" part of Cologne. For years, the "in" place to meet was the relatively rundown Südstadt area, around Chlodwigplatz and Bonner Strasse. That came to an end with the days of "Saturday Night Fever", when young people from outside the city started making regular visits to the smoke-filled "Opera" and the no less tobacco-ridden "Spielplatz". Today, the Südstadt is certainly a lively area for pubs and clubs – but it's no longer "the in place to meet". The city's young artists, aspiring and otherwise, meet up in the "Broadway Café" on Ehrenstrasse. Dressed in black, and looking pale and serious, they spend the mornings there over a cappuccino before possibly switching later to the "Spitz" (Ehrenstrasse), a "cool", American-style bar with its shiny counter and pale green leather armchairs. And in the evenings they may show up at the "Königswasser" in Flandrische Strasse – if it's still "in", that is – or at the "Café Central" in the basement of the Chelsey Hotel on Jülicher Strasse.

Older boys and girls still swear by the "EWG" in Aachener Strasse, a very fifties-looking establishment, with its black-and-white tiled floor, and its rather miserable-looking rubber plants on the window-seats. On the other hand, everyone adores the "XX", or "Dos Eckies" in Friesenstrasse. Its design – red plush and subdued lighting – is a reminder of its original function: it used to be a "Kontakt-Café".

The most original place to meet: Anyone keen on seeing such Cologne greats as TV personality and talkaholic Alfred Biolek having his lunch should pluck up their courage and take a trip to the "Alter Wartesaal". Since its renovation, this former dining-hall at the main station, built in 1915, is now generally regarded as the most original place to meet in all of Cologne. Actors, journalists and artists jostle for a place at the counter, and the cuisine isn't bad either, while the younger generation leaps about in the disco of the same name next door.

It's also worth visiting the "Keule", too, at the Heumarkt, the No.1 meeting-place for Cologne's VIPs. "See and be seen" is the motto here in this restaurant with its black facade; Hans Dietrich Genscher is just one of many famous names to have downed a beer here.

The man who brings the beer is called the *Köbes*.

KÖLSCH

"Kölsch", Cologne's most famous beer, has been continually breaking its own records year in, year out. The breweries that produce it are in a totally unassailable position. Where draught beers are concerned, "Kölsch" has a market share of 90 percent, and the share in the bottled beer market is 70 percent. The 24 Kölsch breweries produce around 3.5 million hectolitres a year, and Cologne has long led the rest of Germany in per capita consumption of beer, as well as having more breweries than any other city in the country.

What is Kölsch exactly? Hard to say. Gustav Hamacher had this to say about it in dialect: "*Wenn su e Jlas Kölsch vör meer steit, dann jeit meer et Hätz op. Ich striche ens üvver et Jlas, hevven et andächtich an der Mungk – un dann läuft dat Kölsch wie jeölt durch der Stroß erav en der Mage.*" ("When a glass of Kölsch stands before me, my heart gives a leap and a bound. I run my hand across the glass, lift it reverently to my mouth – and then that Kölsch flows like oil down the passage leading to my stomach.")

Once it has reached the stomach it soon meets up with several others, for Kölsch is a sociable drink. Quickly consumed, it is swiftly followed by several more, and they all foster an atmosphere of togetherness: "*Mem Nohber am Desch fängk mer ne Verzäll an, un dann wedd dat esu jemötlich, als wammer uns allt johrelang kännte.*" ("My neighbour at the table starts talking to me, and then there's this cosy feeling that we've been friends for years.")

Kölsch is an exceptionally "fast" beer; it's ready the moment the glass has been filled, unlike a "Pils", which takes seven minutes. A Kölsch is there the moment you've ordered it – and in some of the beer-halls, even before you've done so. There it is sitting in front of you the moment you've emptied your glass.

In simple terms, Kölsch can be described as follows: it is a light and slightly bitter-tasting brew, very pleasant to drink, consisting of just water, barley malt and hops, like any other German beer in fact. But Kölsch gets its unmistakeable flavour from the fact that it is "top-fermented" (fermentation takes place at a higher than normal temperature, and a special yeast is also used, which rises to the top during the fermentation process, whereas with "bottom-fermented" beers such as Pils or Export, it sinks to the bottom).

Top-fermented beer was still the most common type of beer as late as the 18th century. It was only when Carl von Linde invented refrigeration towards the end of the century that beer could be produced at a lower temperature, which at the time also meant more hygienically.

Today, the higher sensitivity of top-fermented beer no longer poses any problems due to the cleanliness of the vats and pipes. And today no one, at least in Cologne, can stop the victorious advance of Kölsch. It scarcely has anything in common with 19th-century beer, though: it tastes different (the beer of the last century was "improved" via the addition of grated nutmeg); it doesn't have the same alcohol content (in those days beer was a basic source of nourishment and contained a lot less alcohol); and 19th-century beer wasn't even called "Kölsch" either (the name only appeared a lot later, probably in the form of a secret codeword like the "Halve Hahn").

The amount of Kölsch produced annually has increased 10 times over since 1960, despite the fact that the number of breweries has actually decreased. Even though the top breweries sell their beer in bottles these days, it still tastes far better on draught. And it's at its very best when it gets brewed and consumed under the same roof. There's just one place left in Cologne where this is still possible: "Pfäffgen", on Friesenstrasse.

Back in the 19th century Cologne was still considered very much a wine city: indeed – a fact that has been forgotten – it was north-west Europe's largest wine trading city next to Bordeaux, and the most popular drink here was wine from the Moselle region. With the triumph of Kölsch, Cologne has proved once and for all that, among the other records it holds, it also boasts the oldest brewing tradition in Germany – whatever boasts the Bavarians may make.

In The Heart Of The City

The people of Cologne tend towards sentimentality. They're aware of the fact, and aren't in the least ashamed of it. The Old City (Altstadt) may thus be defined, without further ado, as "the heart of Cologne". Not in a hectic, big-city business sense, though; rather, it's the emotional centre of the city, the part of it which gives the people of Cologne the strongest sense of "home".

The term "Altstadt" is rather confusing, anyway. Many experts think it means the area bounded by the medieval city walls in 1180. It was over 400 hectares (1,000 acres) in size, making Cologne the largest city in Europe for much of the Middle Ages. If one subtracts the areas within this walled enclave that only properly became part of the city in the 19th century, the "Old City" notion is really almost reduced to the original Roman square between the Neumarkt and the Roman Tower on the one hand, and the Cathedral and the Capitol Hill on the other.

But even that is not what today's inhabitants have in mind when they refer to the Old City. The general opinion is that the Hohe Strasse and the Schildergasse, even though they symbolise the hectic, pulsating city centre, are not part of the "Altstadt" at all. Years ago, Cologne's famous actor Willy Millowitsch once tried to sing a song in praise of the Hohe Strasse ("*Wer eimol durch die Huhe Stroß jejangen is...*") – but it never caught on. No, these consumer thoroughfares have nothing to offer when it comes to defining the city's identity, and what life in Cologne is really all about.

The heart of Cologne: The Old City only really starts just beyond the Hohe Strasse, in the direction of the Rhine. Here we see the major showpieces of the city all clustered together in one small area: the Town Hall tower with its glockenspiel and its *Platz-Jabbek* (a grotesque 15th-century figure which sticks out its tongue every time the hour is struck), the *Kallendresser* (a rather disrespectful-looking piece of sculpture in the Old Market) and the Jan von Werth Fountain; the magnificent panorama of the city; the "Martinsviertel" (the area around Great St Martin's), with the monument to those two legendary Cologne characters, Tünnes and Schäl, and the Schmitz Column; the Hänneschen Puppet Theatre, the Ostermann Fountain and all those picturesque little alleyways, filled with restaurants and bars, where business life in Cologne likes to wind down after a long day in an atmosphere of *Gemütlichkeit*.

All these attractions have the **Old Market** (Alter Markt) as their point of reference, with its colourful houses and those magnificent glimpses one catches of the Cathedral towers between them.

It is here that the Carnival reaches both its optical and its topographical climax every year. Here, we are at the true heart of Cologne.

Left and right, the people of Cologne are known for their *joie de vivre*.

This area has twice been the "cradle" of Cologne. In Roman times, an arm of the Rhine used to branch through here. Today's "Martinsviertel" was once an island. The Romans took advantage of this and used the area as a harbour, which must doubtless have affected daily life in Cologne even then. Harbours were always very lively places, full of hard work, hard trading, with colourful goings-on and generally loose morals.

Jupp Engels, a Cologne *Jrielächer* (a dialect word meaning "rogue"), whom the "Martinsviertel" has to thank for its **Schmitz Column**, claims in the inscription on the column that Roman legionaries met up with the beautiful Ubian (i.e. Cologne) girls on the harbour island and thus became the forebears of the noble Cologne family of Schmitz (the city's commonest name).

The Roman city wall passed below the city terrace, situated higher up, and still marked today by the Town Hall tower. The Roman **Praetorium** used to stand on this terrace, too. After the Romans moved out, only its ruins were left behind. Soon afterwards a Frankish princes' court was built a short distance away, on the site of today's Cathedral. In 1959, archaeologists made a sensational find below the Cathedral: the graves of a 6th-century princess and her son, lavishly equipped and completely untouched. Today the find is one of the attractions of the **Diocesan Museum** on Roncalliplatz, which also has a valuable collection of medieval religious art on display, best accompanied, for those interested in art history, by a walk through the Cathedral and its Treasury.

The Frankish princes provided little momentum as far as developing the city was concerned, but they did pave the way for the rule of the bishops.

The Jewish Quarter: Long after the Roman Praetorium had been reduced to ruins, however, it was the Jews who kept the final remnants of civic life together. The quarter of the city in which they lived was the chief centre of

Chilling reminder of the past: cells in the basement of the El-De-Haus, former headquarters of the Cologne Gestapo.

Northern European Jewry for centuries. In the 14th century, the number of pogroms practised by the Christian City Parliament began to increase, until the Jewish Quarter was mercilessly destroyed in 1424 and its final denizens driven out of the city without compensation. It was only in 1794, when the French had taken control of Cologne after the Revolution, that Jews were allowed back in the city.

The "**Jewish Quarter**" contained a "Burghers' House" – which later became the **Town Hall** – as early as the 12th century. Its site was probably chosen with conspiratorial care, for the Jews had their own area of jurisdiction, and the archbishop was unable to simply intervene whenever he wished. As the concept of a City Parliament gained in popularity, a palace-like structure developed from the initial hotchpotch of houses; much of it survives today in the shape of the **Hansasaal**, which is definitely worth a visit.

Self-confidence: Once the City Parliament had achieved its political aims it documented its triumphant self-confidence with the construction of the magnificent **Town Hall tower** (1407–14), visible from far and wide, still very much in the style of Gothic church towers. Inside it is the **Senate Chamber**, with seating and intarsia work by Melchior von Reidt, one of the artistic masterpieces of the Rhineland.

After the pogroms of 1424 the City Parliament, without any apparent scruples, extended its political centre to include the destroyed ghetto. The **Town Hall chapel** was built on the site of the former Synagogue directly opposite the Town Hall only two years later, in 1426, and given the tell-tale name of "St Mary's in Jerusalem". Stephan Lochner created his famous **Altar of the City's Patron Saints** especially for the chapel.

Fate smiled on the old City Parliament for quite a long time: however, 350 years later Lochner's altar had to be taken to the Cathedral – where it can still be admired today – in order to protect it from the French; and World War II destroyed the Town Hall chapel almost without trace.

It was only when the rubble was cleared away that deeper historic connections were laid bare: today the remains of the **Aula Regia**, which formed part of the Roman Praetorium, can be visited beneath the Town Hall (in the newer section known as the "Spanish Building"); the Jewish Quarter and the former positions of its various buildings can be made out via markings on the paving as well as the old street-names; and a glass pyramid marks the site of an ancient Ritual Bath known as the **Mikvah**, which still has a staircase leading down into it.

Those familiar with the origins of the Town Hall will realise why its actual facade faces the Town Hall Square (Rathausplatz) and not the Old Market (Alter Markt). All the important political decisions in the Free Imperial City took place in the Town Hall, one reason why one of the finest examples of Ren-

A detail of the bronze doors Ewald Mataré designed for the cathedral's south portal.

aissance architecture in all Germany can be admired here: Wilhelm Vernukken's **Loggia** (1569–73). By some miracle it was the only section of the building to survive World War II relatively unscathed. The Town Hall itself was rebuilt between 1966 and 1972 according to plans by architect Karl Band, and the tower was modelled on the old original one.

Cologne's industrial prosperity, on the other hand, began for different reasons. Its origins lie not in the Jewish Quarter but in the "Rheinvorstadt", or Rhine Suburb, the area between the old Roman walls and the river. In the 9th and 10th centuries, merchants and artisans settled on the former island, and grew extremely rich. Only one house dating from the 13th century bears witness to this period: the **Overstolzenhaus** in Rheingasse. Today it houses the recently-founded "College of Media Studies".

A trading suburb: Closer proximity to the Rhine as a natural supply route wasn't the only reason why the traders chose to settle between the old Roman city and the river; they also did so because they had turned the Rhine Suburb into their own area of jurisdiction, defying any and all encroaches by the archbishop, who had his residence in the upper part of the city. The *Schreinsbücher* of the Old City, the oldest land registers in the world, are still one of the most valuable assets of the city's archives, and have been kept uninterruptedly since the 12th century.

The former arm of the Rhine had silted up long before it was settled in medieval times. But the area contained no buildings. This link between the upper and lower part of the city became the cradle of newly-flourishing Colonia: the **Old Market** (Alter Markt). As a trading centre, it gradually supplanted the **Hay Market** (Heumarkt) further to the south, which according to reports from travellers in previous centuries used to be one of the largest and finest in Europe. Down by the Rhine lay the

The gables of the double-house "Zur Brezel" and "Zum Dorn" on the Old Market.

customs-houses and warehouses, and one of them, the **Staple House**, came to symbolise the independence of the Free Imperial City. Although only one of its towers – a later addition – survived the war, the Staple House itself has now finally been rebuilt. It forms an original addition, both in terms of its dimensions and its situation, to the line of buildings along the bank of the Rhine which, since their reconstruction, now make up one of the finest city panoramas in Europe (best appreciated from either the bridges or from the other side of the river).

Thus, not only the city's harbours but its markets, too, determined life in today's Old City for over a thousand years, since the 10th century. This lively and colourful mix of people – even more so than in Roman times – soon overflowed the narrow confines of the "Martinsvorstadt", which was swiftly incorporated into the city along with the former Roman boundary, and spread as far as the Neumarkt. Thus it was that the whole area of the Roman city moved a few hundred metres in the direction of the new bank of the Rhine. The markets formed the heart of the city, and the river its main artery. And the situation remained like that all the way up to the last war.

Former focal points: The city's ancient parishes succeeded in retaining a large degree of independence for a long time, and originally even had a say in the appointment of the city's archbishops. Not much was left intact by the French and the Prussians in the 19th century, and World War II took care of the rest. There are only ruins left to remind us of the parish churches which, as former focal points, once played such an infinitely important role in the city's development: the tower of **Klein St Martin** at the "Heumarkt" tram stop; the church of St Columba, locally known as the "Madonna in the Ruins"; and Old St Alban's Church next to the Gürzenich, with its *Grieving Parents* by the artist and sculptor Käthe Kollwitz (1867–

Ewald Mataré's "Kallendresser" (gutter-defecator) squats over the Old Market.

1945), a memorial to the dead of the two World Wars. The only reminders of the former parishes of St Lawrence and St Brigida are street names.

In the ruins of Old St Alban's, by the way, one notices that the city so famous for its cheerful love of life also has an underlying awareness of suffering and injustice: the windows of the neighbouring Gürzenich, the banqueting hall where the Carnival reaches its climax, give a clear view of the ruins of Old St Alban's and of the *Grieving Parents*. The figures are actually copies, but they were created in the workshop belonging to the equally distinguished artist Ewald Mataré (1887–1965); Käthe Kollwitz considered the originals, which she created for the military cemetery in Roggevelde, Belgium, to be one of her greatest works.

And this is not the only piece of work by Käthe Kollwitz in Cologne by any means: the city contains an important collection of her art. One of Cologne's banks, the "Kreissparkasse", having been both fortunate as well as wealthy enough to be able to do so, opened its own Käthe Kollwitz Museum in the Neumarkt quite recently. It contains what is probably the largest single collection of her graphics, and also features a few rare posters as well as several sculptures.

A memorial of horror: If this museum leaves its visitor a certain amount of room to reflect on social misery or on its portrayal in artistic form, another of the city's museum-like memorials will stun him with its reminders of human suffering as a result of merciless human cruelty: the former torture chambers in the basement of the building used as Gestapo headquarters during the "Third Reich", the so-called **El-De-Haus**, at the corner of Appellhofplatz and Elisenstrasse. No one can really say just how many people suffered and died here in these 10 cells. Twelve hundred inscriptions remain on the cell walls, hundreds of them in Cyrillic script as well as in many other European languages. Even those that are illegible still testify to the despair and suffering that has turned this place into a memorial, one from which it is all too difficult to return once more to the streets of lighthearted Cologne and its long history.

The Old City itself contains a lot of attractive details that are not simply there for show, but instead hint at deeper-lying associations. The boundaries between the mercantile "Martinsvorstadt" and the episcopal upper part of the city, between the religious foundations of the nobility and the parishes, were delineated by a complex network of regulations to which people must have been highly sensitive very early on. One instance of this has to be the "**Kallendresser**" figure up on the wall of house number 24, "Em Hanen", in the Old Market. Translated, this word actually means "the gutter-defecator", and the figure can be seen pointing its naked rear end at the square.

Of the many explanations in circulation as to the origins of this figure, the

Left, street performers. Right, these horses' heads are the subject of a popular Cologne legend.

one that comes nearest the truth is the one that treats it as an expression of civic protest. Legend has it that during the Middle Ages, a thief once took refuge from his municipal pursuers in Great St Martin's Abbey. The abbot there did not, however, grant him asylum under the law of that time, but instead handed him over to the patrician municipal council, whereupon the citizens of the Old City protested, both against the secular authorities and against the priests of Great St Martin's – at first via a rude gesture which then probably slowly fossilised into this small statue on the facade.

The fact that the old **Platz-Jabbeck** (derived from the verb *japsen*, meaning to gasp for air), under the clock on the Town Hall tower directly opposite, sticks its tongue out at the Kallendresser each time the hour is struck may just be coincidence, but there again one shouldn't put anything past the people of Cologne, then or now.

The original stone statue of the Kallendresser was lost beneath the rubble of World War II. When Jupp Engels, the "Jrielächer" mentioned earlier, rebuilt his "Em Hanen" house in the 1960s, he had the figure redone in bronze by Ewald Mataré. By the way, house number 24 itself is a listed building, certainly worth seeing for its consistent application of *Bauhaus* principles. Its external features (Kallendresser on the gable, mosaic above the main doorway, bronze plating along the pavement, grille and entryway at the rear next to Great St Martin's) are all the work of Ewald Mataré, whose most famous works include the bronze doors of the Gürzenich and those of the Cathedral's south portal.

Typical Cologne characters: The "Martinsviertel" and the city as a whole also have Jupp Engels to thank for his **statues of Tünnes and Schäl**. These figures, the work of sculptor Werner Reuter, are also among the most-photographed sights of the Old City. The statues refer to two puppets that originated in the 19th century, in the Hänneschen Theatre two blocks away.

Tünnes is a farm labourer from one of the farms that could still be found within the large city walls at the beginning of the 19th century. He can be recognised by his rural clothing, and particularly by his wooden clogs. His nose is unusually large and reddened by alcohol, and his red hair falls straight down. Schäl, taller and more gaunt altogether, is the epitome of elegance with his bow-tie and hat. He joined Tünnes only in the middle of the 19th century, and he symbolizes the city element which gradually took the place of the rural way of life in Cologne during those years. The feature of Schäl that strikes you immediately is his squint, which makes him look rather sly and is quite in character with him, in contrast to the harmless and amiable expression of his companion.

Another popular expression of collective identity is the statue of **Jan von Werth** on his fountain in the Old Market. Here, history and legend combine to produce a heart-rending story. First of all the historical side: the real Jan von Werth was a farmer's boy from the area around Neuss, who succeeded in becoming a famous mercenary leader and cavalry general during the Thirty Years' War. Cologne had him to thank for saving it from destruction, and acclaimed him as a war hero in the 1630s. The **Municipal Museum**, which after World War II was shifted to the medieval Arsenal on the street known as An der Burgmauer (north of the Roman wall), still has some of his original possessions on display.

The Legend of Jan and Jriet: The legend tells us more than the history books: apparently while still a young man, Jan von Werth once worked as a labourer on a farm near Cologne, and courted a pretty maid named Jriet (short for Margaret). She rejected his advances because she wanted to marry a rich farmer instead, whereupon he went off to war and made his fortune. Apparently they saw one another again as he was

The City of Tomorrow

After World War II, during which 85 percent of the city centre was destroyed, Cologne regained its identity only relatively late as city planners finally worked out their vision of the future. For a long time, the planners wandered aimlessly through a thicket of "pressing needs" and "functional requirements". They left the Heumarkt behind as a testimonial to just how confused they were. Here, one of the city's finest squares was mercilessly squandered on road traffic.

It was only in the 1970s that people began to realise that a city structure that had taken centuries to develop could not suit absolutely every modern traffic requirement, and that culture and commerce could actually co-exist quite happily. "A proper balance of the city's functions" has been the watchword of the city planners since then.

And their plans have worked, too. Despite the fact that Cologne is becoming increasingly prone to traffic congestion, more and more people are streaming into the city; despite the increasing number of shopping areas and recreation areas that are closed to traffic, business is really booming; and despite a strong concentration of "business" in the city centre, it still has 133,000 inhabitants – most of whom really enjoy living there.

The people of Cologne readily seize upon any excuse for a festival, and highlights in city planning over the past 10 years have provided ample opportunity: there was the restoration of the Romanesque churches, the redevelopment of much of the "Ring" system, the opening of several brand-new shopping arcades and above all, the redevelopment of the Old City (Altstadt). The focal point of all the efforts made here was the Cathedral/Rhine area with its museums, the Philharmonie and also the Rhine Gardens: the busy Uferstrasse was moved to a tunnel underneath them, at a cost of DM 120 million, which means that one can now take an unhindered stroll yet again between the Old City and the river, just like the good old days.

Work on the outward appearance of the city centre has not been completed yet, however. As a result of the general increase in traffic, the central U-Bahn network is having to be extended, and the area around the main station, as well as the Neumarkt, need basic redevelopment work too. Major traffic arteries, such as the "Nord-Süd-Fahrt" between the Schildergasse and the WDR, are to disappear inside underground tunnels.

A whole new section of the city has recently been under construction: the new "Media Park", on the site of the former Gereon freight depot. The aim behind this ambitious project is to secure for Cologne a key role in the fast-developing fields of information and communication technologies, while simultaneously contributing towards further revitalising the Inner City.

Two more highly promising projects are the redevelopment of the Heumarkt, and also of the city's harbour area. A cultural centre is planned for the site, one that will fulfil the expectations of the many artists living in the Südstadt section of the city, and that will also contain two new Cologne attractions: a "German Sports Museum" and a Transport Museum.

In the Heumarkt, the new building housing the Rautenstrauch-Joest Museum of ethnology is to fill the last remaining gap in the Old City panorama. The museum building will be constructed at the head of the Deutz Bridge, thus forming a link with the Heumarkt. The plans are the result of work by architect Gottfried Böhm. The new museum, with its 45-metre (150-ft) high tower above the ramp leading to the bridge, will provide the city with a whole new look.

The Heumarkt, too, is to be given a facelift. Gottfried Böhm has drawn up plans for this, too, and they include moving the traffic underground and putting a market back in the square – a solution to please motorists *and* pedestrians. After that, most of the damage Cologne sustained during World War II – apart from the area in front of the Town Hall, for which no plans exist as yet – will have been removed.

Considering the city's financial situation, though, it's still not certain whether these expensive plans can be realised. These visions of a more attractive Cologne may remain just that: visions, and nothing more.

being proclaimed a hero; she was still poor, and he said to her: "*Wer es getan hätte!*" ("If only you had married me, Jriet!"). She answered, quick as a flash: "*If only I'd known!*"

This famous Cologne scene has been immortalised in the relief beneath the statue, and also forms the basis of the annual Carnival play *Jan and Jriet,* performed on "Weiberfastnacht" (the Thursday prior to the seventh Sunday before Easter) by "Jan von Werth's Cavalry Troop" at St Severinus's Gate (Severinstor) in the Südstadt.

In 1884, a problem the city had been having with its identity ever since it had become Prussian in 1815 finally rose to the surface. The former Free Imperial City of the West was Catholic, but had now ended up under the authoritarian control of the Protestant state from the East. This naturally brought several economic advantages along with it, but unfortunately it also led to continual clashes in which Cologne's particular idiosyncrasies – above all Catholicism and the Carnival – became more and more pronounced.

In 1855, when a mayor of Cologne suggested that an equestrian statue should be erected in the Old Market in honour of the king during whose reign the city had been taken over by Prussia, the Roman-Catholic opposition became incensed, and immediately applied for permission to erect a column dedicated to the Virgin Mary in the Old Market instead. The Mother of God's Immaculate Conception had been made an article of faith in Rome only a short time beforehand.

A typical Cologne solution: Hefty disputes ensued, and it was actually decades later that a typical Cologne solution was finally devised: the **Column dedicated to the Virgin Mary** was erected in front of the archbishop's residence in Gereonsstrasse, where it can still be seen today; and the **equestrian statue** of Prussian king Frederick William III was erected in the Heumarkt in 1878 – and yet again in 1990 after its destruction in World War II. And in order to protect the valuable site at the "heart" of Cologne from any future intrusions, the decision was made to place the statue of Jan von Werth in the Old Market.

Another of Cologne's many legends has also been rendered in stone, in the shape of the two horses' heads visible on an old tower in the Neumarkt. Since every child always asks about them, just about everyone in Cologne now knows the legend of "**Richmodis of Aducht**". She was a woman who apparently died of the plague at an early age. However she had only been in a state of suspended animation, and at night she came back home and knocked on the door. When the butler brought the news to her grief-stricken husband, the latter is meant to have said that he thought it more likely that his horses would climb the steep staircase to his house than his wife would come back alive from the cemetery. Whereupon the horses actually did come up the stairs. Then he

Left, resting the legs after the bustle of the Schildergasse. Right, the statues of Tünnes and Schäl are among the most-photographed sights of the Old City.

believed it, ran to the door and put his arms round his wife, with whom he spent many more happy years.

One of the old buildings that has remained a firm favourite with the people of Cologne is the **Gürzenich**. The City Parliament built it here around the year 1440 as a "dancing-house". This is where the great banquets used to take place when emperors – the Holy Roman ones as well as the Prussian rulers many years later – were visiting the city. It is here that the proclamation of the Carnival "Prince" still takes place annually. In the 19th century, the Gürzenich was also turned into a concert hall, which is how the Gürzenich Orchestra got its name; and it has retained it, too, despite its move to the new Philharmonie next to the Cathedral in 1986.

Redevelopment of the Old City: The entire Old City, and not just the Gürzenich, has had quite a bit of redevelopment work done on it in the past. The most important restructuring activity took place in the 1930s, when new squares were laid out. The Hänneschen Puppet Theatre was moved to the newly-created Eisenmarkt, and the **Ostermannplatz** received its large **fountain** with its stone figures immortalising the archetypal Cologne characters from the songs of Willi Ostermann (1876–1936), the city's most famous songwriter.

Back in the 1930s, the city's Rings, and its suburbs of Lindenthal, Rodenkirchen and Marienburg were already among the more desirable places to live for the middle classes. The Old City trod the thin line between popularity and social decline. And even after the almost total destruction wrought by the war and the subsequent reconstruction work, things didn't really get much better. Hardly anything was done to make the area any more useful or attractive. It was only in the early 1970s that a new generation began to rediscover the special attraction of the Old City.

Restaurants began to make use of the historic backdrop it provided. By the time the city planners decided they wanted to replace the rubble-strewn area around Great St Martin's with a large multi-storey car park, people had become so fond of the Old City that there was a wave of popular protest. The plans were thus altered, and one of the most delightful and internationally acclaimed inner-city residential areas in Germany was created instead: the **Martinsviertel**.

Old Cologne was thus gradually resurrected. The redevelopment work reached its peak in 1986 when the busy Uferstrasse was moved into an underground tunnel, the Rhine Gardens were laid out anew and the new complex containing the museums and the Philharmonie was opened next to the Cathedral. Since then, for natives of Cologne just as for visitors, even though the Old City's two-thousand-year history is really only fully documented in museums, it can always be experienced any day, and the citizens' emotional life has found a focal point once more.

Left, steps lead down to the Mikvah, or Jewish ritual bath, near the town hall. Right, witness to medieval prosperity: the Overstolzenhaus dates from the 13th century.

COLOGNE'S ANCIENT DISTRICTS

If Cologne draws most of its identity from its historic Old City (Altstadt), then the Cologne way of life and its unique qualities are primarily to be found in the so-called "Veedeln" (dialect form of the German word *Viertel*, meaning "districts") which form several circles around the Old City. The translation of the word simply as "districts", however, conveys very little of its real significance, and of the associations it evokes in its dialect form: it conjures up a sense of neighbourly belonging, a close-knit feeling of "one big, happy family", and it also conveys a sense of community not only as far as local life and local welfare are concerned, but also embracing beliefs and even destiny.

Life in the "Veedeln": Most of the "Veedeln" in Cologne were destroyed in World War II. What remains of them can hardly be traced to where the old streets used to run, but has instead survived in so-called "Veedel clubs" which were all founded back in the 1940s and 1950s, and whose members often live in widely separate parts of the city. Onlookers can get a good impression of them when they take part in the *Schull-und Veedelszöch* procession on Carnival Sunday.

The "Veedeln" that have been revived, and which are being celebrated today may be based to a certain extent on their historic forerunners, but in most respects they are a new development, dating from the 1970s or so. Since that time, the "Veedeln" have come to life again, and are developing their peculiar powers of integration, giving people a sense of belonging and giving Cologne – quite independent of the gloss of its Old City – that everyday, cosy, homely feel that ties people so strongly to their native city.

A smile from Cologne city.

Absolutely typical "Veedeln" today are the "Vringsveedel" and the "Eigelsteinveedel". The former begins in front of the Roman southern gate, the "Hohe Pforte" at the Waidmarkt, and its name is derived from the early Christian bishop St Severinus, known in Cologne dialect as "Zinter Vring". The latter, the "Eigelsteinveedel", at the other end of the Hohe Strasse, gets its name from the eagle, a symbol of Roman domination, which used to mark the military road in front of the city's ancient northern gate.

Both "Veedeln" have several features in common: both are grouped around the former arterial roads of Roman Cologne, which today are among the liveliest, flashiest and yet still reasonably-priced supply centres of the city; both are bordered by the mighty gates of the medieval city wall which have been preserved to this day; both still contain monasteries that are still intact; both contain several Romanesque churches; both still have highly active Catholic communities, which celebrate their popular *Kirmesse* (fairs) every summer according to an ages-old, fixed tradition; and both of them are home to the oldest forms of Carnival celebration.

A mixed population: Alongside the "qualified minority" of old-established inhabitants here, there are also a lot of newcomers: the majority of them are foreigners, but there are also alternatives and artists, rich and poor, workers and intellectuals, famous people and not-so-famous people, believers and atheists, upright citizens and also several dubious individuals for whom the Cologne dialect has several drastic-sounding names. A distinctive feature of this community, however, is that the people here are all one colourful mix and that no one group dominates at the expense of the others; there's an admirable measure of mutual tolerance.

The topographical as well as emotional centre of any and all "Veedeln" is – as it has always been – a church. In the "Vringsveedel", this applies to **St Severinus's**, **St George's**, **St Mary's in Lyskirchen** and the **Church of St John the Baptist** (known as "Zint Jan" in Cologne dialect), and in the "Eigelsteinveedel", to **St Cunibert's** and **St Ursula's**. Even though the old popular piety has been somewhat diluted by secular developments these days, people do still go to these venerable churches for family celebrations and feast days, and continue to treat them with much familiarity; the heart of many an atheist has been known to beat faster at the magnificent sight of the procession of *heilije Knäächte un Mägde* ("holy farm hands and maids") at St Mary's in Lyskirchen.

These remnants of folklore within the city are clues to the strong traditions that the "Veedeln" still thrive on. From 1180 to 1815 there used to be a large rural area between the boundaries of the Roman city and the oversized medieval wall. This resulted in an unusual phenomenon: many farmers actually farmed within the city itself. They did not live in closed-off, conservative village communities, but instead in (relatively) broad-minded parishes, and were organised into special unions, too, known as "Bauernbänke". They were therefore far more inclined to treat the city-dwellers, rather than the inhabitants of the surrounding rural areas, as their brothers.

Successful assimilation: As the 19th century progressed, industrial development began to spread across the fields: factories sprang up, and commercial enterprises were extended. This in turn swelled the ranks of the workforce, and during the course of only three generations, a massive population explosion took place, with the city gradually becoming more and more overcrowded.

Meanwhile, the original farming population had to assimilate a whole new social class made up of workers, with all the issues that entailed. The social misery that followed hot on the heels of this development, the cramped living conditions that forced many people to resort to refined techniques of survival, and group solidarity in the face of the unwelcome Prussian authorities

Left, the Ulre Gate (Ulrepforte), home of the "Red Sparks". Right, the Hahnen Gate on Rudolfplatz.

all combined to produce a remarkable human bond between people as they experienced joy and suffering together, helped one another or fell victim to baseness, dreamed sentimental dreams or had to learn to be tough to survive; and all of this has left its mark on the character of the city's "Veedeln" – on their dialect, their cuisine and their customs. Whatever its drawbacks, though, the assimilation has succeeded.

Love of life and a taste for festivals: The **"Stollwerck Girl"**, a statue by Sepp Hürten that has been standing at the fountain in front of St Severinus's Church since 1989, is a present-day reminder of this historical background. Stollwerck was once world-famous for its sweets and chocolates, and is still a big name in the business today.

In the second half of the 19th century, the Stollwercks built their factory in the "Vringsveedel", providing work and bread for the population. And since good capitalist exploitation of human labour went very much hand in hand with a patriarchal attitude where social and cultural welfare were concerned, the "Vringsveedel" found itself a lot better off than other sections of the city. The Stollwerck "upper crust" – as the firm's workers were referred to – radiated a straightforward love of life, an attitude that is still typical of the "Vringsveedel" today. It is here, on Carnival Sunday and on the Monday before Lent, that the city's Carnival reaches its climax.

The **Berbuer Fountain** opposite "Zint Jan" also testifies to the city's love of life and its taste for festivals. Karl Berbuer (1900–77) was Cologne's most important 20th-century songwriter, and gave a convincing account in his songs of life as seen through the eyes of the simple man in the street. His most famous one was the "Trizonesien Song", a cabaretist's comment on the situation facing the inhabitants of the three post-war occupied zones in West Germany. The song was even occasionally played as a substitute for the na-

Left, fruit seller in the Weidengasse. **Right**, detail of the famous Stollwerck chocolate factory.

tional anthem – because the state did not yet exist. Artist Bonifatius Stirnberg has decorated the fountain with motifs based on Berbuer's songs.

Distinctive-looking buildings: Despite having sustained much wartime damage, the "Vringsveedel" still retains several distinctive-looking buildings. The church and the gate have already been mentioned. Just in front of them is the **Balchem House** (Haus Balchem), Cologne's finest surviving Baroque mansion, with its picturesque oriel window. Halfway towards the Rhine, the **Bottmühle**, one of the four windmills built on the city walls in the 16th century, also provides a romantic sight; and right down by the harbour, the wall's southernmost corner tower, the **Bayentürm**, has been undergoing restoration work.

In the other direction, at the other end of the "Veedel", the **Ulre Gate** (Ulrepforte) is also a picturesque sight. This old tower, once part of the city wall, is today the home of the descendants of the old city guard, the "Red Sparks", who have survived as a Carnival association. Between this tower and St Severinus's Gate (Severinstor), there is an impressive-looking assortment of sacred buildings on the site of the former Carthusian monastery, today serving as the administration centre of the city's Protestant community.

The "Vringsveedel" hasn't lost a trace of its vitality – despite the destruction wrought by the war, despite the fact that Stollwerck has now shifted into a brand-new, fully-automated factory out in the countryside, and despite the fact that the area experienced an enormous amount of redevelopment during the 1980s. The many bars which have survived in the area, however, bear eloquent witness to the close bond between life and pleasure here.

And the "Vringsveedel" has also been enriched by artists who have settled in the former "Cologne factory schools" area on the Ubier Ring during the last few decades. **St Severinus's**

Street festival and flea market in Severinsstrasse.

Gate, which once marked the boundary of the "Vringsveedel", has thus become the centre of a new, extended "Veedel" which now includes quite a large chunk of the Bonner Strasse (i.e. the New Town): the Südstadt. The artists' dives and specialist restaurants in this area are even more popular with the people of Cologne than the various gastronomic experiences on offer in the Old City.

The Südstadt area is also a modern-day example of the integrating power that the former "Veedeln" used to have: many foreigners live here, and they have not only introduced a whole new range of goods and food to the city – their children also speak Cologne dialect, and they enjoy celebrating Carnival too. The city's traditional life is thus being carried on in new ways. Another example is the rock-group BAP, which became world-famous with its songs in Cologne dialect.

Flashpoints: Not quite as special as the "Vringsveedel", though just as lively, is the "Eigelsteinveedel". This area was a lot more miserable than the "Vringsveedel" during the 19th century, and social flashpoints developed which even today haven't quite been completely eliminated. The **Stavenhof** near the Eigelstein Gate once used to be a red-light district, and was not the subject of any polite discussion in the city until comparatively recently.

The trends of the times haven't been as kind to the "Eigelsteinveedel" as they have to the "Vringsveedel", either. The war destroyed as much on the outside as the aggressively ambitious Federal German mentality has on the inside; modern traffic, in the shape of numerous dual carriageways and railways, has carved up this formerly large "Veedel" quite a bit.

Large numbers of foreigners have filled the ensuing social vacuum, so much so that here – in the Weidengasse, for example – the concentration of Turkish inhabitants has reached almost ghetto-like proportions. They are valued by many of the locals, however,

Below, Balchem House, Cologne's best-preserved baroque building. Following pages: St Severinus's Gate.

because the food they provide has enriched the choice available to gourmets in the city. Others are afraid of the area, though, because Mediterranean male pride is easily injured, and problems here tend to get resolved permanently with the aid of knives and guns.

As far as buildings are concerned, it very much resembles the "Vringsveedel": Romanesque churches, the old City Gate, the **Weckschnapp**, a tower built into a house down by the Rhine, at the end of the old city wall; and at its centre, rather than drawings and paintings, it has music. The **State College of Music** is an important institution, even if its oversized dimensions have been plonked right in the middle of what once used to be an area full of small-scale workers' tenement buildings. One place definitely worth seeing is the **Ursuline Monastery Church** in Machabäerstrasse, a secondary school for girls founded by the Ursulines.

A picturesque backdrop: Despite its rather depressing history, much of the urbane charm of the "Eigelsteinveedel" has been rediscovered recently. It has provided a picturesque backdrop for many films – and detective films in particular. Redevelopment work is making visible progress here, too. The "Veedel" is once again in great demand as a place to live in the city, and a lot of the pubs here are a private tip for those in the know. Like the "Vringsveedel", the "Eigelsteinveedel", too, has already spread beyond its original borders: directly on the other side of the Ring, the equally lively "Agnesveedel" begins, with the Church of St Agnes, the second largest in Cologne, at its centre.

Just two of the city's most representative "Veedeln" have been described here. Anyone interested in them will certainly be able to find more. There's something rather jungle-like about them, which means it's a good idea to find someone who actually lives in one to show you around.

Fresh vegetables for sale.

2309403
A3797N
REVENIR

decision is final) wil
days for notification
£1000 winners and
TEST BATTE
AFTER STORA
WHEN READ
1. Open pack ca
DO NOT RE
2. Place battery i
3. Squeeze top a
following leve
Replace all batter
To be used only
Do not use wi
For best perfo
BATTERY SAFETY CO
Follow equipment instru
If leakage comes into
amounts of water ● Inst
batteries at the same tim
different types of batterie
of batteries in fire as they
may cause a short circuit
Patented.
Made in E.E.C.
Duracell U.K.,
Duracell Hous
Church Road,
Lowfield He
WEST
KD Köln-Dusseldorfer
NIR

THE RHINE

"To the north of Bonn, where the Rhine flows out of the narrow hills into the plain, it widens considerably as it rolls past frightened villages, threatening even Cologne, its secret queen" – thus did Heinrich Böll ruminate on the river upon whose left bank the Roman general Agrippa resettled the Germanic tribe of the Ubii more than 2,000 years ago, thereby laying the foundations of Colonia Agrippinensis, today's Cologne. The mighty river Rhine, 400 metres (1,300 ft) wide at this point, flows in a gradual arc up from the south and through the city, leaving it only 40 km (25 miles) further north.

Rather disrespectfully, the river here divides its "secret queen" into two different parts, which have never really made friends with one another. Traditionally, the left bank feels it is the "wahre Kölle" ("true Cologne") and looks across at the right bank, which it refers to by the rather nasty-sounding name of "Schäl Sick", with some degree of sympathy. Some of the sections of the city on the right bank, though, such as Deutz or Mülheim – once independent towns in their own right and retaining many individual features, despite having been incorporated into Cologne with its population of almost one million – look on their neighbours from the other side of the great river with a certain degree of condescension.

Preceding pages: the Rhine is Europe's busiest waterway. Left, making fast: a statue in the harbour area. Following pages: pleasure cruise on the Rhine.

For centuries, only one ferry service connected the two sides of the river. Today, between Cologne-Rodenkirchen and Cologne-Merkenich, there are eight bridges. The first permanent bridge across the Rhine was only built as late as 1859, on the site of today's **Hohenzollern Bridge** between Cologne-Deutz and the main railway station. The high trussed arches of Germany's most often-used railway bridge can be seen from far and wide, and the trains come out of the darkness of the station straight onto the bridge. Pedestrians have to content themselves with a narrow walkway. The **Süd Bridge**, which also has impressive arches, is reserved for rail traffic too, while the **Rodenkirchen Bridge**, and the **Leverkusen Bridge** which was built in 1965 are both motorway bridges. Most impressive of all, though, is doubtless the **Zoo Bridge**, built in 1966, the most recent as well as the longest (1,300 metres/4,200 ft) of all the eight bridges. Designed by Gerd Lohmer, this bold, box-girder construction held up by heavy cables seems to be hovering above the water.

The pedestrians' favourite, however, is probably the **Deutz Bridge** leading from Cologne-Deutz directly into the Old City (Altstadt). Originally, it was meant to be a suspension bridge, but World War II robbed it of that honour. Instead it was resurrected between 1947 and 1948 as a plate girder bridge with box-girders, over 400 metres (1,300 ft) in length. From here, one gets what is easily the best view of the left bank of the Rhine: the narrow houses of the Old City in the foreground, and behind them the pointed silhouette of the Cathedral and the massive towers of Great St Martin's church.

On New Year's Eve thousands of the city's inhabitants congregate here on this gently sloping bridge to see in the New Year with plenty of fireworks: a festival which has long since become a Cologne institution.

Heinrich Böll called the Rhine "both filthy and majestic". River traffic never stops in Cologne. Up to 300 ships pass the city every 24 hours, and traffic on the river is only stopped when the water level is too high. Around 4½ million tons of goods are handled annually in Cologne's five harbours – oil and petrol in the **Niehl II** oil terminus, general and bulk cargo at Niehl I, Cologne-Mülheim, Cologne-Deutz and the **Rheinau Harbour** opposite.

The people of Cologne refer to their river affectionately as "Father Rhine", and it plays an important role in their lives. There is scarcely a single person in Cologne who has not spent at least one hot summer afternoon in the **Rhine Gardens** between the Hohenzollern and Deutz bridges. This long-neglected area at the foot of the Old City was transformed only a short while ago into an attractive park, with flower borders, trees and bizarre-looking fountains. Broad flights of steps lead up to Heinrich-Böll-Platz and to the ultra-modern Wallraf-Richartz Museum/ Ludwig Museum complex, while enticingly narrow alleyways lead off into the Old City.

Another attractive place for a stroll is along the river-bank in the chic suburb of Rodenkirchen, a few kilometres upriver. There are also several restaurant-ships on the river, the best of which is the *Alte Liebe*, as well as a large number of restaurants and bars along the river bank with their inviting terraces affording fine views of the Rhine.

The best way of discovering Cologne from the river is to take a trip on one of the "Köln-Düsseldorfer" excursion boats. The boat known as the *MS Domspatz*, based at the Frankenwerft (the embankment by the Old City between the Deutz and Hohenzollern bridges), also does hour-long trips, several times a day, from April onwards. First it goes past the houses in the Old City and the tall buildings of the Rheinau Harbour, then under the Süd Bridge and along the length of the Oberlander shipyard, and all the way up to the Rodenkirchen Bridge, where it does a huge turn. The way back leads past the meadows and fields of the right bank, past the vast Rhine Park and as far as the Mülheim Bridge, where the *Domspatz* then makes another turn.

There are also "coffee cruises" that go further upriver as far as Porz, and take roughly two and a half hours: they leave from the Frankenwerft every afternoon at 3.30 p.m. And during the journey, the loudspeakers on board keep booming out the famous song "*Warum ist es am Rhein so schön?*"

COLOGNE'S NEW TOWN

In the 1870s, Cologne was on the point of bursting out of its tight girdle of medieval walls. Just how crowded the city had become is clear from the statistics: in 1870 there were 345 people per hectare of land in Cologne. In Paris at that time there were more than 100 fewer, and in London the figure was 96 – not even a third.

A century of expansion: Cramped living conditions are by no means foreign to the Cologne lifestyle. But those who wanted to live well, and who thought ahead, were forced to expand – and it was a century of expansion. The city's time-honoured wall stood in the way, however, and eventually, it fell – the victim of extensive town-planning and an accompanying lack of insight into the significance of a monument that was unique in all Germany. All that was spared were a few grandiose gates.

There again, only two decades later the people of Cologne – who had all previously been in favour of the wall being removed in order to usher in a supposedly better, more open and freer future for their city – were already ruefully singing the praises of the "*ahl schön Stadtmur*" (fine old city wall) they had sacrificed to the ideal of progress.

But once it had been removed there was certainly a lot more space, for the area that had previously been occupied by the wall was now turned into a broad boulevard called the **Ringstrasse**, with trees and colourful flowers. Starting off as the Ubierring in the south, the "Ring" extends in a broad arc around the Old City today just as it did then.

The city's rings have historical names: first there is the Karolinger Ring, followed by the Sachsen, Salier and Hohenstaufen Rings. Then the Habsburg and Hohenzollern Rings lead on to the Kaiser Wilhelm Ring, which forms a transition to the Hansa Ring and the Theodor Heuss Ring (formerly the Deutscher Ring).

The city's new Ring of those days was only the beginning, and today it is still the most obvious symbol of the expanding city of Cologne during the 1880s and 1890s. For since that time, the New Town (Neustadt), the first ever thoroughly-planned urban extension on German soil, has been nestling close by the "Ring". Joseph Stübben was the chief architect behind the New Town area, which lay like a broad belt around the city's old medieval core.

Whether the much-vaunted "chain of festive spaces", made up of streets, squares, apartment blocks and fountains, ever became reality, or whether it ever has to this day, is doubtful. Not all that much is "festive" these days between the northern and southern part of the Rhine, the Rings and the inner "Green Belt" with its railway ring. But the region is lively all the same, with its active "Kwartier Lateng" between the city centre and the university, its innumerable

Preceding pages: a work of art: hydrokinetic sculpture on the Ebertplatz. Left, taking in the sun. Right, St Agnes, the second largest church in Cologne.

private theatres and art galleries, discotheques and pubs, and last but not least, its two parks: the People's Gardens (Volksgarten) and the Municipal Gardens (Stadtgarten).

A home from home, out-of-doors: The **People's Gardens** aren't all that large, nor are they what one would usually call "elegant", though of course that doesn't mean they're "vulgar" at all either. It's just that people here do whatever they want: in the company of their families, over a drink, out in a boat, playing out on the meadows or breaking open their *Pittermännchen* (small beer barrels) beside the pond. In brief, the place smells of Eau de Cologne and dogs, and contains a mixture of Cologne's young, would-be yuppies and people from the "Vringsveedel", students and tramps, all of them peacefully coexisting in a small area.

The idea of these gardens glowing with health and being a fine example of a well-kept municipal park is one that nobody would ever seriously entertain – and therein, perhaps, lies their charm and the secret of their success.

Joseph Stübben described the gardens while they were still being laid out in 1888: "This area, almost rectangular in shape, is 590 metres (2,000 ft) in length, 285 metres (900 ft) wide with a total surface area of 15.3 hectares (38 acres)." The gardens contained all the best features of parks laid out in the 1880s: a place where beer was served, a children's playground, a rose garden, and the groundwater level was also artificially raised so that it seemed to be gushing out of a grotto and flowing into a pond.

These days the gardens still contain the pond, the fountain, the playground and the place that serves beer. However, the racetrack, the concert hall beside the restaurant and the ice rink have long since vanished. The fine street that runs north-east of the People's Gardens, and which contains some of the finest examples of buildings dating from the *Gründerzeit* (the period of rapid indus-

Newly redeveloped, the city's "Rings" are once again an inviting place for a stroll.

trial expansion at the end of the 19th century) is named after the gardens: the "Volksgartenstrasse".

What the People's Gardens are to the south-western part of the New Town, the **Municipal Gardens** (Stadtgarten) are to the north-western section of it. In fact they are and they aren't: they're smaller, closer to the least industrialised section of the Ring system and the Old City, and also a great deal older than their Südstadt counterpart, the People's Gardens. The Municipal Gardens were out in front of the city walls 50 years before Stübben's plans were drawn up. Originally planned as a nursery, they were enlarged in 1865 before being cut back by more than 50 percent in the 1880s to make way for the planned railway.

Cool and cosmopolitan: The gardens were given a facelift and totally altered at the same time, and with the addition of a new restaurant – on the Venloer Strasse side – they also gained some cosmopolitan flair. This is even more true today, because ever since the "Kölner Jazzhaus" began here – between the railway, Venloer Strasse and Spicher Strasse – the atmosphere's been cool and highly international.

On 22 April 1882, the foundation stone for the first house in the New Town was laid, at No. 60 (today No. 58), Hohenzollern Ring. This Ring later became a magnificent boulevard, then after the war it deteriorated into a cinema, fast-food and junk-shop area; it was only at the end of the 1980s that the whole region, which had seen its first house (of what would eventually be a total of 4,000) completed only 100 years previously, was reasonably spruced up once more.

If the area's construction was unique over a century ago, so was its destruction during – as well as after – World War II. One quarter of the buildings were destroyed in the bombings, and just as many were destroyed by the pickaxes of enthusiastic property developers in the 1950s and 1960s. The stucco

A popular meeting-place in the New Town: the municipal gardens.

on the facades was all too often smashed, and figures and projections vanished – along with much of the character of this part of the city.

Nevertheless, over 2,200 of the original buildings are still standing, and what remains still gives one a good impression of what the New Town must originally have looked like.

New Town Renaissance: Had the 1970s not witnessed a reappraisal of the architectural achievements of the "Gründerzeit", Stübben's work might have been further "modernised" out of all recognition. But after having been long scorned, if not rejected out of hand by modernism, the old buildings changed for the better again and their "Renaissance" began.

Stucco was in demand once more, the facades were painted new colours, and came to life. And it hasn't stopped since. These days, many sections of the New Town contain magnificent town houses – especially those in the west, in what was once called the "west end" – that look much as they did at the turn of the century when the area to the north and the south of the New Town, near the Rhine, was still very much the home of "upright citizens". In between, in the south-west and north-west, the atmosphere was a good deal rougher, and the buildings were more modest – these areas were mostly populated by working-class people.

There's one thing Stübben would never have suspected back then, though: the university, which was later built away to the west, directly behind the railway line and thus outside the New Town, has given the area its own very special "student" flavour.

The most unusual and original pubs in the city can be found here around Zülpicher Platz and Zülpicher Strasse, between the Ring and the railway. You can find everything here, from every conceivable kind of pub, serving all manner of food, to beer halls that offer a lot more than just Kölsch; from student bars filled with deafening heavy

Left, the "Colonius" telecommunications tower. Right, the synagogue on Roonstrasse.

metal music all the way to "in" discos. Anyone who considers Cologne a lively place must have paid at least one visit to the "**Kwartier Lateng**".

Right at the centre of the student area lies Walter Bockmayer's "Filmdose", a fun pub which also shows films. Indeed, most of the city's innumerable free theatres and miniature cabarets can be found here in the New Town.

Good food, good art, good pubs: The New Town is more than just an attractive collection of late 19th-century buildings between the eastern, medieval, Cathedral section of the city on the one hand and the western, "Green Belt", suburban section on the other. It also contains numerous art galleries, which have made Cologne the artistic metropolis it is today.

But is the New Town stylistically coherent? – it was designed by one man, after all, and completed within 20 years. Hardly: even Stübben had to make compromises, and World War II as well as the post-war period left deep scars. It was only at the end of the 1980s that streets like Volksgartenstrasse and Moltkestrasse were once again transformed into avenues that were to some extent worthy of their name. And the Ring itself, run-down and sacrificed to traffic long since, is also more reminiscent now of the magnificent boulevard it once used to be – especially along the 2-km section between Kaiser Wilhelm Ring and Barbarossa Platz, with its shops, banks, cinema and pubs. Traffic-free zones have also gone some way towards restoring some of the area's former dignity.

But a lot of scars still remain, many of them deep: the Aachener Strasse and the Richard Wagner Strasse, for instance, the roads leading to and from the western part of the city, have degenerated into overcrowded traffic arteries. To sum up the problem, it is the squares, avenues and open spaces that have suffered the most. It's a painful realisation, and one that is not only true of Cologne and its New Town.

Curious shop-window display in a side-street.

PC 4010

lady braun
WRIGLEY P.K.
KAUGUMMI
Langnese
EISKREM
COLA

EXCURSIONS ON THE LEFT BANK

As far as most tourists are concerned, Cologne is generally limited to the area between the Rhine and the Ring, though perhaps the New Town (Neustadt) area, and Deutz on the right bank of the Rhine also receive a certain amount of attention as well. Nevertheless, there's also a lot to be discovered in Nippes and Ehrenfeld, and in Lindenthal and Rodenkirchen too.

Riehl-Niehl-Nippes: One of the biggest attractions on the left bank of the river, outside the city centre, is the **Cologne Zoo**. Founded in 1860, it is the third oldest zoo in Germany. Despite heavy bombardment during World War II, some of its former buildings have still survived: the elephant house, built in the "Moorish" style, dates back to when the zoo was founded. Around 1880, the cattle house was erected in log-cabin style, and the "South American House", modelled on the city's Russian church, was built in 1899. In 1914, the huge island for the apes was built, and even at that time, modern methods of animal-keeping were being applied: first of all, lemurs were successfully bred, and only recently, a modern house for primates was opened. Another big attraction is the aquarium, which contains not only exotic species of fish but insects as well.

If you cross the old Stammheimer Strasse you reach the so-called **Flora**, and also the **Botanical Gardens**. For its 125th anniversary in 1988 the Flora was – almost – restored to its former splendour. In 1862, a dozen rich burghers of Cologne decided to create an "ornamental pleasure garden", and in 1863 the king of Prussia gave permission for it to be constructed. No less a person than master landscape architect Lenné was responsible for planning the garden, and the "conservatory" was based on Paxton's Crystal Palace at the World's Fair in London. The Flora landscape garden blends into the Bo-

Preceding pages: flea-market knick-knacks. **Below**, a touch of personal grooming at the Cologne Zoo.

tanical Gardens, which were laid out alongside it in 1914.

Church-building in Cologne is not only a medieval affair: the 20th century, too, has its share of important edifices. One extremely talented family of architects, already in its third generation, is the Böhm family. The eldest member was Dominikus Böhm (1880–1955). In 1931 he built **St Engelbert's**, a mighty brick building on the Riehler Gürtel (beyond the Flora), with its eight parabolic conches arranged in a circle.

If you take the Amsterdamer Strasse out to the Niehler Damm you will find a small and very old Romanesque church on the bank of the Rhine: **Old St Catherine's** (Alt St Katharinen). The building was mentioned as belonging to the religious foundation of St Cunibert in 1238; its choir was consecrated in 1260, and the nave was later given another storey and a vault.

Anyone who feels like a swim can make a detour from here to the lake known as the **Fühlinger See** in the district of **Chorweiler**. A few attempts have been made recently to improve the appearance of the area surrounding the skyscrapers here. One delightful place, though, is the **Casimir Hagen Collection** (Sammlung Casimir Hagen) on Pariser Platz. Hagen, a simple post office employee, collected a great deal of ancient artefacts, but also made his rooms available to progressive Cologne artists. Much of the collection was donated to the city in 1957.

From Niehl to Nippes: Another Cologne churchbuilder is Rudolf Schwarz. He designed **St Christopher's**, on Waldfriedstrasse (reached via Königsberger Strasse), a strictly Cubist church, with a free-standing bell-tower.

Cologne also achieved much in the field of housing development in the early part of this century. If you take the Neusser Strasse to Friedrich Karl Strasse and travel along it, on your left you will see the housing estate built between 1922 and 1924 known as **Mauenheim**, designed by Cologne ar-

The good life.

chitect Wilhelm Riphahn. It has a large courtyard area in the middle and is based on Dutch models.

Nippes is a typical Cologne district, with its own shopping centre on the Neusser Strasse and also a daily market on the Wilhelmplatz, with its happy mixture of German and Turkish life-styles. There are some fine houses on the Erzberger Platz, dating from the years of rapid industrial expansion at the end of the 19th century. Something else that shouldn't be missed is the "Goldener Kappes", a popular beer-hall at the entrance to Florastrasse.

Ehrenfeld: A trip to Ehrenfeld should be either started or finished off with a ride up to the top of the **Colonius**, Cologne's telecommunications tower. Once you're up there you can take a seat in the revolving restaurant, and enjoy the panorama of the city below. In good weather the view stretches as far as the Ville chain of hills, and the Bergisches Land. One also gets a very good impression of how Cologne is laid out.

The Cologne suburb of **Ehrenfeld** was founded in 1845, and it quickly developed into a flourishing industrial centre. It has always been an industrial suburb, something that still has an influence on its layout even today. The Neo-Gothic **Church of St Joseph**, one of the first churches in Ehrenfeld, is situated on the Venloer Strasse, the main shopping street. If you take Neptunstrasse opposite you'll reach the recently restored *Jugendstil* glory of the **Neptune Swimming Baths** (only club members can swim there, but visitors are allowed). The square in front of the building is where Ehrenfeld's colourful weekly market takes place.

To the right of the baths is the **Friedenskirche**, rather a rare piece of churchbuilding in Cologne, with its brick walls and semicircular arches, very much in the Berlin style. If you take Vogelsanger Strasse towards the town centre you'll come to **St Mechtern's Church**, a rival of St Gereon's for the city's roll of holy martyrs. The

The "Uni-Center", the highest apartment building in Cologne.

church was badly damaged in World War II, and rebuilt between 1953 and 1954 by Rudolf Schwarz. Nearby are the **4711 factory buildings** (Wilhelm and Rudolf Koep, 1950), fine examples of the city's first period of reconstruction. And a particularly delightful part of town is the area around **St Anna's** (Eichendorffstrasse, Försterstrasse and Ottostrasse) with its fine late 19th-century residential buildings, some featuring luxurious *Jugendstil* decoration.

Lindenthal: Lindenthal (which also includes Sülz, Klettenberg, Braunsfeld and Müngersdorf) is a place that should really be discovered in several stages.

The best place to begin is the **Museum of East Asian Art**. After you've taken your trip through the ancient cultures of China, Korea and Japan, follow the magnificent avenue of chestnut trees along the Lindenthal Canal until you reach Brucknerstrasse. Towering above you at the end of the canal is the **Church of the Resurrection**, a concrete and brick structure built between 1967 and 1972 by Gottfried Böhm. Its interior is an example of the almost brutal sparseness of decoration and that concentrated spatial and spiritual intensity that is so characteristic of much of Böhm's work.

The Brucknerstrasse takes you northwards, straight to the **Melaten Cemetery**, founded by Napoleonic decree in 1810. The cemetery lies on the site of a former leper asylum, which was mentioned as far back as the year 1180. This is also clear from the cemetery's name: it was the *Maladen*, the sick people, who used to live here. The existence of a chapel on this spot was mentioned as early as 1245; it stood on the site of the small church (in use today as a Greek-Orthodox church) set against the wall that separates the cemetery from the Aachener Strasse.

After its destruction in 1474 it was rebuilt as a hall basilica ("Hallenkirche") with two naves of equal height (no entry to the public). The Melaten Cemetery is neoclassical in design, and

Car manufacturing at the Ford works in Niehl.

laid out in a strict grid pattern; the tombs of the great Cologne families can be found along the main axes. Today, many of the gravestones are under preservation order.

Our second tour also begins at the Museum of East Asian Art. To the south of it lies the **university**. Various institutes are dotted along the Universitätsstrasse: next to the museum there is the Japanese Cultural Institute, with the Italian one over the road (built by Hans Koerfer between 1954 and 1955), and also the first major extension to the university after the war: the Faculty of Economics, built by Wilhelm Riphahn.

The university itself was newly founded in 1929, and opened in 1935. The main building, designed by Adolf Abel, has a massive portal in its facade, with the institutional buildings fanning out behind it across the "Green Belt". The artificial lowering of the road in front of the entrance has created a small forum. The bronze statue of **Albertus Magnus** (Albert the Great) by Gerhard Marcks (1956) is a monument to the famous theologian. The new university library and the auditorium were built on the other side of the forum in the 1960s by Rolf Gutbrod.

Our trip takes us past the library to the **Geusen Cemetery** (Weyerthal). This is where the city's Protestants were buried, and it was first mentioned in 1576. "Geusen" is an old word for "beggar", and was a name once given to the Protestants, many of whom had fled here from the Netherlands. The sign of the cross is absent from the gravestones; instead we see familial coats-of-arms, often surrounded by symbols of death: hourglasses, skulls, and oil-lamps.

Something else not to be missed is the **Church of St Lawrence** (reached via Gyrhofstrasse) by Emil Steffan. Built out of broken bricks, it is a unique example of the modest style of much post-war architecture. The small courtyard, enclosed by the church's outbuildings, is an oasis of tranquillity (closed between midday and 3 p.m).

The Albertus Magnus memorial in front of the University's philosophical faculty.

The next trip begins at Decksteiner Strasse. Right at the beginning of it is the church of **St Thomas More**, built by Fritz Schaller between 1962 and 1963. Now turn off into Werthmannstrasse, and you'll reach **St Elizabeth's Hospital**. Dominikus Böhm built the church here, a mighty, triple-naved structure, between 1930 and 1932, and sick patients are allowed onto its upper balconies during services. In the ambulatory is the simple tomb of prelate Johannes von Acken, with the impressive Man of Sorrows created for it in 1939 by Ewald Mataré.

Decksteiner Strasse leads past the **Jewish Cemetery**, with its beautiful old trees, to the Deckstein Mill, a popular excursion destination in Cologne as early as the 19th century, and today a much-frequented garden pub, especially in the summer.

If you take Gleueler Strasse in the direction of the town centre you'll reach the **Krieler Dömchen** and the **Church of St Albert the Great**. The latter was rebuilt after the war from the rubble of its former basilica, and the paintings in the choir were created in the early 1960s by Peter Hecker. The "Krieler Dömchen" of St Steven nearby is a real jewel. Built on the site of a Carolingian wooden church, the present structure was built between the early 10th and 12th centuries, originally with just one nave. It is a magnificent example of a harmoniously-proportioned Romanesque village church.

Following the Mommsenstrasse will take you to the **Municipal Forest** (Stadtwald), the starting-point of your tour. On the way there you'll pass several large, handsome-looking town houses dating from the early part of the century.

Castle route: Lindenthal is also the best place to begin a real live castle route: start off from Barbarossaplatz and follow Luxemburger Strasse as far as **Schloss Weisshaus** (car parking is in Leybergstrasse), mentioned as early as 1145. This delightful little Baroque cas-

Boat-house in Rodenkirchen.

tle, with its extensive grounds, served as a summer residence for the abbots of St Pantaleon's. It changed ownership several times after secularisation. The castle is closed to visitors, but there's still a fine view of it to be had from Luxemburger Strasse.

Further out of town, the **Komarhof**, which also used to belong to St Pantaleon's, can be most easily reached via Geisbergstrasse. This well-preserved building is open to visitors from Monday to Friday.

On the Militärring, change over to Berrenrather Strasse and you'll reach **Burg Efferen**, which was once used by the city of Cologne to defend itself against an archbishop it had expelled. The facade, with its seven windows, faces the street, and the gable bears the coat-of-arms of the Bourscheid family. The side with the castle gate facing the town has a mighty tower above it, capped by a slightly wonky-looking Baroque dome.

Continue driving out of town, following signs to Hürth-Gleuel. Opposite the church is the painstakingly restored **Burg Gleuel**. It is now surrounded, along with its outbuildings, by a modern housing estate.

The route continues to Frechen-Bachem, and if you turn into Mauritiusstrasse just before reaching the church you'll see **Haus Bitz** directly in front of you. Unfortunately, the Baroque manor-house is all that remains; today it contains an art gallery.

Follow the road a bit further and soon you'll come face to face with **Burg Bachem**, which dates back to the Hohenstaufen period. This elegant Baroque building, and especially its interior, underwent generous extension work in the 19th century, and restoration work has been going on since 1970 (no entry to the public).

Take the 264, and you'll reach **Haus Forst**, a magnificent, privately-owned manor-house. Then, between the two autobahns, a road signposted to "Horbell" branches off to the left. In a wooded area (follow the sign saying "Autobahnmeisterei") can be found **Burg Hobell**, the last castle on our route. The inner courtyard of this castle, with its wooden galleries, is particularly charming.

Rodenkirchen and Marienburg: You can reach Marienburg by taking the Bonner Strasse. In front of the roundabout stands the Anglican **Garrison Church of All Saints**, built between 1951 and 1952 by Rudolf Schwarz for the English occupation forces. The high, austere brick building is supported on all sides by buttresses. Here, Schwarz has adapted Romanesque formal elements to match modern requirements.

On the northern side of the Südpark lies **Maria Königin**, the last work to be completed by the great churchbuilder Dominikus Böhm (1853). Rather inconspicuous when seen from the outside, the structure possesses a surprising lightness and brightness inside. The south wall consists of almost nothing but window, and floral motifs form a strong connection between the sacred room and the natural scenery surrounding it.

Marienburg has successfully managed to retain its character of an elegant suburb filled with villas (Leyboldstrasse, Marienburgstrasse, etc.), even though much of the building space here was filled by large residential blocks in the 1980s.

On the Rhine Embankment, drive straight under the motorway bridge to **Rodenkirchen**, and turn off down the Rathausstrasse in the direction of the Rhine. The way leads along the embankment past artists' villas from the 1920s (Richard Seewald, for example, used to live in No. 11), and up to the picturesque part of town around **Old St Maternus's**. The chapel, which dates back to the 11th century, lies high above the Rhine and is surrounded by some very smart-looking half-timber buildings that also double as restaurants – a favourite destination with the people of Cologne.

Right, Memento Mori: in the Melaten Cemetery.

Nesquik

THE RIGHT BANK OF THE RHINE

Since 1888, the Rhine has flowed through Cologne. Up until then it actually flowed past the city. In the summer of 1888 Cologne decided to finally loosen its tight belt of fortifications in order to keep step with the increase in its population, and later on in the same year, the city incorporated the municipalities outside its gates.

Cologne grew rapidly in all directions, also eastwards for the very first time, across to Deutz and Poll on the right bank of the Rhine. The city was now almost 11 times its original size. As businesses established themselves in the newly-acquired regions, the standard of living in the outlying areas rose considerably.

In retrospect, this incorporation certainly seemed to have been justified, and it also seemed the best argument in favour of further ones: at the beginning of 1919, Vingst and Kalk, on the right bank, were swallowed up, and in 1914, after Mülheim and Merheim with all their territory had also been incorporated, Cologne was the largest city in the whole empire, with 20,000 hectares (80 sq. miles) of land.

In 1975 the city expanded once more, this time swallowing up a large area of the right bank yet again: Porz, Cologne's former neighbouring city on the Rhine. More than 40 percent of Cologne's entire surface area (40,000 hectares/160 sq. miles) is now on the right bank of the river.

Wrong side of the river: Of course, statistical harmony conceals the true relationship between the two sides of the Rhine that has developed over the years, best summed up in the nasty-sounding expression "Schäl Sick", which literally means "squint side", though that gives one no clue as to its real meaning: it means the "wrong" side of the Rhine, and originated on the "correct" one i.e. the left one. Indeed, animosity is so widespread that Adenauer used to claim that Walachia began on the other side of the Rhine, and once when plans were made to shift some people from some slums on the left bank across to much more attractive housing on the opposite side of the river, the cry went up and promptly became famous: *"Mer wolle nit no Yokohama!"* ("We don't wanna go to Yokohama!")

Whatever unpleasant things are attributed to the Deutz side of the river, the fact remains that people there don't squint any more than anywhere else. Indeed the phrase itself, and not only its slanderous intention, originated on the Cologne-city side: in the old days, ships going up-river had to be towed, and each horse used for the purpose had its eye facing the river blinkered, which made it *schäl* (squint), and the side of the river it could no longer see was the *schäle Seite* i.e. Deutz.

However, the people of Deutz have learned to live with their reputation, and in 1952 they self-confidently referred to their own Carnival society as "Schäl Sick". In 1990–91 the Carnival's "big three" ("Dreigestirn") was composed exclusively of Deutz inhabitants.

Barbarians: The right bank of the Rhine at Cologne has had rather a bad name in historical times, too: under the emperor Constantine, around AD 310, the Romans built a military camp on the opposite bank in order to secure their bridge over the Rhine and their "Colonia". The camp was known as *Castrum Divitium* (today's Deutz), and measured less than 150 sq. metres. Beyond it lay the land of the Franks, whom the Romans regarded as barbarians.

In the year AD 700 or thereabouts, St Boniface complained that the "town opposite Cologne" was still a pagan stronghold, and in the 16th century the Cologne City Council lamented the immoderate amount of "drunkenness" among "the foreigners of Deutz".

Finally, perhaps it is best to content oneself with what Victor Hugo felt while he was staying in Deutz in 1838,

Preceding pages: Rhine bridges; at a riflemen's meeting in Deutz. Left, mother and child in the Rhine Park.

and later recorded for posterity: "The windows of Cologne face Deutz, and those of Deutz face Cologne; and it is better to live in Deutz, with a view of Cologne, than vice versa." So it's all a question of how you look at it! At that time the Prussians had already been in charge for quite a while, and Deutz was a fortified city just like Cologne, both of them together forming the country's strongest bastion against the French enemy. In 1817 almost every third inhabitant of Deutz was employed by the *Preussen* ("Prussians") – the rather disrespectful term applied since then, by Cologne's older inhabitants, to the military as a whole.

It was in Deutz, in 1840, that the founder of German social democracy, August Bebel, was born. The house at No. 8 Kasemattestrasse still bears traces of this opponent of Bismarck's, whose reference to Cologne in a speech in 1893 probably gave many people more than they had bargained for: "If any city in Germany… can claim the honour of considering itself the birthplace of socialism, then that city is certainly Cologne."

A fortified city: Deutz even has a "Bebelplatz", though it's pretty hard to find. Far more noticeable, even from as far away as Cologne, is Deutz's military past. The tall **Equestrian Statue** beside the river was erected in memory of the Deutz cuirassiers from the 8th "Graf Geller" regiment, who had to draw their sabres more often against revolutionaries and rioters than against enemy soldiers during their time in Deutz, and more of whom were killed by disease, between 1870 and 1871, than by the enemy.

Over here, on the "Kennedy Embankment" with the world-famous panorama of the Old City opposite, the history of Deutz is concentrated into quite a small area. The site of the Roman fort during the emperor Constantine's time has been occupied since 1970–78 by the 20-storey **Lufthansa Building**. The Roman remains were sifted through one

Equestrian statue of the Deutz Cuirassler in front of the Lufthansa Building.

last time during the construction of the 95-metre (300-ft) high building, and some Roman remains survive: the east gate of the fort, for example, situated between the Lufthansa Building and the old people's home inside the restored monastery walls, on the way to Old St Heribert's church.

A permanent bridge used to lead from here across to the left bank. Later, small boats, barges and ferries had to be relied on, and it was only in 1959 that another permanent Rhine bridge, the "Dom Bridge", was built, which because of its box-girder construction is also known as the "Muusfall" (mousetrap).

After the decline of Roman rule, their fort became part of the Crown lands of the Franks, and Otto III presented it to Cologne archbishop Heribert, who subsequently founded a Benedictine monastery within its old walls in 1002. In 1816, after secularisation and the Wars of Liberation, Prince Augustus of Prussia considered the fact that the royal artillery had settled within the monastery walls and turned St Heribert's church into their smithy as an expression of his "goodwill" towards Cologne.

The church's outer walls have meanwhile been reconstructed, after its destruction during World War II. The church's greatest treasure, the magnificent reliquary of St Heribert, was transferred in 1896 to the neo-Romanesque New St Heribert's church, situated at the entrance to the busy shopping street of "Deutzer Freiheit". It dates from 1160 and is the best-preserved reliquary of that time in Germany.

A greenhouse with a view: We continue on down the Rhine, along its embankment, past the less obtrusive "**Landeshaus**" belonging to the Rhineland Landscape Association (1957–58), and next to it, the **Hyatt Regency Hotel**, built in 1988. Its colourful granite-and-glass facade reflects the cityscape opposite for passers-by, and inside, the whole place is rather like a greenhouse – indeed, one of its restaurants is called

Kite-flying on the Rhine Meadows.

exactly that. "Belle Vue" was the name of the hotel in which Victor Hugo so enjoyed the panorama of the city, and this luxury hotel now provides just the same *belle vue* for its guests.

Beyond the Hohenzollern Bridge and north of the Trade Fair Complex is the **Rhine Park** (Rheinpark), originally called the "Kaiser Wilhelm Park" when it was first laid out in 1913, but fully democratic these days; it is the largest park area in Cologne, one that everyone can enjoy, with its unspoilt Rhine meadows, its sculpture parks and its flower borders.

It's possible to travel round the large meadows by narrow-gauge railway, or admire the shrubs and flowers from above on the chairlift. Best of all, though, is the trip across the Rhine and high above the Zoo Bridge inside the gently rocking cars of the **Rhine cable railway**, 900 metres (2,950 ft) long with a 45mm thick cable, and originally opened in 1957. In the summer, one cable car leaves every minute. On the other side of the river the same ticket allows the passengers a trip to the zoo, naturally without any parking-space problems. A footpath leads from the Rhine Park along the harbour and all the way to Mülheim; otherwise the path leads back to Deutz, past the railway station building dating from 1914.

In front of it, on the Ottoplatz, a four-stroke motor on a pedestal (1931) stands as a reminder of its inventor Nikolaus August Otto, whose "Gasmotoren Fabrik Deutz AG" of 1872 later became the famous firm of "Klöckner-Humboldt-Deutz AG". One can gain some inkling of the great importance of that Deutz factory when one considers that its employees included a certain Gottlieb Daimler as well as a Karl Benz.

Jewish tradition: In 1907 the fortifications at Deutz were dismantled, and in front of the defensive installations the street known as Gotenring emerged. The zig-zag course of the Wallstrasse, today known as the "Helenenwall-

A popular place to meet in Zündorf: the island of "Groov".

strasse", is the only reminder of the strategists' former layout. The police station that stands at the end of this street where it broadens out into the Reischplatz once used to house the Deutz Synagogue. Deutz had had a strong Jewish tradition ever since the 15th century, largely due to the restrictive policies in Cologne.

The main synagogue on the Rhine Embankment was torn down in 1914 to make way for the construction of the "suspension bridge", and the premises on the Reischplatz were destroyed during "Kristallnacht" under the Third Reich. Since then there has been no Jewish community in Deutz.

The Nazi plans for the reconstruction of Deutz after the war were, thank God, never realised: a "regional Forum" was to have been built here, a massive deployment zone on Cologne's east-west axis. Cologne of all places, where the Nazis couldn't even get a majority in March 1933, a bastion of Fascism. These plans luckily only got as far as the drawing-board. Today, Deutz, so close to the heart of the city, is having a huge sports and leisure centre planned for it, which will regularly make the headlines.

Once the fortifications had been taken down there was also room for a new harbour. Industrial settlements grew up along the Schnellert, a disused arm of the Rhine. The entrance to the harbour is still spanned by a swing bridge from that time. The long, lime-tree-lined Rhine Embankment adjacent to it is named after the tool factory in the background: "Alfred Schütte Allee".

Poll: Poll, formerly a fishing village, and the same size as Deutz, contributed a lot to the growth of Cologne. The winding streets around the church still contain several clues to this suburb's rural past: many streets are named after fish, such as "Salmstrasse" and "Maifischgasse", and people still refer affectionately to "Poll fisher boys" and "milkmaids".

A favourite meeting-point on Sun-

Nature still has a chance to shine in this park landscape.

days in the summertime is the **Poll Meadow** ("Poller Wiesen"), along the embankment, with its many sports facilities; shepherds can often be seen tending their flocks here. And in autumn, young and old frequently meet here to fly their kites, too, because the wind blows at its strongest down the Rhine itself.

Kalk: Kalk, together with its neighbouring districts of Buchforst, Vingst and Höhenberg, is an industrial suburb, and the fact that a farmstead is documented as having been on this very spot as early as 1003 is all too easily overlooked. Yet Kalk only became a parish, town and mayoralty in its own right at the end of the last century. Growth at that time was unbelievably rapid: it was transformed from a Sunday picnic destination into Prussia's largest industrial centre within less than a century. It also received a suitable coat-of-arms: an anvil, a hammer, a cog-wheel – and a chapel, too.

The chapel's successor still stands today, in Kalk's main street. The 15th-century Pietà inside it had turned Kalk into a place of pilgrimage. In 1941 the **Chapel**, built in 1704, was destroyed by an air raid during the course of a single night, but no one believed that except the Nazis: with its 30,000 pilgrims a year, the chapel had always been a thorn in their side anyway, symbolising as it did not only piety but also resistance – so much so that it is widely believed that they blew up the chapel themselves during the bombardment.

Many of Kalk's original factories still survive: the "Chemische", the local name for the Kalk Chemical Factory ("CFK"), still puffs its white smoke into the sky, and even if the odd factory here is forced to close down now and then, its buildings are usually kept preserved.

Buchforst: Until 1932, Buchforst (the name means "beech forest") was known as "Kalkerfeld". It then decided to bask in its own past glory, even though the people of Mülheim had chopped down all the vast beech forests in the south of their city as long ago as 1797 in order to help repay their war debt to France.

A market here on Wednesdays and Saturdays in the Waldescher Strasse livens up this suburb, and from here, on sunny days, one can see the shining contours and cubic structures of the still very modern-looking "**White City**", built between 1929 and 1932 by Wilhelm Riphahn (who later built the Opera House) and Caspar Maria Grod.

Mülheim: For centuries, Mülheim was the mainstay of the pastoral region now known as the "Bergisches Land", which was formerly the Duchy of Berg. The inhabitants of Mülheim erected a monument in their Municipal Gardens (Stadtgarten) in grateful memory of the most popular of their regents, "Jan Wellem", who as Johann Wilhelm II became Elector Palatine and Duke of Jülich Berg, and in so doing seem to have forgotten all about the stiflingly high taxes they had to pay in order to finance the Baroque splendour of the court in Düsseldorf.

There again, they were probably in a much better position to pay than their neighbours. An edict of toleration proclaimed by its Catholic rulers had made Mülheim an attractive destination to believers suffering persecution elsewhere – believers who were not only pious but also very industrious.

"The industrious one" ("Die Fleissige"): This was also the epithet given to the tiny river Strunde, which used to turn several mill-wheels on its brief journey from Herrenstrunden, near Bergisch Gladbach, to the Rhine. Indeed, it was the mills along the banks of the Strunde that first gave the town its name: mention was first made of "Mulenheym" in the year 1098.

Just as with Deutz, Mülheim's proximity to Cologne forcibly hindered its urban development for a long time. Civic autonomy and a civic constitution in 1322 were very little help either, since there were no town walls. Fortifications were planned on several occasions only to be blocked by Cologne

Cologne's Trade Fair Centre

Even though Konrad Adenauer liked to close the curtains of his compartment just after the train had pulled out of the main station in Cologne and crossed the Hohenzollernbrücke, there was still one thing on the right bank of the river he was eager to keep: the "Messe", Cologne's Trade Fair Centre, near the station in Deutz which is now known as "Messebahnhof". The Rhineland was still under British occupation, and most people in Cologne probably had more urgent things on their minds when their mayor first began making the idea of a "Rhine Trade Fair" in Cologne sound attractive to the members of the City Council.

It would mean continuing an old tradition that had its roots in the 14th century. The trade fair association was founded on 1 April 1922, and construction work based on plans drawn up by Hans Verbeek began soon afterwards on the right bank, on the site formerly used for the 1914 Werkbund (Craft Union) exhibition. On 11 May 1924 Cologne's first ever Spring Trade Fair, with 2,800 exhibitors occupying more than 65,000 sq. metres of space, opened its doors. There were more than 600,000 visitors, including the President of the German Reich, Friedrich Ebert.

Similar trade fairs elsewhere during the post-war era were relatively short-lived, but the "Kölner Messe", as it was now called, very soon developed into an economic enterprise of immense European significance.

Soon it had to be divided up into subsidiary trade fairs, and the original plan is still faithfully adhered to today: there are separate exhibitions of furniture, household goods and clothing; "food, beverages and tobacco", better known as "Anuga", takes place every two years in the autumn, alternating with the famous "Photokina" trade fair. Confectionery and sports goods are other important branches, and there are also two art fairs: the rather classically oriented "Kunstmesse", and the art market, known as "Art Cologne".

The Trade Fair Centre assumed its present-day appearance in 1928, when it was re-designed by Adolf Abel for the "PRESSA" exhibition. Since then it has been characterised by its vertical brick facades and its austere expressionism. The five million visitors to the international press exhibition were also most impressed by the new symbol on the Rhine, the 85-metre (280 ft) high trade fair tower, which is still referred to today by the city's older inhabitants as the "PRESSA tower". It was in the restaurant up here that Oskar Kokoschka painted his "View of the City of Cologne" in 1956 (on display in the Ludwig Museum).

Today, the Trade Fair Centre is one of the most important in the world. Cologne is now the leading trade fair metropolis for over 20 different branches and sectors of the economy; 37 international trade fairs and exhibitions every year attract up to 29,000 firms from over 100 countries, along with 1.8 million buyers and trade visitors from all over the world. Annual turnover has been galloping ahead, reaching DM 250 million. To ensure things stay that way, a lot of investment activity is taking place which will soon turn the Trade Fair Centre in Cologne into one of the world's largest, with 260,000 sq. metres (311,000 sq. yards) of exhibition space.

However, the darkest chapter in the history of the Centre, during the "Third Reich", should not be forgotten. An "SS construction brigade" was stationed here, and more than 1,000 of the prisoners in it had been sent to Cologne and to the industrial areas of the Rhineland for bomb clearance and bomb disposal, and then on to France to build the starting-ramps for the new "wonder weapon", the V2 rocket. Gipsies, above all, were deported from the "Messelager", as were roughly 12,000 Jews, to concentration camps in the east.

Finally, the buildings also served as a so-called "re-education camp" in which the politicians of the Weimar Republic – the ones who could still be hunted down, that is – were held after the attempt on Hitler's life in 1944. Among them was the city's mayor, removed from office long since, whose far-sightedness had originally made the construction of the Trade Fair Centre possible: Konrad Adenauer.

each time, and whatever walls were already in existence were razed to the ground by imperial decree. Flooding and drifting ice were just a few of the resulting problems. It was only in the 18th century that prosperity finally reached the town; the grand-looking burghers' houses on "Mülheimer Freiheit", some of which can still be seen today, bear witness to those times.

In those days, when Mülheim was still a small barge town, the church of St Clement's used to be at its centre. And it was here, where the white excursion boats still moor, that the holy custom of the *Mülheimer Gottestracht* first began.

A pilgrimage on the Rhine: If one is to believe the legend, it all started with a miracle: after stealing some chalices from the church, a thief had attempted to flee down the Rhine. But in the middle of the river his boat suddenly failed him and remained perfectly still: there was still a Host inside one of the chalices. The chalice was brought back again to the church in a solemn procession, and ever since then, on Corpus Christi Day, the barges leave one by one from the embankment in front of St Clement's. The procession, complete with fire-crackers and rifle-bearers, is a mixture of seriousness and fun, a pilgrimage on the Rhine that has become a real Rhenish spectacle.

The barges of Mülheim (*Müllemer Bötche*) have long been featured in Cologne songs: Just say "*Heidewitzka, Herr Kapitän*" – everyone'll sing along immediately. For a long time the barges provided the only means of access to the left bank.

Mülheim also had a pontoon bridge as long ago as 1888, of course: the mayor had acquired it second-hand in Mainz, and it did its duty until 1926, by which time it had become more of a traffic hindrance than anything else. In 1925 the bridge had to be opened roughly 31 times a day, and was thus open for a total of five hours a day altogether. That was the most important argument in favour of a new, artistic bridge which – restored after the war – still spans the Rhine near Mülheim. At its opening in 1929 it was the largest cable suspension bridge in the world.

Flittard: If one follows the course of the Rhine along the Stammheimer Embankment (Stammheimer Ufer) one eventually reaches Flittard, a town continually threatened by flooding (its name is derived from the German verb *fliessen*, to flow, referring to the mud there). Here, at number 152, Egonstrasse, one can admire a monument to 19th-century communications: the "optical telegraph", one of the final traces of a signalling system that once used to extend through the whole of Prussia. After it was completed, in 1833, it passed on signals from Schlebusch to St Pantaleon's in Cologne.

When visibility was good, the stretch from Berlin to Koblenz was quickly covered by 55 such stations. The electric telegraph, however, was significantly faster, and also operated independently of daylight, and so this opti-

Left, the main thing is, it tastes good! Right, burning the "Nubbel" – an old Carnival custom.

cal connection with Berlin was finally abandoned in 1849.

Merheim: When it was incorporated into the city in 1914, Flittard, along with all the other parishes between Dünnwald, Brück and Rath, belonged to the mayoralty of Merheim, a vast rural region with farmsteads and country houses, many of which – including Burg Herl, Haus Mielenforst, Haus Thurn and others – are still in good condition.

Although in those days the mayor actually had his headquarters in Holweide, the central town was Merheim. And while Holweide and Dellbrück, along the road to Bergisch Gladbach, developed into closely-knit settlements, Merheim – at least the very heart of it around the church of St Gereon – has largely retained its village character. The old "Fronhof", built in 1775, and the restaurant opposite, "**Em ahle Kohberg**", built in 1665, both still nestle among its meadows.

Another part of Merheim runs along the length of the major A-road in the area, and here, quite unexpectedly, at No. 421, Olpener Strasse, we find the "**Goldener Pflug**" restaurant, one of the top gourmet establishments in all of Germany. The Merheimer Fliehburg extends away eastwards like a peninsula in the middle of a former arm of the Rhine; from the Stone Age until the Middle Ages, the inhabitants used it as a place of refuge whenever danger threatened.

Rath: One of the castles in the region on the right bank of the Rhine, Haus Rath, had an entire suburb named after it. Rath, on the edge of the Kings Forest (Königsforst), and united with the suburb of Heumar, has retained quite a lot of historical interest despite its swift development.

Porz: Porz, too, has been part of Cologne since 1975. This town on the Rhine, with its highly cosmopolitan centre, has also brought Cologne two very attractive excursion destinations: the **Leidenhausen Estate** (Gut Leidenhausen) with its Forest House ("Haus des Waldes"), and the **recreation island of "Groov"** (Freizeitinsel Groov), at Zündorf. The Forest House is a remarkable nature museum, with a game park as well as a bird of prey reserve in which several rare birds can be observed at close quarters. Anyone who finds the place too much of a crush at the weekend can wander off to the "Wahner Heide" nature conservation area nearby; on weekdays it is used as a military training area.

Zündorf is the most attractive part of Porz. This town, with its old Rhine island of "Groov", was mentioned as far back as the Middle Ages, and even today many medieval buildings, spruced up affectionately for the visitors, still remain between its church and its market. Zündorf's **fortified tower** (Wehrturm) still looms above the town; it was built during the 13th century out of basalt, a substance that medieval weaponry had not yet found a way of destroying.

Left, the Rhine cable car. Right, the Trade Fair Tower.

4711
RESTAURANT

Cologne and Environs
4 km / 2.5 miles
Uedesheim
Himmelgeist
Hilden
Ohligs
Schaberg
Höhscheid
Solingen
Auf der Höhe
Urdenbach
Altrhein
Rhine
Kuckhof
Stürzelberg
Balkhausen
Zons
Zons Citadel
Nievenheim
Langen-feld
Wupper
Herscheid
Sengbach Dam
Dormagen
A59
A3
Leichlingen
Diepen Dam
Knechtsteden Abbey Church
Monheim
Reusrath
Burscheid
Hackenbroich
Hüscheid
A57
Hitdorf
Opladen
to Burg Castle
Lützenkirchen
Worringen
Niederblecher
NATURPARK KOTTENFORST-VILLE
Thenhvn.
Quettingen
A1
Bürrig
Altenberg Cathedral
Fühlingen
Schlebusch
Regatta Lake
Morsbroich Castle
Stommeln
Sinnersdorf
Fühlinger Lake
Merkenich
Odenthal
Dhünn
Lever-kusen
Heimersdorf
DÜNN-WALD
Pulheim
Auweiler
Longerich
Höhenhaus
Bergisch Gladbach
Stamm-heim
Widdersdorf
Cologne
NIPPES
MÜLHEIM
DELBRÜCK
BENSBERG
Abbey Church
Brauweiler
BICKENDORF
LÖVENICH
Cologne Cathedral
LUSTHEIDE
to Bensberg Castle
A4
WEIDEN
Roman Burial Chamber
KALK
LINDENTHAL
MERHEIM
JUNKERS
Hücheln
DEUTZ
HEUMAR RATH
FORST KÖNIGSFORST
Frechen
SÜLZ
ZOLL-STOCK
Benzel-rath
Neu Grefrath
Effleren
Röttgen Palace
A559
WESTHOVEN
PORZ
N.S.G.
Leidenhausen Estate
Berrenrath
Hürth
RODENKCHN.
URBACH
GRENGEL
Türnich
HAHNWALD
ZÜNDORF
Vochem
Knapsack
MESCHE-NISCH
WAHN
Cologne-Bonn Airport
Kierdorfer See
Godorf
Kierdorf
Bleibtreusee
Langel
WAHNER HEIDE
Augustusburg Castle
Berzdorf
Libur
Köttingen
Heider Bergsee
Wesseling
A61
Brühl
Falkenlust Hunting Lodge
Niederkassel
Spich
Troisdorf
Liblarer See
Blessem
Phantasialand Fun Park
A553
Keldenich
Erft
A555

THE CITY'S GREEN BELTS

Inhabitants of Cologne in search of rest and relaxation were still having quite a hard time of things as early as the beginning of the 19th century: apart from a few tree-lined squares, the city, enclosed in its Prussian fortifications, had no parks to speak of at all. Today, however, Cologne is one of the "greenest" cities anywhere in Europe. The two so-called "Green Belts" that run through it are an unmistakeable feature, and were the inspiration of the city's former mayor Konrad Adenauer. A total of 8,700 hectares (21,000 acres) of parkland can now be found within the city's borders.

Unlike many other cities in the last century, Cologne never possessed a royal residence of its own, surrounded by parkland. There were only a few orchards and stretches of farmland just beyond the gates of the medieval city, which were hardly suitable for country walks. This made the creation of various park areas within the city virtually essential. Cologne's first and oldest park – the Municipal Gardens (Stadtgarten) – was laid out across an area measuring 11 hectares (30 acres) between 1827 and 1829.

It was only 40 years later, in 1863, that an attractive new destination for excursions and relaxation came into being with the Flora, which in those days was far outside the city gates, and to which the Botanical Gardens were annexed in 1914. But after this, progress was rapidly made because of the need to extend the city boundaries. From 1881 onwards, further areas of green were added: the Ringstrasse and the People's Gardens (Volksgarten), as well as the Municipal Forest (Stadtwald), impressive for its sheer dimensions.

The Municipal Forest: With its large pond (where boats can be hired), its game enclosure and its old trees, the Municipal Forest, situated between Dürener Strasse and Aachener Strasse near the suburb of Lindenthal, is a favourite hiking area. Around the turn of the century, horticultural director Kowallek had over 300,000 trees, plants and bushes planted, and also laid out various winding paths, ponds and meadows.

Today the Municipal Forest, extended several times (it measures around 200 hectares/500 acres), is an integral part of the city's Outer Green Belt. Avenues of chestnut-trees and mixed forest alternate with areas of pine and birch. Extensive meadows and forests, numerous lakes and ponds with rowing-boats, café-restaurants and small kiosks add variety to this recreation area. The Cologne F.C. football ground here is a big attraction for the fans, and the professional players can often be observed training.

The Inner and the Outer Green Belts: It was largely thanks to the Treaty of Versailles that Cologne's Inner and Outer Green Belts were created at all. Under its provisions, the ring of military fortifications around the city had to be dismantled after 1919, and this was a good opportunity to gain valuable land close to the city for town planning purposes.

Konrad Adenauer, who was mayor at that time, made use of this opportunity and had several large areas (11 large farms, to be precise) of the outer fortifications and the field of fire cleared and turned into parks, despite hefty opposition from the families who owned the land. The work was carried out according to plans drawn up by the landscape architect Fritz Ecke, and his successor Josef Giesen.

The **Inner Green Belt** runs along the Inner Kanalstrasse, past the Aachener Weiher (pond), the Museum of East Asian Art (well worth a visit) and the university area, all the way to the People's Gardens (Volksgarten) and the Hindenburg Park. The **Outer Green Belt** extends for nearly 30 km (18 miles) from the Fühlinger Lake (Fühlinger

See) water sports area north of Cologne, near Chorweiler, right down to the Forstbotanischer Garten south of the city on the Rhine near Rodenkirchen.

The sections of the Outer Green Belt on the right bank of the Rhine begin at the river itself, at the Poll-Westhovener Rheinufer and the Gremberger Forest. Some way past the Severinus Bridge, the Rhine meadows begin, and here one can often see shepherds grazing their sheep in the summer. Tennis courts and football fields border on a hiking trail which leads via two campsites, and one or two interruptions, all the way to Porz-Zündorf and the Groov peninsula.

The Fühlinger Lake: As the city was extended further to the north towards Volkhoven and Chorweiler, it became necessary to create parkland for recreation purposes in this region too. The Fühlinger Lake region, with its mixture of woods, meadows and its man-made lake area (with seven lakes) is an all-year-round attraction. This local recreation area, which covers nearly 300 hectares (700 acres), was completed in 1982. The region formerly contained gravel and sand quarries for use in industry.

Those keen on water sports certainly get the best deal here on the Fühlinger Lake: it has a 2,000-metre (6,500-ft) long regatta course for canoeists and rowers. Riding stables, a tennis hall and outdoor barbecue areas are also available. In the summer, surfers and swimmers throng in their hundreds alongside the lakes, and this is not doing a lot to help the ecological balance. Nature-lovers and those in search of peace and quiet will only feel really at home here outside the swimming season. That's when the extensive network of footpaths and trails, and benches to relax on around the lakes are at their most inviting for people looking for quiet walks.

The Beethoven Park: The green finger of the Beethoven Park stretches from the Outer Green Belt into Sülz, a part of the city much favoured by the student community. It ends up at the Auerbach-

A field of poppies.

platz, where flea markets take place regularly (except in the winter months). Broad meadows, shady trees and enchanted footpaths make the Beethoven Park an idyllic place, in which everyone can find what they are looking for, whether it's somewhere to daydream, play or stroll. There's also a popular beer garden (the "Birkebäumche") situated in the middle of some allotments separating the Outer Green Belt from the city.

A particular attraction for children is the **Children's Zoo** in Sülz, which belongs to the Association of Aquarium and Terrarium Owners. The area once only contained a few ponds; today even such exotic animals as apes, chinchillas, raccoons and porcupines, as well as many varied species of birds, can be observed at close quarters.

The Forstbotanischer Garten: To the south of Cologne, near the suburb of Rodenkirchen, lies the Forstbotanischer Garten, well worth an excursion, with its wealth of rare plants, trees and bushes. It lies on what actually used to be an old rubbish-tip, and it was opened in 1964. Over 3,000 different types and species of trees from Japan, China, America, the Balkans and the Caucasus have made their home here, along with roughly 550 conifers, 2,000 deciduous trees and over 500 different types of rhododendron.

The focal points of the garden are the Rhododendron Ravine, the Japan Park and the Peony Meadow. But the Heather Garden is also worth a visit with its dwarf shrubs, most of them evergreen, which bloom at every season of the year in some form or another. There is also a 10-km (6-mile) long network of footpaths for walkers.

The special theme park known as the **Friedenswald**, in the southern part of the Forstbotanischer Garten, was added in 1979. Across an area of 26 hectares (65 acres) trees have been planted symbolising all the countries with whom Germany has diplomatic relations. The colourful mixture of different types of

Free-time fun on the Fühlinger Lake.

wood makes the park an exciting experience the whole year round. Red maple from Canada, weeping birch from Finland, wild pine from Sweden or the gingko tree from China are just a few examples. The entire park can be walked around along a 4.5-km (3 mile) long footpath. Roughly 100 different kinds of shrub roses and climbing roses can be enjoyed along the park's inner footpath.

The King's Forest (Königsforst): The King's Forest, on the right bank of the Rhine in Cologne, is a fine example of an area of green which, though very close to the city itself, features an impressive variety of possibilities for hikers, walkers and cyclists. The King's Forest is one of the most attractive forest regions of the Lower Rhine basin. It covers an area of 3,000 hectares (7,500 acres) and was originally a part of the crown lands of the Frankish kings. In the year 958 the emperor Otto I gave the forest to his brother, archbishop Bruno of Cologne, as a present. Later on, the abbeys of Deutz and St Pantaleon shared in its ownership.

During the Napoleonic era, the forest was badly damaged: most of its ancient oak trees were felled and the wood taken to France. It was only in 1815, when the Rhineland was retaken by the Prussians, that the area could be properly reafforested. Swedish fir, Japanese larch and Douglas pine were planted. Today, native coniferous and deciduous trees are preferred.

Numerous hidden ponds, long paths through mixed woodland, and groves of pine and oak provide something for everybody in search of rest and relaxation. The footpaths can be walked or cycled along for hours, right up to Bensberg in the north or to Rösrath in the east.

The Brück game preserve: The Brück game preserve lies to the west of the King's Forest, near the suburb of the same name. The preserve, which covers an area of 50 hectares (120 acres), is open until dusk every day of the year. Wild boar and Dybovsky deer in particular can be observed roaming wild here in their natural habitat. A 700-metre (2,000 ft) long **nature trail** at the main entrance to the preserve (on Flehbachmühlenweg) provides visitors with information via notice boards about more than 100 different kinds of trees and shrubs. Picnic tables, shelters and benches are spread about invitingly. In the Erkermühle area, idyllic footpaths lead along the edge of the Flehbach pond.

The Dünnwald game park: The Dünnwald game park, roughly half the size of the one in Brück, lies to the north. Wild boar predominate here, too, as well as fallow deer. One can also go for a refreshing dip nearby in the delightful Dünnwald open-air "forest swimming pool", and nearby there is also a minigolf course as well as a restaurant.

The Leidenhausen Estate (Gut Leidenhausen): Situated to the south of the King's Forest, the Leidenhausen Estate is definitely worth a visit. At the **bird of prey sanctuary**, which by the way is only open to visitors on weekends, one can see eagles, falcons, buzzards, capercaillie and also pheasant. Injured animals are cared for here and then set free again. In the adjoining Forest House ("Haus des Waldes"), the history of the forests in the Cologne area and their ecology is graphically described with the aid of slides, models and original exhibits.

And since 1989, the estate now has a further attraction: a **fruit museum** has been set out on a stretch of open land. It is a living museum in which different varieties of fruit have been planted which are no longer available from the usual fruit-growing industries.

Even further to the south of the King's Forest is the **Wahner Heide State Forest**. This military training area is, however, only open to the public at weekends. Here, the sandy heathland with its many pine-trees as well as mixed forest creates an interesting contrast to the King's Forest.

Autumn in the municipal woods.

Into The Country

The countryside outside Cologne is attractive and varied. To the east are Burg Castle, Altenberg Abbey and Bensberg with a fascinating combination of modern and historic architecture, and to the west are the monastery churches of Knechtsteden and Brauweiler, as well as the medieval walls of Zons. To the south lies Brühl with its castles and its large amusement park.

Burg Castle, Altenberg Abbey and Bensberg: Our first trip takes us into picturesque rolling countryside of the "Bergisches Land" to the east of the city. Take the A1 motorway as far as the turn-off to Wermelskirchen/**Schloss Burg**. The castle's history goes back as far as the 12th century: Count Adolf I of Berg handed over his ancestral seat in Altenberg to the Cistercians in 1133 and built a new castle on the plateau above the **River Wupper**, which is surrounded by steep slopes on all sides and can only be approached on the castle entrance side.

Between 1218 and 1225, the castle was considerably extended during the rule of Cologne archbishop Engelbert II, who was also the closest adviser of Hohenstaufen emperor Frederick II. A particularly impressive feature dating from this period is the castle hall; its sheer size (10 metres/30 ft wide, 25 metres/80 ft long) is also a telling symbol of the power wielded by those who had it built. Towards the end of the 14th century the Von Berg family stopped using the castle as a family seat, and from then on it was used only for banquets, and as a hunting lodge. Düsseldorf, then a small village on the Rhine, had become more important and this duly became the capital of the new Duchy of Berg. The old castle was besieged unsuccessfully on several occasions during the Thirty Years' War, but was only actually fully destroyed after the war was over, by imperial troops. The castle then fell into disrepair, and was dismantled and sold in 1850.

But then in 1887 the "Society for the Restoration of Burg on the Wupper" was founded, and reconstruction work began under the supervision of the head of a weaving factory from Wermelskirchen. In 1914, the work was completed. Famous painters from the Düsseldorf Academy were invited to do the magnificent historical frescos. The "**Bergischer Museum**", which moved to the castle in 1904, features various interesting aspects of local history.

Even though very little remains of its original walls, Burg Castle is still definitely worth a visit, with its picturesque setting, its various gates, its battlements and its keep, and especially because of the magnificent view across the Wupper Valley.

Should you be interested in monuments to technology, take the road in the direction of Solingen as far as the **Müngsten Bridge**. This railway bridge was built as a cantilever steel construction between 1894 and 1897. It spans a distance of 160 metres (520 ft) and the summit of the arch lies at a height of 107 metres (350 ft) above the valley below. Technically speaking, this daring construction is considered a pioneering achievement.

Our next destination is **Altenberg Abbey**, also known as the "Bergischer Dom" (cathedral). The landscape is far more attractive if you go via Wermelskirchen instead of via the motorway (Burscheide exit). As you enter Wermelskirchen the road forks off to Dabringhausen, then it's signposted. About 20 km (12 miles) further on the valley starts to widen, and then the mighty Cistercian Gothic abbey towers among the green meadows.

The abbey is also connected with the Counts of Berg: when they handed over their old ancestral seat to the Cistercians in 1133, the monks, who busied themselves with reclaiming swampland, fishing and agriculture, and led lives of austerity, devoid of all show, decided to

Augustusburg Palace in Brühl.

build their church and their monastery somewhat further down the Dhünn Valley. The first Romanesque pillared basilica was started on as early as 1135, the choir was consecrated in 1145, and the nave in 1160. Thanks to generous donations, the monastery, known by historians as Altenberg I, flourished.

Then, in 1222, an earthquake shook the monastery and caused considerable damage. Construction work thus began in 1259 on what was to be an even more magnificent church, one which would also serve simultaneously as a burial-place for the Dukes of Berg.

As early as 1276, the choir, with its corona of chapels and 11 altars, built according to plans by the monk Walter, was ready to be consecrated. The transept was completed by the end of the 13th century, but then construction work came to a standstill, and the nave was only consecrated in 1379. After secularisation in 1803, and a fire in 1815, the building fell into disrepair, and in the following year parts of the cathedral and the monastery caved in. It was only in the mid-19th century that reconstruction plans were drawn up. The abbey was reconsecrated in 1847, and since that time has served as a church for both confessions: the restoration work lasted until the 1970s.

The building is impressive for its simple clarity of design; any extra ornamentation has been dispensed with, thus allowing the magnificent space and its architecture to have its full effect. The mighty nave has no bell-tower, only a modest roof turret containing a small bell to summon the monks to prayer. A distinctive feature is the leaf ornamentation on the capitals, based on plants native to the Rhine region.

The stained glass windows still survive, and are unusually beautiful. The ones in the choir chapels employ geometric motifs; the large window in the northern transept is decorated with stylised floral patterns in grisaille and already contains a small amount of colour; it is only the massive west window (dating from the end of the 14th century) with its tracery and gold-tinted glass, that is resplendently colourful. This results in a bright, clear light, made even more intense by the limewashed stone of the walls. The Baroque additions to the cathedral have been lost, but the tombs of the abbots and dukes of Berg still survive.

Little remains of the monastery. The Baroque entry gate and the outbuildings opposite the western portal, however, have been preserved, and there is still a charming bar-restaurant there today, the "Küchenhof", with St Mark's Chapel, one of the oldest buildings, on its southern side. The chapel's exterior walls date from the time the monastery was founded, and after the earthquake of 1222 it was given a new vault – a particularly fine example of Early Cistercian Gothic architecture.

A **Fairytale Forest** ("Märchenwald"), in which the tales of the Brothers Grimm come to life at the touch of a button, is a few minutes' walk away.

Keeping old traditions alive in front of Altenberg Abbey.

Bensberg rounds off our trip into the Bergisches Land. Anyone interested in modern church architecture should make a detour to Schildgen (in Odental, turn right in the direction of Cologne) and visit the **Church of the Sacred Heart** there, designed by renowned Cologne architect Gottfried Böhm. One of his first ever buildings, it was consecrated in 1960, and its six conical towers make it easily recognisable. The interior is successful both in terms of its simplicity and its spiritual tranquillity.

The road to Bergisch-Gladbach forks off just beyond the church. It leads past the red Burgher's House – also by Böhm, though designed in 1970 – and then on to Bensberg. The first street signposted to the town centre (Zentrum) leads straight up to Elector Johann Wilhelm's Baroque **Hunting Lodge** (Jagdschloss), built between 1700 and 1716 by Matteo Alberti. Now that the rubble masonry has been whitewashed once more, the edifice has regained something of its Mediterranean grace. The generously laid-out building, with its three wings, today houses a boarding school (no entry to the public).

Off to one side lies the **Goethe House**, with a good view of the Rhine Valley from its terrace, and only a few steps away from here is the **Town Hall**, a daring exposed concrete structure built by Gottfried Böhm between 1965 and 1970. It has the basic shape of a historic round castle, and aspects of Romanesque architecture have been incorporated into its modern structure.

Brauweiler, Knechtsteden and Zons: Our second trip takes us to the Lower Rhineland. Anyone keen on visiting the abbey church at Brauweiler should make sure he chooses either a Thursday morning or a weekend to do so, because those are the only times it's open. **Brauweiler Abbey**, dedicated to SS Nicholas and Medardus, is best entered via the door beneath the mighty westwork, which is flanked by two towers.

The abbey's history dates back to the year 1024, but nothing remains of the

Clear proportions give the interior of Altenberg Abbey its special atmosphere.

original building. A second building, which included the church's magnificent crypt, was started in 1048, and consecrated in 1061. The church then underwent several alterations until 1226; the westwork dates from the first half of the 12th century. The Late Romanesque nave with its fine niched triforium was given a Gothic ribbed vault in 1514. The building features several interesting examples of different styles, from Romanesque all the way to Baroque.

The abbey has had quite a changeable history. In its structure, the "Marienhof", situated near the back of the building, dates from as long ago as the end of the 12th century. The capitals in the cloister are particularly fine, and there is an important cycle of Romanesque wall-paintings in the chapter house.

The front courtyard, the "Prälaturhof", was built in the mid-18th century and in the following century another storey was added. A very fine imperial hall in the rococo style still remains (all the inner chambers can only be entered on guided tours). In 1809 Napoleon decreed that the abbey should be used as a doss house, and then in 1811 it fell into the hands of the Prussians, and was used for a long time as a prison, eventually by the Gestapo. After a brief and inglorious spell as a mental hospital, the abbey was then thoroughly renovated by the Rhenish Office for the Restoration of Public Monuments.

To reach Knechtsteden, travel via Geyen, Pulheim and Rommerskirchen, and then turn off towards Neuss. It's signposted at Frixheim.

Knechtsteden Monastery was founded in 1132 and handed over to the Premonstratensian Order. Construction work on the eastern end of the church began in 1138; between 1151 and 1162 the nave and the western apse were built, and the crossing tower as well as the towers flanking the choir were extended. In 1477, the east choir was redone in the Gothic style. After flourishing for a brief period, the abbey then

Entrance lodge to the monastery at Knechtsteden.

sank into obscurity. Construction work only began again in the 17th century: the church was given a new roof and the monastery buildings were extended considerably. In 1802 the monastery was dissolved, and both church and monastery were destroyed by a fire in 1869. Reconstruction work began again in 1878. Since 1895, the building has been used as a missionary training school by the Congregation of the Holy Ghost. Restoration work began on the church at the end of World War II.

The building, with its two choirs, conveys a strong feeling of tranquillity. It has two distinguishing features; one is the way the buttresses alternate in the nave. Here, the vault is not only held in place by several main supports but also by a series of small intermediate pillars. The cupolae are also unusual: they finish off the crossing and the transepts in place of the usual vault. The western apse is dominated by the 12th-century fresco of *Christ as Pantocrator*, and the font also dates from the same period. There is also a 14th-century Pietà.

From the abbey, turn left in the direction of Strabag, and when you get there follow signs to Dormagen. Beyond the motorway, keep on going straight ahead until you reach Zons.

Zons, sometimes known as *Feste Zons*, and originally a fortified customs post, was built by Cologne archbishop Friedrich von Saarwerden between 1373 and 1400, after the Rhine customs post had been moved there from Neuss. But after mismanagement by archbishop Dietrich von Moers, the fortified post had to be pawned off to the chapter of Cologne Cathedral. In 1620 the town was destroyed by a major fire, then in 1794 Zons became French and was confiscated from the Cathedral chapter. The castle, the customs tower and the customs house itself were all then sold in the following year. Today Zons is a part of Dormagen.

Large sections of wall, as well as many gates and defensive towers still survive from this fortress, which was originally constructed on an almost rectangular ground-plan measuring 300 metres (980 ft) by 250 metres (820 ft). After the fire, the houses were rebuilt, and since 1908 the town has undergone elaborate restoration work. Today it is a popular tourist destination, with all that that entails, including good food.

Friedenström Castle is largely in ruins, but some of its buildings have now been restored, and the handsome manor-house ("Herrenhaus") contains the **local museum**, with its impressive specialist collection of *Jugendstil* art. Fairy-tales are performed on an open-air stage here in the summertime.

Brühl: Our third excursion leads to Brühl. To get there, take the Luxemburger Strasse. Then follow the signs beyond Hürth. This route first takes you to **Schloss Augustusburg**.

There was another building on the site before this magnificent palace was built: in 1284, Archbishop Siegfried von Westerburg began building a moated castle, which was completed in

A matter of taste: Gottfried Böhm's Town Hall building in Bensberg.

1298. For the archbishops, the castle served both as a magnificent country seat – the area was very good for hunting, with plenty of game nearby – as well as a fortress. Louis XIV then captured Cologne and Brühl, but it was only when the fortress was recaptured by troops from Holland and Brandenburg, in 1689, that it was blown sky-high.

Elector Joseph Clemens already had plans for its reconstruction in the French style as early as the beginning of the 18th century, but it was his successor Clemens August, from the Wittelsbach family, who began the work in earnest. He was most impressed by the suggestions he received from Westphalian architect Johann Conrad Schlaun, and the latter went on to complete the initial shell construction between 1725 and 1728.

After that, French architect François Cuvilliés was entrusted with the construction work; he removed the final traces of the original moated castle and shifted the state rooms to the southern wing of the building. In front of the new palace, an elegant parterre was laid out according to a design by Dominique Girard. The stairwell was also shifted to suit this, and in 1740 no less a person than Balthasar Neumann was successfully enlisted to design it. In 1768, after 40 years' construction work, the palace was completed.

In 1794 French troops occupied the palace and its magnificent contents were sold off cheaply; the palace and its surrounding gardens then fell into disuse for many years. In 1815 the palace became Prussian. Renovation work took place between 1876 and 1877, and renowned garden architect Lenné was enlisted to remodel and to extend the palace gardens. During World War II the palace was badly damaged, but over the years it was restored once more, and has now regained its former splendour.

The guided tour takes three-quarters of an hour (it's impossible to get into the palace without going on it) and starts off in the north wing. After going through the well-preserved winter rooms one reaches the generous stairwell, which separates off into two flights of stairs on the central landing, leading up to the state-rooms on the upper floor. After the "Gardesaal" and the music room one then reaches the audience chambers on the south side, with their magnificent view of the park. Luxuriant and elegant stucco, magnificent painted ceilings and richly ornate wood panelling lend the whole place a festive atmosphere. The summer rooms on the ground floor, with their blue-and-white "de Bloempot" Dutch tiles, are somewhat more austerely furnished.

Close by is the **palace church**, connected to the palace itself via an orangery; the church is a simple Franciscan Gothic structure, with a magnificent Baroque altar by Balthasar Neumann in its choir.

Only a few kilometres from here – and well signposted, too – is **Schloss Falkenlust**, a rococo jewel that is not to be missed. The house was built according to plans by Cuvilliés – and also commissioned by Clemens August – between 1729 and 1733 as a *maison des plaisances*, and its tastefully laid-out rooms have a very intimate feel to them. The decoration in the rooms is both more reserved and more delicate than that of the larger palace.

After the revolutionary troops had retreated, this small palace fell into private hands and was only acquired by the German state of North Rhine-Westphalia in 1960, before being brilliantly restored.

On the way to Schwadorf it's also worth taking a look at the **Schallenburg**, a well-preserved 12th-century fortress in the form of a moated castle.

Take the autobahn to Brühl-Süd, and you'll come to **Phantasialand**. Go through the "Brandenburg Gate", and you've reached Europe's largest amusement park, with mountain railway, white-water rafting, cable-car rides and Wild West attractions. The park is closed from 1 October to 1 April.

A nice day out: the fortified medieval town of Zons.

TRAVEL TIPS

Getting There

220 By Air
220 By Rail
220 By Bus
220 By Road

Travel Essentials

221 Visas & Passports
221 Money Matters
221 Health
221 What to Wear

Getting Acquainted

221 Government
222 Economy
222 Geography
223 Population
223 Time Zone
223 Electricity
223 Business Hours
223 Holidays
223 Events
223 Religious Services

Communications

224 Media
224 Postal Services
224 Telephone & Telex

Emergencies

224 Security
224 Lost & Found
224 Medical Care

Getting Around

225 Airport Transfers
225 Orientation
225 City Maps
225 Public Transport
225 Taxis
225 Rental Cars
226 Map: Transport
227 Rhine Cruises
227 On Foot/By Bicycle

Where to Stay

228 Hotels
229 Pensions
229 Youth Hostels
229 Camping

Food Digest

230 Cuisine
230 Beverages
231 Restaurants
233 Pubs
233 Cafés

Nightlife

234 Discos
234 Night Cafés & Bars
234 Gambling

Things to Do

234 Sightseeing
236 Tours
237 City Tours
237 Excursions
238 Gardens & Parks

Culture Plus

239 Libraries & Archives
239 Museums
241 Exhibits/Galleries
241 Concerts
242 Opera & Ballet
242 Cinema

Shopping

243 Shopping Tips
244 Markets

Sports

245 Spectator
245 Participant

Special Information

246 The Disabled
246 Children
246 Women
247 Business People
247 Students

Useful Addresses

247 Tourist Information
247 Consulates

246 *Art/Photo Credits*

247 *Index*

Getting There

BY AIR

The Cologne/Bonn Airport is organised on the drive-in principle and has the reputation of being an airport of conveniently short distances. It is situated about 17 km (10 miles) from the city centre and is easily accessible by motorway. Due to its sophisticated safety equipment and extensive landing facilities, during especially troublesome and unfavourable weather conditions it is frequently used as an alternative airport for Düsseldorf and Frankfurt. All large airline companies offer flights into the Cologne/Bonn airport and there are a number of non-stop connections to various other cities, for example to New York.

The Airport Information Office is open 24 hours a day; its telephone number is (02203) 400. Independent airline companies maintain business hours between 8am–6pm Monday–Friday and 8am–noon on Saturday.

BY RAIL

The main railway station is centrally located right next to the Cologne Cathedral. During peak traffic periods there have been as many as 100,000 passengers counted on any one day. This particular railway station is the busiest traffic junction in all of Germany and its main terminal is classified as a historical monument. Trains operated by both the Deutsche Bundesbahn (German Federal Railways) as well as those run by other large international lines pull into the main station. The shops, restaurants and International Press Agency located in the main terminal remain open quite late. The Tourist Information Office is only about 200 yards away from the main station.

BY BUS

Numerous tour buses make stops in Cologne for one or even several days. The main bus station for regular public buses is located between the main railway station and Rheinuferstrasse.

BY ROAD

A circular motorway with seven major intersections makes it relatively easy to leave Cologne in just about any direction. There are two motorways which lead directly into the city itself, thus helping to relieve the congestion on general inner-city traffic. The best routes to take into the city if you're driving in from the circular motorway are as follows:

If you're coming in **from the North** (A 3), turn off at the motorway intersection Köln-Ost and head in the direction of Cologne. Drive over the Zoobrücke until you reach the exit marked "Rheinuferstrasse" (get into the right lane after going over the bridge), and continue driving south until you reach the cathedral.

If you're coming in **from the East** (A 4), drive across the motorway intersection Köln-Ost in the direction of Cologne and continue over the Zoobrücke. Keep going until you reach the Rheinuferstrasse Exit (get into the right lane as soon as you leave the bridge), and continue in a southerly direction until you reach the cathedral.

If you're coming in **from the South** (A 3), at the Dreieck Heumar (Heumar intersection) take the A 4 in the direction of Aachen. At the very next motorway intersection (Köln-Gremberg) turn onto the A 559 and head towards Köln-Deutz. From here, follow the signs which will lead you over the Severinsbrücke into the city centre. The first exit after the bridge will bring you to Rheinuferstrasse. From here the cathedral lies to the north.

If you're coming in **from the West** (A 4), at the motorway intersection Köln-Süd turn onto the A 555 and continue in the direction of Köln-Süd. At the next roundabout take the first exit towards Rheinuferstrasse and follow this northwards until you reach the cathedral.

A computerised parking system informs car drivers as to the current situation in the car parks located within the inner-city area. Fifteen multistorey car parks are open 24 hours a day including the Parkhaus am Dom (an underground car park located beneath the cathedral square), the Aral-Parkhaus Augustinerplatz (close to Neumarkt), the underground car park situated beneath the Hotel Intercontinental (Helenenstrasse) and the Parkhaus at the corner of Hohenzollernring and Maastrichter Strasse. As not all car parks remain open at night it's a good idea to keep the aforementioned in mind before setting out for an evening stroll or bout of entertainment.

The same laws apply to foreigners (if they have not been living in Germany for more than a year) as to German citizens with regards to driving: both are required to be in possession of a valid driver's licence and car registration papers.

Travel Essentials

VISAS & PASSPORTS

Citizens of the following countries (amongst others) are required to have a visa: Eastern European countries (with the exception of Poland, Hungary and Czechoslovakia), China, Turkey, the Near East, many countries in Africa, Thailand, the Philippines, India and Vietnam. As current policies pertaining to obtaining a visa are subject to change at short notice, it's wise to check first with the German Consulate in your own country.

MONEY MATTERS

Many hotels, restaurants and larger shops accept credit cards. Due to sliding work schedules, banks often maintain different business hours. However, it is pretty safe to assume that banks are generally open from 9am–4pm Monday–Wednesday, 9am–6pm Thursday and 9am–3pm Friday. The exchange offices located in the main railway station are open daily 7am–9pm.

HEALTH

On the whole the standard of hygiene is good and you can drink the water without giving it a further thought. Be that as it may however, *Kölsch* (lager beer) tastes better and *Kölnisch Wasser* (Eau de Cologne) smells sweeter.

WHAT TO WEAR

When packing your bags keep in mind that it can get quite hot in summer and very cold in the winter (with temperatures sinking to as low as minus 15°C/5°F), so choose your wardrobe accordingly.

Getting Acquainted

GOVERNMENT

Since the end of World War II the city of Cologne has nearly without exception been governed by the SPD (German Social Democratic Party). The very first chancellor of West Germany, Dr Konrad Adenauer (a member of the Christian Democratic Union [CDU], was not only the mayor of Cologne from 1917 to 1933, but also held this office from 4 May to 6 October 1945. Norbert Burger (SPD), the 1991 successor to this position, is assisted in his office by Hans-Josef Blum (CDU) and Renate Canisius (SPD). The city council is composed of 84 members. In 1991, 41 of these belonged to the SPD, 30 to the CDU and six to the FDP (Free Democratic Party). In addition to these there are three members belonging to "Die Bürger" (The Citizens), three from the Republican Party (the far right-wing party), and one independent member.

In Cologne the City Council and Administration are separate entities. The mayor presides over the former while the town clerk is in charge of the latter. He is assisted by 11 town councillors, each of whom is responsible for a different department.

Since the beginning of 1975 Cologne, like many other large North Rhine-Westphalian cities, has acquired yet another division of local administration, the District Government. Cologne is divided into nine districts; the very first district representative were elected on 4 May 1975. The districts have the power to make decisions concerning matters of local importance.

ECONOMY

Cologne has been a significant economic and trading metropolis (with an emphasis on the latter attribute) ever since the Middle Ages. This has been mainly due to the city's fortuitous geographical position at the intersection of European traffic routes and the Rhine. Today Cologne boasts a ring motorway, unlike any other to be found in Europe, with 10 major intersections leading off from it into all four directions, a city motorway, eight bridges spanning the Rhine, the busiest railway junction in Germany, an intercontinental airport as well as the biggest river port in Europe. Around 1,100 trains pass over the Hohenzollernbrücke each day, making it the most frequently travelled railway bridge in Europe and the Cologne/Bonn Airport is the veritable centre of air freight transport in Germany. At the present time the airport is under construction, which will increase its passenger traffic capacity. The Rhine has always been a vital European economic thoroughfare. It is therefore no wonder that Cologne has developed into an important trading and economic centre.

The Cologne Trade Fair can be described as the "turntable" of foreign trade. Altogether 37 international trade and specialised fairs take place regularly in the city. Many of these specialised fairs are the largest of their kind in the world, for example ORGATEC, PHOTOKINA, IFMA (International Bicycle and Motorcycle Exhibition), ANUGA (Nutritional Foods and Luxury Edibles), the Furniture Fair and Confectionery Fair. The exhibition centre comprises 14 different halls, the dimensions of which taken together add up to a total of 150,000 sq. metres, plus a further 52,000 sq. metres of open space. In addition to all this, two convention centres provide the framework for the 1,100 exhibitions put on as part of the annual Cologne Trade Fair. Around 29,000 exhibitors, hailing from 102 different countries, and 1.8 million visitors – about a third of them from foreign lands – congregate every year at the Cologne exhibition grounds.

Cologne is ranked third (after Hamburg and Munich) as the city with the highest number of insurance companies. There are about 60 insurance agencies maintaining offices here and many important companies have made the city their main headquarters.

In the realm of automobile manufacture Cologne occupies the Number One position in Europe. Since the year 1931 the Ford factory situated in Niehl on the left bank of the Rhine has been producing cars. Today 1,200 completed vehicles leave the assembly line per day. In addition, the car manufacturers Citroen, Mazda, Toyota and Renault have all established main German branches in or around Cologne.

A momentous event in the city's history took place in 1876 when Nikolaus August Otto developed the internal combustion engine, which was later named after him. His memorial is located in front of the Deutz Railway Station. And in Deutz, located on the right side of the Rhine, the firm Klöckner-Humdoldt-Deutz continues to manufacture diesel engines of every shape and size, as well as tractors for export throughout the world.

Numerous retail trade and speciality associations maintain headquarters in Cologne and the some 6,500 different trades businesses are based here. Last but certainly not least, Cologne is proud of Glockengasse No. 4711, home of the world-famous eau de toilette of that same name.

GEOGRAPHY

Cologne is situated at an altitude of 55 metres (183 ft) above sea level and is almost completely flat. The only visible waterway is the mighty Rhine, which makes an enormous curve to the left through the middle of the city. All other waterways are contained within subterranean channels and are thus more or less hidden from sight.

POPULATION

According to a census taken in 1991, Cologne numbers about 1 million inhabitants. Of these 524,000 are Catholic and 215,000 Protestant. The remaining quarter of the population is divided into adherents of the Moslem, Jewish or Old Catholic faiths. Approximately 16 percent of the total population is composed of foreigners, the highest percentage of these being Turkish, followed by Italians and Yugoslavians.

TIME ZONE

The time in Cologne corresponds to Central European Time. Daylight Savings Time is in effect from the end of March until the end of September.

ELECTRICITY

The electrical supply in Cologne is AC 220 volts and 50 Hz. Outlets are designed to accommodate three-pronged safety plugs.

BUSINESS HOURS

Due to sliding work schedules, office hours vary. However, generally speaking, the core time falls between 9am and 4pm. In the city centre shops are open from 9am to 6.30pm except on Thursdays, when most remain open until 8.30pm. In the suburbs stores are usually closed for lunch in the afternoons from 1pm to 3pm. On the first Saturday of every month during Daylight Savings Time shops in the city centre stay open until 4pm; at all other times of the year they are open until 6pm. Beginning four weeks prior to Christmas, stores in the city centre remain open every Saturday until 6pm. In the suburbs many shops close for the day at 1pm on Mondays or Wednesdays.

Official buildings and offices are open to the public only until noon and are always closed on Saturdays.

Shops located in the main railway station and airport stay open later than others.

HOLIDAYS

In addition to the federal holidays celebrated throughout all of Germany, public officials in Cologne are also given a break on the Feast of Corpus Christi (held on the Thursday in the second week following Whitsun) and on All Saints' Day (1 November).

During the peak periods of Carnival in Cologne there isn't much going on in the way of official business, but this lack is more than made up for by the enthusiasm of celebrating civilians. The Thursday before Shrove Tuesday is *Weiberfastnacht* – the day during Carnival when the women take control of things. On this day many offices and shops close around lunchtime. Work also comes pretty much to a standstill on *Rosenmontag* (the Monday before Lent) in both the city itself and in the surrounding countryside. When the regional parades take place on Shrove Tuesday (in most suburbs), you can count on the shops and offices in the city being closed.

EVENTS

Each month the Tourist Information Office issues a list of all up-coming events. The Cologne Carnival Festival Committee publishes a calendar of festival events at the beginning of every year.

RELIGIOUS SERVICES

CATHOLIC

The Cathedral: Masses are held at 6, 7, 8, 9,10 (High Mass), and 11.30am. Evening masses take place at 5 and 6.30pm. The well known cathedral choir, the only boys' choir in Cologne, usually sings at the High Mass.
St Columbia, Kolumbastrasse 4: Masses are held Saturday at 6.30pm and on Sunday at 8 and 9.30am.
Minorite Church (Minoritenkirche), Kolpingplatz: Masses are held on Sunday at 9 and 11am.
Great St Martin's (Gross-St-Martin), An Gross-St-Martin 9: Mass is held on Sunday at 11am in Portuguese and again at 12.30pm in Spanish.

PROTESTANT

Antonite Church (Antoniterkirche), Schildergasse: Services conducted on Sunday at 10am and 6pm. At 6pm Monday–Friday "10-minute devotionals" are held.
Church of the Cross (Kreuzkirche),

Machabäerstrasse 26: Service conducted on Sunday at 11am.

Church of Jesus Christ (Christuskirche), Werderstrasse 16: Service conducted on Sunday at 11am.

COMMUNICATIONS

MEDIA

Cologne is home to three radio stations (Westdeutscher Rundfunk, Deutschlandfunk, Deutsche Welle), two TV stations (Westdeutscher Rundfunk, RTL plus) and many studios.

Print media are represented by the daily newspapers:

Kölner Stadt-Anzeiger, Breitestrasse 70, tel: 2 24-0.

Könische Rundschau, Stolkgasse 25–45, tel: 16 32-0.

Express, Breitestrasse 70, tel: 2 24-0.

POSTAL SERVICES

The big post offices located in the city centre are open throughout the day 8am–6pm Monday–Friday and on Saturday 8am–noon. The post office in the main railway station is open on weekdays 7am–10pm and on Sundays and holidays 10am–10pm. In the suburbs most post offices close for lunch between noon and 3pm.

TELEPHONE & TELEX

Local calls cost 30 pfennigs; for long-distance calls 0.10 DM, 1 and 5 DM coins may be inserted. You'll find a number of yellow, public pay-phone booths located at various places throughout the city. Round telephones can only be operated with telephone calling cards. For information on calls within Germany dial 11 88; for calls placed to countries outside Germany the number for information is 0 11 88. The dialling code for Cologne is 0221. It is possible to send a telegram 24 hours a day. If you want to send one from within the city limits dial 11 31; if you're placing the telegram from any adjoining area, the number is 0 11 31. At many post offices there is a public telefax service.

EMERGENCIES

SECURITY

Several car parks provide parking places near the exit which are especially reserved for women. They are usually well-lit and monitored by video cameras.

LOST & FOUND

The Lost and Found Office located at Herkulesstrasse 42 in Cologne-Ehrenfeld can be reached by dialing 221 63 12. It is open 7.30am–noon Monday–Friday and can be contacted by phone between 7.30am and 3.45pm Monday–Thursday and 7.30am–noon on Friday.

MEDICAL CARE

There is a University Clinic, three municipal and 18 private hospitals in Cologne. In exchange for a special health insurance paper, patients from other European Community countries are given a certificate necessary for obtaining medical treatment at no extra cost. It is recommended that visitors hailing from non-EC countries get medical insurance from their private insurance agency before leaving home. The telephone number for emergency medical aid is 72 07 72. Under the number 1 15 00 you can find out which dentists, vets and chemists are currently open for emergency duty.

Getting Around

AIRPORT TRANSFERS

The number 170 bus leaves at 20-minute intervals to transport passengers between the Cologne/Bonn Airport and the city. (Departures from behind the main station and from the Deutzer Station.) A taxi ride from the airport to the city centre takes about 20 minutes and will cost around 30 DM.

ORIENTATION

Because the streets of Cologne are laid out in the form of five concentric rings, getting oriented is a relatively easy process. The innermost ring is called simply the "Ring", the middle one "Innere Kanalstrasse", the next the "Gürtel", which is followed by the "Militärring" and, finally, the Autobahnring (the aforementioned circular motorway).

Main arterials radiate outwards in a star shape along both the right and left sides of the Rhine from the city centre.

On the left side of the Rhine Neusser Strasse leads towards the north (Neuss-Düsseldorf), Venloer Strasse towards the northwest (Grevenbroich, Venlo), Aachener Strasse towards the west (Bergheim), Luxemburger Strasse towards the southwest (Hürth, Zülpich), and Bonner Strasse towards the south (Wesseling, Bonn).

On the right side of the river Siegburger Strasse heads towards the southeast (Troisdorf, Siegburg), Olpener Strasse towards the east (Bensberg, Bergisch Gladbach), and Bergisch-Gladbacher-Strasse towards the east (Bergisch-Gladbach, Wipperfürth).

CITY MAPS

Large maps of the city are provided at prominent points throughout the city centre. They are often displayed on the back of advertisement billboards.

PUBLIC TRANSPORT

Well-developed bus, tram and subway systems make it fairly convenient to get around in Cologne. The subway includes sections which run at street-level. As there are no conductors present on any of the various forms of local transport operated by the Köln Verkhersbetriebe (KVB) (Cologne Transport Services), tickets must be purchased before boarding – at ticket machines, from the special counters located at subway stations, or from the vehicle driver. At some specially marked stops and in the subway trains, however, drivers are not permitted to sell tickets. Tickets must be cancelled just prior to or after boarding (either before leaving the platform or actually in the vehicle).

An all-day ticket costs 8 DM and is valid for a full 24 hours. Single-journey tickets are 1.50 DM for shorter distances and a three-day pass is available for 14 DM.

TAXIS

You can find a taxi parked at any of the taxi-stands located at all the particularly busy places in Cologne. Other alternatives include hailing one on the street, or ordering one by calling 28 82. Taxis are usually beige in colour. The base rate is 3 DM with each kilometre thereafter costing 1.80 DM.

RENTAL CARS

The following is a selection of regional and international car rental agencies:

Avis: City office. Tel: 23 43 33
Airport office. Tel: (0 22 03) 40 23 43
International reservations. Tel: (0 130) 77 33

InterRent: City office. Tel: 13 20 71
Airport office. Tel: (0 22 03) 5 30 88

Hertz: City office. Tel: 51 50 84
Airport office. Tel: (0 22 03) 6 10 85
Reservations. Tel: (0 130) 21 21 or (0 69) 73 04 04

Braun: Open day and night. Tel: 32 20 32

Colonia: Open 7.30am–6pm Monday–Friday and 8am–noon Saturday. Tel: 25 30 28

Cologne Public Transport

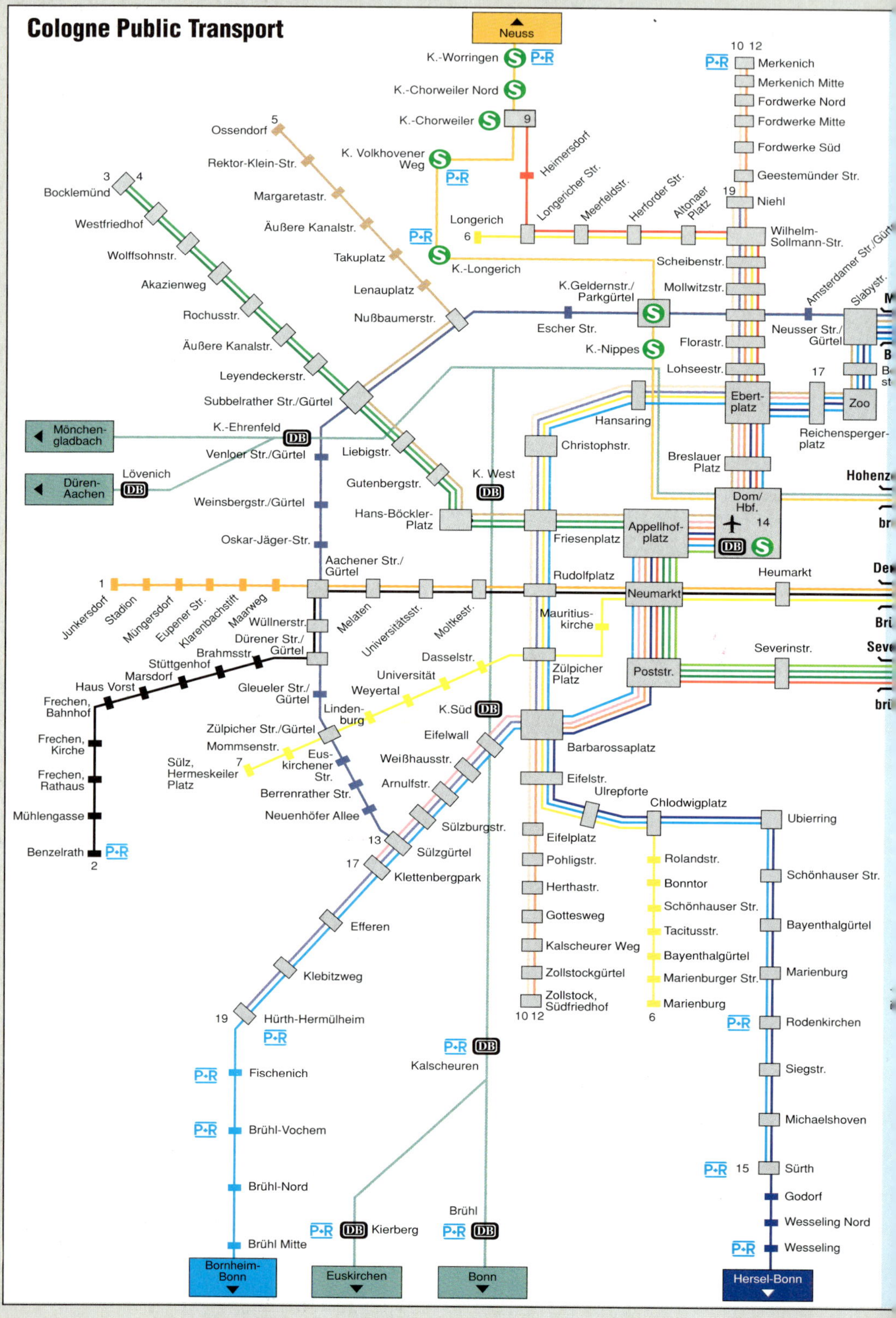

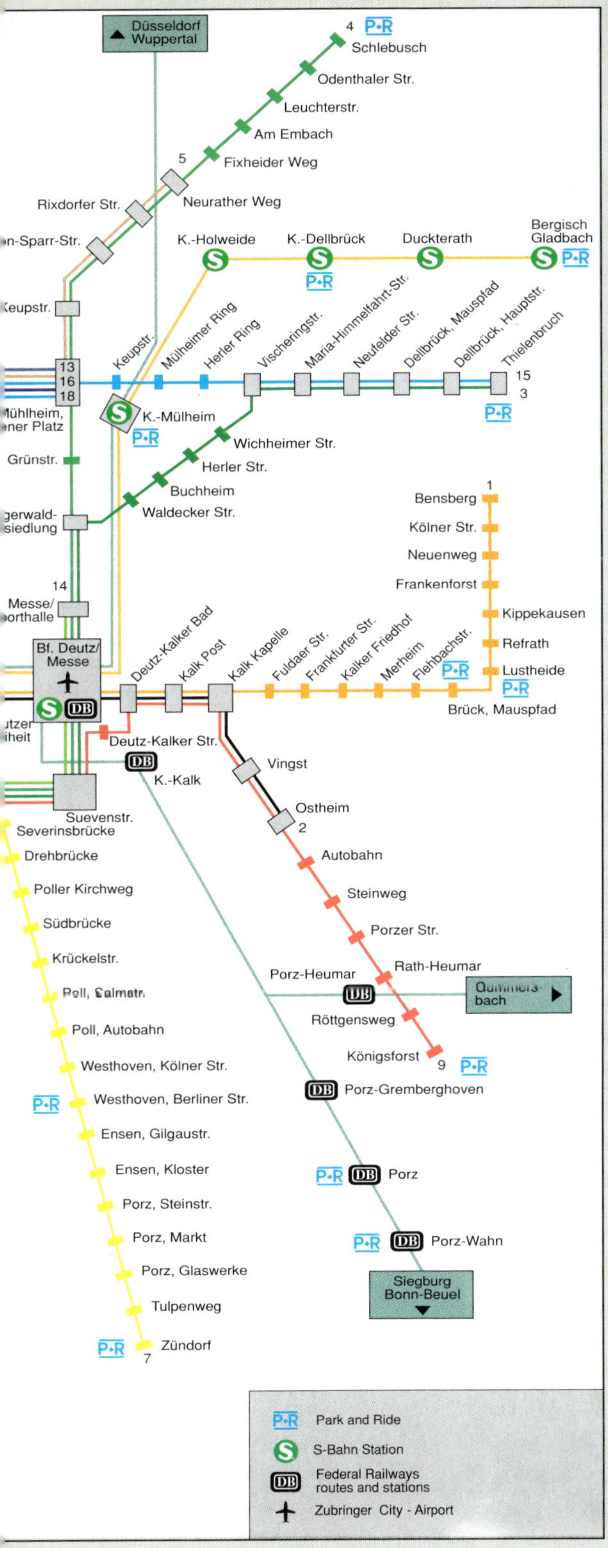

RHINE CRUISES

If you're planning on visiting Cologne during the summer, don't miss the opportunity to take a boat trip along the Rhine. There are several different types of cruises available, including short trips which take place within the space of an afternoon or evening and longer voyages which may last all day, for instance the journey to Koblenz. The hydrofoil *Rheinpfeil* (a member of the Cologne-Düsseldorf German Rhine Steamer Company) provides a speedier means of boat travel and will even take you as far as Mainz (a mere four hours). The return trip to Cologne via the German Federal Railway takes a good two hours.

Day excursions, for example one that ferries you by Bonn and past the Siebengebirge ("Seven Hills"), or even one that just cruises within the Cologne city limits, are quite worthwhile. The boats are in operation from Easter until October. Tickets can be purchased at the mooring located between Hohenzollernbrücke and Deutzer Brücke.

Köln-Düsseldorfer Deutsche Rheinschiffahrt AG (Cologne-Düsseldorf German Rhine Steamer Company): Tel: 21 13 25
Steamboat Colonia: Tel: 21 13 25
Passenger Boat Linden: Tel: 38 47 38
Rhine-Mosel Passenger Boat: Tel: 12 16 00

ON FOOT/BY BICYCLE

The numerous sightseeing attractions in Cologne's city centre can be explored conveniently on foot. There are three pedestrian zones located in the very heart of the city: Hohe Strasse, Schildergasse and Breite Strasse. Roncalliplatz (situated next to the cathedral) and the Rheingarten (adjacent to Roncalliplatz) are also devoid of car traffic, as are many streets and alleys in the old part of the city.

The paths running along the banks of the Rhine are especially suitable for cycling, as is the outer green-belt containing the city forest. The following touring maps are recommended for those wanting more extensive bike riding excursions both in and around Cologne:

Radwanderkarte Stadt Köln (Cologne Bicycle Touring Map), published by Landkartenhaus Gleumes, 1:50,000.

Rad-und Wanderkarte Köln/Bonn (Bicycle and Hiking Map for Cologne/Bonn), published by RV-Verlag, 1:50,000.

Radtourenkarte Nr. 40 (Bicycle Touring Map No. 40): around Cologne and Bonn, 1:100,000.

WHERE TO STAY

Lodgings in Cologne run the gamut from simple youth hostel quarters to luxury-class hotel suites. There are over 16,000 beds available in more than 200 different hotels. When the huge international trade fairs take place in Cologne in the spring and autumn, it's a good idea to book accommodation well in advance. If you want to make a reservation by mail, make sure you send in your request sufficiently far in advance to receive a written confirmation. If you're in need of help or advice in the matter of finding a hotel room, contact the Verkehrsamt der Stadt Köln (the City of Cologne Tourist Information Office), Unter Fettenhennen 19, D-5000 Cologne 1. Tel: 221 33 45. They're open from 1 May–31 October on regular working days 8am–10.30pm and from 1 November–31 April on workdays 9.30am–7pm.

HOTELS

UPPER PRICE CATEGORY

Double rooms starting at 300 DM:

Dom-Hotel, Domkloster 2a. Tel: 20 24-0
A first-class hotel enveloped in a wealth of old tradition located directly across from the cathedral. It's quiet, lavishly decorated and contains 181 beds.

Excelsior Hotel Ernst, Trankgasse 1–5. Tel: 27 01
Another top-class hotel of long-standing located right by the cathedral. It's quiet, exclusively furnished and contains 255 beds.

Holiday Inn Crowne Plaza, Habsburger Ring 9–13. Tel: 20 95-0
A luxury-class hotel housed in what used to be an administration building. It's situated just a few short minutes away from the cathedral, has a swimming pool, sauna and 420 beds.

Hyatt Regency Köln, Kennedy-Ufer 2a, Deutz. Tel: 82 81 234
Located as it is on the right bank of the Rhine, not far from the Trade Fair Centre, this hotel provides its guests with the most superb view of Cologne. It was first opened in 1988, has a swimming pool, sauna and 614 beds.

Hotel Im Wasserturm, Kaygasse 2. Tel: 20 08-0
An old water tower, extensively renovated in 1989 and located just a few minutes away from the cathedral, is the site of this top-class hotel. It boasts a modern French interior, a roof-top restaurant with an all-around view and 170 beds.

Inter-Continental Köln, Helenenstrasse 14. Tel: 22 80
Situated directly in the city's historical centre, the Intercontinental is furnished to please those with the most discriminating of tastes and is well-suited for accommodating conferences and conventions. It has a swimming pool, sauna and 530 beds.

Maritim, Heumarkt 20. Tel: 20 27-0
This noble hotel, opened in 1989, is located directly along the Rhine in the old part of Cologne. Its enormous, glass-ceilinged atrium housing a variety of shops and eating establishments is unique in Germany. Within the hotel is a large hall suitable for both celebrations and conventions, a swimming pool, sauna and 900 beds.

Ramada Renaissance Hotel, Magnusstrasse 20. Tel: 20 34-0
First opened in 1989, this hotel is situated right next to the recently renovated Friesen Quarter and boasts a swimming pool, sauna and 300 beds.

MIDDLE PRICE CATEGORY

Double rooms starting at 200 DM:

Altea Hotel Severinshof, Severinsstrasse 199. Tel: 20 13-0
Located right by the Severinsbrücke about 10 minutes from the centre of town. Both the bus and subway stop nearly at the door. Long-term guests are given the option of having a room fitted with a tiny kitchen. There's an atrium beer garden in the inner

courtyard and the hotel contains 519 beds.

Ambassador, Barbarossaplatz 4a. Tel: 23 51 81

This hotel is located just on the edge of the old part of the city. The windows are made of special noise-prevention glass and the hotel boasts high-quality service, is furnished quite comfortably and has 70 beds.

Consul, Belfortstrasse 9. Tel: 77 21-0

Despite being only 10 minutes away from the old part of the city, the Consul is exceptionally quiet. It is ideal for both conventions and large celebrations, has a swimming pool, sauna and 230 beds, 20 percent of which are reserved for non-smokers.

Dorint Hotel Köln, Friesenstrasse 44-48. Tel: 16 14-0

Although this hotel is located right in the middle of the lively Friesen Quarter, it is nevertheless quiet and comfortable. Decor is modern and there are 213 beds.

Pullman Hotel Mondial, Kurt-Hackenberg-Platz 1. Tel: 20 63-0

A hotel recently renovated in a way that will please even the most discriminating of guests. It was built in 1963 and is located just opposite the Philharmonie. The Symphony Restaurant provides exactly the right ambience in which to meet with friends after a concert and wind down the evening over a quiet drink. There are 350 beds.

Viktoria, Worringer Strasse 23. Tel: 72 04 76

Just a few metres from the Rhine in the new part of the city, this Art Nouveau-style villa, which is officially under protection as a historical monument, possesses a wonderful atmosphere. Breakfast is included in the room price and the hotel has 75 beds.

LOWER PRICE CATEGORY

Double rooms starting at 100 DM:

Hotel am Augustinerplatz, Hohe Strasse 30. Tel: 23 67 17

A comfortable hotel with good service located in a shopping centre. It has 105 beds.

Coellner Hof, Hansaring 100. Tel: 12 20 75

This well-known establishment is located at the edge of the old part of the city and boasts comfortable rooms and a good cuisine. There are 110 beds.

Domgarten, Domstrasse 26. Tel: 12 03 03

A small hotel with a nice atmosphere situated along a quiet street in the old section of Cologne. There are 22 beds.

Haus Marienburg, Robert-Heuser-Strasse 3. Tel: 38 84 97

This peaceful hotel is housed in an old Art Nouveau-style villa with a lovely garden in the distinguished suburb of Marienburg. It has 22 beds.

Hotel Rheingold, Engelbertstrasse 33–35. Tel: 23 65 31

A well maintained hotel which has a sauna and bar. It's located quite near to Rudolphplatz and contains 130 beds.

Stapelhäuschen, Fischmarkt 1–3. Tel: 21 21 93

This simple, homey hotel is in an old medieval house which is classified as a historic monument. It is located directly on the banks of the Rhine in the old part of the city and has 57 beds.

PENSIONS

There are several pensions that offer single rooms with running water in them starting at 25 DM per night. Two of these are the "Jansen" (Tel: 25 18 75) and "Kirchner" (Tel: 25 29 77), both located near Rudolphplatz at Richard-Wagner-Strasse 18.

YOUTH HOSTELS

Probably the most inexpensive overnight arrangements to be made in Cologne are at its youth hostels. The only prerequisite for staying here is a valid Youth Hostel Membership Card.

Jugendgästehaus (Guest House for Young People), An der Schanz 14. It's located in the suburb Riehl (on the left-hand side of the Rhine) near the Mülheimer Brücke.

Jugendherberge (Youth Hostel), Siegesstrasse. This hostel is located in Köln-Deutz at Hohenzollernbrücke. Tel: 81 47 11.

CAMPING

Municipal family camp site in Poll, Weidenweg. Open: 1 May–30 September.

Young peoples' camp site in Poll, Alfred-Schütte-Allee. Open: only during the summer holidays.

Campingplatz Berger in Rodenkirchen, Uferstrasse 53a. Open: 1 March–30 October.

Campingplatz Waldbad in Dünnwald, Peter-Baum-Weg. Open: all-year round.

FOOD DIGEST

CUISINE

Cologne natives prefer good, substantial fare when it comes to dining out and in many restaurants you'll find a number of regional dishes on the menu including:

Rheinischer Sauerbraten mit Klössen (braised beef with dumplings in the traditional Rhine style). Though this dish was originally prepared with horsemeat, nowadays it is almost always made of beef. However, there are some places which still serve it in its original form.

Himmel un Ääd (Heaven and Earth). Stewed apple (heaven) and mashed potatoes (earth) are mixed together and eaten with fried blood sausage (called *Flönz* or *Bloodwoosch* by Cologne natives).

A dish that frequently serves to confuse many out-of-towners is *Halve Hahn*, which is assumed by most to refer to half a fried chicken. Contrary to expectations, however, what will actually be brought to your table is a *Röggelchen* (a roll made from dark rye flour) with butter and some aged Dutch cheese. The history of the "Halve Hahn" can be traced back to the 19th century and is as follows: Parsimonious businessman invited some friends over for a "Halve Hahn" (half a chicken), but, unbeknown to his guests, he gave instructions to the innkeeper that the aforementioned rye roll, whose dark, crispy surface is faintly reminiscent of a fried chicken, should be served with cheese instead. At first his guests were, understandably enough, disappointed, but in no time at all the the culinary invention caught on throughout the entire city. The "Halve Hahn" tastes especially delicious when accompanied by *Kölsch* (the local beer) and is frequently consumed as a snack rather than a full meal.

Rievkoche, a kind of potato pancake, are sold by the threes with or without apple sauce at snack bars and are also served in restaurants at special times during the year. The fragrance alone emanating from these little pancakes made of freshly grated potatoes and fried in oil with a generous amount of onions is irresistible. At the very least, every tourist will be confronted with these savoury morsels on the square just outside the railway station; in one of the pavilions here *Rievkoche* are prepared according to an original recipe.

Hämmche met suure Kappes refers to pork knuckles served with sauerkraut and mashed potatoes. This is the ideal dish if you've got an especially hearty appetite, even taking into account that the bones contribute significantly to the size of the portion.

Äázezupp is the code word for a tasty pea soup which is cooked with onions, lamb or rendered bacon. There are still many families in Cologne that maintain the tradition of serving *Äázezupp* on Saturdays. It is also a very popular dish at street and folk festivals.

BEVERAGES

All of the aforementioned specialities have something in common; they all taste best when washed down with the national beverage *Kölsch*. In Cologne Kölsch is the Number One beverage. Every year about 3.9 million hectolitres of this delicious brew are poured down thirsty throats. Cologne natives prefer to swill a glass down while standing at the counter in a favourite bar, and of course, as one thing often leads to another, a second (or third or fourth) glass frequently follows. Because this fermented beer must be as fresh as possible, it is typically served in tall, narrow glasses which, although swiftly emptied, can be just as quickly refilled. This "liquid bread" is also said to be quite healthy as it purifies the body, normalises blood pressure and aids the digestive process. There are even some people with kidney stones who swear that drinking *Kölsch* prevented them from needing an operation.

In the Cologne breweries *Kölsch* is brought to you by a waiter called *Köbes*, wearing black trousers, a blue cardigan and blue apron made of linen. His purse is generally concealed under the apron, and usually under his overhanging belly as well.

Of course there are also other beverages available in Cologne. Those who prefer drinking good wine have a number of different and excellent wine bars to choose from. The proximity of the city to the wine-growing area that begins 30 km (19 miles) to the south beyond Bonn, is an advantage. At one time grapes were also cultivated in Cologne itself. Today, all that's left of this heritage is a tiny vineyard located near the government buildings.

RESTAURANTS

For a really superb dining experience, choose one of the gourmet temples that have been awarded either stars, chef hats, or spoons. There are more than two dozen of these fine eating establishments in Cologne.

Keep in mind, however, that an exceptional meal is enjoyed at a characteristically exceptional price.

EXPENSIVE

As a rule, you can expect to pay at least between 40 and 50 DM for a main dish at the following restaurants:

Chez Alex, In der Mühlengasse 1. Tel: 23 05 60
Fine French cuisine served in an elegant atmosphere.

Ristorante Alfredo, Tunisstrasse 3. Tel: 24 43 01
A small restaurant serving Italian cuisine. Specialities include fish and pasta in a multitude of variations.

Bastei, Konrad-Adenauer-Ufer 80. Tel: 12 28 25
Excellent French and international cuisine. A splendid view over the Rhine.

Em Krützche, Am Frankenturm 1. Tel: 21 14 32
A restaurant with over 600 years of tradition behind it. Specialities are based on traditional Rhineland cuisine, and include brain of calf, sweetbread and game.

La Poele d'Or, Komödienstrasse 50–52. Tel: 13 41 00
French cuisine prepared with a light, fine touch. The specialities of the house are based on different kinds of top-quality fish.

Goldener Pflug, Olpener Strasse 421. Tel: 89 55 09
French cuisine at its finest. The speciality is the "menu surprise".

Rino Casati, Ebertplatz 3. Tel: 72 11 08
This restaurant is known for its imaginative Italian cuisine and top-quality wines. Home-made pasta dishes are the speciality.

Restaurant Wack, Benesisstrasse 57. Tel: 21 42 78
An especially noble dining establishment which specialises in fine Alsatian cuisine.

Weinhaus Im Walfisch, Salzgasse 13. Tel: 21 95 75
This restaurant, located in a house dating from the year 1626 which has been classified as a historical monument, is known for its exquisite international cuisine. The wine list contains more than 300 different kinds of wine. Fish dishes are the speciality.

Bergische Stube, (Hotel Inter-Continental), Helenenstrasse 14. Tel: 22 80
Excellent French and international cuisine are served here amidst classy surroundings.

Dom-Hotel Restaurant, Domkloster 2a. Tel: 20 24-0
High-quality international cuisine served in exquisite surroundings. The menu boasts a wide assortment of different kinds of fish; in the evenings diners are entertained with live piano music.

Hanse-Stube (Excelsior Hotel Ernst), Trankgasse 1–5. Tel: 27 01
This subtly and tastefully decorated restaurant serves creative international cuisine. The wine list is truly outstanding.

MODERATE

Due to the fact they haven't been honoured with any particular badge of culinary distinction, the following restaurants of the middle-class price range are less expensive than the aforementioned ones. A main dish in one of these eating establishments will cost between 25–35 DM.

Amabile, Görrestrasse 2. Tel: 24 60 17
This restaurant serves gourmet French food. The speciality of the house is lamb filet in a basil-garlic crust.

Artischocke, Moltkestrasse 50. Tel: 25 28 61
A cosy restaurant well known for its fine French cuisine and in particular for its raw salmon marinated in raspberry vinegar and olive oil.

Colonius Turmrestaurant, Innere Kanalstrasse 100. Tel: 52 20 61
While enjoying their meal, diners have a view of Cologne and the surrounding countryside. International cuisine is served here.

Daitokai, Kattenbug 2. Tel: 12 00 48
Gourmet Japanese restaurant where the specialities are prepared at your table.
Haus am See, Bachemer Landstrasse 420. Tel: 43 43 21
A much-frequented restaurant located on Decksteiner Pond in the Stadtwald (City Forest), a short drive beyond the city. Both international cuisine and regional specialities are available here.
La Baurie, Vorgebirgsstrasse 35. Tel: 38 61 49
A small, French restaurant. The house speciality is potato pancakes served with marinated salmon.
Le Bouquet (Holiday Inn Crowne Plaza Hotel), Habsburger Ring 9–13. Tel: 20 95-0
A light-filled, friendly restaurant with excellent French food and a diverse wine list.
Le Moissonnier, Krefelder Strasse 25. Tel: 72 94 79
Lovely Art Nouveau-style restaurant. The tasty French cuisine is complimented by an outstanding selection of wines.
L'Osteria De Donatis, Eigelstein 122. Tel: 12 33 73
This small Italian restaurant specialises in pasta made on the premises.
Maharani, Komödienstrasse 40. Tel: 13 76 52
A well-known Indian restaurant which has recently moved from the Ring to premises near the cathedral. Tandoori specialities cooked in a real Tandoori oven are served.
Marienbild, Aachener Strasse 561. Tel: 49 31 66
An elegant dining establishment specialising in "New German Cuisine".
Poncho's, Salzgasse 9–11. Tel: 24 65 65
Here you can sample Argentine dishes of the finest quality. It specialises in huge steaks that melt in your mouth.
Ratskeller, Alter Markt. Tel: 21 83 01
German cuisine served in surroundings with a markedly historical ambience. Fish and game are the specialities.
Restaurant Der Messeturm, Kennedy-Ufer. Tel: 88 10 08
This restaurant offers fine French and international cuisine and a splendid, panoramic view out over the old section of the city.
Wirtshaus Schwejk, An Gross St Martin 2. Tel: 21 67 30
An eating establishment known for its Bohemian specialities including Prague ham in bread dough and Pilsener Urquell on tap.
Zorba the Buddha Oscho Restaurant, Brüsslerstrasse 52. Tel: 57 40 745
Diners can enjoy exquisite vegetarian specialities from all over the world here. There's a vegetarian pizzeria adjoining the main restaurant.

INEXPENSIVE

It is also quite possible to eat well and relatively cheaply in the breweries where traditional Cologne specialities are served with *Kölsch*. Tasty fare both here and at numerous other restaurants serving foreign cuisine will cost about 10 DM per main dish.
Bier-Esel, Breite Strasse 114. Tel: 24 85 59
Cologne's oldest mussel house. During the summertime instead of mussels a large assortment of salads are offered.
Bizim, Weidengasse 47. Tel: 13 15 81
A small restaurant specialising in fine Turkish cuisine, in particular lamb and fish dishes.
Brauerei zur Malzmühle, Heumarkt 6. Tel: 21 01 17
An old and venerable brewery serving traditional Kölsch cuisine.
Brauhaus Päffgen, Friesenstrasse 64–68. Tel: 13 54 61
A restaurant rich in tradition specialising in fare indigenous both to Cologne in particular and the Rhineland in general.
Consülchen-Pub, Belfortstrasse 9. Tel: 77 21-0
"New German Cuisine" served here. The house specialities include homemade brawn served alongside potatoes fried with bacon and potato pancakes with pickled salmon.
La Barrière, Aachener Strasse 569. Tel: 49 32 56
French cuisine with an emphasis on vegetarian dishes.
La Fattoria, Severinstrasse 8–10. Tel: 32 72 43
This Italian restaurant offers a large selection of pasta dishes and delicious antipasto.
La Lavallier, Am Hof 20–26. Tel: 23 38 91
A bistro serving international cuisine. There's a great view of the cathedral from the terrace and a good bar.
Früh am Dom, Am Hof 12–14. Tel: 21 26 21
This cosy brewery serves Kölsch specialities, its own home-brewed schnapps and, of course, *Kölsch* on tap. They also have a beer garden.

Früh em Veedel, Chlodwigplatz 28. Tel: 31 44 70
Typical Kölsch dishes such as "Halve Hahn" and lamb.

Mandalay, Brüsselerstrasse 53. Tel: 52 74 73
An Indonesian restaurant where many dishes tend to be piquant and spicy. Specialities include "Fire Pot" and "Shanghai Duck".

Oasis, Kennedy-Ufer 1 (in the Lufthansa building). Tel: 81 44 41
From this Greek restaurant diners have a lovely view of the old part of Cologne and the cathedral.

Osho's Place, Venloerstrasse 5–7. Tel: 57 40 745
This vegetarian restaurant is a congregating place for friends from all over the world.

Spaghetti-Palast, Hahnenstrasse 37. Tel: 21 17 09
The specialities here are spaghetti dishes. Guests are entertained by a pianist.

Stadtgarten-Restaurant, Venloerstrasse 40. Tel: 51 60 37
This Italian restaurant has a large beer garden and puts on well-frequented jazz concerts. Specialities here include salads, pasta and, in summer, fare grilled on the barbecue.

Taj Mahal, An St Agatha 27. Tel: 24 11 12
An Indian restaurant where vegetarians are well catered for. Curries are the speciality.

Theatre-Schänke, Schwertnergasse 1. Tel: 21 57 31
Both actors and audience of the nearby theatre meet after performances in this small Greek restaurant.

Tchang, Grosse Sandkaul 19. Tel: 21 76 51
A cosy Chinese restaurant of long-standing tradition.

Zum Treppchen, Kirchstrasse 15. Tel: 39 21 79
A popular restaurant with a large beer garden located some distance away from the centre of things in the suburb Rodenkirchen. Specialities include Mainzer Käse (Mainz Cheese) and Cologne liver sausage.

PUBS

When the conversation turns to pubs in Cologne, the historical breweries are generally the first places that come to mind. However the usual place to down a beer after a long day's work is at one of the corner pubs located in the middle of just about every neighbourhood. If you stand at the counter, it probably won't take long before you get into a conversation with one of the many regulars.

Things tend to get a little more lively in the pubs located in the old part of the city. Starting from the posh pub **Keule**, Heumarkt 56, you wil find drinking and eating establishments in just about every building. **Papa Joe's Biersalon Klimperkasten**, Alter Markt 50–52 is especially worth mentioning. The pub houses a valuable collection of musical instruments, one of which is played every hour. Between these special performances jazz bands play live music.

A number of different jazz musicians take turns playing daily at **Em Streckstrump**, Buttermarkt 37. On Sundays at 11am, there's a *Jazzfrüschoppen* – the first beer(s) of the day accompanied by jazz and free peanuts.

Mostly students tend to congregate in the area around Zülpicher Strasse in Sülz, with its picturesque ensemble of pubs and cafés. People associated with the radio and television business meet at the **Orgelchen**, An der Rechtschule, while the clientele frequenting the **Kleinen Glocke**, Glockengasse 58–60, tends to be members of the literary guild.

Directly opposite the cathedral is **Alt Köln** with its splendid facade and carillon. Moving figures strike the hour throughout the day. Inside you'll find a veritable warren of cosy rooms, corners and balconies.

The **Alte Wartesaal**, located in the main railway station, is a real original. Predominantly journalists and artists congregate here.

CAFES

Cafés, both those where you can and cannot dance, have a long tradition in Cologne. Nowadays however, the *Tanzcafé* is pretty much extinct. At the head of the list is the place with the very best view of the cathedral, **Café Reichard**, Unter Fettenhennen. During summer it seems as though the whole world meets on the terrace here; during the winter months guests can enjoy a view of the west facade of the cathedral from inside a glass pavilion. Violinists and pianists playing discreetly complete the atmosphere of grandeur. Other cafés include:

Café Jansen, Obermarspforten 7
Café Riese, Schildergasse 103
Café Zimmermann, Herzogstrasse 11. The speciality here is Havannatorte.

Café Fassbender, Mittelstrasse (in the Bazaar de Cologne)
Café Cremer, Breite Strasse 54
Café Schmitz, Breite Strasse 87. The specialit is *Printen* (a type of gingerbread). (You can also get a replica of Cologne Cathedral made from the same dough.)
Café Wahlen, Hohenstaufenring 64. The speciality is *Baumkuchen*.
Café Steudter, Kaiser-Wilhelm-Ring
Café Füllenbach, Ebertplatz
Café Eigel, Brückenstrasse. The speciality is *Pilztorte* (mushroom pie).
Café Franck, Rudolphplatz.
Trödelcafé, near St Agatha. Doubles as an antique shop.

NIGHTLIFE

Cologne is neither Hamburg nor Las Vegas when it comes to nightlife. Nevertheless, there are several streets in the city where night owls can enjoy themselves until dawn.

DISCOS

Alter Wartesaal im Hauptbahnhof
Coconut Grove, Salzgasse 5
Lord's Inn, Roonstrasse 7
Omas Schnapshaus, Alter Markt 36–42
Wicküler im Römer, Kleine Budengasse 1
Show-Boat, Hohenzollernring 16–18
Clou, Hohenstaufenring 58
Ekkstein's, Ubierring 24
Zorba The Buddha Osho Diskothek, "die Grosse", Hohenzollernring 90
Zorba The Buddha Osho Diskothek, "die Kleine", Brabanterstrasse 15

NIGHT CAFES & BARS

A substantial part of Cologne's nightlife takes place around Friesenplatz on both sides of the Hohenzollernring. Very few of the night cafés and bars open before 9pm, but they compensate for this fact by staying open until the small hours of the morning.
Blue Night, Im Klapperhof 48
Chez moi, Palmstrasse 38
Chez Nous, Große Budengasse 13
Kokett, Altenberger Strasse 11
Intermezzo, Unter Käster 5
Karibik, Gereonshof 36
King George, Sudermannstrasse 2
Apropo, Im Dau 17
Tiffani, Venloer Strasse 19
Bonotel, Bonner Strasse

GAMBLING CASINOS

Although Cologne has its own gambling casino, the roulette balls roll in a more fashionable atmosphere in Bad Neuenahr 45 km (28 miles) to the southwest and in Aachen 80 km (50 miles) to the west.

THINGS TO DO

SIGHTSEEING

At numerous places scattered throughout the city centre you can see a variety of sights attesting to Cologne's 2,000-year-old history. New evidence of both the Roman and medieval cultures emerges with each excavation. Many of these finds have been integrated into the surroundings, for example in the Parkhaus am Dom (the multistorey car park located beneath the cathedral).

Any sightseeing tour through the city should be devised with the specific interests of its participants in mind. The emphasis of such a tour might be archaeological sites, or sacred medieval or modern architecture. The following are a few suggestions.

The area around the cathedral has changed quite a bit over the past few years, especially when the Wallraf-Richartz and Ludwig Museum, Philharmonie and Rhine Garden came into being. This complex has created a car-free network of pedestrian zones running from the cathedral to the Rhine. As a result of the Rheinuferstrasse being lowered and routed through a tunnel between the cathedral and Heumarkt, Cologne is once again actually situated "on the Rhine".

The first stopping point of nearly every tour is, naturally, the **Cathedral** itself. Its High Gothic architecture alone is enough to mesmerise just about every out-of-town visitor. A number of remarkable sights are also to be found inside the cathedral, for example the Shrine of the Three Magi, the Altar of the City's Patron Saints by Stephan Lochner, the modern painting beneath the organ gallery by Peter Hecker, and the Treasury. A truly panoramic view of the city and surrounding countryside can be had by climbing the 504 steps leading up from the visitors' floor. On the way up take a minute to catch your breath by looking in the belfry where you'll see the "decke Pitter", the biggest bell in the world. The tower is open from 9am to 5pm.

If you continue on your way over the cathedral plaza and Roncalliplatz, you'll pass the venerable Dom-Hotel and the fascinating Roman-Germanic Museum before entering the **Altstadt** (the old part of the city) with its many historical houses, cafés and restaurants. This particular section of Cologne extends all the way to the Rhine where a number of boats are moored.

Hohe Strasse, the most famous shopping street in Cologne and the very first pedestrian zone in Germany, can likewise be reached from the cathedral plaza. Here you'll find boutiques, speciality shops and restaurants strung like a row of beads, one right after the other. Street musicians, wandering salespeople and fruit vendors serve to make the already colourful scene even more brilliant. At the point where the attractiveness of Hohe Strasse dwindles, the wider **Schildergasse** begins. In this street there are a number of giant department and clothing stores as well as speciality shops, a butcher's and a church.

Schildergasse ends at **Neumarkt**, a large square surrounded by surging traffic. One of the 12 Romanesque churches in the city, **Church of the Holy Apostles** (St Aposteln), is situated on the west side of the square. This also marks the start of yet another shopping area full of exquisite boutiques, jewellery shops and the **Bazaar de Cologne**, an especially classy shopping arcade. Mittelstrasse runs into Rudolphplatz, where you'll see the **Hahnentor**, one of the three preserved medieval city gates in Cologne. Heading off to the right is Pfeilstrasse with its many galleries and trendy shops. This street leads right to St-Apern-Strasse, where you'll find quite a few good antique stores.

Rudolphplatz is bordered on the west by **Ringstrasse**, called here Hohenzollernring and a bit further on Hohenstauffenring. This street follows the course of the former medieval city wall and thus encloses the oldest part of the city centre. The biggest cinemas in Cologne are mostly concentrated north of Rudolphplatz. This particular boulevard is a real promenade where people stroll with the intention of seeing and being seen. Along the northern part of Ringstrasse, in front of Ebertplatz, and along the southern part, in front of Chlodwigplatz, you can see preserved sections of the city's medieval fortifications. **Eigelstein-Torburg**, the northern city gate, is located at Ebertplatz and the **Severinstorburg**, its southern counterpart, is situated at Chlodwigplatz. At one time there were no fewer than 12 fortified major and minor gates built into the city wall. These served to protect the 40,000 citizens living within and constituted one of the largest medieval fortifications. Of all the smaller gates, the Ulrepforte is the only one still in existence today. Currently, the Carnival society "Rote Funken" (Red Sparks) has set up its domicile there.

If you head out in a westerly direction from the cathedral, you'll pass a number of different buildings which are all affiliated with Westdeutscher Rundfunk (West German Broadcasting). Continuing along this route will lead you by the **Kunstgewerbe-Museum** (Museum of Arts and Crafts), which was formerly the home of the Wallraf-Richartz Museum, over busy Tunisstrasse to the **Opera House** with its own theatre. To the right of this is the reconstructed original factory **Glockengasse 4711**, the famous eau de Cologne company established by Ferdinand Mülhens.

By going over the cathedral plaza and Roncalliplatz, you'll get to the **Alter Markt**, characterised by narrow houses with pointed gables, the **Jan-von-Werth-Brunnen** (Jan von Werth Fountain) and the **Rathaus** (Town Hall). It's here at the Alter Markt at 11.11am on 11 November, in what's known as the fifth season in Cologne, that the Carnival period is officially opened. Stairs lead to the Rathausplatz and to the front side of the Town Hall where there's an exquisite Renaissance gazebo and, inside, the sumptuous Hansesaal, dating from the year 1349. The carillon in the Town Hall Tower can be heard daily at noon and again at 5pm. A ritual Jewish bath, the **Mikwe**, has been unearthed in front of the Town Hall. It dates from the Middle Ages and can only be reached by going down through a 15 metre (50 ft) shaft. This bath, which is now filled with ground water, was at one time used for ritual ablutions. The bath is open for public viewing during Town Hall working hours; the key can be obtained from the gatekeeper in the Town Hall gazebo.

The **Gürzenich** is about 100 metres (335 ft) further to the south. The citizens set up this building as a dance hall between 1437 and 1444 and it is still used today in its original capacity. Celebrations, dance events, conventions and Carnival activities all take place in what's fondly referred to as "Cologne's living-room". Behind the Gürzenich are the ruins of **St Alban's Church.** In the nave is a copy of the sculptural group by Käthe Kollwitz entitled *Grieving Parents*. There is, moreover, an entire museum in Cologne devoted to Kollwitz where many of the artist's sketches, sculptures and printed graphics are on display. (Neumarkt 18–24, in the Neumarkt Passage.)

As far back as the Middle Ages Cologne was described as "hillige Cöllen" (holy Cologne). Doubtless contributing to this reputation is the fact that there are **12 unique Roman Romanesque churches**, all located in quite close proximity to one another within the medieval city's perimeters. These churches are considered to be 12 of the most important in all of Western Europe. Nearly all the holy edifices are closely tied to the names of the city's archbishops. The oldest of the garland of Romanesque churches is **St Pantaleon's**, which was consecrated in the year 980 and contains the gravestone of Kaiser Theophanu. **St Andrew's** (St Andreas), situated directly to the northwest of the cathedral, houses the tomb of the Doctor of the Church Albertus Magnus and **St Ursula's**, located a bit further to the north, holds the relics of the city's patron saint and her 11,000 madonnas, whose memory has been preserved for ever by the 11 flames visible on the city's coat of arms. The other churches attesting to the magnificence of Romanesque architecture include **St Gereon's,** the **Church of the Holy Apostles** (St Aposteln), **St Cecilia's**, **St George's**, **St Cunibert's**, **St Mary's in the Capitol**, **St Mary's in Lyskirchen**, **Great St Martin's** and **St Severinus's**. It was through these 12 churches that Cologne gained the reputation of being the "Rome of the North". All were badly damaged during World War II and it was only with great effort that their reconstruction was completed by the year 1985. Only the west tower of St Cunibert is still under construction at this time.

There are other churches of significance in Cologne in addition to the aforementioned Romanesque churches and the cathedral. These include the Gothic places of worship, the **Minorite Church**, containing the tomb of the "father of apprentices" Adolf Kolping, the **Antonite Church** (Antoniterkirche), which houses Barlach's *The Angel of Death*, and the **Church of the Assumption** (Maria Himmelfahrt), erected by the Jesuits between 1618 and 1678. The latter is located in Marzellenstrasse, not far from the cathedral and main railway station.

The **Church of Mary in the Kupfergasse**, which sustained serious damage during the war, has been restored in its original Dutch Baroque style. Cologne natives have grown especially fond of the scaled-down reproduction of the Holy House of Loretto and its "Black Madonna", a statue attributed with miraculous powers.

A sacred jewel is the **Chapel of St Columbia**, located on Brückenstrasse. The chapel was erected from within the ruins of the parish church by Professor Gottfried Böhm in 1950. The windows were made by Georg Meistermann. The chapel is popularly referred to as the "Madonna in the Ruins".

TOURS

City Tours: Further information and exact times are available directly from the Tourist Information Centre near the cathedral, tel: 221 33 32.

Cathedral Tours: Weekdays at 10am, 11am, 2.30pm and 3.30pm. During the summer there is an additional tour offered at 4.30pm. Tours are conducted Saturdays at 10 and

11am, and on Sunday and holidays at 2.30 and 3.30pm. Occasionally, due to special circumstances, these tours begin a little later.
Town Hall Tours: Monday, Wednesday and Saturday at 3pm.
Ubii Monument: near der Malzmühle 1; Thursday 4.45pm–6pm.

CITY SIGHTSEEING TOURS

Throughout the entire year the Tourist Information Centre organises city sightseeing tours. During the winter these tours commence at 11am and 2pm; during the summer they begin at 10 and 11am, 1, 2 and 3pm. Each lasts approximately two hours and includes all the major sights of Cologne. There is a 20-minute stop planned in either the Schnütgen or Municipal Museum.

Explanations of what you are seeing are given in German, English and French. Tickets can be purchased directly from the driver for 20 DM per person. The bus departs from the southern side of the Tourist Information Office.

In the months of July and August additional **Abendfahrten** (evening tours) are also on the agenda. These begin with a bus tour of Cologne by night, followed by a boat trip along the Rhine and take in two short detours to see the Dance Fountain and TV Tower "Colonius", which affords the most beautiful view by far over the twinkling city. The evening tour is concluded with a glass of *Kölsch* or wine, a bite to eat and some lively entertainment in a restaurant or bar. This particular variety of evening pleasure lasts about 3½ hours and costs 45 DM (subject to change).

Taxi-Guide is a special taxi service which can be ordered by calling the number 28 82. It has 25 taxi drivers who, after having been especially trained to be city tour guides and passing the necessary test, have received a licence permitting them to guide tourists round the historical sights of Cologne. Visitors interested in hiring this service can request that their driver speak German, Italian, Dutch, English, French or Turkish. A tour lasting just short of two hours will cost you about 60 DM. Taxi drivers are also happy to fulfil any special sightseeing wish. Naturally, these out-of-the-ordinary requests will cost you a bit more. Air Service Teuberg, tel: (0 22 03) 40 24 53, offers **City Sightseeing Tours by Plane**. These tours take about 15 minutes and cost 160 DM for up to three persons.

EXCURSIONS

Whether you choose to travel by bus, tram, rail or by boat along the Rhine there are several interesting excursions which will lead you into the surrounding countryside.

Brühl lies to the southwest between the cities of Cologne and Bonn. The main attraction here is the **Augustusburg Castle**. Hours: 9am–noon and again 1.30–4pm every day except Monday. Closed: during the months of December and January. Guided tours of the castle are available on the hour or half-hour, depending on demand. For further information tel: (02232) 42 471. In the summer the castle provides an elegant backdrop for the well-known **Brühler Castle Concerts**, conducted by Helmut Müller-Brühl. It is necessary to reserve tickets for the concerts in advance; they are also available at the usual ticket outlets in Cologne.

Other attractions in Brühl include:
Falkenlust Hunting Lodge. Hours: 9am–noon and 2–4pm. Closed: Mondays. For further information tel: (02232) 121 11.
Phantasialand, the biggest recreational and adventure park in all of Europe. Hours: 9am–6pm daily from 1 April–31 October. Tel: (02232) 361 01.

Bensberg lies to the east just short of Cologne's city limits and can be easily reached via the A 4 (motorway), or by tram in about 20 minutes. Today a part of Bergisch Gladbach, this little town became famous throughout the world for its modern **Town Hall** built of concrete and glass by Gottfried Böhm. The remains of the old castle on the site have been integrated into the new construction. From a good distance away you can catch a glimpse of the mighty **baroque hunting lodge**. Unfortunately the building is not open for public viewing as it now houses a boarding school.

If you continue on beyond Bergisch Gladbach you'll come to the **Altenberg Cathedral**, an immense Cistercian abbey situated in the heart of the picturesque Bergisches Land. Some of the cathedral's stained-glass windows are over 700 years old and the western window with its brilliant colours and beauty is especially breathtaking. The old cloister compound has been carefully renovated and currently houses seminar buildings, restaurants and a cloister shop in which you can purchase recordings of the cathedral's organ. The cathedral contains one of the largest organs in all of Germany, with 6,000 pipes, four manuals and 82 registers. Concerts take place here at various times throughout the year.

Zündorf, situated along the right side of the Rhine on Cologne's southernmost outskirts, has preserved its village character despite the fact it is actually a part of the city. The narrow streets and alleyways lined with half-timbered houses, the medieval market square and three old churches all contribute to give the visitor the impression that time has stood still here. The town has gained in attractiveness by the "Groov", a recreational area located directly along the banks of the Rhine encompassing meadows, bicycle paths, ponds where you can rent rowing boats, mini-golf and a combination indoor and outdoor swimming pool. Several different eating establishments within the old walls and having large terraces provide for hospitality.

The largest **brown coal mining area** in Europe and, consequently, the densest concentration of energy production generated at coal power plants is located to the west, between Cologne and Aachen. The coal-mining company Rheinbraun operates an information centre in Paffendorf Castle near Bergheim/Erft.

Other excursion destinations include:
Burg Castle on the Wupper. Hours: 9am–6pm daily and 1pm–6pm Monday 1 March–5 November, and between 10am–5pm daily except Monday 13 November–end February. For further information tel: (0212) 4 20 98 or 4 20 99.
Brauweil Church. Hours: all day during the weekend and on Thursday until 1pm. The abbey courtyards are open 10am–4pm. To book an appointment telephone Frau Kunz at (02234) 80 52 49.
Knechtsteden Monastery. Hours: open all day.
Zons. Sightseeing tours of this medieval fortified city are available upon request at the Heimat-und Verkehrsverein (the Local and Tourist Information Agency). Tel: (02106) 37 72.

GARDENS & PARKS

Despite the fact that there are over one million people living in Cologne, the city is remarkably green; for every inhabitant there are about 75 sq. metres (800 sq. ft) of green area. Citizens have their long-standing mayor Konrad Adenauer (who later became the Chancellor of Germany) to thank for the **Äusseren Grüngürtel** (the Outer Green Belt) in the west part of the city. Within this 12-km (8-mile) stretch of forests and meadows there are a number of extensive footpaths, areas for playing or sunbathing, ponds where you can rent rowing boats and the Müngersdorf Stadium.

To the north of the city a recreational area encompassing 200 hectares (500 acres) of land has developed around **Fühlinger Lake**. Seven lakes (former gravel-pits) have been connected to one another. The 2,000-metre (6,670-ft) regatta course, an outdoor swimming pool surrounded by a large lawn for sunbathing and a lake for surfing provide the main attractions for thousands of people during summer.

Visitors will be delighted by the variety of flowers, trees and plants from all four corners of the earth to be found in the **Botanical Garden** in Cologne-Riehl. A population of rare trees has been cultivated here since 1864. Tropical and subtropical plants are on display in the greenhouses. In the immediate vicinity of the Flora is the **Zoological Garden**, spread out over spacious parkland. Visitors are drawn at all times of the year see more than 7,000 different kinds of animals from all over the world living here. The zoo includes an aquarium with an insectarium for reptiles, fish and insects. Hours: 9am–6pm during summer and 9am–5pm during the winter.

There are well over 4,000 different kinds of plants growing in the **Forst Botanical Garden**, located in Rodenkirchen (a suburb in the south of Cologne) at the intersection of Schillingsrotter Weg and Rondorfer Strasse. The variety of plants and trees here encompasses everything from the North American giant redwood tree to exotic specimens from Japan. Adjacent to the garden is the **Friedenswald** (the Peace Forest), where each country of the world is represented by examples of its indigenous trees.

The **Rhine Park** extends along the right side of the Rhine, directly opposite the city centre. This park has twice been the site of the German Garden Show. Large flower beds, and lawns provide enough room for more than 5,000 different kinds of plants to grow. A chairlift crosses the park, the separate seats spaced at intervals of a few metres. Playgrounds, cafés, fountains and sculptures punctuate the landscape and the panoramic view of the city centre from the Rhine's banks is unique. There's a funicular which goes from the north end of the Rhine Park up and over the Rhine itself, over the Zoobrücke to the left-hand river bank where it finally deposits its passengers directly in front of the entrance to the Zoological Garden.

The **Tanzbrunnen** (Dance Fountain), a unique open-air area used for a variety of entertainment events, is located at the southern end of the park by the exhibition grounds. During the summer season international show stars perform here. The spacious grounds offer room enough for approximately 2,500 visitors to find seats, some of which are under cover. The area is called "Tanzbrunnen" due to a dance floor and large fountain, both enclosed under a tented roof. Further information and a calendar of events are available from the beginning of May onwards at the Tourist Information Centre.

Indigenous wild animals can be seen in the **Stadtwald** (City Forest) near Cologne-Lindenthal, in the **Wildpark Brück** and in the **Wildpark Dünnwald**. The German Association for the Protection of Forests has also established a display of different kinds of trees here.

The **Leidenhausen Recreational Area** (Cologne-Porz Eil), located at the edge of the Königsforst in the east of Cologne, offers a variety of hiking trails, open spaces for sunning or recreational activities, a big playground for children, a bird of prey sanctuary and the forest museum "Haus des Waldes".

Groov, a "recreational island", is situated on the right-hand bank of the Rhine in Cologne-Porz Zündorf. There's a little lake (where you can rent a rowing boat), marina, mini-golf course and swimming pool, as well as a number of eateries where you can sit down and have a snack. When the weather is good, the island is particularly popular.

CULTURE PLUS

LIBRARIES & ARCHIVES

HBZ – Hochschulbibliothekszentrum (Rhineland-Westphalia University Library Centre): maintains a comprehensive catalogue of books available at all other university and college libraries. Classen-Kappelmann-Strasse 24. Tel: 40 10 05
Historisches Archiv (City of Cologne Historical Archives): Severinstrasse 222-228. Tel: 2 21-23 27
Dom-und Diözesan-Bibliothek (Cathedral and Diocesan Library): Kardinal-Frings-Strasse 1. Tel: 16 42-8 62 21
Evangelische Bibliothek (Protestant Library): Karthäusergasse 9. Tel: 33 82-318
Stadtbücherei - Zentralbibliothek (City Library – Central Library): Josef-Haubrich-Hof 1. Tel: 221-38 28

Other libraries and archives located in foreign cultural institutes include:
British Council, Hahnenstrasse 6
Amerika-Haus, Apostelnkloster 13
German-Finnish Association, Albertus-Magnus-Platz
Institut Français, Sachsenring 77
Institute for Italian Culture, Universitätsstrasse 81
Institute for Japanese Culture, Universitätsstrasse 98
Belgisches Haus, Cäcilienstrasse 46

MUSEUMS

With its eight municipal, numerous privately-run and ecclesiastical museums, Cologne is one of the most significant cities for art in all of Europe. This status has been re-emphasised by the construction of the new Wallraf-Richartz and Ludwig Museum between the cathedral and the Rhine in 1982.

The largest gallery devoted purely to painting in the entire Rhineland can be found at the **Wallraf-Richartz Museum**. The heart of this collection is composed of works by artists of the Cologne Painting School. On display at the **Ludwig Museum** are a selection of relatively recent works dating from the Expressionists through to the Moderns. The museum's focal points are provided by both the Haubrich and Ludwig Collections. The museum is located at Bischofsgarten 1. Hours: 10am–8pm Tuesday–Thursday, 10am–6pm Friday–Sunday. Closed: Monday. Guided tours take place Tuesdays at 6pm and Saturdays and Sundays at 11am.

Located right next to the aforementioned museums, the **Roman-Germanic Museum** is devoted to an account of culture and life beginning from the period following the death of Christ. The Roman settlement CCAA (Colonia Claudia Ara Agrippinsium) was established around the year AD 50 and the many exhibits include glassware, vessels, coins and jewellery, as well as the Dionysos Mosaic, the tomb of Lucius Poblicius, mural paintings, various other tombstones and holy stones date back to this period. Adjacent to the southern side of the museum at its original location, a Roman harbour road has been reconstructed. The address is Roncalliplatz 4. Hours: 10am–5pm Tuesday–Sunday, 10am–8pm Wednesday and Thursday. Closed: Monday. Guided tours are available upon request.

Just a few metres further on the **Diözesanmuseum** (Diocesan Museum) provides its visitors with an overview of sacred art. Here precious burial objects extracted from the tombs of Frankish princes are also on display. The address is Roncalliplatz 2. Hours: 10am–5pm Monday–Saturday, 10am–1pm Sunday. Closed: Thursday.

The **Stadtmuseum** (Municipal Museum) is housed in what was once the old municipal armoury which dates back to the 16th century. The museum contains exhibits depicting middle-class life as it was experienced from the Middle Ages until modern times. The address is Zeughausstrasse 1–3. Hours: 10am–5pm Tuesday–Sunday, 10am–8pm Thursday. Closed: Monday. Guided tours are available Saturdays at 3pm.

In 1952 the **Schnütgen Museum** was moved into the Romanesque basilica of St Cecilia. Christian art from the Middle Ages until the present day with an emphasis on the Romanesque and Gothic periods is displayed in surroundings truly worthy of such works. The museum is located at Cäcilienstrasse 29. Hours: 10am–5pm Tuesday–Sunday, 10am–8pm on the first Wednesday of every month. Closed: Monday. Guided tours offered on Sundays at 11am.

The most extensive collection of Chinese, Korean and Japanese art in Germany is on view at the **Museum für Ost-asiatische Kunst** (the Museum of East Asian Art). The museum is located at Universitätsstrasse 100. Hours: 10am–5pm Tuesday–Sunday, 10am–8pm on the first Friday in every month. Guided tours are offered on Sundays at 11am.

Around 60,000 different articles from a number of distant lands and continents can be numbered within the permanent holdings of the **Rautenstrauch-Joest Museum**, thus making it one of the largest ethnological collections of its kind to be found anywhere. In the special section "Spielzeugwelten" (World of Toys), there are several thousand examples of handmade toys from the Barbara Schu Collection. The museum is located at Ubierring 45. Hours: 10am–5pm Tuesday–Sunday, 10am–8pm on the first Wednesday in every month. Closed: Monday. Guided tours are offered on Sundays at 3pm.

The **Museum für Angewandte Kunst/** Kunstgewerbemuseum (The Museum of Applied Arts/Museum of Arts and Crafts) has now found a home in what was formerly the Wallraf-Richartz Museum. Examples of artistic trades from the Middle Ages as well as design, glass and porcelain are displayed here. The museum's address is An der Rechtschule. Hours: 10am–5pm Wednesday–Sunday, 10am–8pm Tuesday. Closed: Monday.

The **Josef-Haubrich-Kunsthalle** (Josef-Haubrich Art Gallery) on Neumarkt presents changing exhibits from all areas of art and art history. The Kölner Kunstverein (Cologne Art Association) is located right next to it and devotes its changing exhibitions to well-known artists of the 20th century. It's located at Josef-Haubrich-Hof, Kunsthalle. Hours: 10am–5pm daily and 10am–8pm Tuesday and Friday. Guided tours are held on Tuesdays and Fridays at 6pm. The Kunstverein is open 10am–5pm Tuesday–Sunday and is closed on Monday.

In the westernmost suburb of Cologne, **Weiden**, Roman excavations in a subterranean **burial chamber** are on public view.

The address is Aachener Strasse 1328. Ring for the attendant; groups should call to book an appointment in advance. Tel: (0 22 34) 7 33 99. Hours: 11am–1pm Tuesday–Thursday, 10am–5pm Friday and 1–5pm Saturday and Sunday. Closed: Monday and national holidays. There are also **Romanesque tombs** on view in the crypt of St Severinus's church. On every Monday and Friday at 4.30pm there is a guided tour conducted through both the excavations and the church. Those wishing to join a tour should call in advance Tel: 31 68 70.

The **Praetorium**, located underneath the Town Hall, is a Roman palace originally belonging to the governor and can be visited daily except Monday 10am–5pm. If you'd appreciate an extensive tour it is necessary to call and request one in advance. Tel: 221-34 68 or 221-41 98.

The city's automatic information service will provide you with a summary of all the exhibits currently on view in Cologne museums, tel: 221-43 43.

EXHIBITS/GALLERIES

There are more than 100 galleries and art dealers as well as auction houses in Cologne. Until the middle of the 1960s the city was most noted for its old art. This changed, however, with the advent of the first art market held in 1967. From this point onwards numerous galleries and artists established themselves in Cologne and, as a result of this, an international art scene emerged. Many of the galleries are located in the triangle created between Neumarkt, Rudolfplatz and Friesenplatz. The Kreishausgallerie (at the corner of Albertus-Strasse and Magnusstrase) is actually an arcade where several galleries specialising in modern art are grouped together.

The most important, internationally active galleries include:

Galerie Boissere, Drususgasse 7–11
Galerie Ricke, Volksgartenstrasse 10
Galerie Werner, Gertrudenstrasse 24–28
Galerie Zwirner, Albertus-Strasse 18
Galerie Max Hetzler, Venloer Strasse 21
Galerie Monika Spüth, Maria-Hilf-Strasse 17

Two other galleries also deserve special mention. The first of these is the **CCAA Glasgalerie Köln,** Auf dem Berlich 24, which deals in modern glass creations and replicas of Roman glassware. The second is the **Naive-Kunst-Galerie** in Dellbrück, Roteichenweg 5, where a permanent exhibit of works by internationally acclaimed naive artists is complemented by a variety of special exhibits. If you'd like to visit, it is necessary to call and make an appointment, tel: l: 68 83 38.

Every year in November the art market "Art Cologne" draws artists, gallery owners and visitors from all over the world.

CONCERTS

Advance Booking Office: Tickets for all important concerts and events which take place in Cologne can be purchased in advance at the following outlets:

The theatre box office at Neumarkt. Tel: 21 42 32
The theatre box office in Kaufhof (a large department store). Tel: 21 66 92
The Rudolphplatz Theatre Ticket Box Office. Tel: 23 83 57
Saturn Theatre Ticket Box Office. Tel: 12 19 12
KölnTicket, Roncalliplatz. Tel: 28 01

The quantity of musical events offered in Cologne has increased due to the construction of the **Philharmonie** (Philharmonic Hall), located in the Wallraff-Richartz and Ludwig Museum complex. The subterranean, ultra-modern concert hall can accommodate audiences of up to 2,200. At home here are the Gürzenich Orchestra, West German Radio Symphony Orchestra and the Köln-Musik. The repertoire encompasses everything from jazz to folk and chamber music, to symphony productions and contemporary music. Occasionally on Sundays at 11am Viktor Lukas presents the tremendous tonal richness of the Klais Organ.

The Rhineland Chamber Orchestra primarily performs baroque music and compositions from the classical period. Concerts take place in the Philharmonie or in the Schnütgen Museum.

The Gürzenich Choir, Kölner Kantorei, Männer-Gesang-Verein (Men's Choral Society), Philharmonic Choir, Kölner Kammerchor (Cologne Chamber Choir), Mülheimer Kantorei, Bach-Verein Köln (Cologne Bach Society) and the Kölner Kurende all put on vocal performances throughout the city.

Classical music venues:
Philharmonie, Bischofsgarten 1. Tel: 23 38 54
Gürzenich, Martinstrasse 29/37. Evening box office: Tel: 221 23 85
Musikhochschule Köln, Dagobertstrasse 38. Tel: 12 40 33
WDR Grosser Sendesaal, Wallrafplatz. Tel: 220-1

Rock, Pop and Jazz venues:
Luxor, Luxemburger Strasse 40. Tel: 21 95 06
Em Streckstrump, Buttermarkt 37. Tel: 21 79 50
Subway, Aachener Strasse 82-84. Tel: 51 76 69
Stadtgarten, Venloer Strasse 40. Tel: 51 60 39

OPERA & BALLET

The performance seasons of both the opera and ballet take the various school holidays into account and generally commence at the beginning of September and last until the middle of July. The Opera House repertoire includes both classical and modern works. The building, designed by Wilhelm Riphahn and constructed between 1957 and 1962, can accommodate 1,300 people. The municipal theatres support their own ballet ensemble, the Kölner Tanzforum. In July dancers from all over the world meet here to participate in the traditional "Sommerakademie des Tanzes" (Summer Academy of Dance).
Opernhaus, Offenbachplatz, evening box office, tel: 221 82 52

THEATRES

Schauspielhaus, Offenbachplatz. Evening box office: Tel: 221 82 48
Schlosserei in the Schauspielhaus. Tel: 221 83 21
Kammerspiele, Ubierring 45. Evening box office: Tel: 32 79 90
Theater am Dom (light theatre), Glockengasse 11, Kölner Ladenstadt. Tel: 21 99 21
Senftöpfchen (cabaret), Grosse Neugasse 2-4. Tel: 23 79 80
Die Machtwächter (cabaret), Gertrudenstrasse 24. Tel: 24 21 01
Theater der Keller (contemporary theatre), Kleingedankstrasse 6. Tel: 31 80 59
Bauturm (contemporary theatre), Aachener Strasse 24. Tel: 52 42 42
Urania-Theater (contemporary theatre), Ehrenfeld, Venloer Strasse 265. Tel: 56 15 96
Comedia Colonia, Löwengasse 7-9. Tel: 26 76 70
Freies Werkstatt Theater, Zugweg 10. Tel: 32 78 17

The **Volkstheater Millowitsch**, Aachener Strasse 5. Tel: 25 17 47, is an institution which is particularly close to the hearts of many Cologne natives. At the present time the 6th generation of Millowitsch family members are performing theatre in Cologne; the company has performed here since 1936.

The **Puppenspiele der Stadt Köln** (Cologne's Puppet Theatre), Eisenmarkt. Tel: 21 20 95, is not a theatre just for kids. Both children and adults are sure to enjoy the performances. Typical Cologne characters like Hänneschen, Bärbelchen, Tünnes, Schäl and many other city originals are brought to life here as puppets.

In both theatres the local dialect is spoken: in the Millowitsch Theatre you'll hear the Rhineland dialect and in the Hänneschen Theatre the real Cologne dialect.

CINEMAS

The largest concentration of cinemas in Cologne is found along the Ring between Christophstrasse and Rudolphplatz. These are usually cinema centres, housing just a few large and small movie theatres under one roof.

The **Autokino** (Drive-in cinema) is in Porz, on Frankfurter Strasse. In Höhenberg (Im Weidenbruch 4) there is what's called **"Filmdancing"**; films are shown on a big screen while you're dancing. The **Lupe 2** on Mauritiussteinweg 102 and the **Cinemathek** in the new Wallraf-Richartz and Ludwig Museum both show avant-garde and old films.

In Hürth, situated east of Cologne and reached via Luxemburger Strasse, the new **Kinozentrum "UCI"** is in operation. This centre contains no fewer than 14 separate movie theatres and can accommodate a total of 2,800 people. Over 40 films are screened daily in these state-of-the-art cinemas. It's a good idea to reserve tickets in advance, tel: (0 22 33) 79 91 23.

Shopping

SHOPPING TIPS

The pedestrian zones in Cologne are perfect for undisturbed strolling and shopping. The covered arcades are ideal for shopping too, and not only when the weather leaves something to be desired. The **Bazaar de Cologne**, for instance, houses 63 shops and cafés, restaurants, ice-cream parlours, fountains and a glass elevator.

Olivandenhof is the name of the new shopping centre situated in the middle of the old business district between Neumarkt and Breite Strasse. Since 1988, 30 retail stores and a number of eating establishments have been conducting their business under a single glass roof. A number of oval galleries, connected to one another via glass escalators and a glass elevator, furnish a total of 4 x 160 metres (535 ft) of prime window space. All in all, this high-class shopping centre is designed for customers with good and expensive taste.

The art galleries and classy shops housed in the **Kreishausgalerie** also share a common roof. The **Kölner Ladenstadt** is the oldest shopping arcade in Cologne. In addition to stores which specialise in more sophisticated, luxurious items, there are also those which sell posters in general and film advertisement and art reproduction posters in particular. The Theater am Dom and the Pfeffermühle, (a restaurant serving crêpes to appeal to everyone's taste), are also located here. In the basement, "Colon" (a kind of a beer village) has spread out and a car park takes up the entire upper floor.

Without a doubt the most famous shopping street in the city is **Hohe Strasse**, the very first pedestrian zone in all Germany. Boutiques, trendy shops, department stores and speciality shops interspersed with restaurants suitable for either a quick bite or a leisurely meal are all strung out along the narrow North-South axis running through the city centre.

During the summer street painters and musicians take over the area where Hohe Strasse begins in the north, Wallrafplatz and the adjacent cathedral plaza. **Schildergasse** branches off from the southern end of Hohe Strasse towards Neumarkt. This broad street is lined with department stores like Kaufhof, Woolworth, Kaufhalle, Dyckhoff and Hertie, as well as with cinemas and cafés. **Breite Strasse** (Karstadt) runs parallel to this thoroughfare and offers a (nearly) car-free pedestrian paradise. Over the past few years **Ehrenstrasse** has developed into a modern shopping and entertainment street. A number of unusual boutiques have sprung up around the Sartory Theatre.

Eigelstein and **Weidengasse** (the latter branches off from the former), located in the northern part of the city centre, have fallen practically completely into Turkish hands. This is the place to buy excellent, top-quality Turkish culinary specialities like mutton, sheep's milk cheese, traditional round loaves of flat bread and exotic spices.

With a sales area encompassing 3,500 sq. yards, "Gonski" (Neumarkt 18), and its branch store located at Domkloster 2, is the largest **bookshop** in Cologne. Other big bookstores in the city centre include "Herder am Dom", Komödienstrasse 11, the "Bücherstube am Dom", which is located not at the cathedral, but rather at Neumarkt 2, "Sieger am Dom", Komödienstrasse 7, the railway bookshop "Ludwig", located in the main railway station and the "Buchhandlung am Barbarossaplatz", Barbarossaplatz. The bookstore "Gleumes", Hohenstaufenring 47–51, specialises in maps and travel literature.

Good antiques can be purchased in St Apernstrasse, near the Intercontinental Hotel. You can have works of art restored here as well as an expert's report drawn up. Mittelstrasse is distinguished by its exclusive **fashion boutiques**.

You can get nearly any **record** and **CD** that you can think of at "Saturn" on Hansaring. For those more interested in rock and pop, the place to go is WOM (World of Music), located in the basement of the Hertie department store at Neumarkt.

Unusual jewellery, for example Finnish designer pieces by Lapponia, can be found at Klaus Kaufhold (Quatermarkt 5 – near the intersection of Hohe Strasse and Schildergasse, or at Apostelnkloster 17, between Neumarkt and Mittelstrasse). In 1980 he established the first platinum workshop in his store at Quatermarkt and was thus instrumental in helping this relatively new material become popular in the world of jewellery production. Juwelier Hölscher (Hohe Strasse) carries a good selection of classic jewellery and Josef Becker (Hohe Strasse) specialises in silver articles.

Souvenirs of all shapes and sizes can be found in the small shops around the cathedral. An especially popular gift always was and still is, of course, Eau de Cologne 4711. This can be purchased in literally every perfume shop, but is also readily available in the speciality stores clustered around the cathedral and in the Glockengasse. (The latter address is where the firm had its original quarters.) If you're looking for a really special souvenir from Cologne, pay a visit to Brüggelmannhaus in the Mühlengasse. Here Lilli Balg-Baur sells her handmade puppets of original Cologne characters like Tünnes, Schäl, Hänneschen, Bärbelchen, etc. Each puppet is unique down to the tiniest detail. Lilli Balg-Baur received a first prize in the USA for her original Cologne waiter, the *Köbes*.

Balloons large and small, costing anywhere from 20 pfennigs for the smallest to a whopping 50,000 DM for the largest inflated decoration, can be found at Frau "Balloni" in Cologne Ehrenfeld, Gutenbergstrasse 10. Sybille Hartung makes dreams come true out of feather-light rubber. If you're looking for **magic tricks and equipment**, make sure you stop by the "Zauberkönig", Grosse Budengasse 3, near Hohe Strasse. In addition to magic articles they also carry a large selection of joke gimmicks. The "Postkarteladen" located at Breite Strasse 93 has the largest assortment of **postcards** around.

MARKETS

Although there is no main outdoor market in Cologne, there are about 37 different ones with over 80 events that take place on various days during the week in the Altstadt-Nord (the old part of the city in the north) and in a number of suburbs. Between 7am and 1pm you can stock up on fresh fruits, vegetables, meat, cheese, butter and eggs, as well as on spices, herbs and textiles. The Nippeser citizens have held their **Markt am Wilhelmplatz** ever since the turn of the century. Over the years it has become the oldest and biggest outdoor market in the city. It is held every day except Sunday. The **markets in Lindenthal and Klettenberg** each have more than 50 years of tradition behind them. Both are located in the "Belt"; the former on the third Cologne Ringstrasse and the latter in Buchforst on Waldecker Strasse.

Flea Markets take place every two months in the old part of Cologne, as does the **Antique Market**, in Cologne Ladenstadt. In spring and autumn there's a **Trödelmarkt** (a combination junk/flea market) held at Neumarkt. From the middle of April until the middle of May numerous visitors are drawn to the colourful, fragrant **Flower Market** at either Neumarkt or Rudolphplatz. Already from the middle of May until the beginning of June, just before the other wine festivals get rolling, the **Kölner Weinwoche** (Cologne Wine Week) is organised at Neumarkt. Growers from wine-producing areas all over Germany come together here to present their products and you can count on things getting at least a little wet and wild.

Neumarkt is also the site for **Bücherherbst** (Autumn Books), a book fair attended by some 60 different publishing houses and bookstores. It is held 10–18 September. The exhibits are complemented by a variety of interesting poetry readings, singing and cabaret performances. Things start taking on that Christmassy-feeling from around the end of November until the 23 December. The stands which make up the traditional **Weinachtsmarkt** (Christmas Market) are open for business on Alter Markt and on Neumarkt.

SPORTS

SPECTATOR

Cologne has acquired quite a good reputation as a "sports metropolis". Numerous athletes from the city have made it to the very top of their respective athletic fields. There are several arenas in Cologne suitable for staging large events. All are located conveniently and can be easily reached. The New Year is ushered in with the Cologne Six-day Cycle Race, held at the **Sporthalle in Deutz**, Deutz-Mülheimer-Strasse. Tel: 88 20 31.

The **Müngersdorf Stadium**, Aachenerstrasse 703. Tel: 49 83-224,. A generously laid-out athletic complex situated on the western perimeter of the city, this was erected in 1923, thus making it Cologne's very first stadium. It includes fields for soccer and track events, an area for horse shows, tennis courts, hockey fields, a large outdoor swimming pool, physical fitness course, gymnasiums and various open spaces. The German Sports College is also located here. The modern main athletic stadium offers covered seating to as many as 60,000 spectators and is the home ground of Cologne's first division side 1 FC Köln. Still in the second division, Fortuna Köln is based at the **Südstadion** (South Stadium) in Zollstock, Vorgebirgsstrasse. Tel: 36 20 43.

The Sport-und Bäderamt (municipal office for sports and swimming) has up-to-date information regarding events scheduled for both stadiums. Tel: 49 83 222.

The Cologne ice-hockey club "Die Haie" (The Sharks), several times over German Champions, fights out many of its battles in the **Eissporthalle** (Ice Sports Arena) of the Cologne Ice and Swimming Arena (Lentstrasse 30, on the road that leads over the Zoobrücke on the left side of the Rhine. Tel: 72 60 26).

Turf fans will find themselves irresistibly drawn to the **Horse Race Course** in Cologne-Weidenpesch, Rennbahnstrasse 152. Tel: 74 80 74. Horse racing began here on the 3 March 1898.

PARTICIPANT

Nineteen indoor and 10 outdoor swimming pools, the Ice and Swimming Arena with its 61-metre (203-ft) long slide, two 30 x 60-metre ice-skating rinks (which are only in operation during the wintertime) and numerous private swimming pools provide a variety of opportunities to satisfy your urge to swim or participate in some type of athletic activity.

A few of Cologne's swimming pools are:

Martinsbad, located in the Altstadt, Lintgasse 10. Twelve 10 x 20 metre pools filled with water heated to 30°C. Hours: 10am–10pm Monday–Friday, noon–7pm Saturday, 11am–6pm Sunday.

Kurbad Marienburg, Marienburger Strasse 70. This 10 x 20 metre pool contains sea water heated to a pleasant 32°C. Hours: 10am–9pm Monday–Friday, 7am–8pm Saturday.

Familiensauna "El Paradiso", located in Rösrath-Hoffnungsthal, east of Cologne. Options offered here include Finnish, panoramic, organic and steam saunas, indoor and outdoor swimming pools, massage and physical fitness training equipment. Hours: 10am–10pm daily.

From the middle of 1991, **Aqua Land**, an extensive recreational water-world boasting ultra-modern facilities, is open for fun of the wet variety. It is located at the northernmost outskirts of Cologne, near Chorweiler, Merianstrasse 1 (at the corner of Merianstrasse and Neusser Landstrasse).

Bowling buffs should be sure to check out the modern alleys at **Alpha-Bowling** in Cologne-Klettenberg, Luxemburger Strasse 299. Open: 4pm–1am Monday–Friday, 2pm–1am Saturday and Sunday. A second option right in the city centre and maintaining four alleys is **City-Bowling**, Moselstrasse 44.

Tennis and squash aficionados can work up a sweat at any one of the four tennis and 16 squash courts at **City-Sport** in Cologne-Sülz, Rhöndorfer Strasse 8–10. A swimming pool and sauna on the premises round the options off nicely. Hours: 8am–midnight daily. There are 10 courts, a sauna and solarium at **Squash-Park** in Cologne-Weidenpesch, Neusser Strasse 718a. Hours: 10am–midnight Monday–Friday, 10am–8pm Saturday, Sunday and holidays.

If horseback riding is more your style, get into contact with the **Kölner Reit-und Fahrverein** in Cologne-Müngersdorf, Aachener Strasse 800. Tel: 49 14 32.

Golfers have a choice of two courses: **Marienburger Golf-Club e.V.**, Militärringstrasse. Tel: 38 40 53, or **Golf-und Landclub Köln e.V.**, Refrath. Tel: (02204) 6 31 14. Both clubs require that you have a valid membership card for another golf club.

Special Information

THE DISABLED

Most theatres, museums and public facilities in Cologne are equipped with special entrances and lavatories to accommodate disabled visitors. Additional help is also available upon request. Many subway stations can be reached by either escalator or elevator. Some of the pedestrian traffic lights also provide acoustic signals for the blind. The City of Cologne prints a brochure entitled "Freizeit – Bildung – Ferien" containing information regarding all the facilities in the city suitable for disabled people. The brochure is free and can be obtained at the Tourist Information Centre.

CHILDREN

Most children will enjoy a visit to the zoo or one of the wild animal parks in Brück or Dünnwald. In Gut Leidenhausen there are different birds of prey to see along with big game animals and wild boar. You can rent a rowing boat in Groov, in Zündorf, and on Decksteiner Pond in the western green-belt. A trip high over the river on the Rhine funicular or with the chairlift across Rhine Park is sure to please.

During summer well-known fairy tales are performed on the open-air stage in Zons, the fortified medieval city located to the north of Cologne. There are two **children's theatres** which are especially tuned into what might be entertaining to younger audiences. At Ömmes & Oimel the emphasis is on fairy tale-like performances that tend to stimulate a child's own fantasy. The theatre is located at Löwengasse 7–9. Tel: 24 76 70. The spectrum of children's and young people's theatre performed in Die Kugel in Rodenkirchen, Industriestrasse 170. Tel: 31 99 60, extends from adventure stories all the way to musicals.

Statt Reisen, a non-profit organisation, offers two different **tours**, each lasting about 1½ hours, for groups of 12 children or more. The emphasis here is on fairy tales, sagas and legends native to Cologne. For example at the Heinzelmännchen Fountain the story of the Wichtel (magical cleaning elves) is told. Games and a quick bout of painting on the cobblestones keep even the youngest members of the tour happy. Further information is available at: Statt Reisen, Herwarthstrasse 22. Tel: 52 64 64.

WOMEN

The Women's Historical Society organises **city sightseeing tours for women**. The tours lead primarily to those places where women played a special role in Cologne's history. Anyone wishing to participate should book in advance by writing to the: Frauengeschichtsverein, Marienplatz 4, 5000 Cologne 1. The Piccolo-Theatre, Zülpicher Strasse 28. Tel: 23 27 04, is a **theatre by women for women**. Most productions are plays which focus on women, for example *Antigone* by Anouilh, *Nora* by Ibsen, etc. Plays revolving around women-oriented topics such as *Die Töchter der Hexen* (The Witch's Daughters) or *Hören Sie mal* (Listen For Once), a female monologue, are also performed here.

George Sand, in Mauritiussteinweg, is a **café for women** which offers an extensive cultural programme oriented towards women's interests.

The **Frauenbuchladen** (Women's Bookshop), Moltkestrasse 66. Tel: 52 31 20, carries a selection of books dealing with specifically female themes, fiction and poetry works by women, as well as an assortment of biographies about particular women.

BUSINESS PEOPLE

Industrie-und Handelskammer (The Chamber of Industry and Commerce), Unter Sachsenhausen 10. Tel: 1 64 00
Köln-Messe (Cologne Trade Fairs), Messeplatz 1, Deutz. Tel: 82 11
Amt für Wirtschaftsförderung (Bureau for Economic Promotion), Richartzstrasse 2–4. Tel: 221 33 12

STUDENTS

University of Cologne, Albertus-Magnus-Platz. Tel: 470-1
University students in possession of a valid student identification card can eat relatively cheaply in the "mensa" (the student refectory) and are also permitted to use the student library, which stocks a selection of newspapers from all over the world (Universitätsstrasse 12, Cologne-Lindenthal).

The brochure "Studieren in Köln" (Study in Cologne) is available for free from the Kölner Studentenwerk (Student Administration Office), Universitätsstrasse 16, 5000 Cologne 4. Tel: 47 29 152 or 47 29 157. The Student Administration Office also has information regarding inexpensive student housing.

USEFUL ADDRESSES

TOURIST INFORMATION

Information of interest to tourists is available from the **Verkehrsamt** der Stadt Köln (The City of Cologne Tourist Information Office), Unter Fettenhennen 19, 5000 Cologne 1. Tel: 221 33 45.

CONSULATES

Belgian Consulate General
Cäcilienstrasse 46
5000 Cologne 1
Tel: 21 53 64

Costa Rican Consulate
Neumarkt 41
5000 Cologne 1
Tel: 23 00 08

Icelandic Consulate
Spitzweg 16
5000 Cologne 1
Tel: 48 78 78

Italian Consulate
Universitätsstrasse 81
5000 Cologne 41
Tel: 40 08 70

Dutch Consulate
Sechtemerstrasse 12
5000 Cologne 51
Tel: 37 14 23

Austrian Consulate
Glockengasse 1
5000 Cologne 1
Tel: 24 74 75

ART/PHOTO CREDITS

Photography by

Page 63, 84/85, 86/87, 16/17, 162/163 166, 168/169, 180, 184, 185, 188/189, 190, 191, 194, 201, 203, 206, 218	**Michael Bengal**
Cover, 12/13, 14/15, 27, 31, 32/33, 35R, 39, 40/41, 42, 44L, 54, 56, 57, 58, 76/77, 80, 98, 104, 106, 107, 105, 110/111, 117, 112, 118, 127, 130, 132, 133, 134, 141, 145, 146, 147, 151, 155, 156, 158L, 172, 178/179, 182, 192, 199, 207L, 207R, 209, 210, 216	**Wolfgang Fritz**
7, 26, 28, 30, 35L, 37, 38, 44R, 52/53, 74/75, 81, 82, 88, 94, 95, 100, 101, 102, 103, 109, 122, 123, 125, 126, 128/129, 136, 139, 142, 143, 144, 148, 149, 152, 153, 154, 158R, 159L, 170/171, 173, 174, 176L, 176R, 177, 181, 187, 200, 202	**Günther and Margarete Ventur**
1, 97, 159R, 160, 161, 175, 197, 214	**Heinz Mülow**
34, 36, 43, 50, 119	**Rheinisches Bilderarchiv**
78, 79, 164/165, 196	**Bodo Bondzio**
68	**Klaus Barisch**
51	**Bundersbildstelle Bonn**
71	**Electrola**
183	**Ford-Werke**
114, 115, 120, 121	**Rainer Gaertner DPGh, Bergisch Gladbach**
137, 212, 213, 215	**Karin Hackenbroich**
62L, 62R	**Dieter Klein**
66	**Klaus Lefebvre**
72	**Lindenstrasse/D. Krüger**
67	**Willy Millowitsch**
60	**Peter Peitsch**
70	**WDR**
45	**4711**
Maps	**Berndtson & Berndtson**
Illustrations	**Klaus Geisler**
Visual Consultant	**V. Barl**

INDEX

A

Abel, Adolf 184, 199
Acken, Johannes von 185
Adenauer, Konrad 47, 50, 51, 65, 83, 193, 199, 205
Agfa-Foto-Historama 120, 122
Agnesveedel 163
Agrippa of Nettesheim 61
Agrippa 25, 167
Alberti, Matteo 213
Albertus Magnus 33, 61, 184
Alfred-Schütte-Allee 197
Altar (of St Agiluph) 96
Altar of the City's Patron Saints 35, 96, 145
Altenberg Abbey 211–212, 213
Altstadt 44, 89, 101, 120, 131, 143, 151, 157, 167
Andreae, Otto Gustav 123
Anno II, Archbishop 29, 106
Aquinas, Thomas 33, 61
Archbishops 29–31
Arnsberg, Count Gottfried von 96
Arsenal (Zeughaus) 38, 39, 114
"Art Cologne" 126
Art dealers 126–127
Art Exhibition Hall 120
Art galleries 126, 177
Art 120–122, 126–127
Artisans 31
Artists 126–127, 160, 161
Augustus 113
Augustusburg Palace 211
Aula Regia 145

B

Balchem House 160, 161
Band, Karl 146, 106
Banking 49
BAP 70, 71, 161
Barlach — *Angel of Death* 49
"Bartholomew's Night" 35
Battle of Worringen 31, 33
Bauernbänke 158
Bavarian Windows 96
Bayenturm 160
Bazaar de Cologne 132
Bebel, August 194
Becker, Jürgen 61, 62
Beer-houses 135
  Bieresel 136
  Früh am Dom 131, 135
  Goldener Kappes 182
  Malzmühle 135
  Päffgen 135, 141
  Sion 135
Beethoven Park 206
Beethovenstrasse 133
Bender, Hans 61, 62
Bensberg 213
Berbuer Fountain 159
Berbuer, Karl 159
Bernard, Josef 119, 123
Bertram, Ernst 62
Beuys, Joseph 93, 121
Bild-Zeitung 73
Biolek-Alfred 140
Bismarck 42
Blum, Robert 61
Bläck Fööss 70, 71
Böhm, Dominikus 181, 185, 186
Böhm, Gottfried 124, 151, 183, 213, 215
Böll, Heinrich 55–57, 61, 62, 63, 167
Bookshops 132–133
Borger, Hugo 116
Born, Nicolas 61
Botanical Gardens 180, 205
Bottmühle 160
Brauweiler Abbey 213–214
Brecht, Berthold — *Threepenny Opera* 65
Breite Strasse 132
Brinkmann, Rolf Dieter 61
British occupation 47
Broadcasting 50, 73
Broelman, Cathringin 36
Bruno, Archbishop 29, 108, 208
Brück game preserve 208
Brühl 215
Buchforst 198
Building boom 31, 43
Burg Bachem 186
Burg Efferen 186
Burg Gleuel 186
Burg Hobell 186
Burgher's House (Bensberg) 213
Burghers 21, 29, 30, 31, 35, 37, 119
Buschulte, Georg 103
Busmann, Peter 69, 120
Bütenredner 81

C

Caesar, Julius 25, 113
Cafés 138, 140–141
Capitol 113
Car industry 48
cardo maximus 25, 113
Carnival 21, 55, 65, 79–81, 193
Carstanjen Collection 121
Casimir Hagen Collection 181
Castrum Divitium 27, 193
Cathedral 21, 31, 36, 42, 44, 55, 56, 57, 89, 93–96, 144
Catholicism 40, 153
Chapel (Town Hall) 145
Charlemagne 29, 93
Chemical industry 49
Children's Zoo (Sülz) 207
Choirs 70
Chorweiler 181
Christianity 27, 29

Churches
Augustusburg palace church 216
building boom 31
Garrison Church of All Saints 186
Great St Martin's 29, 101, 102, 103, 105
Jesuit Church 35
Kalk Chapel 198
Krieler Dömchen 185
Maria Köningin 186
of the Assumption (St Maria Himmelfahrt) 38
of the Holy Apostles 29, 101, 102, 103, 105, 106
of the Resurrection 183
of the Sacred Heart (Bensberg) 213
Old St Alban's 147
Old St Catherine's 181
Old St Heribert 195
Old St Maternus 186
St Agnes 163, 173
St Albert the Great 185
St Andrew's 29, 101, 105
St Cecilia's 101, 106
St Christopher's 181
St Clements (Mülheim) 200
St Columba 147
St Cunibert's 31, 101, 102, 105, 108, 158
St Engelbert's 181
St George's 101, 102, 103, 106, 108, 157
St Gereon's 29, 56, 101, 102, 103, 105, 106
St John the Baptist 157
St Joseph's 182
St Lawrence 184
St Mary's in Lyskirchen 101, 102, 157, 158
St Mary's in the Capitol 29, 101, 102, 103, 105, 113
St Mechtern's 182
St Pantaleon's 29, 101, 103, 108
St Severinus's 29, 101, 103, 105, 106, 157
St Thomas More 185
St Ursula's 29, 101, 106, 158
St Ursula 158, 29
Ursuline Monastery 163
City Council 33, 34
City Parliament 145
City Wall 30, 44, 173
City-Treff 133
Civic Theatre 65
Clares Altar (cathedral) 94
Clemens, August 216
Clemens, Elector Joseph 216
Clemens, Wilhelm 123
Clubs
Basement 71
Cauri-Club 70
Luxor 70, 71
Popocatepetl 70
Rose 70
Underground 70, 71
Wartesaal 71
Cockerel Gate 44
Code Civil 40
"Coffee Cruises" 168
College for Media Studies 73
Cologne F C 205
Cologne Philharmonie 69
Cologne Radio Symphony Orchestra 69
Cologne School of Painters 96, 120
Cologne Sports Hall 70
Cologne Zoo 180
Cologne-Deutz Bridge 47
Colonia Agrippinensis 167
Colonia Claudia Ara Agrippinensium (CCAA) 25, 113
Colonius 182
Column of the Virgin Mary 153
Craft businesses 49
Crones, Edwin 124
Cuvilliés, François 216
Czukay, Holger 71

D

Dassel, Archbishop Rainald von 30, 93, 95, 96
Deckstein Mill 185
decumanus maximus 25, 113
Deter, Ina 71
Deutz Bridge 167
Deutz 27, 29, 43, 47, 50, 167, 193, 194, 196, 197
Dionysos Mosaic 25, 116
Dom Bridge 195
Drinking water canal 115
Dünnwald game park 208

E

Eau de Cologne 44, 45, 49, 65, 183
Eburones 25, 113
Ecke, Fritz 205
Eckhart, Master 61
Economic decline 38
Ehrenfeld 182
Ehrenstrasse 132
Eifel Hills 25, 115
Eigelstein Gate 39, 44
Eigelstein 133
Eigelsteinveedel 157, 158, 161, 163
El-De-Haus 47, 144, 148
Emperor Claudius 25, 113
Emperor Constantine 193
Engelbert II, Archbishop 211
Engels, Friedrich 43
Engels, Jupp 144, 150
Englebert, Archbishop 31
Equestrian Statue of the Deutz Cuirassier 194
Ernst, Max 55, 122
Essenwein, August von 94
Express 73

F

Fairytale Forest 212
Farina, Johann Maria 45
Fasching 55
Fassadenriss F **(Cathedral)** 96
Fastelovend 79
Felten & Guilleaume 43
Feminis, Giovanni Paolo 45
"Fifth season" 21, 79
"Filmdose" 177
Fischer, Adolf and Frieda 124
Flimm, Jürgen 65
Flittard 200
Flora 180, 205
Food 135–140

Football 83
Ford Company 48, 49
Ford, Henry 48
Forstbotanischer Garten 207
Franks 27, 29, 193, 195, 208
Frederick II 211
Frederick William III 38, 153
Frederick William IV of Prussia 40, 42, 93
Free Imperial City 31, 38, 39
Freie Werkstatt Theater 66
French domination 39, 40
Friedenskirche 182
Friedenström Castle 215
Friedenswald 207
Fühlinger See 181, 206, 207

G

Galleries 126–127
Gerhard, Master 114
German Christian Democratic Union (CDU) 51
Gero Cross 94
Gero, Archbishop 96
Geschlechter 33
Gestapo 144, 148, 214
Geusen Cemetery 184
Giesen, Josef 205
Girard, Dominique 216
Gleichschaltung 47
Glockengasse 44, 45, 49, 65, 132, 183
Goethe House 213
Goethe, Johann Wolfgang 45
Gottfried, Hermann 102, 106
Gottwald, Christoph 62
Green Belts 51, 205–208
Greene, Graham 62
Grielächer 57
Grod, Caspar Maria 198
"Groov" 196, 202
Gründerzeit 174, 176
Grönemeyer, Herbert 71
Guilds 33
Gutbrod, Rolf 184
Gülich, Nikolaus 36, 37, 39
Gürzenich Orchestra 69, 154
Gürzenich 35, 38, 43, 48, 69, 80, 148, 154

H

Haberer, Godfried 69, 120
Hahnen Gate 158
Hansasaal 145
Hanseatic League 33–34
Haubrich, Josef 119, 120
Haus Bitz 186
Haus Forst 186
Hay Market 146
Hecker, Peter 185
Heinsberg, Archbishop Philipp von 96
Henoth, Katharina 38
Heribert, Archbishop 195, 29
Heumarkt 151
Heuser, Klaus 71
Heuss, President Theodor 123
Heyme, Hansgünther 65
Hildebold, Archbishop 29, 93, 94
Hillinus Codex 93
Hitler, Adolf 47
Hochstaden, Archbishop Konrad von 93, 96
Hockey 83
Hohe Strasse 25, 89, 113, 131, 132, 143, 157
Hohenstaufen period 101, 106, 108
Hohenstaufen wall 96
Hohenstaufenring 133
Hohenzollern Bridge 21, 40, 47, 48, 167
Hohenzollernring 133, 175
Holzmeister, Clemens 102
Horse racing 83
Housing 43, 181
Hugo, Victor 193
Hunting Lodge (Bensberg) 213
Hürten, Sepp. 159
Hyatt Regency Hotel 195

I

Ice hockey 83
Inner Green Belt 205, 47
Institor, Henricus 36
Insurance 49
International Sport Festival 83
Investiture Controversy

J

Jan von Werth Fountain 33, 143
Jazz 70
Jecken 79
Jesuits 39
Jewish Cemetery 185
Jews 35, 40, 47, 144, 145, 197
Joest, Carl 43
Jugendstil art 215
Julia Agrippina the Younger 25, 113

K

Kaiser-Wilhelm-Ring 133
Kalk 198
Kallendresser 143, 147, 148, 150
Kettenbach, Hans Werner 61, 62
Kiel mutiny 47
Kiepenheuer & Witsch 61
King's Forest (Königsforst) 208
Klein St Martin 147
Klingelpütz 57
Klöckner-Humboldt-Deutz 43, 49, 196
***Klüngel* (Nepotism)** 37, 39, 56
Knechtsteden Monastery 214
Köbes 135, 140
Koch, Werner 61
Koep, Wilhelm and Rudolf 183
Koerfer, Hans 184
Kokoschka, Oscar 199
Kollwitz, Käthe — *Grieving Parents* 147–148
Köln-Düsseldorfer excursion boats 168
Kölner Jazzhaus 175
Köln-Krimis 62
Kölner Stadt-Anzeiger 73
Kölnisch 55–57
Kölnische Rundschau 73

Kölnische Volkszeitung 73
Kölsch 49, 71, 135, 136, 137, 141
Kölsch (dialect) 71
Kölschrock 71
Komarhof 186
Kreishausgalerie 132
Krämer, Günther 65
Kuene, Konrad 96
Kwartier Lateng 177

L

Ladenstadt 132
Lady Chapel 96
Landeshaus 195
Leidenhausen Estate 202, 208
Lenné 180, 216
Leverkusen Bridge 167
Life-Musik-Hall 70, 71
Lindenthal 183
Little Theatre 124
Lochner, Stephan 35, 96, 119, 120, 145
Loggia 146
Lohmer, Gerd 167
Lom von 123
Lortzing, Albert 65
Lower Rhine Music Festival 1821 69
Ludwig I of Bavaria, King 96
Ludwig, Peter and Irene 119
Lufthansa Building 194

M

Maahn, Wolf 71
Madonna in the Rose Garden 119, 120
Maisch, Herbert 65
Malleus Maleficarum 36
Marcks, Gerhard 184
Marienburg 186
Markets 133
Marsil Stone 114
Martinsviertel 143, 144, 154
Marx, Karl 43, 61
Mass production 43
Mataré, Ewald 93, 145, 147, 148, 150, 185
Maternus 27, 93
Mauenheim 181
Mayekawa, Kunio 124
Media 50, 73
Meistermann, Georg 103
Melaten Cemetery 183, 186, 38
Merchants 31, 33, 34
Merheim 202
Merovingians 29
Meshow, Anton 37
"Messe" 199
Mikvah 145, 154
Millenium Exhibition of 1925 47
Millowitsch, Willy 65, 66, 67, 143
Mittelstrasse 132
Modern art 126–127
Moers, Archbishop Dietrich von 96
Mohr, Christian 93
Municipal Forest 185, 205
Municipal Gardens 174, 175, 205
Museums
  Applied Art 119, 120, 123
  Bergischer 211
  Diocesan 144
  East Asian Art 124, 183
  fruit (Leidenhausen Estate) 208
  Käthe Kollwitz 132, 148
  Ludwig 119, 120
  Municipal 114, 119, 150
  Rautenstrauch-Joest 123, 124, 151
  Roman-Germanic 25, 26, 27, 113, 115, 116, 119
  Schnütgen Museum of Medieval Art 101, 119, 122, 124
  Wallraf-Richartz 113, 119, 120, 21
  Zons local museum 215
Music Academy 69, 70
Music 69–70
Musica Antiqua Köln 70
Mühlens family 45
Mülheim 167, 198, 200
Mülheimer Gottestracht 200
Müngersdorf Stadium 47, 83
Müngsten Bridge 211

N

Napoleon 40, 119, 208, 214
National Socialists 47
Nazis 47, 51, 63, 119, 148, 198, 197, 199
Nepotism 34–35, 37, 39
Neptune Swimming Baths 182
Neue Rheinische Zeitung 43, 61
Neumann, Balthasar 216
Neumarkt 40, 89, 106, 116, 131, 151
Neumarkt-Passage 132
"New Bible" window 96
New Town (Neustadt) 44, 173
Newspapers 73
Nicholas of Verdun 30, 95
Niedecken, Wolfgang 71
Niehl II terminus 167
Nippes 43, 44, 133, 182
Nägeli-Harald — *Death* 106

O

Offenbach, Jacques 65
"Old Bible" window 96
Old City (Altstadt) 44, 89, 101, 120, 131, 143, 151,157, 167
Old Market (Alter Markt) 143, 146
Olivandenhof 132, 133
Opera House 65, 69
Optical telegraph (Flittard) 200
Ostermann, Willi 62
Ostermannplatz 154
Otto I 208
Otto III 195
Otto, Nikolaus August 43, 196
Outer Green Belt 47, 205
Overstolzenhaus 123, 146, 154

P

Paintings 120–122
Papa Joe's 70

People's Gardens 174, 205
Phantasialand 216
Pilgrim, Archbishop 29
Platz-Jabbek 143, 150
Poll Meadow 198
Poll 197
Population 44, 48, 158, 173, 193
Porz 202
Postumus of the Rhine 26
Praetorium 26, 116, 144
Preilstrasse 132
Press Exhibition (PRESSA) 1928 47, 199
Protestants 40
Prussian era 42
Prussians 194
Puppet theatre 66, 67
Purple Schulz 71

R

Radio 73
Raschdorf 119
Rath 202
Reconstruction 48, 151
"Red Sparks" 80, 81, 158, 160
Reidt, Melchior von 145
Relics of the Three Magi 30, 93
Religious beliefs 27
Restaurants
Alfredo 137
Alte Liebe 168
Ambiance am Dom 137
Artischoke 138
Baba 138
Bali 138
Bandirma 138
Bizim 138
Bosporus 138
Café Especial 138
Chez Alex 137
Em ahle Kohberg (Merheim) 202
Goldener Pflug 137, 202
Graugans 137
Il Bagutta 138
Kuchenhof 212
La Barrière 138
La Baurie 138
Mandalay 138
Moissonnier 138
Rino Casati 137
Tapabo 138
Wack 137
Reuter, Werner 150
Revolution of 1848 43
Revolution of 1918 47
Rheinau Harbour 167
Rhenish School of Music 70
Rhine cable railway 196
Rhine Gardens 168
Rhine Park 196
Rhine Suburb (Rheinvorstadt) 146
Rhine 48, 89, 167–168
Richartz, Johann Heinrich 119
Richerzeche 30, 33, 34
Richmod's 132
Richmodis of Aducht 153
Rings 132
Ringstrasse 173, 205
Riphahn, Wilhelm 182, 184, 198
River Strunde 198
River Wupper 211
Rock music 70, 71
Rodenkirchen Bridge 167
Rodenkirchen 168, 186
Roman aqueduct 114, 115, 116
Roman burial chamber in Cologne-Weiden 116
Roman Fountain 114
Roman North Gate 27
Roman stone wall 113
Roman Tower 113, 114, 27
Romans 25–27, 79, 93, 106, 113–116, 144, 193, 194
Rosenmontag Parade 79–81

S

Saarwerden, Archbishop Friedrich von 96, 215
St Anna's (Ehrenfeld) 183
St Apernstrasse 132
St Elizabeth's Hospital 185
St Gereon 27, 96
St John's Chapel (Cathedral) 96
St Maternus' Chapel (Cathedral) 96
St Peter's Door (Cathedral) 94
St Severinus's Gate 31, 44, 160, 161
St Severinus 27
St Ursula 27, 96, 123
Sancta Colonia 30
Sax, Abraham 37
Schäl 57, 67, 143, 150, 153
Schallenburg 216
Schaller, Fritz 185
Schallück, Paul 61
Schildergasse 25, 89, 113, 131, 143
Schiller — *Die Räuber* 65
Schlaun, Johann Conrad 216
Schloss Augustburg 215–216
Schloss Burg 211
Schloss Falkenlust 216
Schloss Weisshaus 185
Schmitz Column 143, 144
Schnütgen, Alexander 122
Schuh, Oscar Fritz 65
Schumacher, Fritz 47
Schwarz, Rudolf 119, 123, 181, 183, 186
Schürmann, Joachim 102
Scotus, Johannes Duns 61
Secularisation 40
Senate Chamber (Town Hall) 145
Senftöpchen 66
Service sector 49–50
Severinus Bridge 48
Shopping 131–133
Shrine of the Three Magi 30, 95
Siegburg Madonna 123
Silvanus 27
Six-Day Cologne Cycle Race 83
Spee, Friedrich von 61
Sport 83
Sports Academy 83
Sprenger, Jacob 36
Stadthalle at Mülheim 70
Staple House 146, 38
"Staple Right" 31
State College of Music 163

Stavenhof 161
Steam power 42
Steffen, Arno 71
Steguweit, Heinz 62
Stern, Carola 62
Stirnberg, Bonifatius 160
Stockhausen, Karlheinz 69
Stollwerck chocolate factory 49, 65, 158, 160
"Stollwerck Girl" — statue 159
Stollwerck, Franz 43
Street performers 131
Sturm, Vilma 62
Stübben, Joseph 44, 132, 173, 174, 176, 177
Suburban development 43, 44
Sugar industry 49
Süd Bridge 167
Südstadt 161
Sülzer, Bernd 62

T

Television 50, 73
Temple of Mars 113
Teutons 26
Theatre 65–66
Theatres
  Bautürm 66
  Comedia Colonia 66
  Hänneschen 66, 143, 154
  Kammerspiele 65
  Keller 65
  Millowitsch 65–67
  Schauspielhaus 65, 66
  Schlosserei 65
  Theater am Dom 66
  Volkstheater 66, 67
Third Reich 47, 199
Thirty Years' War 36, 39, 150, 211
Three Kings' Chapel 96
Tomb of Poblicius 25, 27, 116
Tourism 30, 50
Town Hall (Bensberg) 213, 215
Town Hall Tower 35
Town Hall 38, 145
Toy collection 124
Trade Fair Complex 50, 126, 199
Trade Fair Sports Hall 83
Trade 26–27, 39
Traffic 151, 177
Trajan 26
Transfixbrief 35
Transport network 48
Treasury 96
Treaty of Versailles 205, 47
Turkish districts 133, 138, 161, 182
Turner, Tina 71
Tünnes and Schäl 57, 67, 143, 150, 153

U

Ubii Monument 113
Ubii 25, 26, 113, 167
Uferstrasse 151, 154
Ulre Gate 158, 160
Uni-Center 182
University 33, 184

V

Veedeln (districts) 89, 157
Verbeek, Hans 199
Verbundbrief 34, 35
Vernukken, Wilhelm 146
Vier-Scheiben-Haus 48
Villeroy & Boch 94
Vitellius 26
Vogt, Albert 62
Voigtel 93
Vringsveedel 157, 158, 160

W

Wahner Heide State Forest 208
Wallraf, Ferdinand Franz 119, 120, 123
Wallraf, Günter 62
Wand, Günter 69
Waveren-Stina 36
WDR Big Band 69
WDR radio station 48, 50, 69, 73
Weavers' uprising 34
Weckschnapp 163
Weidengasse 138, 161
Weinsberg, Hermann von 116
Wellershoff, Dieter 61, 62
Werth, Jan von 150, 153
White City (Buchforst) 198
Wine trade 141, 31
Winters, Christoph 66
Witch hunts 36
Women 36
Working conditions 43
World War I 47
World War II 47–48, 101–108, 119, 151, 175, 177
Worringen 47
Writers 61–62

Z

Zeltinger, Jürgen 71
Zons 215, 216
Zoo Bridge 167
Zwerenz, Gerhard 62
Zwirner 93
Zündorf 202